Principal Works of Upton Sinclair

The Journal of Arthur Stirling, 1903
The Jungle, 1906
The Metropolis, 1908
King Coal, 1917
100%, 1920
They Call Me Carpenter, 1922
Oil!, 1927
Mountain City, 1930
Roman Holiday, 1931
Co-op, 1936
Little Steel, 1938
World's End, 1940
Between Two Worlds, 1941
Dragon's Teeth, 1942
Wide Is the Gate, 1943
Presidential Agent, 1944
Dragon Harvest, 1945
A World to Win, 1946
Presidential Mission, 1947
One Clear Call, 1948
O Shepherd, Speak!, 1949
The Return of Lanny Budd, 1953

BOSTON

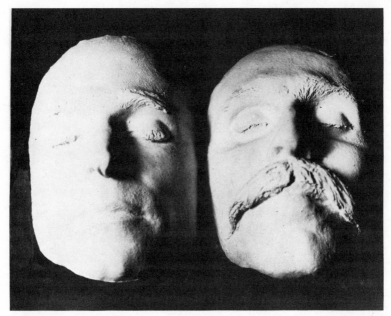

Plate 1.
**The death masks of Sacco and Vanzetti
(1927)**

*"The current was turned off, and the medical
men made their examination, and at twenty-
six minutes and fifty-five seconds past midnight they pronounced that the last spark of
anarchism had been extinguished from the
august Commonwealth of Massachusetts."*
Page 742

BOSTON

A Documentary Novel of the
Sacco-Vanzetti Case
by

UPTON
SINCLAIR

With an Introduction by Howard Zinn

1978
ROBERT BENTLEY, INC.
872 Massachusetts Avenue
Cambridge, Massachusetts, 02139

Copyright © 1928 by Upton Sinclair
Copyright © 1978 by Robert Bentley, Inc.
Printed in the United States of America
Library of Congress Catalog Card Number 77-86279
10 9 8 7 6 5 4 3 2 1

Library of Congress Cataloging in Publication Data
*SUMMARY: A Boston dowager becomes involved in the social upheaval
generated by the trial of Nicola Sacco and Bartolomeo Vanzetti.*

1. Sacco-Vanzetti Case Fiction [1. Sacco-Vanzetti — Fiction]
I. Title PZ3.S616 Bo 1978 [PS3537.185] [FIC] 77-86279
ISBN 0-8376-0420-6

CONTENTS

PHOTOGRAPHS

INTRODUCTION

Upton Sinclair's novel, *Boston,* has been out of print too long, and it is a gift to have it back. Fifty years have passed since Nicola Sacco and Bartolomeo Vanzetti were strapped into a chair at Charlestown Prison, near Boston, and electrocuted. There is a need to recall what happened, and to understand why *Boston,* classified as fiction, is so true an account of that case, that time, and so unsettling in its closeness to our case, our time.

The story of Sacco and Vanzetti, whenever revived, even after half a century, awakens deep feelings. In the summer of 1977, Governor Michael Dukakis of Massachusetts officially pronounced that the two men had not had a fair trial, and immediately there were outcries in the state legislature, letters to the newspapers.*

One citizen wrote: "By what incredible arrogance do Governor Dukakis and Daniel A. Taylor, his legal adviser, dare to put themselves above Gov. Alvan T. Fuller of Massachusetts, who declared that Sacco and Vanzetti had a fair trial, were fairly convicted and fairly punished for their crime?"

Another, signing his letter "John M. Cabot, U.S. Ambassador, Retired," expressed his "great indignation" and noted that Governor Fuller's affirmation of the death sentence was made after a special review by "three of Massachusetts' most distinguished and respected citizens — President Lowell of Harvard, President Stratton of MIT and retired Judge Grant."

Heywood Broun put it a bit differently, in his column in the *New York World* fifty years ago: "It is not every prisoner who has a President of Harvard University throw on the switch for him. ... If this is a lynching, at least the fish peddler and his friend the factory hand may take unction to their souls that they will die at the hands of men in dinner

* See Appendix for the *Report to the Governor in the Matter of Sacco and Vanzetti.*

xi

jackets or academic gowns...."[1]

Governor Fuller's son, Peter Fuller, Boston's leading Cadillac dealer, as well as a racer of thoroughbred horses, called Dukakis' statement "an attempt to besmirch a guy's record that we believe in and love, whose memory we cherish." He added: "We're sitting here in the last building my father built, and it's the most beautiful car agency on the Eastern Coast and perhaps in the United States."[2]

In New York, a few days before August 23, 1977, the 50th anniversary of the execution, the *New York Times* reported: " 'Plans by Mayor Beame to proclaim next Tuesday "Sacco and Vanzetti Day" have been canceled in an effort to avoid controversy,' a City Hall spokesman said yesterday."

There must be good reason why a case fifty years old, its principals dead, arouses such emotion. It is not the kind of history that can be handled comfortably, in harmless ceremonies, like the Bicentennial celebrations of 1976, in which the revolutionary doctrines of the Declaration of Independence were lost in a Disneyland of pageantry. Sacco and Vanzetti were not Washington and Jefferson, not wealthy insurgents making a half-revolution to exchange a limited monarchy for a limited democracy.

They were, as Upton Sinclair reminds us, using the harsh word so often as to irritate us, to make us feel the insult ourselves, "wops," foreigners, poor workingmen. Worst of all, they were anarchists. As anarchists, they were not only opposed to the capitalist economic system, but to any form of state power, any situation in which power was centralized in a small number of people, whether in a monarchy or a representative body. They believed, as anarchists generally do, that the resources of the earth should be distributed fairly equally among all people, that decisions should be made collectively in small groups in touch with one another, that such a system of equality in wealth and political power would make crime, punishment, and prisons unnecessary. They thought that without the provocation of economic profit or nationalist spirit, war among nations would end for all time. But to have all this happen, the rich would have to be fought in a series of struggles, leading up to a general strike to take away their power. Such a way of thinking, to the officials of the government, was not a crime like payroll robbery or murder. It was much worse. And so, the story of two such men cannot be recalled without trouble.

Therefore, let us recall it. But let us not concentrate on that question which is the center of most discussion of the Sacco-Vanzetti case: were they guilty of the robbery committed April 15, 1920, at the Slater and Morrill shoe factory in South Braintree, Massachusetts, and the murder of the paymaster Frederick Parmenter, and the guard, Alessandro Berardelli? Let us go beyond that question to ask others, more important, more dangerous. That is what *Boston* does.

Not that we can neglect the question of guilt or innocence: the trial, the witnesses, the defendants, the judge, the jury, the lawyers, and all those appeals to the higher courts, the governor, the presidents of Harvard and M.I.T., to the Supreme Court of the United States. It is, indeed, the suspiciousness surrounding all that which leads us further.

Why, three weeks after the holdup at South Braintree, were Sacco and Vanzetti arrested on a streetcar in Brockton? True, they had been at a garage to pick up a friend's car, and a getaway car had been used in the robbery, but no one knew what kind of car that was. True, they were both armed when picked up, but they had some reason to be worried for their safety. They were aliens and anarchists, and for months there had been raids carried out by order of Attorney General A. Mitchell Palmer, in which Department of Justice agents all over the country invaded meetings of suspected radicals, broke into homes in the middle of the night, held people incommunicado and without warrants, beat them with clubs and blackjacks.

In Boston, five hundred were arrested, chained together, and marched through the streets. Luigi Galleani, editor of the anarchist paper *Cronaca Sovversiva,* to which Sacco and Vanzetti subscribed, was picked up in Boston and quickly deported.

Something even more frightening had happened. A

fellow anarchist of Sacco and Vanzetti, also a follower of Galleani, a typesetter named Andrea Salsedo, who lived in New York, was kidnapped (the proper word for illegal seizure of a person) by members of the Federal Bureau of Investigation, and held in their offices on the 14th floor of the Park Row Building. He was not allowed to call his family, friends, or a lawyer, and according to a fellow prisoner, he was questioned and beaten. During the eighth week of his imprisonment, on May 3, 1920, the body of Salsedo, smashed to a pulp, was found on the pavement near the Park Row Building, and the Bureau announced that he had committed suicide by jumping from the 14th floor window of the room in which they had kept him. (In 1977, one recalls an incident of the 1950s, disclosed recently: the mysterious death-fall of a scientist named Frank Olson from a 16th story hotel window in New York, after being surreptitiously dosed with LSD by the Central Intelligence Agency.)[3]

It was May 5, 1920, having just learned of Salsedo's death, that Sacco and Vanzetti were found, armed, on a Brockton street car, arrested, and interrogated. They responded to police questions with lies, and these would later, at the trial, be considered as "consciousness of guilt," and would form an important part of the evidence that would send them to the electric chair.

What did the police question them about, and why would they lie? Here is a sample:[4]

> Police: Are you a citizen?
> Sacco: No.
> Police: Are you a Communist?
> Sacco: No.
> Police: Anarchist?
> Sacco: No.
> Police: Do you believe in this government of ours?
> Sacco: Yes. Some things I like different.
> Police: Do you subscribe for literature of the Anarchist party?
> Vanzetti: Sometimes I read them.

Police: How do you get them, through the mail?
Vanzetti: A man gave one to me in Boston.
Police: Who was the man?
Vanzetti: I don't know him.

Were the police intent on finding two robbers, who then turned out to be anarchists? Or two anarchists, who turned out to have enough that was suspicious about their behavior — carrying guns, lying to the police — to make them vulnerable. Conviction would be easy if they were Italians, and almost everyone who placed them far from the scene of the crime on that day — six of seven who testified they saw Sacco in Boston, all of the five who testified they saw Vanzetti in Plymouth — were Italians, speaking in broken English to a totally Anglo-Saxon jury, before an Anglo-Saxon judge who declared his hatred for radicals several times during the trial, outside the courtroom.

It would be helpful, too, if the judge consistently overruled the defense and supported the prosecution, and if he misstated the evidence in summing up the case for the jury, especially on so crucial a question as: did the fatal bullet come from Sacco's gun?[5] Felix Frankfurter, then a professor at Harvard Law School, would describe one of Judge Webster Thayer's opinions as "a farrago of misquotations, misrepresentations, suppressions, and mutilations."[6]

The trial began immediately after Memorial Day, a year and a half after the end of that orgy of death and patriotism that was World War I, the newspapers still vibrating with the roll of drums, the jingo rhetoric. Twelve days into the trial, the press reported the bodies of three soldiers transferred from France to Brockton, the whole town turning out for a patriotic ceremony. All of this was contained in newspapers which the jury could read, only the reports on the trial having been cut out. On the fourth of July, in the midst of the trial, the papers reported a gathering of 5000 veterans of the Yankee Division, in Plymouth.

This mood would be sustained during the crossexaminations of Sacco and Vanzetti by prosecutor Katzmann:[7]

Katzmann (to Sacco): Did you love this country in the last week of May, 1917?

Sacco: That is pretty hard for me to say in one word, Mr. Katzmann.

Katzmann: There are two words you can use, Mr. Sacco, yes or no. Which one is it?

Sacco: Yes.

Katzmann: And in order to show your love for this United States of America when she was about to call upon you to become a soldier you ran away to Mexico?

At no point in the trial did the prosecution establish any motive that Sacco and Vanzetti may have had for the robbery. The stolen money was never found.

It is not hard, however, to establish a motive for the prosecution. After the trial, two long-time agents of the Department of Justice, Weyand and Letherman, gave affidavits saying: "The names of Sacco and Vanzetti were on the files of the Department of Justice as 'radicals to be watched,' the Department was eager for their deportation... the case against Sacco and Vanzetti for murder was part of a collusive effort between the District Attorney and agents of the Department of Justice to rid the country of these Italians because of their Red activities. ... For it was the opinion of the Department of Justice agents that a conviction of Sacco and Vanzetti for murder would be one way of disposing of these men."[8]

The affidavit said a deal was made: federal agents were to help the prosecutor get evidence on the criminal charge, and the prosecutor in turn would try to get information from Sacco and Vanzetti which might help deport their associates. Twelve agents were at one time assigned to the case, and an informer was placed inside the Sacco-Vanzetti Defense Committee.

All of this rings even more true in the 1970s than in the 1920s. We know now, on the basis of F.B.I. records disclosed reluctantly in recent aggressive lawsuits by black and radical groups, that the F.B.I., in its war on radicalism, has resorted to informers and spies, forged letters, thievery, and murder. We know that the F.B.I. collaborated with a local District Attorney in 1969 in planning an armed attack on a Chicago apartment, in which police shot to death two black militant leaders.[9]

Too many defenders of Sacco and Vanzetti are embarrassed by their radicalism and concentrate on the who-done-it? of the robbery-murder. But the determination to get rid of the two anarchists was too persistently fanatical to be an oddity of Boston or Harvard, an unfortunate judicial slip, a prejudice of one person or another. It is best explained by the powerful resolve of the American Establishment after World War I and the Russian Revolution to eliminate all radical threats on the eve of a new and uncertain era in world history. This fear of opposition seems exaggerated to anyone who knows the weakness of revolutionary movements in America, but there is considerable historical evidence that the American power elite with so much at stake — control of the greatest aggregate of wealth and power in the world — takes no chances.

Consider the situation in the United States in 1920, when Sacco and Vanzetti were first arrested on that streetcar in Brockton. Between 1877 and 1914, the nation had experienced the most violent rebellions of working people in the history of the modern state: the railroad uprisings of 1877 (including a take-over of the city of St. Louis), the anarchist-led demonstrations in Chicago in 1886, the Homestead steel strike of 1892, the nationwide Pullman strike of 1894, the victorious Lawrence textile strike of 1912, and, finally, the bloody warfare in the Colorado mine districts in 1914, where federal troops had to be called in after the Ludlow Massacre to control a state-wide insurrection of armed, angry miners.

In the years before the First World War, the Industrial Workers of the World was born — militant, revolutionary, uniting all sorts of workers the system had worked so hard to separate (skilled and unskilled, black and white, native and foreign), resisting vigilantes and police, arousing nationwide attention with its work in the Lawrence strike. In the electoral counterpart of those labor struggles, the Socialist Party, its magazine *Appeal to Reason* read by 500,000 people, was winning a million votes for Eugene Debs as president, and electing socialist officials in hundreds of towns throughout the country.

The concentration of huge fortunes in the hands of large corporations like the Standard Oil Corporation, U.S. Steel Corporation, and the banking house of J.P. Morgan, along with miserable conditions in factories and mines and city slums became especially evident in the early years of the 20th century. This made it easier for socialist and revolutionary movements to grow.

The war in Europe created an opportunity for a patriotic assault on radical movements. Congress legislated, President Wilson signed, the Supreme Court sanctioned, the Justice Department moved, and two thousand dissenters from the war were prosecuted, nine hundred sent to prison. Virtually the entire leadership of the IWW was put on trial and jailed; the socialist and anarchist movements were crippled by jailings and deportations.[10]

With the war over, the repression did not end; indeed, it intensified, for in the meantime the Bolsheviks had taken power in Russia. Also, there were revolutionary movements in Germany, Hungary, and Italy. The post-war atmosphere was full of fear of communism, of anarchism.

Had not this atmosphere cooled between 1920 (the trial of Sacco and Vanzetti) and 1927 (their execution)? Somewhat. But by now the case was a national cause, an international issue. It had become a test of will, of class strength. We'll show them! "Did you see what I did with those anarchist bastards the other day? That will hold them for a while." (The words of Judge Thayer, spoken at a Dartmouth football game after he had turned down a defense motion for a new trial, quoted in an affidavit by Dartmouth Professor James Richardson.)

The American system keeps control not only by a lottery of rewards (only a few make it, but everyone has a chance), but also by a lottery of punishments (only a few are put away or killed, but it's better to play it safe, be quiet). The determination to get a few obscure Communists, or a few obscure Italian anarchists, only becomes comprehensible as part of such a system, a scheme only partly understood by those who carry it out, but with the accumulation of more than enough parts to make the plan whole. What is perhaps not seen at all by the jury, and only dimly by the prosecutor, is seen more clearly by Governor Fuller, the wealthy auto dealer, and Lowell, the textile millionaire president of Harvard.

Upton Sinclair wrote *Boston* in nine months, in what seems like a barely-controlled anger, right after the execution of Sacco and Vanzetti in August, 1927. He had become famous twenty years before, instantaneously, when his exposé of the Chicago stockyards, the novel *The Jungle*,* appeared serialized in the socialist magazine *Appeal to Reason*, and then, within a few months of its publication as a book, became a national success and was reprinted in seventeen translations all over the world. *The Jungle* influenced Bertolt Brecht's play *Saint Joan of the Stockyards*, was praised by George Bernard Shaw in England, and in America by the feminist Charlotte Perkins Gilman and the socialist Eugene Debs. It became the prime example of "muckraking" literature for generations of Americans.

Sinclair went on from *The Jungle* to become one of the most productive and widely read American writers in the history of the country. Before his death in 1968, at the age of ninety, he had written ninety books and thousands of articles. His correspondence (collected at the Lilly Library of Indiana University) totaled 250,000 letters to and from people all over the world, famous and obscure.[11]

Born in Baltimore of southern parents, his father an itinerant, heavy-drinking salesman, his mother the proper puritanical daughter of a minor railroad official, Sinclair grew up in vermin-infested boarding houses in Baltimore, and then, after the age of ten, in dingy rooms in Manhattan. He learned about class differences first-hand by observing the financial manipulations of a banker uncle. He was on his own at seventeen, already writing professionally. He

* Available in hardcover from Robert Bentley, Inc.

went to City College and Columbia, taught himself French, German, and Italian, and, early on, read the anarchist poet Shelley.

He first turned to socialism in his early twenties, when he met socialists, and began reading books like Kropotkin's *Mutual Aid,* Veblen's *Theory of the Leisure Class,* Edward Bellamy's utopian novel *Looking Backward,* and Jack London's *People of the Abyss.* His own writing was always incorrigibly political. His dissections of the educational system, the press, the arts, the politics of oil (his novel *Oil!* was banned in Boston, oddly enough, for its mild sex passages rather than for its outrageous political viewpoint), were intended to bury capitalism under a barrage of facts, and to present socialism in a way that Americans could accept.

Sinclair was something of an activist, too. He was arrested in New York in 1914 for picketing Rockefeller's office after the Ludlow Massacre (the burning to death of eleven children and two women in a miners' tent colony after a machine-gun attack by the Rockefeller-controlled National Guard). And in 1923 he was arrested for reading the First Amendment to striking IWW transport workers in San Pedro, California.

In 1922, after the trial of Sacco and Vanzetti, during the period of endless motions and appeals, Sinclair visited Vanzetti in Charlestown Prison. Perhaps this was the beginning of that thinking process which led to *Boston.* Certainly, the portrait of Vanzetti in the novel is more poignant, more textured, than can be found anywhere in the literature on the case, except in the letters that Vanzetti and Sacco wrote from prison. I cannot resist quoting something Vanzetti (still trying to master the English language) wrote, which suggests as much about him as it does about Sacco:

> Sacco is a heart, afaith, a character, a man; a man lover of nature and mankind. A man who gave all, who sacrifice all to the cause of Liberty and to his love for mankind; money, rest, mundain ambition, his ownwife, his children, himself and his own life...

Oh, yes, I may be more witfull, as some have put it, I am a better babbler than he is, but many, many times in hearing his heartful voice ringing a faith sublime, in considering his supreme sacrifice, remembering his heroism I felt small small at the presence of his greatness and found myself compelled to fight back from my eyes the tears, quanch my heart trobling to my throat to not weep before him — this man called thief and assassin and doomed.[12]

When, seven years after that visit to Vanzetti, Sinclair began to write *Boston*, just after the executions, he chose to tell the story through a sixty-year-old grandmother. Perhaps he was impelled by his own experience with women. His first marriage was a failure. He seemed unable to give his wife, Meta Fuller, the passionate love she wanted, and they were divorced. It was Meta who read Charlotte Perkins Gilman's *Women and Economics* and gave it to him, after which he went on to Bebel's *Women and Socialism* and the writings of Havelock Ellis. While this did not make him an ideal husband and father to their son, it made him conscious of the subjugation of women, and he later became a strong supporter of feminist programs, including birth control and pay for housewives.

Sinclair's heroine in *Boston* is Cornelia Thornwell, who deserts her Brahmin-banker family to live with poor Italians, work in a factory, walk a picket line, become a friend of Vanzetti. She becomes totally involved in the case. Such a heroine, improbable as she is, makes the book a pioneering literary work. Its feminist impulse is clear, through Cornelia Thornwell, who walks a wide arc around her proper daughter to embrace her radical granddaughter, thinking, saying: "What was the reason women were always bound by fear? Because they were afraid! Why were they obedient? Because they obeyed!"

We are a bit uneasy with such a person — the kind of patronizing blue-blood-sympathizer-with-red-causes it is easy to poke fun at. But there is wisdom in the device, because through Cornelia's family connections, Sinclair can show us the Brahmins of Boston and America, their opulence as owners, their poverty as people, compared to the family of Beltrando Brini, with whom Cornelia lives.

Of course, there is simplification and romanticization, beneath which rests an undeniable truth about the effects of a capitalist culture on both its beneficiaries and its victims. In one of Sinclair's brilliant juxtapositions, he contrasts Nicola Sacco and Elbert H. Gary, chairman of the board of directors of the U.S. Steel Corporation. As Sacco and Vanzetti were awaiting execution, the press reported that Gary had died, and left a dying message for his loved ones, his last will and testament:

> I earnestly request my wife and children and descendants that they steadfastly decline to sign any bonds or obligations of any kind as surety for any other person, or persons; that they refuse to make any loans except on the basis of first-class, well-known securities, and that they invariably decline to invest in any untried or doubtful securities of property or enterprise or business.*

As Sinclair puts it: "At this same time, two anarchist wops, one of them an avowed atheist, the other a vague deist of the old-fashioned sort, were writing their last words to their beloved ones." Nicola Sacco wrote to his son, Dante:

> So, Son, instead of crying, be strong, so as to be able to comfort your mother.... take her for a long walk in the quiet country, gathering wild flowers here and there, resting under the shade of trees, between the harmony of the vivid stream and the gentle tranquility of the mother nature, and I am sure that she will enjoy this very much.... But remember always, Dante, in the play of happiness, don't you use all for yourself only.... help the persecuted and the victim because they are your better friends.... In this struggle of life you will find more love and you will be loved.*

Observing the Thornwell family up close, and the Brini family up close, Upton Sinclair shows us America in the way it does not want to be seen, as a class society, its poli-

* page 672

tics as class politics, its justice as class justice. It is an old-fashioned view, obscured and complicated today by the material and ideological possessions of middle-class America, and yet still fundamentally true.

In the midst of the Sacco-Vanzetti case, a wealthy man in Milton, south of Boston, shot and killed a man who was gathering firewood on his property. He spent eight days in jail, then was let out on bail, and was not prosecuted; the district attorney called it "justifiable homicide." Upton Sinclair reports it in *Boston*, but it could be a news item from any period in American history, including our own.

When *Boston* came out in 1928, some reviewers, while admiring it as "propaganda," scorned it as art. But most praised it. The *New York Times* called it "a literary achievement.... full of sharp observation and savage characterization...." The chairman of the Pulitzer Prize Committee of 1928 said later that *Boston* would have received the prize were it not for its "socialistic tendencies" and "special pleading." (When Sinclair did finally win a Pulitzer Prize in 1943, for the third of his eleven "Lanny Budd" novels, *Dragon's Teeth*, it was for a rather toothless novel about a heroic world wanderer, offspring of a munitions maker and a beauty queen, an art dealer, secret agent, sexual and political adventurer, a kind of left-of-center James Bond who waded through the mud of international politics with clean strides, a man not likely to consort with the likes of stockyard worker Jurgis Rudkus of *The Jungle*, or the fish peddler Vanzetti in *Boston*.)

Boston, along with *The Jungle*, is generally considered to be among Sinclair's best novels. He had not the literary gifts of a John Steinbeck, who combined verbal artistry with political passion. But he was a compelling storyteller, and he has his moments of real eloquence. Against so many contemporary novelists, bubbly with style, cynical about human possibility, pretentiously psychological, and ultimately empty, the power of Upton Sinclair's protest in *Boston*, the clarity of his viewpoint, seem refreshingly healthy.

George Bernard Shaw wrote Sinclair from England, praising his artistry in recreating historical fact:

> I have regarded you, not as a novelist, but as a historian; for it is my considered opinion, unshaken at 85, that records of fact are not history. They are only annals, which cannot become historical until the artist-poet-philosopher rescues them from the unintelligible chaos of their actual occurrence and arranges them in works of art.... When people ask me what has happened in my long lifetime I do not refer them to the newspaper files and to the authorities, but to your novels.[13]

Boston does not fit orthodox library categories, which insist on the boundary between fiction and non-fiction. It is a history of the Sacco-Vanzetti case truer than the court transcript, more real than any non-fiction account, precisely because it goes beyond the immediate events of the case to bring the reader close to the historical furnace in which the case was forged, to the atmosphere in the country breathed in by all participants, despite the closed doors of the courtroom, judge's chambers, and jury room, poisoning the verdict. It puts the straight lines of neutral type in the lawbooks under a microscope, where they show up as rows of trenches in the war of class against class.

It may be objected that it is a distortion of the facts to go outside the record of the case to the record of the system. But why should the historian who really seeks the truth about an event recapitulate the strictures of the courtroom, which focuses only on "the facts," scrupulously keeps out the "irrelevant" and then places in charge of determining the facts and judging what is relevant a black-robed agent of the system.

The greatness of *Boston*, in distinction to all the books arguing the guilt or innocence of Sacco and Vanzetti, is that it raises a far more important question: the guilt or innocence of the system of economics, politics, and culture which created factories like the Slater and Morrill shoe factory at South Braintree, millionaires like the Lowells and the Fullers, robbers like the Morelli gang (which may have done the job at South Braintree) and radicals like Sacco and Vanzetti, and lets them all loose, in a war to the death, where the rich control the armaments of bullet and law.

With such a view of the case, expectations of "justice" become as naive as expectations of winning at roulette, for in both cases, while there are exceptions, to keep the suckers coming, the structure of the game insures that everyone will be kept in place. If a case like that of Sacco and Vanzetti is seen, not as an objective weighing of evidence, but as an instance of the struggle between the classes, then Sacco's insistence from the beginning, waving aside all lawyers' promises and friends' hopes, makes profound sense: "They got us, they will kill us." So does his statement to the court, on sentencing: "I know the sentence will be between two classes, the oppressed class and the rich class.... That is why I am here today on this bench, for having been of the oppressed class."

That viewpoint seems dogmatic, simplistic. Not all court decisions are explained by it. But, lacking a theory to fit *all* cases, Sacco's simple, strong view is surely a better guide to understanding the legal system than one which assumes a contest among equals based on an objective search for truth.

Then on whom can the Saccos and Vanzettis of any era depend, when the judicial system, however frocked to disguise its shape, is made of the same stuff as the larger system to which it connects? Certainly not, Sinclair shows us through Cornelia Thornwell's shattered innocence, on judges, juries, higher courts, governors, committees of notables. Governor Fuller was polite but firm. The intellectual Lowell was calm but unyielding. The Massachusetts Supreme Court, the Justices of the U.S. Supreme Court, Holmes and Brandeis, reacted with coldness, the technicalities falling from their lips like icicles.

Nor could they count on the lawyers and committees for the defense, who depended on legal arguments, on the investigation of facts, always deluding themselves that more facts, better arguments would win, not understanding that this was one of those moments in history when a nation's rulers, feeling insecure, become ruthless. At such moments, the liberal press retreats into cowardly cautiousness. And the customary niceties of free speech and assembly, so proudly paraded before the world as proof of America's goodness, are withdrawn, the permits cancelled for meetings on the Boston Common, and the police called to club and arrest those who gathered in defiance.

At such moments it does no good for an indefatigable investigator, the young lawyer Herbert Ehrmann, to follow up the confession of Sacco and Vanzetti's death-row partner, Madeiros: "I hear by confess to being in the south Braintree shoe company crime and Sacco and Vanzetti was not in said crime. Celestino F. Madeiros," and to find a pile of astounding evidence pointing to the Morelli gang of Providence, Rhode Island.[14]

Vanzetti had the answer. Unless a million Americans were organized, he and his friend Sacco would die. Not legal arguments, only mass action could save them. Not words, but struggles. Not appeals, but demands. Not petitions to the governor, but take-over of the factories. Not lubricating the machinery of a supposedly fair system, to make it work better, but a general strike to bring the machinery to a halt.

That never happened. Thousands demonstrated, marched, protested, not just in Union Square, Boston, Chicago, San Francisco, but in London, Paris, Buenos Aires, South Africa. It wasn't enough. In the 1960s, when a great national movement against the Vietnam war was created, involving millions of people, the vibrations shook some courts, some juries, into acquittals for political defendants. But there was no mass movement for Sacco and Vanzetti.

Still, Vanzetti's idea held. If people struggled, organized, understood that it was not a court case, but an epic encounter, then, even if two men died, something good would come out of it. As Vanzetti told a reporter in the last days, foreseeing the effect: "This is our agony, and our triumph." Indeed, Americans of every generation since that time have learned, and some become more radical, by the recollection of the case of Sacco and Vanzetti.

When Vanzetti was arrested, he had a leaflet in his pocket, advertising a meeting to take place in five days. It is a leaflet that could be distributed today, all over the world, as appropriate now as it was the day of their arrest. It read:

> You have fought all the wars. You have worked for all the capitalists. You have wandered over all the countries. Have you harvested the fruits of your labors, the price of your victories? Does the past comfort you? Does the present smile on you? Does the future promise you anything? Have you found a piece of land where you can live like a human being and die like a human being? On these questions, on this argument and on this theme, the struggle for existence, Bartolomeo Vanzetti will speak.

That meeting did not take place. But Vanzetti did speak, and so did Sacco, over the years of their imprisonment, in their letters, in their legacy, in the literature carrying their message, their spirit forward. As in this book, *Boston*.

Howard Zinn, 1978

Howard Zinn, historian and Professor of Political Science at Boston University, is active in civil rights and anti-war movements. He is the author of *Vietnam: The Logic of Withdrawal, Disobedience and Democracy, The Politics of History*, and other books. He is also the author of a play, *Emma*, about the anarchist-feminist Emma Goldman, produced in Boston in 1977.

Notes

1. Broun's column can be found in his *Collected Edition of Heywood Broun* (Harcourt, 1941). He was fired by the *World* soon after this column appeared. Broun was a marvelous writer, a socialist, and, in

the 1930s, an organizer of the first national union of journalists, the American Newspaper Guild.

2. *Boston Globe,* August 10, 1977.

3. For more information on this and other activities of the C.I.A., see the multi-volume report of the Senate Select Committee on Intelligence (Government Printing Office, 1976).

4. This is drawn from an excellent article on the Sacco-Vanzetti case, "Remembering Sacco and Vanzetti," which appeared in *WIN* magazine, August 4, 1977, written by Rev. Philip Zwerling, Minister of The Community Church of Boston, which helped in the defense of Sacco and Vanzetti.

5. Ballistics experts at the trial disagreed on whether the bullet came from Sacco's gun, and one of them, a Captain William Proctor, later claimed that the prosecution had arranged with him to mislead the jury. It is on the basis of ballistics evidence that Francis Russell, in his book *Tragedy in Dedham* (McGraw-Hill, 1962) pointed the finger of guilt at Sacco (but not Vanzetti). In an article in *The New Republic,* March 2, 1963, Michael A. Musmanno, who had been a young lawyer working for the defense, took apart Russell's evidence, and left nothing standing, certainly not Russell's own credibility.

6. See Felix Frankfurter's book, *The Case of Sacco and Vanzetti* (Little, Brown and Company, 1927), which was based on his article of the same title in the *Atlantic Monthly,* March, 1927.

7. This appears in Volume II of the trial transcript, entitled *The Sacco-Vanzetti Case; Transcript....* which appeared in five volumes and one supplemental volume (Holt, 1928-29). It is reproduced in a book especially rich in all sorts of information, *The Legacy of Sacco and Vanzetti,* by G. Louis Joughin and Edmund M. Morgan (Harcourt, Brace, 1948).

8. See Zwerling article (note 4).

9. See *New York Times,* Sept. 26, 1975, for story of 238 illegal burglaries committed by the F.B.I. from 1942 to 1968, figures released by the Senate Select Committee on Intelligence.

See Volume 6, *Hearings Before the Select Committee to Study Governmental Operations with Respect to Intelligence Activities* for information on the participation of F.B.I. operatives in acts of violence against civil rights workers.

See Volume 4 of the same hearings on illegal mail openings by the F.B.I.

See Book II of the Final Report of the same Committee, p. 212, in which the Committee concludes that the F.B.I. "secretly took the law into its own hands . . . to act outside the legal process altogether and to covertly disrupt, discredit and harass groups of individuals." This was in the COINTELPRO (Counterintelligence Program). On p. 139, the report says: "The abusive techniques used by the F.B.I. in COINTELPRO from 1956 to 1971 included violations of both federal and state statutes prohibiting mail fraud, wire fraud, incitement to violence, sending obscene material through the mail, and extortion."

On F.B.I. forgeries of letters, see the *New York Times*, October 6, 1975, reporting on newly-disclosed documents in a Socialist Workers Party suit against the government.

On p. 141 of the Church Committee's Final Report, Book 2, there is the report of "black bag jobs" by the F.B.I., what the committee called "warrantless break-ins."

The *New York Times*, January 11, 1976, carries a report, based on information "placed on the public record or gathered by the Senate Select Committee on Intelligence," in which an F.B.I. informant said that agents of the F.B.I. had instructed him to kill a San Diego economics professor and radical activist named Peter Bohmer.

The *New York Times*, Sunday, May 9, 1976, tells of a report to the Senate Committee in which the F.B.I., according to the report, "pointed with pride" to its involvement in "shootings, beatings and a high degree of unrest . . . in the ghetto area of southeast San Diego."

A *New York Times* dispatch of July 11, 1976, based on government sources, reported that F.B.I. agents had committed "widespread acts of unauthorized lawlessness, including the burning of automobiles, assaults and illegal wiretapping, while conducting internal security investigations in the last five years . . . ."

See *New York Times* March 13, 1975, and May 25, 1975, for stories of depositions in a civil suit in Chicago which revealed that the F.B.I.

had supplied a floor plan to Chicago police of the apartment in which Fred Hampton and Mark Clark, two Black Panther leaders lived, shortly before the police attacked the apartment in a pre-dawn raid and killed the two men, Hampton as he lay on his bed.

10. For a fascinating account of this period see Murray Levin, *The Politics of Hysteria* (Basic Books, 1972).

11. My biographical information on Upton Sinclair comes mostly from Leon Harris, *Upton Sinclair: American Rebel* (Crowell, 1975).

12. From *The Legacy of Sacco and Vanzetti*, p. 468-469 by Joughlin and Morgan.

13. From *Upton Sinclair: American Rebel* by Leon Harris.

14. It is an exciting story that Herbert Ehrmann tells in his book *The Untried Case: The Sacco-Vanzetti Case and the Morelli Gang* (Vanguard Press, 1933).

Reading List

Ehrmann, Herbert B. *The Case That Will Not Die: Commonwealth Vs. Sacco and Vanzetti.* Boston: Little, Brown and Company, 1969.

Ehrmann, Herbert B. *The Untried Case: The Sacco-Vanzetti Case and the Morelli Gang.* New York: Vanguard Press, Inc., 1933.

Feuerlicht, Roberta Strauss. *Justice Crucified: The Story of Sacco and Vanzetti.* New York: McGraw Hill, 1977.

Frankfurter, Felix. *The Case of Sacco and Vanzetti.* Boston: Little, Brown and Company, 1927.

Frankfurter, Marion D., and Jackson, Gardner, eds. *The Letters of Sacco and Vanzetti.* New York: Octagon Books, 1971.

Joughin, G. Louis, and Morgan, Edmund *The Legacy of Sacco and Vanzetti.* New York: Harcourt, Brace, 1948.

Levin, Murray. *The Politics of Hysteria.* New York: Basic Books, Inc., 1972.

Lowenthal, Max. *The Federal Bureau of Investigation.* Westport, Connecticut: Greenwood Press, Inc., 1971.

Sacco and Vanzetti Chronology

April 15, 1920	Murders of Berardelli and Parmenter at South Braintree.
April 17, 1920	Inquest at Quincy with regard to South Braintree murders.
May 5, 1920	Arrest of Sacco and Vanzetti.
May 6, 1920	Interview of Sacco and Vanzetti by District Attorney Katzmann.
September 11, 1920	Indictment of Sacco and Vanzetti for South Braintree murders.
May 31-July 14, 1921	Trial of Sacco and Vanzetti at Dedham before Judge Webster Thayer.
November 5, 1921	Motion for new trial as against the weight of the evidence argued before Judge Thayer.
November 8, 1921	First supplementary motion for new trial filed.
December 24, 1921	Motion for new trial as against the weight of evidence denied.
May 4, 1922	Second supplementary motion filed.
July 22, 1922	Third supplementary motion filed.
September 11, 1922	Fourth supplementary motion filed.
April 30, 1923	Fifth supplementary motion filed.
October 1, 1923	Supplement to first motion filed.
October 1-3, 1923 November 1, 2, 8, 1923	All five supplementary motions argued before Judge Thayer.
November 5, 1923	Motion relating to Proctor affidavit filed.
October 1, 1924	Decisions by Judge Thayer denying all motions.
November 18, 1925	Madeiros confesses to South Braintree murders and exonerates Sacco and Vanzetti.
January 11-13, 1926	Argument of appeal of Sacco and Vanzetti from conviction and from denial of first, second and fifth supplementary motions.

May 12, 1926	Conviction of Sacco and Vanzetti affirmed by Supreme Judicial Court.
May 26, 1926	Motion for new trial based on Madeiros statement filed.
September 13-17, 1926	Madeiros motion argued before Judge Thayer
October 23, 1926	Decision by Judge Thayer denying Madeiros motion.
January 27-28, 1927	Appeal from denial of Madeiros motion argued before Supreme Judicial Court.
April 5, 1927	Denial of Madeiros motion affirmed by Supreme Judicial Court.
April 9, 1927	Sentence of death imposed by Judge Thayer on Sacco and Vanzetti.
May 3, 1927	Petition for clemency addressed to Governor Fuller.
June 1, 1927	Advisory Lowell Committee appointed by Governor Fuller.
July 11-21, 1927	Hearings held before Advisory Committee.
August 3, 1927	Decision by Governor Fuller denying clemency.
August 10, 1927	Petition for writ of habeas corpus denied by Justice Holmes of the United States Supreme Court, and by Judge Anderson of the United States District Court.
August 19, 1927	Exceptions overruled by Supreme Judicial Court.
August 20,1927	Petition for writ of habeas corpus denied by Judge Morton of the United States Circuit Court of Appeals.
August 20,1927	Petition for stay and extension of time in which to apply to the United States Supreme Court for writ of certiorari denied by Justice Holmes of the United States Supreme Court.
August 22, 1927	Similar petition denied by Justice Stone of the United States Supreme Court.
August 23, 1927	Sacco and Vanzetti and Madeiros executed in Charlestown Prison.

AUTHOR'S PREFACE

The decision to write this novel was taken at nine-thirty P.M. (Pacific Coast time), August 22nd, 1927: the occasion being the receipt of a telephone message from a newspaper, to the effect that Sacco and Vanzetti were dead. It seemed to the writer that the world would want to know the truth about this case; and his judgment proved correct, because there began a flood of cablegrams and letters from five continents, asking him to do the very thing he had decided upon.

A "contemporary historical novel" is an unusual art-form, and may call for explanation. So far as concerns the two individuals, Nicola Sacco and Bartolomeo Vanzetti, this book is not fiction, but an effort at history; everything they are represented as doing they actually did, and their words have been taken from their letters, or from the dictation of friends and enemies. All others who played important parts in this drama likewise appear as they were, and under their own names.

Paralleling the Sacco-Vanzetti case throughout the book is a story of business and high finance which will be recognized as a famous law case recently carried to the United States Supreme Court. I have used the incidents of this case as material for my fiction; but the characters which I have invented to enact this story are wholly fictitious, and bear no relation whatever to the real persons in the case, who are entirely unknown to me. There is one simple rule for guidance in reading the novel: the characters who are real persons bear real names, while those who bear fictitious names are fictitious characters.

The writer has been visiting Boston off and on for twenty-five years. The first visits had to do with the novel "Manassas," and involved meetings with the city's old-time heroes, such as Thomas Wentworth Higginson, Frank B. Sanborn, Julia Ward Howe. The later visits, having to do with "The Brass Check," "The Goose-step" and "Oil!", involved a change of view-point not without its interest to students of our history. Nevertheless, it should be said at the outset that what is great in Boston finds due recognition in this story. Those who have made the city's glory have never been its rulers, but always a "saving minority," and that minority is there to-day, and it is active.

The task has not been approached in a spirit of grudge; on the contrary, the writer regards with a mixture of gratitude and amusement those Boston officials who provided for "Oil!" an advertisement which went around the world several times. To them he owes the fact that he is almost out of debt to his printer, for the first time in twenty-five years as publisher of his own writings. An honest effort has here been made to portray a complex community exactly as it is. The story has no hero but the truth, and its heroines are two women, one old and the other young, who are ardently seeking the truth.

The complete legal record of the Sacco-Vanzetti case is soon to be published in six volumes. I would have checked by this record every statement having to do with legal proceedings, but unfortunately a few documents were not accessible at the time of writing. I had the 3,900 pages of the Dedham trial testimony, but the Plymouth trial testimony, of which only one copy existed, was withheld from me. I have checked my narrative by many documents derived from the record, and had the manuscript read by a dozen persons who have made an eight-year study of the case. I have omitted every statement concerning which doubt has been voiced, and the story contains no errors of any real significance. It so happens that the important thing in connection with the Sacco-Vanzetti case is to know, not what a certain witness testified, but how he came to testify at all. Those who read my story attentively will get the meaning of this remark.

I wish to make clear that I have not written a brief for the Sacco-Vanzetti defense. I have tried to be a historian. What I think I know, I have told the reader. What is uncertain, I have so portrayed—and have let the partisans of both sides voice their feelings and beliefs. My book will not satisfy either side completely; both have already expressed dissent—which I take to mean that I have done my job.

I desire to acknowledge my great indebtedness to James Fuchs and Floyd Dell for valuable literary criticism, and to many Bostonians and ex-Bostonians for advice and help. So many of these prefer to have their thanks in private that I confine myself to this general acknowledgment. Also I owe apology to persons active in the Sacco-Vanzetti case, whose letters and adventures I have purloined and assigned to my fictitious characters. Extraordinary adventures—let no one say that romance is gone from the world! Also, let no fiction-writer imagine that his powers of invention can rival those of the Great Novelist who makes up history!

I think I should add that "Cornelia," the heroine of this story, is a lady eighty-six years of age, an old friend of mine, who ran away from her family at the age of sixty as I have described. But this lady never had anything to do with the Sacco-Vanzetti case, and my character, "Cornelia," bears no relation to any of the ladies who interested themselves in that case.

BOSTON

CHAPTER 1

THE RUNAWAY GRANDMOTHER

I

It was the parlor-maid who found Old Josiah in the morning, seated at his desk, his head fallen forward upon his arms. He might have been asleep, but his dinner-coat told her that he had not been to bed. She stood in the door-way, whispering his name feebly; then she fled to Addicks, the butler, who was privileged to make intrusions. He touched his master's hand and found that it was cold. So Cornelia Thornwell was awakened and told of her release.

She had had a right to expect it many years ago. Now that it had come, it seemed too late. Fright seized her, an indescribable sense of loneliness. What would life be like, without a husband to direct it? How would her grandchildren know what to do, without Josiah to incarnate the Thornwell tradition?

But she must not show emotion to servants. She slipped into her dressing-gown and came down to her husband's study. "Call Dr. Morrow," she said to the man. "And then notify Mr. James or Miss Clara." Her youngest daughter, wife of James Scatterbridge, lived upon the estate, in a house just visible through the distant trees. At this hour Clara would be getting her brood of seven started on the day, and James would be dressing for his work at the mills. Both would drop everything and hurry over to relieve Cornelia of care.

The daughter arrived in three or four minutes; very emotional, as always—it seemed as if she had come to be one more of the large brood she was raising. She was growing continually in bulk, as they did; she was chattering as eagerly as they, and her mind, like theirs, would fly from one small topic to the next.

1

But she had a strong sense of what was proper, and was shocked to discover no tears in her mother's eyes.

James Scatterbridge came with her. He ordered the body taken upstairs and called up his two brothers-in-law and gave the news; then he came to Cornelia. "Now, Mother, you are not to worry about the practical details. We'll attend to it all." James was solidly made, both in body and mind; a plain-looking and plain-thinking business man, with nothing of what he called "frills." He ran the great cotton-mills in the valley below them, and a little thing like a funeral presented no difficulties to his mind. "I'll notify Hobson, the undertakers; also, there will be the press to see to." He moved away; and Clara, drying her tears, started off upon the subject of a dressmaker for her mother's mourning costume and her own.

Such things had to be attended to, Cornelia realized. "But, Clara, I'm not going to wear a veil."

"Oh, Mother! Whoever heard of such a thing!" Clara's large china-blue eyes grew even larger and rounder with dismay.

"I am not going to be a Hindoo widow and jump on the funeral pyre."

"Mother, don't start making jokes! You of all people cannot afford to be eccentric."

"Why, my dear?"

"Because everybody knows you weren't happy with Father— you didn't really love him."

"Because I didn't really love him, must I pretend that I did?"

"But Mother, we don't want to set everybody talking! Surely you owe him one last tribute!"

The telephone rang in Cornelia's room. It was her oldest daughter, Deborah. "Mother, Henry and I will be right over. We'll be there in an hour, and meantime I want to make sure nothing is done about practical arrangements."

"How do you mean, dear?"

"I mean the funeral."

"James said he would notify Hobson's."

"Oh, Mother, how perfectly atrocious! Don't you know that nobody has Hobson's?"

"I don't know anything about it, Deborah."

"Well, I do think we ought to be allowed to manage our own

father's funeral without having our in-laws take everything out of our hands! Clara has no more taste than a sack of potatoes, and she lets James run her, and put the stamp of his commonness on everything in our lives. Won't you please see to it that those undertakers don't get into the house?"

"My dear," said Cornelia, "I shall follow my usual policy of letting my children do their own disputing." And she hung up the receiver.

It was not merely a matter of the social standing of undertakers, she realized; it was a deep-seated, bitter quarrel among her children, never to be assuaged. Deborah and Alice, the two oldest, considered that the husband of Clara had robbed them of their patrimony, and that Clara had compounded the felony by failing to make his life miserable. Originally the Thornwell mills had been Thornwell; established by Josiah's father and extended by the son, with James Scatterbridge an employee of low standing. But James had forced his way to the front, and after the panic of 1907, when a reorganization had been necessary, it had been he who possessed the confidence of the directors and bankers. So now a great block of shares, instead of being a family inheritance, were tucked away in James's safety-vaults.

Nor had the ex-employee helped matters by marrying the youngest daughter; that was a scandal, which the world would never forget. Three generations from now, you would hear whisperings at Boston dinner-tables: "Oh, but, my dear, don't you know that story? The original Scatterbridge was a clerk in the plant and he got all the stock away from them, and they had to marry him to get it back!"

It was not as if the other two sons-in-law had needed the money. Rupert Alvin was a banker who counted the year a failure if he had not added a million to his fortune; and Cornelia had heard Henry Cabot Winters boast that his law firm never had less than twenty-five millions in litigation. But apparently this money game was one in which it was not possible to be satisfied. Rupert and Henry, who composed a team, would have liked to take in Jerry Walker's felt-plants and the Thornwell cotton-mills, each in one bite. They had their "lines" on so many other properties that Cornelia could not keep track of them; the names were to her like those of ancient battles, famous in story, but which she had never looked up on a map.

II

Dr. Morrow came; the pink of fashion, rosy-faced and silver-haired, with sharply trimmed, dapper white mustaches. His manner reminded you that good breeding asserts superiority to every weakness of mortality. He went to the big four-poster bed, felt the cold hands, listened for the non-existent heart-beats, and then turned to the widow. "Well, Cornelia, old Josiah had fourteen years more than the Bible promised him. So we can't complain." He knew there had been no love between them.

Hearing the verdict, the efficient James instructed Josiah's secretary to notify the papers. Some went to press early, and would need time to handle this important story. The secretary would begin with the *Transcript,* the family organ of all the families that "count" in Massachusetts. The mischievously-minded assert that mortality records show a great increase upon Fridays, due to desire of the socially elect to appear in Saturday's obituary columns.

Meantime the efficient James was closeted in Josiah's study with the efficient head of the Hobson undertaking establishment, and these two were learning to understand each other. It was to be a great funeral, a matter of state, which would mean prestige and advertising to the concern which secured the contract. The family was wealthy, and would pay for the best, but there must be a distinct understanding that they were to get what they paid for. Mr. Hobson listened politely and replied that he understood Mr. Scatterbridge's position perfectly. There was no reason why a funeral should not be dealt with as any other matter of business; and certainly his firm appreciated the importance of social prestige and would be prepared to adjust its price accordingly. After which he produced a portfolio about caskets, revealing that there were art-modeled items of burnished bronze for which it was possible to pay from twenty-five thousand up. James Scatterbridge gulped once and composed his features, and did not reveal his plebeian astonishment.

Meantime Deborah Thornwell Alvin was descending from her limousine, tall and stiff, always ready for a funeral, because she dressed in black, with only a touch of white at the neck and a double necklace of white pearls. She had her father's lean and stern features, and had served as his deputy in keeping the family traditions in effect. As soon as she was in the house she began objecting in decorous whispers; and presently there arrived her sister, Alice, her ally in war on the Scatterbridge clan. Who had given James authority to bring those vulgar Hobson people into the case? Who had taken the responsibility to rush the family into print, from who could tell what cheap and sensational angle?

"Mother," said Deborah, "do you know anything about Father's will?"

"Nothing, my child; he never spoke of it to me in his life."

"We're going to find, of course, that James has got this house and the land. You know he took a mortgage on it when Father lost his money in the New Haven jam."

"Let me remind you, Mother," put in Alice. "Father promised me my pick of the old furniture. He knew I was the only one that appreciated it—he told me that again and again."

"Yes, my dear. I hope he put it into the will."

"I can only say this, if James and Clara get that Mayflower cradle that I was rocked in, they may bury me in it." Alice Thornwell Winters's fair blonde features were set in a look which her beauty-specialists would have deplored, because it made sharp lines on each side of her mouth. Alice was the adventurous one of the family, going in for costly culture, inviting poets and artists and people of that dubious sort to her home. She had been painted several times and hung in exhibitions, and had learned to regard herself as a work of art, a feature of the social landscape. The fact that she could appreciate the old treasures of the family was a moral reason for a family quarrel: something which Boston quarrels require.

III

If Cornelia had realized the previous night that she was hearing her husband's last words, no doubt she would have paid more attention. There is a certain importance attaching to finality as such, even when it applies to the words of a man who has been your husband for forty years, and whose every mental reaction is known to you in advance.

Cornelia had been reading about the destruction of the Rheims cathedral; there was an engraving of it among the works of art she had brought back from her honeymoon, and she had gone into her husband's study, and seated herself upon a hassock, and begun rummaging in the drawers of a chest which had belonged to Great-grandfather Thornwell, holding the records of his ships in the East India trade. In a drawer bearing in faded gold letters the label, "Sylph of the Sea," she had found the portfolio of engravings and sat turning them over for an hour or two.

And meantime Josiah was conversing with Rupert Alvin,— oldest of his sons-in-law. They paid no more attention to Cornelia than if she had been a mouse. They were talking about Jerry Walker and his felt-business; and Cornelia, even while thinking about cathedrals, could not help catching the drift of their remarks. Jerry Walker had been an errand boy in an institution of which Cornelia had been a patroness; and now it appeared that he was on the way to monopolizing the felt-business of New England. Rupert Alvin, who ran the Pilgrim National Bank, objected to monopolies in the hands of other people, and was of the opinion that Jerry was dangerously impulsive—he had paid over a million dollars for the Atlas hat-works, while Rupert was in the midst of making up his mind whether the concern was good for a small loan.

Cornelia glanced at her son-in-law, who sat very straight, as he always did, in the big leather armchair; his dinner-coat bulging, his tucked shirt-front puffed out, so that he looked like a black and white pouter-pigeon. Rupert's face ran to bulges: his forehead a great pink bulge, with two minor ones over the eyes, his cheeks half a dozen rosy-red bulges, and his neck and chins a number of bigger and redder ones. To Cornelia there was something comical in his indignation that some one else had dared to think more quickly than he. But that was the kind of thought she had spent forty years learning to keep to herself.

Josiah gave his decision, in his old man's voice that was beginning to crack. Jerry Walker might break himself some day, but not now; these were the days to buy anything at any price; hats were necessary to armies and felt slippers were worn in hospitals. That led them to the subject which all men of affairs were discussing in this summer of 1915. Josiah repeated his well-known opinion that it would be a long war and that it was the part of wisdom to buy and buy. Cornelia sat thinking of human lives while they were thinking of money.

Rupert was of the opinion that the war couldn't last over the year, because the warring nations were heading for bankruptcy. But Josiah told him not to worry; we would lend them the money, provided they spent it for our goods. How would we get the money back? And Josiah said we wouldn't have to get it back—it would be like Jerry Walker's felt-business. "When Jerry can't pay what he owes us we'll take over his plants."

Cornelia got up, carrying her engraving. "Good-night," she said, and they answered in a perfunctory way; and that would have been the end of it if she had been the right sort of a wife. But she could not resist the impulse to stop in front of her son-in-law and remark, "It'll be fine, Rupert, when we can bring Europe up to date." Rupert, a practical-minded man, assented; and Cornelia held up the picture of the cathedral. "We can widen out this Angel Tower and make it the branch office of Jerry Walker's felt-plants."

For forty years, even during the two that Josiah Quincy Thornwell had been governor of the Commonwealth, Cornelia had been saying things like this, and some people had found it roguish. But never Josiah; always he would frown, and remark, as now, "Your sense of humor is untimely, Cornelia." She put her hand lightly on the top of his white wig and said, "Some day, my husband, you will tell me the proper time for my sense of humor."

So she tripped out, the little old lady who had seen so much that was funny in this big household that the wrinkles around her eyes had got set in a pattern of laughter. Not even the destruction of the Rheims cathedral, not even the thought of the peasant-boys in the trenches, could wipe out her amusement at the moral impulse of Boston, which was driving Rupert Alvin to take charge of Jerry Walker's felt-business, and likewise of the geography and finance of Europe. Her last thought was "He'll do both those things." And, in his own time and at his own convenience, he did.

IV

In the offices of half a dozen evening papers the "rewrite" men had dug out a column or two of copy which had waited for thirty years, being brought up to date every year or two. They

inserted at the top the information that Josiah Quincy Thornwell, twice governor of the Commonwealth of Massachusetts,
leading manufacturer and philanthropist, for twenty years a
member of the Republican State Committee, had been found that
morning dead at his desk in the family home in the town of
Thornwell, the probable cause being heart failure. The more
sensational papers added how the body had been found by a
parlor-maid; the sort of thing for which Deborah would hold
James Scatterbridge responsible. Also they said that the
funeral services would be held at Trinity Church, Boston—
whereas Deborah and Alice were determined that they should
be at the family home, so that the undesirables might be excluded.

Upstairs in the ex-governor's apartments Mr. Hobson's shirt-
sleeved assistants were spreading their rubber-sheets and placing two tables end to end, at the same time listening to their
employer set forth his conviction, that "ninety percent of this
business is psychology. You meet a hard-boiled guy like that one
downstairs and you have to let him talk himself out, and then
he's ashamed of himself and you can do what you want with him.
After all, what does he know about funerals and how a swell one
ought to be conducted?"

And at the same time in Cornelia's sitting-room Deborah and
Alice had brought up the subject of the Shah of Persia's rug.
"It really is my property," Deborah was saying. "I only left it
in the house because I knew Father liked to have the heirlooms
all together. For years I have seen to the cleaning of it every
spring and sent a servant to make sure it was safe. You know
that is true."

"Yes, of course," said Alice.

"And now if James and Clara think they are going to move in
and let their children trample it—"

Cornelia went downstairs and met Great-uncle Abner, Josiah's
youngest brother; Abner Quincy Thornwell, burly and slow-
moving, stoop-shouldered and very deaf. Like many thus af-
flicted, he considered it necessary to hear his own voice. "Well,
Cornelia," he boomed, "well, well—so it has come at last! A
hard day for you, I know! We'll stand back of you, my dear.
Anything I can do?" There was a look of concern on his bland
and rosy countenance—something that happened rarely, for he

gave most of his time to chess and would sit for hours lost in a problem.

Clara appeared, and greeted her uncle. When he asked her what he could do, she shouted into his ear, "Make Mother wear a veil."

"Veil?" said Abner. "Of course she'll wear a veil! Aren't veils made for widows?"

"Mother doesn't care, she wants to advertise to the world that she isn't grieving. I don't believe she has shed a single tear."

Said Cornelia, "I have read that moving picture actresses make tears out of glycerine. Perhaps I may do that for the funeral."

"Oh, Mother, how can you say such horrid things?" Clara began wiping real tears from her nose and her uncle peered from one to the other, with the uneasiness of the deaf. "Glycerine?" said he. "I hear it cures cancer, but I don't know if it's true. What did Josiah die of?"

"Dr. Morrow called it heart failure."

"Heart failure, hey? Well, that's respectable enough. Where is he, up in his room? Poor old boy! But he had a long life, and he got what he wanted."

He ambled off, and Cornelia found herself escorted into the library for a formal conference with James Scatterbridge. This son-in-law did not possess the worldly art of concealing his purposes, but had to come directly to the point, like a business man. "Mother, I suppose you haven't had time to think what you are going to do, but I want to be the first to tell you that you'll be welcome to live with Clara and me. Nothing will give us greater pleasure, and we'll do everything we can to make it the same as your own home. Things will stay just as the governor loved to have them."

The meaning of that was plain enough: Deborah and Alice were right in their fears! "I suppose, James," she said, "this house will come to you?"

"It is already mine, Mother. The governor gave me a deed several years ago. You know how his New Haven stock went all to pieces; and the money I advanced to him was more than the place was worth. The governor felt a little nearer to me because I had so much to do with managing the mills."

"Yes, of course, James. But the girls are going to be vexed. Does the deed include the furnishings?"

"Yes, Mother; but Clara and I will do our best to satisfy the others. What I want to make clear to you is, it will be your home just the same. You need never know that anything has been changed."

"That is kind of you, James." She said this with her lips, but at the same time her mind was flying on. Clara would bring her brood of seven to this stately old house and they would possess it; she could hear their shouts resounding through the halls, their heels clattering on the stairs; she could see them sliding on the polished floors, using the Shah of Persia's rug to play marbles on. Against the wall of the library in front of her was a book-case some ten feet tall and seven feet wide, of French walnut, hand-carved over every inch of its surface with rose-vines and blossoms; the morning sun streamed upon it, and a thousand facets shone like burnished gold. There was a companion-piece farther down the wall and Cornelia knew that the last dealer who had inspected her husband's treasures had mentioned eight thousand as a price for that pair.

"There are some valuable things in this house, James."

"I know, Mother, and don't you worry. We'll add a wing back of the conservatory and keep the children there till they've learned manners. I haven't been used to fine things, but Clara has and she's the boss of this family. You stay and help her."

"I don't know, James. I am sixty years old, and all that time I have done what other people have told me. Now I might want to please myself."

A troubled look appeared behind the large round spectacles of James Scatterbridge. He had a literal mind, adjusted to the production of seventy million yards of low-priced cotton goods per annum; this production was the real religion of his life, and, for the rest, he left everything to his wife, satisfied that he had done the best possible in the matrimonial line. And now here was this little old lady with the laughing eyes, bearing the sacred name of Thornwell, hinting at the revolutionary idea of pleasing herself. In his heart James was afraid of this great family, with its implacable pride and dignified cruelty; they were sons of pirates and privateersmen, while James was a farmer-boy, whose ancestors had worked and produced.

v

He had no chance to question Cornelia. The bell rang and through the wide double doors of the library he saw Addicks in conference with several well-dressed youngish men. Presently the servant came with a message which, repeated from one dinner table to another, became a standard jest of the inner circles of Boston. Addicks had been with the family more than fifty years and understood all possible social relationships. Now, after due meditation, he came to his master with a formula precisely adjusted: "Mr. James, there are three reporters and a gentleman from the *Transcript.*"

James went out, took the three reporters and the gentleman into the privacy of the governor's study, and proceeded to enjoy the fruits of his own distinguished marriage. He reminded them that the Thornwell line went back to the Mayflower; there was in the mansion a cradle which had been brought over in that greatest of ships. He reminded them that there had been two colonial governors in the line, and two governors of the Commonwealth. He reminded them of the deeds which Josiah had performed in office, how he had sent the public thieves to jail. He verified the names of the ex-governor's children and gave the names of the grandchildren, not forgetting the seven of James, all of whom carried the blessed name: Josiah Thornwell Scatterbridge, Cornelia Thornwell Scatterbridge, James Thornwell Scatterbridge, Quincy Thornwell Scatterbridge—and so on. He was in the midst of telling them how the Thornwell mills were to be closed for a half day during the funeral, when a tap was heard on the door of the study, and there entered in full majesty Mrs. Rupert Alvin, *née* Deborah Quincy Thornwell.

"James, do I understand that these are representatives of the press? Good morning, gentlemen, I am Mrs. Alvin, the governor's oldest daughter. You will wish to know that I have been in communication over the telephone with the Reverend Doctor Wolverhampton, rector of St. Luke's Church here in Thornwell, which the governor built and endowed. He has agreed to officiate at the funeral services, which will be held in the family home. I understand that some of the papers have a report that the funeral will be held in Trinity Church, Boston, but that is a mistake; they will take place in this house on Friday afternoon at two

o'clock, and be sure you get it correct so that our friends will
be under no misapprehension. Yes, the name is pronounced
Woolton, but spelled W-o-l-v-e-r-h-a-m-p-t-o-n—the Reverend
Doctor James Lowell Wolverhampton, rector of St. Luke's
Church, Thornwell. He will be assisted by the Reverend Mr.
Quincy Adams Thornwell, a cousin of the governor's. The in-
terment will be in the family vault at St. Alston's Cemetery."

After which Mrs. Rupert Alvin, *née* Deborah Quincy Thornwell, seated herself firmly upon the sofa, knowing that so long
as she was there not even her plebeian brother-in-law would dare
to contravene her. It was a legend of the family that in one of
Deborah's disputes with her own husband she had said: "Take
me into the closet and spit on me if you will, but when we are
in public show me the respect that is due to my station."

The three reporters and one gentleman took their departure
in a taxi-cab which they had hired jointly and were whirled
down to the village, where each annexed himself to a telephone
receiver and spelled out these details, which were first rushed
out on a typewriter and then upon a linotype machine and then
upon a printing-press. So in less than an hour after James had
spoken and Deborah had revised him, the newsboys were crying
the second edition of the afternoon papers, with all possible
particulars about the life and death and impending funeral of
the ex-governor of the Commonwealth. They had a generous-
sized picture of him on the front page; a lean face with thin,
tight-shut lips and a long thin nose tapering to a point; a face
that had reappeared continuously in the course of three centuries. In panels on the walls of his music-room were four oil
paintings, life-size, of four different governors, in four different
costumes, but unchanged in soul; personally incapable of wrong-
doing and merciless to all wrong-doers. Statesman, manufacturer, philanthropist, said the newspapers in their editorials: a
model to posterity, an exemplar of all things dignified and
worthy of emulation—

And meantime, up in the big room with the four-poster bed
and the windows shrouded with dark curtains, Hobson, the psychologist, was remarking to one of his assistants, "If you don't
stop pumping on that carotid you'll have this old gent's face dis-
colored and have to paint him."

VI

Rupert Alvin arrived, having stopped at the Pilgrim National Bank just long enough to glance at his mail and order his engagements postponed. Now he emerged from his purring limousine, drew himself up to his full height of six feet, composed all the bulges of his face, straightened his waistcoat and went in. He listened with politeness to James's account of the arrangements made, and then, in a room apart, he listened to his wife's emphatic opinions of Hobson, and rugs, and the determination of James to become the Thornwell family.

Finally he sought out Cornelia. "Mother. I want to tell you that Deborah and I will be more than glad to have you make your home with us and will do everything in human power to make you happy."

"Thank you, Rupert. I really can't say yet; I haven't had time to get myself together."

But her mind was quick, and was busy picturing life with Rupert and Deborah. They had a big house on Commonwealth Avenue, where they lived three months of the year; the rest of the time they occupied a castle on the rocks of the North Shore. Deborah had the lean face and thin nose of her father and held herself in the same stiff manner; for her that variety of chair is made, of which the backs go up in a straight vertical. She would be her father's successor in understanding and preserving the Thornwell traditions. She was very devout, and gave her spare time to the management of charities—certain special ones; she did not like other people to make contributions to them, because they would then expect to meddle with her administration. It was her complaint that there was no such thing as an efficient subordinate to be hired; impossible to delegate any responsibility, so she managed everything.

As for Rupert, he was running a great banking industry which carried a general supervision of other industries and the gradual taking over of many of them. In between times he would advise about his wife's charities and their religious affairs. His hobby was church architecture; the rectors of parishes in eastern Massachusetts would come to him for advice about the proper proportions of an apse. Cornelia realized that if she went to live

with them she would indeed feel "at home"; she would be told
what to do, exactly as if Josiah were there.

Rupert was summoned to help his wife revise the list of the
guests to be notified of the funeral; and Cornelia wandered into
the music-room, where the services would be held. But she could
not stand those four life-size governors, each with the same lean
face and tightly shut lips and nose tapering to a point. She went
into the conservatory, where there were beautiful plants and
flowers, and benches for young lovers listening to music—even
in the suburbs of Boston they did that. Cornelia's children had
been young here and now her grandchildren were at the age of
love, yet she had never felt at ease in the house; she had never
been able to have her way, it always had to be the Thornwell
way. A public career had not been enough for Josiah; he had
insisted upon managing his household and had had the support
of brothers and sisters, a whole phalanx of righteous people.
Great-aunt Deborah had lived in the home until her death,
quite recently, and had been the real mistress of the family,
with the duty of teaching the daughters what Thornwell daughters ought to know and think.

For Cornelia there had been a little music and a little painting,
a rose garden and some books, a few friends, a play now and
then and symphony concerts. Gradually the family got used to
the fact that they could expect no more of her than this—that
she should conceal from them the fact that she found any element of fun in their sober traditions. They did not understand
her smile, and it never occurred to them to want to understand
it; what made them "Boston" was the fact that never by any
possibility would it cross their minds that they had anything to
learn from what was "not Boston." Cornelia's father had been
a professor in a small college, which was decent enough, but his
father had been a common immigrant; and three generations
from now at Boston dinner-tables people would still be whispering to their neighbors, "Oh, yes, but, my dear, her grandfather
came over in the steerage; they say he was a bog-trotter—the
name was Irish, anyhow."

Nor had there been any fun in being the wife of a governor.
Let those who wanted fame and prominence help themselves
to Cornelia's share! It had meant long speeches to listen to, bores
to talk to, indigestible dinners to eat. It had meant never speak-

ing a natural word, never laughing a merry laugh; everything calculated, everything a matter of policy, to enhance a career which loyalty required a wife to believe in. Cornelia put her hands to her ears to drown out the roaring of crowds shouting victory on election night. She could hear a nasal. drawling voice pledging zeal for the public interest. "Fellow-citizens of the Commonwealth, upon this solemn occasion when you have summoned me by your suffrages—" and so on. Nowhere any charm, or humor, or touch of simplicity! Nothing but heavy pageantry and play-acting, from the cradle to the coffin!

Even now, when in the darkened bedroom the psychological Mr. Hobson had charge of Josiah's affairs. Said the assistant, "How shall I get this old buster's wig to stay in place? Can I ask one of the servants for some glue?" Said the psychologist, "No, you can't ask for glue in a house like this—what would they think? Look on that bureau for a couple of safety-pins."

VII

The news had spread, the telephone was ringing, messages of condolence were arriving—a constant coming and going and whispering in the house of death. The dressmaker to consult Cornelia about her costume; also the old lady who sold bonnets in the town and was patronized as a matter of charity. Cornelia was willing to be charitable—but Clara was using this old lady to persuade Cornelia to don a veil. A dozen other questions: who was to provide the flowers, and what kind? What was to be the music, and who was to play it? Should the mill-hands be given an opportunity to look upon the features of their employer and just how was that to be managed? Two keys of the organ failed to sound and must be seen to. Such details served to break the monotony of mourning.

Also there were relatives arriving: Quincy Thornwell, Great-uncle Abner's son, a clubman of fifty or so, prematurely white-haired, his wizened face full of gossip; he had the reputation of a ladies' man, in a decorous Boston way, and Cornelia liked him because he was not so proper as the others and would tell her funny stories about the city. Quincy had grown rich by using the family information on the stock-market. He spent his days in board rooms, watching the prices of stocks chalked upon a wall; and in the evening, when he was not visiting the ladies, he was playing chess with his deaf old father. They talked about poor Josiah for a while, and then Abner could not keep off his hobby. He tried unsuccessfully to whisper: "The fellow that won the last round is a Jew, but they say he's French—kind of funny, ain't it?"

And then Priscilla and Elizabeth, the daughters of Deborah. Priscilla, the elder, was a perfect replica of her mother and planning at the age of twenty-one to devote herself to settlement work. Betty, the younger one, gave Cornelia thrills; a little round face, a nose trying its best to turn up, soft brown eyes that shone with tenderness, and little puckers when she laughed. She sat in the councils of the women, demure and silent, as became a miss of seventeen, whose right of entrance might be challenged. Later, when Cornelia left the room, she followed. "Oh, Grannie, I wish they didn't have to quarrel so!"

"So do I, Betty."

"Sister is just beside herself over that old Shah of Persia's rug. Of course it's interesting to know that your grandfather traveled in Persia and had the Shah give him presents; but after all, there are plenty of rugs you can buy. But Mother says if Aunt Clara doesn't let us have it, she'll never speak to her again. Do you suppose she means that?"

"Such things have happened, dear. Your Great-uncle Abner has not spoken to your Great-uncle Ahab for fifty years."

"Oh, Grannie! What extraordinary things in a family! Will Great-uncle Ahab come to the funeral?"

"Of course."

"And he won't speak to Great-uncle Abner?"

"In public he will, but not otherwise. Abner married the girl that Ahab was engaged to, so Ahab has stayed a bachelor all his life. Don't you remember that big house down at the shore that they sawed in half?"

"Oh, was that it?"

"They quarreled and divided it exactly, and Ahab moved his half to another part of the town."

Said Betty, "I'm so glad you're not going to cover yourself with a horrid black veil. It wouldn't become you a bit. And I'm glad you're not crying when you don't feel like it. I say for you to do what you want to."

"Thank you, Betty dear."

"It's a fact that Grandfather never felt the need of personal affection—or at least he never showed it—so why should other people show it?" Betty stopped for a moment, and then caught the old lady's hand. "Oh, Grannie, you're crying now! I've hurt your feelings!"

"No, dear, not that! It's just that I was thinking how much unhappiness I'd have saved if it had been the fashion for people to say what they mean."

"Well, Mother is cross with me; she says I'm an unnatural child, and she can't understand me. Do you find me so?"

"No, dear." And Cornelia smiled through her tears. "Don't mind me, I was really looking for a chance to cry. It's a great strain when you break the habits of forty years, no matter what they are."

"Oh, Grannie dear. I wish you'd come and live with us, and wake up the family. I wish Mother wasn't so terribly strict with me. I wish I had a car of my own. Dear me," said Miss Betty, "what a lot of things I wish!"

VIII

There came Henry Winters, husband of Alice; later than the others, because he had had to appear in court. It is not customary to adjourn court for the death of fathers-in-law, but when it was Governor Thornwell the case was different. Henry had been conscious of doing a distinguished thing when he asked for adjournment and the judge of doing a distinguished thing when he granted it, with a gracious little tribute to the eminent departed.

As Alice Thornwell Winters was a model of social elegance, so Henry Cabot Winters was a model of legal insouciance; a lawyer who was also a man of the world and of fashion. Four years in Harvard and three in the law-school had not sufficed to suppress his sense of humor and for this reason he was the nearest to Cornelia of her sons-in-law. He was a slender and rather dark man, fastidious, dressed in the pink of fashion, his graying hair combed in a picturesque wave. He commanded enormous fees for his inside knowledge of the financial affairs of New England; and after business hours he became the man of pleasure, yachtsman, fox-hunter, favorite in the ballrooms. He knew the right people and brought in the business; and left it for his partners to do the tiresome work of looking up the law and winning cases.

Henry now had need of all his urbanity. First he had to listen to his wife raging in whispers on the subject of the Mayflower cradle; and immediately afterwards he was trapped in the drawing-room by his sister-in-law, Deborah. "Henry, there is something that some member of the family simply has to speak to you about. I hope you understand that I have no wish to intrude upon your private affairs, but I have spoken to Alice and it seems that I can accomplish nothing—she absolutely insists that she will let Joyce Edgerton attend the funeral if he wishes."

"Why shouldn't she, Deborah?"

"Henry, the way you and your wife work out your marital problems is no affair of mine—"

"Exactly, Deborah!"

"—until it threatens to become a public scandal. Don't misunderstand me, I am not casting any doubts upon my sister's virtue—she assures me that her relationship to Joyce Edgerton is innocent and maybe it is—but there is a limit to what you can expect the world to believe—and when Alice continues to have some young man tagging after her everywhere she goes—and when she changes them so frequently—and they all go to the devil afterwards—you know what I mean, Henry! And of course it may be true that Joyce Edgerton is a great poet—or that he is going to be some day, and all that—nevertheless it seems to me that this is one time when the family has some rights and when the sacredness of our grief ought to be respected—and I really think we have a right to ask you to use your authority and see to it that Joyce Edgerton finds some other way to amuse himself on Friday afternoon—surely he can find an unmarried woman to go somewhere with him—just this one day, that's all I am asking—"

And so on; until Henry Cabot Winters got up and excused himself and went up to his mother-in-law's sunny rooms, where none of the curtains had been drawn, and he could sink into an easy chair and laugh. Cornelia knew about it, of course; Deborah had not failed to put the problem up to her. They discussed it for a while and Henry remarked that Alice deserved much more admiration than any one man could supply. Later on he made the same little speech as the others, offering Cornelia a home and assuring her that everything they had would be at her disposal. The Winters had a great deal: a town house and a suburban estate and a camp on a lake up in New Hampshire. They had only one son, a lad who was preparing to enter St. Mark's school, so there would be plenty of space and freedom for Cornelia. She could laugh about life with Henry; but what would she do about Joyce Edgerton and about the young man who had preceded him and the one who would follow him?

Alice had her side, of course; it was pretty generally known that Henry was keeping a woman in an apartment in the Fenway. Also, Alice was "virtuous"—meaning that she never gave herself to any of her adorers. But living in the house with Alice meant that you had to know the details of these emotional entanglements; just what the new young genius found in the soul of Alice that was so especially wonderful and why he preferred it to what he found in any of the available unopened buds who had not been beaten upon by the storms of experience. You had to know whether these young geniuses were happy or unhappy, whether they were coming or going; and after they were gone, you had to know just why they had been so disappointing to Alice, so unworthy of the high faith she had placed in them.

"Henry," said Cornelia, "I suppose I'm going to have a little money left me out of the wreck of Josiah's fortune?"

"I hope so."

"I suppose James will tell me about it in due time. If it's enough, maybe you'll advise me about renting an apartment in the Fenway, where I understand things don't have to be so proper." And Henry laughed—he couldn't help laughing, of course; but at the same time he was somewhat shocked. How much did his mother-in-law know about such matters? How much should he admit to her that he knew that she knew? He had an impulse to glance behind him at the open door.

"Henry," said Cornelia, suddenly, "I am ashamed of the way this family is behaving. But, you know, the Thornwells have not been exactly what you call 'nice' people."

"No," said Henry, "they have been 'great' people."

"Which means," countered the woman, "they have been greedy—and with a streak of insanity."

IX

The heavens, regardful of the dignity and standing of the late governor of the Commonwealth, sent rain on the night before the funeral to wash the air and make every blade of grass to shine. They sent the sun especially early to chase away the clouds, all but a few fleecy ones, setting off the deep blue of the sky. The expanses of lawn that stretched out on every side from "Hillview" were smoother and cleaner and brighter than any rug that a Shah of Persia ever trod. Under the great dark oaks a flock of sheep were feeding, and behind a steel fence a herd of deer. On the opposite slope in the distance were the white columns of the Scatterbridge home, and at one side the cottages of the tenants who worked the thousand acres of farmland. To the east, underneath the newly risen sun, were glimpses of the great mills, red brick stained with coal smoke; also of the river through the trees, and day and night came the music of water pouring over the dams.

The mansion had tall columns in front, going up over the second story, covering both the veranda and the graveled driveway. The house was painted white, the paint, like everything else, being decently old. Wings had been added on each side, and in the rear the music-room, and beyond that the conservatory: nothing regular, because the architects had had to adjust themselves to the elm trees which bowered the structure.

All morning there was the sound of wheels on the driveway, and delivery men and chauffeurs in uniform ringing the bell, bringing wreaths and floral designs. "Say it with flowers," ran the formula; and every saying had a card attached, to identify the sayer: the Governor of the Commonwealth and his lady, the Bishop of the Diocese and his wife, the members of the Republican State Committee, the Society of the Sons of St. Andrew, the Society of Colonial Dames, the Class of '58 of Harvard University, the employees of the Pilgrim National Bank, the executives and managers of the Thornwell Mills Company, the Chamber of Commerce of Boston, the Board of Trade of Thornwell—so on through a long list. Addicks, the perfect family servant, received each offering with grave thanks, deposited the cards on a silver tray and handed the flowers to the footman, who took them to the music-room and placed them under Deborah's direction.

The room had been made into a church, the "highest" possible. There was an altar with a large cross made of white roses and at each side a seven-branched candle-stick, with tall candles burning. The casket was in place, holding the lean body of Josiah, his face upturned to the light for his last few hours, the long thin nose seeming longer and thinner than ever could have been possible in life. The skin was a pale waxy color, tinted with great skill—since Mr. Hobson was not merely a psychologist but a "cosmetologist" also. In his advertisements he said "Every funeral is *my* funeral"; which was why Deborah considered him so vulgar. Boston—the real Boston—does not wish its advertisements "peppy."

The three reporters and the gentleman from the *Transcript* came again; and this time there had been an understanding between James and his sister-in-law. It was like the case of the man who said that he and his wife had worked out a solution of the domestic problem; on all major issues he was to have his way and on minor issues she was to have hers; and so far, no major issues had arisen. The three reporters and the gentleman were received by James and Deborah, and James got the cards from the silver tray and dictated the names of those who had sent floral tributes; while every now and then Deborah would say, quietly, "Omit that name, if you please." Not every one was entitled to send tributes to a Thornwell funeral!

The organist from St. Luke's Church arrived, and Addicks knew exactly what to say to him. "This way, if you please, sir. The choir will robe itself in the little room back of the governor's study. The ceremony will begin promptly at two." Attired in a flowing white day-gown, the visitor proceeded to test the organ, and mysterious vibrations crept up and down the timbers of the building. "Jesus, lover of my soul, let me to thy bosom fly," whispered walls and ceilings; and at the same moment Deborah Thornwell Alvin was standing with her two hands clenched, addressing Clara Thornwell Scatterbridge: "I wish to say once for all, I consider one-third of the family heirlooms are my property; and if they are taken from me because of any mortgage I shall regard the taker as a pawnbroker for the rest of my days."

X

Members of the family arriving. The ladies went upstairs to put their hair and complexions in order, while the men stood about, exchanging phrases in soft whispers: a beautiful day, yes, ideal for the occasion, most fortunate; a fine editorial in the *Transcript,* the press had been dignified; a great man was gone, we don't have that kind any more; a very convincing tribute from the party, yes, they would find it hard to replace him; looked as if the Germans might get to the channel; amazing the way the market continued to boom.

There came John Quincy Thornwell, another son of Abner, with his father's heavy frame and his uncle's long nose; soft-voiced, semi-bald, president of the Fifth National Bank. And Grandfather Porter Alvin, father of Rupert, and Andrew Alvin, his younger son, a polo player and sport, tanned as brown as a Kanaka, with a puffy checked necktie and every shiny strand of his black hair in exactly the right position. He stood in the library, listening to Great-uncle Abner shouting "Who will read Josiah's books now?" Andrew ran his eyes over the shelves of heavy works on political science and history and economics and law, and knew that he was not the one.

Two automobiles deposited six pairs of choir boys, subdued in voice but eager of eye; they were herded into the robing room by the Reverend Mr. Quincy Adams Thornwell, the cousin who was to assist in the ceremony; tall, flat-flooted, with large bunion shoes and black suit and flat black hat like an English curate—its ugliness excused for the reason that it had ritual significance. Also came the rector and his lady; the Reverend Dr. James Lowell Wolverhampton, pronounced Woolton, physically and phonetically equipped to become a bishop; he gathered up the letter "rs" which the Boston Brahmins all drop, and saved them and rolled them out two or three at a time in his sermons.

He received the final advice from Deborah: "The family will descend at one-fifty-five." After which he retired into Josiah's study, to instruct his assistant concerning the service. "First I recite, 'Lord, let me know mine end,' and you make the responses. The choir sings, 'Lord, Thou hast been our refuge,' and then, before the Lesson from the Epistle of St. Paul, we intone the anthem—"

"Then I will need both books?" broke in the Reverend Mr. Thornwell.

"No, no! You don't understand." And with Christian patience the rector said it all over again, but more slowly, pointing out the passages. He would have added the word "Dunce!" but that would not have been a Christian thing to say to a cousin of a governor.

XI

The guests arriving. They stepped onto the veranda and the chauffeurs parked the cars in a long line down the driveway. There were three policemen in blue uniforms stationed in front of the house, but in this well-trained community they had only to confer dignity. The guests did not chat, merely murmured a few greetings, after which they went to the music-room, which most of them knew well; walking softly, on padded feet, and not permitting their eyes to show signs of animation. They were old people for the most part; gentlemen with white heads or gray, flesh-colored or rosy; they wore black broadcloth, some with black stripes of braid down the side of the trousers. The ladies were in black, with now and then a touch of white at the collar and cuffs; many of them wore black-dotted veils and fur neck-pieces even in summer weather. They were much wrinkled and the older ones had hanging mouths; they let themselves carefully down the three polished steps into the music-room and took their seats, seeing only what it was possible to see without moving the eyes.

The place was open and airy, full of sunshine; divided into four sections by an aisle down the center and a cross aisle with open doors at each side. It had white Doric columns set in the walls, and panels with the stern ancestors painted. There were tall windows, with dark red curtains at the side, and seats upholstered in red velvet to match. The front of the room had a bower of flowers and in the center, where the two aisles crossed, stood the casket with the body of the great man, white carnations at his head and white roses at his feet; if you looked down through the glass, as a few did, you saw his thin nose of pale waxen color, and his white wig, resting securely in position with no trace of safety-pins.

Across the aisle was stretched a purple ribbon, marking the seats reserved for the family and the family servants; in this solemn hour class distinctions were abolished, there was only Thornwell or not-Thornwell. The governor of the Commonwealth—the living one—came in with his lady, but no one did them special honor; they seated themselves among the guests. So with the lieutenant-governor and his lady, and the senator who represented the Commonwealth in Washington; a "scholar in politics" with a very famous name, a dapper little gentleman with sharply trimmed mustaches and beard. If you knew the "blue-bloods" of this community, you would recognize great bankers and lawyers, the presidents of two universities and several scholars of fame. You would not know the timid old ladies dressed in rusty black, who had got out of cars some distance down the driveway and walked about for a while so as not to get there too early; poor relations, who had been in receipt of pensions from Josiah, and were trembling with anxiety until the will should be read.

Through the side door you saw a throng of humble people; the employees of the mills, which were shut down for the afternoon. They came streaming up the path from the road below, dressed in their pathetic best; they would stand patiently for an hour or two, listening to the strains of the organ and waiting their time to file through the room. A rare occasion for them; one might work in the mills another generation and gaze up at the white-painted castle amid its sheltering elm trees and never climb the path to glimpse the splendor. The rest of the village, which did not work in the mills, was clustered along the roadside to stare at the shining limousines and their stately occupants. It was feudalism in frockcoats.

The grandfather's clock at the head of the stairs pointed to one-fifty-four, and the organ was pealing a magnificent heavy tune. Every person in the room knew the words, and beheld the same magnificent picture—

Ten thousand times ten thousand
In sparkling raiment bright,
The armies of the ransomed saints
Stream up the steeps of light:

'Tis finished, all is finished,
Their fight with death and sin:
Fling open wide the golden gates
And let the victors in.

At which sublime moment, with all heaven thundering in her ears, Alice Thornwell Winters, black of dress and white of face, was confronting Clara Thornwell Scatterbridge, demanding, "Once more and for the last time, do you admit that the Mayflower cradle is my property?"

Said Clara: "I think this a most unsuitable moment—"

Said Alice: "There could be no moment more suitable. It marks the break-up of our family, if you so decree. That Mayflower cradle has been the cradle of our destiny, and the symbol of our position. I was rocked in its arms, and the generations before me. I bore the first man-child—"

Said Clara: "Well, I have borne five boys and two girls, even though a little bit late."

Said Alice: "I have Father's pledge and I stand on that. Give me your answer!"

Said Clara: "It is a matter about which James must be consulted—"

Said Alice: "You have had opportunity to consult James, and you have done so. If you do not answer my question, I understand that your answer is no."

The clock had moved one minute, and Cornelia came, saying, "It is time to descend. I hope my children are not going to advertise our family shame to the world."

XII

The procession of men and women and children was formed in the proper order, and down the stairs, two by two, they went: Cornelia first, with no veil over her features and no tears in her soft brown eyes; her gray hair was smoothed flat, and her little round face was solemn, her little nose facing straight ahead, her gaze fixed upon nothingness. One hand rested upon the arm of Great-uncle Abner; and behind her came Great-uncle Ahab, escorting Great-aunt Priscilla. Then Deborah, the oldest daughter, with her husband, Rupert Alvin; then Alice, the second daughter, with her husband, Henry Cabot Winters; then Clara, with her husband, James Scatterbridge; then the son of Alice, and the two daughters of Deborah and the seven children of Clara tapering to a small pair with a governess between them. The miscellaneous uncles and aunts and nephews and nieces and cousins had already been seated inside the magic purple ribbon, so the procession ended with the personal servants; Addicks, with his venerable black suit showing slightly green in the bright sunlight; the governor's private secretary, and his Negro valet, and Cornelia's Negro maid, and the handy man, and the gardener, and the cook—all persons who had been with the family so long that they alone knew the dates.

The six pairs of white-robed choir boys came down the center aisle, their cherub voices proclaiming, "Now the laborer's task is o'er; Now the battle day is past." The last and tallest bore a high jeweled cross and behind it strode the two clergymen, robed in white and black. All found their proper places, and the rector lifted his hands and pronounced, "Peace be upon this house." And, truly, whatever spells he might command were in order at this moment, with Clara Scatterbridge sitting with her teeth clenched on the thought, "They are ours and we shall keep them!" And Alice Winters glaring before her at the sentence, "They got it by a mortgage, like pawnbrokers!" And Priscilla Alvin, elder daughter of Deborah, shutting her fists tight upon the conviction, "When it comes to a show down, Mother will give up, but I will never give up!"

"I am the r-r-r-esur-r-ection and the life!" proclaimed the Reverend Dr. Wolverhampton; and then, exactly as if he had known about Mayflower cradles and Shah of Persia's rugs, he added, "We brought nothing into this world, and it is certain we can carry nothing out." The choir chanted, "Lord, thou hast been our refuge: from one generation to another"; and then the clergyman began to read the extract from the fifteenth chapter of the First Epistle of St. Paul to the Corinthians. It is very long and somewhat involved, so there was no matter for surprise if here and there a member of the congregation found his attention straying. Rupert Alvin had seen, as he came down the aisle, the face of Jerry Walker gazing from one of the side seats; thus it was inevitable that Rupert should be thinking about the felt-plants and the hat-works which Jerry had bought, and would he be able to meet his notes, and how far should the Pilgrim National Bank lead him on? And Great-uncle Abner, who in the next match was to meet the French Jew, and could not help wondering about the fellow's tricks. And young Josiah Thornwell Winters, the infinitely precious son of Alice, who had a date with a girl and wondered how soon he would get off. And Betty Alvin, who sat behind her grandmother, thinking, "If only she'd come stay with us and liven things up!"

The voice of the rector was wrestling with the complicated Pauline metaphysics. "For this corruptible must put on incorruption, and this mortal must put on immortality. So when this corruptible shall have put on incorruption, and this mortal shall have put on immortality, then shall be brought to pass the saying that is written, Death is swallowed up in victory." Cornelia was thinking "Can all that really be true? Shall I really ever see Josiah again? Is he alive somewhere now, and does he know what I am thinking? If he does, am I really free?"

In the casket, within three feet of her, lay what St. Paul called the "natural body" of her husband. For three days it had been preserved by formaldehyde solutions; but an hour or two more and it would be shoved into a vault, and there would begin a process extremely unpleasant to think about. Cornelia had been reading Fabre, and had come upon the details, which now forced themselves upon her shuddering thoughts. St. Paul, thinking the same thoughts, had said, "This corruptible must put on incorruption."

XIII

The clergyman was praying; and Cornelia, down upon her knees, said a prayer of her own, "Oh, Lord, let my children stop quarreling!" Then she was back in her seat, listening to a eulogy of the great departed. "When the state was in peril, he was as a rock of refuge . . . to every need, public or private, he gave freely . . . the greatest of his generation . . . we of the new time call in vain for his like—" and so on, a discourse that was Boston in every tone and accent. But Cornelia's mind was occupied with the realities of this household, to whom the glory of Josiah was not a crown to be worn but a carcass to be rended. For years she had prayed "O Lord, take worldliness out of their hearts." But something must have been wrong with her technique of prayer; it had failed entirely of effect.

"The services will be continued at the place of interment," said the rector; and the six pairs of choir boys marched out, singing "The church's one foundation," and the guests moved slowly into the library and the drawing-room, or to the front lawn, to await while the mill-hands filed across the room. The executives of the company were in charge of this, but Cornelia considered it her duty to remain, and her daughters, not to be outdone in ceremony, stood by her side.

The workers came in single file, slowly and hesitatingly: men and women, old and young, foreigners for the most part, pathetic figures, the more so because of their efforts to look proper. It was not often, under this system of feudalism in frock-coats, that the two kinds of people met in the same place; but here they were, the masters, tall and elegant, and the toilers, stunted in form and scarred in features, with shoulders bowed and limbs crooked and hands knotted and calloused. They had stood upon weary feet for hours in order to see this splendor, but now they were too timid to look at it; all but a few of the young ones kept their eyes straight ahead. A few saw Cornelia—persons whom she had visited in sickness—and these made faint signs of recognition, which she acknowledged.

Then came the pall-bearers; the honorary ones, whose names were in the papers, walking honorably alongside. The casket was slid into the hearse; the relatives entered their cars and so did those guests who cared to follow, and the long line of vehicles set out, with two motorcycle officers at the head and all traffic waiting respectfully. So they came to the family mausoleum, with the costly bronze receptacle waiting for its tenant. The group stood about with heads bowed, and again the choir sang and the Reverend Dr. Wolverhampton lifted up his rolling voice. "Man that is born of woman, hath but a short time to live, and is full of misery." The casket was set in place and sealed, and the doors of the vault were shut and locked; the blessings of the Lord were conferred upon those present; and all was over. The hearse went back to its garage to await the morrow's passenger and the guests scattered to their homes; the members of the family returned to "Hillview" for a ceremony which concerned them alone—the reading of Josiah Thornwell's will.

XIV

Behold them waiting in the library: every one, from the highest to the lowest, the richest to the poorest—even the older servants, who were certain of being remembered. Every one—save two. Clara, looking about, missed her sister Alice and, becoming suddenly suspicious, went into the entrance hall. There, coming down the broad staircase, was a sight the like of which had never been seen by any Thornwell since the days—well, a long time ago, when the ancestors had been privateersmen. Alice was marching, her cultivated features set in grim defiance and her deep-souled eyes staring before her; behind her a French maid, and between them a piece of furniture of brown varnished wood, much scarred and scratched.

Clara stood, all but paralyzed. "Alice Thornwell! What are you doing?"—as if it were not evident enough! Then, seeing Alice go straight by without a word: "If you take that cradle out of this house, I will never speak to you while I live!" And then, "I will denounce you for a thief to the world!" And when even this most dreadful of maledictions failed of effect, Clara could only stand with fingernails dug into the palms of her hands and face white with fury, whispering over and over, "Oh! Oh! *Oh!*"

They went through the front door and Clara rushed into the library, whispering to her mother "Alice is stealing the cradle!" Cornelia hurried outside in time to see the heirloom being loaded onto the Winters limousine. It would not go through the door, but the two women set it on the running-board on the right-hand side, away from the chauffeur; the maid sat on the front seat and held it through the front window and Alice sat on the rear seat and held it through the rear window; and the car rolled away down the drive, leaving the Thornwell family like a nest of ants which has been stepped on.

And even that was not the end! A dreadful idea flashed through the mind of Clara, and she rushed into the rear reception room, which the ladies of the family used for their tea-parties. In the center of this room, upon the seldom-trodden floor, had reposed the Shah of Persia's rug; and now it was gone! Clara gave one glance, and fled back to her older sister. "Deborah Thornwell, you have stolen my rug!"

Deborah drew herself up to her utmost height of amazement. "I have not touched my rug!"

"But it's gone!"

"It has not been taken by me." Still whispering, of course.

Clara looked, and saw that Deborah's elder daughter, Priscilla, was missing. She asked no more but turned to Addicks, the perfect servant, who never in his fifty years of devotion had encountered an emergency like this, nor in his maddest nightmare had dreamed it. "Addicks, Miss Priscilla has taken the Shah of Persia's rug. Search for it and bring it to me. Run!"

In the two hundred and eighty-five years of Boston's history, no such un-Bostonian thing had ever been known to happen, so there could be no Bostonian way of dealing with it. Clara Thornwell Scatterbridge became an ordinary woman in a rage. With tears in her china-blue eyes she appealed to her husband, to her mother, even to her older children and the governess. Ignoring her husband's efforts to restrain her, she ran from room to room, flinging open doors and looking into cupboards and behind sofas. As it occurred to her to look outside, she rushed through the doorway, breathless, red of face, forgetting her stoutness, her laboring heart, her varicose veins, forgetting even that institution which through so many generations had stood inviolate, the Thornwell dignity. A civilization in ruins!

The mystery was solved at last. Word spreading among the servants, a chauffeur reported that he had seen Miss Priscilla with the rug in her arms, going towards the apple-orchard. So across the fields marched Clara, followed by Deborah, at Clara's insistence. The other members of the family, suddenly realizing that this was a scene which must not be admitted, ordered the lawyer to begin the reading of the will.

Out under an old apple-tree, in the exact geographical center of the priceless Persian rug, sat the new generation, "young Boston," which was going to think and act for itself—and bring back the days of the pirates and privateersmen.

"Priscilla!" commanded Clara. "Get up!" And then: "Priscilla, you hear me speak to you! Get up off that rug!"

Silence. And Clara turned to her sister. "Deborah, will you order your child to obey?"

Would she? There was a pause, while history hung in the

balance. "Priscilla, I disapprove of what you are doing. Please get up."

And so the rug-sitting sphinx revealed a voice. "Mother, I am the person who will inherit this rug and I have made up my mind what to do. I shall sit here until Grandfather's will has been read. If he gives it to us, as he promised, all right. If not, Aunt Clara may call the police to remove me from it."

"Priscilla! You defy your mother?" Clara's voice was trembling. "Deborah, make her obey you!"

"Priscilla, obey me," said the mother. Was it possible that the voice lacked just a little of its usual firmness? Anyhow, Priscilla Alvin continued to sit, her eyes fixed on space.

"Obey your mother!" commanded Clara.

"Priscilla, obey me!" echoed Deborah.

"Mother," said the rug-sitter, "I was twenty-one years of age last week and I have taken legal advice and learned that I am no longer compelled to obey any one but the law. I am here and I shall stay here, and I serve notice now that if any one but a policeman removes me I shall get a warrant for the person's arrest."

"Oh!" cried Clara. "What is this new generation coming to?"

"Aunt Clara," said the rug-sitter, "you will save time if you go back and hear the will, because you won't accomplish anything meantime. Do not worry, I shall stay right here till the question is decided. I could have gone farther if I had wanted to, but I like this orchard, which you got away from us."

XV

And meantime Cornelia had gone to her rooms and locked the door behind her; and then into her bedroom and shut that door, to make doubly certain. She was pacing up and down, beset by a storm of emotion. As they say a drowning man lives over the experiences of his whole life, so she was living the repressions of forty years. All the rages she had felt and never voiced! All the disappointments, the despairs! The experiences she had longed for, and never dared to have, and now could never have, because it was too late! She had been caught, a wild young thing in a trap; she had lived, a prisoner in a cell. She had had dreams, and seen them suffocated; she had had

children, and seen them taken from her, and made into strangers. Forced into the mold of this family—this solid phalanx
of iron people—with iron souls, iron wills which broke you!

This crowning indignity, this outbreak in the very presence
of death—this was an accident, Cornelia told herself. They had
never done anything like this before, nothing so open, so undignified. They would repudiate it themselves, they would be
ashamed of it to-morrow. This was not "Boston"! But to
Cornelia, who had been on the inside of "Boston," it seemed an
outbreak of reality, a revelation of hidden natures. Petty
jealousy, petty greed, masked with dignity, and wearing the
solemn costumes of historical tradition! Other people, living
people, would quarrel over real things; the Thornwells quarreled over the dead rags and relics of their ancestors!

Once there had been real people in this family! Once there
had been men and women who had acted, who had dared to
think for themselves—and to care about something else than
rags and relics! Memories surged into Cornelia's mind, of the
old days when the Thornwells had been smugglers and priva-
teers—not thinking about the proprieties then! There had been
revolutionary leaders among them—men who had gone into the
"pot-houses" and incited mobs! There had even been women
who had dared to think, and to act, instead of obeying the men!
Didn't they worship the memory of a Great-great-aunt Deborah,
who had been one of the anti-slavery pioneers? Not frightened
by the horrible name of "Black Abolitionist"—no indeed, she
had made her home one of the stations in the "underground
railway" which had carried fugitive slaves to Canada! She had
taught Negroes to read and write—not only black women, but
black men! Such was the tradition they thought they worshiped; but really they only worshiped the rags and relics of it!

Suddenly this storm of emotion culminated, and Cornelia,
who had been pacing back and forth in her room, suddenly
stopped still. What was the reason women were always bound
by fear? Because they were afraid! Why were they obedient?
Because they obeyed! When they wanted to act, they did not
know enough; and when they knew enough, then they were too
old! But who could say you were too old to act, if you acted?

Cornelia, trembling with excitement, but at the same time calm inside, went to her desk and sat down, and took pen and ink and began to write.

"My dear Children:
"For forty years I have been doing what other people wanted me to do, and I have never had any fun. Now I think I have done everything I can for you, and that you can get along without me. I hope that I am old enough to take care of myself. I am going away for a while, to remain until I choose to return, if ever. I am not taking any property, because there has been too much of it in my life, and I believe I shall be happier without it. I am going to prove to myself, for my own satisfaction, that I can take care of myself, without any advice or assistance from any one. I have only one request, that you will waste no time or money in efforts to find me. It will only irritate me and do no good whatever, because I shall continue to do exactly what I please. I have heard of runaway children; I am going to be the runaway grandmother.
                              "With best wishes,
                                        "Mother.
"P.S. I enclose a respectable letter which you may show to our friends."

And the second letter:

"My Dear Children:
"Your father's sudden death has shocked me deeply, and after the strain of the funeral I realize that I am run down and in need of rest. I have received a telephone call from an old school friend who is starting on a camping trip and begs me go along. I think such a complete change will help me, so I am taking a night train, and write this to explain and leave you my dearest love and wishes for a happy summer.
                              "Affectionately,
                                        "Mother."

Having sealed these two letters in one envelope and marked it "For Deborah, Alice and Clara," Cornelia laid it in the middle of her bed. She then changed her mourning garb for an ordinary street-dress, and took her handbag with some ready money in it, and unlocked the two doors, and slipped down a back stairway, and out by a rear door, and down the path which led to the main road. There was a trolley stop, and a car labeled "Boston," and she stepped aboard.

CHAPTER 2

PLYMOUTH ROCK

I

THE "jitney bus" from Boston came speeding down the highway, and when it got into North Plymouth it stopped in front of the cordage company's plant. There climbed out a little old lady, carrying a straw suitcase, and dressed in humble workingwoman's clothing, with a worn gray shawl over her head. From beneath the shawl peered a pair of twinkling brown eyes, and these remained, taking in the landscape, after the bus had rolled on its way.

There was a two-story brick building, seeming to extend forever along the bay-front; built in the fashion of a fortress, with a steel fence in front, and a pond which had been turned into a moat in medieval style. High up in the blue sky floated an American flag, to let you know that this was not a Rhine castle of the middle ages, but a center of industry in the land of the Pilgrim's pride. The old lady stood wondering what to do next. Finally she approached the steel gates and inquired of the keeper, "Please, Mister, where I go for job?"

The man pointed to a building on the other side of the highway. "There's the employment office," he said. "But you're too late; we're closing in five minutes. Come to-morrow."

The old lady looked at the red brick walls and the blue sky and the white clouds and the starry flag, all made to go upon a picture postcard. The windows of the long factory were open, and she heard the roar of spinning-machinery, and saw the figures of men and women moving about. Suddenly a siren boomed; and as if by magic, the various buildings began to belch human figures. Apparently they had been lined up just inside the doors, like runners at the start of a race; they behaved as if the building were on fire, or full of poison gas. More and more dense grew the throngs of escapers, until the roadway was gray and blue with the shirts of men and the multi-colored dresses of girls. For the most part they were foreigners, Italians, Portuguese, and other dark peoples. They were small and stunted, the older ones bent with toil, walking mechanically, looking neither to right nor to left. The younger ones chatted in twos and threes, and some had a friendly smile for the little old lady with the brown eyes peering from under the shawl.

Two thousand or more came through the gates, and then gradually the procession thinned out, and the old lady turned back to the highway and along the tree-shaded street. Smaller streets went off it, lined with the homes of workers, four-family wooden tenements, square and plain, with dingy worn paint or none at all. The old lady found herself walking beside an Italian boy, seven or eight years old, a slender child with bright black eyes; he whistled cheerfully, and was reasonably clean. So the old lady said, "Hello, little boy; what is your name?"

"My name is Beltrando." He spoke in good English.

"Do you know anybody who would like to take a boarder?"

The boy thought, and then said, "Come see my mamma." He led her down a street labeled "Suosso's Lane" to a two-story house of unpainted shingles. They went in by the rear door, and Cornelia Thornwell found herself in the kitchen of Mrs. Vincenzo Brini.

"I come from Boston," she said. "I look for job in cordage plant. You know anybody got room for boarder?"

Alfonsina Brini was a young woman, small but strongly made, with kind motherly face and quick intelligent eyes. She examined her visitor with some curiosity, and said, "You Yankee lady?"

"Why, yes," said Cornelia Thornwell—her pitiful effort at concealment collapsing at once.

"Why you talka lika foreign?"

"Well, I thought maybe you understand better." Her smile was friendly and disarming, and won the other's heart.

"Me no onderstanda good," said Mrs. Brini. "Trando, here, he talka like Merican boy, he tella me." Mrs. Brini was in working clothes, and had not yet taken off her hat. "Me joosta get home," she said. "Me worka by woolen mill. You gotta job by cordage?"

"I want to ask for one," said Cornelia. "Do you think I can get it?"

"Shoore, plenty jobba now. Plenty shippa get—how you say, Trando, afondato—shippa sunk, maka new rope, plenty cordage job. But harda work, you very olda lady for cordage job."

"Oh, I won't mind hard work," said Cornelia, with the serenity of complete ignorance. "What will I get?"

"You no skilla work, you getta six dollar week. Some day you learn skilla work, you getta maybe eight, nine dollar week. My osband he work by cordage, getta twelve dollar half."

"And what will I pay for board?"

"You boarda maybe two dollar half, maybe t'ree dollar. You boarda by me, you go in room wit' my big girl, I make it two dollar quarter. You take little rooma for self, I maka two dollar half."

"I think I'd like to have room to myself," said Cornelia, timidly.

Mrs. Brini escorted her into the parlor. It was perhaps twelve feet square, with one of those plush-upholstered sets of furniture which are advertised at special bargains—$38.50, and you sign a blank on the dotted line, and once a month the agent collects three dollars, with interest on the unpaid portion. Also there was a phonograph, bought in the same way; and before Cornelia had been in the house half an hour, Beltrando had produced the big red record which had cost a week of Cornelia's board, and took the place of an icon or shrine in this family. "You listen to Caroos'," said the little boy; and Mrs. Brini stopped washing the vegetables for the salad and stood with hands wet and rapture in her eyes, while a mighty voice spread its wings and bore her soul to Italy.

II

The room assigned to Cornelia was five feet by eight, and held a wire cot and a chest of drawers. Her straw suitcase would go under the bed, and her clothing would hang on hooks behind the door. There was a window with home-made curtains in front of it, and on the chest of drawers a hand-woven lace cover, held in place by two figures in tinted glass, one a shepherd, the other his sweetheart, in Italian costumes. "This is lovely," the boarder said, gallantly; "it will seem like home."

And now, with the door shut, Cornelia Thornwell stood in the midst of her empire, trying to grasp what her new life would be like. She wanted to bathe her hands and face, and realized with dismay that she would have to use a bathroom in common with half a dozen other persons. No doubt she could replace the Italian shepherd and his love with a tin washbasin and pitcher. But would she be able to afford such luxuries on six dollars a week? And especially when she had not yet earned the six dollars, nor even the chance to earn them!

She put the contents of her straw suitcase away in the drawers and started to shove the suitcase under the bed, but discovered that the way was blocked by a couple of boxes containing books. This surprised her, and she sat on the bed and examined them. "Manzoni," was the first name, and she had heard it somewhere; but the title "I Promessi Sposi," told her nothing. The next was "A. O. Olivetti: Azione Diretta e Mediazione"; and that told her nothing either. The next was "Le Scuole Clericali," and she judged that must be a religious book; the next, "G. Most: La Peste Religiosa," must be the same. These people would probably be devout, and would they expect a "Yankee lady" to go to church with them? The next was "Ernesto Renan: La Vita di Gesu." She had heard of that, but had the impression that it was an agnostic book; surely her rector had spoken of it as taking Jesus for a man pure and simple. However, these people would not expect her to know about their authors.

She went outside to enjoy the evening. There was a vegetable garden in back of the house, all green and shiny after recent rains. A man was working here, with his coat off; a big fellow, with long arms flying vigorously as he threw the dirt. Cornelia was pleased by his diligence, because it promised fresh food for the table. She walked down the path and said, "Good evening," and he stopped his labors. She had given her name as "Mrs. Cornell," and now he greeted her as "Miz' Cornella." Just as the London working-classes drop the "h" where it belongs and put it where it does not belong, so these Italians did with vowels; they would say, "You lika da spagett'?"

"I am Mist' Brini," said the gardener; and Cornelia said, "I am glad to know you"—which was true enough, for she had been timid on the subject of foreign men, and this one, her future landlord, was reassuring. He was of middle age, and sometimes his face would be puzzled, and sometimes it would be amused, but always it was honest. His arms were hairy, and his large head set on a long neck. "Plenty gooda vegetable," said he. "You lika da minestrone?" He waved his arm with a gesture which seemed to sweep the whole garden into a pot, and offer it for her evening meal. Cornelia was to observe, as time passed, that Vincenzo Brini would never lose a chance to make a gesture; he would invent a whole pantomime to convey the meaning of a single word, and there was no trouble too great to be taken in these demonstrations.

"You lika da cipolla?" he inquired, pointing to another row.

"Onions?" inquired the other.

"You teacha da Eengleesh, I teach Italian." Brini grinned like a boy, and pointed to another row. "Ravanelli."

"Radishes," said Cornelia.

"Bietola," said Brini.

"Beets," said Cornelia.

This educational game went on until it was interrupted by the appearance of another man; a laborer arriving from his day's toil, with his coat over his sweat-stained arms, and a dinner-pail in his hand. Brini forgot his rows of vegetables and called, "Hello, Bart!" He added a torrent of words in Italian, evidently explaining the strange lady. "You meeta my frienda, Bart, he boarda by us, long time board."

The newcomer was a tall and somewhat stooped man; Cornelia was puzzled, because he seemed to be young, yet his face had many lines of care. He wore a brown mustache, which was left to nature, and drooped to a long point on each side of his mouth, giving him the appearance of a grave and amiable walrus. He was a dignified person, and did not indulge in the Brini fervors. "I pleased to meet you, lady," he said. "My Eengleesh ver' bad, I shame for heem."

"She teacha da Eengleesh!" put in Brini. "You teacha heem plenty, Miz' Cornella, he learna queeck, a bigga stúdent, got plenty book, read all time."

"Oh! Those must be your books under my bed!" said Cornelia.

"I taka heem out, lady," said the newcomer, at once, and started towards the house. Cornelia, with her woman's intuition, noted that this young laborer thought about others before he thought about himself.

"Fermati!" exclaimed Brini. "You no go in lady's room, you waita!" He grinned, and explained to Cornelia, "He no onderstand politess, he reada da book, molto studioso, all day. Getta da job, maka da little mon', give up job, reada book. He greata man, my frienda Bart—" and Brini's hairy arm went around the other's shoulders in a hug—"he gooda man—besta man—you ask all Italian in Plye-moot'—dey tella you—never soocha gooda man in all state Massachusett like my frienda Bartolomeo Vanzett'."

III

The family sat down to supper. It was not a big kitchen and they were crowded, with elbows touching: Papa Brini at the head of the table, Mamma at the foot, the three children on one side and Cornelia and her fellow-boarder on the other. She had been wondering what she would eat among these foreign people; she found a big bowl of salad with plenty of oil and vinegar, a chunk of parmigiano cheese, a loaf of bread in Italian fashion, shaped like a letter H, and finally a bottle of red wine, of which the children had a little and the women had one glass; the men were supposed to finish the rest. But she learned that Vanzetti would take no wine; out of the books he had got ideas about health and was a vegetarian most of the time. He explained to the new guest in his struggling English: "Poor people molto fortunato—how you say, lucky—no can buy richa food. You eata simple t'ing, you keepa da healt' all lifa long." After which ensued an argument with Papa Brini, who made it clear both by words and action that he looked upon the wine when it was any color whatever. He laughed gayly and explained to Cornelia the most elementary of Italian puns, "divino da vino."

It is customary in Italian gatherings for the women, and especially old women, to keep in the background; but these humble people were showing especial honor to their guest, including her in the conversation and making her feel at home. They had to struggle with strange words and call upon the children; and Cornelia was interested to observe these latter and their behavior. The oldest was about ten, small, dark-eyed, quiet and pretty; her name Lafevre, which they shortened to "Fay." She was going to public school, as was her brother Beltrando, and it was curious how completely Americanized they were, with the quiet reserve of the New Englander and even the broad "a" and the murdered "r." Boston was having its way with them!

"Fay" served as the dictionary for their conversation; an abridged one, needless to say. She was teaching Vanzetti English, he explained, and he was teaching her Italian—that is the Tuscan dialect, the Italian of literature. The Brinis came from the neighborhood of Bologna and spoke the dialect of that region; Vanzetti spoke as a Piedmontese, but since he had begun to educate himself he had learned the classical language and wanted Fay to know it too. It would be a poor exchange for a child to acquire American newspapers and magazines and give up Dante.

Cornelia had come among these foreign people with no little trepidation. It was the common phrase among her social set that the Italians, or "wops," as they were called, "lived like pigs." She had been prepared for dirt, degeneracy, brutality, even crime. Would she be able to stand it? Would she be physically safe in the midst of it? And now she sat, nibbling a clean salad and good bread and butter and cheese, and sipping an acceptable claret, listening to an Italian ditch-digger, who had washed at least his hands and face and put on a clean dry shirt in her honor, and now was holding forth upon the subject of the "Divina Commedia"!

Cornelia stated that she had read the poem—in Longfellow's translation; and from that moment he and she were friends. "Oh, da greata poet, da greata man! You reada heem, you know Italia, you lova da people! He was frienda da people, Miz' Cornella, he was—what you say it—ribello." He turned to little Fay, but she did not know long words, and he had to explain a "ribello" by frowning and shaking his fist. "De reecha men drive heem out, he live long time esilio, he suffer, he speaka da trut'. I no read heem till I come America. I younga man, worka by cloobba New York—great reecha cloobba, I washa da deesh. And such filt' I see, it maka you seek; you no eata da suppa if I tell it you what I see in soocha place. Beeg dining room, granda—marmoreo, how you say it? All reecha, much light, bigga men all dressa beeg shirt"—the speaker made signs to indicate an open shirt-front, and puffed himself out so that

Cornelia decided her son-in-law, Rupert Alvin, must have been to dinner in that "cloobba"!

"Evening dress," said she, helping him along.

"Joosta so—aristocratico, eccelso! And in pantry, in place for washa da deesh, soocha filt'! I gotta little room, alto, high up, povero. Come home, I moocha tired, go sleepa queeck. But I come by Italian book-store, I see Dante, ver' cheap for poor man. I say, greata poet, for shame I be sooch—what you say it—ignoranza. So I take heem home, I read, forgetta da sleep, forgetta da greata reecha cloob, da padrone maledirante—I live wit' da greata soul in olda time, I fighta da priest, clericali, I see heem in da hella—scusa me, lady—we say it in Italia more polito, l'inferno."

The speaker paused long enough to gulp a mouthful of bread and cheese; then he began again: "I say Fay, I say Trando, not forgetta greata poet of old country. You reada heem, you have greata soul, you be strong, never 'fraid, you bear it—what you say it—infortunio, calamita. I go by Italian book-store, I say, You give me ever'ting Dante, I read heem all. I reada book—not poem, how you say?"

"Prose?"

" 'Il Convito.' That is, you sitta down for suppa, lika dis, but gooda suppa—plenty friend come—maka feast."

"The Banquet?" said Cornelia.

"So," said Vanzetti, and he recited a passage, and then, with many gestures, and mixing of Italian words with English, he conveyed to the Yankee lady what his great teacher had to say on the subject of riches. The widow of Josiah Quincy Thornwell, mother of three millionaires' wives, now learned upon authority of one of the world's great seers that it is the amassing of wealth which imperils and slays cities and nations; that riches do not come to the good man, because his mind is upon weightier matters; that the man of right appetite and true knowledge never loves them.

"You learn little bit," said Vanzetti, "I maka you onderstand heem Italian. No can make Eengleesh, spoil beautifool sound. You hear heem—listen, Miz' Cornella." He began to recite, lingering over every syllable, sounding all the vowels broad and long, as the Italians do:

Per me si va nella città dolente;
Per me si va nell' eterno dolore;
Per me si va tra la perduta gente.
Giustizia mosse il mio alto fattore.

"He sadda man," said Vanzetti; "never soocha sorrowful man live on eart'. He call it l'inferno—lika you say American, 'hella,' but not for curse-word, Miz' Cornella, you know what da priesta teach, da place for punish badda men."

"I understand."

"But you no believa da priest, it is all same hella here, what badda men maka for poor man, killa da people in war. You reada Dante, you no t'ink l'inferno, you t'ink Italia, you t'ink America, here, now. So he say"—and the speaker repeated the verses, and painfully worked out their English equivalent:

By me you go into da sadda city;
By me you go into da endless sorrow;
By me you go among da losta people.
Joostice it mov-èd him, my greata maker.

It is a fact that much great poetry has been written in the dialects of the poor and humble; it is a fact that Dante's own dialect was that, until he made it a world-language. But Cornelia did not know this, and did not realize that the Italian ditch-digger was making good poetry of his own. She only knew that she was managing to understand what his teacher meant to him: "Perduta gente, Miz' Cornella—it is not people what have deny da priest and go hella, it is people what is poor and no got friend, go for be shot, and kill-èd in bigga war. Dat is perduta gente, losta people; for soocha people it maka me tears in da heart."

IV

The family was stirring early. Brini did an hour's work in the garden before he went to his job, and his friend Bart insisted upon helping. Mrs. Brini made the coffee and "frittata" for breakfast and would not let Cornelia help, but instead made her listen to good advice. "You no try be foreign woman, dey glad for have Yankee lady worka by cordage. You tella heem osband

die, you harda luck, musta get job. But you no be 'fraid,
plenty coraggio, plenty odder job. You say got to have day work,
no letta heem give nighta job. Wartime maka plenty job, you
no be 'fraid."

Vanzetti was working for the cordage company, "—worka
picka shov," was the way he phrased it; digging a ditch for a
pipe-line they were laying. So he walked with Cornelia, and
gave her more advice. "You have harda time, Miz' Cornella,
olda lady, no giovane, molta affaticata—harda work. You go
easy, no be scare of boss, he no die hungry if you no killa self
for heem. You worka slow, taka time. You losa job, we help, no
let gooda lady hungry."

So Cornelia went boldly into the employment office and looked
the clerk in the eye and said, "I would like employment."

It was the first time she had offered herself for sale, and it
was a new sensation to be looked over from the market point of
view. "Ever worked at cordage?"

"No, sir."

"What have you done?"

"I taught school. Then I married. Now I am a widow, and
must support myself."

"This work is pretty hard for an old lady."

"I'm not afraid of hard work. I'll take care of that. But I
want a daytime job."

"You might do wrapping," said the clerk. He consulted a
chart. "We have no vacancy, but we might move somebody on."

"Thank you," said Cornelia. "Arrange that, if you please."
She was trying a little "psychology" on him, and it appeared to
work. He asked her questions and entered her replies on a card;
and presently she found herself in charge of a messenger, passing through the high steel gates.

It was a long walk to her destination; this greatest cordage
plant in the world extended three-quarters of a mile along the
bay-front, with a covered dock to which the ships came to unload their cargoes of sisal, and railroad tracks and switch-yards
for the cars which carried away rope and binder twine. The
roar of machinery was everywhere, and men hurrying about like
busy ants. Cornelia stayed close to her guide, who knew his
way through the labyrinth of labor, and would deliver her safely
to her little niche.

The ceiling of the wrapping-room was low—no space was wasted. The coils of rope came through upon an endless platform and a row of women sat sewing burlap covers with long needles and hempen thread. Cornelia's escort spoke to the foreman, who took another woman off the job, gave her seat to Cornelia and showed her the work. She had to turn the coil of rope a certain distance, take up a threaded needle, turn in the edges of the burlap cover and sew a certain number of stitches; all this within a calculated time, before the motion of the platform took the coil of rope out of her reach and brought a new one to her.

It took an intelligent person above five minutes to learn all there was to the job; after that it was just the same motions over and over. At first it was agreeable; Cornelia's problem was solved, and she could take glimpses at the other women in the line and at the room and the machinery. But after an hour or two the unaccustomed muscles and nerves began to make protest; she was tired and her hands were trembling. The hempen thread was long and so was the motion of her arm; if you think it is not tiresome to wave your arm for several hours—try it! She began to feel dizzy, and the coil of rope which had at first moved normally, now seemed to be glued to the platform and refused to turn. She had no way to tell the time; she was at the mercy of this enormous machine which had run wild and forgotten the clock, and would go on until the row of arm-waving women were paralyzed!

But at last the siren sounded; and then Cornelia understood, without any sociological discussion, why it was that the workers leaped up in a flash and hurried outdoors. For herself, she did not move; all she wanted was to lie back against the wall and close her trembling eyelids and let her tired hands drop. She had brought lunch in a little box, but she did not want it; she only wanted to be still. She answered faintly the other women who sat near and expressed their sympathy. They knew how it was at first and sought to reassure her; it would be easier by and by, her fingers and back would get used to it. But she was an old lady, to be tackling a job like this.

Yes, Cornelia was old; she had never felt so old in her life before. She had been foolish to attempt such a thing; she might have known she couldn't see it through. But then she shut her

tired fists and clenched her teeth. She had made up her mind
to get a job and stick to that job, whatever it turned out to be.
Now this was it, and it was do or die. People in New England
did things like that—strange, eccentric, and terrible things, because their consciences drove them to it, or just because they
had said they would, and were too stubborn to change.

v

The siren sounded again and the great machine started to
rumble. Cornelia picked up the threaded needle with her shaking
fingers, and began making the motions against which her being
rebelled. She saw her future stretching out to infinity; every
morning from seven until twelve she would sit and make these
motions; then she would rest an hour and make them again
from one until six. And those ten hours would be ten hours,
and no nonsense about them, no fine sentiment. Cornelia recalled
her reason for selecting the Plymouth Cordage Company as her
first employer. Old Mr. Perry—J. Lawrence Perry, a director
of the company—was such a kindly old gentleman; she had
heard him talk so much about the "welfare work" they were
doing and what a beautiful plant it was and how happy and
contented the workers were. It had sounded quite idyllic and
Cornelia had swallowed it whole. Mr. Perry gave money to
various charities, and also gave time to running them, and
everybody admired him so. But now it came to Cornelia in a
flash that she didn't care in the least what he did with the money
he got by selling these coils of rope; what she wanted was for
his machinery to stop for a few minutes! All the love and fine
sentiment in the world didn't matter a particle, so long as you
had to sit here ten hours out of twenty-four making the same
motions over and over!

Nor did it matter that rope was clean and even romantic,
having to do with ships! Cornelia had pleased herself by that
vain imagining; but now she realized that she wasn't going to
see any ships, nor have anything to do with the rope, except to
take eighteen or twenty stitches around the edges. She wasn't
going to know what became of the product after it left her
fingers; she wasn't even going to know, except by hearsay, how
it came to be what it was. The dear, gentle, white-haired old

Mr. Perry hadn't provided any system for escorting his employees through the plant and showing them the process. Each one went to his own appointed spot and was standing there when the siren blew and stayed there until it blew again five hours later. One job was the same as the next—except for one difference, the amount of money in the pay envelope when it was torn open. Some day Cornelia would point that out to dear old Mr. Perry and see the shocked look on his placid face. The idea gave her satisfaction, helping to drive from her consciousness the clamor of aching muscles and nerves.

When at last the siren blew again, one of the other women had to help Cornelia from her seat. She was the last to escape from the building, and the last to reach the gates. Brini and Vanzetti were waiting for her and they ran quickly and put their strong arms under her feeble, trembling ones—and what dear, good, honest, kind Italian laborers they seemed! They could read in her face how exhausted she was and they half carried her along the street. All the way, Vanzetti was murmuring, "Poor Miz' Cornella! Too harda job for olda lady! You no keep so harda job!"

And when they had got home and she said that she did not want any supper, but just to lie down on the bed, it was the disciple of Dante who brought her a glass of milk and forced her to drink it, whether or no. While he watched her, he said, "Miz' Cornella, you no go back for cordage jobba. You do little housework, you helpa da seeck little bit, no try mill work, you too olda lady, no usèd so harda work! I got little money in bank, I helpa you little bit, we all help, you get little job wit' Yankee family—"

But Cornelia said "I'll be all right in the morning. I'm not going to give up my place."

VI

Cornelia had hoped to find it easier the next day, but was disappointed. She slept badly and woke up with every muscle in her back and arms and fingers sore. It was a continual effort of the will to make these aching muscles do their work, and each hour of labor was a new ordeal. It was many days before these pains began to diminish and she paid for the effort by a sensitiveness in the shoulders and back for the rest of her life. The doctors called it "articular rheumatism" and were satisfied when they had given it such an impressive name. The patient was expected to be equally satisfied with the achievement.

Cornelia ought to have been flattered by her social success in Suosso's Lane. Each morning she had two able-bodied men to escort her to work, and the same two and a small boy to bring her home in the evening. The whole family would baby her, putting her to bed, insisting upon bringing her supper, and refusing to let her do any sort of work. She could eat lying back on a pillow, and they could talk to her from the kitchen where they ate. They made a regular function of it, with no end of fun and laughter.

Why did they do it? Was it the innate kindness of the poor? Would any Italian family have done the same for an elderly woman who was in trouble? Cornelia hoped it was true; but she began to suspect that there were special factors in her case. She was a "Yankee lady" and these people knew themselves for "wops" to the rulers of a strange rich land. It must have been evident to them that this mysterious elderly person with the slight frame and soft muscles, the gentle voice and sensitive feelings had been used to a different kind of life. She had come out into the cold world at the age of sixty, alone and friendless, to fight her own way. And why? She told them she had been left a widow, and their imaginations had done the rest. She had been thrown into destitution; cruel relatives had deprived her of her inheritance! Some such simple and naïve story they had made up for her and so she stood for romance to them.

Vanzetti insisted upon heating a glass of milk hot for Cornelia because it was nice and soothing that way and easy for a tired lady to digest. Later, when he went outdoors, Mrs. Brini remarked, "He so kinda heart, no can let anybody hurt. One time we got baby cat—how you say, kitten—poor little kitten getta seeck. He molto seeck, my osband he say, no good for suffer, he sure die, I keela heem. So he taka kitten by neck, for go outside and hitta heem on head. And Bart, he near go crazy. 'No, by Godda, you no keela kitten?' 'Buttalo giu!' say my man. 'What you t'ink, I gotta time for seecka kitten all time?' 'You giva heem me, I got plenty time,' say Bart, and he taka da kitten, he maka little box, he put heem in wit' grass for soft, he maka heem bed, and joosta soon he come homa night, he feeda da kitten wit' warm milk."

Cornelia laughed. "So that is where he learned it! I am his sick kitten!" And when Vanzetti came back, she called herself that and it gave great glee to Fay and Trando, who told her the Italian word, "gattina," and it would have become her nickname, only their mother made them stop because it was not dignified.

To help them out, Cornelia told them that at home she had gone by the name of "Grannie," and they told her the Italian equivalent, which was "Nonna," and began to call her that. Everybody had nicknames in this family and wanted Cornelia to call them by these, so that she would really belong. Alfonsina Brini was "Cicadet," the meaning of which was not clear. The youngest child was called "Dolly," because of the rag-doll she was never without. Vanzetti had a special name for Beltrando, a high-strung little fellow, who frequently did not get along with the boys outside; he would come in crying, and Vanzetti, to tease him out of it, would call him "Magoon," the Bolognese word for "sorry."

Papa Brini did not understand his sensitive child very well, so the boarder had taken over the task of his moral guidance; Vanzetti would sometimes romp with him and sometimes scold him, and sometimes explain life to him in serious discourses. The boy adored him and would follow him about, watching his every move. Vanzetti liked to go for long walks after his supper, to lose himself in thought; when it was stormy, he would walk back and forth in the kitchen, four steps of his long legs one way, and then four steps the other, completely oblivious to everything in the house. Perhaps because of the shortness of the space he would now and then take little steps, as if he were dancing; and Trando would follow behind him, back and forth, doing his best to reproduce each motion. The others would smile, but Vanzetti never seemed to know about it. What was he thinking at these times? What were the guiding ideas of this unusual Italian ditch-digger?

VII

One evening Cornelia sat on the steps of the porch, drinking in the soft breeze, watching the fire-flies and listening to the crickets. In the garden of the next house a woman was working and she came to the fence and said, with a substantial Irish brogue, "Good evenin', mum."

"Good evening," said Cornelia, politely; then to her surprise the woman said, "Would ye come over here, mum? I have somethin' to say." So Cornelia moved her stiff joints and limped over to the fence. "My name is Mrs. O'Dowd," said the neighbor, and Cornelia said, "I am Mrs. Cornell."

"Pleased to meet ye, Mrs. Cornell." She lowered her voice as she went on: "I have been watchin', and 'tis evident to me yez are an American lady, and perhaps ye do not know these Eyetalians. So, no offense, but I thought it might be good to give a bit of warnin'."

"Of what, Mrs. O'Dowd?"

"Likely ye did not know these Brinis before ye come to board with them—is that so?"

"Yes, it is."

"Sure, and I knowed it; says I to me man, 'She's picked them up on the street or somethin' '."

"I met the little boy on the street."

"Sure I was of it. 'Tis a good lad he is, I've nothin' agin him, barrin' that now and then his ball will bounce into me garden. Well, Mrs. Cornell, ye'd ought to know that ye have fell into a bunch of dangerous people—the worst there is in this town or many another—arnychists, the lot of them."

"Arnychists?" said Cornelia, puzzled.

"The very bad kind, mum, the Eyetalian kind, the murderin' and bomb-throwin' arnychists."

"Oh, Mrs. O'Dowd! You really think they do that?"

"I've never saw them do it, mum, but 'tis what the neighbors say, and the priest he is forever preachin' agin them, warnin' us that we shall not speak to them for any reason. For, ye see, 'tis not only the bombs, but 'tis atheists they are; they do not go to any church at all, mum, and their childer have never been baptized, they are lost souls the lot of them."

"Lost souls," said Cornelia, "how terrible!" And in the back of her consciousness was an echo of a melodious phrase—"Per me si va tra la perduta gente!"

"Mrs. O'Dowd," she said, "you surprise me. They have been so kind to me!"

"Yes, mum, but a lot of us would be that if we had a chance. 'Tis easy to know a lady when ye see one, and when she's in trouble, and tryin' to make her own way, 'twould be no great thing to give her a helpin' hand. But we would do it in the Blessed Name, mum, so it would count for somethin'."

"Well, I thank you very much," said Cornelia. "I am glad to know, of course."

"I hope ye will not say that 'twas me that told about it, because I have childer of me own, and I'd not like to find meself blown out of bed by no bombs."

"I'll surely not mention it," said Cornelia. "I'll need time to think what to do. It may be the kindest thing would be for me to stay with them and help convert them from their bad ways."

" 'Twould be a blessin' for fair," said Mrs. O'Dowd, "for 'tis a sore disgrace to Suosso's Lane to be havin' such a family in it. But be careful, mum, while ye argue, for ye might be the one to be converted yeself."

"Are they as dangerous as all that?"

"Well, Mrs. Cornell, 'tis somethin' I do not know of meself, because I don't know a word of their lingo and never hope to. But Father O'Brien says they have the divil in their hearts, and that makes them hard to deal with, so ye had best take warnin' and be careful."

"I will, Mrs. O'Dowd, and you may pray for me if you don't mind." So Cornelia went back to her seat on the porch.

After a while she went inside, and there was Brini, with a twinkle in his eyes and a wide grin on his good-natured face. "You talka wit' Miz' O'Dowda—what she tella you? She say, no live wit' anarchista, badda people, maka di bombe, t'rowa heem in da church"—and Brini made a violent upward motion with his hands—"blow uppa da Sancta Trinità and Benedetta Vergine!" Then he lowered his voice to a whisper. "Molto secreto—no tella heem—he putta di bombe nella mia casa, he blow bambini alla hella!"

Seeing from the expression of Cornelia's face that his guess was correct, Brini burst into uproarious laughter. "Ho, ho, ho! You tella Miz' O'Dowda, Vanzett' he moocha badda man—diavolo—furfante—maka di bombe, molte bombe, sicuramente! Bombe di zucchero"—and Brini made motions of sucking his fingers and finding delight in the sweet taste—"bombe di pistachio—di crema—bombi di gelati—What you say it?—ice crema—di pasticceria—in Italia he what you call pastry-cook— granda gooda pastry-cook!"

The end of the week came; and very surely Cornelia did not fail to remember the Sabbath day to keep it holy. It was a day of rest—and for remembering the old hymn about every day being Sunday by-and-by.

But then came Vanzetti. "Very gooda day, beautifool sunshine, Miz' Cornella. You come wit' me, see somet'ing molta bella."

"I'm too tired to walk, I'm afraid."

"No walka far—little way, I help. Show bella campagna, maka happy, gooda sentimento. You come, I carry."

At the foot of Suosso's Lane was a round knoll, blocking the view; Castle Hill, it was called, and beyond it, Cornelia realized, must lie the bay. They stooped under a fence and there was a little path and Vanzetti put his strong arm under her weak one and half lifted her up the slope. Bushes and a few pine trees grew upon it, but not enough to interfere with the view when you got over the rise. "Oh, lovely!" she exclaimed, and Vanzetti was delighted. "Shoore, moocha pretty!"

The bay was sparkling blue in bright sunshine; bounded by a long sand-spit, and a couple of rocky islands. In the distance ran the low misty line of Cape Cod and close at hand on both sides was the town, white-painted houses in a setting of green. One shore-line was occupied by the long brick buildings of the cordage plant, with tall chimneys out-towering the hill. Cornelia did not care for that, so they seated themselves on the other side, facing the monuments of Plymouth.

"Somewhere on that shore is Plymouth Rock," said she.

"I show you!" said Vanzetti, and pointed out the landmarks. "I worka one time by heem, bringa feesh from boat. Plenty people come for see all time. He looka same like any rock."

"You know what happened there?"

"Shoore, I read in schoola-book, Fay got heem. People come in ship for liva here, maka state Massachusett."

"That was nearly three hundred years ago; not so long ago as your Dante, but it seems long to us."

"Plenty long for make istoria," said Vanzetti. "Sometime I t'ink it mistake for teach istoria. People study tempo passato, make conservativo, timido—you onderstand?"

"Yes; but it depends on how you study it. The Pilgrim fathers were really quite wonderful. They came in little boats— so little you could hardly believe it. Perhaps you've seen the bones of that old boat in Pilgrim Hall."

"Shoore, I see ever't'ing."

"There was nothing here but a wilderness, full of wild Indians, savages. A stern and rock-bound coast, the poet described it; and winter coming, they had to hurry and build huts for shelter. They had poor food—only what little grain they had brought and the game they could kill, and the fish. That first winter was frightful, half of them died; yet they stayed on— when the next ship came, the following summer, not one of the survivors would go back to England. That showed the kind of people they were."

"Shoore," said Vanzetti, "greata people—ribelli—fighta priest, fighta king—come for joostice, come for liberty. But get liberty for self, no give for odder. I say liberty for all."

"Of course," replied Cornelia; "but that is not so easy. How can everybody have liberty, when maybe there are some who won't play fair?"

"Is no soocha people, signora."

"You don't think there are bad people?"

"Some badda, sure, seecka people, must helpa soocha people, teach, put in—what you say—ospedale, 'ospital for seecka men. But mosta people be good, wanta joostice, you give heem chance. No, no, Miz' Cornella—" the speaker became eager, the Italian in him came to life, he began to make gestures and raise his voice—"what is trouble wit' people is not badda heart, it is badda teach', badda sistema—it is power, it is go-vernment"— he accented this word on the second syllable. "It is priesta, king, capitalista, padrone—taka men, maka fight, maka war for profit."

"You think that explains the war in Europe?"

"No t'ink—I know, signora. I live Europe, I see come dissa war, I come America for evitare—how you say—get away. It is war for padrone, for master—for bigga capitalista!"

"You don't think the people's hearts are in it?"

"Shoore, some—but why? Is it not teach in school? Who maka da school? Who maka giornale, da newspaper? Always padrone, he teacha da war, he wanta da profit, he maka da people for slave, for machine—what he care for worker life? What he care for poor lady here by cordage? You liva wit' worker, you see heem! You t'inka for self, you reada book I geeva you!"

And suddenly Cornelia remembered Mrs. O'Dowd and her warning! "Be careful, mum, while ye argue, for ye might be the one to be converted yeself."

IX

White sail-boats dotted the bay in front of them, and majestic clouds sailed overhead, making slow sweeping shadows on the water. Church-bells sounded and little birds sang in the trees about them and wild flowers bloomed; so much peace and beauty—yet Cornelia had to remember that men were slaughtering one another by the thousands, using hideous machines they had spent years in building and generations in learning to build. She closed her eyes and whispered, "Let's be happy for a few minutes!"

The controversy died out of the other's voice. "I know, signora! I say, be happy, I no t'ink war no more, no t'ink rivoluzione, politica laida! I go picka flower. Soocha sweet flower grow here—you know heem? Mayflower—it is not only ship, it is flower. I learn time of year, I looka for heem. I taka Fay, Trando, odder piccoli, go looka flower, getta moocha bigga— what you say—gobba—bunch. I taka heem home, give Alfonsina, she happy, make home so nice, pretty. I say, get gooda book—roman—what you say, lova story—reada nice, be happy. I come here, Sunday morning, quiet, church-bell—gooda place for read, nobody here. I come holiday, all day; sometime I got no job—no needa so moocha work, so moocha money, no got family—I what you say lonely man. Alla right, I reada book, look outa for self. I healt'y man, stronga man, plenty time, gooda life—I laugha, say, war no get America—I no care Italian, let heem look outa for self. You onderstand?"

"I understand. Most men take it that way."

"I say, No be crazy, Vanzett', you no maka da world, no

can changa heem. I say, You no maka da war, Vanzett', you no stoppa heem. But Miz' Cornella, no can t'ink, no can forget. T'ink alla time fossi—what you say it—digga place in ground for fight war."

"Trenches?"

"Joosta so, I see alla time trench, see men killa brodder, see men die orribile, wounda, scream, agonia. I say, Vanzett', you no do somet'ing, you traditore, you—how you say, betray somet'ing?"

"Traitor."

"Trait'! I say, Vanzett', you no be trait', you speaka da trut', you maka da protest, da propagand', you getta da meeting, you calla da men, getta da speaker. No can speak self, Miz' Cornella, joosta lavorante, workman, molta ignoranza, povero. But we got speaker for denounca da war, Italian speaker, he come—Galleani—you know heem?"

"I never heard of him."

"All Italian man know heem—olda man, granda man, he speaka for poor man, maka da propagand'. One time I helpa heem for speech in Plye-moot'. He come, bigga meeting, molto popolo. My boss—I worka for contractor—he no like, he say 'Abbastanza for anarchista propaganda, no more jobba for you, getta da hella!' So I looka for new job, but I feela moocha good, I helpa da cause."

"What is it you expect to do?"

"Teacha da people! Maka heem no fighta da war, no fighta for padrone, for capitalista! Say people, fight real nemico, fighta capitalista! He maka war for heemself, for hees money, bigga money—alla right, let heem fighta hees war, workman no fighta hees war, giammai, never! When capitalista no can maka fight workmen, so queeck you see stoppa da war, signora, is it not so?"

"I don't know," said Cornelia, sadly. "Sometimes I think men like to hate, they get a thrill out of it. The capitalists send their own sons to the war and they get killed, a lot of them."

"And de women—you t'ink dey lika war?"

"Some of them do—they cheer for it, and hate—even worse than the fighting men. There are women in Boston who want to get America in this war the worst kind of way."

"It is propagand', Miz' Cornella—capitalista propagand .

Why for could we not live happy in dis bigga countree—why for moosta we go fight odder countree? You go Italia, you hear say, countree too moocha people, moosta have rooma, more land, taka from odder people. You t'ink, too moocha people, too moocha bambini—alla righta, no hava so many bambini—what you say it, baby. Scusa me, signora, you olda lady, I talka plain for you—you know what I mean, no have so moocha baby?"

"We call it birth control," said Cornelia, smiling.

"Shoore, birt' control, alla right. Now, you say birt' control Italian woman, no have so moocha baby. Butta come priesta, he say, diavolo, inferno, moosta have baby, you no have baby you go to hella! He no letta you teacha da people, he driva you out, putta jail, maka propagand', calla name, scare people, no listen. For why? Priesta say he talka for God. God, he say moosta have baby, maka beega popolazione! Den God he say, no got rooma for popolazione, moosta taka land, moosta maka war! You onderstand?"

"Yes, I understand."

"Sooch imbecillità! Follia! Moosta have war for maka room, moosta have baby for filla room! More war for maka more room for more baby! E la donna, woman, what for is woman? Animal for maka more baby for war-man, militarista, kill. Keepa da woman for slave, for ignoranza, for priesta, for super-stizione—for maka da plenty baby for soldier! Soocha countree is Europe, signora, and soocha like America if capitalista have way. But anarchista say, No have way! Anarchista say, No die for soldier, fighta for worker, for self! Anarchista say to woman, Stand up, no be fraid da priesta, he no can hurt! Is no soocha god lika priesta preach, is gooda God, lova da people, lova da baby, no wanta heem kill-èd in war! Is it not trut', signora? Is it not joostice?"

And Cornelia realized how wise had been the warning of Mrs. O'Dowd, concerning the subtlety of the devil, and the perils of entering into contest with him! For here the devil was managing to present what appeared to Cornelia a quite reasonable argument; nor did his propagandist appear at all devilish, but rather a dreamer of dreams, so simple of mind as to have no conception of the odds against him, the forces of colossal cruelty that would sweep him away as a leaf before a hurricane.

x

Time passed, and Cornelia became a completely established member of the Brini family; also a completely disciplined worker for the Plymouth Cordage Company. Now and then she lifted her eyes from the task of needle and thread and got to know the people about her—their faces, their names, their nationalities and modes of speech. She would chat with them during the noon hour and hear the gossip of their lives, the hopes which moved them and the fears which held them back.

Also she became aware of the plant, the gigantic complex of labor which surrounded her. She learned the names of different buildings and picked up an idea of what went on inside them; the "hackling," the "cleaning," the making of the "sliver," the spinning of the yarn, the "forming" and "laying" of rope. Technical terms began to take on the shadow of a meaning; she got glimpses through door ways of "spinning-rooms" with hundreds of "flyers," as far as the eye could see down a vista, and of powerful "laying-machines" which took a hundred threads of yarn and wrought them into a heavy four-strand rope at a single process. Little by little there soaked into her mind a realization of the technical complexity of an industry whereby trainloads of hemp from the Philippines and shiploads of sisal from Yucatan evolved into cordage of every size from wrapping and binder-twine to towing-lines and sixteen-inch cables for battleships.

The human cogs who made up this machine were—at least in the lower ranks with Cornelia—very slow of wit; they labored under a load of handicaps—poverty, ignorance, a foreign language, new and bewildering customs. There were agencies supposed to lift them up, such as public schools and night schools, but it seemed to Cornelia these were countered by forces far stronger, interested to hold them down. Landlords and loan-sharks, peddlers of shoddy goods, fake patent medicines and adulterated foods, smooth-tongued agents inducing them to put their savings into non-existent gold-mines and oil-wells—there were few among these workers who managed to escape such plunderers.

And chief among the agencies of exploitation was, of course, the great rich concern under the administration of the benevolent Mr. J. Lawrence Perry. The company owned most of the houses in which the workers had to live; it owned most of the land about, and was, of course, not entirely without influence upon the government of the town. It paid six dollars a week to its unskilled women workers and nine to the men, and manifestly a family could not be supported on such a wage; the tacit assumption was that the women of the family would work, and the children as soon as they could pretend to be old enough. The home would be kept by the old people and the young children and the invalids and cripples. It would not be a well-kept home, nor very attractive; and the ladies and gentlemen whose incomes came from cordage stocks and bonds would remark, some with pity, some with contempt, "Dagos, wops, hunkies—they live like pigs!"

XI

Now something more than ordinarily maleficent was befalling these humble wage-workers. It was happening all over the world, but they did not know that—they only knew Plymouth. The cost of everything they bought was going up day by day. Because of the war in Europe, the allied nations were borrowing money in America, and spending it for American goods. Exactly as Josiah Quincy Thornwell had foretold on the night of his death, it was making enormous and incredible prosperity for American manufacturers and stock-speculators; but also it was making higher and higher prices for the poor. And there was no corresponding increase in the wage, so close to the border-line of want; there was no authority charged with the task of calculating living costs, and adjusting earnings to them. The great industries which owned and rented tenements to their workers would raise the rents a dollar or two a month and tell the tenants that this was necessary; but they would overlook what might be necessary to the tenants.

The cordage-workers were slow of wit, yet they did know whether they had any money in their pocket-books at the end of the week. Pay-day was Thursday and when the money ran out on Tuesday night instead of Wednesday night they grumbled to one another and speculated about it; and gradually an understanding spread, a kind of crude mass-consciousness, a thing as it were separate from the individual minds, with a life of its own. These workers were entirely unorganized; cordage was one of the "open shop" industries, having the sacred "American plan" in its full and ideal perfection. The fact that the workers had no way to voice a grievance was a matter without significance, because in a land so great and prosperous it was impossible for a grievance to arise. Any one who went to the foreman and complained was obviously a "sorehead," and the foreman would tell him to take his troubles somewhere else. That would be the end of him for the cordage industry; whatever skill he might have acquired he could throw into Plymouth Bay.

Cornelia knew little about labor matters, but the elementary thought came to her that these ill-paid workers ought to have a union. She said it to the Brini family and greatly to her surprise discovered that her words gave distress to Vanzetti. "No say sooch a t'ing!" he cried. "Organizazione is trappa for worker, make heem slave! Union is joosta same as go-vernment! Bigga, reech offeesh', putta feet on desk, smoka bigga cigar, tella worker go hella!"

Now Cornelia knew that Vanzetti had helped to unload fish and in her efforts to understand his torrent of words she had a vision of a "feesh" which had feet and put them on desks and smoked cigars. She asked an explanation, and the family burst into laughter and with Fay's help it was made clear that Bart was talking about not "a feesh," but "offeesh," the officials of labor unions. There were hordes of them in New England and they paid themselves good salaries and did nothing for the workers, so Vanzetti declared; therefore the workers not yet organized must be saved from their snares.

"But then what are you going to do?" asked Cornelia, greatly perplexed.

"Moosta teacha worker—t'ink for self—no need offeesh' t'ink for heem. Can all stand togedder, all lika one, but no offeesh', no salary, no graft."

Cornelia had thought that a labor union was an elementary idea, upon which every kind of radical would agree. She asked and it was explained to her, with the translation of long words, that Vanzetti's kind of anarchistas did not permit organization. There were other kinds, who called themselves "comunisti anarchici," and would support revolutionary unions like the I. W. W., and even back the old-line unions in time of strikes. But Vanzetti called himself "anarchico individualista," and would have no kind of organization, except a purely temporary kind to manage a strike—a "comity," as he pronounced it, to represent the strikers, and not be paid any salary, and be changed at any time the strikers saw fit.

Moreover, it was apparent that he was distressed because his friend, whose education he had taken so earnestly in hand, was dallying with the evil thought of a union. "Who talka soocha t'ing wit' you?" he demanded; and when she assured him that the notion had come of itself, he was not comforted. Cornelia laughed—it seemed to her deliciously funny; she told him he was just like "Mrs. O'Dowda," afraid she might imperil her soul by taking up with dangerous new ideas!

Censorship of course exercised upon Cornelia's mind its customary effect of awakening curiosity. She pressed her teacher for more facts, and so learned of the existence of obnoxious characters known as "riformistas"; persons who believed it possible to improve the present social system, or to change it little by little. This kind of thinking was a trap for the wage-slaves, because it led them into politics. "Politica ě un perditempo!" declared Vanzetti, and the way he said the word and the expression on his face made clear that it was something very bad. "Riformista is traditore," he went on, and repeated the English word which Cornelia had taught him, "Riformista is trait'!"

"Traitor," corrected Cornelia, and Vanzetti said, "Shoore, trait.' He is trait', because he get elect' butta no do notting, he is offeesh', he got salary, he liva by graft, he maka da promessi, he tella da bigga lie, he keepa da capitalismo. No, no, mia frienda, have notting do wit' riformista, wit' socialista, he is giallo—how you say it, color of flower—not red, not blue, what you call heem, golden-rod—yes, yellow! Socialista is yellow, he is badda frienda for worker."

XII

Soon afterwards Cornelia made actual contact with one of these dangerous characters. On Saturday evening there came a caller: a short, solidly-built young Italian, marble-cutter by trade, introduced as "Compagno" Culla. He had come to see the two men upon a matter of business and they discussed it in their own language, while Cornelia and Alfonsina sat placidly sewing. Cornelia caught several times the word "picanic," but did not realize that this was an English word, until Mrs. Brini whispered that this Culla was one of the socialistas of Plye-moot', and that they were getting up a picanic. Cornelia saw that the talk was becoming more and more animated; the three men were gesticulating and raising their voices, and presently she heard a familiar word, that wicked word "riformista." Vanzetti pronounced it in a tone of scorn and lest Compagno Culla should fail to understand to whom it was applied, the speaker pointed at him, and exclaimed, "Riformista e giallo e traditore—"

Now Compagno Culla had a newspaper in his hand, partly opened; he lifted it and with sudden vehemence hurled it to the floor. In the course of the journey it came all the way open and made a great racket. "Eh via, puh!" he exclaimed. "Parlate sfacciatamente!"

Whereupon Vanzetti started to his feet, with a sweep of his arms embracing the surrounding atmosphere. "Riformista e traditore!" he shouted.

"Diffamazione!" protested Compagno Culla.

"Traditore di lavoratori!" persisted Vanzetti. They began pouring out two torrents of vehement Italian, which met in the middle and formed a whirlpool of words, with four waving arms in the vortex thereof. The arms were coming nearer and nearer and must inevitably have met, had not Brini stepped between, shouting louder than both the orators put together. At the same time Mrs. Brini sprang up and caught Vanzetti by the sleeve, saying something which contained the word "Nonna!" Cornelia had got out of her chair with a frightened look on her face—not being used to Mediterranean methods of conducting political discussion. Vanzetti glanced at her and then turned sharply on his heel and walked into the kitchen; while Brini and Culla exchanged a few laughing words and the latter went away.

Vanzetti came back and sat down, looking not a little embarrassed. "I shame-èd for bad temper, Nonna," said he—he was calling her now by the children's pet name, and she was calling him Bart. "I try for not getta so angree, but riformista is soocha badda fellow."

He explained what it was that Compagno Culla had wanted—the list of names of the anarchistas of the vicinity, so that they could be invited to the socialista picanic. Some time ago the anarchistas had given a picanic with an anarchista speaker and all the socialistas had been invited and many of them had come; now they thought the favor ought to be reciprocated—quite overlooking the difference in the situation. For the socialistas, being riformistas and gialli, were let alone by the polizia; but the anarchistas, being real and true rivoluzionarii, were always fearing trouble with the polizia and naturally could not give the names of their friends and supporters to any gialli riformisti. So now Compagno Culla was angry and thought his party was not getting a square deal.

The discussion that followed brought out a further point— that the socialistas of Plymouth had a great advantage over the anarchistas, because they believed in organizations and had a good and lively one, with perhaps fifty members; whereas the anarchistas, not believing in organizations, had a weak one, in fact little more than a list of names. Therefore the socialistas could do things which the anarchistas could not do, they were distributing their literature regularly every week and seducing members away from the anarchistas. Vanzetti said this without seeing anything humorous in it and was perplexed when Cornelia began to tease him, suggesting that it sounded like an admission that organization was sometimes useful. Her teacher would laugh and joke about all other matters except his doctrine; that was sacred, that was a way of escape from slavery, war and horror for the workers, and about it he was fanatical, implacable—he who was so gentle and soft-hearted in all other relations of life!

That was a Saturday evening; and next morning Cornelia and her teacher went for a walk in the woods and coming out met a group of four children who had been gathering flowers. Each had a bunch which they offered for sale—two cents apiece. Vanzetti bought all four and the children went off happy. Then he said, "Too many flower, I giva you one bunch, taka one for Cicadet, no wanta more." He threw two bunches into the bushes. "Why did you buy them all?" asked Cornelia, interested in his reaction; and he was a little shocked by her lack of perception. "No could buy joosta two, make odder children onhappy, dey worka so hard, da money is like so moocha more for dem."

XIII

The bright days of summer passed quickly, and the bracing days of autumn, and then came the first threats of winter. It is nothing to joke about on this stern and rock-bound coast, where icy gales blow in from the ocean and snow piles up and blocks the streets, and the temperature goes to considerably below zero. Cornelia found that she had to take every cent of her savings to buy herself a warm coat, and then it was not so warm; she learned to live in it all day while she worked in the factory, a good part of the time in the home, and at night she made it into a bed-cover.

There came days when the trip to her work and back again were infernal experiences, recalling those regions of Dante where the lost souls are frozen solid in ice. But in the great poet's story it is possible to see the damned, while here they stumbled through pitch darkness, at half past six in the morning and the same hour in the evening. Cornelia would get her coat buttoned tight over a sweater and the family would pin her shawl fast over her head and ears, leaving just a peep-hole for the eyes and nose. Then with her hands in mittens, and these tucked under the shawl, she would start the long journey, with Brini's big hand grasping her under the arm. They would go staggering through snow-drifts, sliding on the ice and packed sleet; her hands would be half frozen, yet she would have to jerk them out to catch Brini and keep from breaking her bones. The pitiless winds would howl and buffet her and stab through her flimsy garments: the whirling snow would blind her—yet there was not much danger of getting lost, there being a stream of bundled figures plodding to the same goal. It was January of 1916, and out across the storm-lashed ocean the ships were being sunk, so there must be more cordage to keep the world at war. Any woman who failed to complete the journey twelve times per week would not have her pay-envelope with the six dollars on Thursday night; and how then would she pay for food and bed and shawls and coats and mittens and rubber shoes and cough medicines and dentistry and surgical operations and opera-tickets?

Cornelia was changing not merely her ideas but her appearance and personal habits. She no longer took a bath every morning before she dressed. Getting up at a quarter before six, by the light of an oil-lamp and in rooms where she could see her breath, she found that her one thought was to get into the warmest clothes she had, and as many of them as possible; her second thought was to get two cups of the hot boiled chicory which serves for coffee in the homes of the poor. Thereafter she had no impulse to take off her clothes until she got into bed—and not all of them then, because her bed-covers were made of cotton, and even with all her clothing piled on top there were nights when she could not sleep for the cold. And now and then she would remember the formula she had heard the prosperous ladies repeat—that at least the poor might keep clean!

Another principle of hygiene which had been taught to her was plenty of fresh air at night. It was easy for the doctors to say it, sleeping in rooms with heat, and layers of woolen blankets and eider-down quilts. But now Cornelia adopted the custom of the poor, to seal up windows at the beginning of winter and breathe such air as happened to get into the house. If this, combined with a poor diet, brought tuberculosis, it would be called the will of God. In Cornelia's case it would be the stubbornness of a woman who had made up her mind and would not admit defeat. She had signed a declaration of independence—and here was her Valley Forge!

The cordage workers lived in their dark holes, forgotten by the world except on rent day. They grumbled and complained, because the cost of living kept on going up and in winter it was so much worse—there were no gardens with fresh vegetables, nor trees with apples and pears on them, nor berries which the children could gather in the woods. Now everything had to be bought in stores and the housewives picked over the meager supplies; and when they could no longer make ends meet, what were they to do?

Some voiced their complaints to their bosses and were told to go elsewhere; and every time that happened the pot of anger boiled faster. Brini and Vanzetti came home at night, voluble and gesticulating; sometimes they would hurry off after supper—"meeting by Giuseppi," they would say, or whatever name it might be. Several times Cornelia went to such meetings, and a mass of people packed themselves into a little parlor, with overflow into the kitchen, and complained and argued and gestured for an hour or two. Such was Vanzetti's solution of the labor problem, the workers to gather in little groups—"gruppi autonomi," was his phrase; each of these gruppi would decide what it wanted and appoint a representative to meet with others from the Portuguese, the French-Canadians, the Germans, the Irish.

The believers in politics and organization, the socialistas, held a meeting in a hall, with more than a thousand workers, and a speaker in English, one in Italian and one in Portuguese; those who did not understand any of these languages understood the excitement of the rest. Also came the I. W. W. with their speakers, and their program of "direct action," the taking over of the industries by the "one big union." They were strong among these New England mill-workers, having the prestige of a great victory in the woollen mills of Lawrence three or four years ago.

And of course that stirred Vanzetti and his anarchistas. They too must have a meeting and summon their leader, Galleani, to point out to the workers the dangers of organization, and how it was possible to win freedom from both capitalistas and labor union "offeesh'." There was a gathering of the "gruppo autonomo di Plyemoot'," and money was subscribed to pay for the hall and for what Vanzetti called the "expensit." He contributed ten dollars himself, and explained to Cornelia that his share was greater for the reason that he was a "lonely man."

XIV

That was a Tuesday night; and next day, preceding pay-day, there appeared mysteriously at the cordage plant a force of two hundred and fifty "private police" to guard the property. Where did they come from, this hired army of capitalism, and where were they kept when they were not working? Did they travel about the country, putting down labor troubles? Had the masters got trouble so systematized that they could count upon a regular supply of it to keep this army at work? Nobody knew; but here they were, big husky fellows, bundled in over-coats and arctics and fur-topped gloves, with clubs in their hands and revolvers in holsters at their belts—in plain sight, where nobody could miss their meaning. They paced before the gates and the doors of buildings, and to make them comfortable when they were off duty the town's most fashionable summer hotel sprang into activity.

The various "gruppi" had agreed upon their demands, eight dollars a week for unskilled women and twelve for the men. They appointed a committee to present the demands to the company, and the meeting took place, and the company ex-plained that such an increase, twenty-five percent, would bank-rupt it, and then no one would have any job. The company offered a raise of five percent, and the committee rejected this; there were more meetings, and crowds of people standing about stamping their feet in the snow, and the guards commanding them to move on, and getting surly answers. There were work-ers who said that if the company would pay the cost of these guards in wages it would help quite a little; they were even ungrateful enough to suggest that old Mr. Perry's "welfare work" be stopped, so that the people could have the money for food.

As usual, this big magazine was fired by a little spark. On Thursday morning, pay-day, one of the men in number three spinning-room got into a dispute with his foreman; the foreman told him to take his coat and hat and get out, and instead of obeying, the man turned and started yelling to his comrades. The foreman took him by the shoulder to put him out, and others came rushing to his help, and there was a tumult, and above it rose the word, "Strike!" It spread like wildfire down the long spinning-room; what had been at one moment an industry became in the next a mob. "Sciopero!" yelled the Italians. "Folga!" echoed the Portuguese. "Grève!" shrieked the French-Canadians. "Streik!" bellowed the Germans. And "Strike! Strike! Strike!" roared Americans and English and Irish and Welsh, and all others who had learned the word. A hundred Paul Reveres set out in every direction, spreading the wildfire from room to room. The openers of the bales threw down their knives, and the feeders turned from the "breakers," and the spinners deserted their "flyers," and the engineers shut off the power, and the wheels stopped turning, and two thousand workers grabbed their clothing and tumbled outside, pouring into a few minutes' clamor the pent-up anger and misery of many silent years.

The storm reached Cornelia's wrapping-room, and the women had to quit whether they wanted to or not, because the platform stopped moving. She got her things and streamed out with the rest. The crowds were milling about, the frightened guards shouting, "Move along, keep moving there!" In various places impromptu meetings started, and the stream would be blocked. Cornelia saw a man leap upon the corner of a loading platform —a man in a worn blue "reefer," with a storm hat pulled over his ears, and a pair of brown walrus mustaches hiding half his face. "Compagni! Lavoratori! L'ora della riscossa è scoccata! Essa darà la libertá agli oppressi"—whereupon another man climbed upon the platform and gave the orator a shove which sent him flying. "Get out, you blankety-blank, and don't show your face in here again!" And the company detective sought out one of the foremen, inquiring, "Who is that wop they call Bart —the one with long mustaches like a walrus? We'll have to keep our eye on him, he's one of the trouble-makers."

CHAPTER 3

DAGO RED

I

Snow in the air, whirled here and there by unpurposed winds; snow on the ground, thrown back from sidewalks and turning them into trenches. Guards and policemen, pacing in front of the cordage company gates, making long puffs of steam as they breathed; and workers, huddled on the other side of the road, stamping their feet and dancing about, blowing on their fingers or tucking them under their arms. Sky lowering and light dim—it seemed a good time to be indoors, yet nobody went. In leather arm-chairs in the Union Club of Boston were comfortable old gentlemen who had agreed to pay the guards five dollars a day and board at the hotel, to stand in the cold and drive strikers back from the gates; while the strikers had the hope that by standing in sufficient numbers and with sufficient menace they might get a dollar more in their pay envelopes every Thursday; also the certainty that if they gave up and went away, some yet hungrier wretches would sneak in and take their jobs. So the two groups confronted each other, the living presence of the class struggle. "Get back there! Move along now!" "What's the matter? Ain't I got a right to walk on the street?" So it went, the ceaseless wrangling of the picket-line; the most perfect of all civilizations engaged in dividing the product of its industry.

Two thousand had gone out, men and women, a huddled mass, speaking a dozen different languages, and without guidance. Whoever had an impulse towards leadership, a theory as to how labor might be aided, now found his chance; the unorganized mass began to grow organs—a miracle of mutation while you watched. The socialists had a meeting-place in North Plymouth, Rispicci Hall, and this was thrown open, and was swarming with strikers. Impromptu meetings were held, and committees named, and speeches made. In the evening came the sympathizers and propagandists, summoned hastily from Boston; Felice Guadagni, a journalist, orator of the socialists, and Paul Blanshard, a very young assistant clergyman from a Congregational church. There was a bigger meeting-place, Humberto Ferrari Hall, and this was packed to the doors, and the eager audience learned in several languages the meaning of solidarity, and the details of how to conduct a strike.

First of all they must get up a circular and mail it out to lists of names, and raise funds for support. The greater number of these workers lived close to the border-line of want, and their money would soon be gone. Those who had savings would contribute, and more would come from the labor movement outside. On the first day a hundred strikers put up five dollars each; which would pay for rent and telephone calls and telegrams, stamps and typewriters. The socialists and anarchists and I. W. W. brought their mailing-lists, and a feeble little machine of working-class publicity began to function.

Next day there was a parade; eighteen hundred workers marching the whole length of the main street of Plymouth, passing the cordage company's plant, despite all the guards and the "cops." Three days later came another parade, twice as big, with women and children carrying poles from which dangled clams and mussels, with the sign, "We are tired of living on these all the time!" That amused the newspaper reporters, and brought good publicity.

Organizers came: one representing the American Federation of Labor, the conservative union, which was ready to help them get shorter hours and higher wages; also one from the Industrial Workers of the World, which would help them to take over the cordage industry. The strikers listened to both, and were pulled and hauled between them; their minds being still further confused by the anarchists, who clamored that both organizations were traps for the workers, contrived by shrewd officials who wanted to live without working. Let the workers run their own strike, and let those who sympathized be content to raise funds and feed the children.

So thought and spoke Bartolomeo Vanzetti. In this crisis he forgot his timidity and humility, and developed into a full-fledged orator. So did many another worker, who found himself making a speech before he knew it. You would get into an argument with some one, and others would gather to listen, and soon there would be a crowd. When the cops drove you off the picket-line, you would stop at the next street-corner and voice your indignation, and when they moved you on, you would stop at the corner beyond that. There were always plenty willing to listen; it was the process by which the workers got their education, and developed their solidarity. You would learn more in one day of idleness than in a month of labor. In this crisis realities were unveiled, and you saw them in their nakedness. If there was anything you could not understand, there were others willing to explain. In the day by day consulting among the workers, it was surprising how clear everything became.

II

Not so many years ago, though it now seemed ages to Cornelia Thornwell, there had been a strike in the Thornwell Mills, and it had been broken in the usual way. But Cornelia's husband had sent her away to the country-place of their daughter Deborah on the North Shore; so she had not heard the shouts of the mob and the crack of revolvers, nor seen the guards patrolling the family mansion on the hilltop. All she knew were newspaper accounts, and the pictures, drawn by Josiah and his son-in-law James Scatterbridge, of the desperate unreason of the strikers. One cause of her evolving into a runaway grandmother had been a lurking suspicion that their way of breaking a strike had not been entirely ethical.

And now here she was, in position to see with her own eyes; if she needed theories, here were A. F. of L. and I. W. W., socialists, anarchists, syndicalists, right and left wingers, even a few single-taxers and vegetarians. In the strike headquarters she met the young clergyman, Paul Blanshard; a new kind of clergyman, with a religion meant to work here and now. He was barely out of his teens, yet he saw the whole struggle so clearly that Cornelia felt herself his junior. He had got his training through the Intercollegiate Socialist Society; and as she watched the effect of his leadership upon the inert mass, a new vision dawned upon her. The idea of the workers taking over industry and running it for themselves had seemed a fanatic's dream; but now she began to wonder, might it not after all be possible—some day in the far-off future?

To her friend Vanzetti it was a cause of grief that she was seen to be talking with this young clergyman. Vanzetti had taken her for his pupil and favorite, this unusual Yankee lady who was willing to learn from an Italian; and here she was falling into the snares of the "riformistas"! Again and again he explained to her what a waste of time it was to deal with "politeesh." He struggled with long polysyllables, half way between Italian and English. "Twenty year, t'irty year, worker go politica, elect deputati for parliament—get elect', do notting, traditor', sell out! Sama t'ing wit' union, worka hard, maka bigga union, grande, potente—never do notting—joosta graft! All rispettabilità, onorevole—you onderstanda me? Worker, he work joosta same—all time. Politeesh, he no work, liva good, dressa genteelman! He is like—I no can say Eengleesh, it is somet'ing in ocean, he get on ship, on shell of crab—" and Vanzetti resorted to his dictionary for the word "barnacool," so that he might apply it to the rosy-cheeked young Congregational clergyman. Yes, the Reverend Blanshard would find a place on the backs of the workers, and stay there like the rest! "You see, Nonna, he joosta sama priest—new kinda talk, but all sama for worker. Riformista is—what you call it—trait'!"

"Traitor," said Cornelia.

"Shoore, trait'," replied Vanzetti.

The State Board of Arbitration and Conciliation took up the grievances of the cordage workers, proposing to adjust them. And here was the trap in action—to lure the workers into the hands of "politeesh" and "offeesh." The more conservative strike leaders insisted upon presenting their case before this board, and Vanzetti opposed them with all his energies. He rushed about from one gathering to another, arguing, protesting; when he saw that the proposition was going to carry, he became frantic, and there was another row between him and Compagno Culla.

The socialist was trying to explain the wishes of the Italians to the English-speaking workers, when Vanzetti climbed onto the platform and thrust the speaker away. "Worker, have notting do wit' commish! It is trap! It is for breaka strike! It is for maka slave! It is for bringa you, for bringa wife,

bambini, for be slave for cordage companee! Why musta worker
get politeesh for settle strike? Why musta get go-vérnment for
settle strike? Why musta have owtoritee? Always owtoritee
for worker! But let worker settle strika for self. Soocha man
lika dis—" and Vanzetti pointed an enraged finger at Culla—
"soocha man is trait' for worker—he is more bad as capitalista—"

There was a storm of controversy, some shouting on one
side, some on the other. But the majority did not want to
listen to anarchist propaganda just then; they called for Compagno Culla, and he got the floor again, and shook his fist at
his rival and demanded: "Why for he talk owtoritee? Anarchista no like owtoritee, he tella you; but I tella you anarchista
is heemself owtoritee! He taka da platform, he maka da speech,
he musta have hisa way or he maka da vee-ólence! Is it not so,
comradda?"

III

The great rich company, the biggest cordage company in
the world, which now in the second year of the great war was
doing more business and making more money than ever in its
history before, sent its officials before the state board to argue
that wages of six dollars a week for unskilled women and nine
dollars for unskilled men were abundant and generous. It
proved that this meant an average wage of twenty-five dollars
a week per family, by the simple device of having fathers and
mothers and half-grown children all at work—which was the
best thing for them, because it kept them from idleness and
dissipation. The strikers countered by putting on the witness-
stand the head of one of these families, John Corsini, who had
a wife and nine children, the oldest fourteen years of age; John
was paid nine dollars a week, and the interpreter quoted: "He
says they sometimes make a meal that would not be fit for a
pig to eat. He is heavily in debt. Goes in debt about five dollars
a week. Friends bring in food and stockings now and then to
help out, otherwise the children couldn't go out in the street."

It was shown that in nineteen years past, the company had
raised wages three times, each time only five per cent; while
in ten years the cost of living had gone up more than fifty per

cent. This moved the company, out of the generosity of its corporate heart, to risk another five per cent increase; more than this would mean inevitable ruin. Its highly paid lawyers argued, and their eloquence was reproduced in the newspapers; smooth-tongued agents came among the workers repeating the arguments, and promising many sorts of favors to leaders who would be tractable. The most expensive secret-service agency in the world was at work. Dissension and doubt and fear spread among the pitiful bewildered masses. The company gave out the announcement that unless its terms were accepted at once, strike-breakers would be brought in. At the same time there appeared a number of head-breakers, the state police, who rode ruthlessly into the crowds.

Also there came autobuses from Boston and other places, with loads of ordinary policemen; they stood three ranks deep in front of the gates, and could have joined hands along the three-quarter mile of steel fence. Any time they saw a crowd gather, they would come at double-quick. "Move along there now—step lively!" If you tried to argue as to the rights of people to the use of the streets, they would not argue back, but jab their clubs into your stomachs or your backs and run you along. If you failed to run fast enough, you would get a thump; and next day in the police-court you would be sentenced as a rioter, and newspapers would tell how the mob was getting out of hand, and the company was requesting the governor to call out the militia.

But the strikers stood firm; they would not accept five per cent advance, and, urged on by the radicals, they requested the state board to withdraw its intervention. The company was worried, because the agents of other cordage concerns were in Plymouth, hiring away their best workers. Something must be done; so one or two hundred "scabs" were got into the plant, around the fence by the seashore, and an effort was made to start one department. The struggle became more tense; the picket-lines drew closer, and the rate of Cornelia Thornwell's education was speeded up.

A picket-line was no place for an old lady—so her Italian friends argued and pleaded; but she had come in search of experience, and insisted upon getting it. The first time she saw an unarmed worker struck down by a policeman's club, she gave voice to her indignation: "Oh, you brute! How dare you!" And when he turned and came at her, there was a moment before she realized that she was no longer a lady, able to give orders to a policeman. Only when he thrust his club into the abdomen of a woman in front of her, and sent the woman reeling into a snow-bank, did Cornelia realize her danger, and turn and run. Yes, she, the widow of an ex-governor of the Commonwealth—she who had lived for forty years in a palace, and been waited upon by servants and honored by all the world—she ran! And in good earnest, as fast as she knew how, because the "brute" had heard her cry, and meant to get her if he could. That she escaped was only because her friend Brini and others crowded in and took the blows. Incidentally they took the club from the policeman, and got away with it, and were very proud of the souvenir!

But that did not comfort Cornelia. The ignominy of her experience had brought tears of rage into her eyes; she would never forget it, and for the rest of her life she would be an illustration of the fact, well-known in the labor movement, that members of the leisure class who take an interest in the cause are apt to become more radical than the workers themselves. Of two thousand participants in the Plymouth cordage strike, only one had ever thought of a policeman as a servant to whom she might give orders.

Cornelia had been born in Massachusetts, and had lived all her life there. She had really believed about her state, or commonwealth, as it prefers to call itself, all the fine things its leaders and rulers had told her. She had listened to orations about Pilgrim fathers and New England town-meetings, the cradle of liberty and the hub of the universe and all the rest. Here she was only forty miles from Boston, for practical purposes in its suburbs; within sight of Plymouth rock, a shrine so sacred that it had a miniature temple built over it; and to her consternation she found herself with no rights that any policeman or private detective was bound to respect. Unless, of course, she chose to declare herself, to cease to be a cordage worker on strike, and become a member of the ruling caste! She went to a police-court, and heard workers testify as to unprovoked assaults, and heard a judge give the police a mild rebuke for their conduct; and then she went back to the picket-line, and saw the same thing going on, precisely as if no judges or courts existed.

And here was the significant thing—out of several thousand people, she was the only one who was surprised! The rest, no matter how angry and excited they became, always mentioned that much worse had happened at Lawrence and Lowell and Fall River and Milford and a string of other places! "My gosh, what you t'ink?" said Alfonsina Brini. "You t'ink dey let worker win strike if can help?" And when Cornelia wanted to know if the police belonged to the cordage company, her landlady's response was, "Who else is it for belong?"

IV

Cornelia, of course, had been on the inside of her city's affairs, and she knew the history of the Boston police force. The Irish-Catholics had carried an election and captured the city; whereupon the old New England element had passed a state law, taking control of the police away from Boston, and vesting it in the governor of the Commonwealth, who was still an Anglo-Saxon gentleman. It was the practice to rent out this force to neighboring towns; and they had developed a strike-breaking department, subject to call by all manufacturers and mill-owners. The force worked hand in glove with the private detective agencies, exchanging records and information. So had been evolved a complete technique of labor-smashing; and all in darkness—the newspapers proceeding upon the principle that what the public didn't know wouldn't hurt it.

Cornelia Thornwell, watching this system in operation, found herself crying out in bewilderment. How could the rich, her kind of people, be so blind? How could they overlook the consequences of teaching the workers such contempt for law? What was the use of talking about Americanization, when, in a time of crisis, you denied every right of citizens, and even of human beings? You herded them like cattle, you beat them like dogs—and then you were surprised and shocked if they turned and bit you in the back of the leg! Before this month's strike was over, Cornelia had come to feel that she would never blame these working people for anything they might do.

The case of Vanzetti was before her day by day. This

dreamer-idealist was so built that he suffered more with other people's pains than with his own. When he half-carried a shuddering body off the picket-line, and washed a torn and bloody scalp with a basin of water and a rag, the tears ran down his cheeks, and his hands shook. And then, that evening, he turned up at the Brini home with a gun! He, the apostle of brotherhood —the tender-hearted one who had refused to let a sick kitten be killed—he was getting ready to kill policemen! To be sure it was not a very efficient weapon, a five-chambered revolver of an old type, much rusted; and Cornelia could see from the way her friend handled it that he hardly knew which end was which. When she tried to dissuade him from his course, Mrs. Brini laughed and told her not to worry, Bart would not shoot anybody; he had once gone hunting with another young fellow, who had shot a bird, and Bart had been so affected by the sight of the dying creature that he had been unhappy for days, and had never gone hunting again.

"But if he's not going to use it, why carry it?" protested Cornelia. "If they catch him with it, they'll send him to jail surely."

To which Vanzetti made answer, "When I go jail for worker, I helpa cause." Which seemed to Cornelia a dark and obscure saying. How could it help the cause of the workers, for a poor Italian ditch-digger, whom nobody had ever heard of, to be sent to jail?

v

The real meaning of the gun was the coming of Galleani. The anarchists were determined that the fallacious arguments of the "riformistas" must be answered, and they had summoned their great leader and teacher to state their side. There was opposition to this among the other strike-leaders, and at first they refused to have the Galleani meeting in their hall; they were trying to avoid provocation, not wanting the newspapers to portray them as extremists. It was only after Galleani had promised to tone down his utterances and to avoid incitement to violence that they agreed to let him be heard.

He came to the Brini home the afternoon of the meeting, so Cornelia got a good look at him: a benevolent and paternal figure, who might have been dressed up for Santa Claus; broad-shouldered and stout, dressed in a long frock coat like a clergyman, with an "alderman" in front, and bushy white whiskers spread above it. He was at once hero and granddaddy to the Italian workers; they would gaze at him in awe and call him "Maestro," and then they would feed him on cakes and wine, and pat him on the sleeve, and call him "Nonno." He was their thinker, their great student, who read everything and knew everything, and told them about it once a week in their paper, "La Cronaca Sovversiva," the "Revolutionary Chronicle," which had a circulation of ten thousand, the fighting organ of the Italians of New England. Its elderly editor lived in honorable poverty, supporting a wife and four children upon a salary of eight dollars a week, eked out by gifts from those who had more. His overcoat was frayed, and fastened at the neck with a large safety-pin, but that did not keep him from being a very dignified gentleman.

In his train came a bodyguard of a score or so of Italian workers, some of them not yet out of their teens, but all in grim earnest. There were rumors that the police meant to break up the meeting and arrest the orator, and these young fellows were here to see about it—every one with a gun in his overcoat pocket, and some with two, and a dirk for good measure. Among them was a Jewish lad out of the slums of New York, at that time employed on a Boston newspaper, and later to be known as Michael Gold. He saw a dingy New England town, with dirty snow trodden underfoot and gray clouds overhead turning soon to night, and—so it seemed to the visitor—not less than a million of policemen. The little band of rebels came like Daniel into the lion's den; they were determined to fight, rather than let their leader be taken. Fortunately no trouble occurred—else America might have exchanged a proletarian playwright, a very scarce article, for a revolutionary martyr, of whom it has had far too many.

Cornelia went with her Italian friends to the meeting. She could not understand what the orator was saying, but she enjoyed the powerful vibrant voice, and shared the thrill of the audience; afterwards her friends would tell her what had been said, for as long as she cared to listen. Luigi Galleani advised them to build up their moral forces, opposing to the brutality of the police their iron will to brotherhood and solidarity. He told them that they were the sole creators of wealth, and that some day, not so far away, they would take possession of their own. He told them to beware of self-styled leaders, persons who set themselves over the masses and presumed to control them. He told them to free their minds from superstition, reverence for gods and priests and judges and policemen; for they themselves were their own gods, their own judges, and the enforcers of their law; that was right which their conscience and sense of brotherhood justified to them. Once as a girl in Boston Cornelia had attended a lecture by a certain well-known Mr. Emerson; she had heard about a queer New England recluse, Mr. Thoreau, author of a pamphlet entitled, "On the Duty of Civil Disobedience." So there was nothing strange to her in these high-sounding ideas; the only trouble was, that the higher they sounded, the more difficult it was to bring them down to earth. One and all, the leaders in this strike preached solidarity, but they were not able to achieve it among themselves, and so their followers were scattered and their energies wasted.

VI

The state board was pleading with the workers to accept a ten per cent raise; and some wanted to say yes, and others no, and some said it was a trap, because the company had not offered ten and surely the offer should come before the acceptance! There was more wrangling in the meetings, and Vanzetti would leap upon the table and shout, "Traditore! Trait'!" and others would outshout him and drag him down. He would come home, heartsick, declaring that the spokesman for the Portuguese had sold out to the companee, and all the sufferings of the strikers were going for nought.

The strike had lasted a full month, and the workers' money was exhausted, and some were sneaking back to work, and the rest were desperate with fear. The police had come and broken up their meetings and closed their hall, and what more could they do? The Italians met secretly, here and there, to decide whether they should trust the board. All but a few extremists wanted to give up, and it was plain that these few could never get jobs with the cordage company anyhow.

Cornelia, exhausted by the long ordeal, went home and crept

into bed, and was just falling asleep, when she was disturbed by loud voices in the house. It was Vanzetti and Culla, with Brini trying to pacify them. Cornelia was going to sleep in spite of the noise; but suddenly she heard Vanzetti shout, "Spee-a! Spee-a!" Culla yelled something in reply, and there was a scuffle and a crash, and Cornelia leaped out of bed and rushed into the little parlor, to see Vanzetti lying on the floor, making desperate efforts to get up, but in vain, because the mighty Brini was on top of him, holding him down. All that could be seen of Compagno Culla was a pair of coattails disappearing speedily through a doorway.

Vanzetti promised to behave, and was let up. He was too angry this time to make apologies to Cornelia. But he told her volubly what that abbominevole Culla had done; after voting to deliver the workers back into slavery, he had had the insolence to come here to the house, to ask for some fifty dollars of relief money, which Vanzetti had collected from the anarchistas of a neighboring town, and which Culla, as a member of the strike committee, was supposed to take over. Vanzetti had refused to give the money up; never would he trust anything to gialli socialistas, riformistas and traditori of the working class! He would take the money back to those who had contributed it, or he would turn it over for the use of some other strikers. Culla, very angry, had threatened to brand Vanzetti for malversazione, embezzlement of the workers' funds; and thereupon Vanzetti shouted, "Spee-a! Spee-a!"—which is to say, "Spy," the most dreadful of all accusations.

Such was the ending of Cornelia's career as a striker. Next morning she got up at a quarter to six, and was duly pinned up in her shawl, and stumbled through the darkness to her place in the wrapping-room of the cordage plant. The bosses were very polite—good morning, glad to see you—it was almost like a social function, an extraordinary change. The workers had shown that they had some power after all, and the lesson would not be soon forgotten. And the State Board of Arbitration and Conciliation set to work, and after two months of deliberation it succeeded in finding a formula which would save the face of the company officials, enabling them to do what they had declared was impossible. Cornelia would find more money in her pay-envelope thereafter, and it seemed quite wonderful—until she stopped and figured that it would take nearly half a year for the increase to make up what she had lost during her weeks of idleness. It was the most perfect of social systems.

VII

There was no more work for Vanzetti in or near the cordage plant; his reckless agitation had cost the company a couple of hundred thousand dollars a year in extra wages, and so he was stopped when he tried to pass the gates. Some one set detectives to follow him everywhere he went. He managed to find himself a job cutting ice: a safe, outdoor activity, where he was in plain sight, and there was no harm he could do. So he remarked to Cornelia, with a twinkle in his eye, "I putta bombe da dinnameet under da ice, he freeze again nexta night queek!"

Ten hours a day he pushed a long saw on an ice-pond, and slid heavy blocks onto wagons. He liked the work because it was picturesque and lively, and gave him a chance to look about. He would come home exhausted, but with adventures to tell. He got himself a pair of rubber boots; they were expensive, and he was proud of them, and so was Trando, who could almost get into one of them, and was a comical spectacle staggering about the room in two. But three days later Vanzetti came back without these treasures, and at supper-table he said, "I must get nodder two boot."

"What's the matter?" Everybody asked at once. "You lost them?"

"No losta," said Vanzetti, "butta no got. I take heem off for go wit' wagon. I come back, see feller, Pietro, you know heem— Guasti, I t'ink he name."

"I know heem," said Brini. "No gooda feller."

"He poor feller. He got wife, four bambini. No can live soocha familee for what you get cutta da ice. I see he got my boota, putta heem on for work. I t'ink I go heem say, 'You giva me boot, you worka no boot.' But I senta shame for do it. I t'ink, Vanzett', you lonely man, no gotta bambini for buy suppa, you worka little bit more, get nodder boot."

Later on, towards spring, came another incident that Cornelia never forgot. The ice was gone now, and Vanzetti was back at "picka shov'," and one day he reported that he had lost his purse on the street. How much did he have in it? Not sure, but he thought maybe thirteen dollars. That was a whole week of hard labor, and everybody was concerned. The family discussed it all through supper. Vanzetti said that he was sure there was plenty honest people in Plymouth, maybe one of them had picked up the purse; he would put up signs, the way they did in Italy. So Cornelia helped him to phrase a notice, "Lost, small purse," with his name and address; he went out that evening with a hammer and some tacks, and put up the notices on telegraph poles along his route.

This was while he was still being watched by detectives—in fact they did not entirely let up until eighteen months after the strike. So everybody was startled when, next evening after supper, there came a blue-uniformed policeman. "You advertised a purse?"

"Shoore," said Vanzetti; a little uneasy, as the poor always are in the presence of the law. Might this method of advertising be illegal among these strange Yankees?

"What kind of purse?"

"He is rounda blacka purse, not very moocha beeg."

"What did you have in it?"

"I t'ink I got t'irteen dollar, notta more."

"Is this your purse?" The policeman held it out.

"I t'ink it is heem, looka like heem."

"But it's got eighteen dollars in it."

Vanzetti hesitated. "No t'ink had eighteen dollars. Shoore no got so moocha mon'. Musta be odder purse."

The members of the Brini family had crowded to the door to listen, and now broke into protest. "What you say, Bart?" cried Alfonsina. "You no can tella ah mooch you got?" And to the policeman, "He no can tella ah mooch mon' he got! He giva da mon' all time. He giva da mon' to little one, children all time— he buy somet'ing, giva present all time, never t'ink for keepa da mon'. My osband here, he tella you, Mister Polissman. Tella heem, Vincenzo!"

"Shoore," said Brini, "He bigga fool for money. He giva me for keep, forgetta, never know ah mooch he got."

"Me know his purse," persisted the woman. "Me see alla time in room, me fixa room. Could taka half his mon' all da time, he not know it. It is hee's purse, Mr. Polissman."

They discussed the time and place where the purse had been

found, and everything fitted. So the policeman said, "I guess you better take it. Nobody else has claimed it." But Vanzetti was stubborn, he was quite sure he couldn't have had so much as eighteen dollars in his possession. He would not take it, and the policeman went off, much puzzled at this singular kind of "wop."

Also there were further developments of the affair Culla, curious and touching to the Yankee observer. Compagno Culla had been blacklisted by the cordage company—despite the fact that he was one of the moderates. He was doing some kind of sedentary work, and complained that he was suffering from indigestion. Vanzetti, enthusiast for the back-to-nature way of life, advised him that it was because of sitting still all day. Said Bart, telling Cornelia about it, "Come wit' me, worka picka shov', you maka you self new man." And sure enough, Compagno Culla gave up his indoor work, and went to digging ditches, and after he had got used to it, he found that his indigestion was better. He mentioned it once at the Brinis, and Bart patted him on the shoulder, proud and benevolent.

After the visitor had gone, Cornelia said, "You don't want to kill him any more!" And Vanzetti grinned, as he had learned to do when "Nonna" was teasing him. "Wanta kill so long he try for be offeesh', maka union, be secretary da union, maka jobba for self. When he come lika me, worka picka shov', maka fight capitalista, padrone, den he is compagno, comradda, gooda feller, I lika heem." So, little by little, Cornelia came to understand the type of idealist-fanatic, which could be gentle as a child in all personal relationships, but fierce and dangerous when roused by social wrong.

VIII

Springtime! You dressed by the light of dawn, and the good old sun was shining over the sea as you went to your day's work. As if ashamed for the suffering his absence had caused you, he gave double measure, and the snows melted, and little rivers ran from every hillside, and in sheltered corners you saw green things sticking their timid heads from the ground. Brini hurried home from the factory and tore off his coat and seized his spade and went to work, a man possessed by the common or garden variety of frenzy. Even Vanzetti, after ten hours "picka shov'," could not escape the disease, and joined in with the rake. So must the Pilgrim fathers have behaved after that first long winter, when so many had perished upon inadequate rations, and they dreamed the miracle of green things growing from this strange new soil.

One lovely brown bed after another was leveled and raked smooth, and laid out with strings by the eager children. They could hardly wait for their father to get home in the afternoon to start planting. They set up labels on little stakes—it was a miniature graveyard of seeds, and everybody cherishing the religious hope—"Resurgam!" The children would come hurrying home from school, and there were the tiny green threads of onions, and little green points that would be radishes, and pink-tinged ones that would be beets! When, a couple of weeks later, there were some big enough to be pulled and washed and made into a baby salad, that was a regular religious ceremony, a Dago thanksgiving.

Out in the woods you could find tiny flowers of fragile and unearthly beauty, such as ravish the souls of children, and of prophets and dreamers and fanatics. On Sunday mornings Vanzetti and Cornelia and Fay and Trando would set out, and if it had been left to the man they would never have stopped wandering the whole day long, and by night time they would have been lost. The woods were his temple, full of infinite mysteries. He would point out signs of nature's cunning; he would speculate about things he did not understand, and ask Cornelia if she knew; if nobody knew, perhaps they could watch and find out. He would get down on his knees over an ant's nest, and be happy for an hour with the frenzied labors of these tiny bundles of energy. Then he would spring up and start walking again; come on, it was almost time for mayflowers, perhaps they would find some in the next little valley.

And the seashore! So many strange things that you had never seen before! The children would scramble about on slippery rocks at low tide, and gather more treasures than their hands could hold. Better leave them where they were, said Bart, and carry off knowledge about them. They would sit on the high rocks to rest, and watch the sailboats and the ships, and speculate about where they came from and what they brought. Bart

was curious as to other parts of the world, and how men lived
there. When he discovered that Cornelia had read books about
such things, he would ask her questions, pretending that it was
for the education of the children—but it was like the father who
enjoys the circus more than the children do!

The mayflowers came, and you could gather bunches of them,
and turn the humblest worker's home into a bower. The vegetable rows were shining now, and the salads on the supper-table
were explosions of green, and the soups were steaming sym-
phonies in red and green and white and yellow. The rising sun
ran you a race in the morning, and the evenings were so bright
and lovely that you hated to go to bed. It was what you had been
waiting for, through the black and bitter winter; Cornelia quoted
the one-eyed Kalandar of the Arabian Nights: "This indeed is
life! Pity 'tis 'tis fleeting!"

In the house across the street lived Signor Prezzolini, who
earned his living by teaching the violin. When he gave lessons
to his young pupils it was not so pleasant, but sometimes he practiced for himself, and in warm weather he would have his windows open, and what could be more wonderful than to sit on
your front porch in the twilight, and gaze up at far-off mysterious stars, and listen to strains of ravishing beauty? In those
hours the little Brini boy's life-destiny was determined; he was
only eight and a half years old, but he made up his mind one
evening, and announced it gravely, "I am going to be a violinist."

Cornelia was moved to tell him something out of her own
childhood. She had lived next to the home of rich people, who
gave many balls and parties, and would have an orchestra to
play. Cornelia's mother would put her to bed, and the child
would creep to the window and listen. Then a bold idea occurred
to her, and she took a blanket and stole downstairs, and into the
neighbor's garden, and crawled under a bush, where she was
safe from discovery; there she lay for hours, wrapped in the
blanket, listening in such ecstasy that even now she would shiver
as she remembered it.

Little Trando nestled closer to her, and put his sensitive
hand into hers. In between the playing, he begged for more
stories about her girlhood. She told him how she had believed
in fairies, and would run out into the garden in the early dawn,

and hunt under the prettiest flowers, trembling with the delicious hope that a fairy might be hiding there, and what would she say if she met one. But here Bart, the serious one, intervened; he did not approve of fairy-stories. "No should tella children what is not true, Nonna. It plenty lovely t'ing what is real, plenty miraculosa—how you say it, wonderfool. When you teach somet'ing true, is usefool too, but fairy is lika diavolo, like angioli, superstizione, no gooda for teach."

IX

Cornelia had by now got hardened to her job. Her hands were skinny, with whipcords standing out on the backs; her fingers were knobby at the joints, and covered with tough calluses. Her shoulders were bowed to meet the coils of rope upon which she sewed, and one shoulder sagged lower than the other. But they did not ache, and she could work peacefully, and have time for a bit of gossip with her neighbors, and for long thoughts about the life she was living, and the people she had come to know.

The circle of her acquaintance had been greatly widened by the strike, which had the effect of bringing the workers together and breaking down barriers of language and creed. Mrs. O'Dowd, Cornelia's pious neighbor, had been on strike, with her husband and several relatives, and they had learned that the "wops" next door were also capable of loyalty, and that their jabber of sounds might mean something of importance to Irish aristocrats. Cornelia served as go-between, and got so well acquainted that she ventured to hint perhaps the heavenly powers might find some way to accept good works as a partial substitute for good doctrine. That was contrary to Father O'Brien, of course, but even so, one might think about it, and one might pray for the lost souls.

That was actually being done, Cornelia learned; it was Mrs. Lavatelli, the neighbor on the other side, who was so much distressed by the sight of three bambini who had never been baptized, that she made it a practice to burn a candle before the image of the virgin every night before she went to bed. And Cornelia said, surely that ought to be enough. God was being properly reminded, and it must be assumed that He, in His infinite wisdom, would take whatever steps were necessary.

There was naturally a great deal of curiosity among the neighbors as to this mysterious Yankee lady who had lost her husband and home under circumstances to which she never referred. They would come and call, or avail themselves of opportunities to gossip over the back fence while hanging out clothes or working at the vegetables. And Cornelia would make use of her social training to divert the conversation, so that presently the neighbors would be talking about their affairs, and Cornelia would be learning something of the things for which she had come here.

What struck her most frequently—and always on the funny-bone—was the complete identity of spirit between these ladies of the back fence and those of the "Back Bay." If Cornelia had imagined that by evolving into a runaway grandmother she was going to find freedom from conventions, from the petty restrictions of collective femininity, then she had made a great mistake, and wasted the sixty-first year of her life. For these working women and wives of working men had their very strict notions of what was proper, and they had the same system of government by gossip. The only difference which Cornelia noticed between them and the "Sewing Circle," the body which had ruled the social destiny of Boston for two generations, was that the ladies of the back fence did not lower their voices when they came to the worst part of their stories; they had not cultivated the use of the shoulders and the eyebrows as substitutes for words in the circulation of slander.

The ladies of the back fence did not have so much money as the ladies of the Back Bay, but they made up for it by having more children, and they used these for conversational purposes in the same way. They would tell the charming things the little ones had said, and just as in Boston, it never occurred to them that this might bore the listener. Also they would tell about the children's ailments, and what the doctor said, and whether or not the doctor knew what he was talking about. Apparently the unsatisfactoriness of doctors, at the present stage of their development, had been discovered by the poor as by the rich. There was the same experimenting with unorthodox remedies, and the same talk about results—Cornelia might as well have been back in the nursery with her daughter Clara Scatterbridge.

And then clothes. There were fashion magazines passed from hand to hand, and when Mrs. O'Dowd's younger sister made herself a party dress, she cut it upon a pattern you would have seen at the Friday evening dances of the socially elect. The material here was sleazy, but that did not enter into the conversation, because nobody knew it was so.

And then ancestors! Strange as it might seem, the ladies of the back fence talked about family, and who was who, and why. To be sure, they could not go so far back; they had no family-trees and colleges of heraldry, no pages of genealogy in the *Evening Transcript* every Wednesday. But there were so many more families, that it made an equal supply of conversational material. Strange as it might seem, there was the same amount of hostility and the same amount of pride in the family talk. Cornelia never met any woman so low that she could not find some other women to look down on; she never found any woman so high that she was not eager to know a Yankee lady, and to repeat to her neighbors what the Yankee lady had said.

x

Also Cornelia got to know Vanzetti, with the intimacy inevitable in the crowded homes of the poor. She knew him standing in front of a little cracked mirror, tying his cravat and singing songs of his old home. She knew him teaching songs to the children, and learning American songs they brought home from school. She knew him keeping watch in the kitchen, to make sure that Alfonsina did not have to carry coal or wood. She knew him sitting up long after the rest had gone to bed, reading by the light of an oil lamp, his brow furrowed in thought. At such times he would be lost to her and to all the world; she, who had always taken comfort for granted, was awed by the spectacle of a man who robbed himself of sleep to get knowledge.

He taught her some Italian, and she taught him English. She explained that mystery, so difficult of comprehension to an Italian, that it is possible for certain consonants to follow each other without a vowel between. One said "a great big house"; one did not have to say "a greata bigga house." She explained the simple idioms, one after another. One did not say,

"I no can"; one said, "I cannot." Vanzetti wrote this down, and presently had made such progress that he would stop in the middle: "I no—cannot." She labored to teach him the mystery of the sound "th"; showing him how the tongue was placed, stuck out a little, and pressed against the lower part of the upper teeth. The children were fascinated by that; they had learned to make the sound, but without knowing how they did it. They would watch Bart's efforts; he got so that he would stick his tongue out, but alas, he could not always time it right, and he would stick it out and then pull it in and make the wrong sound! The children laughed merrily—such pleasure it gave them, to find themselves superior to the grown-ups! But that was all right with Bart—it was his dream that the children would be superior in all things.

Once or twice a month he would disappear for a day or two. The irregular character of his work made this possible—and anyhow, there was no job that could hold him when it was announced in "La Cronaca Sovversiva" that Galleani was going to lecture on the effects of the war upon the revolutionary movement in Italy, or Carlo Tresca upon syndicalist versus individualist anarchism. Vanzetti would come back brimming over with arguments, and news from the "Gruppo Autonomo di East Boston," as the Galleani followers called themselves. He and Brini would have vociferous arguments, and later Vanzetti would explain to Cornelia what it was about. Or perhaps there would be a "picanic" in a neighboring town, and Vanzetti would get a bundle of literature to "distriboot." Or there would be a strike in the shoe factories of Lynn, and he would compose an appeal, and take it round among the anarchistas, and collect fifty cents from one and a quarter from the next, and in a couple of days would have twenty dollars to be forwarded by postal order.

Little by little Cornelia was coming to understand his doctrine. He would pick out passages from the paper and explain them to her, and answer her questions and objections. It was one of those high perfectionist doctrines, which assume in human beings a quantity of virtue which few as yet possess. Those who succeed in living up to this doctrine are sublime; but those who fail may break their necks. Might there not be persons using Vanzetti's lofty phrases as a pretext for evading duties, or as a means of preying upon their fellows? So Cornelia asked, and the other answered that this might happen, but there could be no progress without some risk, and neither men nor women could learn to swim unless they entered the water.

He was determined to read English, and from one of his trips he brought back a book called "The Conquest of Bread," by P. Kropotkin. Cornelia, with her woman's wit, did not fail to divine that there were two people going to be educated out of that book! Curiously enough, it was not until later that she connected its author with a very famous scientist from Russia, whose visit to Boston had made a great stir in intellectual circles some eight years previously. A high-up nobleman escaped from exile in Siberia, Kropotkin had been a social lion. A Harvard professor who was in the next year to become president of the university—than which there is no higher station in the world—had introduced him for a course of lectures at the Lowell Institute. How could it have occurred to Cornelia that this learned foreigner with the bushy gray whiskers whom she had met among the most exalted of the Brahmins, could be the author of a tract recommending the overthrow of government by mass insurrection of the proletariat? How could she have imagined that Mr. Lowell would have consented to further the propaganda of anarcho-syndicalism? How could she have imagined it—or, for that matter, how could he?

XI

There was a good-sized grape-arbor behind the house, and it came slowly into leaf, and then into blossom, and spread upon the air a marvelous sweet perfume; you could stand and drink it, almost as if it were the reality of autumn instead of the promise of spring. "Divino da vino!" said Vincenzo Brini; it was in the days before prohibition, of course. "Gooda redda wine," he said, pointing to the blossoms. "You calla heem 'Dago Red.'" And then with his good-natured grin he pointed to himself. "Nodder kind Dago Red!" He pointed to Vanzetti. "More Dago Red!"

It was a joke to which they were much accustomed. The children would hear it called after them when they went to school: "Dago Red! Dago Red!" Even Father O'Brien had taken it up, and in one of his sermons had advised his flock to avoid any and all kinds of "Dago Reds." "What you t'ink of dat?" said Alfonsina, outraged; and Cornelia answered. "Tell him what they did to Jesus. He too had a nickname, 'King of the Jews.' They wrote it on the cross—'I.N.R.I.'—Jesus of Nazareth, King of the Jews."

"I know," said Vanzetti. "I read heem. He was not what priest say, he was worker, same like me and you, ribello, rivoluzionario! Da priest in his time want him kill-èd—say he make trouble. I no—cannot say it Eengleesh—"

"'And they were the more fierce, saying, he stirreth up the people.'"

"Joosta so! He was gooda man, povero. I sorry when he die. I make tears for heem. I say compagno—Comradda Gesu, die for make joostice for worker."

So it was when you were talking with Bart. You would begin by smelling the grape blossoms and making jokes about the wine you were going to drink; and you would end by making tears for Comradda Gesu.

"Summer is y-comen in!" sang the pair of wrens on top of the grape-arbor; putting in an extra vowel, just as if they had been Dagoes! It was a time for coming outdoors, a time for beauty and joy. But alas, the hideous slaughter in Europe was mounting to frenzy, becoming an extermination of the human race. The exploiters and imperialists whose greed had dragged Italy into the conflict were sending propagandists over here, to lure the Italian youth back into the slaughter-pit.

And so there was a bugle call in the soul of Bartolomeo Vanzetti. He heard it all the time, he could never cease talking about it. He must not spend the warm summer days lying on Castle Hill, reading Dante and Manzoni; he must help to organize meetings in one town or another; he must go the day before and distribute handbills from house to house, and beg the people to come; he must be on hand to take up a collection and forward it to Galleani, so that more papers might be printed, to hold the demon of militarism at bay, and expose the lies of piety and patriotism. That was his duty, his martyrdom—his way of following the example of Comradda Gesu!

CHAPTER 4

YOUNG AMERICA

I

THE days passed; and one of them rang a bell in the soul of Cornelia Thornwell. She had kept her vow, she had won the wager with herself. For a whole year she had taken care of herself, asking no advice and no favors from any one. She had got a job as a manual worker, and held it for a year, and lived on her earnings, and had twenty-five dollars put away. Now she might go home if she wanted to.

Did she want to? It was hard to be sure; at one time she would find herself thinking about this one and that, and what had happened to them all this time. But then she would remember the desperate determination of everybody to dominate her life; all those highly disciplined and rigid people who knew what she ought to do at every moment of her life, and would never cease from telling her! Well, she would have a way to escape, a city of refuge!

She had made up her mind to tell no one where she had been; it would be a scandal, a mystery with which they might torment themselves for the rest of her life; a skeleton in the family closet—the bones of a runaway grandmother! The imp of mischief kicked up his heels in the depths of Cornelia's soul; she thought of each person she knew, and what that person would make of the problem. The secret would be a club she would hold over their heads, to make them behave. "Let me alone, or I'll disappear again!" Like her daughter Alice's hysterics, which had developed at the age of three, in a lovely and much petted child who wanted to have her own way, and which continued in a social queen of forty, who had to have a platonic lover in addition to a husband.

Now Alice's mother would also have a platonic romance! Cornelia, aged sixty-one, would have an adopted son, an Italian

91

ditch-digger, aged twenty-eight—agnostic, anarchist, and "Dago Red!" She might be sure of its being safe and innocent, for she had watched him a year, and never seen him look at a woman, nor heard him voice such an idea. Also she had the word of Alfonsina: "He never t'ink woman, he joosta t'ink joostice."

Such was Cornelia's tangle of moods, when, on an evening in July she was coming home from work with another woman, and down the main street they saw, walking toward them, two girls of the leisure class. There was nothing unusual in this, for the summer-hotels were open, the "season" at Plymouth was in full swing. To be sure, the daughters of the rich did not prefer this part of the town for walking; their part lay to the south, where the shore-road was lined with villas and splendid estates. The workers would see them roaring by in fast motor-cars, radiant, exquisite, with veils floating; snatches of laughter and song would be wafted back, reminding you of the paradise of freedom and happiness you had lost by being born in the wrong half of Plymouth.

The two girls came on; one in pink chiffon, one in white, both lovely and gay, chatting, not heeding the swarm of tired laborers, drab and dusty. Cornelia saw them coming, and her eyes rested on them carelessly—until suddenly she started, and the blood leaped into her face. That one in pink, with the lovely little round face framed in soft brown hair and crowned with a pink chiffon hat with flowers—that was her grandchild, Betty Alvin! Little Betty, grown two or three inches taller, and miraculously blossomed into womanhood, rounded and ripe.

Cornelia was in a panic. What must she do? Look straight ahead—no, she must turn to the other woman and talk—about anything, the first words that came into her head—"That foreman is too bad-tempered, he's not fit for such a job, there'll be trouble in our wrapping-room if he stays, there ought to be some way we could make a protest—" and so on, while the girls came nearer. And suddenly—Cornelia must not look, but out of the corner of her eye she saw Betty stop and stare. The two working women passed by, and went on quickly, Cornelia chattering about anything, anything.

Betty had recognized her grandmother! Would she turn and follow? Cornelia ventured a swift glance behind, and saw that the two girls were going on. It was the Thornwell training; Betty, assuming she were sure of the recognition, would understand that Cornelia might not want to be recognized, might not want the truth to be known to Cornelia's companion or to Betty's. But what a tumult must be in the child's young heart! Her long-lost and prayed-for "Grannie," in the shape of a poor old working-woman in a faded calico dress, with a pitiful remnant of a black straw hat stuck on her head. No, it couldn't be true! Yet it could not be doubted!

Betty would come back, Cornelia felt certain. She thought it over and decided to take the child into her secret. Betty was the one for whom she cared most; it would be like a visit home. So next evening Cornelia lingered on the way from work, and walked by herself; and presently here came Betty, in the same pink dress, but with no companion. Seeing her coming, Cornelia turned off the main street, up a more or less deserted lane, and presently she stopped, and turned and met her grand-daughter.

II

"Grannie! It's you!" And then, "Oh, Grannie! How could you?" And then, "Grannie! What on earth have you been doing?"

"I've been taking care of myself, dear."

"Oh, Grannie, but how!" And then, "Oh, you poor dear! Why, your shoulders are bowed! And your poor hands, your fingers! Who ever saw such things?" Betty became speechless; but the tears gushed into her eyes and ran down her cheeks.

"Don't worry about me, dear. I've been having a very good time; and I've learned a lot."

"What have you been doing?"

"I've been working for Mr. J. Lawrence Perry. Don't you remember that nice old gentleman who comes to dinner?"

"Does he know it?"

"No, of course not; I'm just a cordage worker."

"But, Grannie, what ever put such an idea into your head?"

"I wanted to know that I could take care of myself, and I wanted others to know it, so they would let me alone. I wanted to be independent."

There came a flash of fire behind the rainclouds in Betty's

eyes. "Oh, Grannie, I know exactly how you feel! Sometimes I've thought I'd do the same thing! If I'd known where you were, I think I'd have come to you."

Cornelia dodged that suggestion. "How is everybody at home, dear?"

"Why, they're all right, I guess—the same as they always are. They're very much worried about you, of course."

"Are they really that, or do they just have to pretend it?"

"They have to pretend not to be; because it is supposed to be all right, you know."

"Everything is always supposed to be all right," said Cornelia. "What am I doing?"

"You went to California for the winter; and you've been ordered to a rest-cure."

"I see. The neighbors will take that to mean that I'm in an asylum."

"Well, Grannie, that wouldn't shock them any more than this. Oh! I never heard of such a thing in my life. How do you *stand* it?"

"Well, it hasn't always been easy, but it's been good for me. I'll be myself from now on, and not what any one else wants me to be."

"How are you living?"

"I'm boarding with an Italian family, very good kind people. I'm comfortable there, and I've learned all sorts of things. I went through the strike last winter."

"Grannie, how perfectly thrilling! I never heard anything so romantic!" The girl was aglow with excitement, and Cornelia would have liked to take her in her arms and hug her. But what would the neighbors think, seeing a working-woman on such terms of intimacy with a young lady of fashion? Even in North Plymouth, one must remember the neighbors!

"Betty, I'm taking you into my secret, and you must keep it for me. I'm not going to tell anybody where I have been."

"Of course, Grannie, whatever you say. But are you going to live here always?"

"No, I shall come back; but I don't think I'll live with the family." Then, after a moment: "What did they do about their quarrel?"

"You mean about the cradle and the rug? Well, you see, they

forgot it when they found you had gone; they were so shocked, and ashamed of themselves. Now they don't speak about it—in fact, they've persuaded themselves it didn't happen. Aunt Alice took the Mayflower cradle out of the house because she knew that grandfather had left it to her in the will."

"Did he really do that?"

"Yes, and he left the Shah of Persia's rug to Mother; and so they didn't have to have a row, and they didn't; it's the sort of thing that couldn't happen in Boston, so it never did. If anybody mentioned it, they'd deny it—and they'd be very angry about the denial."

Cornelia laughed. "You little monkey! Are they teaching you psychology at Miss Wilson's?"

"No, but naturally I listen and think. They've got another quarrel now, that I'm not supposed to know about; but I can't help hearing—and then Priscilla tells me a lot."

"What is it?"

"Well, it's Aunt Alice; there's a gentleman who admires her very much, and it's all right, of course, only she drove somewhere with this gentleman, and somebody else saw them, and there was a lot of gossip about it, and mother had to lie for Aunt Alice at her Sewing Circle, and she vows she will never do it again. And Aunt Alice cried, and they haven't been to each other's house for several months."

Cornelia thought for a space. "I don't believe I'm ready to go home yet, Betty!"

III

They strolled to the edge of the woods, where they found a seat covered with pine-needles, and Betty told more gossip of the Thornwell clan. Aunt Clara had had another baby; that made eight, and Aunt Alice called it a positive indecency—if they were looking for scandals, there was a real one. And Great-uncle Abner had had a bad attack of the gout; and his son, Uncle Quincy—you must pronounce it as if it were another disease—had won a chess cup. And Uncle Henry Winters and Uncle James Scatterbridge had made no one could say how many millions buying ships and things and selling them to the allies; and Betty's father had made a speech at a banquet of the bankers, declaring that the interests of civilization required that America should enter the war. "On which side?" asked Cornelia; and the girl looked at first puzzled and then shocked. "Oh, the allies, of course."

So Cornelia told the decision which had been forming in her mind during her year of independence. She was a pacifist. She believed that the interests of civilization required that men should stop killing one another. When Betty said, "Oh, but if the Kaiser should win!" Cornelia answered that it didn't matter who won, the interests of civilization would lose. She quoted one of the founding fathers, Benjamin Franklin, to the effect that there never was a good war nor a bad peace.

This was a subject they might have discussed for quite a while; but Betty's conscience began to trouble her. "It is time I was dressing for dinner, and I mustn't be late. Mrs. Walker has to be so careful with me."

"Mrs. Walker?" said Cornelia; and the other explained that she was spending a couple of weeks with the Jerry Walkers. Cornelia could hardly believe her ears. "How does that happen?"

"I know, it sounds funny; but you see, Lucile Walker, the oldest daughter, is at Miss Wilson's, and I like her better than any other girl in the school—in fact we just adore each other. She really knows more than six of me, Grannie, and why does one always have to be thinking about family and ancestors? The way it seems to me, we Thornwells have got so much pride and money that we don't really need to amount to anything or to know anything. Honestly, I get bored with it; and Lucile interests me, so why shouldn't we be friends?"

"Certainly; only I'm surprised that Deborah would let you visit them."

"Well, we had a time, of course. Mother says she simply cannot understand my vulgar tastes. She couldn't figure out where I got them, but now she's decided that it's from you, Grannie!" And Cornelia spread out her knobby knuckles, and said that she had gone back to her ancestors; and Betty caught those knobby knuckles and cried over them, and they had a fine sentimental time.

Betty told more about the people she was visiting; she knew the whole shameful story from her mother—how Jerry Walker had been employed as an errand boy in St. Andrew's hospital, of which Cornelia had been one of the supporters; and later he had worked as a felt-salesman, and Grandfather Thornwell had helped to put up the money so that he might buy his first plant. Now he owned about all the felt-plants there were in New England, and was getting to be as rich as anybody. But he could never be forgiven for being a nobody, and it was preposterous that his daughter should have been admitted to a fashionable school with the daughters of the Thornwells.

"You can see how it is," said Betty. "If anything were to go wrong with me while I'm at Mrs. Walker's, she would never be forgiven; so I mustn't cause her any worry. If I could tell her about you, Grannie—but then I don't know"—and again laughter lighted up the eager face of the girl—"I'm afraid maybe you are not respectable any more!"

Cornelia replied, "I'm lost forever. The people I've been living with are far worse than the Walkers. They are called Dago Reds."

"Dago Red?" said Betty, puzzled. "I thought that was what the college boys call wine."

"Yes, but this is another kind of Red, those who don't believe in religion, or in government; they are anarchists, in short."

This time Miss Betty was really shocked, and all the laughter died out of her eyes. "Oh, Grannie, but you're joking!"

"No. But they're really quite charming people. I'll introduce you to them, maybe, and you can see. One of them is called Bart, and he is a saint."

"A saint?" echoed Betty, still more puzzled. "But you said they didn't believe in religion!"

"It appears that many saints don't, any more," was Cornelia's reply. "There are what you might call secular saints."

IV

They walked towards Betty's dinner, and on the way discussed the problem of how she was to meet these dangerous and thrilling friends of Grannie's. Betty could not be absent from the Walkers' without giving some excuse, and she did not want to tell any fibs to a hostess who carried such a grave responsibility. It would not do to tell Lucile, because secrets

didn't last long with her, and anyhow, she was not old enough
to be a chaperon. Betty bethought herself of Miss Mehitabel
Smith, the unmarried sister of Mrs. Walker. Miss Mehitabel
was very, very upright; "almost as good as Mother," said
Betty. She did a great deal of visiting among the poor, and if
Betty were to be seized with a desire to go visiting with her,
that would be perfectly proper; Miss Mehitabel could visit her
own poor, while Betty visited Betty's—and it would be no fib,
because anybody had only to look at that frightful get-up that
Grannie wore—"How on earth do you stand it?"

It would be necessary to take Miss Mehitabel into the secret;
but Betty was sure it would be safe, for no one could be more
conscientious. Cornelia said all right, but of course Betty must
not give any hint of the reason why Cornelia had left home;
family quarrels were family skeletons, never taken out in public;
and Betty said, "Oh, of course!" She would say that her grandmother was engaged in sociological research, and her secret
must be kept because otherwise her conclusions would be invali-
dated. Miss Mehitabel would be thrilled to death by that, and it
would be such a very, very little fib, it would hardly count at
all. It was agreed that Betty was to pay a call in Suosso's Lane
on the following evening.

And meantime, what must the little mischief do but arrange
with Miss Mehitabel to inspect the cordage plant! Miss Mehitabel was a stockholder in the company, so it was easy for her,
and at 10 o'clock in the morning the two of them suddenly
appeared in Cornelia's wrapping-room. They did not speak, but
stood for a long time and watched the work, and Cornelia stole
glances at them out of the corner of her eyes. The other women
workers did the same, the young ones especially; for Betty was
as good as a fashionplate or a visit to the movies. As for Miss
Mehitabel—well, Cornelia tried to imagine what an Italian
or Portuguese worker would make of her solid Norfolk jacket
fastened with a belt, and her plain tweed skirt without a pleat
or fold, and her plain brown stockings and "ground gripper"
shoes. Miss Mehitabel wore her hair short—this in the days
when it was an act of heroism—and parted in the middle and
covered by a Swiss guide hat with a small feather in it—the
only ornamental thing in the whole costume.

Miss Mehitabel's face was serious, even stern, and her eyes

looked out through large horn-rimmed spectacles. In short, she was a perfect imitation of a certain very common type of Beacon Hill lady who has got through with nonsense once for all, especially the nonsense of men, and wishes to advertise the fact, especially to the men. In the case of Miss Mehitabel, who was a rank outsider, it was a very bold, even presumptuous thing to do; but that, of course, would be something beyond the comprehension of a cordage worker, who would take Miss Mehitabel to be the real thing, and have enough to do trying to imagine what that thing might be. After the two ladies had walked on, Cornelia heard the foreman of the department standing behind her seat, discussing the problem with the subforeman. "Now what do you suppose a woman gets herself up like that for?"

"Search me," said the subforeman.

"Well, they tell you the reason there is so many old maids in New England, because the men goes west. But what I say is, if the women tried hard enough, they could get the men to come fetch them." It was what is known as "Yankee humor."

v

Cornelia had decided not to give the Brinis any explanation of Betty. She would just say that one of her grand-daughters was visiting in Plymouth, and wanted to meet them. There was a mystery anyhow, and the presence of a grand-daughter would neither add to it nor take away.

Betty put on her least fashionable costume for the occasion; but the gulf between the lowest of Betty's and the highest of an Italian cordage worker's was not to be bridged at one day's notice. Alfonsina had barely time after supper to put clean clothes on the children, and to smooth her own hair and put on her necklace of beads. Papa Brini came in from the garden and washed his hands and put on his coat. As for poor old Bart, his clothes hung on him as if they had come from a pawnbroker's, and he didn't even know enough to trim his walrus mustaches when a young lady was coming to call.

But all the stiffness and embarrassment was soon forgotten; because Betty set out to be loved, and there was no resisting her. "Nonna?" she said, when she heard Cornelia's name.

"What does that mean?" When they told her it was the Italian word for grandma, she said, "Oh, how cute! Nonna. I'll make it my pet name for her," and she began to do it right away.

She got one arm about Trando, and said, "You will teach me lots of lovely Italian words. And Nonna tells me you are going to be a violinist. I play the piano a little, and you can come to see me and we'll play duets; only you are going to be famous, and you won't waste your time with me." So then, of course, Alfonsina beamed, and Vincenzo was so touched that he got out one of the last of his precious bottles of "Dago Red," and they all had a glass—even Bart drank a little when it was a matter of courtesy. They made the jokes about "Dago Red," and the one about "divino da vino," and explained it to Betty. And then she turned to Bart and said, "Mr. Vanzetti, Nonna tells me that you have made her into a pacifist."

Now Bart, of course, had never seen anything so lovely as this in all his life; at least, never close at hand, and paying attention to *him*. He who would walk a whole afternoon in the woods searching for the first mayflower, now saw one come laughing and chatting into the parlor where he boarded. Of course he was awe-stricken; but even so, not for a moment must his proletarian conscience be drugged. "No, Meess Betty," said he. "Nonna is very good lady, mooch lovely lady; but if she is made pacifista"—he pronounced it Italian fashion, "pachifeesta"—"if she is pachifeesta, it is not by me. I am never sooch t'ing."

"Oh, then what are you, Mr. Vanzetti?"

"I am anarchista."

"And what is the difference?"

"Moocha differenza, Meess Betty. Anarchista is fighting man. He will not fight in war for capitalista, for padrone, what you call master, but he will fight for worker, for joostice, for make freedom of slave."

"Oh! So then you and Nonna don't agree!"

"I t'ink it is maybe good for Nonna be pachifeesta, she is olda lady, no—cannot fight. She has got sooch kind heart—"

"But then you have a kind heart, too, Mr. Vanzetti. She told me how you would not let the sick kitten be killed."

"Seeck kitten not do harm, I not like for kill helpless t'ing. But capitalista is not helpless, Meess Betty, he is fighting man,

is most fighting man in whole world. If you study, you onderstand what is cause of great war. What for must million men
go fight, be kill-èd, miseramente, cruel? It is for get market
for rich capitalista; it is for get coal, iron—what you call it for
burn in lamp?"

"Oil?"

"It is for sooch t'ing worker must die. It come go-vérnment,
take you per forza, like slave, put in uniform, say go kill. If
you say no—cannot kill, you go prigione—prison, you get torture, maybe shot. I say, what for talka pachifeesmo for soocha
men? No, worker must fight, is never men get free wit' out
fight for freedom. Is it not trut', Nonna?"

"I wonder," said Cornelia. "The Negro slaves were freed
without having to do much fighting—"

"Oh, but Grannie!" It was Betty who broke in. "Other people
had to fight for them; and if they aren't really free yet, maybe
that is the reason, because they haven't done their own fighting."

So Cornelia confronted the problem of the younger generation. She sat back and listened, while small talk and efforts at
charm were forgotten, and the idealist-dreamer set forth his
vision of the better world to be. She realized that Betty had
come there, with her mind made up to probe to the bottom this
phenomenon of a "secular saint"; to know exactly what he
thought, and judge it, not according to what Miss Wilson's
school was teaching, nor according to what the Back Bay would
approve, but according to the facts. "You can understand, Mr.
Vanzetti," said she, "I don't hear very much about these ideas,
and they are strange to me. But I'd like to know all I can.
Maybe you would let me come Saturday afternoon, and you
and I and Nonna would take a long walk in the woods, and you
could explain to me."

Never in the year that Cornelia had known Bart had she seen
him so happy as then! "Meess Betty," said he, "is notting in
whole world I like so much as for explain."

VI

It was a warm, still afternoon, and a hundred pleasure-boats
made holiday upon Plymouth Bay. Motor launches chugged
here and there, and fishermen drew their nets and set their

lobster-pots; while on the top of Castle Hill Bartolomeo Vanzetti sat under a wind-beaten tree and with many gestures told the story of his life to Cornelia Thornwell and her granddaughter.

He had been born in a peasant home in the village of Villafalletto, on the banks of the river Magra, in northern Italy. He had yearned for an education, but as fate would have it, his father read in a newspaper how forty-two lawyers had applied for a position in Turin which paid only seven dollars a month; and that ended the hope of culture for little Bart! At the age of thirteen he was put to work as a pastry cook's apprentice, and slaved for fifteen hours a day, from seven in the morning till ten at night, seven days in the week, with the exception of three hours on Sunday. Thus passed six years of his pitiful youth, until at last his health broke under the strain, and he was brought back to his village home. Through those years he had been a devout Catholic, and had solaced himself with the faith that his sufferings were God's will. "I make fist-fight for church," said he, with a laugh. "Fellow he say somet'ing very bad, I make heem sorry."

Then the will of God inflicted a still more dreadful sorrow upon him. His mother fell ill. He had loved her more than he could find words to tell, in either English or Italian. "It is why I so glad for have Nonna come here. Always it make me memory my modder. It is story I not tell her, sooch terrible story. She is so sick, sooch agonia, she screama, long time no —cannot sleep; I must go ask men on street for not sing, make noise. It is so bad, nobody in family can stand for see her, not osband, not daughter. It is me must help her—must hold her in arm, must—what you say, nurse—for two mont' I not undress for sleep. One day she die in my arm, she suffer so, not know me, not my tears. It is me must put her in coffin, must walk to grave, must shovel dirt onto my modder. Sooch miseria! You know what is Dante say, Nonna—'nessun maggior dolore'—it is no sooch greater grief in world as to remember happy time in miseria. But for me it is no sooch grief as to remember what my modder musta suffer. Always I see it, and each old lady in world is my modder."

There was a pause, while the ditch-digger blinked a tear out of his eyes; then he went on. "Could no more be happy in home.

No can ever laugh. My fadder, he get gray, very old. I no can —cannot work, must go walk in wood, stand by river on little bridge and look down in water, t'ink maybe I fall in, not have so mooch sufferance. So I t'ink maybe come America; is new country, great country, I start more life; is what you say in song, 'sweet land of liberty'—Fay she sing in school. It is what you say, full dinner-pail. So I say, I come America, not for get rich, get little money, no work so hard, have time for read book. I joosta readed De Amicis, great writer, what you say 'Cuore,' it is story of his heart. I t'ink maybe I be socialist now, little bit socialist, sentimentale, genteel, good, ever'body be kind, make new world, ever'body be happy, maybe by vote. I come America for sooch pretty—what you say, dream."

Vanzetti paused, and closed his eyes in pain. "Next to lose modder, next most badda t'ing in whole life is lose America. You 'Merican lady cannot onderstand, no never, not if talk all day. Hear about Statue Liberty—beautifool, wonderfool—paradiso. Come Ellis Island, all sudden knock on head, like badda dream, inferno—brutale, treat people lika beast—little ones cry, hide in modder's dress. What for is reason for treat poor people sooch way? Why make sooch fear, sooch hate? I go on street, stand look, strange city, mooch automobile, big train upstair—bang, bang, make fright. I go look for home; no got one friend, ever'body try cheat, rob poor straniere—what you say, foreign. Must go sleep in room, twenty people, is filt' ever'- where; must hunt job, washa da deesh, must sleep wit'—you scusa me, Meess Betty, is not gooda story for tell sweet young lady—"

"Go on," said Betty. "If it's not too bad to happen, it's not too bad to hear."

"It is t'ing what bite in bed—it make you onhappy—cannot sleep. I live in room upstair, top of house, mooch people, very hot. I go for work restaurant—it is mooch famous place, you read about in book; all time go artist, writer, take lady for supper. I not know what is now, but eight year back I washa da deesh, mosta bad dirt, steam all time, grease on roof drop on food, on clean deesh; all slop on floor, drain get stop, you stand t'ree inch water all day washa deesh, like work in sewer. I talk many men, it is same plenty big restaurant, all for show, not care be clean. But worker he cannot tell story—who would hear heem?

"I work fourteen hour one day, twelve hour next day. I get five, six dollar week. Get food very bad, dirty, like dog. I no can stand, t'ink maybe get seeck, I stop, go country, look for work outdoor. But is very bad time—you know, Nonna, is what you call panic joost come, make very bad for job. Must go hungry, beg job, get food out of garbage-can maybe, some-day starve, so weak cannot work more. It was farmer give little job—two week—he not need me, but he sorry for poor wop—it is first time I get kind word from any one American, I never forget that farmer.

"It is long story, Meess Betty, you no want hear heem all. I get work by brick furnace, shovel coal, it is job for kill man, sooch heat. But I near die hungry, so I stay, ten mont' I shovel coal. I go Conecticut, get job by stone quarry, work a year. Is better so, meet plenty Italian, got home, see people dance, play violin evening. I no dance, but like see friend be happy. I read mooch book, I read paper, t'ink about worker, hees life, I see is not land of liberty, is all same, whole world is slavery for worker. It is few people own land, own factory, is capitalista, sooch people maka da profitt, it is for profitt musta be all indus-tree. Worker is—I cannot say Eengleesh, is what you buy and sell, comodità—is not human, is joost somet'ing for be sold for profitt. You onderstand, Meess Betty."

"Certainly."

"It shock you, maybe—"

"Not at all. I've thought about it a lot. What do we do for all this money we have? We young people, especially—we can work if we want to, and that's very kind of us; but if we prefer we can lie back and loaf the rest of our lives. No, Mr. Vanzetti, don't be afraid to talk to me!"

"You must onderstand, I not have sooch idea when I come America, no what you call foreign red. I learn heem here, I see wit' eye, I talk wit' worker, I t'ink what is way for free-dom. I am anarchista long time before to see anarchista paper, hear anarchista speaker. When I hear heem, I t'ink, it is olda story, it is my word from mout' of odder man!"

And Betty, sitting with her eyes riveted upon him, re-marked, "That is a little the way I find it, listening to you!"

VII

There was more to this talk; a discussion of Vanzetti's ideas, and his answers to many questions. When it was over, Cornelia walked part of the way home with her grand-daughter, taking one of the back streets. "Oh, Grannie, what a wonderful man! Grannie, I never dreamed of such a thing—why don't they tell us there are men like that among the working-people? Do you suppose there are many?"

"He says there are; but maybe he is being modest."

"So polite and so kind—he really is a gentleman, Grannie, and without any family, or any one to teach him."

"He is a gentleman if the word is worth using, dear."

"And think what that man has read, stealing all the time from his sleep! Grannie, I was never so ashamed in my life! I'm going to get that book by Kropotkin—I'm going to read and understand for myself. I've known it was all wrong, I've been saying it to myself for a year or two. What am I doing— except to show how to wear clothes?"

"You're supposed to be studying, dear. I thought you had to work hard at Miss Wilson's."

"Oh, yes, we're Spartan enough, but it's all so remote from reality, so academic and so tiresome. We listen to Miss Wilson talk a lot, and it's not good form to ask questions, because she is deaf, and we don't want to reveal the fact. I'm bored with it, Grannie—and I'm bored with society before I get in! Does that sound like a prig?"

"No, dear, of course not."

"Well, you can't imagine such idle boys! I suppose when I'm a deb, and meet older men, it won't be so bad; but I was invited to one of the Brattle Hall dances—and you talk about the Dickie and who made it and who didn't, and about football, and last year's scores and this year's prospects; and after that it's time to stroll out into the moonlight and get sentimental. Down here you go sailing and you go to garden parties, and you never hear anything worthwhile. The one serious thing in Plymouth is the pulling and hauling between the descendants of the Pilgrims and the descendants of the Puritans. One claims social precedence, and the other won't grant it, and they gossip dreadfully. Mrs. Walker doesn't belong to either set, and she ought to be glad—but she isn't." They walked on, until suddenly the girl burst out, "Do you know what I'd really like to do, Grannie?"

"What, dear?"

"Stay right here the rest of the summer, and get a job in the cordage plant with you, and prove that I'm some use."

"No, dear, you can't do that, it would make your mother and father too unhappy. And besides, it would be giving away my secret."

"Yes, I suppose so. But anyhow, I am going to do something worthwhile before I get through."

"Where you going the rest of the summer?"

"Camp Putnam for August; and of course that's exciting, in a way. Did they have Camp Putnam when you were a girl?"

"No, people didn't go as far as the Adirondacks; and besides, I wasn't a fashionable person."

"Well, anyhow, they found some way to get you married off to an eligible man!" And Betty laughed. "Oh, yes, we know what Camp Putnam is for! The old people think they are being so sly, they get together and plan the list every summer, and rule out the least desirable ones—it's as select as if it was God we were visiting. They even try to arrange the partners, but it doesn't work out to oblige them. I know Mother wants to put me off on Ebenezer Cabot, but Grannie, he's an out-and-out moron."

"Don't say that, dear!"

"But it's true! You know perfectly well that most of us old families have feeble-minded ones, and regular lunatics, with keepers watching them, somewhere off in a remote wing of the house. Isn't it true that Great-uncle Ahab was that way for years?"

"Yes, dear, but you mustn't speak of it."

"Only to you, Grannie. But I'm telling you there'll be no Ebenezer in my young life. But I think before this summer's over I'm going to have to deal with a proposal."

"Who from?"

"Roger Lowell. He was there last year, and he almost did it, but it wouldn't have been proper, because he was only a sophomore then, and they're not supposed to be engaged; but this year he's a junior, and so it'll be all right."

"Do you like him?"

"Well, I do and I don't, Grannie. He's a dear, in a way, and very good, but so awfully stiff and prim, so conscious of his great family, and what it's correct for him to do. If I were to marry him, I think I'd be like you and Grandfather Thornwell, I'd hardly dare crack a smile the rest of my life. I've already shocked him by some of the things I've said. I told him a woman should promise to stay with a man so long as she loved him, not any more. He said she ought to promise to love him forever, but I said that would be silly, because how could you tell? Did you ever meet him, Grannie?"

"The first time I met him, he had his pink toes up in the air."

"Oh, I'll tell him that, and humiliate him to death! No Lowell should be seen in such a position!"

"And the second time he had a bib around his neck, and porridge running down it. The last time I met him, he was in evening dress, and his collar was stiff and his tie was puffy, and his sober round face looked over the top like a big pink chrysanthemum."

"Oh, Grannie, that's Roger exactly! And I'm his ideal of womanhood—if only I wouldn't make jokes! Now I'm going to read Vanzetti's books, and be really serious, but I'm not sure if he will like me as an anarchist. And Grannie, I'm supposed to go home to-morrow, but I hate to leave you like this—honestly, I'm ashamed of the food I eat."

"I'm having a very happy time. dear."

"How long do you plan to stay?"

"I'm not sure—I keep changing my mind. When I read in the paper about that speech your father made, trying to get us into the war—then all of a sudden I think I'll come back and take up a pacifist campaign."

"Oh, Grannie! How perfectly appalling! You'd be like old Mrs. Abigail Webster Adams—she made a speech at a socialist meeting, and Father said she ought to be locked up in an asylum."

"No doubt he'll say that about me," said Cornelia. It was a prophecy.

VIII

Betty went away, and the rest of Cornelia's stay was enlivened by letters, addressed to Mrs. Nonna Cornell—it was Betty's little joke. They were highly confidential letters, full of family information. "Uncle Quincy has found the perfect chess player, a man who can foresee all possible combinations. Uncle James is building a whole new house on the back of 'Hillview.' And Father says the Boston banks have got a hundred million dollars of British and French bonds. They sold them to the public, but had to take them as collateral, and if the allies should lose, not a bank in Boston could keep open. So you had better come on up and make that pacifist speech."

And then: "I have been to the book-store that Mr. Vanzetti told me about. It is kept by a nice dark-eyed young Russian who was eager to undertake my education. I have a number of books which I keep hidden in the bottom of a trunk, they are lots worse than the 'Cosmo' with Robert W. Chambers. One is called 'Vindication of the Rights of Women,' by Mary Wollstonecraft Godwin. The preface says it is a hundred and twenty-five years old. The world has not caught up with her yet. I am very much excited about this book, because it is just what I had been thinking. But Roger will not like it."

Then: "I am at Camp Putnam, ready to be paired off for life, with no possibility of its not being good family. It really is the loveliest country, and impossible not to have a good time. It is so nice to wear sensible camping clothes; how I wish that women might wear short skirts all the time. But if I were to walk down Tremont street this way, I suppose I'd have a crowd of boys hooting me. There is much in the world to be changed. I think the Mary Wollstonecraft book has made me into a suffragette. Would that shock you?

"I am going out now to climb a mountain. We shall all spend the night on top and see the sunrise, and come home to-morrow, and then we shall eat most tremendous quantities of cakes and syrup. We seem to be hungry all the time. Aunt Betty, who runs the camp and us, has put a big block of chocolate in the pantry, and a little hatchet with which we knock off pieces. Mother says it was exactly the same in her day— the same hatchet, but I don't suppose the same block of chocolate. At least, we shall not leave much for our children."

And then: "We have climbed many mountains, and are having our good time in a sober, conscientious way. We are really very serious young people. Did I tell you that we have a way of testing any newcomer? We have a funny story that we tell him; at least it is said to be funny, but really it has no point, and we watch to see if he laughs. If he does, we know that he is not sincere. It is very ingenious, but after you have watched the procedure two or three times it strikes you as a little self-conscious. I suppose it is our Puritan blood that makes it necessary for us to be always consciously and deliberately righteous.

"It would not be a very good test with Roger, for he might not laugh even if the joke did have a point. We have had some long talks and I thought I would break the news gently, so I said, 'I have met several radicals, and am much interested in their ideas.' Roger. said, 'That is all right, I am the same way, I had a prof last year who was quite terribly radical.' I asked, 'What did he say?' and Roger answered, 'Oh, all sorts of things. He kept talking about the "lost books of the Bible," and he said that the substance of the ten commandments was found in earlier writings, and the story of the flood was derived from Babylonian sources.' You might tell that to Mr. Vanzetti and shock him!"

The climax of the courtship: "Oh, Grannie dear, my dolly is stuffed with sawdust! Roger and I have had a heart to heart talk and a most terrible quarrel, and it is all over—my name is never going to be Lowell. I told him I had come to realize that marriage was a form of slavery for women; and he said he knew what I meant, it was the word obey in the ceremony, but there were some clergymen who would leave that out if you asked them to. And I said it wasn't only that, it was the idea of a woman's parting with her autonomy; that every woman ought to have the final say about the children she bore; she ought to be free—especially if she were willing to earn her own way, as I meant to do.

"So then he was much puzzled, and asked me what I thought we ought to do, and I said I believed in a free union, with our own promise to each other, to be true to our best selves, and to do our best to love each other, but not stay together if we

couldn't. And Roger said, 'You mean—you mean you wouldn't
really—you wouldn't get married at all?' and he turned red to
the tips of his ears, and I said, 'You don't understand my feelings.' But he couldn't talk about it any more—he said, 'Betty
Alvin, if I had made such a proposition to you, it would have
been a deadly insult.' And I said, 'Maybe so, but I am making
it to you, and that is something different,' And he wanted to
know where I had got such outrageous ideas, but when I tried
to tell him he didn't really want to know, and wouldn't look at
the book. He tried to talk to me about my soul, and I laughed
at him, and so now we are most fearfully polite to each other
when anybody else is present, because of course we don't want
to have a scandal in the camp. Oh, Grannie, I wish you would
come back home, because I am going to be so lonely!"

IX

The "Gruppo Autonomo di Plymouth" gave a "picanic" that
fall, and from all the neighboring towns came swarms of
Italians, by train and bus and second-hand automobile. And
then it was announced that the "Circolo Drammatico Mario
Papisardi" was going to give a play in Stoughton, a "shoe-
town" some thirty miles away. They had quite a fine dramatic
organization, and Bart laid off work for three days to travel
round and place tickets for them. Illness kept the Brinis
from going, but some neighbors, the Angelottis, invited Cornelia.

A young anarchist comrade called for them in his car;
Mike Boda was his name, and he told Cornelia that he was a
macaroni salesman, and raced about the country in his little
Overland car, hopping in and out at Italian homes. He was
a chipper little fellow, about five feet two inches high, and
it was just as well that he was no heavier, because when you
had Bart on the front seat with a boy on his knee, and Mr.
and Mrs. Angelotti and Cornelia on the back seat, with another
boy on the father's lap and another on the mother's, you had
about as much weight as the springs of a low-priced car could
be expected to stand.

But the roads were good, and they rolled along singing
songs, and it was a gay party that swept into the shoe-town.
The children had been to the movies, of course, and they

had seen a play at school, but this was their first grown-up play, and they could hardly contain their excitement. They drove to the home of a comrade whom Vanzetti had recently met at one of the East Boston gatherings. Nicola Sacco was his name, and he lived in a fine cottage, which had formerly belonged to his boss. "Great feller, Nick," explained Bart. "He work shoe-factory, is edge-trimmer, mooch skill work, he make so mooch fifty, sixty dollar week, that boy—smart feller, got lovely wife, you see."

Their host ran out to the gate to meet them, a chap of twenty-five, with even, regular features and black hair and eyes; very active, like a cat, a figure all of steel springs. He had come from the ankle of the Italian boot, while his wife, Rosina, came from the north—young and dainty, with vivid auburn hair and an eager face full of sunshine and freckles. They had a little boy, about three years old. "Hello, Dante!" called Bart. "Someday we have nodder poet!" But the new poet was shy, and hid behind his mother's skirts.

Nick and Rosina were to act in the play to-night, so the guests refused to go into the house and disturb them. The visitors had their supper all in a box, and would make a "pic-anic" on the Saccos' front lawn. But nothing could prevent the host from showing them his garden; next to his family, it was the pride of his life, he worked at it every night till it was too dark to see. He led them down the rows of tomato plants, and lifted the branches and showed the big red globes under-neath. He knew only a few words of English, but Cornelia did not need a translator, because for forty years she had seen her husband showing off his flowers to visitors, and she knew every expression and gesture that goes with the ceremony.

x

They went to the hall where the play was to be, and met most of the Italians of New England, it seemed. There were Nick and Rosina on the stage, magically transformed into peasants of the home country. Cornelia had one of the young Angelottis on each side, and they were supposed to whisper into her ear what was happening; but they became so enthralled that they forgot there was anybody in the world but the figures in the play. However, Cornelia knew many Italian words, and all possible Italian gestures; and the story was so simple, and so full of action, it was easy to follow.

Nick was a peasant, whose son had been taken from him and forced to fight the Arabs in Tripoli. Meantime the father was in dire straits—"Militarism and Misery" was the title of the drama. His wife was ill of a fever, and he had no money, and the cruel landlord threatened to turn them out. When Nick offered to work for the landlord, his plea was refused, because, as an anarchist, he would lead the other workers to revolt. A good doctor came to visit the wife, and he and Nick had a debate, in which Nick set forth the principles of his faith with most wonderful eloquence. His comrades brought him money, and threw out the landlord, calling him "affamatore" and "assassino"—starver and assassin: whereat the doctor was so much impressed that he declared himself a convert to anarchism. "The new comrade am I"—and the other comrades burst into cheers, and the audience was not slow to follow.

Then came the soldier-boy, home from the wars. He boasted of the Arab women and children he had slain, and his father, a true internationalist, threw his pay into his face and ordered him from the home. "Get out, get out of here, robber and assassin!"—a painful scene. In the next act, the soldier-boy sat in the barracks, brooding over his shame—to such good effect that when he discovered another soldier with a load of antimilitarist literature, he let the guilty one escape. And when in the last act he was ordered home, in charge of a file of troops, to shoot down the striking peasants, he refused, and went over to the side of his father, and died from a shot fired by the mayor. It was a tragic and sensational ending, and Nick as the revolutionary father rose to heights of eloquence. "Yes, to the barricades! Farewell, my son—victim of bourgeois imperialism, repose in peace! To-day is not the day to mourn the dead. It is the day of battle and vengeance. Let us hasten, comrades, where the struggle is more fierce, to avenge not only him, but all the obscure martyrs fallen through capitalist greed." And as the comrades rushed out and the firing began off-stage, you would have thought you were in La Scala—such storms of applause, such tears and raptures, so many bouquets on the stage, so many "evvivas" and "bis!"

It was easy to smile at the naïveté of such a story. But when you saw how deeply it moved the audience, then you had to stop and think, and realize that it was the stuff of the lives of Italian peasants. If the drama and its emotions were simple, it was because the reality was the same. Even the conversion of the doctor might have happened—for, after all, there were anarchist doctors, well known in Italy. And the struggle against militarism—that was the religion and martyrdom of the peasant all over Europe. Everything in the drama was true, except the revolution—and what was needed to bring that, but the very fervor and impulse of this peasant audience?

The family discussed all this as they drove home. It was late and the children went sound asleep, but the grown-ups never wearied of talking, and explaining matters to Cornelia. Vanzetti told more about that wonderful fellow "Sacc' "—who was, in real life, exactly as he had been on the stage. "He come America same year like me. Was young feller, seventeen. Got brudder wit', brudder no can stand, is too hard work, musta go home Italy. Nick, he work water-boy, carry water for gang all day. He work Hopedale, is beeg strike by foundry-shop—you read about heem maybe. Police is rough, mooch bad. Nick he is on picket-line, get hit plenty time. Is way for make red, make anarchista—you see, joosta like dramma. Nick is not speaker, but gooda man for organize. Work now by little shoe-factory, is good friend wit' boss, do day-work, night watchman too, make plenty money. But never he change, stand always by worker. Some day it come odder beeg strike, Nonna, you see Nick Sacc' be leader, he do joost what you see for make rivoluzione. He cannot fear, is brave—like what you say —leone—lion."

And Bart went on to tell about something which had happened a month or two ago, when the young hero's mettle had been tested. "He get arrest—he musta go jail for hold meeting. It is protest for beeg strike in copper country—you know maybe—Mesaba range—out West. Is plenty rich people in Boston own copper-mine not like for have worker hear how they beat people, t'row in jail. Try for stop meeting, shut-up Nick and not let him tell about it."

Cornelia said nothing: but a procession of "bluebloods" began to move with stately dignity through her thoughts: the

Paynes, the Shaws, the Agassizs—yes, she knew "coppers," and the owners thereof. She remembered a scandal that had made awe-stricken whispers in the Sewing Circle—an old man had died, and it appeared that for twenty years or so he had been keeping eight thousand shares of his copper stocks hidden under a dummy name in New York, signing the name of this dummy. The executors of his estate failed to report these shares to the government, to avoid paying taxes on them; they had been caught, and some of the brightest legal lights of Boston were nearly disbarred. Nobody had gone to jail, of course—only "Nick Sacc'," who had tried to tell the Italians of Massachusetts how the "copper kings" were beating and killing their Michigan miners.

XI

The grapes on the Brini arbor had become dark purple globes, and had been harvested and converted into "Dago red." The leaves had turned, first yellow and then brown, and had dropped off and been blown into the corners of the garden. The cabbage and turnips were stored in the cellar, and the tomato-vines grew mushy after frost, and then dry and hard. All that beautiful garden was a wreck, and the sun was going away on his long pilgrimage. Very soon Cornelia would be getting up by lamplight, and shivering while she dressed, and being pinned up in her shawl for the journey to the cordage-plant. Could she stand another of these winters?

Betty was back at Miss Wilson's school, and begging her grandmother to come to Boston. Surely she ought to be taking part in the campaign to reëlect Woodrow Wilson, who had kept us out of war, and said we were too proud to fight. How Boston—the Boston of State Street and fashionable society—loathed that phrase, and how they jeered and raged in their *Transcript!* But there was another Boston, which had crossed the seas a generation ago to escape the potato famine; it had found an abundance of potatoes in New England, and had converted them into a crop of young Irish voters, pledged to the worship of the Virgin Mary and the extermination of the British lion. In vain did "Pro Bono Publico" and "Hundred Percent American" write letters to the *Transcript,* summoning the new world to the rescue of down-trodden Belgium. Irish-Catholic Boston did not read the *Transcript*, and it thronged to the polls and elected an Irish-Catholic mayor, who would see to it that Irish and Germans and pacifists might hold all the peace-meetings they wished, and parade through Park Street and spit when they passed the Union Club.

Wilson was reëlected; and it seemed that the war-danger was over. He would go on writing notes to the Germans, as he had been doing for a year or two, and the Germans would go on ignoring them. Cornelia decided that she would not be needed as a pacifist agitator, nor would Vanzetti have to take refuge in Mexico, as he had made up his mind to do in case America should enter the war. "Capitalist I will fight some day," said Bart, "but never will I kill German worker, Austrian worker, for make good no banker bond." Cornelia had not mentioned the highly confidential subject of Boston high finance and its commitments to the allied cause; but apparently the "reds" had their own sources of information, for the "Cronaca Sovversiva" was full of talk on the subject, and details of the intrigues of State Street and Wall Street.

XII

The first snow of the year was in the air, and Cornelia came hurrying home in the darkness, with half an inch of snow melting upon her shoulders. She was surprised to see a large limousine in front of the Brini door, its two long streams of light making day in Suosso's Lane, and revealing the million-footed dance of the snowflakes. As she came nearer, the door of the car opened and a bulky man stepped out; Cornelia could not see his face, but his voice caused her to stop dead in her white tracks. "Is that you, Mother?" It was Rupert Alvin!

In a certain musical comedy it is set forth how the founder of Columbus Day landed in the new world, and the Indians came eagerly, inquiring, "Are you Christopher Columbus?" When he admitted his identity, they exclaimed, "At last we are discovered!" So now it was with Cornelia. The jig was up, she knew—and took but a moment to get herself together. "Hello, Rupert!" she said, with an air of nonchalance—there are times when the Thornwell training comes in handy! She accepted her son-in-law's outstretched hand, and let him help her into the limousine, where sat her eldest daughter, Deborah. "Oh, Mother! Mother! How could you?" Yes, even the stately Mrs. Rupert Alvin wept when she saw those bowed shoulders and that pitiful working-woman's shawl covered with a load of snow. She had snapped on the light in the limousine; but Rupert snapped it off again quickly.

"Control yourself, Deborah," he commanded—having in mind the chauffeur, who would overhear, in spite of the glass partition. "Mother, we want to have a private talk with you. Will you not please come home with us—at least for a day or two?"

"I can't, Rupert. I have a job."

"Can't you get excused temporarily?"

"One does not get excused from jobs, one gets fired."

"But Mother, you have a little income from the estate!" It was Deborah, breaking in.

"Wait, Deborah!" insisted the husband, again. "Mother, will you let us take you to some hotel here in Plymouth, where we can discuss matters quietly?"

"Certainly I will do that. But first I must tell my friends. They will be expecting me to supper and will worry."

"I will see to that," said the man, quickly, and he got his majestic bulk out of the car, and Cornelia wondered vaguely, was he afraid she might make her escape? Was she being kidnaped? Inside her something fluttered like a bird in a trap. "Don't be caught! Don't let them get you!"

"Oh, Mother, you are all wet!" Deborah was lamenting. "Take off that shawl!" She drew it off, and began to wrap Cornelia in a big fur robe. Cornelia submitted, because it was easier than to argue. Her mind was busy with another problem: how had they found her? Could it have been Miss Mehitabel? Impossible to believe that Betty had revealed the secret!

Rupert returned, and gave his orders to the chauffeur, and got into the car, which began to sway on luxurious springs down the unpaved and rutted lane. It turned onto the main street, and sped to a hotel, where they got out, and Rupert engaged a room, and Deborah hurried her mother through the lobby. Presently they were locked in a place where family secrets might be safe —after Rupert had stepped to the door once or twice and opened it, to make sure there were no eavesdroppers.

"I am perfectly all right," said Cornelia, in answer to her daughter's clamor that she was wet and that she was cold and that she was exhausted. "I have been very happy," she declared, in answer to laments about the state of her shoulders and her hands. And when Deborah had got to the question of how her mother could have been so cruel as to treat them this way, Cornelia broke in with the demand, "How did you find me?" She had to repeat the question before Deborah answered, "We got your address from Betty."

"You mean she told you? I can't believe such a thing, Deborah!"

"I don't mean that. She wrote you a letter, and we got it."

"Oh, I see." A great load was lifted from Cornelia's heart. After a moment she said, "I would like to have the letter." Seeing them hesitate and look at each other, she said, "Give me my letter, please." So Rupert took from his pocket an envelope, which Cornelia could see at a glance was very bulky.

Balancing the letter in his hand, the great man began, in his most solemn tones, "Mother, I wish to explain that when we opened this letter we did not know it was to you. If we had known that, we should have brought it unopened. But you will see, it is addressed to Mrs. Nonna Cornell, and that meant nothing to us, except that our unhappy daughter was communicating secretly with some unknown woman. Only when we opened the letter, did we discover that it was to you."

"Neither of us read it, Mother," added Deborah. "It may be we had a right to, but we didn't feel sure."

"I will read it to you at once, my child."

"I don't think it will be necessary. We had a talk with Betty, and I think we know the situation."

Cornelia held the letter in her hands. How pathetic seemed the little joke, "Mrs. Nonna!" She took the letter from the envelope, and saw why Deborah had suggested not hearing it—the last page was numbered forty! But Cornelia had to read only two sentences to know the whole story.

"Dear Grannie:

"I am in the most dreadful predicament you can imagine, because Roger Lowell, the tenth descendant of a line of theocrats, spent three months laboring with his conscience and finally made up his mind that he must save my soul by telling father of the indecent proposition I had made at Camp Putnam! So now here I am shut up in my room and forbidden to go out, until I have promised to reform—and so I am forced to smuggle this letter to you by one of the maids."

XIII

The antagonists squared off for battle—two against one. It would be none the less deadly, because it would be carried on under the forms of courtesy, even of love.

The first thing was for Deborah to weep some more. This was not easy, for she was haughty, self-contained—the last word in aristocratic reticence. But there was that pitiful figure—gray-haired, bowed and bent, in wretched shapeless clothing wet with melted snow—that was her mother! And even though she told herself that her mother had become insane, it was none the less terrible. Also, impossible to forget that certain scenes which Deborah forbade herself to remember had had something to do with her mother's mental disorder. So the tears streamed down Deborah's cheeks—and she had one of those long, half-masculine faces, which are not improved by weeping.

In Cornelia's own being the trapped bird was still fluttering. "Fight! Fight! Don't let them get you!" She had had a year and a half to think matters over, and she knew all the devices of families to break people down. She remembered Cousin Amelia Quincy, who had sought to marry the wrong man, and how Cousin Amelia's mother had fallen violently ill—a complete nervous breakdown—which had lasted until the wrong man had given up and married some other girl.

So now Cornelia made her voice stern, and said, "It is silly for you to behave that way, Deborah. There is nothing the matter with me, and I assure you my children are not going to get their way by tears."

Then Deborah drew herself to her full height. "I will not annoy you any further. I have of course no right to object to your living your own life—"

"None whatever, my child."

"But I have a right to object to your ruining the mind and character of my young and impressionable daughter."

"I hope I have not done that."

"Unless our daughter tells us what is not true, you introduced her to a band of anarchists and atheists—"

"Not atheists, Deborah, you have got the wrong word."

"You mean that Italian man, whatever his name is, is not an atheist?"

"He has explained to me carefully his beliefs. He worships one God, the God of nature, of love and justice. He worships only one, so perhaps that constitutes him an infidel."

Deborah declined this challenge to theological controversy. "And free-lovers!"

"That is still less accurate. I doubt very much if Vanzetti has ever been any kind of lover in his life. He is a saint who believes in free love."

"Is that one of your jokes, Mother?"

"It sounds like it, I know, but you will have to learn that there are new ideas loose in the world, and it is not practicable to keep people from knowing about them—not even by shutting them up in their rooms and confiscating their mail."

Rupert Alvin was silent, considering that free love is not a theme for mixed conversation; and anyhow, in family disputes the less an "in-law" has to say, the safer for him. When the two ladies began exchanging views upon the efficacy of a church ceremony as a purifier of lust, Rupert arose and went to the door and opened it and peered out. It was a delicate hint, and the ladies took it, and discussed anarchism. Or rather, Cornelia discussed anarchism, while Deborah discussed anarchy, and refused to recognize the difference. Cornelia asserted that she had lived among Italian anarchists for a year and a half, and had not seen a single bomb—except those which Brini described as "bombe di pistacchio."

They were on the subject of foreigners and their alleged resemblance to pigs, when Rupert decided that it was time for a man to interpose his authority. "Mother," he said—and went on, in spite of his wife's angry signals—"we are not getting anywhere by arguing over subjects like this. The question is, what are we going to do. I know that our mutual esteem and affection will bring us to an understanding in the end; so what I am hoping is to persuade you to come home and stay with us a while. I know you will be able to induce Betty to—well, to moderate her expressions. That is all we ask, and I am sure you agree that we do not want an open scandal in our family."

"Certainly not, Rupert."

"Well, then, come with us, and in time we can work it all out happily."

"That is easy to say, Rupert, but it seems to me you are taking a serious risk. Suppose that while I am your guest I should consider it my duty to appear on some public platform and say that the effort to bring America into the war is a crime against civilization, and that the motive power behind it is our big bankers, who have loaned so much money to England and France and Italy that they cannot face the prospect of losing their investments?"

To Rupert Alvin, president of the Pilgrim National Bank of Boston, and directing head of the most powerful financial group in State Street, it was as if his mother-in-law had taken a sharp rapier and brought the point of it close to one of his waistcoat buttons. The many large bulges which composed Rupert's face and neck became still larger, the pink ones turning red, and the red ones purple. His large round eyes opened wide, and the hands which clutched his large round knees tightened until they showed the tendons. Either Rupert's tongue refused to make a sound, or else Rupert's brain did not know what sound to tell it to make.

XIV

"My children," said Cornelia, "I want to be fair, and make myself understood if it can possibly be done. For forty years I did what I was told was my duty, and let other people guide my life. I was very unhappy—how unhappy I did not realize until Josiah was dead, and I had begun to do what I wanted to do. Now for the rest of my life I am going to be an individual, and not a cog in the family machine. And while that will seem terrible to you, you can comfort yourself with the fact that it is real 'Boston'—'old Boston,' the very best there is. Everything that is glorious in our history has been made by people who have 'come out,' and fought some prevailing sentiment. I never realized that until I got alone and thought it over. Take Wendell Phillips—you cannot say anything against his ancestry, there was never any one more completely 'Back Bay.' Yet he turned into an abolitionist and labor agitator, the same as a pacifist and 'red' at the present time. It has always been that way, and the ones you honor now, the ones whom the rest of the world knows about—Samuel Adams and John Quincy Adams, Emerson and Thoreau and Phillips and Garrison and James Russell Lowell— yes, there was even a Lowell, Deborah—and Thomas Wentworth Higginson—even a Higginson, Rupert, tell that to State Street! Boston history has been made by the 'saving minority.' You must know that is true?"

"Yes, but Mother"—it was Deborah protesting—"that was all in the past!"

"And now the world is perfect, and we don't need any more changes! Well, my dear, all I can tell you is, I have looked the world over and made up my mind that it has never been worse than right now—with some ten or twenty million men lined up on opposite sides, using all the machinery and brains of civilization to slaughter one another. No, I think we need changes, and there is going to be a Thornwell among the 'come outers,' and you will have to put up with the humiliation of it. I don't think I shall be lonely—I've been able to recollect the names of a number of old ladies who have left their families and are living in apartments and hotels, interesting themselves in one queer cause or another. I never paid much attention, because Josiah wouldn't have approved of my associating with them. But now I shall look them up—I suppose I shall join the Twentieth Century Club."

"Oh, Mother! How horrible!"

"And the suffragettes, whatever they call their organization —there are two, I believe. And the socialists have a local—I am not an anarchist, Deborah, comfort yourself with that—and anyhow, the anarchists don't have any organizations. I suppose the pacifists have one; I hear that Mrs. Abigail Webster Adams has come out for them, and that Rupert thinks she ought to be locked up in an asylum. Well, Rupert, that has been the idea of the comfortable people for a long way back—I remember they accused Socrates for corrupting the youth. But even though you put people in an asylum, their ideas get out—you cannot always be sure that the maid will turn their letters over to you."

Cornelia paused; and then, seeing the look on her daughter's face—"Yes, my dear, that was a mean one. But you must realize that Mother is going to fight from now on; Mother holds her convictions with just the same intensity that you hold yours, and something inside her compels utterance. It is that stern terrible thing we call our Puritan conscience. It is out of fashion at the moment, but it takes new forms, it has a rebirth, and does not rest until it has made some impression on the world—some change such as the independence of the colonies, or the abolition of slavery, or the outlawing of war, or the setting free of labor. And then the next generation forgets about the conflict, and says how famous Boston is, what great people it has produced! And their grandchildren become the aristocracy, and want everything to stay as it is!"

XV

Cornelia had her own proposition, which she had been thinking over for several months. "I will come up to town at once and get a little apartment, and Betty can come live with me. That will be respectable—it will even tend to make your runaway grandmother all right. And I'm sure I can guide Betty and keep her from going to extremes. It is what she herself has been begging me to do, and I know she will be happy."

"Thank you," said Deborah, with a touch of sarcasm. "To make the children happy is the one duty of parents under the new dispensation. But some of us parents are old-fashioned, and think about our children's souls."

"Yes, my dear, and it may be that the saving of Betty's soul depends upon her believing everything that is preached at Trinity—even though, as I suspect, the preacher does not believe it himself. But let us be practical about the matter. What will you do with the child? Ordinarily, when daughters threaten to run wild you send them off to Europe with an aunt, and they look at cathedrals and paintings for a year, and that is cultural. But now your war is in the way, so the only place to send her is out west, and she would see only rocks and rivers, which are not so cultural. Of course you can keep her shut up— make a prisoner of her by force—but that would only harden her spirit and drive her to extremes. Also, it would mean an open scandal, because your servants would know, and it would be all over the Back Bay in a night, and everybody would be certain the child had done something far worse than talk radicalism. Moreover, you can only keep her for a short while—then she will be of age, and you will lose your hold on her."

"We can disinherit her."

"Yes, of course; but she would have my property—"

"I think, Mother, you ought to be informed about that." It was Rupert breaking in—since it was a banker's affair. "You have no property, only an income of five thousand a year from the estate."

"Well, Rupert, I have lived upon four hundred a year for the past year and a half—"

"Mother, you don't mean it!" Impossible for the most reticent daughter to encounter such a statement with silence!

"What else have I had? I have lived on it, and even saved a little. And now if I come up to town and take my income of five thousand a year, with what has been accumulating, Betty and I will be rich."

"You would not be able to pay for the child's clothes!"

"Well, Deborah, maybe you know your daughter better than I, but my guess is Betty would learn to make her own clothes quite cheerfully. Will you give me a chance to ask her?"

"Most certainly not! In spite of your ridicule, I believe in my religion, and in a little decency and decorum. I shall not give up my daughter to become an anarchist and atheist—nor even a socialist and infidel—nor yet a saint who believes in free love."

"Well put, Deborah—we are both of us developing what Broadway would call the 'punch.' But put yourself in my place just a moment. I served your father faithfully for forty years, and conscientiously refrained from doing any of the things which made him angry. I gave life to three of you girls, and helped to find you husbands of the sort I knew your father wanted you to have. If you have any complaint as to your share in husbands, you have been too proud to make it to me. Have you, Deborah?" Cornelia paused, and looked at the solemn Rupert with a twinkle in her eye. Then she continued, "You both have what you want. But I have very little; I am old and lonely, and an object of sympathy. There are eleven grandchildren—no one of whom would have been in the world except for me. I put it to your sense of justice—may I not ask for one of the eleven to keep me company in my old age?"

It was turning Deborah's own weapons against her, and Deborah could not help being disturbed. "I think you would have shown better judgment if you had chosen one of Clara's eight, rather than one of my two."

"Perhaps that is so. But I did not choose Betty—she chose me; or rather, some fate did it, there is an affinity between us. I assure you, Deborah, upon my honor, I had no thought of causing this to happen. But it has happened, and we have to admit it."

"Never!" cried Deborah. Her lips were set in that expression which Cornelia had seen ten thousand times upon the face of Josiah Quincy Thornwell. It was recorded for all time in the paintings of four governors in the music-room at "Hillview."

Cornelia turned to her son-in-law. "Is that your decision also?"

Rupert hung on to that caution which is such an excellent thing in "in-laws." "Mother, I hope you will not go to any extreme—"

Cornelia laughed. "First I have to make sure what you and Deborah plan to do to Betty."

"We plan to do our duty as parents, to compel our child to behave herself!" It was Deborah, with great vehemence.

"Do you mean that she must believe what you believe—even though she doesn't? Or do you mean that she must say that she believes what she doesn't believe? Or will you be content if she agrees to say nothing about her beliefs?"

"That is what we commanded her to do, and she refused."

"Are you sure you made the distinction? Are you sure you didn't ask her to stop believing? I suspect you were so horrified and angry, you didn't know exactly what you were demanding." And Cornelia rose, saying, "I will try to supply a little wisdom and good temper for you. To-morrow I will go up to town and put up at a hotel, and get some clothes, so as not to disgrace you, and in the evening I will call at the house, and have a talk with my grandchild, and persuade her to be more fair than her parents."

"You must not feel that way about us, Mother!" It was Rupert, still trying for a compromise.

"There is no sense in saying any more to-night, Rupert. We have argued too much, for Thornwells. It is because I am not really 'Boston,' that I do this vulgar thing of trying to talk things out. But I love Betty, and cannot bear to see her spirit bruised. I will do the best I can, and advise her to suppress her eager young ideas on marriage, and private property, and war, and whatever else you object to—until she is of age, and her own legal mistress."

Cornelia took her shawl and started to put it on. "Mother! That thing is all wet! Let me give you my coat!"

"It is quite all right, there will be a good hot stove where I am going."

"But Mother, you must have dinner with us!"

"My friends will give me something to eat when I get home. I could not eat now."

She saw tears start in Deborah's eyes again, and that was as it should be. When Rupert labored to persuade his mother-in-law to ride to Boston with them, she answered that she had reasons for preferring the train; then she started towards the door. "Good-by, my children."

Rupert took up his coat and followed her. "At least you will let us drive you to where you are living, Mother."

"Thank you, but I am able to walk."

"But Mother, that is absurd—it is storming!"

"I have walked to my work for a year and a half, through every sort of storm—at six-thirty in the morning, and again in the evening—and have not yet missed a day."

So Cornelia unlocked the door and went out; Rupert and Deborah both following, arguing and pleading with her in low, decorous tones, all the way to the street. But she set her lips tight, and when Rupert tried to take her hand and lead her to the car, she withheld it, saying once more, "Good-by, my children," and hurrying away into the snow-haunted darkness.

XVI

The next evening, according to her promise, Cornelia called at the Alvin mansion on Commonwealth Avenue, dressed like a nice, quiet old lady of the social reform or "blue-stocking" type. She rang the bell with some trepidation, not quite certain whether she would be admitted; but she found an amazing situation—the family rows all settled, Betty out of prison and back at Miss Wilson's, and the entire Thornwell clan assembled to welcome home the runaway grandmother! To overwhelm her with kindness, with beauty, tact and charm, to afford her a demonstration of respectability, and make her realize its advantages over anarchism, atheism and free love!

There was Clara, in the radiance of her eighth maternity, and her husband, James Scatterbridge, shining with the extra millions he had made; and Alice, never more elegant, never more gracious, with no trace of a scandal or a hysteric about her; her husband, Henry Winters, jewel upon the finger of the legal profession; Deborah and Rupert, all courtesy and smiles; Betty, a little pale after a cyclone of emotions, but none the less lovely for that; Betty's older sister, Priscilla; Great-uncle Abner, and his son, Uncle Quincy—pronounced as if he were a disease of the throat. All of them in their most honorable costumes, all so amiable—not one hint of rebuke or complaint, not even a tactless slip—unless you count Great-uncle Abner, whose deaf man's voice boomed through the drawing-room; "Well, well, Cornelia, they tell me you've been making money!"

They had learned their lesson, that was the long and short of it; they would return to dignity and reserve and good manners—to "old Boston"; and Cornelia would return with them, and Betty also. There would be no more quarrels, no more scenes, no more scandals and "talking out" of things, no more anarchism, atheism, or free love!

There was a buzz of conversation, family news, compliments and courtesies. When would Cornelia come to see her new grandson? Had she heard of the fine record Alice's son had made at St. Mark's? Would she hear about Uncle Quincy's chess wonder? "How is your gout, Abner?" "How is the new wing coming on, James?" So many polite and pleasant things to talk about, that it was only near the end of the evening that she got a few words alone with Betty.

"Oh, Grannie, how on earth did you do it?"

"I don't know, dear—what did I do?"

"You completely tamed Mother and Father. They came back this morning as nice as pie."

"I guess they just had a little time to think things over, and realize how much they loved you." Cornelia was going to be tactful too!

"Well, yesterday Mother wouldn't hear to reason at all: I must promise to never believe anything she disapproved of, I must never talk about such things to anybody, and must never look at such a book! Of course I couldn't promise all that, could I, Grannie? You can't imagine how dreadful I felt, to have to tell Mother and Father that I wouldn't obey them! So I thought I was going to have to stay in my room till I didn't know when. But after they had talked with you, all they wanted was for me not to disgrace them publicly."

Cornelia was tempted to say that Rupert and Deborah had found the older generation so much worse than the younger, that it had frightened them. But no, she was going to be tactful! "I plan to get a little apartment, dear, and you can come see me, and we'll keep our thoughts to ourselves, and not give the family anything more to worry over." Thus Cornelia Thornwell, in December, 1916, while the German government was preparing its new submarine policy, which was to rouse all the warlike elements in America, and force all the pacifist ladies of Boston to make public speeches, and break with their families, and be raided by mobs and arrested by the police! With the Bolshevik revolution less than a year in the future, and the "white terror" following close upon its heels!

CHAPTER 5

I

CORNELIA declined three invitations, to live in three different mansions, and got herself an apartment on the north side of Beacon Hill, where the poor live near enough to the rich to come as servants, and to be visited as objects of charity. She had three rooms and a tiny kitchen and bath; one room being planned for her grand-daughter, in the hoped-for course of events. Cornelia did not mention this, but announced that she was going to live alone, to the great dismay of her family. Betty was in the secret, and helped fix up the little room, which was a great joke, because it had perhaps the twentieth part of the floor-space she enjoyed at home. But what is floor-space, compared with adventure, romance, the tasting of forbidden fruit? "Oh Grannie, it's so cute! And it's going to be such fun! Do you suppose they will really ever let me come?"

"I don't know, dear; if we're both very good and proper— if you don't have any more love-affairs—"

"Oh, Grannie, I am off for life! That horrible little monster of propriety, Roger Lowell—it makes me blush just to think of him!"

"The same effect that you had upon him," said Cornelia.

They discussed the technique of self-suppression, so fundamental to life in Boston. For forty years Cornelia had gone about her daily affairs, thinking her own thoughts, and seldom even venturing to make jokes about what the others did. Now Betty must learn the art. She must say, "Yes, Mother," and "Certainly, Father," and let it go at that. In an extreme case she might say,"I think, Mother, it would be wiser if we did not discuss that question." She might be firm and say, "I really think, Mother, you ought to excuse me from saying any more." If she would do that, politely but persistently, her family would

128

have a great respect for her; and some day, she might remark casually, "Mother, I think I will invite Grannie to go to the symphony to-morrow afternoon." Later she might phone and say, "Mother, I'm having supper with Grannie, and spending the evening with her." It would be hard for a mother to say, "No, you must come home at once"; or even to ask, "Are there going to be any anarchists present?"

Of course it all depended upon Cornelia's "behaving herself." But alas, the imperial German government announced its new policy—the submarines were going to sink passenger vessels without warning; and forthwith the Back Bay declared war on Germany, while South Boston, the Irish quarter, declared war on Britain. There was a symbolical insurrection when the Irish paraded down Beacon Street; the Back Bay shut up its houses and drew the blinds, but the cooks and dining-room girls and parlors-maids and chambermaids threw wide open the basement doors and windows, and stood in the area-ways and cheered themselves hoarse. For a generation it had been one of the diversions of the "Sewing Circle," to whisper harrowing stories of the conduct of these Irish maids with Irish policemen in the kitchen; but now it was even worse—the policemen were replaced by German spies, and nobody was safe any more!

Among the activities of the Kaiser and his agents was to persuade deluded sentimentalists into organizing groups with high-falutin names to preach pacifism. There was a "Fellowship of Reconciliation," and a "Women's League for Peace and Freedom," and a "People's Council for Peace and Democracy," and a "Jackasses' Association for Flubdub and Buncombe"—so Rupert Alvin described it in one of his purple-faced rages. The *Transcript* had been publishing atrocity stories in twelve editions every week for a hundred and twenty weeks, and the Back Bay had believed every word it read; so now imagine the sensation when one of these organizations of long-haired men and short-haired women listed among its abettors a former "first lady" of the Commonwealth!

And Mrs. Josiah Quincy Thornwell was going to make a public speech in favor of America's taking it lying down! When that announcement appeared, the entire family came, one at a time or in groups, to argue and plead and scold. Clara wept, in the name of her whole precious brood; if the Germans took

Boston, they would cut off all sixteen of those sweet chubby hands. Alice used the arts which she had practiced for forty years, ever since she had made the discovery that her beautiful face would cause others to yield their will to hers. Deborah had never had a beautiful face, so she had gone in for character, and now declared that she must consider her duty to her children, and protect Betty from the contagion of German and anarchist propaganda.

II

Also Henry Cabot Winters gave his mother-in-law an entire evening of his socially precious time. She was pleased at that, because Henry had a sense of fun, and would talk about realities. She got in a Negro maid, and prepared him a good dinner, and he came in full regalia, with his gray hair composed in a graceful wave and held there by a cylinder of stiff and shiny black silk. And while she fed him, she told him her adventures as a runaway grandmother, her work in the Plymouth cordage plant, and how she had lived on six dollars a week, and about the Italian anarchists who made bombs of pistacchio, and the rebel saint who had been the cause of Betty Alvin's reading Mary Wollstonecraft Godwin on the rights of women. Impossible to imagine a more diverting story—and especially the climax, which had come only last week—Cornelia's meeting with Mr. J. Lawrence Perry, and telling that elderly philanthropist how it felt to be an unskilled worker in his mighty plant, and be chased off the picket-line by his special policemen!

And later on, when dinner was over and the maid dismissed, the great lawyer settled himself in an easy chair with an ash-holder on the arm, and with the utmost tactfulness steered the conversation onto the subject of German propaganda; with the result that his mother-in-law put him on the griddle. "Tell me, Henry, how much do the Boston banks stand to lose if the Germans win?"

"Is this for publication, Mother?" The cloud of cigarette smoke did not obscure the twinkle in Henry's fine dark eyes.

"Your name is not for publication, Henry. I'm told it's a hundred million dollars."

"Round figures are generally exaggerated. As a matter of fact it would be everything the Boston banks have, because when a panic like that got started, nobody could say where it would stop."

"And that's why we have to go in?"

"We live under a system, Mother. Maybe you know how to change it, I don't."

"And what's this I hear about you and Rupert taking over the Haupt electric works?"

"Jehoshaphat! Where did you get that?"

"Well, I have sources of information. I suppose that is the system too—our leading bankers getting back the cost of their war-propaganda!"

"Well, Mother, we can't expect the Germans to pay it for us; and if we do go in, we surely can't leave the manufacture of our war-supplies to the enemy!"

"The fact that you and Rupert and James are getting your lines on Haupt Electric means we really are going in, then?"

"Of course, Mother, we're going in; that is what I want to tell you—it is unwise of you to waste your strength and happiness trying the impossible. You know, I don't fret about appearances like the rest of the family; but I'm fond of you—we used to have jolly little chats, and I missed them when you ran off. I thought maybe, if you wanted to blow off steam, you might blow it at me, instead of at an audience. Believe me, public life is wearing—not all the millions of all the Boston banks could get me into it! I imagine you've found that out, since you put your name on a letter-head, and set yourself up as a target for all the cranks in New England. How many begging letters have you received this week? How many associations have you joined to reform our spelling and put a stop to vaccination and vivisection?"

That was Henry Cabot Winters, genial, shrewd, playfully cynical. But do not let his social charm fool you; underneath the "Harvard manner" there was a wolf. He would nose among the banking secrets of Boston—he called the biggest bankers in the city by such names as "Ted" and "Winnie" and "Jimmie"; he had been to college with them, and met their wives and daughters in the evenings; he had access to their records, he could call up on the telephone and ask how much so-and-so was borrowing, and what were his assets and connections; and presently he would catch a scent of blood, and put himself upon the trail of a wounded caribou, and track him down—for years, maybe, never resting till he had drunk the last drop of blood from his veins. Both bankers and industrialists dreaded him, yet they could not get along without him; there was vigorous competition between two big banking groups in New England, and Henry's crowd needed his cunning, at any price he chose to ask. His fee was seven hundred dollars a day, but that was merely for overhead; his real reward was part of the carcass of each caribou.

Now he lounged in a faded Morris chair out of a second-hand shop, and lighted one cigarette after another and gazed at the feeble art-effects which Cornelia had been able to produce without spending money. He sounded like a schoolboy as he said, "Gee, Mother, I wish I could get off by myself and live the simple life!"

"Why not, Henry?"

"Well, I've got a costly wife, and a son to put through the education mill—"

"Rubbish, Henry, you know you laugh at Alice and her elegance, and your money will probably ruin your boy. There is some real reason."

"Well, I guess it's a game, Mother; you have to do something. When I rowed on the Harvard eight—it wasn't really so important, but we'd have broken a heart-valve to keep six inches ahead of the Yale boat. Life is like that. If you stop to ask for a reason, you spoil the fun, so you just shut your eyes and pull the stroke."

"So that's how we're going into the war, and kill one or two million of our boys—to win a game we don't really believe in!"

"No, Mother, it's different there. Some fellows won't play the game according to the rules, and we're going to put them out."

"Who made the rules, Henry?"

The great lawyer laughed. "You ought to come into my office, and learn to cross-examine witnesses. That would be a new stunt for a runaway grandmother—to become a lawyer at the age of—what would it be, about sixty-five!"

"But answer my question—who made the rules of the game?"

Henry laughed again. "England, I suppose; she has made the rules of all the games, hasn't she?"

III

Mrs. Josiah Quincy Thornwell sat at a long table, running lengthwise across the head of a room, and raised up a foot or so like a dais. The seat at the center was occupied by an elderly gentleman, with Cornelia at his right, and at his left a Chinese lady with slit eyes and coppery skin. The rest of the table was occupied by a dozen persons of prominence in Boston intellectual life. The great room was filled with tables, running at right angles to the head-table, and occupied by four or five hundred members of the Twentieth Century Club.

Luncheon was in progress, with colored waitresses hurrying here and there, amid a rattle of knives and forks and a subdued murmur of conversation. But every now and then each of the four or five hundred pairs of eyes would steal a glance at the head-table, and particularly at Cornelia. As a matter of mathematics, it is obvious that this meant a number of eyes upon her all the time, and she was aware of it, and her answers to the president's remarks were absent-minded, and her efforts to consume a proper quantity of lamb chop, peas and potatoes were intermittent.

It is a bad thing to eat solid food when you are excited, but Cornelia had not yet learned that lesson so important to orators. As "first lady" of the Commonwealth she had now and then been compelled to say a few words of thanks to the lady chairmen of visiting delegations; but this was the first time she had been a "headliner," her début as pacifist and rebel. The story of her adventure had of course been whispered all over by this time; and not ten generations' training in austerity and reticence could keep the four or five hundred pairs of eyes from manifesting interest. There was not a vacant seat at any table; after the dessert and coffee had been served, and the tables piled back out of the way in a corner, there were not folding chairs enough for the throng, and all the doorways were packed with standers.

The lady with the slit eyes and the coppery skin was a native graduate of a Chinese mission school supported by Boston money. She was introduced, and told them about life in this school—employing a pure and perfect Bostonese, with the broadest possible "a" and no "r" at all; she even referred to "that cradle of liberty, Funnel Hall"—just as if her name were Cabot or Lowell, instead of being Wang-Sin-She! American school-histories tell about a place called "Fanueil Hall," and you know how it looks, but unless you visit "old Boston," you don't know how it sounds.

Every Saturday through the fall and winter the Twentieth Century Club held these luncheons, and you would hear the head of a Negro school in Mississippi or maybe in Liberia; a woman who had been studying the opium trade in the Orient, or white slavery in the Argentine; a physician who had been curing the Eskimos of trachoma, or a strike-leader who had been jailed in Colorado. It did not matter where you came from or what you had, so long as it had to do with making the world better. This was the only organization of elderly liberals in the whole world; they were always ready to join something new, and if you were persuasive enough they would write you checks. Nowhere else in the world were appearances more deceptive; nowhere did fine feathers so fail to make fine birds. The old lady in front of you, dressed in rusty black silk and carrying an umbrella frayed at the edges, might be the owner of a mountain of copper in the Northern Peninsula of Michigan, or of six city blocks of tenements in East Boston.

Cornelia saw many persons whom she knew, and others whose faces were familiar—perhaps because they were types. The very same kind of old ladies made up the "Sewing Circle"; but there they had made long yellow flannel petticoats for the poor, while here they remade the world. Old ladies with little round faces, like Cornelia herself; old ladies with long faces; dimply faces, wrinkly faces with mouths drawn down at the corners; little bustling ladies, large ample ladies, timid shy ladies, grim determined ladies—row after row of them, with eyes fixed upon the copper-colored speaker. It would not have been polite for Cornelia to look at any one of them too long, so her eyes moved from one face to the next. She saw hair drawn up in tight little topknots, hair pitifully thin, with pink scalps showing through; hair in curls, hair in waves, hair neatly plastered down at the sides. An old lady with a benevolent boy's face, and one with bulgy rosy cheeks; one with deeply graven mouth and double lines at the side, one with wide outstanding ears, one with round white forehead, one shiny in new silk and ropes of pearls, one tinkling with chains and medallions.

And scattered in between, old gentlemen! Bald ones whose scalps were pink, and bald ones whose scalps were white; some with thin white hair, some with bushy gray hair; some with neatly trimmed military mustaches, with droopy mustaches, with grandfatherly beards, with chin-whiskers, round like a quarter-moon, relics of old New England. Old gentlemen with saggy cheeks, or portly, like bishops, or military and erect; rosy clubmen; earnest, ascetic preachers with clerical collars; one with a red nose; one very fashionable, with glasses hanging from a black silk cord; one famous scholar with no hair on top of his head, but covering his collar in back. These, no more than the ladies, could be judged by appearances; the poorest-looking might be the richest, the mildest-looking might hold the most revolutionary opinions. One thing alone was certain— you could never voice an idea too strange, a course of action too dangerous, for some of these elderly idealists to applaud! There would even be one or two ready to follow you, to act upon their convictions, even to the death. It was "old Boston"!

IV

Cornelia made her little speech; very gently and quietly, even humbly. She found many who were with her; and many, of course, furiously opposed to her—though etiquette forbade them to show it except by looking stern and grim. Next morning the newspapers reported the event, briefly but with dignity; yes, even the most rabidly patriotic were respectful—it was the right she had acquired on the day she became a Thornwell. Nothing she could do, short of murder, would forfeit that immunity. If she became a maniac, and had to be shut up in an asylum, the papers would decorously cease to mention her; but no opinion held or expressed would ever cause them to insult a sacred Brahmin.

And curiously enough, the rest of the clan were proud of that fact; in a perverse kind of way they gloried in the eccentric old lady who had told the world to go to the devil. Much as they hated her ideas, they would have been ready to stamp their heels hard on any miserable shrimp of a journalist who dared to deal impolitely with her. The fact that no such shrimp appeared, helped to reconcile them to what had happened; they realized, as families frequently do, that the reality was not so bad as the anticipation. So, after a week or two, Betty was permitted to take her grandmother to a symphony concert.

But Cornelia did not succeed in preventing the war. The great machine rolled on, flattening out all opposition. The Irish of Boston might parade and spit, they might hold meetings that turned into riots, they might make the city a scandal throughout the nation—but the great machine would flatten them out in the end, their mayor, their police force, and their cardinal. It would do the same with socialists and anarchists, pacifists, sentimentalists, all other varieties of cranks. Clear the way for Juggernaut!

And meantime Rupert Alvin, Henry Cabot Winters and their "crowd" were busy taking possession of the electrical manufacturing plant of Haupt. All this "crowd" were active Republicans, and this was a Democratic administration; its promise to be non-partisan and patriotic was a kind of chaff that would not catch old birds like Rupert and Henry. They got hold of a prominent Democratic statesman, close to the administration, and took him in with them, on the basis of a ten per cent "cut"; and he had a nephew whom he installed in the office of the "Alien Property Custodian," who had charge of robbing the enemies of America at home.

So Rupert and Henry got possession of the great property for one-twentieth of its market value, and turned out the German-American executives, and put in some younger sons of the "blue-bloods," and were ready to manufacture war supplies and sell them to the government at the highest possible prices. And the government was ready to buy with patriotic fervor. If the business men of the country made big profits, they could pay high wages, and enlarge the plants, and increase the product, and there would be prosperity for every one except the Kaiser.

Billions of money and millions of men—such was the slogan. Congress passed a conscription act, ordering all men between the ages of twenty-one and thirty to register for the draft: soon after which there was a ring at Cornelia's doorbell, and when she answered, she saw her friend, the maker of pistacchio bombs. She had sent him her address, but not telling him of her change of name. Sooner or later he would find out who she was, but meantime she would put both names on the door of her apartment, and let her Italian friends go on using the name they had learned.

So there stood Bartolomeo Vanzetti, hesitating a little, not sure if she would want to see him, since she had given up being a working-woman. "I come for say good by, Nonna."

"Where are you going?"

He came in. "Anybody here for hear me?" Then he told her, "I go Mexico for keep out from war. I go wit' Nick—you know, young feller you see in dramma one time, Nick Sacc'. Is good feller, we go Mexico togedder for not get draft. Never will fight for capitalista, Nonna."

"Of course not, Bart."

"You no t'ink I am coward for run away, Nonna! You see me and Nick, we fight when time come, but is not yet. You see worker get in war, he get his eye open, he learn what is capitalismo. You see great t'ing come when dissa war is done, Nonna. Come greata change, come rivoluzione. I know, you cannot believe, joosta wait, you see what I tell. Come bad time, come unemploy-èd, come big strike, lika war. Maybe it come great richa countree, like Britain, maybe it come poor countree like Russia—go what you say—cannot pay debt—bancarotta—"

"Bankrupt."

"Maybe come Russia, you see tsar get kill-èd, grand duke run away. Maybe come Italy, plenty chance for Italian anarchista make fight. I go Mexico, wait soocha time."

"How will you get along, Bart?"

"I get along, all time. Got two good arm, good back, worka picka shov', make living. Some odder Italian come, we not get lonely. I write letter some time, maybe get book, learn write Eengleesh, get educate, shoore! I never forget you, Nonna, besta friend, good lady, help workingman—onderstand heem. It is best t'ing of all, Nonna, it is better for onderstand as if you give million dollar. It is t'ing what come from heart. I want you know"—and here the maker of pistacchio bombs laid his hand gently on her shoulder—"I want you know, Nonna, I have for you the sentiment. I not know to say Eengleesh—is Italian word, sentimento—mean kinda feeling."

"I understand, Bart." There were tears in Cornelia's eyes. "I

shall think of you often. You have taught me more than you
realize—perhaps more than I realize myself."

A curious circumstance, that neither Vanzetti nor Sacco
needed to run away to Mexico. As Italian subjects, they were
not liable to the draft. But they believed they were—and so
did Cornelia. They became draft-dodgers in thought, which to
New England, home of Transcendentalism, was exactly the same
thing as draft-dodgers in reality.

They went; and a few days later Cornelia picked up her
morning paper, and there on the front page was a startling
story: a revolution in Russia, the tsar a prisoner, and a democratic, popular party in control! An amazing, an incredible
event; making it possible once more to have hopes, to believe
that changes were possible, that evil systems, entrenched for
generations, might at last be broken down. Also, it raised
Bartolomeo Vanzetti from the status of a dreamer to that of a
prophet. Cornelia had listened to his phrases, and smiled gently
at his peasant simplicity of mind; but here suddenly his ideas
became reality, made known upon the front pages of every
newspaper in the world!

V

The pacifists had failed to keep America out of the war, but
there was still the question of peace terms, upon which depended
the duration of the fighting. So the agitation in Boston went on
—until July, when the marines at the navy yard took matters
out of the hands of the Irish mayor. There was a parade organized by the socialists, in support of their program of no
conquests and no indemnities; the police had given the necessary
permit, but all the same, the marines raided the parade and
broke it up, tearing the banners away from the marchers. They
finished by raiding the socialist headquarters, and dumping its
contents into the street. Cornelia was in this parade, and once
more encountered violence; but now she was panoplied in her
dignity as a "blue-blood," and did not have to run.

Also—most dreadful circumstance—Elizabeth Thornwell
Alvin, daughter of the president of the Pilgrim National Bank,
was in that riot! She did not get into the papers, and it was
a couple of days before some thoughtful friend brought the

news to her father. There were more scenes, and Betty, in spite of all tears and protestations, was again forbidden to visit her runaway grandparent. A program was proposed to keep her in remote country places during the summer; but she vowed that she would not go to that foolish Camp Putnam. "You might as well give up, Mother; there's no chance in this world of my marrying one of those dull young men!"

"Betty, don't be vulgar!"

"I am being honest, Mother. You know what Camp Putnam is for. But you'll have to realize once for all—my opinions make it impossible for me to be a social success—there, or anywhere else."

"What is it you want to do, child?"

"I want to go stay with Grannie—all the time."

"But you wanted to go to college!"

"I've changed my mind. I realize that you don't learn anything at college."

"Betty! What a silly thing to say!"

"Well, you don't learn the things I want to learn. I got more from being in that one parade than I did in a whole year at Miss Wilson's."

"So you want to study to be a leader of street-mobs!"

"Grannie is trying to find out the causes of modern war, and found a society to teach them. It's too late this time, she says, but next time perhaps we can avoid being caught. And Mother, you must know that is important—just as much so as the feminine endings in Shakespeare's plays, and whatever else you learn in college. And it's the right kind of thing for Boston people to do. When you've succeeded, then people recognize it, and build a monument to you."

"Oh! So you're going to have a monument in Boston!"

"Not for myself—but for Grannie, yes indeed! Look at that Shaw Memorial, Mother—people come from all over the United States to see it. Those Negro troops are dead and turned to bronze, so they are safe and respectable; but when they were live Negro troops, and Colonel Shaw marched them down Beacon Street, the members of the Somerset Club pulled down the shades. That was how the Union Club came to be founded— some of the people on Beacon Hill were loyal to the Union cause, and Grandfather Thornwell was one of them. That is history, Mother; but I didn't learn it at Miss Wilson's, and I wouldn't learn it at Radcliffe. The Union Club is top-hole now, and it pulls down the shades on us. But we shall have a 'Peace Club,' or something like that, and fifty years from now we'll be the highest high-hat in town, and there'll be an oil painting of Grannie in the lobby, and the family will be proud as Punch!"

Thus Betty, citing precedents, according to precedent. It all seemed so reasonable to her—and to her mother raving nonsense. Was it not obvious that Colonel Shaw had upheld the hands of Abraham Lincoln—the president, even though nothing but a vulgar rail-splitter! Now here was Woodrow Wilson —a gentleman and a scholar, even though he did come from the wrong university—here he was fighting for civilization, and Cornelia and Betty were trying to stab him in the back.

"Yes, Mother"—for Betty had not yet learned Cornelia's technique of self-suppression. "It all depends on what history decides about this war. Did we have to get in? Or could we have brought the nations to better terms if we had stayed out?"

So they wrangled, until the tempers of both were frayed, and Deborah exclaimed, "Your Father has lost all patience with you! You run a grave risk that he will cut you off!"

"But, Mother, do you seriously think I should spend my life sitting round waiting for you and father to die?"

"Oh, what things you do say!"

"But that's what you said! I'm not to do any thinking of my own until you are dead and I've got the money. But what good would it be to me then? I wouldn't know any better to do with it than to make yellow flannel petticoats for the poor—so ugly that the poor can't be persuaded to wear them!"

That was a dreadful utterance—a jeer at the most sacred institution of feminine Boston, the "Sewing Circle": a group of ladies of the highest social rank, who met for luncheon at one another's homes, and afterwards sewed for the poor and gossiped for the rich. A fresh layer was recruited every year out of the débutante set, and they constituted the basis of selection for all other social activities; if you didn't get into the Sewing Circle, you never got into anything. And it was really true that up to quite recently they had made yellow flannel petticoats for the poor, and had stopped because it was no longer possible to find any one to wear their product. Mrs. Rupert Alvin was indignant at the presumption and ingratitude of the inhabitants of East Boston and South Boston slums, and had favored going on making the petticoats according to tradition, and sending them to Europe, where the lower classes knew their place in life.

VI

Betty went to Plymouth, to spend a couple of weeks with her friend Lucile Walker. She wrote, begging Grannie to come, and Mrs. Walker added a formal invitation. But Cornelia did not want to visit rich people; to her Plymouth meant Italians and the simple life. She wrote to the Brinis, and found they had no boarder, so she went down for a few days. A strange sensation, reëntering that so different world! She would keep it as a place of refuge, a stimulus to the imagination, a cure for the mental diseases of affluence. Here people said what they meant, and it was possible to understand what they were doing. When Vincenzo Brini got up at dawn and shoveled and raked and grubbed in the dirt, he did not have to tell you, like Henry Cabot Winters, that life was a game, and you must play it without thinking; no, Vincenzo would say, "Moocha gooda vegetable!"—and escort you from row to row of his treasures, and tell you the Italian names, and remember the English names —after you had reminded him! Alfonsina wanted a wash-tub, for perfectly sound economic reasons. Beltrando wanted a violin, and some one to teach him to play it, and was going to earn the money by picking berries.

The boys were playing baseball on top of Castle Hill, and the birds sang, and the sun sparkled on the bay, and the pleasure-boats made diverging tracks on the water. There were flowers in the woods again—but alas, no Vanzetti to explain them and explore nature's mysteries. Incessantly they talked about him, the things he had said and the things he had liked. He had gone away without saying good-by to Trando and Fay, afraid lest their children's prattle might reveal his secret. Their mother had explained matters later—but it was hard for them to be reconciled to his lack of trust.

Alfonsina had got a letter. Both Sacco and Vanzetti were in Mexico, and the latter had found work as a baker. The Mexicans came to America for jobs, and the Italians took what they left behind. Then came a letter for Cornelia, and the family sat round the table and read and discussed it. "I have obtained book for English education. I shall be greatly cultured. Each word as I investigate in dictionary I secure in mind." They could picture him, sitting in a laborer's hut, patiently looking up long words by the light of a candle, and putting them together. not always in the right order.

"It is primitive country, much hospitality of people, much to approve, but not developed industrial. The great America has depraved us, we feel in nature's wildness lonely. I will be glad for receiving English books for education reading, it is great limitation to obtain Italian reading. Nick and me endeavor for improvement our companions of exile. It is necessary for information of world developments. You have seen Russian rivoluzion, but is necessary for explanazion that such is lacking in true rivoluzionairy significance. It is of bourgeois nature, for making country like capitalistic America. It is not of workers or peasants, but Kerensky is tool of business men, and you will see that the desires of Russia for acquirement of Constantinople will not be abandoned, and the participating of Russia in the war will have this significance. I will not proceed in this discussing because is possible for letter to be censured, but will say that all nation in most cruel conflict have imperialist ambition which will not abandon for beautiful sentiments. I have long walk for obtaining stamp for letter so will conclusion with expressing of sincere esteem, your Bartolomeo Vanzetti."

VII

Cornelia went to call on the Jerry Walkers—she could not fail to do so, being no longer in hiding. They lived in a big remodeled house on a hilltop looking over the bay, and you would have thought them very fashionable, if you had not known the dreadful fact that Mrs. Walker was the daughter of a Pittsburgh steel manufacturer. Startling to realize how one could have all this comfort, and even elegance, and yet be totally non-existent from the social point of view. Mrs. Walker was a fair, buxom lady, her manner to Cornelia a curious mixture of deference due to a "blue-blood," modified by the need of not seeming too eager for social promotion. A strange world, in which a motor-ride of six minutes brought you from Suosso's Lane, where things were simple and natural, to this hilltop mansion from which simplicity and naturalness had been banished as by an enchanter's spell.

But, a spell for ladies only! Jerry Walker, who had begun life as an errand-boy, liked to talk with Cornelia about those days; and how the Governor had helped him to a start. He liked to talk about his enormous business, which he was organizing upon a new system. Not content with owning all the felt-plants of New England, he had got a chain of establishments to manufacture the things that were made of felt— shoes, hats, hospital supplies; he had a jobbing business to distribute them, and was not going to stop until he had retail stores, and even the sheep to make the wool. He was eager about all this—a bouncing little man with bristly yellow hair, standing up like a bull-dog's. He was extremely self-confident, a great business organizer, who knew it, and frequently said it, adding prophecies. A highly dangerous state of mind in New England, where all is secrecy, and instinctive repugnance toward anyone who talks. Cornelia remembered that last discussion she had heard between her husband and Rupert Alvin, when Jerry Walker and his felt-plants had been the subject. It was easy to understand why Rupert was so antagonistic to this talkative outsider, and resented his control of a great New England industry, accusing him of all crimes in the business list.

Just now Jerry Walker needed to expand his business for war purposes, and needed to buy stocks of raw material for government contracts. He ought to buy quickly, because the price of wool was leaping day by day; but he could not get the banking credit. Everybody else was getting it, all along the line, but from him the bankers demanded practically the taking over of his business.

It was the working out of a situation which Cornelia understood clearly; but she did not have the right to talk about it, not even to Betty. The latter had learned of Mr. Walker's troubles from Lucile, and was embarrassed, because among those who held the whip-hand were her own father and her uncle, John Quincy Thornwell, president of the Fifth National Bank. "Grannie, I don't know much about banking, and I don't suppose you do, but I can't help thinking it seems to go by favor. Mr. Walker never wore the hat-band of a Harvard club, and his wife isn't in the Sewing Circle! Do you suppose that is why they say such bad things about him?"

Cornelia answered, "I once heard Great-uncle Abner say that banking is the private preserve of the blue-bloods, a feeding-crib for the sons and nephews and cousins."

"But, Grannie, that isn't fair! There's Father and Uncle John, who can get all the money they need from their own banks—"

"No, dear, they can't do that—it would be against the law."

"It wouldn't be against the law for them to lend to each other, would it? Or to Uncle James, or other members of the family? Certainly you never hear of the Thornwell mills having to scuffle for credit. And Mr. Walker is a capable man, who has built up his business by hard work and not by family favors. I would talk to Father about it, if I thought it would help."

"No, dear, you'd better not meddle. Your parents would say the Walkers were trying to use you."

"I suppose that's why they hate to have me come here. I must only know the people who come to our dinner-table."

Cornelia laughed. "Dear child, it is embarrassing to know those who are coming to your dinner-table on a platter!"

VIII

The fall of 1917. All about Cornelia a gigantic stir of war preparation, but very little intellectual preparation to match it. She did not have to go far in her studies to learn that the various peoples of Europe had been fighting among themselves for centuries, and in this fighting had frequently shifted partners. Whatever enemy they had at the time, they hated that enemy just as heartily, and accused him of atrocities, and did not hesitate to have priests and bishops invoke the aid of God to overcome him. Always the real cause of the war was a desire to take land from the other nation; plus the fear that the other nation would reverse the procedure—as indeed it would.

Could the same situation exist in this greatest and most cruel of all conflicts? To have that question answered, Cornelia had to get in the Negro maid, and invite Quincy Thornwell to dinner. Do not confuse Quincy with his older brother, John Quincy, for these two sons of Great-uncle Abner were very different beings. John, the banker, had the reputation of being the closest-mouthed person in Boston, which was like being the tallest mountain in the Himalayas. But Quincy lived by gossip, quite literally; for twenty years he had listened to the talk of his family and friends, and turned their advance knowledge into a comfortable fortune on the stock-market. His wizened features were set in mockery, and if you were in the family he would tell you most outrageous and delightful anecdotes.

Quincy went everywhere, and met everybody. He could tell you what the British ambassador had said to Major Higginson last week. The evening before last he had dined at Fenway Court, the palace of the eccentric but brilliant Mrs. "Jack" Gardner, and had there met Sir Leslie Buttock, the latest of the procession of British propagandists who were coming to fascinate and thrill the American plutocracy. Sir Leslie was making the transcontinental tour, and after he had praised the champagne of a Minneapolis banker, or the cigars of a Seattle ship-builder, each of these provincials was an insider and social equal for the rest of his life, and the price was five—ten—twenty billions—no one knew just how much—to be used in doubling the area of the British empire.

A generation or more ago "Mrs. Jack" had set out to cut a swath through Boston society with the millions of a big department store. A vivid little creature, with the continental standard of manners and morals, she had horrified the Back Bay beyond utterance; when she lost her temper, she would break into cursing like any British aristocrat. But she went abroad and hobnobbed with royalty, and was cabled back home; she bought famous paintings, and built herself a palace in what was then the suburbs of the Fenway, and thumbed her nose at the prudes. Now she was an old lady, with decades of notoriety behind her, the acknowledged leader of the smart set.

A British diplomat once gave the official definition of a lie— a falsehood told to a person who has a right to the truth. All diplomats and propagandists who came to Boston did "Mrs. Jack" the honor of admitting her into the inner circle. At her dinner-parties you took off your propaganda-coat, so to speak, and lounged in your military shirt-sleeves. So Quincy Thornwell could tell his aunt exactly why the war was lasting so long. The price of Italy's repudiating her alliance with Austria and Germany had been the Trentino and Trieste, which meant the mastery of the Adriatic. Japan's price was Shantung from China. Russia was to have Constantinople. France was to have Alsace-Lorraine, and if possible the Rhine. Britain was to have all the German colonies, an empire in themselves. When you talked to Quincy about any of these powers giving up their spoils because of the beautiful speeches of Woodrow Wilson, he showed his good manners by pretending it was your idea of being humorous.

And yet there were a hundred million or so of good Americans who really believed that their President was somehow going to achieve that miracle! Deborah, for example, and her serious elder daughter, Priscilla, who was going in for Red Cross work of the higher, administrative kind. When you talked to them about peace terms, you discovered that they were trusting the country entirely to a man who was a Democrat, and came from the wrong university! If you mentioned the secret treaties, they would say that these matters were too delicate for public discussion; the President of course had sources of information that were not open to us—

"But why not?" cried Cornelia, and could get no convincing answer. Either the allies were going to give up their predatory aims or they were not. If they were, why not publish the fact? Such declaration would save millions of lives and billions of treasure—for manifestly, one reason for enemy resistance was fear of the consequences of defeat. But if you tried to point this out, you were called pro-German, and people turned their backs on you. They had adopted a slogan, "Win the war!"—which meant that they found it easier to fight than to think. And Cornelia, who had gone out into public life, now had the duty of laboring with them, and suffering because of their blindness. No more could she be content with the troubles of three daughters—their diseases in childhood, their moral training, their love-affairs and marriages, their fourteen pregnancies and eleven children. Now she had a million sons in France, and must agonize with them all—even when they were wayward sons and spurned their foster-mother's care!

IX

Betty was going to Radcliffe. It was a compromise that had worked itself out with her parents; provided she would put herself under respectable instructors, and read the sound and wholesome books they would indicate to her, she might go and live in the apartment with her grandmother, and meet anarchists and socialists and atheists and pacifists and German agents in her off hours. It had been a losing fight for Deborah and Rupert, because they had other things they must think about, while Betty had nothing but the determination to get with Grannie. After all, what could be more respectable than a grandmother? What more laudable desire for a young girl than to comfort an elderly widow, alone and poverty-stricken? It was really a scandal to balk such an impulse; it was advertising to the world that Cornelia was a shady character!

So Betty installed a few of her books and her clothes in the little room, and the pair of them were as happy as honeymooners —they gave each other a hug every time they met. The Negro maid came every day—because the Alvins insisted on Betty's paying half the household expenses. Betty's runabout was in a garage nearby, and any time it was raining or snowing, a man from the garage would bring it over, and Betty would drive Grannie to anarchist or socialist or atheist or pacifist or pro-German meetings. Or they would sit at home in the evenings and study subversive books with red bindings, of which there were now a hundred or so on Grannie's shelves—Mr. Longfellow and Mr. Emerson and Dr. Holmes having been relegated to a box under the bed. Betty would give her college studies "a lick and a promise," and then take up Bertrand Russell on world imperialism. Most convenient to have a respectable aristocrat, brother of an earl, to quote against Sir Leslie Buttock and Sir Syphon Scotch!

It was well that this idyllic menage had got definitely under way before the second, or Bolshevik, revolution in Russia. Possession is nine points out of ten in family affairs, as in revolutions, and it was no more possible to get Betty out of Grannie's apartment on the north side of Beacon Hill than it was to get Lenin and Trotsky out of the Kremlin. But what agony of soul for the Alvin family, and for the Winters and the Scatterbridges, and the whole Thornwell clan! The face of the war changed in ten hideous days! The eastern front gone all to pieces, and a million or two of Germans set free to overwhelm the western front! Russia out of the war, and no one but America to take her place! And red revolution on the rampage over a sixth of the surface of the globe! Insolent, low-down workingmen daring to take possession of a great government, and calling on their fellows in other lands to follow suit!

Every property interest throughout the civilized world rallied against that peril, and the greatest machine of propaganda in history went into action. To meet the immediate emergency, Lenin and Trotsky must be German agents; so a mass of documents were forged, endorsed by the state department, and spread upon the front pages of the newspapers. Then came the atrocities—for which little Belgium had been a dress rehearsal. Bureaus for the construction of horrors were set up in every border city from Helsingfors to Vladivostok, and the cruelty and bloodshed inevitable to a great revolution were magnified a thousand fold. It was St. Bartholomew's Eve in Russia every time an American newspaper went to press. The Soviet government collapsed once a week, and Lenin jailed Trotsky, or was murdered by Trotsky, in alternating afternoon editions. The "free love" element became the basis of the most obscene hoax of the ages, and fifty million women were "nationalized" in one colossal orgy. Every decent woman in America believed it—and so it was possible for President Wilson to begin his private war upon the Russian people, in defiance of the Constitution which he had spent his life in expounding.

From that time on the advocacy of reasonable peace-terms ceased to be a society function, a diversion of after-luncheon orators, and became a criminal conspiracy, conducted by little groups in upstairs rooms with the shades drawn and admission by pass-word. It became, in short, "Bolshevik plotting." Did not the Bolsheviks prove it by proceeding themselves to make peace with Germany, an act of treason to democracy and liberty? Did they not make matters worse by ransacking the archives of the tsar, and publishing the secret treaties whereby the allies had agreed to divide large sections of the earth, without any democracy or liberty for the inhabitants thereof? There is a story of a Kentucky colonel who was asked why he had knocked a certain man down. "Did he call you a liar?" "Worse than that, he proved it."

With one exception the American newspapers ignored these treaties, and to Cornelia and the pacifists that seemed treason to the national welfare. But what could the pacifists do? For any group to circulate them meant to have offices raided and property destroyed; for individuals to agitate them meant to be mobbed, to be jailed and held "incommunicado," tarred and feathered, beaten with blacksnake whips, in a few cases strung up to telegraph-poles.

Nor was it protection that you lived within sight of Bunker Hill monument and "Funnel" Hall. The grandsons of that "broadcloth mob" that had dragged William Lloyd Garrison through the streets with a rope about his waist were now out to preserve their French and British bonds. Nor was it any longer of avail that your city had an Irish-Catholic vote; the Catholic church was one of the property interests which had rallied against "Bolshevism." City policemen, federal secret agents, and an army of spies and informers in the pay of wealthy patriots, would break into offices and homes at any hour of the day or night, and spirit people away and hold them for as long as they saw fit; in short they would commit all the crimes they were trying to prevent, and destroy beyond repair the Constitution they professed to worship.

x

Into this valley of midnight shadow walked Cornelia Thornwell and her grand-daughter, clasping each other's trembling hands. They were in no personal danger, as it turned out; the patrioteers would seldom trouble rich people, especially those who had "family" behind them. Seen from the outside this "white terror" appeared a mad frenzy, and it was hard at first to understand that there were cunning brains guiding it, that mob-outbreaks were planned by shrewd gentlemen in swivel-chairs. These gentlemen would be glad to scare the widow of Governor Thornwell and make her shut up; but failing in that they would not advertise her treason by arresting her. The reason was that the decision rested with Henry Cabot Winters and Rupert Alvin, who were contributing large sums to the defense societies, and sat in at the councils where lists were gone over and policies determined.

No, what would happen to Cornelia was that her janitress would be instructed to preserve the contents of her trash-basket every night; and one of her old-time friends of the Sewing Circle would turn up and announce herself as a convert to pacifism, and join all the societies to which Cornelia belonged, and go to meetings with her, and get on the executive committees, and turn in a detailed report of everything that went on there, with lists of the members and subscribers, and manuscript copies of what was being considered for publication. Included in this mass of information appeared the fact that Mrs. Josiah Quincy Thornwell was in touch with Italian anarchists of Plymouth, and exchanged letters with one of the group, a draft-dodger—though so far there was no evidence that she had helped him to get away. He wrote to her under the code name of "Nonna," and a letter she had received from him, entered in the secret service files under the index number of 1842T36, read as follows:

"Dear Nonna:

"It will be great rivilation for you to see the coming of my prophecy, the real rivoluzion prevail in Russia. This is greatest event of history and is to be recognize for beginning of epoch. It is first opportunity for liberty for worker and peasant of world. It is hope which can be very brief to endure, and will depend entirely what shall happen in other country. If will come rivoluzion in Germany, Austria, Italia, France, England, then will be possible for building worker society without exploitation; but if is impossible for achievement rivoluzion in other country, is little hope for freedom for Russia, and you will see ending of worker's control. When Russia must defend self in war, it will be militarismo, and is impossible for liberty with militarismo. It will then become Russia government of force like all other gouverment, and rivoluzion will be perished. Whatever you can do for rivoluzion of American worker, that is only way for assistance of proletarian power in Russia. In Mexico is not much activity, for lack of language speaking, so Nick and me will make secret return for propaganda. With sincere esteem and fraternal greetings, Your friend, Bartolomeo Vanzetti."

XI

It was in the spring of 1918, with the last German drive in France under way, that this stolen letter was placed in the hands of Rupert Alvin. It caused great mental disturbance in a loyal citizen, and he came to the apartment and, standing in the middle of the floor, announced that Cornelia stood in great danger of a term in state's prison for persistent and contumacious disloyalty; also that Betty would bundle up her things and accompany her father to his car immediately. Whereupon occurred one of those scenes which are so essentially un-Boston that all Bostonians deny they ever happen. Perhaps they would not have happened, had not old Josiah married a bog-trotter's grand-daughter, and thus introduced an element of hysterics into the family.

Betty declared that she would not, could not desert her Grannie. The more sternly she was commanded to obey her father, the louder she wept and the tighter she clung; even when Grannie herself advised her gently to go, she relaxed her grip no particle, but sobbed, how could they demand such a thing of her? The greater the peril in which Grannie stood, the less possibility that she, Betty, would desert her! So it appeared that Rupert had overspoken himself, and he hemmed and hawed and admitted that the danger of arrest and imprisonment was not immediate, his influence had been able to avert the calamity; whereupon Betty said that if that was the case, what was the reason for her going? And what can a man do in the face of logic like that?

What Rupert did was worthy of his Puritan ancestors, and proved that the old stock was still sound. He adjudged his daughter guilty of domestic sedition, and pulled out his watch and gave her three minutes in which to capitulate; at the end of that time he would go home and write a will in which she would have no share, and would be forever forbidden entrance to his home. For three minutes he held the watch, and Betty clung to her grandmother with such frenzy that not a finger could be pulled loose. Rupert snapped to the watch—it was the old-fashioned kind with a gold case and a lid on a hinge—and stalked out of the room without a word. And Betty wept for an hour or two, fully convinced that her father meant every one of those cruel words, and that she was forever an outcast.

Until the doorbell rang again, and there came Deborah, and behind her, silent and somewhat sheepish, the ponderous and impressive president of the Pilgrim National Bank. From which it appeared that the old stock was degenerating in spots! Rupert could rule a board of directors with an iron rod, but he could not rule the tongue or spirit of his wife. She declared that he would not do the cruel thing he had threatened; his sense of patriotic loyalty had caused him to forget the love they all bore for one another. What Deborah would do was to throw herself upon the mercy of her mother and her child, and implore them to spare the family the horror of having either go to jail. So, of course, there was more weeping—still that Irish blood. Betty cried, what was the use of trying to talk about it, when they didn't know what they were supposed to have done? How could they promise not to do it, until they knew what? So Rupert had to give hints which nearly betrayed the secret; he told them they were known to be consorting with anarchists and draft-dodgers.

So it was a question of their giving up Vanzetti! But they did not agree with Vanzetti's ideas, and Vanzetti knew they did not, they had tried to argue with him, to persuade him to a more American point of view! Was that treason? Were they forbidden to try to reform the anarchists, or even to know what anarchists thought? If so, who was to answer their arguments? Rupert snapped out that the way to answer such dogs was to string them up to lamp-posts; and then, of course, the fat was in the fire. What was the use of a Constitution if it didn't work in war-time? What was the use of free speech if it applied only to the things you wanted said? If public questions were to be settled by stringing people up to lamp-posts, who was to be strung, and who was to string—how could you decide? Betty cried, and Cornelia cried, and Deborah cried. Ideas are extremely trying things, devastating in their effect upon the female nervous organism; there is something to be said for the point of view of the Clara Scatterbridges, who have nothing to do with ideas, but stay at home and have eight babies.

Betty and Cornelia laid down their joint program. They had never advocated violence and never would; but neither

would they support a war. They would advocate the ending of
this present war upon terms of justice to all parties, which included the rights of those peoples whose lands were going to
be handed over as spoils of battle. If it had become a crime in
America to advocate such ideas, then there would be an old
Thornwell lady and a young one in prison. Rupert and Deborah
took their departure, as solemn as if it were an execution
they had attended; and five minutes after they left, the doorbell rang again, and there stood a humble Italian laborer, wearing a worn suit of clothes two sizes too big for him, and droopy
walrus mustaches equally out of proportion. That very anarchist draft-dodger who had been the cause of the family scene!

XII

He stood embarrassed. "I not know if should come—"
"Of course you should come!" and they drew him in.
"Could make trooble for ladies."
"We are not afraid of trouble," said Cornelia; and Betty
chimed in, "You are a sight for sore eyes!"—that was the way
the new generation was learning to talk, in spite of Radcliffe.
Vanzetti's face lighted up—so glad he was to see them, so
pathetically eager for friendship. He was haggard from his
wanderings, more somber than ever with the pressure of the
war upon his spirit. His age at this time was thirty years, but
unconsciously Betty took him for old enough to be her father,
while Cornelia took him for her equal. At the same time he
was a little of the child to them—the way of every woman with
a poet and a dreamer, who cannot get himself adjusted to a
harsh world.
He had been a wanderer for a year, and had not liked it.
He was going to make propaganda, and take whatever came
to him; going back to Plymouth, to live near the Brinis—not
in his old room, because the children were growing up and
would need it. One could not be sure, but he thought he would
not be arrested; the government had plenty of soldiers, but
needed laborers for war construction.
They discussed the world situation. The propaganda for
intervention to put down the Russian revolution was on the
point of success. A shameful thing, said Cornelia. But to her

surprise she found that Bart had already given up interest in
Russia; the revolution there was lost, he said. "Is joost like
I write, Nonna—is militarismo, is one more go-vèrnment for
rule worker. Maybe you do not read what soviet have done
for anarchista in Russia? They stop propaganda, shoot heem,
put heem in jail—is joost like capitalista—is what you say
—tirannia—make worker obey, make work, make fight in
army—"

"But, Comrade Vanzetti, aren't the soviets to defend themselves?" It was Betty breaking in.

"Must defend, Comradda Betty, but defend like free men.
If man not want fight, nobody got right for make heem fight.
Nobody got right for make heem slave, for stop hees mind,
hees right for speak."

"Wouldn't it be hard to keep an army going on that basis?"

"If you got joostice, will find plenty men for fight, plenty
free men. You wait, Comradda Betty, you see Italy, you see
somet'ing happen! Is poor countree, Italy, if war stop, will
be much bad time, much trooble—will come rivoluzion, I t'ink
shoore. Italian is not so easy man for control, like Russian
peasant, he is man will fight for right, will be free man. You
see different kind revoluzion, different sistema for manage
countree. It is our job now, make money in America, make all
money we can, send home Italy for anarchista propaganda."

"I'm afraid you'll have trouble," said Cornelia. "They have
spies, they know what everybody is doing, and they get rougher
every day. I fear you'll be arrested."

"Is no matter, Nonna, no worry for me. Is business of
anarchista make propaganda, musta make, wherever go. You
get putted in army, all right, make propaganda wit' soldier.
You get putted in jail, make propaganda wit' jailer, wit' prisoner—is all same, is men, like me, like you. Sometime he come
out, is always some way for new idea spread—is no way for
stop, not jail, not bullet! In whole world is notting can stop—
is biggest, most strong dinnameet."

He sat in his chair, half out of it, with the eagerness of his
emotion. His face wore a strained look, and his eyes had that
light of stubborn fanaticism which Cornelia had come to know.
He turned to Betty, the younger one, guardian of the future.
"Wit' anarchista is lika dis, Comradda. He say: Capitalismo is

injoostice, I will not stand heem! Say, I will break heem, will fight heem, will never stop—never what you say, surrender. I will speak—will say strong word—shock person, make heem t'ink. Will speak all time, everywhere—make men hear—even when he not want hear!"

Suddenly Vanzetti stopped, a little embarrassed. Even an anarchist must be a gentleman! And perhaps so much vehemence was not in order in a lady's drawing-room. "It maybe seem like crazy talk?" he asked.

Cornelia said, "Wait." She went to the bookcase, to a shelf which contained a few old books, not yet stowed under the bed. She took one out. "I will read you something, Bart. We had a young New Englander, of old Puritan stock, who took up the notion that chattel slavery was wrong, and set out to preach it, and very nearly got lynched in Boston. His name was William Lloyd Garrison—learn it, Bart, a good name to quote in this part of the world. He started a paper called the 'Liberator'—that was in 1831, eighty-seven years ago. In the first issue he stated his program. Listen." And she read:

"I will be as harsh as truth, and as uncompromising as justice. On this subject I do not wish to think, or speak, or write with moderation. No! No! Tell a man whose house is on fire to give a moderate alarm; tell him to moderately rescue his wife from the hands of a ravisher; tell the mother to gradually extricate her babe from the fire into which it has fallen—but urge me not to use moderation in a cause like the present. I am in earnest—I will not equivocate—I will not excuse—I will not retreat a single inch—and I will be heard. The apathy of the people is enough to make every statue leap from its pedestal and hasten the resurrection of the dead."

Said Vanzetti: "What is name?" He said it over, so as to remember it—William Lloyd Garrisoon. "I never hear heem before, but I feel heem brudder; am joosta sooch man like heem!"

CHAPTER 6

WHITE TERROR

I

THE day of glory, sung in the "Marseillaise," had arrived; the American troops stopped the first German onslaught, and began their counter-advance which was to end the war. The whole country thrilled with it—all but a few perverse persons, so constructed that they could not think of glory, but only of boys crawling about in burning forests, dragging shattered limbs and protruded entrails. "Ah, but the broken bodies, that drip like honeycomb!"

Cornelia and her grand-daughter went to Plymouth to rest for a week, Betty staying with her friend, Lucile Walker, and Cornelia with the Brinis. The little room which had been Cornelia's for a year and a half now belonged to Fay, but she was glad to vacate it. Vanzetti had a room with a neighbor, but came in for his meals, and stayed to do his studying in the evening. He was digging more ditches, and reading diligently the few radical papers he could get. There had been a revolt in the Italian armies; it had been suppressed, but more was coming, and he watched for every scrap of news.

Also he told Cornelia of his experiences in Mexico: what a fine fellow that Nick Sacc' had proved to be, and how they had settled down with a colony of Italians, all draft-evaders, living upon a rough communistic system. Bart had helped to feed them, baking bread, and also he had fed them "anarchista propaganda"—bread for the spirit. There had been several in the group whom Cornelia knew: Boda, the little macaroni salesman who had driven them to see the drama; and Coacci and Orciani, two others whom she had met on that same occasion.

Nonna, like Christmas, came but once a year, so it was a holiday for everybody. Papa Brini showed his garden, and Cornelia recited the Italian names, and he tried to say the Eng-

156

lish names, and the children laughed at his blunders. They had their walk in the woods on Sunday, and gathered bunches of flowers, and Fay and Trando remembered things about nature which Bart had taught them, and were proud of it. Bart had resumed charge of the boy's development, and would give him advice and help. One day Trando had a cold, and Bart said the way to cure it was to sweat; so he got down on his knees, which made him about a match for a nine-and-a-half-year-old boy, and the two of them had a wrestling match, in which the big man was floored several times, and the small boy whooped with delight. Pretty soon he was perspiring profusely, and Bart put him to bed with no supper but a drink of hot lemonade. In the morning he would be all right, said the amateur doctor.

Trando wanted a violin, and had worked all last summer to earn the money; but then he had had to spend it, because the family went down with "flu." Cornelia wanted to give him a violin, but Bart said no, that would spoil it all; let the little fellow earn it, and then he would really value it; the achievement would give him courage, a sense of power. This was the time for berries, and there was nothing better for youngsters than to wander in the fields all day.

Trando's relations with the boys of the neighborhood made a problem. They would not play with him, because the priest had warned them to have nothing to do with a bad boy who did not go to church: there was a place in hell for such as he. The other boys called him "socialist," and when he went off and read a story-book, or played with his sister, they called him "sissy." It was hard to please them. Bart told him to make of his persecution a source of strength. Many a great man had done that, and those who had spurned him in boyhood would see him leap above their heads when they were grown.

Vanzetti told him what was true about religion. There was a great and good God, the God of nature, whose laws we must understand if we would be happy. This God loved all human beings alike, and it was not His will that some should be slaves to others. We might pray to Him for courage and strength; but we did not need any priest to intervene for us. The priest was nothing but a man like other men; he might be good, or he might be bad, like Father O'Brien—but in any case he represented a system which helped to keep the poor in subjection to the rich, and so was a trap for their minds.

Then Trando wanted to know about how we got born, and how we got married. It is the custom of Italian parents to say they buy the babies; but Bart explained those things seriously to Trando; and he talked to Cornelia about it, and asked her to talk to Fay, because children ought to know the truth, and parents had a foolish shyness about talking to their own little ones. All the questions of children ought to be answered; they should connect the idea of shame only with actions that were harmful to themselves or to others. A wise man speaking, always; a man gentle, full of spiritual insight—yet turning into a lion at a moment's notice when confronted with "injoostice." Some of the bigger boys found that out when they undertook to torment the "sissy."

II

Betty Alvin's relations with the Walker family were peculiar. They were all extremely patriotic, and shocked beyond utterance by the opinions and behavior of Betty and her grandmother. But they were fond of Betty, and if she had come to Plymouth and not stayed with them, it would have been emphasizing an estrangement. Of course Betty's mother put the worst construction on their invitation, saying that the Walkers would rather know a "red" blue-blood than none at all. But Betty would not believe that, and kept up the friendship with Lucile at Radcliffe and at home, carefully avoiding any utterance that would displease her hosts.

Mr. Walker appeared only once during the visit. He was in greater trouble than ever, and showed it in every line of his features—a really terrible example of what the fierce pace of business can do to its victims. Mrs. Walker was silent and preoccupied, and Lucile hesitated to say anything; but Betty got it out of her finally—Mr. Walker was convinced that there was a determination on the part of a Boston banking-group to put him out of business, and the man who was at the head of the campaign was Betty's uncle, Henry Cabot Winters. This information was coming to Mr. Walker from many different sources: in all the troubles of the felt industry, it was

Mr. Winters who stood behind the scenes and pulled the strings.

Just think of it, exclaimed Lucile—here were enterprises that had made a million and a quarter dollars in net profits last year, and were going even higher this year; yet the owner could not get half a million dollars' credit from any bank in Boston or New York! They all stood together; if the banks where you had your accounts, your banks of deposit, as they were called, refused to "check your paper," why, then no other bank would accept it. The felt-industry was peculiar, in that the sales were made early in the year, but payments were not made until the fall, which meant that the business was helpless without credit; the bankers knew that perfectly well, and Mr. Walker had always had the credit, year after year, as a matter of course. This year he had to have more, because of his war contracts, and the increased production; the wicked thing the bankers had done was to make promises, and lure him along from month to month, giving him no hint there was anything wrong until the last moment, when one or two hundred thousand dollars' worth of notes came due, and suddenly he was told that he must "take them up." There must be some reason for such things, said Lucile; and Mr. Walker was convinced that it was Henry Cabot Winters plotting to ruin him.

The bankers had put accountants on Mr. Walker's books, and insisted that he would need three million dollars to carry him until the fall. They were going to make him pay twenty-seven per cent for the use of that money. He didn't mind that so much—his profits could stand it; but he didn't believe he was really going to get the three million. When the time came, there would be more excuses and delays, and he would be compelled to turn the stock of his companies over to the bankers. He had twenty big plants of one sort or another, all working day and night, employing more than eight thousand men; he was doing what was supposed to be patriotic war-work—but the government wouldn't help him with a dollar, and wouldn't protect him against these banking conspiracies.

Betty took that story to Cornelia. "Can it possibly be true, Grannie? Can Uncle Henry be doing such a thing?"

"I'm sorry to say, dear, he has that reputation."

"But Grannie, he doesn't seem that kind of man!"

"Men have different standards for their friends, and for outsiders. Uncle Henry has grown rich, and he has never produced anything that I know of."

"But Grannie, that would be a wicked thing to do to Mr. Walker!"

"It's the way of the business world. I watched it, and held my peace—for forty years. I used to hear things that Henry and James and your father would talk over with your grandfather. Josiah did it to others—and then at last somebody did it to him. He trusted the big bankers in New York—the Morgan crowd, because they had such a respectable name. He put everything he had into the securities of the New Haven Railroad, and those New York bankers simply gutted it, they stole every dollar, and the stock fell from two hundred and forty-six to sixteen, if I remember. I've heard your grandfather say, he had enough New Haven paper to fill up the music-room, but it wasn't enough to pay his debts."

"Is that why Uncle James has the mills and 'Hillview'?"

"That's the reason. There were tens of thousands of people left in worse plight, widows and children and old people. All this decline of New England industry that you hear about really dates from that time when we trusted the Morgan crowd; for they took something like five hundred million dollars away from this part of the country."

"But Grannie, if Uncle Henry is doing that to Mr. Walker, it is really the same thing as banditry!"

"Yes, of course; but you mustn't say it to your father or your uncles; they wouldn't take it kindly from a twenty-year-old girl."

"I'll be older some day," said Miss Betty.

III

The first thing when Cornelia got back to town, she went to call at her son-in-law's office. "Henry, what is this I hear about you and Jerry Walker?"

"What do you hear, Mother?"

"That you are taking his plants away from him."

"Has Jerry told you that?"

"No; but Betty has been visiting Lucile, and naturally hears about their troubles."

"Jerry tells his wife, and she tells Lucile, and Lucile tells Betty, and Betty tells you, and you tell me!" Henry laughed.
"Is it true, Henry? Are you after him?"
"It is absolutely untrue, Mother."
"You're not interested in his affairs?"
"I didn't say that. Jerry comes to certain bankers—including Rupert and John Quincy—and tries to borrow money. The bankers are my clients, and ask me to investigate, and draw up papers, and perform other legal services, which I do. Because the decisions of the bankers don't please Jerry, he takes up the notion that I'm an arch-conspirator, plotting his ruin. But that's all rubbish."
"Henry, you have the reputation of not being a very gentle enemy."
The other laughed again. "Well, Mother, have you come to convert me to pacifism? But seriously, I got through with Jerry Walker years ago. I was a stockholder in two of his felt-companies, and a director. I found that his way of doing business didn't agree with mine, so I let him buy me out at a fair price, and washed my hands of him. But he's been afraid of me ever since—because he knows I know too much about him."
"Henry, I've always had an interest in Jerry, ever since he was an errand-boy at the hospital, a bright little fellow that I saw had a future. Josiah helped him to get a start, you know."
"Yes, of course. But he's grown up now, and learned many tricks, and he plays the business game pretty roughly."
"I can't pretend to know all about his affairs—"
"Naturally not, Mother; only an expert accountant could do that—and he'd have trouble, because Jerry has hidden some things cleverly. It's a complicated matter, I assure you, and you make a mistake if you let the Walkers use you, or even worry you. Nobody can believe a word Jerry says."
"I just want to ask you to give him a square deal, Henry. Give him what you give other business men."
"Well, Mother, it's up to the bankers, and you are talking to a lawyer. There are many bankers interested in the Jerry Walker problem, and they all agree that he wants much more than any other business man—he wants everything in sight. There's only so much credit to go round—only about two per

cent of what people holler for—and Jerry is getting more than his share, and using it without any sort of scruple."

"He's paying a high price for it, I understand."

"He thinks so, naturally. It seems a simple matter to him, for the banks to check all the paper he can sign. He never figures on the risks the banks may be running."

"Is it true he's paying twenty-seven per cent, Henry?"

"That is a question you'll have to ask the bankers, Mother. I can't discuss my clients' affairs. But I'll say this as a general principle—two men seldom agree about the value of a horse, when one of them is selling and the other is buying."

"Henry, I want to ask it straight. You're not planning to take over Jerry's business?"

"Absolutely not, Mother!"

"You're telling me the truth?"

"When have I told you anything else?" And the telephone rang. Henry took down the receiver, listened, and said, "Yes, Rupert, I'll be right over. I'm having a consultation on the matter with Mrs. Thornwell, and I'm telling her you are the banker, and the real villain in the case."

So later in the day Cornelia went to call on this "real villain," and found him, a large island completely surrounded by statistics and charts relating to the felt business. He was polite, but reluctant to give her his precious time. If she had come to ask about investing a thousand dollars of her own, he would have taken an hour off to advise her—he would do that any day for any member of the family, even the poorest fifth cousin. But when she came about Jerry Walker he told her frankly that she was letting herself be used by a family of adventurers. She was deceived if she thought that Rupert had anything more to do with the matter than a score of other bankers; it was a council of the financial leaders of Boston who were deciding the future of the felt industry, and even if Rupert were to go before them and say, "Gentlemen, I have promised my mother-in-law that out of my affection for her we will agree to let her former errand-boy have all the money he wants"—still the other bankers might refuse to assent. "And I don't carry three million in my own wallet, Mother."

IV

Both Henry and Rupert had told Cornelia what was not true; and only two or three weeks later she found it out. Mrs. Jerry Walker came to Cornelia's apartment, and broke down and wept, and told the terrible story of what was happening. Jerry Walker was being stripped of every dollar he owned in the world; and it was Rupert Alvin and Henry Cabot Winters who were driving the other bankers to the job, sometimes against their will, and even without their knowledge. The loan for three millions had been agreed upon, and Mr. Winters had been instructed to prepare the papers; but instead of doing so, he had got one of the big banks in New York to call a loan suddenly, and Mr. Alvin had brought up demands that the other bankers had not known about—in short, everything had been tied up for a month.

Finally, in order to get half a million dollars in a hurry, poor Jerry had had to turn over to the bankers all the stock of all his companies. It was supposed to be a trusteeship—he had the right to get the properties back any time within two years by paying a million and a quarter; but the very day they got the securities, the bankers, with Mr. Winters at their head, had set to work to plunder the properties. They put in their own directors, and barred Jerry Walker from access to the books, and even barred him physically from the plants. They were disposing of all the assets of the subsidiary companies, and loading them up with debts and claims—everywhere Jerry turned he found that some unknown lawyer had mysteriously appeared with liens and suits. Everything was tied up, so that the real owner of the properties could not get a dollar, and was going to have to sell his home to get money to live.

So that was that. The caribou was down, and his blood was being drunk. Cornelia might wring her hands, and be very sorry; she might shout at the wolves and scold them—whereat they would lift their bloody jaws for a moment and grin at her. "Of course, Mother," said Henry, quite blandly and good-naturedly, when next she met him—"of course, I told you an untruth. What did you expect me to do?"

"I expected you to have a sense of family loyalty."

"You have too good a mind to fool yourself with such an

argument, Mother. I have plenty of Thornwell family loyalty, but not the least particle of Walker family loyalty. If you had come to me for the truth about affairs of your own, you would have had it; in case of need you might have had the last dollar I own in the world. But when you let yourself be used by Jerry Walker, to try to pull wires for him in the midst of a business crisis—then you haven't the least reason in the world to expect me to give you any information to be carried back to him! —Yes, of course, you didn't mean to carry it back, but I assure you Lucile expected to get it out of Betty, and Mrs. Walker expected to get it out of Lucile. They have been cultivating an intimacy with Betty for several years for exactly that purpose, and I didn't intend to let them succeed. When I told Rupert and James about it, they agreed that I had done exactly right to stall you."

"So you're going to put Jerry Walker out of the felt business!"

"Not at all, Mother. He knows felt well, and if he wants a job as manager of one of the plants, we'll pay him a good salary. What he doesn't know is finance, and we're going to fix him so he can't lead the Boston banks into a smash."

"He was making a lot of money, Henry."

"A chimpanzee could make money right now, with the government buying everything at any price you ask. But the war will be over soon, and then will come the storm, and we're going to have a safer man than Jerry Walker at the helm of the ship."

So Cornelia went away, and watched the events of the next few months, and decided no longer to think of her son-in-law as a wolf. From now on she would see him as a large, black, witty, urbane and charming spider. He lurked in a hole and watched the business flies, and once in a while he made a pounce, and sunk his fangs into a victim, and wove him round and round with a ton or two of legal nets, until he could not move a finger; after which he would be sucked dry of his financial juices.

In the case of the too enthusiastic manufacturer of felt, what happened was that he struggled in the nets until his health broke down; his hands trembled so that he could not hold a cup of coffee, and he had to go to North Carolina for the winter and play golf. While he was gone, the bankers sat down with his lawyers, and convinced them that the victim stood not a chance in the world, so the lawyers advised him to sign a release, forgiving his enemies for all they had done to him, in consideration of the sum of six hundred and twenty-five thousand dollars. For this price he gave up properties which earned a million and three-quarters net profit that year, and were worth about ten millions on the market. The six hundred and twenty-five thousand paid a part of his debts, and he sold his home to pay more, and his family gave up their social ambitions and moved into a cottage, and his daughter quit going to Radcliffe and went to work.

"Isn't it nice, Grannie?" said Betty. "When I get older, if I behave, I'll get a lot of Lucile's money, and I can hire her—perhaps to be a governess to my children. And Priscilla will have a share of it too, and can found a charity home to take care of Mr. and Mrs. Walker when they are old. And Cousin Josiah"—that was Henry Winters' one son—"he'll have a bigger share than any of us, to spend on women-chasing—I understand that's what he's doing now. Aunt Alice will be able to retain her adolescence—"

"My child! Don't say things like that!"

"I'm talking in the family, Grannie. We members of the new generation are going to be what you call hard-boiled. They are raising us in war-time, and we're getting used to plain language and messy sights. I read in the paper that Mrs. Henry Cabot Winters is planning a 'little theater,' in which her mystical poet's works are to be shown to the world as soon as the war is over. If Aunt Alice wants to subsidize genius, why does she have to pick out literary lounge-lizards and music-box monkeys?"

Cornelia said, "Dear me, I am really getting old! The new generation shocks me!"

V

There came a day when every able-bodied person in America rushed out of his house, and fell on the necks of passersby and danced and laughed and shouted and sang. Men threw their hats into the air, or tied tin cans to the tails of automobiles and drove up and down the streets. Three days later they all turned out and did it again, because the first time had been a mistake, some news agency had been in too much of a hurry. But it was a big enough war to deserve two armistice days, and even in State Street one saw "blue-bloods" celebrating with bootblacks, and high-hatted bankers forgetting their dignity for the first time in their eighty years.

This was a celebration in which even the pacifists could join. The nation would have one or two hundred thousand cripples to take care of—but at least you didn't have to think of new thousands being made every day! You could again expect people to listen to reason, and could work at stopping the next war without danger of arrest. The Kaiser had fled to Holland, and there seemed a real prospect of that newly-promised world. Such wonderful promises—a world fit for heroes, a world made safe for democracy, a world in which the last war had been won by the forces of justice! So we had been told in a golden glowing speech at least once a week for a year and a half; and now we were to see it made real. As a first step President Wilson packed up his typewriter and his fourteen points, and went over to Europe to oversee the making of a world charter. His packing appeared to be careless, for he lost one of the points in England—that providing for the "freedom of the seas"—and had only thirteen when he landed in France.

The American people had been told to trust him; he was the President, and had sources of information not open to the rest of us—so Deborah had assured her mother. But now it turned out that he hadn't any sources of information, or if he had, he hadn't used them. He had made no bargains whatever with the allies, he had not made them give up a single one of their greedy demands. And now, of course, it was too late; the danger was over, the allies were no longer afraid, and would do exactly what they pleased.

It was a disillusioning experience, and was to produce ten years of cynicism and corruption in every department of American life. The climax came when the President capitulated to the diplomatic ravens, and let them have their prey, and came home and told the public that that was what his fourteen points had meant. He did more than that—he went before a committee of the Senate, and stated that he had not known about the secret treaties until he went to Paris; which one had to take as Pascal took the doctrine of his church, and believe it because it was impossible.

VI

There were a few groups in America whose demands did not depend upon the diplomats at Versailles; and among these were the women. France might grab the Rhine, Japan might grab Shantung—but what was to prevent American women from having their rights at home? Surely the men were not making such a success with their votes that they could spurn the help of wives and sisters! Let us have a world made fit for heroines! So the campaign of votes for women leaped into life in a score of cities. In Washington the ladies began besieging senators and congressmen, and elderly statesmen took to physical flight from urgent feminine tongues. The militant suffragists began carrying placards in front of the White House, and got themselves arrested over and over again. It was most embarrassing, because the jails in the national capital had been made for street-walkers and Negro drunks, and had no accommodations for ladies.

The suffragists were divided into two groups, the respectable ones, who made dignified speeches and circulated petitions and got an inch in the newspapers once a month; and the militants, who set themselves the goal of a front-page story twice a day, and made it most of the time. Each of these two groups was active in Boston—a city full of ladies who felt themselves competent to take charge, not only of America, but of the world. Each group laid siege to Cornelia Thornwell and her granddaughter, and the militants won. Another scandal in the Sewing Circles, and another grief for a great family!

Cornelia's oldest daughter, Betty's mother, was a vigorous "anti." Her enemies told a story about her, that one day when company was expected, and many duties were clamoring, she had locked herself in her study and made no response, and when subsequent complaint was made, the answer was that she had been writing an article on "Woman the Home-maker." Jokes like that gave annoyance to the "antis," because it was so obvious to them that nothing but the wicked activities of the suffragists were dragging them out from the homes they loved, and compelling them to become examples of the evil they feared. Yes, the "wild women" had that power, and rejoiced in it; when the "antis" hired a house on Park Street and opened up offices, what should they see but a group of women marching back and forth before their door, carrying a banner with a strange device:

They say that home is woman's sphere.
What are the antis doing here?

The true "anti" was Cornelia's youngest daughter, Clara Thornwell Scatterbridge, who stayed at home with her eight babies, and loved them and petted them and scolded them and wept over them and saw that their various nurses and governesses kept their noses wiped. Clara had no idea what a vote looked like; but, alas, that didn't get even an inch in the papers! Nor did it have any appreciable effect when Alice Thornwell Winters shrugged her beautiful white shoulders and lifted her haughty eyebrows in scorn at the idea of sacrificing her feminine charm. Neither did it help when she wrote more and larger checks to pay for the "little theater" which was to produce the plays of Chauncey Duvillier, dealing with ancient Erse legends about dusky-haired promiscuous queens. The productions came off, and were at once very "high-brow" and very "high-hat," but they did not seem to reduce the attendance at suffrage meetings.

President Wilson had set his stern Presbyterian face against the program of national suffrage. It was a question for the individual states; thus spoke Sir Oracle, and when the female dogs barked, he said it again. But such a thing had been known as a great statesman changing his mind when made uncomfortable enough. It was a fact that the women out west had got the vote and were using it; Woodrow could not forget that it was California which had elected him the last time, and might defeat his party and his world policies the next time. A terrible thing to contemplate having women vote, but a still worse thing to contemplate having them vote Republican!

The President came back from Europe in February, and the suffragettes prepared a hearty welcome for him in New York. It was more than he could face, in his nervous condition, with that incredible statement he had to make to the Senate; so at the last moment the route of his ship was changed, and it landed at Boston. That put the burden onto the Boston suffragettes, who had to organize a demonstration almost overnight. They came rushing to Cornelia and Betty; would they help? Banners must be got ready, asking urgent witty questions, and these must be carried by ladies of absolutely indigo-colored blood; they must be carried as close to the President as the police would permit, and then a little closer; also the great man's latest anti-suffrage speech was to be burned in effigy on Boston Common.

VII

"Old Boston" is a city which has been laid out by cows. They made tracks, and these became lanes, and the lanes have now become narrow canyons of concrete and steel, made immutable for all time by a court-house full of deeds with intricate specifications. You may still see on Beacon Hill a house which has a narrow archway built under one room—because in selling the land the owner specified that access must for all time be left for his cow to reach the Common. Now, instead of a cow, there was coming a high-powered automobile bearing a long-featured Presbyterian gentleman in frock coat and silk hat, under military escort, with all the trappings of glory, and that unending roar of applause which he had heard even from the billows in mid-ocean. Patriotism in Boston was to have its day of rapture; Democratic patriotism, taking in even the Irish-Catholics, and marred only by the antics of twenty-two contumacious females, who refused to accept a great statesman's own definition of what he meant by democracy.

Among these twenty-two lady-pests was the widow of Josiah Quincy Thornwell, former governor of the Commonwealth; also Elizabeth Thornwell Alvin, daughter of the president of the Pilgrim National Bank. But the names of these two were not on the list furnished to the press; in that case the two would have been spotted by the police, and denied the honor they craved. They sallied forth with the other women, carrying placards aloft, in the route of the procession; and promptly they were snapped up, and hustled into a patrol wagon, and landed in Joy Street police-station—most beautifully named of public institutions in the home of the bean and the cod.

The police had them—and what was to be done with them?

The police had no idea. The one thing desired was to keep them out of the newspapers; which was the one thing impossible to achieve. They spent the entire day sitting in a room in the police-station, with no food—save the knowledge that they would be on the front page of all the afternoon newspapers! In the evening they were taken to the "House of Detention" under the Court House, where they slept on board benches covered with black oil cloth. They rolled up their coats for pillows, and spread newspapers to cover the dirt—but alas, the worst part of the dirt had powers of locomotion. Cornelia, sitting up awake, watched Betty sleeping, and counted twenty-one round black objects on her newspapers, and in the morning some of the women's ankles were so swollen that they could not get on their shoes. Also sleep was interfered with by the constant bringing in of drunken women, who howled in loud voices what appeared to be a popular song, "I love you as I never loved before." In the morning they filed out to a rusty iron sink to wash, and everyone had to answer the question, "Are you a drunk or a suffragette?" But these woes vanished in a blaze of glory when they discovered that they had got a quarter of a million dollars' worth of publicity on the front pages of the morning newspapers—while the respectable lady suffragists, who had presented a dignified petition, had got one inch in each paper!

Now they were going to be taken into court, and would refuse to employ lawyers, and would make twenty-two eloquent suffrage speeches. So they thought, but their captors thought otherwise. For these publicity-seekers the constitution of the Commonwealth was to be suspended, and trials were to be in secret in one of the rooms of the prison! When they learned this, there was a hasty consultation among the prisoners, and an agreement not to recognize such an illegal tribunal. Until they were in open court, no woman would say a word.

Their enemies had a still more dastardly scheme; they were going to deprive the little band of their most brightly shining star. A jailer came in and demanded, "Which is Elizabeth Alvin?"—and of course all the prisoners knew instantly what that meant. Papa Banker had got busy and pulled some political strings, and his daughter was to be bailed out, or spirited away, or something—a vile plot! Betty made no sound or sign, and neither did any one else; and presently came the young Irish policeman who had arrested and "booked" her. He had been ordered to pick her out of the bunch—and a fine mess he made of it!

It so happened that in the course of a year and a half, Betty was to be deeply concerned with the problem of identifications. To what extent was it possible for bystanders, witnesses of a crime, to describe the men who had committed the crime, and to recognize them some time later? Human lives have depended upon this problem, and not for the last time. Whenever Betty and her grandmother thought about the matter, the first thing that came to their minds was this experience in the Joy Street police-station. Here was a policeman who had arrested Elizabeth Alvin on the street, and marched her along for some distance, in the meantime having a considerable argument with her as to his right to destroy her banner, and his right to squeeze and hurt her arm. He had put her into a patrol-wagon, and sat opposite her during a ride of several blocks through crowded streets, meantime gazing at her and speculating, what kind of crazy loon was this that wanted a vote, when so many people that he knew were glad to sell theirs for two dollars. Arriving at the station-house, he had stood at the desk and booked her for sauntering, loitering, disorderly conduct and resisting arrest —enough offenses to keep her in jail until President Wilson's successor had been elected.

And now, next morning, came this young policeman to pick that young person out of a group of twenty-two, most of whom could not possibly be the right one, because they were old like Cornelia, or large and matronly, or tall and masterful, or in some other obvious way not the young and sweet and lovely Betty. She was the youngest in the crowd, and there were not more than half a dozen others near her age. All she had done to make the policeman's task harder was to take off her brown coat with beaver fur trimmings, and appear in a blue silk dress. What all the women did was to stand or sit, completely unaware of the policeman's existence, while he wandered about, peering into one face and then into another, obviously perplexed. He had all the time he wanted, he had everything his own way— and he got the wrong woman!

He picked out a fashionable young matron, mother of two blossoming babes, and said, "That's the one." The jailer commanded, "Come with me, Miss"—and when the young matron remained unaware of his existence, he stooped in front of her, and put one sturdy arm about her knees, and lifted her over his shoulder, and carried her like a sack of meal, out of the room and upstairs into the presence of the secret judge. He arrived there, somewhat red and out of breath, and the young matron no less so. Set down upon her two feet, she stamped one of them, and glared at the judge and the jailer, and clenched her two fists. "I will say just this and no more—I am *not* Betty Alvin!"

VIII

The night that Betty and Cornelia spent in jail there was a gathering of the Thornwell clan: not summoned, but just happening, because every Thornwell who got the report knew instantly that it was his duty to repair to the Alvin home on Commonwealth Avenue to offer aid and counsel.

There was a general agreement that it would be useless to get the two renegades out of jail until the President was out of the city, because they would only get in again and make another scandal. There was also agreement as to what should be done with Betty; she must be shipped abroad by the very first steamer. The war was over now, and while passports were not being given for any but official purposes, it would be an easy matter for Rupert to get what he wanted, and Betty would be put in charge of some elderly respectable relative, and subjected to the refining influences of Westminster Abbey and the Tower of London and the National Gallery and the Nelson Column, and later on to the Louvre and the Eiffel Tower, and would doubtless come back at the end of a year a lady like all the other ladies who lived on Commonwealth Avenue, home of the least common and most exclusive wealth in America.

About Cornelia there was a sharp difference of opinion. One group declared that the thing to do was to excommunicate her and ignore her existence; while the other group wanted to have her committed to an institution, where she would be treated with the utmost kindness and consideration, but prevented from bringing further disgrace upon an honorable family. The head of this group was Uncle Abner, whose deaf man's voice would boom out in the drawing-room at intervals, "Lock her up!" The others would try to explain objections to this plan, but he would only say again, "Lock her up!" There are some advantages to being deaf, it is so much easier to keep your opinions unchanged.

Great-aunt Priscilla joined Abner's group. She was tall and thin, and suffered from anchylosis of the spine, which made it painful for her to sit erect, but she never sat any other way in public. She had the long lean face of her dead brother, Josiah, and of Betty's mother, Deborah; it sagged now, but the pouches disappeared as she set her jaw in anger and declared, "It is the proper thing to do in such cases. Everybody will agree that we are justified."

"Not quite everybody, Aunt Priscilla," said Henry Cabot Winters. "Surely not the suffragettes."

"I am talking about people one mentions," said the old lady.

"But the suffragettes would say it was persecution," objected Deborah, "and they would make a great fuss."

"We should have them picketing this house!" added Rupert.

That horrible idea silenced all of them but Abner. "Lock her up!" said he; and when his son Quincy shouted into his ear, "The suffragettes would object," he answered, in good old Puritan style, "Lock 'em all up!"

There were many precedents that could be cited for this procedure, and the old people did not fail to cite them. All you had to do was to find a judge and a couple of doctors who sympathized with the family predicament—and it would be easy enough for Thornwells to do that. Great-uncle Ahab had become violent at one time, due to his disappointment in love, and had spent ten years alone in a wing of the Thornwell mansion, with a keeper by day and another by night; he still had spells of brooding, when similar action had to be contemplated. Such emergencies arose in all "blue-blood" families—it was one of the mysteries of the Lord's mercy—and all physicians to the rich were accustomed to signing certificates, and judges to issuing commitments.

Some such action might have come of this conference, had it not been for Henry Cabot Winters, that witty, urbane and charming black spider. He was nothing but an "in-law," and not really entitled to speak, but he did it none the less. "Cornelia is eccentric, but she is not insane, and we all know it; she has many friends who know it, and one of them is Morrow."

"Morrow?" said Great-aunt Priscilla. "Who brought Morrow into it?"

"Well, Morrow as Cornelia's physician would naturally expect to be consulted; and I'm pretty sure you'd have him against you."

"What makes you think that?" It was James Scatterbridge, the great mill-owner, who had made some millions of yards of bandages for soldiers who were not going to be wounded, and was now very busy making clear to the government that he was not going to give up his profit on these contracts. He had postponed an important conference this evening, and if his mother-in-law was going to be locked up, he wanted it done quickly.

Said Henry, "Cornelia told me that Rupert dropped a hint of something of the sort to her, and she decided she would take the precaution to have a chat with Morrow, and tell him her story, and all her ideas. He was very much amused, of course— at least that is what Cornelia reported."

"Oh, yes, it is *most* amusing!" snapped Great-aunt Priscilla. "The newspapers are finding it so, and no doubt their readers. But is that what we have been paying Morrow for—some fifty years, I believe?"

"Well," said the lawyer, "you certainly can't offer to pay him to declare Cornelia *non compos;* at least, I don't think he would take the money. So it looks as if we'd have to forget our black sheep."

"Well, at least let her take her own Irish name!" This parting shot of the old lady made Deborah and Alice wince—because, after all, the black sheep with the Irish name was their mother. That is the difficulty in these family councils—there are so many toes to be trod upon! It was safer to be deaf, like Great-uncle Abner, and go on saying, over and over, "Lock her up!"

IX

Three days after this conference Great-uncle Ahab was walking home on a stormy night, and fell and struck his head. He lay in the snow for some time before he was found, and a few hours later he was ill with pneumonia, and next day was in a critical condition. The family came in haste—including his brother Abner, somewhat embarrassed after fifty-three years of estrangement. He tried to refer to the matter, but Ahab was in a delirium. That was "old Boston's" idea of drama—an old man who could hear very little shouting to another old man who would never hear anything. They talked about it in the clubs for quite a while.

Also they talked about the funeral, which was an imposing affair, the same as Josiah's—for after all, Thornwells were alike in the eyes of the Lord, even though in the eyes of the world one might be a governor and the other a manic depressive. The ceremony was held in the house which Ahab had sawed in half in order to get away from his brother; and all through the ceremony you heard the dead man's half dozen hairless Chinese dogs howling their heads off in an upstairs room—it was most uncanny. When the will was read the family kept it secret—which of course put everybody on tiptoe with curiosity, and caused the newspapers to give it special prominence when it was filed for probate. One provision read, "I leave my beloved dogs to my sister Priscilla, whom they remind of newly born mice." Another said, "I leave my half house to serve as a home for elderly gentlemen of good family who can prove that they have been robbed by their relatives." Finally, his income from stocks and bonds of the Thornwell Mills Company was to be used to establish a chair at some New England theological seminary which would agree to have a course of lectures delivered every year under the auspices of "The Ahab Adams Thornwell Foundation for the Precise and Final Refutation of the Lyman Beecher Interpretation of the Doctrine of Infant Damnation as Expounded in Holy Writ." Ahab had heard Lyman Beecher at the age of twenty-five, and had waited sixty years to have him precisely and finally refuted.

At family funerals the hardest hearts are softened and the fiercest prides are humbled. Betty remembered that Great-uncle Ahab had once given her a pony, riding it all the way to her home, with his long legs reaching to the ground. So it was a good time for her mother to plead with her. Yes, Betty would promise to engage in no further public disturbances until she had finished that year at Radcliffe; and thereafter she was willing to spend a year abroad and become cultured—could

Grannie go with her? The little minx asked it quite soberly; and Deborah, equally without trace of a smile, explained that the family was under great obligations to Cousin Letitia Adams Quincy, who had nursed Betty once as a little girl, while Deborah herself had been in Europe.

Cousin Letitia was a third or fourth cousin—one of those who had arrived too early for the funeral of Josiah, and got out and walked about the estate for half an hour, in order not to make herself conspicuous. Because of such behavior she was known as a perfect lady, and now was to receive the poor relation's ultimate reward. Deborah had interviewed her and ascertained that she had read nothing since "The Marble Faun"—except the "Sunday School Examiner's Bulletin" and the religious and genealogical pages of the *Transcript*. She was judged immune to the contagion of redness, and the right person to chaperon Betty's grand tour. The girl accepted her with a meekness which would have made Deborah suspicious, if the latter's natural shrewdness had not been smothered under a heavy load of self-sufficiency.

x

It was high time to get excitable young rebels out of the country; the family realized that more and more clearly every day. For it appeared that the signing of the armistice was not going to mean peace; not even the signing of a treaty would mean it. Our troops were to stay in Germany; worse yet, they were to stay in Siberia and Archangel, and wage President Wilson's private war upon the Russian people. The American army and navy were to serve as a world police-force for the capitalist system. Exactly what Cornelia had seen the Boston police do in Plymouth, the national police were going to do all over Europe and Asia, sometimes under our command, sometimes under British command. And any persons at home who objected to this program would be hit over the head with the so-called espionage act; a law enacted to punish enemy spies, and now serving to jail American citizens for protesting against attacks upon a friendly people without a declaration of war.

It was the White Terror. Conducted partly by mobs, and partly by police and government agents acting as mobs, it had for its aim the destruction of every means through which the American people might learn how their blood and treasure were being wasted. It stopped at no crime; the law-enforcers of city, state and nation became the leading criminals. In New York four Russian boys and a girl, all of them under age, attempting to distribute a circular protesting against the invasion of Russia, were seized by the police and tortured until one of them died; the rest were prosecuted in the federal courts and received sentences of twenty years' imprisonment.

Such things were happening all over the country, and made trouble for well-meaning persons like Cornelia, who sought to argue for constitutional methods. How could she ask her friend Vanzetti to settle the grievances of the workers by political action, when again and again socialist candidates were thrown off the ballot, or, when elected, were denied their seats? How could she urge him to obey the law, when the law-makers and law-enforcers themselves defied it? A year or two ago Vanzetti had made to her the statement, "Capitalist is most fighting man in whole world"; and never did the capitalist work harder to prove that the anarchist was right.

The victims of this White Terror would strike back; and if they struck blindly, it was the way the lesson had been taught them. May Day was an occasion for celebration of the Russian revolution by all who believed in it; and on the day before May Day, a package arrived by mail at the home of a United States senator in Georgia, especially conspicuous for his "red-baiting." The package was opened by a Negro maid, and exploded and blew her to pieces. That led to hurried searches, and the finding of a score or so of bombs in the New York post-office, addressed to various persons of prominence, and detained because they had not enough postage paid.

May Day came in Boston, with that terrible news upon the front page of the papers. The socialists had several meetings scheduled—and they were a legal party, not advocating violence in any form. But this was a distinction the newspapers and those who controlled them were anxious to conceal. When the audience emerged from one hall, and attempted to march down the street to another hall where there was another meeting, they were set upon by three hundred policemen and a mob of soldiers and sailors, thoroughly "americanized" by a year in

Europe. The socialists, and many innocent passers-by who happened to look foreign, were chased through the streets, hunted out in stores where they sought refuge, and pummeled and clubbed into insensibility. The police loaded them into patrol-wagons, and then beat them over the heads while in the wagons; they loaded them into trucks, and permitted the soldiers and sailors to beat them—there were even cases of policemen lending their clubs to members of the mob who thought some victim insufficiently mishandled. They raided the second hall and beat up the audience; the fighting went on for two or three hours, until four persons were killed, and a hundred and sixteen dragged off to jail. Among them was a son of Boris Sidis, of Harvard, and H. W. L. Dana, a grandson of Henry Wadsworth Longfellow and of Richard Henry Dana.

So once more Cornelia heard the thud of hickory clubs on human flesh and bone. This time Betty heard it too, and both of them had to run for their lives. They got into a cab and drove home, both trembling so that they could hardly use their hands, both white and tearful, with a mixture of fear and rage. They spent hours of anguish together, telephoning to find out who had been killed and who had been hurt and who was in jail; then to get lawyers, and persons with property for bail-bonds—all the routine so familiar to the seasoned "radical," and so startling to the newcomer who still believes in his country.

In the morning Cornelia would go to court, and perhaps serve as a witness. Betty could do nothing but return to college and keep quiet, and hope that no one would report her to her parents. She had not meant to break her promise—but how could one know that going to a socialist meeting was disorderly conduct?

Judge Hayden was the magistrate presiding at the trials, a majestic gentleman, as they all tried to be. But under the strain of his intense patriotism, he forgot his dignity, and broke loose and delivered tirades—and not at the police for lending their clubs to be used in beating socialists. He did not punish a single one of the assailants, but sent the victims to jail for varying terms. "The uneducated and the overeducated," was one of his sneers—which sounded peculiar in Boston.

It was to be expected that when the next lot of bombs went off, one of them should tear out the front of Judge Hayden's home. In Constantinople under the rule of the sultans it was said that the state of social discontent could be ascertained from the number of fires which occurred in the city; when the number increased unduly, some grafting officials would be strangled, and the fires would grow fewer. But Boston is not an easy-going place like old Turkey; Boston is a Puritan stronghold, and its rulers are stiff-necked. The more numerous the bombs, the more they would increase the causes of bombs. The answer of the authorities to the bombing of Judge Hayden was to put Galleani on a steamer and ship him back to Italy; also to plant several spies among the Boston anarchists.

XI

This was while Betty was saying good-by to her friends, including these same anarchists. Without a word to the family, Betty and her grandmother stole away to visit a band of desperados who were at that time the theme of thousands of words in the files of the Department of Justice, the American Protective League, and the million-dollar detective agencies. They actually spent a night in an anarchist home in Plymouth, and listened to jokes about "bombe di pistacchio," and heard Vanzetti's story of old Galleani's parting from his wife and four children.

This was one of the ingenious new methods of torture which the White Terror had devised. They would grab a man in the middle of the night and lock him up in a police cell, and badger him there until he admitted that he did not believe in government, or that he regarded government as an affair of violence—something they made it easy enough to admit! They would then present the confession to the immigration authorities, and a warrant of deportation would be signed, and the victim would be taken secretly on board a steamer—his wife and children left behind, with no money to follow him, and nothing but to beg or starve.

Vanzetti had given up his "picka shov'." His friends had urged that the work was too hard for him, and he had invested his savings in a fish business belonging to an Italian who was going home. "Fish-business" sounded most impressive—until you learned that it consisted of a hand-cart, a pair of scales, and a route. Twice a week he got a barrel or two of fish, either from the docks or by express from Boston, and shoved his hand-cart about, ringing a bell and calling, "Pay-shee! Pay-shee!" He had had this same kind of business once before, said Alfonsina, but had not been successful, because he let everybody owe him money. This time he had promised to run it on a strictly cash basis. Vanzetti grinned, and said that it was a "mosta good business," because he met all the Italian women and children in Plymouth, and they got to know him and feel friendly, and he would say a few words about "joostice," and when there was to be a meeting or a "picanic," no one could "distriboot" circulars or sell tickets so well as he.

Trando had saved up his money and bought himself a three-quarter size violin for ten dollars, and a bow for two and a half, and had had several lessons and learned to play a tune. Of course he was made to exhibit this accomplishment, with Bart serving as master, keeping the time with an erect fore-finger, cocking his head on one side and judging critically the pitch of the notes, which were apt to vary slightly from the normal. It was "Old Black Joe," a very sad tune, and there were tears in Alfonsina's eyes at the finish—though perhaps they were tears of pride, that this marvelous thing should be coming from her precious little boy. Through the years that were to come Trando was to play that tune many times for Bart, under circumstances that would bring tears into the eyes of all who heard it.

XII

They climbed Castle Hill, and picked a few of the wild flowers, and watched the sail-boats on the bay. It was a part-ing for Betty and Bart, and both of them were moved, though Bart said, "Maybe I come see you in Europe pretty soon. I think I not be let in this countree mooch time; get shoore catched and sended home. Pretty soon it come trooble in Italy, maybe rivoluzione—make American afraid for have Italian here."

"Well, you won't mind going back to Italy." It was Betty speaking.

"Shoore not, get free tickets, mooch pleas-èd. I glad for

be lonely man, no family for suffer. I fraid for man like
Vincenzo, like Nick Sacc'—they catch heem, send away—mooch
trooble for family. Come mooch spy—come spy in cloob in
East Boston—all time spy watch. But he not tell true story,
tell bombe, make people hate anarchista."

Vanzetti paused, and watched the sail-boats for a while.
"Sooch a lovely place, is hard to t'ink so ugly thing can be
in the world. You meet Yankee man, he is a good feller; you
laugh, you make joke, he is please, he think wop is all right,
pretty good. But next day he take you, put you in jail, beat
you with rubber hose, hang you up by finger, torture you
terrible. Is hard to believe, but it happens all time, plenty
fellers in cloob can tell. I say, I not give up, not stand sooch
thing, I fight. I keep gun all the time now." And Bart patted
his hip, where a large lump was evident.

"Have you shot that gun off yet?" inquired Betty.

"Shoore, I take it in wood, I practice, he shoot pretty good."

"Well, it's not only the gun, it's the gunner. You need a
lot of practice, Bart, if you're going to shoot it out with the
police." It was Betty again, and her grandmother was dis-
mayed. Where on earth did she pick up slang—"shoot it out!"
And where had she acquired that matter-of-fact smile, discussing the mad idea of resisting arrest? Truly, the new generation was traveling fast, and their elders had to "keep on the
jump."

Cornelia knew that if you objected to what the new generation did or said, it would refrain from arguing with you, but
would relegate you to the storeroom of the "has-beens," and
forbear to take you in its confidence. But in her own head
she pondered and worried. Betty's pacifist convictions had apparently not been able to stand the strain of that "May Day
riot" in Boston.

One of the children came up to report that there were men
at the house to see Bart. There were two Italians with a motor-
cycle and a side-car. Cornelia recollected their faces, from
the night of the dramatic performance in Stoughton. She was
introduced to them again, Coacci and Orciani, workingmen
and anarchist propagandists. The former had just recently
been arrested for deportation, and was now under a thousand-
dollar bond. They talked in Italian, and then drove off, and

Bart brought in from another room a package which the two had left; he laughed and told Betty and Cornelia that it was a bomb, and these two had advised him not to let the strange Yankee ladies into the secret, because, after all, who could say they might not be spies?

The package was big enough for a bomb, to blow up a whole cordage-plant. It was heavy; and when Bart cut the string and opened it, they saw what his joke meant—it contained what he liked to call "mental dinnameet." There were a dozen copies of a book, bound in red paper covers, brilliant enough to send a man to jail for ten years in Massachusetts. Bart handled the books with loving pride, because they were published by the "Gruppo Autonomo di East Boston," and he had helped raise the money to make the enterprise possible. "Faccia à Faccia col Nemico" was the title, "Face to Face with the Enemy." It was a series of biographies of the anarchist martyrs, with their pictures. It was needed in this crisis, to remind the comrades how the heroes of past times had been able to withstand torture and persecution, almost as bad as the White Terror in America. Bart had taken orders for this book among the Plymouth comrades, and now he said, "I take heem queeck, I get him distriboot, never let policeman catch heem, giammai!"

XIII

Cornelia went back to Boston to raise funds for the families of the May Day victims; while Betty and Cousin Letitia went to New York, accompanied by Deborah, and with a proper amount of tears and handkerchief-waving were started on their grand tour. The Thornwell clan breathed a sigh of relief when the young madcap was actually at sea.

For the first month it seemed all right. Betty was in London. "And Mother," she wrote, "it is quite like Boston; New England is really Old England. I look out of my hotel window and see thousands of brick buildings stained with smoke, and chimney-pots and dormer-windows through a haze—I might be looking north from Beacon Hill. I really do not see that one has to leave Boston to get culture, but I am doing what you wish. We are going to-night to study the British labor party at a big mass-meeting in Albert Hall. I am assured that the police will not club the audience as it comes out. It was kind of you not to tell Aunt Letitia too much about my 'redness'; she is so gentle and innocent, everything is educational to her. I am going to learn a lot, and only hope you and father won't mind if I study live people instead of dead ones."

That was a hint of trouble; but it was nothing to what came a week later from Cousin Letitia. "Dear Cousin Deborah: We are having a *most delightful* time in London—I will *never* be able to find words to express my gratitude to *you* and *Cousin Rupert* for affording me this greatest and *undreamed of* opportunity—for such it was, I assure you—though perhaps in some *secret* corner of my soul I did cherish the *dream*. Betty is the *dearest* child, and *most* companionable, and tractable in every way. To add to the *perfection* of our happiness, who should turn up in London yesterday but dear Aunt Cornelia Thornwell! It was Betty who saw her, in the lobby of our hotel. 'It is *Grannie!*' she exclaimed; and at first I could hardly believe my *eye-sight*. *Imagine* such a coincidence—here in far-off London! *Truly* the world *is* getting smaller. She was called over here unexpectedly upon business. We have decided to go to Paris, and put off seeing London Bridge and the Tower until later."

And then, a week after that, another letter from Betty. "I hope you and Father will not be too much annoyed by Grannie's following us to Europe. She says she just got too lonesome and couldn't stand it. The older generation is very stubborn, I find, and difficult to control. I will try hard to keep her out of trouble. She has letters of introduction to leading statesmen, but we are going to see the Eiffel Tower first, so as to be regular tourists. It was very good of you to leave our itinerary to our own choice, and we are availing ourselves of this freedom. Next week we leave for Buda-Pesth. There are some officials whom Grannie wishes to meet, and they may not be there long, because governments change swiftly in Europe nowadays. Cousin Letitia has read that there are very fine gypsy orchestras in Hungary, and this thrills her repressed Puritan soul. I hope you and Father will not blame this poor dear lady for anything that may go wrong with our tour, because she is really as good as gold, though too naïve to cope with the present world situation. She is invited to lunch with a prominent editor or member of the house of deputies, and it does not occur to her to ask whether he is royalist or communist. She says, 'I suppose it is not the custom for these European men to trim their beards or their finger-nails.' But do not worry about us, because we are learning a great deal."

That letter alarmed Deborah, but it seemed worse yet when Rupert came home that evening and read it and told her about Hungary. There had been a Bolshevik revolution in that country, and the "officials" whom Cornelia and Betty were going to meet were no doubt some blood-thirsty "commissars," Jews and ex-convicts who were slaughtering the men and nationalizing the women of several empires. Rupert knew all about it, because he had before him a proposition for financing the overthrow of these "officials" in the interest of European stability; he had that very day been investigating the prospects for having the bonds of a new counter-revolutionary government absorbed by the Hungarian population of New England. He had lunched with a man who had explained the details of the plan, and had prepared a schedule of the subsidies required to obtain the support of the Hungarian-American press. The world was growing more and more complicated, and the tasks of a leader of high finance made him sit up nights and study geography.

"My God," said the tormented father, "I suppose there's only one thing left—they'll be going to Russia!" Which showed what a great mind he had. For two weeks later came another communication from Mistress Betty, as follows:

"I suppose you poor dears are going to be truly shocked by this news, and I am sorry, but there is no helping it. Grannie and I are leaving to-morrow for Saratov, which is in Southern Russia. It is the place where that crazy yarn about the nationalizing of women got its start, and we are going to see for ourselves. We had the extraordinary good fortune to run into a man whose head Grannie bandaged up after it was broken by the police in the Plymouth cordage strike. Now he is to take charge of the railroads in a province as big as the whole of New England, and says he has an underground way to get through the allied lines without danger. It is just like Boston here, you can do anything if you have money. It is going to be

a most educational experience, and you must not worry about
us. The world is changing rapidly, and nothing could be more
important than to watch the new political forms in the act of
evolving. When these changes come to America, somebody will
have to understand them.

"Please do not worry about Cousin Letitia, who is perfectly
safe and happy in Buda-Pesth. We have taken the precaution
to introduce her to influential people on both sides, so she will
be all right whichever comes out on top. Meantime she is handing out half loaves of bread to the starving children of war-
refugees. That is charity, and she understands it. In the evenings she hears a gypsy orchestra, in company with an elderly
Hungarian playwright who speaks fluent English, and has become completely absorbed in the maiden-lady from Boston. I
think she is the first one he ever met, and he has the idea she
will be wonderful in a play; the only trouble is that European
audiences would consider it a fairy-tale. I do hope you will not
blame Cousin Letitia because of Grannie. She could not possibly have the idea there is anything wrong about a grandmother. When she was in school, she was taught to admire the
revolutionary leaders of New England, and now that she meets
those in Europe, she finds them highly educated men.

"We only plan to stay in Russia one or two months. Grannie
has promised to return in the fall, to teach a course in the causes
of modern war at the labor college which will be opened in
Boston if the police do not smash it. I expect to come back to
Buda-Pesth and take a job with some relief organization—any
one that will accept a person who has been in Russia. At present
the Interallied Food Mission is refusing all aid to the starving
children of Red Hungary. That is Mr. Herbert Hoover's
amiable method of bringing back the Whites, and it should earn
him everlasting infamy in American and Hungarian history.

"I hope you won't mind if I find some way to earn my own
keep; there is a hard time in the relation between parents and
children, when the parents have to realize that their little ones
are grown up. I will continue to let Father send me money if
he wants to; I will not refuse a dollar that will keep some child
alive for a month. The suffering in all Eastern Europe is
atrocious—I have seen sights that would make any darling of
luxury grow up in a hurry. Be patient with Grannie and me,

and realize that we love you all, in spite of not doing what you want; we are acting according to the dictates of our consciences, and where would New England be in history if some people had not done that?

"Affectionately your daughter,
"Elizabeth."

CHAPTER 7

DEPORTATION DAYS

I

RUPERT ALVIN would have worried more about his runaway daughter, if he had not had so many troubles at home to keep him occupied. It seemed as if all the devils in Puritan New England broke loose that summer of 1919. There were a couple of million soldier boys turned out of the training camps, and flotilla loads returning from France, and no jobs to go round. They took to crime, to bootlegging, to striking, to demanding bonuses, to all kinds of behavior which kept bankers lying awake at night. The war-orders, the great prop of prosperity, had been pulled from underneath, and business was like a man waking up on the morning after a celebration.

The cost of living had been going up all through the war, but now it went faster than ever; there was a shortage of everything, and nobody could live on his salary. Out in Seattle there was a general strike, almost a revolution; while close at home, in Lawrence, a strike of the mill-workers had to be put down by kidnaping the leaders and beating them insensible with brass "knucks" and blackjacks. And then, in Boston, the most incredible event of all—a strike of policemen! Of the safest "cops" in the whole of civilization, Irish-Catholics trained in humility and obedience in parochial schools especially established for the purpose! Truly, it seemed the end of Rupert Alvin's world.

The policemen had been grumbling about their wages all through the year. Some were getting as low as ninety-two dollars a month, and how could a man keep a family on that? They grumbled about the way they were housed—many of them in that old Joy Street station, which had been built before the Civil War, and was dirty and verminous. They went on grumbling, and the authorities went on putting them off—for if you paid living wages to policemen, what would be left for

187

politicians? In August the grumblers formed a union, and joined the American Federation of Labor. Treason and red rebellion under the very shadow of Bunker Hill monument, on the very steps of "Funnel" Hall!

There were at this time two great banking groups competing for the mastery of Boston's affairs; like the wars of the Guelphs and the Ghibellines in ancient Florence. Parker, Jones and Company, one of these concerns, stood in with the city administration, and their Democratic mayor appointed them as a committee to sit down with the leaders of the union and work out a settlement. The policemen were to get their "raise," and everything would be polite. But they had omitted to consult Rupert Alvin and the Pilgrim National crowd; and Rupert was incensed that his dignity should thus be flouted. Also, he had religious convictions on the subject of labor unions. For policemen to organize and wring concessions by threats was a challenge to the very being of the state. If a Democratic mayor were allowed to bargain with Democratic Irish-Catholic labor leaders, and pay out the city's money under duress, the Republican Rupert might as well retire from his job of running Massachusetts and Europe.

He consulted first with Henry Cabot Winters, as was his custom; then he got his associates together and told them his plan. Never would there be another such opportunity to teach a lesson to the forces of disorder. The policemen's union must be broken, its leaders driven from the force, and not a man who went on strike should ever again be employed by the city. Rupert carried his point, and the heads of the Chamber of Commerce were called in and won over, and the police commissioner was summoned and told of the decision. Fortunate indeed that this official was appointed by the governor and not by the mayor, and so was a "blue-blood" and not a demagogue!

The business men of the city had rallied to defend their property. The president of Harvard had offered a thousand students, and all these volunteers were ready to go on patrol-duty the moment they were called. The policemen had given ample notice; they would strike at five forty-five o'clock on the afternoon of September ninth; and moreover they left four hundred of the old men to protect property. But it was Rupert's plan to teach the city, and indeed the whole country, a lesson by a demonstration of what it meant for policemen to form a labor union. To that end the old policemen were kept shut up in headquarters, and the volunteers were not summoned until nine o'clock the next morning. For one whole night Boston was to be without any police protection whatever; and to make assurance doubly sure, one of the big detective agencies supplied a few men to throw bricks through the windows of department-stores and start things moving. That the plotters had actually done this was never proved, but you would meet many "blue-bloods," familiar with the gossip of the clubs, who were certain that it had been done; and several years later, when Boston saw its leading bankers on the witness-stand in the case of Jerry Walker, and heard them lying about how they had got possession of the felt-industry of New England—then Boston was ready to believe anything about bankers!

II

Whoever started it, the windows were smashed, and men and boys jumped through the holes and helped themselves to what they wanted; you saw women sitting on the curb-stones, fitting themselves with expensive shoes. There were many hold-ups that night, and some rape; more horrifying yet, there were crap-games going on the Common—on the very steps of the State House with its golden dome. It is characteristic of Boston that this breach of decorum was the thing which stamped itself upon the public mind, and stands out in unwritten history. Three hundred crap-games in broad daylight—that shows you what the mob is like, and what would happen if there were no hickory clubs to hold it down!

The merchants of the city were in a panic, putting up barricades in front of their shops, arming their clerks and spending the night in a state of siege. The picture of Boston in the hands of its criminal element had gone all over the country; Boston papers had made a fearful panic, and the faithful press agencies had spread it; so Rupert's lesson had been taught, and it was time for the city to be saved. The mayor called out some of the state militia—under an old law he had the right to call the part which belonged to Boston. He wanted to call the rest, but for this an order from the governor was needed; and here came an unexpected hitch in the program of "law and order."

The representative of Anglo-Saxon superiority in the State House happened to be a gentleman by the name of Calvin Coolidge, whose story is one of the oddest ever invented by that Great Novelist who makes up history. A thin-lipped, tight little man, a petty lawyer and bill-collector from the western part of the state, "Cal" had got elected to the legislature, and attracted the attention of the Republican boss because he always did exactly what he was told, and never said a word that could be left unsaid. If a politician has an opinion he is bound to offend somebody; so, obviously, the wise course is to have no opinion on any subject. Strange, that no one ever thought of it before "Cautious Cal"!

The man who ran the Republican state machine through this period was a multimillionaire senator by the name of Murray Crane. He had established for his good political boys what was known as the "escalator system," or the "Massachusetts ladder." So long as they took orders, and kept themselves presentable to the voters, he would promote them regularly, step by step. It was a slow process, and you were old when you got to the top, but Massachusetts liked that, it is old itself. In this case, however, there developed a phenomenon known as "Coolidge luck"; as if the fates were amusing themselves by boosting this feeblest man in the state machine. Among the legislators aspiring to the state senate there existed a "rotation agreement"; there was never any competition at the primaries, each town took its turn. But the man ahead of Coolidge died, and he jumped into the place. Then, as a state senator who had never made a speech, he learned that the man in line for president of the senate had attacked woman suffrage. When the suffragists asked the views of Calvin, he shut the tightest and thinnest pair of lips in Massachusetts. The women attacked the other man and beat him at the polls, and Calvin presented his claims to the boss, and became president of the senate. Clear the way!

Next it happened that the man who was scheduled to become lieutenant-governor made the mistake of speaking in favor of prohibition. Again Calvin kept his masterly silence, and the liquor interests switched to him, and he was nominated. He served two terms as lieutenant-governor, at a time when everybody was sick of politics, and was pleased with a man who said nothing and did nothing. As a reward they made him governor; and now here was a crisis, and two big groups of bankers pulling him this way and that! There was nothing for him but physical flight, and for twenty-four hours no one connected with the government knew where the governor was to be found.

At last Rupert dug him out, on the farm of Murray Crane, who had pushed him up the escalator. They had a night session, and Calvin heard such things as never will be printed in any history-book. When the time came to call out the state guard, he did what he was told; the machine-guns went into action on Boston Common, and fired à whole volley of shots heard round the world.

As for Calvin, he waited several days, until it was evident that Rupert's strategy had been successful; public sentiment had turned against the strikers. Then Calvin rushed forward, waving in his hand a telegram to Samuel Gompers, proclaiming in clarion tones: "There is no right to strike against the public safety, by anybody, anywhere, at any time!" That was, of course, what the capitalist press wanted at the moment; the governor's proclamation took the front page all the way from Boston to Seattle—where there had been a rival strike and a rival hero. One of these two masterful men was destined to become vice-president and then president of the United States on the basis of his heroism; while the other was destined to become a supersalesman of real estate, unloading ten thousand subdivision lots upon admiring "come-ons." Which hero was to be which was a matter of a toss-up in a hotel-room, at the tail end of a long-drawnout political convention. It may have been "Coolidge luck"—and again, it may have been the fact that the Massachusetts leaders were able to certify that here was a man who had never once expressed an opinion in twenty years of public life, and had never once questioned an order from Murray Crane, who had pushed him up the escalator.

III

This police strike cost the community three million dollars; nor did the community make it up out of policemen's wages, because it granted to the new men more than it had refused to the old. But that was all right to Rupert Alvin. In the first place, it wasn't his money; and in the second place, it was not a question of money, but of what he called "principle"—meaning the bankers' right to have their way. The "mob" really had learned a lesson; there would be no more crap-shooting on the Common, and no more labor unions among public servants.

Neither Rupert nor any of his crowd reckoned the dumb resentment smoldering in the hearts of fourteen hundred men, who had thought themselves guardians of law and order, and now discovered that they were pawns in a game of power. These men had been pleading for a living for themselves and their families; they had been polite enough, humble enough—until they saw these qualities unheeded. They had served the city faithfully—some for twenty or thirty years; even the Back Bay admitted the virtues of those whom it knew. You would hear ladies of the Sewing Circle exclaim, "What do you suppose has become of that lovely policeman who used to help us across Boylston Street in front of Trinity Church? The one that got books from the library, and asked for something about the Æneid!" That story, told by the librarian, had been a tradition of the Back Bay forever after. So appropriate to Boston, to have a policeman who got books from the library, and actually appreciated the Æneid!

Cornelia Thornwell came back from Russia to find her city in a grim mood, with armed soldiers patrolling all the streets. The time for nonsense was past, the Bolshevik menace was going to be put down. The word "nonsense" included the fact that an elderly woman, once of high respectability, but now badly "cracked," had run away from her family and spent two months in Soviet Russia. Cornelia found that no newspaper in Boston manifested interest in what she had done; none desired to tell its readers about the condition of women in that city of Saratov where the "nationalization" story had started. No, the Boston papers wanted highly flavored horrors, invented by tsarist refugees in Riga and Helsingfors and Warsaw and Bucharest and Constantinople; they would pay the tolls to have such inventions cabled, but they wanted no facts which could be got by sending a reporter to an apartment on the north side of Beacon Hill.

Privately, of course, some of the "blue-bloods" got a tremendous "kick" out of Cornelia's story. Henry Cabot Winters came to dinner and spent a most interesting evening. Quincy Thornwell came, and loaded up with stories to tell to the guests at Mrs. Jack Gardner's. That was gossip, and gossip has always been the privilege of good society. But when it came to public utterances—to a newspaper interview, or a speech at some meeting—that was a different matter; that was Bolshevik propaganda, undermining the bases of American civilization. The word Bolshevism had become the worst of all terms of abuse, and covered everything in the modern world you did not like. The Massachusetts Chamber of Commerce issued a pronouncement to the effect that the new prohibition amendment was a Bolshevik conspiracy!

Rupert Alvin declined to meet his mother-in-law. He might have got from her first-hand information as to the outcome of his enterprise to overthrow the communist régime in Hungary, but he would not sacrifice his dignity by admitting that Cornelia's crazy jaunt could have even that much use. Rupert proposed to handle his mother-in-law and his daughter as he had handled the policemen's strike. The time for nonsense was past.

Deborah came to see her mother, and listened with painful reserve while Cornelia assured her that Betty was perfectly all right, and there was no need to worry. Betty was turning into a very fine woman, the best of the lot of them; she was doing a useful work in Buda-Pesth, and was justified in ignoring her father's cablegrams. Nor would she suffer because Rupert had cut off her funds. Her salary of thirty dollars a week was quite regal for any part of Central Europe. As for Cousin Letitia, she might become the wife of the elderly Hungarian playwright, Hubay, if the family would put up one or two thousand dollars for a "dot." Cornelia herself had had a most instructive experience; the world was changing, and her children would have to learn, as she had learned, to adjust their minds to new ideas.

Deborah pressed her tight lips together—for she had come with a stern resolve not to wrangle with her poor distracted mother. "We have done considerable adjusting of our minds this fall," she said. "We have seen crap-games on the Common, and machine-guns also. We have known what it feels like to

lie awake all night in fear of the murderous mob." And that
was true—for Rupert had not been able to convince his wife
of his complete mastery of the situation. Not even four private
policemen guarding her home had sufficed. Like most of the
ladies on Commonwealth Avenue, Deborah had looked under
all the beds that night, and had visions of her treasures being looted and her dignified person "nationalized."

IV

But if the capitalist press did not care to hear about the adventures of Mrs. Josiah Quincy Thornwell in Russia, rest assured that there were plenty of socialists, communists and
anarchists who did. Cornelia was besought to come and talk to
this group and that; she was urged to write down what she
had seen, and let it be printed in a pamphlet; and when she
consented, it meant that she had definitely committed herself
as a "Red," and was listed in the card-files of the Department
of Justice as an active Bolshevist. In the month of November
"red headquarters" in Boston was raided, with much uproar,
and everybody in it arrested and "held for deportation." Among
the truckloads of literature confiscated were some of Cornelia's;
and although Rupert was able to keep it out of the papers, he
brought the story home to the horrified family, and Deborah
conveyed to her mother the warning that she stood within the
shadow of arrest, and that her family's influence would not
again be used in her behalf.

Vanzetti spent an evening in the little apartment, and heard
all that Cornelia had to tell, and asked a hundred questions, and
carried her answers to the "gruppo" in Plymouth and the
"clooba" in East Boston. There were fierce debates going on
among the anarchists as to the attitude they should take to
the rapidly spreading soviet movement. Some were disposed
to weaken in their anti-state principles. Government was a bad
thing, so long as it was an instrument for suppressing workers;
but when it became an instrument for suppressing counter-
revolution, then it was no longer so easy to decide. But "in-
dividualistas" like Vanzetti stood immovable, and as a result,
many of them were in trouble in Russia; some had been shot,
and others were in jail. So Vanzetti hated the Russian govern-

ment as much as he hated the American, and was grieved by any good word that Cornelia had to say about it.

A very confusing situation! However, Cornelia had been watching the radical movement for four years now, and could talk the language of the different groups, and understand their reactions. That was more than the capitalist press could do, or the police, or the department of justice agents, or the courts, or any others who had the public ear in this crisis.

The job of "mopping up" the Reds was on in earnest. Congress had appropriated a couple of million dollars—which is the way to make things happen in America. All the big detective agencies were feeding at the trough, and the card-file of suspects now counted a total of two hundred thousand names—so the Attorney-General told a committee of Congress. This gentleman, oddly enough, was a Quaker, and under the combined banners of William Penn and Jesus Christ was instituting a campaign of wholesale terror, the like of which had not been known in America since the Iroquois Indians had been routed from upper New York state.

The prisoners taken in the November raids, together with a number of anarchists such as Emma Goldman and Alexander Berkman, were loaded onto an old government transport, the "Buford," and on the twenty-first of December this vessel, known to the newspapers as the "Soviet Ark," set forth for Russia. It was a beginning of the program recommended by all patriotic orators, "If they don't like this country, let them go back where they came from." Here and there you found one even more ardent—such as the statesman who said that he "would send them in a ship of stone with sails of lead"! Such was the "Christmas spirit," as manifested in America a year after the ending of the war to end war!

v

"Dear Nonna," wrote Vanzetti from Plymouth, "come to see us little bit for Christmas. All Italian anarchista is unhappy and fear will come truble for us after finish Russian. Is no more Cronaca, and no leader in New England since Galleani is deport. Would be good have you come for letting us know one American lady understand worker and is not afraid for speaking. Vincenzo got bottle good Dago Red in cellar, it is not prohibitioned, for was there before. Trando has learn new melody by violin, it is 'When you and I were young, Maggie.' Fay is putting corns on string for decorate, it is word not in book, but is white corns which produces noise on stove. Alfonsina is working now by cordage and I have expection of much business for Christmas, it is time for all Italian eating eel and I have order for barrel of living to be deliver from Boston. Your esteeming friend, Bartolomeo Vanzetti."

Christmas Day was on Friday, and Cornelia wrote that she could not come on that day, but would come Saturday morning and stay over Sunday. Not all the witch-hunts in New England could keep the Thornwell family from inviting her on Christmas Day, and from having their feelings hurt if she failed to appear. Clara, who had a monopoly on young children, was naturally the hostess, and "Hillview" the place. It was one of those great family reunions, when the clan say by their presence those things which are never said in words. Three faces were missing since last Christmas. Ahab would never be seen again; the spine of Great-aunt Priscilla had become solidified to such an extent that not all the pride in New England could bring her to a Christmas party; and Betty was in Buda-Pesth, handing out loaves of bread to the children of war-refugees.

"Hillview" was much changed from the day, now four and a half years past, when Cornelia had run away from it. James had kept his promise to leave the old part intact, but he had put on a monstrous new building in the rear, for the eight young ones and their numerous nurses and governesses and servants, as well as for guests—it was a luxurious hotel. The children were all over the place, racing about, shouting, bumping their heads on the hardwood floors, tramping nuts and raisins into priceless rugs, smearing chocolate candy on white brocaded upholstery. Christmas came but once a year, and one must not find fault; one must exchange sticky kisses, and admire a tree so tall that it went up to the second story, standing in the curve of the winding stairway. It shone with a myriad little lights, red, blue, green and yellow, and was piled around with enormous quantities of expensive toys, really marvels of ingenuity and workmanship, all of which would be broken and thrown on the junk-pile, or forgotten in the attic a month from now.

Also there were the grown-ups to be greeted: Clara, rounder than ever, lamenting that no arts of any specialist helped to reduce her; James, solid and matter-of-fact, expanding with his vast prosperity, and with the importance of himself as host. Not for a million dollars would he have said it in words, but his manner made clear that "Hillview" was no longer "Thornwell," it was "Scatterbridge." Deborah, stately in a creation of purple velvet; Rupert, with complexion to match his wife's dress, and a manner of impeccable cordiality to Cornelia, as if such a thing as a quarrel with a mother-in-law had never been heard of in Boston. Alice Thornwell Winters, whose elegance and grace paid no tribute to the passing years; Henry Cabot Winters, dapper and genial; their son, Josiah, still growing length ways, and pale—perhaps from overstudy, as his fond mother said, perhaps from what the savage Betty described as "woman-chasing." Also there was Deborah's older daughter, Priscilla, tall and dignified; it had been four years and more since she had raped the rug, and the crime was forgotten.

Not a word about Betty, nor anything else to humiliate Cornelia, or to remind her of her fall from grace. Unless you count Great-uncle Abner, poring over the *Transcript,* and commenting on a wireless dispatch from the "Soviet Ark," now four days at sea. "Says it's stormy, and the passengers are seasick." The deaf man's voice of Abner boomed from the library and filled all downstairs. "Well, I'd cure their seasickness if I had my way!"

"They say there's no cure for it known!" shouted Abner's son, Quincy.

"No cure?" Abner's voice broke into a hoot. "I can tell them a cure—dump the two hundred and forty-nine beggars overboard, and they'll be cured in a couple of minutes!"

There was a pause while the old man turned over the paper. When he broke loose again, it was the "crime wave," unfailing topic at all New England gatherings. "Country going clean to the dogs! See that story about the holdup in Bridgewater yesterday? Coming to a fine pass when a shoe-company can't bring its payroll from the bank without having shot-gun battles in the middle of the street! Read that?"

"Yes, I read it," said Quincy.

"Right out in the middle of Broad Street, corner of Hale—you know the place?"

"I know it."

"Big wide street, trees on both sides, trolley-car down the middle. And, by jingo, if two bandits in an automobile don't pop out and open fire on the pay-truck, just after daylight, half-past seven yesterday morning! *Transcript* says the police have no clew to the bandits. Wonder what police are for!"

"To go on strike, father."

"It's these foreigners!" And Uncle Abner leaned closer to his son's ear, which was not in the least deaf. "Infernal foreigners we've let come in and ruin the country! Sixty years I kept telling it to Josiah—ought to have stopped them. First Irish, then Jews, then Dagoes, then Hunkies, then God knows what. They've taken the country from us—the old stock might as well move out, they steal everything we've got. Ought to take every steamer that brought 'em over and make 'em take 'em back free, that's what I say!"

Did Uncle Abner know that Cornelia was in the music-room with the children, and hearing every word he shouted? Maybe so, for he was a shrewd old rascal, and you're only supposed to be polite when you know it. "Ought to ship 'em back where they came from, and all those sentimentalists that encourage 'em go along!"

VI

Cornelia left the palace of Thornwell-Scatterbridge, and went to the humble tenement in North Plymouth. Here too was Christmas, but on a minor scale. The tree was not quite up to Cornelia's shoulder, and the decorations were half a dozen red and yellow baubles, two for five cents at the grocery-store, a few strands of tinsel, some red ribbon off a package Cornelia had sent, and finally, long strings of snow-white "corns," with three pairs of small-sized but ravenous jaws waiting until Cornelia should have seen the spectacle before commencing the work of destruction. The presents, ranged under the tree for her inspection, were few and cheap—with the single exception of three fine story-books which had come from Boston. They were now set up conspicuously, and three children clamored their happy thanks.

The Brinis had long ago found out who Cornelia was; they knew that she came from a great rich family; yet not all the cruel "class consciousness" in the world could weaken their trust in her. It seemed to Cornelia that this offered some hint of how to avoid the stresses of the war between capital and labor; also for the bitter strife between the old Yankees and the new foreigners, and for the "crime wave," and many other troubles of the time. But when she told that theory to her friends of the great world, they called it "sentimental," and went on with their wiser and more practical plan of jailing and deporting and killing. Also most of the so-called "class-conscious" revolutionists would have agreed that Cornelia's program was "sentimental"; so apparently the jailing and deporting and killing had to continue.

They had a grand supper that Saturday night. Alfonsina had made bean-soup, which Vanzetti was "crazy about"—he admitted it; and budino, a kind of custard pudding, and tortellini, a dish of meat cooked in noodles. Vanzetti was a vegetarian on principle, because he thought it wicked to kill animals for food; but once in a while he fell from grace, and the occasion was apt to be tortellini. The animal was already dead, said Trando; but Bart would not permit that sophistry—when we ate meat, he said, we caused another animal somewhere to be killed, it was the law of supply and demand. He spoke of animals as his "fellow creatures," and this gave the children great glee; they would bring home a crab, or perhaps a big spider, and refer to it as "Bart's fellow creature." But that did not trouble the philosopher; he made it the occasion for a lecture on the wonders of nature. All these strange beings did really have a life like us, at least the beginnings of it; each one knew all the things it needed to know in order to take care of itself—and many a man was not so wise.

Vincenzo had given his wife a tiny glass bowl with three gold-fish for a Christmas present; and this stood now on a table in the little parlor, by the window, where the light shone through it. Bart was fascinated by these creatures, he would stand watching them literally for an hour at a time. He was wondering what it was like to be a gold-fish. If you dropped a bit of food into the bowl, the fish would know it and take it into their mouths; if it was not the right food, they would

spit it out again. What told them that? What had taught them
not to flee from a man's hand—though fish in the wild state
would do so? Did the fish know that man existed, and what
did they think about him? Strange questions one could ask about
life!

Trando got out his violin, and played "When you and I were
young, Maggie." So many sweet songs made you sad! The
little boy played it several times, and Bart hummed the words
which the children had taught him. A wonderful act of creation,
making a melody out of the chaos of all the scratchings that
were possible on four violin strings! The Brinis were so proud,
something fine was coming out of their lives, something better
than "working by cordage" all your life, better than "living like
pigs," as the Yankees phrased it.

"Some day maybe we get piano," said Bart. "Fay she learn
play, we have grand music."

"Oh, yes, we'll get a piano!" said Trando, and added, in
school-boy dialect, "I don't think!" He was twelve years old
now, and America was teaching him to be a little "fresh" at
times. "It'll be like that horse you were going to get me!" He
explained to Cornelia, "He promised me a horse to drive the
day before Christmas. He had a barrel of eels to deliver, and
I was to help him, and for two weeks he was telling me I'd
have a horse and wagon, and I didn't think about nothing else
all the time. But when the day come it was the same old push-
cart."

"It is baker got horse and wagon," explained Bart. "He
promise for rent heem one day, but then he cannot, so must
pusha da cart. Trando he see—what you call it, visione—heemself sit in seat, make noise with whip, 'Gittup!'—granda gentleman, all little Italian girl come look, say what is this, something wonderfool! But instead to crack whip, he musta carry
basket with package eel. He is little scare, for eel he is live and
make move—what you say?"

"Wiggle," put in Fay.

"Mooch wiggle!" said Bart. "Little boy tink maybe he come
out from paper, make bite!"

"No, I wasn't scared," said Trando, "but I knew they were my
fellow creatures and I didn't like to have them killed." They all
laughed—even Vincenzo, who did not understand jokes in

English. Bart, with his vegetarian scruples, was hard put to it to justify his conduct in having a barrel of his living fellow creatures shipped to him by express, and turning them over to the murderous fury of two score Italian housewives, who had skinned them alive and put them in salt for the next day's feast, as much a tradition with the Italians as turkey in all Yankee homes.

VII

Sunday morning they went for a walk—on the street, because the woods were full of snow. Coming home, Vanzetti bought a Boston newspaper, because he wanted to know what was happening in Italy. Cornelia read him a brief item, how the Italian workers were forming shop-councils, preparing to take over industry from the capitalists. They talked about this, and how it would happen in different countries. Vanzetti had made a speech in a hall in Plymouth. "I force-èd be spikker," he explained, because the man who was supposed to be "spikker" had such wrong ideas. Bart knew that any one who discussed anarchist ideals in public in these critical days ran risk of arrest, and of deportation or worse. But he would not be silenced, and Cornelia knew that he would not, and did not even suggest it. "Anarchista musta make propaganda!"

The children had got hold of the comic supplement, and were devouring it, laughing over the jokes and explaining them to their mother. This humor dealt with incipient young criminals, who perpetrated every indignity upon their elders. And meantime the elders were reading about the product of a previous decade of comic papers—the "crime wave" and its latest manifestations. There was more news about the Bridgewater holdup, which Cornelia had heard Abner Thornwell discussing. Bridgewater was only twenty-two miles from Plymouth, and in the same county, so the attempted robbery had been much talked about. Now the shoe-company was offering a thousand dollars' reward for the bandits, and Vanzetti remarked, "You offer plenty money, you catch plenty feller. Is always polissmen, witness, for swear poor feller in jail."

He went on to say, how stupid for people to be surprised by the crime wave. "You send million feller to Europe, you put heem in army, give gun, teach heem keell; you bring heem back, he go home, find some odder feller got his job, got his girl; he look for job, cannot find, he is hungry—you think he don't steal? Is foolish for not onderstand, is people do not want onderstand."

"You think the cause of crime is always economic?"

"Shoore, Nonna, I not think all men alike. Some men is strong, is got what you call—carattere—"

"Character."

"He will not do crime, he will die before do crime. But nodder man, he is weak, is too much tempt, he sees friend do crime, get plenty money, he try sometime, maybe get caught, he go jail. Is worst place for make criminal, is jail, is like school, learn how to do it. You go like me, Nonna, you work one job, work nodder job, meet onderd, meet thousand worker, you meet plenty young criminal, young feller vanaglorioso for what he do, think he is smart feller; I hear heem talk, I know what is make crime wave. Is great reech men, spend beeg money— automobile, gooda dress, fine lady—what you say, lusso—luxury. Poor feller, he look, he like to live sooch life, have plenty money, plenty girl. He say, 'How come it reech man he get it, how come in bég-ginnin' "—Bart accented the word on the first syllable—"how come in bég-ginnin' he make the money? Is reecha man honest? Is it sistema honest? He see everywhere beeg thief get plenty money, not ever punish. He see, you steal thousand dollar, you call-èd bandit, you steal million dollar, you call-èd banker. Is it not true, Nonna?"

Cornelia thought of Jerry Walker and his felt-plants. "It is sometimes true, Bart."

"All right, is injoostice. So long you have injoostice, is crime; more injoostice, more crime. Is like something you make in chimica—it come all time the same way. But reech man he not like to hear sooch thing, is better for heem call bad name, make polissman, put heem in blue clothe, give heem big cloob, send heem out to hit poor feller on head, put heem in jail. Big crime come, all right, get more polissman, make thousand dollar what you call it—reward—get plenty stool-pigeon, you onderstand?"

"Yes, I know what you mean."

"Is always rotten feller, swear anything for money, send somebody to jail. All polissman want is catch somebody, all newspaper want is catch somebody, fill up jail, so reecha man is happy, is what you call law and order. You wait, Nonna, you see—thousand dollar will make sure—catch plenty Bridgewater bandit!"

Strange and awful are the fates that dispose of mortals— leading us blindfolded through curtains of black fog. How could it happen that Bart could speak such words, and no shaft of lightning split the fog, no warning finger pierce the curtain, no voice shout in thunder-tones, "You! You! You!" They sat chatting casually, criticizing each other's theories; the children laughed, bringing them pictures of the Goofy Googles; Alfonsina washed the dinner dishes, and Vincenzo, not being able to share in the argument, fell asleep in his chair; the gold-fish wiggled their silken-filmy tails, and the Powers that sent the universe on its course, benevolent or heedless, omniscient or omninescient, sent no smallest hint of the fact that Bartolomeo Vanzetti was himself that "poor feller" whom the thousand-dollar reward was to bring down for the Bridgewater crime!

VIII

Cornelia went back to Boston, and found a letter from Betty:

"I have been having so many adventures, I hardly know where to start telling. I have been experiencing very eloquent and romantic love-making from one of the sons of 'Archie.' That is our nickname for the Austrian arch-duke who came in with the Roumanian armies and put himself on the throne, to the great dismay of the allies. This son is tall and somber and splendidly-idle. I can understand how it is that American husbands are found unsatisfactory. I try to imagine Father or Uncle James making such speeches! He pays endless compliments in carefully perfected English; but the trouble is he doesn't really know me at all. He is content that I am the daughter of a rich American banker; he doesn't guess my political opinions, and I dare not tell him, because I might lose my job! But it will be a good thing for His Highness to have his self-assurance reduced. He says that American girls are made of marble, and I smile and tell him it is his first contact with a social equal. Then I have to explain about the Back Bay!

"Also there is an undersecretary at the legation who is eating his heart out over me. He is quite different, rather tongue-tied, but serious, I fear. He comes from the middle west, and doesn't really know me either—though of course it is possible for him to understand how I can be virtuous though unchaperoned. I am also causing misery to a young lady of our mission, who is in love with the undersecretary. Apparently not all the troubles in Europe are enough to keep people from entanglements of the heart. I think it is rather the contrary, the general disorganization upsets everybody, and leaves the fancy roaming.

"While I am on the subject, I might mention that I was violently besieged by one of the Bolshevik agents before he took flight to Switzerland disguised as a chauffeur. He told me I was not truly a free woman at all, but a wretched little Puritan that would dry up and blow away at an early age. I showed him Cousin Letitia, who is still capable of being thrilled, but not of being seduced, even by the elderly playwright Hubay. There is something inside our marrow-bones, deeper than we realize, and stronger than our ideas. Roger Lowell would be surprised to hear that about me! Anyhow, I am sure there will be no love-affairs for me until I get back to America; it would be like a romance in a morgue.

"The suffering here is dreadful beyond words. I suppose you get news in the papers, but probably not true, because everything is propaganda for somebody or something. It really was the charitable Mr. Hoover who overthrew the Reds here in Hungary. I don't know if it is published at home, but here all his aides are proud of it, and tell the details and boast. We are managed by a California lawyer, one of Herbert's intimate friends, and they not merely blockaded and boycotted Red Hungary, but they bought some of the labor leaders to overthrow the Bolsheviks.

"It has been like a kaleidescope; you never know when you wake up in the morning who is governing you—till you get to the office and hear what happened during the night. The Reds went out, and then came the Roumanian army with 'Archie,' and we had to drive him out and get a White régime—which is rapidly turning into a dictatorship. Those poor fool labor-leaders who let themselves be used to turn out the Reds have mostly been shot or had their skulls cracked, and I wonder what our noble-minded Herbert thinks about it. There ought to be some way to make the White gentlemen come sit in the pools of blood, as we relief-workers have to do.

"It has taught me my lesson; 'law and order' talk will never fool me again. It really seems as if our master-minds want to teach labor that there can be no middle course, and no honesty or decency in the class struggle. The Reds here fell because they were too gentle, and let their enemies plot against them. The Russians made a clean sweep, so they survive. And don't let any one fool you about the amount of killing they did; don't let any one frighten you with talk about the 'mob.' From this time on I take the dear 'mob' to my heart; I am only afraid of dashing young gentlemen in gaudy uniforms, and elderly diplomats and business men in dinner-jackets. There isn't a country in Central Europe where the Whites haven't killed ten for every one the Reds have killed, and in many cases it has been a hundred for one.

"And the worst is, Grannie, these White dictatorships are all American-made—with guns and uniforms from our army and dollars from our bankers. They have got an American loan here in Hungary, and I am wondering if father is in on it. He probably won't tell you, but ask Uncle Quincy—he knows. If it's true, I'll never take another dollar from Father—and I'll tell him so.

"Dear Grannie, do please take care of yourself, because if anything were to happen to you, what would I do, with not a soul to understand me? Sometimes I get frightened, and get alone in my room and have a good cry; because, after all, it is absurd to think that a girl not yet twenty-one should know more than all her family put together. You know what Great-aunt Priscilla says, so very calmly: 'You will be wiser when you are older.'

"Maybe the 'antis' were right, Grannie—women are not meant to meddle in politics! Maybe we ought to stay at home and look after the babies, like Aunt Clara. But when we get the babies raised, the old men step in and send them off to the battle-field, so what's the use? I go over and over it in my mind, and the only conclusion is that this generation of girls must go on strike, and refuse to have babies until the men stop killing. So I shall stick it out, and when I come back the family will

find me worse than ever. I suppose you are having troubles
enough at home; tell me all, but write as if I did not agree with
your ideas. I have a way of getting this letter smuggled out, but
your letters to me may be opened, and I don't want to lose
my job quite yet."

IX

Yes, Cornelia had her troubles. The day after New Year's
there burst upon Boston and the whole country a storm known
as the deportations delirium. To the Quaker Attorney-General
had come a brilliant idea; he would win the Democratic nomination for the presidency, upon the basis of his heroic services
in deporting the Reds. The two million dollars which Congress
had voted him would be turned into a campaign fund for the
glory of Jesus Christ and William Penn.

The ingenious Quaker arranged to lure his victims into public meetings, and have the police appear suddenly and bar the
doors, and sort out all the foreign ones, and load them into
patrol wagons. The problem of getting the Reds all over the
country to come to meetings on the same night was comparatively simple, because the government had put so many spies
into the radical organizations that they had elected themselves
to office, and were in position to call meetings whenever they
pleased. Also they had been able to vote resolutions and adopt
manifestos of such violence as to make the deportations legally
possible. As Federal Judge Anderson of Boston said when the
facts came out in his court: "It is perfectly clear on the evidence
before me that the Government owned and operated a part, at
least, of the Communist Party." It was one time when all business men believed in government ownership!

The raids were scheduled for the night of January second,
1920, and netted some four thousand prisoners. Twenty cities
and towns in New England contributed a thousand—including
thirty-nine who had met for the purpose of organizing a co-
operative bakery. The prisoners were lined up against the walls
of police-stations, searched and beaten by detectives, denied
counsel, denied reliable translators, and sentenced on the spot
by officials of the Department of Immigration. They were loaded
into vans and taken to the immigration station in Boston, and

thence to Deer Island prison. In order to make the utmost possible amount of campaign material for the Quaker Attorney-General, the victims were chained together in pairs, and paraded down State Street, past the old State House, and over the rings of cobble-stones that mark the site of the Boston Massacre. Such a novelty brought newspaper photographers in swarms, and the story stayed on the front page for several days. Never such advertising for a presidential candidate.

Also the Department of Justice agents saw to it that good reading matter was supplied for the pictures. Four bombs had been found at one meeting, said the report; they were taken to a police station and put into a pail of water—and apparently dissolved in the water, for they were never heard of in court. Among the organizations raided was an amateur dramatic society, which had rented some old guns for use in a play; so the newspapers reported a "red arsenal." Apart from stage properties, the police acquired a total of four firearms: this by a search of four thousand persons, and raiding their homes and breaking into their trunks. Apparently they had selected for deportation the least military group of individuals in America.

Here were the troubles for Cornelia Thornwell. Four hundred men and women jammed into cells in Deer Island prison, with broken window-panes in the midst of New England winter, with no blankets, no mattresses, and no adequate toilet facilities. Husbands torn from wives, mothers separated from their babies—and all held according to the genial Spanish custom known as "incommunicado," denied lawyers, denied any information as to their fate. One woman, attending a meeting with her little girl, had been dragged to jail, and the child left to wander alone through the streets of Boston all that January night. One man flung himself over a railing five stories above the ground, and dashed out his brains in sight of the rest of the prisoners. Another went insane, and several others were on the verge. And concerning all this mass of misery no mention in the newspapers, and vilification for any one who dared to protest.

So Cornelia must sit at the telephone for hours, and argue and plead with her friends, and rush off to committee meetings, and get a stenographer and dictate letters, and pay for long telegrams to congressmen and senators and officials in Washington and New York. She must besiege club-women, and plead for opportunities to speak. She must meet newspaper reporters and give long interviews which never saw the light. She must haunt the doors of officials, and waylay them on the street when they would not see her. She must start a subscription list, and go round like a Salvation Army "lassie," irritating bankers and lawyers and merchants, and their wives and daughters in the Sewing Circle, abusing her social position in shameless fashion to get at people, and tell them such harrowing stories that they would put up good Brahmin money to buy blankets for Bolsheviks, and milk for starving babies whose mothers and fathers had committed the crime of belonging to political parties owned and operated by the Department of Justice.

And this no job of a few days, but of months. The Quaker presidential candidate was slow to realize that he could not produce evidence against eighty per cent of all those he had seized. In Boston, through an unfortunate oversight, there was a Federal judge who believed that law-enforcers ought to obey the laws they enforced. He declared from the bench that a mob was a mob, even when it was made up of Department of Justice agents. He would issue writs for one prisoner after another, and when the prisoner was able to prove that he was an American citizen, or that he hadn't actually joined the Department of Justice party, the victim would be turned loose. But all that took time—and meanwhile there were a thousand or two children to be fed, and as many falsehoods to be refuted, and only a small group of rebel ladies to do it.

X

Almost every Sunday during that winter Vanzetti came up to Boston. He was doing well with his fish-peddling, and in between times shoveling snow or cutting ice, so he had money for the trip and for propaganda. In the midst of all this repression he had made up his mind that the anarchistas must have a paper, and he was raising the seven hundred and fifty dollars needed to buy a linotype machine; he had even written a couple of articles to appear in the new paper, and was working hard to "culture himself," studying both Italian and English.

He came to have supper with Cornelia one evening, and when she ventured to point out the dangers of his course, he answered that you could never accomplish anything if you quit in times of danger. The times of accomplishment were bound to be times of danger—trust the capitalistas for that.

Many of the Galleani group had been deported; Coacci had been arrested—one of those two men who had brought a package of books to Bart—Cornelia had met him. The gruppo had raised a thousand dollars' bail for him, and now he was under sentence of deportation. Also Nick Sacco was making his plans to take his family back to Italy. Great events were coming this next summer—perhaps the real revolution—and Nick as a man of action wanted to be there.

Yes, it would not be bad to be sent to Italy just now; but alas, you didn't always get there! Bart told the terrible story of Compagno Marucco, who had been put on a steamer and never heard of again. All the anarchistas believed he had been pushed overboard on the way, because he had detected some of the government spies working among the group. Another man had hanged himself in his cell; had he really done that, or had somebody done it for him? You needed nerves of steel to go on with propaganda in the midst of events like that!

Bart talked about the spies. One had been exposed by Carlo Tresca in New York: Ravarini, who had posed as an anarchista for many months, one of the violent kind, a follower of Ravachol. One of his plans had been to revive "La Cronaco Sovversiva"; he had offered to get the money, and had suggested Bart for editor. But Bart had been too modest, he did not consider himself a well enough educated man.

This Ravarini had been seeking to fasten the bombings onto the Galleani group; for the government agents had apparently convinced themselves that this group was guilty. Bart discussed the idea, and he said there was no such great nonsense in the whole world. He pointed out what had happened—the police had arrested hundreds of anarchistas, and searched their homes, and had never found a bomb, nor anything having to do with a bomb. Some day the truth would come out—the guilt lay with detective agents, "feller get rich by hunting anarchista."

"You think they would kill innocent people?" asked Cornelia.

"Is not many people keell-èd, Nonna! Bombe blow up little piece of house, sometime when people is out, or sleep upstair and not get hurted. You want keell somebody, is not sooch difficultee, plenty people keell-èd all time, plenty Italian keell you cheap—what you call it, black hand. I know sooch feller, plenty, hear heem talk in café, vanaglorioso for what he do. He say, 'No sooch great keeller in whole state Massachusetts; nobody shoot so queeck, so straight.' You pay heem onderd dollar, next night your nemico he die. What for make big bombe, big noise?"

"But they sent bombs by mail, Bart!"

"Shoore, send mail—but he not put on stamp enough—the mail do not go! What follia, Nonna! Think, amica mia, how easy to find out what is postage! You not need take bombe to post-office, no sooch reesk—no, you go any post-office, any town, you say, what postage for take five pound, ten pound, twenty pound, what you like to send. You say, got package for New York, for Chicago, any place. You not go self, send odder man, send child, you get stamp, million people buy stamp. But see, Nonna—anarchista is sooch fool, he get dinnameet, he pay money, make twenty bombe, get address, send to this man, to odder man, send to Boston, New York, Lawrence, Passaic, all place—but not got sense for finding out ow mooch stamp! Is crazy thing, Nonna, is imbecillità!"

"You think government agents did it?"

"Not go-vérnment, but what you call private agent—big feller, make million dollar. He make big scare, Congress vote money, big banker get bad fright, he spend money, he say, you sava my life, you catch anarchista, you put heem in jail, so he not blow up the bank, he not keell me. Look, amica mia, you read paper, you see this morning, big banker make—what you call —notizia—avviso—"

"Advertisement."

"Avvertisament, whole page, scare people, say polissman must catch the red, the bomber, the anarchista, musta deport, must put in jail. Is patriottismo, militarismo—you see in paper?"

Yes, Cornelia had seen it, and not for the first time; it had become quite the fashion for groups of leading citizens, bankers, merchants, the Chamber of Commerce or other civic groups, to publish full-page advertisements warning the public of the imminent danger of red riot and insurrection. "Yes, I read it," she told Bart—but was ashamed to add that among the signers that morning was Rupert Alvin, her son-in-law, and John Quincy Thornwell, her nephew-in-law!

XI

Almost a year had passed since the mailing of those "May Day bombs," and still the police had not succeeded in catching any of the senders; so naturally there was dissatisfaction on the part of patriots. What was the purpose of a huge secret service agency, built up at enormous expense? The loyal newspaper publishers forbore to express impatience in print, but privately they were outraged. A first-class red scare meant millions in increased sales, but how could the most ingenious editors and reporters keep excitement alive without a few facts?

The Department of Justice had one set of clews. A bomb had blown out the front of the home of the Attorney-General, the Quaker gentleman who was planning to move to the White House, and the man who carried this bomb had apparently himself been blown up. The authorities claimed to have identified the fragments as belonging to an Italian anarchist by the name of Valdinoci, one of the Galleani group. He had worn sandals, and in his pockets had been some leaflets in crude English, proclaiming anarchist ideas. The purpose for which the spy Ravarini had been set to work was to find the printing office in which this circular had been set up.

Ravarini sent contributions of money to Malatesta in Italy, and got letters from him, and then appeared among the comrades in Boston and New York, a very ardent Red, with literature to be printed, and precise ideas as to how it was to look. He would hang about an anarchist print-shop for several weeks, and have his stuff set up many times, or would come and set it up for himself. In this way he tried all the type in several printing offices; and at last in a shop in Brooklyn he found, or claimed to find, what the Department of Justice believed was the type from which the Valdinoci leaflets had been printed. It was the office of an anarchist paper called *Il Domani*— "To-morrow"—and the printers of this paper, two Italians by the name of Salsedo and Elia, were arrested and taken to the offices of the Department of Justice in the Park Row Building in lower New York.

The genial custom of holding prisoners without allowing them to communicate with their friends or even with an attorney is one for which we have neglected to invent an American name. But for the custom of torturing prisoners to make them confess, we have our jolly slang, "the third degree," and all judges and lawyers in America know that it is employed, and all pretend not to know it, and when evidence obtained by torture is produced in court, all judges and lawyers solemnly accept it, and at the same time go on believing in the constitutional rights of accused men. It is obvious that in no other way can the system of inequality of property be maintained, and any one who denounces the "third degree" is liable to suspicion of "redness."

Salsedo and Elia were held for three weeks in the Department of Justice offices with no warrant of law. At last Salsedo succeeded in smuggling out a letter to Vanzetti, who took it to the anarchist group in Boston. They knew without being told that the two men were being tortured, for the purpose of forcing them to implicate other anarchists in bombing plots. On Sunday, April 25th, there was a meeting of the group and it was decided that somebody must go to New York to consult with the comrades there and see what could be done for the victims. The choice fell upon Vanzetti, and he went, and called upon Carlo Tresca, editor of *Il Martello,* whom he had never seen before. "Don't you know me, Carlo?" he said, gently. "I am Vanzetti." He had been sending in collections for the support of the paper, and occasionally writing articles. Tresca embraced him and kissed him on both cheeks, Italian fashion.

The two of them set out down the street: Vanzetti no small man, but outtowered by his companion, whom the strike-police used to call "the bull." In Mesaba, where the Back Bay families of Boston were holding onto their hills of copper, they framed him for first degree murder, and kept him in jail for nine months. They put three bullets into him, at different times. One side of his face was disfigured, and during the Paterson strike a newspaper published his picture with the caption, "Who Will Be a Good Citizen and Make the Two Sides of This Face Alike?" Seven times they arrested him during this desperate strike of the silk-workers. Now the Department of Justice was anxious to get him again, and was soon to do it—for the crime of demoralizing Italian Catholic women by a two-line advertisement of a pamphlet on birth control!

Carlo and Bart were going to see an Italian lawyer who had been hired to help Salsedo and Elia; he had offices directly underneath the Department of Justice rooms—an arrangement that Carlo found suspicious. But it was a problem how to change, because Carlo could not get to the prisoners, and Salsedo's wife had been so terrified by the detectives that she did not know what to do. They saw the lawyer, and Carlo wrote a note for the prisoners, and the lawyer took it upstairs, and came back and reported that Elia had refused to read it, and Salsedo was "getting crazy" and would not answer any questions. This confirmed their worst fears, so they consulted an American lawyer, connected with the Civil Liberties Union, who agreed to seek an interview. Bart said he would go back to Boston and send fifty dollars of his own money, and raise more to pay the lawyer.

There was one other thing Bart wanted to do in New York—to see the Statue of Liberty. He had missed the sight when he had come to this country, because his steamer had arrived in a fog. And while it was true that America was not living up to this statue, still it was a world symbol of the cause to which Bart was dedicating his life. But they were too late for the boat which goes out to Bedloe's Island, and Bart was so much disappointed he almost had tears in his eyes. "All the years I have wanted to see it!" he said to Carlo.

XII

The day Vanzetti went to New York Cornelia spent packing two trunks. There had come a quite amazing telegram from Betty in Vienna: "Letitia married Hubay my color discovered job flooey tired need recreation come immediately positively summer Italian lake reply Hotel Royal." Cornelia called up Deborah, and first read the message and then translated it; and after Deborah had voiced indignation at the treason of a poor relation, and horror at the idea of her daughter unchaperoned in a center of notorious gayety, she asked what

Cornelia was going to do, and actually hinted for her to join Betty. So much had four years of defeat tamed the family!

Cornelia had been exerting herself beyond her strength. She was sixty-five years old now—as her daughters never failed to remind her—and for four months she had not rested a day. A summer on an Italian lake with Betty for company sounded very good, and she said she would go, and Deborah undertook to have her husband use his influence to get some kind of special passport immediately, and to engage passage on a steamer, and even pay for it. Cornelia and Betty would be taken back into the family again, and have the services of all-powerful males to make smooth their paths in whatever part of the world they chose to roam.

The *Floritania* was to sail from New York on Saturday afternoon, and on Friday morning Vanzetti telephoned to Cornelia, still in Boston. He had just arrived from New York and wanted to tell her the news. She asked him to lunch with her, and heard from his lips the terrible story of Salsedo and Elia. She knew the former of these two men, who had worked as a printer in Boston, and had come to the "picanics": a frail little fellow, suffering from tuberculosis—"he very bad now," said Bart; "wife she think they keell heem." Bart had been to the savings-bank that morning and drawn out fifty dollars and sent it to Carlo, according to his promise; and Cornelia said she also would contribute fifty, and wrote a check. She felt quite rich that day, having several of Rupert's handsome and impressive bank-drafts.

It seemed a shame to be going away for a holiday in a crisis like this. But Bart said instantly that Cornelia must not think of it; he agreed with her daughters that she was an old lady, and needed a rest, and nothing should interrupt it. He talked about the Italian lakes, not very far from where he had been born. "Sooch lovely countree! Gooda people, work hard, live simple, naturale. You be happy, live outdoor, walk in wood, pick little flower, send to me. I pick you mayflower, send heem in letter." Then he added, "Maybe I come, we take little boat in Italian lake, Comrade Betty she sing little song! I think I like be deport!"

"Take care of yourself, Bart!" said Cornelia. "If you want to come, pay your fare, so then you can return."

Bart laughed, and made his usual answer: "Anarchista musta make propaganda!" She learned that even in the midst of these perils he was organizing meetings and distributing literature. He was working with that Italian, Boda—"you know heem, little feller, macaroni salesman, he drive us one time for see dramma when we go Nick Sacc'."

"I remember him."

"He is got same little car. Is go bust in winter, but now he get heem fixit, pretty soon he drive heem, we distriboot the books!" And Bart laughed, like a bad boy. "Book wit' red cover what so scare polissman—you remember book is bring Coacci and Orciani one time in Plymouth?"

"Yes, very well."

"Is very bad book, molto pericoloso, is red anarchista cover, 'Faccia à Faccia col Nemico.' Is reason for deporting Coacci— they find six copy by heem, he say is the reason. He is gone two week now, maybe is Italy. I get hees what you say—address —he got wife and children leav-èd behind in Brockton. You maybe see heem in Italy."

"Have you got any of those books in your house, Bart?"

"Shoore, two, t'ree copy, sell heem sometime. Nick Sacc' is got more. Nick he is not 'fraid, he go anyhow, is got pass-port, ticket, all fixit. You not see Nick in Italy, he live in Sout', way down in what you call boot. He is happy feller, go Italy. Is got fifteen onderd dollar save in bank—wife, she make heem sava ten dollar all week. Now he go see rivoluzione, maybe help. Is young feller, can not stay here when sooch great time come, can not be happy for trim edge of pretty shoe for fine gentle-man!"

"You really think there's a revolution coming in Italy?"

"You watch, maybe see heem! Great sight for Yankee lady —nobody harm you. Italian worker, he think America is free countree, good countree—he think he make Italy be countree like America! He do not know what happen to poor wop in Massachusett, he not read in paper how Department of Joostice agent take poor seeck printer, torture heem, beat heem, to make heem tell what Joostice agent want to be tell-èd!"

So it was with Bart—difficult to make jokes, or to plan for a holiday, because all brain-paths led to these dreadful cruel-ties and sufferings. Impossible to enjoy a luncheon, neatly served by a much-puzzled Negro maid! No, Bart would begin to twist bread-crumbs into little pellets, which was very bad manners; his look would grow abstracted and far off, and Cornelia would understand that he was up in the fourteenth story of the Park Row Building in New York, where two comrades might at that moment be hanging by their thumbs, or having their arms twisted behind their backs.—As a matter of fact they were being beaten in the face with blood-stained shoes, said to have been worn by the bomber who had been blown to fragments in front of the home of the Quaker Attorney-General. It was a refinement of imagination difficult for an uncultured Italian to foresee.

XIII

That night there was a theater-party, given by Rupert Alvin to serve notice upon the world that all was well between himself and his departing mother-in-law. They sat, very conspicuous, in a box, Cornelia, Rupert and Deborah, their daughter Priscilla, Cornelia's nephew-in-law, Quincy Thornwell, and her second daughter, Alice Thornwell Winters, who had given up her latest adorer in deference to the family's demands, and was now being rewarded in this public manner. They saw an expensive and highly sophisticated comedy from New York, dealing with people of their own social station who did not have to give up anything, not even one another's wives. After which the Alvin limousine rolled to the station, and Cornelia and Deborah took the midnight train to New York.

Next morning they drove in a taxi-cab, and inspected the fashionable shops, and Deborah bought a few things, but Cornelia did not buy, because everything would be so much cheaper abroad. They lunched at one of the fashionable hotels, and took another taxi to the steamer; and on the way Cornelia said to the driver, "Where is the Park Row Building?"

"Way downtown, ma'am, by City Hall Park."

"We don't go near it?"

"Not unless you want to make a trip."

"Never mind," said Cornelia; and her daughter asked, "Why are you interested in the Park Row Building?"

"Oh, nothing; a couple of friends of mine have been tortured there for the past three weeks."

It was like that with Cornelia nowadays—impossible to carry on polite conversation, to enjoy any sort of holiday. Deborah had to shut her lips tight together, and pretend she had not heard. And pretty soon there was the mighty steamer; the crowds, and the partings, and the waving of handkerchiefs, and the promises to take good care of yourself, and to write often, and to give my love to So-and-so; and then a tear or two, and the gangways coming up, and the great steamer sliding out into the river, and the tugs straightening it for the journey. And then the long panorama of towering white and gray buildings, the magical sky-line of Manhattan—

Did ever a dream-city rise from the sea
That was fairer, more fleeting and fragile than she?

But Cornelia missed all the poetical ecstasies, because she was thinking, "Which is the Park Row Building? And which is the fourteenth story?"

But there was no one to ask, and soon the sky-line faded, and there was the Statue of Liberty, and she thought of Bart, and what it meant to him. Then came the ocean, and the rolling of the ship, and she was in her state-room for two days. When she came on deck again, there was the daily newspaper, published from wireless reports for the benefit of the vessel's leisure class; and Cornelia read that at three o'clock on the morning of the third of May, an Italian anarchist by the name of Salsedo, held by the Department of Justice for complicity in the bomb explosions of a year ago, had committed suicide by throwing himself from the fourteenth story of the Park Row Building in New York.

No more details of such a horror, to trouble the sleek and contented passengers of the *Floritania*. But two more days passed, and the ship's newspaper contained another item, this time from Brockton, Massachusetts. Two Italians, leaders of a bandit-gang, had been nabbed by the police, charged with the murder of the paymaster and a guard of the Slater and Morrill shoe factory of South Braintree, and the theft of a payroll of sixteen thousand dollars. It was believed that this band had been responsible for numerous payroll hold-ups in Eastern Massachusetts during the past year, and the police expected to nab the other members within a few hours. Cornelia read this, but it meant nothing special, for there was hardly a day that papers did not report hold-ups from some part of the country; and in this case the news-service had not thought it worth while to mention that the names of the two arrested men were Nicola Sacco and Bartolomeo Vanzetti.

CHAPTER 8

THE DETECTIVE MACHINE

I

O fates that hold us at your choice,
How strange a web ye spin!

Thus the poet; and never more aptly than of that web which the fates wove about the lives of Nicola Sacco and Bartolomeo Vanzetti. Their two friends Cornelia and Betty were to spend the better part of seven years trying to disentangle this web; laying bare a story which for mystery and melodrama has few equals. The narrative goes back to the previous Christmas, two days prior to Cornelia's last visit to Plymouth.

At six o'clock on the morning of December 24, 1919, Bartolomeo Vanzetti had been asleep, when one of his customers, Balboni, coming home from night-work, stopped by to get his Christmas eels. Mrs. Fortini, Bart's landlady, woke him up, and he sold the eels to Balboni, and then dressed, and swallowed his bread soaked in coffee, and got out his little hand-cart and his scales and his basket and his packages of live eels, all weighed and wrapped the day before. He had more than forty orders to fill, because he was selling Christmas eels for thirty-five cents a pound, whereas in Boston the Italians were paying as high as a dollar and a quarter. He delivered several packages before daylight; Mrs. Augusta Niccoli was still in bed, and called to him to put the package on the kitchen table; she would pay later.

Soon after seven o'clock came Beltrando Brini, having gobbled his breakfast, excited because he was to have the baker's horse to drive. He met Bart on the street, expecting to go with him to the baker's; but Bart insisted that the ground was wet, and Trando must run back home and get his rubbers. It took the boy fifteen or twenty minutes to find them in the attic; meantime Bart met the elder Brini, coming home from night-work; and then went to Bastoni, the baker, and was told that the latter

219

could not spare the horse and wagon—a development which caused much grief to the twelve-year-old Trando. This was at seven-forty-five, as the baker remembered, because at the moment Bart entered his home the whistle of the cordage company blew, and no one who has guided his life by that whistle ever thereafter fails to hear and heed it. "The whistle is our bread and butter," said Bastoni.

It was during those same fateful minutes between seven-thirty and seven-forty-five that there occurred what is known to history as "the Bridgewater crime." In the town of Bridgewater, some twenty-two miles from Plymouth, a truck belonging to a shoe-company came rolling down Broad Street. It contained the payroll for the week, and was driven by a chauffeur and guarded by two other men. As it neared the corner of Hale Street, there was an automobile standing, and two bandits sprang out and opened fire. The guards returned the fire, and there was a battle for a minute or two; until a street-car came down the slight grade—the motorman having run back into the car to hide from the bullets. The street-car came between the bandits and the truck, and frightened the bandits so that they ran, and leaped into their auto, and sped away. No one was hurt, so the "Bridgewater crime" was classified as "attempted robbery."

The shoe-company employed the Pinkerton agency, and within a few hours the Pinkerton men were on the spot, interviewing every one who had witnessed the attempt. Their reports were known to the prosecution, but not to the defense in the case until six or seven years later. The reports proved that the witnesses of the crime could not agree upon essentials, not even as to the make of the bandit-car. As for description of the bandits, there was a wide range of choice, and the statements of all four leading witnesses varied greatly from what they were later to testify on the witness-stand concerning the crime.

Being balked of clues, and at the same time hounded by clamor and tempted by rewards, the authorities resorted to that method which is the mainstay of American police procedure— the "stool pigeon." Underworld characters are paid to bring the gossip of their cafés and hang-outs. So-and-so has got a new car; So-and-so-other has given a diamond ring to his girl; So-and-so-else was heard to say that he did such-and-such a job. It is manifest that such clues are open to suspicion; jealousy and revenge play a large part in them; yet, reënforced by the "third degree," they form the method by which a good part of the population of capitalist prisons is recruited. The "stools" were active in this Bridgewater crime; and what they brought affords a problem for students of the occult and the mystical. Let historians investigate and psychologists weigh and philosophers speculate and make what they can of the fact: the Sacco-Vanzetti case, which echoed like a series of detonations around the world, which was destined to cause windows to be smashed in American legations in Buenos Ayres and Geneva, and taxi-cab drivers to throw their fares into the faces of American ladies in Paris—this cause célèbre had its origin in a "detective machine" invented by an underworld character, and looked into by an unnamed Italian woman in East Boston.

To the Pinkerton agents came a "stool" with the rumor that a certain A. C. Barr could tell about the Bridgewater crime. So there was a hunt for A. C. Barr—height five-feet-ten, weight 175 pounds, age forty, eyes dark, hair black, and so on. When found, the person proved to be an Italian—Angelo Christoforo Barragini, or words to that effect. He was questioned, and said, yes, he did know about the crime. How had he learned it? He had invented a "detective machine," with which you could solve crime mysteries. It consisted of a crystal globe into which you looked, and you there saw the crimes happening. A woman in East Boston had used it and had seen the Bridgewater hold-up, committed by Italians who lived in a little house on the outskirts of a town; there were four or five of them, and they were dark, and had a car which they kept in a shed in back of the house.

Now, detectives are paid by the day while they are working, and this has a tendency to stretch out their assignments. They followed up this "detective machine" clue, taking into their confidence Mike Stewart, the worried chief of police who kept the town of Bridgewater in order between bandit-raids. Mike, a burly "small-town cop," red-faced, heavy-lidded, good-natured but not abnormally brilliant, took the detectives in his car, and they drove about inspecting little houses inhabited by Italians on the outskirts of towns. They found several, and were suspicious of one, and caused alarm to the occupants; but they found nothing definite. The Pinkerton reports were turned in, and the Bridgewater crime was listed among the unsolved mysteries in Massachusetts police history. The "detective machine" was stowed away in the subconsciousness of Mike Stewart, ready to pop up again sometime—according to the laws of the subconsciousness, understood in all psychological laboratories.

II

Three months later, on April fifteenth, came another sensation, known to history as "the South Braintree crime." In another "shoe-town," at three o'clock in the afternoon, the paymaster of the Slater and Morrill company took the pay-money, about $16,000 in two steel boxes, and accompanied by a guard, started to carry it from the office to the factory, a distance of a couple of blocks. They were passing another factory, the Rice and Hutchins, when two foreign-looking men who had been lounging by the railing suddenly drew guns and opened fire point-blank. They put four bullets into one victim, killing him at once, and so wounded the other that he died the next day. They picked up the boxes of money, and at the same instant an automobile came rushing up the street and slowed, and the two bandits sprang in and were driven away at high speed, shooting at the bystanders as they went.

This very brutal and successful crime caused great excitement in the factory towns which lie to the south of Boston. So many raids had occurred during the past year, no town knew when its turn might come. Rewards were offered, and again the Pinkerton detectives came and made their investigations and turned in reports. Just as in the Bridgewater case, the numerous witnesses disagreed about essential details of what they had seen. They could not describe the car. One said Hudson, others said Buick; one said green, another said dark blue, others said black; one said shiny, another said spattered with mud. Many witnesses made statements quite different from what they afterwards made on the stand. So here was another unsolved crime —and a great clamor of the public, demanding to know what police were for. There was no clue—save only a memory lurking in the subconsciousness of Mike Stewart, waiting for a chance to pop up!

It so happened that the day after the South Braintree crime, while all the countryside was ringing with the horror of it, there came to see Mike Stewart a Federal immigration officer, looking for an Italian anarchist by the name of Coacci, a shoe-worker sentenced to deportation and out on bail; his time was up, but he had failed to appear, and the officer had come to arrest him, and according to the custom he asked for Mike's help. So Mike sent a man with him to the Coacci home, which happened to be a little house on the outskirts of a near-by village.

They found the shoe-worker with an oval-shaped tin suitcase strapped and ready, the inevitable green umbrella on top. Also there was another Italian, a boarder by the name of Boda. Coacci had pleaded for delay because his wife was sick; but here was his wife, she wasn't sick, and Coacci admitted that that had been a pretext, he had wanted a few more days to settle his affairs. Now he was ready to go. It was late at night, and the immigration officer said to wait till to-morrow; but Coacci said no, he would go now and get it over with. Some one was taking his wife to stay with relatives, and he was all packed up, and would like to get the next day's steamer from New York.

They went, and Mike Stewart heard about it, and sat in his office and thought it over. It was midnight, a time for ghosts and goblins. Strange that a man should insist upon being taken away from a country so great and so rich as America! This fellow Coacci was a Red, and the weekly paper in Bridgewater was running a series of articles, prepared by the Department of Justice, telling the small-town population of America the crimes which the Reds were committing all over the world. Mike pondered; and suddenly there occurred a phenomenon understood in all psychological laboratories—there popped into his memory the woman in East Boston who had looked into the "detective machine"! Here was a little house on the outskirts of a town, occupied by Italians! In a flash the whole story came to Mike: Coacci had been in on the South Braintree crime, and the reason he was so anxious to get away was that he had the sixteen thousand dollars!

With another officer Mike went to the Coacci house, and there was Boda, five feet-two inches high, swarthy, with a little black mustache, soft-spoken, polite, chatty; a macaroni salesman, he told Mike; and his car was an Overland, a small car, just now laid up for repairs. Yes, he had a gun, and he let Mike examine

it—a .32 Colt. There were no signs of crime, so Mike went off
and pondered some more, and then telephoned to New York
and learned that Coacci had sailed for Italy. They found a trunk
which he had left, and they broke it open, but found no payroll
money, only a few pieces of shoe-leather, which some shoe-
workers consider they have a right to "swipe" from the company
when they get a chance.

Mike decided to arrest Boda, so he went to the house, but
now it was empty. Boda had disappeared, and the police found
that suspicious. But his little Overland car was in Johnson's
garage in West Bridgewater, and Johnson was told to detain
whoever came for the car, and thus have a chance at the rewards.

So the trap was set; and two weeks later came an Italian by
the name of Orciani, driving a motor-cycle with a side-car containing Boda. At the same time by street-car came two other
Italians, Sacco and Vanzetti. All four were anarchists, members
of the Galleani group; they had made this rendezvous at Johnson's garage, for a purpose which was to be a subject of controversy for the next seven years.

They went to Johnson's house, and found that the car was
repaired, but had no license plates for the present year, so
Johnson advised them not to drive it; he kept them talking,
while his wife ran to a neighbor's and telephoned to the police.
But the four men became suspicious and went away. Bart and
Nick took the trolley to Brockton, and while they were on the
outskirts of the town a police officer entered the car and drew
a gun and ordered them, "Hands up!" Then was the time for
them to make use of the weapons they carried; for Bart to put
into effect his threat of not being taken alive. But alas, it
was as Alfonsina Brini had predicted, he didn't know anything
about using a gun. Pretty soon came a second officer, and the
prisoners were taken to the police station and locked in cells.

For years Bart had studied the life and death of "Comradda
Gesu," and "made tears" for him. And now came a strange
coincidence. The first action of one of the policemen, upon having got this criminal safe behind bars, was to come to the door
of the cell and call him. Bart came, meekly, and looked through
the bars, whereupon the other spat full in his face.

The reason for this action was that among the documents
found on Bart was a letter from an anarchist friend, referring

to the evil actions of a certain priest, whom the writer called
"a pig." The policeman had spat in defense of his religion, and
turned away, fully satisfied in his Catholic soul. His priests had
not taught him to read the life and death of Jesus; they had
taught him that Jesus was a God, and if you had asserted that
Jesus was a working-class agitator, he would have wanted to
spit in your face also. But Vanzetti knew what had happened
to "Comradda Gesu" on the cross, and he wiped his face clean,
and sat upon the cot in his cell, with cold chills running up and
down his spine.

III

Sitting in their separate dungeons that first dreadful night,
a common thought was in the minds of both Sacco and Vanzetti. Less than three days had elapsed since their comrade,
Salsedo, had thrown himself, or had been thrown, to his death.
Were they going to share his fate? One duty was obvious—to
avoid saying anything that would involve other comrades. So
when they were cross-questioned, they denied that they knew
Boda, denied that they knew Orciani, and told lies as to where
they had been and what they had been doing. These lies were
easily exposed, and constituted the famous "consciousness of
guilt," upon which the prosecution was to insist for seven years.
     In spite of all fears, Vanzetti had refused to give up his
appeal to the workers. "Anarchista musta make propaganda!"
He had planned a meeting for the ninth of May, four days off,
in Brockton, and had drafted a circular, which Nick had in his
pocket. So the police had something else to study and discuss:
a series of questions, crude, yet with a primitive eloquence that
disturbed even the dullest mind. "You have fought all the wars.
You have worked for all the capitalists. You have wandered over
all the countries. Have you harvested the fruits of your labors,
the price of your victories? Does the past comfort you? Does
the present smile on you? Does the future promise you anything? Have you found a piece of land where you can live like
a human being and die like a human being? On these questions,
on this argument and on this theme, the struggle for existence,
Bartolomeo Vanzetti will speak."
     It is an old idea, and has been haunting the minds of dreamers

tor thousands of years; you may find it voiced by the prophet
Isaiah twenty-five hundred years ago. "And they shall build
houses, and inhabit them; and they shall plant vineyards, and
eat the fruit of them. They shall not build, and another inhabit;
they shall not plant, and another reap." It is interesting as a
symptom of the mental state of the time, that shortly before the
arrest of Sacco and Vanzetti, a Christian clergyman in the city
of Winnipeg, Canada, had been indicted for the crime of quoting
these ancient Hebrew words!

Among the questions asked of Bart and Nick was: "Are you
an anarchist? Are you a communist? Do you believe in the overthrow of the United States government by violence?" These
were the conventional deportation questions, and were reassuring to the prisoners in fear of torture. Bart answered them
gently and tactfully. "I like things a little different," said he!
When a friend came to see him next day, he smiled and said,
"Well, I get free trip to Italy!" So it was that Cornelia and
Betty, enjoying their second week of vacation, received a letter
from Fay—fifteen years old now, and quite a cultured young
lady:

"Dear Nonna:

"I write to tell you the sad news that Bart and Nick Sacco
are in the police station at Brockton. Bart asked to tell you he
is not treated bad, except for being spit on once. The lawyer
says he will be surely deported, because the police got a circular
which he wrote about a meeting to protest about the killing of
Salsedo. Bart says tell you he is happy because he will come
to see you soon, and please stay on the Italian lake and do not
worry, because you have worked too hard and should have a
rest. As Nick was going anyhow it will save him the fare so
it is all right. I write in a hurry not knowing when there goes
a steamer, and Bart is afraid you might read it in the paper
and be worried."

That was all for a week; then another letter:

"I am sorry to have to say that the arrest of Bart and Nick
is worse than what I wrote you. The police pretend to think that
they drove an automobile and shot two men and stole a pay-

roll in South Braintree last month. It is so silly that we cannot believe it yet, and Bart himself does not believe it, he says it is just to get something on him to deport. The comrades here have all paid money and engaged a lawyer to get him off. Bart insists that I must tell you there is nothing to worry for, as he was in Plymouth all that day and talked with many people, like Mr. Corl who was fixing a boat. And of course when they know about Bart they will not think he could be a bandit. It will make you laugh to hear the police are quite sure that Bart was the driver of the bandit-car, as you know that he never had anything to do with a machine, and papa says he is so clumsy he cannot drive a wheelbarrow. The comrades have found a rich store-keeper who will put up bail, so we hope to have Bart with us again soon. Please write him a nice letter in our care and tell him you are not worrying, because it is something he talks about each time we see him, that your vacation must not be spoiled for him. You know how like him that is, thinking about everybody else but his own trouble."

IV

From Italian lakes the land goes back by stages, rising higher and higher into the sky, and each stage has been taken in charge by generations of strong arms and backs, and made into orchards and gardens. Every smallest corner of soil has been terraced and buttressed with walls, and dug and planted with a row of olive trees—or a row of onions—up to where the bare rocks stick out and the white clouds gather. Here and there in sheltered places are cabins built of stone, and in them women breed prolifically, and send their progeny to Massachusetts to be known as "wops."

The lakes are blue, and the sky almost as deep a blue; by the middle of May it is summer, and all the land is bursting with vegetation of a thousand shades of green and olive-gray. The air is balmy, and ladies from Europe and America put on gay dresses and wander about in the gardens of villas and hotels, or drift on the water in little boats, holding bright parasols overhead to protect their creamy complexions. Everything is peaceful, and it is possible to float and sing "Kennst du das Land?"—and have no idea that the peasants on the hillsides are

seething with hatred of their landlords, and forming coöpera-
tives and revolutionary societies, preparing to dump off their
backs the age-old burden of parasitism.

Here in a little inn by the water-side Cornelia found her
granddaughter Betty Alvin, carefully chaperoned by Joe Randall,
American socialist journalist aged twenty-eight, and Pierre
Leon, French communist editor aged forty-four. In the days
before the war if a young lady from the Back Bay had traveled
about Europe with two gentlemen, she would have caused herself to be ostracized for life; and maybe it was still so, Betty
wasn't sure—but she was sure that she didn't want to know
any one who didn't want to know her. These two men between
them had much important information, so she had begged them
to come to this Italian lake while she waited for Grannie.

Pierre Leon was stocky and broad-shouldered, with a rosy
face and black mustache twisted to points. He had lived for
years in London teaching French, and in Berlin teaching English; he knew enough Italian to attend labor meetings, and now
was studying Russian because revolutionary events demanded it.
He had been an anarchist, then an anarcho-sydnicalist, for a
long time a left wing socialist, and now was a communist suspected of a right wing deviation. He had read most books that
had ever been published on these subjects, and most good literature besides; he could talk brilliantly about anything, and liked
nothing so much as having some one to argue with until three
in the morning. He was supposed to be resting for his health,
but it was difficult for Cornelia to see where either health or
rest came in, for he lit one cigarette from another, and would
work all morning writing an article, study labor and radical
papers all afternoon, and argue all night about what he had
read.

His qualifications as chaperon for an American young lady
were peculiar. He took toward all women the attitude of the
continental male, and this had caused in the American young
lady a vigorous reaction, which in return had caused in the continental male an amused curiosity. Said Betty, "He thinks the
purpose of woman is to submit herself, and that every woman
will, if the man is fascinating enough. But I have made him
understand that I'm a queer little New England old maid, so
now he's a good sport and studies me." Betty added that Grannie

was not to dislike Pierre on that account, because it was his environment, all European men were that way, especially since the war—the only difference was that the radical men could let you alone, because they had other things to think about, whereas the leisure-class men had nothing to do but chase women.

Joe Randall came from Virginia, and had wavy brown hair and a charming slow drawl. Cornelia had met him in Russia, so she knew his story; he had come as a young college graduate to an attaché's position in our legation at St. Petersburg, and had seen the war, the revolution, and the diplomatic intrigues. This had made him into a radical, he had kicked over the traces, and now was a free-lance journalist, writing mostly for papers which could not pay him anything. But he had a small income, and was expecting to shake the world with a book about the "White Terror," on which he worked diligently every morning, and talked all the rest of the day if any one would listen.

It was evident that Joe's eyes followed Betty wherever they could, and Cornelia, being still an old-fashioned grandmother, wanted to know about it. "He is a dear," said Betty, "and I have to admit that he makes me shiver now and then. But I'm not sure we shall hit it off. I'm trying to make sure."

"What is the problem?"

"Well, several. In the first place, I'll have to propose, because Joe is poor, and he thinks I am going to be rich. I'll have to explain that I'll escape being rich if I marry a Red. Also, there's his wife."

"Wife?" echoed Cornelia—but managing to keep too much surprise out of her voice.

"Didn't you know he had one? She went back to New York several years ago. She doesn't love him."

"Are you sure?"

"Joe is. It seems that she's reactionary, and you know enough to realize that no man and woman can be happy when they hold opposite opinions on the class struggle. That's what I am concerned about—I think I'm turning into a communist, and Joe still ties himself to the old social-democracy that was killed in the war and doesn't know it."

"I see," said Cornelia. Her heart warmed to Joe, because she did not want Betty to go with the fighting crowd. But she must not say so!

"You know," said the girl, "I think it's a form of our Anglo-Saxon egotism, we think we can change our social system by a method different from all the rest of mankind. We have such a marvelous constitution, and such a wise electorate, we can do it step by step—and all the while the truth is we don't intend to change a thing, but to smash anybody that dares a move. No rough stuff—except what the possessing class needs in its business. Pierre quotes Lenin's definition of the state: 'a monopoly of violence.' Don't you see it, Grannie?"

"I am still one of the sentimentalists, Betty dear."

"Yes, I know, and you'll back up Joe in all our wrangles, no doubt. Well, he needs you, for he's got all current history against him—to say nothing of the ruling class of the world!"

v

To this quartette of assorted thinkers came the news about Sacco and Vanzetti. When the first letter was read, Cornelia said it would be pleasant to have Bart here. But Joe Randall smiled dryly and told her not to count too much upon it; for capitalist policemen were not so eager to provide their victims with vacations on Italian lakes. When the second letter came, he said, "I told you so."

"But it's too absurd!" cried Cornelia. "They are innocent!"

"They have to prove it," said Joe.

And Pierre Leon eyed the old lady with a quizzical expression. "Don't forget, comrade," said he, "it sometimes happens that anarchists are guilty." Then, seeing Cornelia's startled look, he added, "I was an anarchist myself for years; and I assure you I wasn't always innocent!"

Said Betty, "You mustn't say that to Grannie. She is soft-boiled."

Pierre was interested in American slang, which he said was a new contribution to the world's poetry. He asked about this phrase, and then went on: "People that are soft-boiled had better not go wandering about in the radical movement, because they may get their shells broken." He went on to say that about anarchists you could never make a general statement, each one was a law to himself. You had to know him before you could say what he would do—and even then you didn't always know.

"Well, we know Bart," insisted Cornelia; "and we know he is no bandit."

"And the other one?"

"I don't know him so well, I only met him two or three times. But he's a gentle, soft-spoken young fellow—"

"Which means absolutely nothing," said Pierre. "Even your American two-gun-men have been that; I think it's a tradition, out on the western plains, that your deadliest sheriffs have been mild-mannered men. The first thing you have to know about an anarchist is what leaders he follows."

"Bart and Nick belong to the Galleani group."

"But Galleani is a militante. If you don't believe that, go down to Milano, or wherever he's living now, and hear him. Who gave you the idea he is a pacifist?"

"I didn't have that idea. Bart told me he was a militant—"

"But then, when an anarchist tells you he's a militant, why don't you believe him?" Pierre's face indicated that this was one more droll aspect of American ladies. "Understand me, Comrade Thornwell, it is good of rich and cultured ladies to take an interest in the exploited workers; but you suffer always from the fact that you can't possibly realize how they actually feel."

"Don't forget, Comrade Leon, I worked for a year and a half in a cordage plant, and lived on the wages."

"I know, Betty told us; and I never heard anything like it. But all the same, if you will pardon me, it wasn't practically real, because if you had been ill or out of a job, you'd have gone back to your family; it wasn't psychologically real, because you always knew you could, and you had the moral support of knowing you were a lady. No worker has that; so don't be shocked if you should some day learn that some workers commit what the bourgeoisie calls crimes in the struggle against their exploiters."

There was a pause, while Cornelia digested these uncomfortable words. At last she said, "Crimes such as banditry, Comrade Leon?"

"Well, that's a question that calls for definitions. If you mean by banditry, robbing for private advantage, the answer is no. If you mean robbing for the cause, the answer is, there have been such anarchists: not many, but a few. Take Ravachol; he robbed the rich and gave the money to the poor, and boasted of it."

"What do other anarchists say of that?"

"I have heard a thousand arguments about it. It's a practical question, whether such a course helps the cause; some say yes, some say no. A few anarchists repudiated Ravachol, others endorsed him—Elisée Reclus among the latter, and he is a god of the movement, a great scientist and a great soul. You see, Comrade, it is difficult for any anarchist to repudiate another who has acted from good motives. There are two things a real anarchist will never do; one is to betray a comrade, and the other is to profit at the expense of the cause. So long as he is loyal, and risks his own life for the cause, nothing he does can be repudiated; that lies in the nature of the doctrine, because he is a law to himself, and has a right to be that, and other anarchists proclaim that right. How can they control him? How can they refuse to stand by him?"

"That ought to frighten me," said Cornelia, "but we New Englanders were raised on that creed—we called it Transcendentalism."

"I know," said Pierre. "There are few anarchist book shops without copies of Thoreau's 'Duty of Civil Disobedience.'"

"But we managed to keep the doctrine from involving the right to kill other people." Thus Cornelia, sure of her Boston.

"Did you really?" asked Pierre. "Stop and think now!" There was something in his tone that told Cornelia he was going to have fun with her. The twinkle was also in Betty's eye and in Joe's, so she knew they were in the secret. "Think hard!" said the Frenchman, and when she gave it up, he said, "Did you ever hear of a practicing anarchist by the name of John Brown?"

"Well," said Cornelia, hesitating; "I suppose he did kill people—"

"Yes, do suppose it! It so happens we have been reading a life of him—and while you are talking about bandit-raids, consider the one at Harper's Ferry. It was a surprise attack, you remember; it was going to give the slaves a chance to rise and get hold of an arsenal with some guns; and to that great end, four white men, quite innocent, harmless fellows, not even slave-holders, were shot dead in the streets of a country town. And remember, they took him and hanged him as a common felon, and were certain that history would agree with them. But up in Boston your Wendell Phillips proclaimed in a public meeting, 'He has abolished slavery in Virginia!' And some anarchist poet wrote four lines—Comrade Betty, can you say those lines that you like so much?"

And Betty, who had been smiling, became suddenly serious, and recited:

> *Not any spot six feet by two*
> *Will hold a man like thee!*
> *John Brown will tramp the shaking earth*
> *From Blue Ridge to the sea.*

VI

Needless to say, there were many questions Cornelia wanted to ask of Pierre Leon. She realized that the time for dodging was past, it was up to her to get clear in her own thinking. She admitted to these three friends what before she had feared to admit even to herself: the doubts as to whether it could be true, as the government and the newspapers took for granted, that some of the Italian anarchists had been doing that wholesale bombing.

Said Pierre, "Set this down for certain at the outset—all militant anarchists believe in bombs. Not all make them—any more than all Christians sell their goods and give to the poor. It is too uncomfortable and dangerous. But the faith calls for it, 'anarchist christenings,' is the phrase—and when some young enthusiast comes along and wants to practice, the preachers can't very well say no. And when the boys get into trouble, then of course the movement has to rally and defend them."

"And that, of course, includes telling the world they are innocent?" It was Joe, with a touch of socialist sarcasm.

"Naturally. It goes without saying that anybody who will fight will try to deceive the enemy. What you have to get clear is the central doctrine of anarchism, that property used for exploitation is theft. That makes capitalist society a gigantic bandit-raid, a wholesale killing; any killing you have to do to abolish it, or to cripple it, always is a small matter in comparison. Twenty years ago, when I used to argue questions like this, they were more or less academic; our generation had never known war. But now take what has happened, and you realize that to the working-class theorist, human life has ceased to have any value, compared with the bringing on of the revolution. We know that capitalism means one more world slaughter after another; it means that inevitably, you might say by definition. Every capitalist society has to compete for markets and raw materials, or else cease to be a capitalist society. It intends to take our lives by the tens of millions; and are we denied the right to save ourselves—because, forsooth, the effort means killing a few capitalists and kings and judges and police spies and what not? You can see that, to an anarchist, such an idea is childish."

"Or to a communist," added Joe Randall, the socialist.

Said the other, "Between the anarchist and the communist it is a question of technique. I once heard an American labor leader put it effectively: 'Never use violence—until you have enough of it!' That will serve for the communist formula—and I leave it for Joe to explain the polite social-democratic program of killing a tiger half an inch at a time."

So they wrangled for a while, saying sharp and bitter things with perfect good humor. Pierre declared that some day he would have the job of putting Joe into jail—and maybe Cornelia, too, because she believed in free speech for capitalists, and might insist upon practicing her theory. Maybe Betty would be putting her own Grannie into jail—stranger things had happened in revolutions. To which Joe replied that it was people of Pierre's way of talking that made a peaceable solution so difficult; they brought on reaction, and set the workers back for decades. So for a while Sacco and Vanzetti were left in the Brockton police-station, forgotten.

Until Betty said, "You are getting poor Grannie so balled up with your theories and your shocking facts that she'll lose heart and be scared out of the movement."

"For God's sake," exclaimed Pierre, "don't let me do that! In the first place, I don't know a thing about your Bart and Nick, they may be two harmless dreamers. And anyhow, innocent or guilty, no working-class rebel ever did a tenth part of the harm to society that society has done to him. No one of them ever carries a tenth part of the guilt that is borne by the judges and officials who prosecute him. Think of the guilt of those who caused the war, in order to extend their markets or to save their investments!"

That was coming close to home for Cornelia and Betty. Said the former, thinking of her three perfectly self-satisfied sons-in-law, "Can there be guilt when there is no consciousness of guilt?"

Pierre answered, "That is the sort of question the Puritan conscience likes to wrestle with. But let us set aside theories, and consider the practical problem of labor defense. Whether an accused worker is guilty or whether he is innocent is a matter you can almost never guess in advance. If he's guilty, he won't tell you, and it would be wretched taste for you to ask. On the other hand, maybe the police have got the wrong fellow; often enough they know it, and don't care, because they figure he's done something equally bad, and anyhow he's the sort that is safer in jail. Then again, maybe it's a provocateur's job—something the bosses have planted, in order to have a pretext for raiding offices and smashing presses and throwing leaders into jail. Either way, you can't know until you get in up to your ears. You may find you've got a chance to expose the police and win public sympathy—or you may have something that will discredit the movement and turn the public against you for years."

"A complicated matter, being a revolutionist!" remarked Cornelia.

And Pierre replied, "You bet your shoes it is—to quote your American slang."

VII

On the morning after the arrest of Sacco and Vanzetti came Mike Stewart, bringing his "hunch," which was destined to control their lives and deaths forever after. Mike himself called it by the more dignified name of a "theory"; he told it to the district attorney, who liked it so well that he rented Mike from the town of Bridgewater, and for a year thereafter the policeman had nothing to do but search out facts to fit his "theory."

A part of it was that the same bandits who had committed the South Braintree hold-up in April had committed the Bridge-

water attempt of the previous December—the one which had
been seen in the "detective machine." The police proceeded to
collect some fifty persons who had witnessed one or the other of
these crimes. Orciani was arrested at his factory, so there were
three bandits to be identified. The usual procedure is to mix
up the suspects with a number of other men and see if the witnesses can pick the guilty ones. But in the dingy old police-
station of Brockton the three suspects were put in a room, and
the witnesses were brought in and told that these were the
bandits, and could they recognize them? Sacco and Vanzetti
were sleepless, unshaved, unwashed, uncombed—a condition in
which a leader of fashion looks like a bandit. But even so, the
witnesses were uncertain, some said they might be the right
men, others said they were surely not.

Several witnesses had seen the bandits in special circumstances, for example with a cap on; so Sacco was ordered to
put on a cap, and did so. Another had seen the bandit crouched
down; Sacco was ordered to crouch, and the witness thought
he looked more like a bandit that way. Another had seen the
bandit pointing a gun; Sacco was ordered to act as if he were
pointing a gun, and the witness was quite sure that made him
look more like a bandit. Witnesses who were obdurate, and
wouldn't stop saying they were the wrong men, were dropped
by the prosecution, and it was up to the defense to find them
if they could. In a great many cases they did so—but too late.

The police had found a Buick car abandoned in some woods,
two miles from Coacci's home, and it was part of the "theory"
that this had been used in the two crimes. This "bandit-car"
was now brought to the police-station, and Sacco and Orciani
were loaded into it, and with a detail of the state police, heavily
armed, were taken for a tour of the shoe-towns. Word went in
advance, "The bandits are coming," and huge crowds gathered.
At the time of the South Braintree crime several workers had
run to the windows of the shoe-factory and seen the bandit-car
driving away. Now the scene was reënacted, with these persons
looking from the windows to judge if Sacco and Orciani looked
like the men they had seen. The crowds, meantime, did not wait
for a decision; they knew these were the bandits, and tried to
beat them, and did spit in their faces. It was a grand public
circus, and by means of it the police persuaded three shoe-

workers to recognize the bandits, and to stay persuaded until the preliminary hearing a week or two later, when they changed their minds and said they couldn't be sure. When the trial came, a year later, they had changed again, and took the stand and identified Sacco and Vanzetti as the bandits, and made three of the five witnesses upon whom the august Commonwealth of Massachusetts relied to the death.

On the day after the arrest of Sacco and Vanzetti the three prisoners were arraigned before a magistrate. Orciani was charged with operating a motor-cycle without a tail-light—although his motor-cycle had had a tail-light and it had been lighted; Sacco and Vanzetti were charged with carrying revolvers without a license. Bail was denied, on the pretext of a war-time law. The three victims were taken back to jail, and the task of fitting the facts to the "theory" was continued.

A week later there was a hearing upon the charge of murder; and here an unexpected thing happened—the number of bandits was reduced to two. The district attorney stated that the identification of Orciani was not sufficient. That seemed strange, because more persons had been willing to think that Orciani looked like the bandit than had been willing to think it about either Sacco or Vanzetti. What had happened was that Orciani had been able to produce an American alibi. Not merely had he punched his time-clock in the factory that morning, but he could produce his boss and several other "white men" to swear that he had been at his machine all day. It was only three weeks back, and he hadn't missed a day.

Also it developed that Sacco was to be let off from the Bridgewater charge—because he, too, had an American alibi. But on the day of the South Braintree affair, according to his own story, he had gone up to Boston to get his passports; he had lunched at a café with friends, and had gone to the consulate, where they remembered him for the comical reason that he had been told to provide a photograph for his passport, and had brought one of great size. A clerk remembered it; but then, he was an Italian, and Italian alibis do not "go" in Yankee police-courts.

As for poor Bart, alas, he had nothing but Italian alibis for both dates. On the day before Christmas he had sold eels to fifty housewives, and during the South Braintree crime he had been digging clams and bait. But such things do not count against a policeman's "hunch," so Bart was charged with both crimes; the prosecution was going to prove that he was the bandit who had stood on Broad Street, in Bridgewater, firing a shotgun at the pay-truck, and also that he was the driver of the murder-car at South Braintree—he who had never touched a steering-wheel in his poor proletarian life! The moral of these developments was clear to sarcastic young radicals such as Betty Alvin—that good little wops had better stay close to the boss, and punch a time-clock four times a day. Instead of going home at night, they would be safer kept in pens.

VIII

A lawyer had been engaged to defend Sacco and Vanzetti at these preliminary hearings, an Irish gentleman by the name of John Vahey. Some lawyers with criminal practice employ what are known as "runners" to bring them business; and whether Mr. Vahey knew it or not, it was an Italian generally known as a "runner" who persuaded the friends of Vanzetti to employ Mr. Vahey. The lawyer himself was no "runner," but a stout gentleman who did not hurry about to find witnesses for his client; he was content to let the Brinis fetch the wops to his office. He was active in the politics of Plymouth County, and intimate with those who controlled its affairs, including the district attorney, Fred Katzmann; he was an "associate judge," and went into an arrangement to share business with Katzmann. It has been said in Vahey's defense that Vanzetti was probably the first innocent man he had ever had as a client. Very possibly Vanzetti was wrong in his fixed idea that his lawyers had "thrown him down." He was a hard client to defend, because he persisted stubbornly in denying that he had been to Johnson's garage with Boda the night of his arrest; he would not permit any capitalist lawyer to persuade him to say a word that might involve another comrade.

The friends of Sacco in Boston had also engaged a lawyer to defend him. Before a month had passed there were three lawyers in the case, and one of them was young and confiding, and told how he had heard one associate say to the other, "See if you can get Sacco to tell where he buried the money, and we'll divide it." A part of the "theory" became that Sacco had buried the treasure in the garden of his home, which belonged to Mr. Kelley, his boss; and in each of the next seven spring-times, when Mr. Kelley's father got ready to plant potatoes, a thrill would go through the Commonwealth of Massachusetts. Sacco's boss was digging for the treasure! It was hard on poor Nick, because it implied that Mr. Kelley thought he was guilty, whereas Mr. Kelley had trusted Nick as night-watchman.

Cornelia and Betty sent money to help interest these legal gentlemen. Cornelia and Betty meant to stay in one place all summer, so they would not need Betty's full allowance. They rowed on the lake, and climbed the mountain paths, and listened to all-day and all-night arguments on the theories of anarchism, syndicalism, communism and socialism, with the history of these movements in a dozen countries for three-quarters of a century. There came another letter from Plymouth, telling of develop-ments, with a message from Bart insisting that Nonna was not to worry, and not to cut short her rest.

The idea of accusing Bart of the Bridgewater crime seemed to Cornelia such madness, she could not take it seriously. It was a case of mistaken identity, which would be cleared up when it was investigated. "They can't make such a charge against a man who has lived in a town for eight years; and when he went about that whole day, peddling eels to all North Plymouth! If it had been any day but the day before Christmas, one might say there was a chance of getting the dates mixed; but every-body knows that Italians eat eels on Christmas, and Bart can prove that he had a barrel of them. It seems as if somebody has gone crazy."

"The bourgeoisie always goes crazy when its property-rights are threatened," said Pierre Leon.

"But I was there the day after Christmas," persisted Cornelia, "and they told me all about what they had done—Bart and Trando, and the barrel of eels, and the baker's horse, and how Trando would never believe Bart's promises again. Surely I could testify to that conversation!"

"They might call it hearsay," said Joe Randall. "And anyhow, the jury would say it was a put up job—to fool you and prepare an alibi. The Italians are cunning, you know!"

They comforted themselves with the thought of the law's

delay. Criminal cases took a long time to get on the calendar in Massachusetts; and meantime, since bail was refused, there was nothing Cornelia and Betty could do. But the law is like a sleeping tiger, capable of swift and deadly leaps when it is roused. The second week in June there came a cablegram; the situation was very bad, and Bart was to be tried for the Bridgewater crime in less than two weeks. There was just time for Cornelia and Betty to get a steamer; so the little radical party broke up at an hour's notice. Pierre Leon would go back to his desk, and Joe Randall decided that he knew enough about the White Terror in Europe, and his book ought to have a chapter on Massachusetts!

IX

Their steamer came in to New York one afternoon, and there on the pier, waving handkerchiefs, were Deborah and Priscilla. Betty's sister was engaged to be married to a young mountain of copper; an enormously important alliance, which had already supplied a column of genealogy to the *Transcript*. The ladies were going to plunder the Fifth Avenue shops of their treasures; also the father, Rupert Alvin, was in town, on business connected with Jerry Walker's felt-plants, now in his care. They were going to a musical comedy that evening, and had planned diversions for several days. Betty had been away a whole year, and any normal rich girl would have brought home several trunk-loads of presents for relatives and friends. But here was this madcap pair, returning precipitately, with no purchases whatever—and very mysterious about it, obliged to decline diversions, and take the night train for Boston. After much nagging, Deborah got it out of them—they were hurrying to attend the trial of an Italian anarchist bandit! And they did actually go—Betty in spite of mother, father, and sister, Cornelia in spite of daughter, son-in-law and granddaughter.

Bart was in the County Farm Jail at Plymouth, and during the afternoon was brought from his cell into the reception room. He had on a coarse gray shirt and trousers, badly shrunken; his outdoor color was gone, he was haggard and thin, and his walrus mustache drooped mournfully. But, oh, so glad he was to see them! His face lighted up, and he came, half running, holding out his hands; the messages of his soul leaped to them, love and pity and heart-breaking grief. Poor old Bart—the greatest lover of freedom Cornelia had ever known—shut up behind steel bars! Tears started into the eyes of both the women, and the prisoner's voice broke as he tried to speak. "Oh, Nonna, I so sorry for spoiling your holiday! Oh, Betty, I so sorry for bringing you to sooch place!"

"It's all right, Bart, we had a good holiday, and now we're here, and we're going to get you out in short order." It was Betty speaking, brave little soul—no melancholy while she was in charge! "Cheer up, old pal, it's going to be easy. This is Comrade Joe Randall, who has followed me all the way from Italy because he thinks I am going to be silly enough to marry him."

Bart turned quickly to the good-looking young fellow. "I glad for meeting you, Comrade Jorandall. If Comrade Betty marry you be very lucky feller."

"Oh, I'm not sure yet," said Betty. "I've got to make a real Red out of him. Now he's nothing but a pale pink, one of those riformistas that we don't trust. But he's going to help get you off, and that will educate him."

Their feeble effort at jollity came to a speedy end, and they talked about the trial, only two days away. "My enemy have got me," said Bart; and they knew without asking who this enemy was, the profit system, embodied in Plymouth by the great cordage company from which Bart had helped to extort two hundred thousand dollars every year, in the form of higher wages to its workers. "I think the go-vérnnent not let me ever get away," said Bart, and Betty's cheerfulness could make no impression on this firm distrust.

"You see what they do," he said. "They cannot prove Nick and me at South Braintree, have not got evidence for sending two men to electric chair. So they think, first we take Vanzett', we fixit him for Bridgewater job, we make him convicted. So when it come trial for South Braintree job, jury will say, one of them fellers is bandit, he is convicted, it is not so hard for believing they both should die."

"But Bart, it's crazy to try to prove that you were in Bridgewater that morning!" It was Cornelia speaking.

"They have got it fixit, Nonna, they prove what they want. I tell all friend not fool self. They have got everything, they are friends with our lawyers."

"Oh, Bart!"

"I sure of it. Come big feller, lazy, smoke big cigar—is what for Italian worker pay money, buy him big cigar. He is funny man, he make joke, he whistle. I say, 'I am innochent.' He make funny face, he say, 'Very bad, they put you wit' Sacc'!' He stick up finger in air, he make it go round, so"—Bart made a spiral motion, his index finger going up. "He say, 'Pfist!' Is hardest work he ever do for poor wop."

"I thought they had an investigator getting witnesses!"

"Have got Italian feller—he is spy for go-vérnment. He get all comrades put up money, buy him automobile, so he can go look for witness. But it pass many days, he not bring witness. Is plenty witness in Plymoot', but it must Brinis find them. Is maybe witness in Bridgewater, could find people say I not look like bandit, but cannot get them."

"Bart," said Betty, "we are not spies for the government, and we're going to rent a car right away, and take the Brinis this evening and see if we can find some witnesses in Bridge-water. Cheer up now, we're really going to help you. Joe here is an expert investigator; he is writing a book on the White Terror in Europe."

"Is same terror here, Comrade Joe, is plenty people could tell I am innochent, but will not dare speaking. Is polissman saw me on street, talk wit' me in morning, ask for price of eel, but will not tell. Is express office man, he knows I got barrel of eel, but he will not let us look for paper—what you call it, receipt. Is superintendent of cordage plant, you know him. He know I was in Plymoot' that day—but see if he come for wit-ness! You saw him, Nonna, always, ever since strike, four year, he walk across street when I come, is not willing for meet me. Is may be hate, may be fear—but see if he help me getting out from jail! No, it is price I pay for eight year I try to educate worker. What is it they have said about Gesu, Nonna?"

" 'He stirreth up the people.' "

"Joosta so! And I am joosta same age, Nonna, I am thirty-two, like it was Comrade Gesu when his enemy put him in jail! I have readed about him—it is book what they give for wop to read in jail, because all church people have not know how bad rivoluzionario was Gesu!"

This was one of the themes Bart liked to talk about; he forgot

his own desperate peril for a few minutes. When the three
visitors went out, Joe Randall said, "This much is certain whatever happens, the police have given us a good martyr!"

x

The little party set out in a car that evening, and going from
house to house at the scene of the Bridgewater hold-up, they
found two Italians who had witnessed the crime, and had told
the police that the bandit who stood on the street and fired a
shotgun was a short man with a closely cropped mustache. These
witnesses had been rejected by the police, as not fitting the
"theory," and they were willing to appear for the defense. There
were other witnesses who might have been found, if there had
been more time, and if the seekers had realized the urgency. But
Cornelia was hugging her notion that the case of the prosecution was bound to break down in court; and what human mind
could have conceived that ghastly eccentricity of the laws of
Massachusetts, which amounted in effect to this: that whatever
evidence was presented to the jury at this coming trial would
count, while everything that was found out later might as well
have been left in the darkness of oblivion? To quote the words
of the Supreme Judicial Court of the august Commonwealth,
handed down in the Sacco-Vanzetti case: "It is not imperative
that a new trial be granted, even though the evidence is newly
discovered, and if presented to a jury would justify a different
verdict." Such is the law of the Brahmins and Blue-bloods, which
altereth not!

O fates that hold us at your choice
How strange a web ye spin!

How strange the plight in which you have placed us—that
we walk backward into our lives, with eyes that see the past,
but are blind to the future! With ears that hear the past, but
are deaf to the future! Betty rented a car, and Joe drove her
and Cornelia and Vincenzo and Alfonsina to Bridgewater, and
along with that little party went a vast throng, made up of
twenty-six hundred and nine days, each one with a separate
burden of griefs and regrets. Days, black-clad and somber, wav-

ing black veils unseen! Days wailing and moaning, shouting
alarms unheard! Cornelia and Betty and Joe and Vincenzo and
Alfonsina got out of the car, and separated and walked up and
down streets, and rang door-bells and went into houses asking
questions of strangers; and into every house with them went
ten million mourners, ten million protestants marching, singing,
carrying banners in a hundred foreign tongues. Mobs roared
their fury, shrieked their imprecations; bombs exploded, sheets
of plate glass were shattered; cavalry charged, clubs fell on
human heads, sabers clove human flesh, men fell and bled and
died—and of all that tumult not one sound reached the deaf
ears, not one glimpse penetrated the blind eyes!

Voices, ghostly voices calling, up and down the streets of the
little town of Bridgewater, all through that warm spring night!
Run, Betty, run, on your swift young limbs that have been
trained by climbing mountains! Run, and rest not, until you
find those other witnesses who will testify that the bandit had
a closely cropped mustache! Run, Cornelia—one last effort of
those old legs, shrunken and withered so that you do not like to
see them—find some one who can bring you to those Pinkerton
men who interviewed the witnesses of the prosecution, and
heard them say they could not identify the bandits! Joe Randall,
driver of the car, don't go back to Plymouth to-night! Turn
your headlights to Boston, an hour or two away, and use your
newspaper introductions to find the reporter who was first upon
the scene, and will testify to what all the witnesses said!
Cornelia, put your family influence to work, get the shoe-company and the insurance company to give up those Pinkerton
reports—now while they will count, and not later, when they
will be thrust into a pigeon-hole and forgotten by a governor's
secretary, who is paid a double salary to see that the great man's
mind is not burdened with details!

Look, Cornelia! Look, Betty and Joe, look at that man, waiting in the future; a man with a smile made of marble, with eyes
like two agates, cold, expressionless, a supersalesman of automobiles who will play the part of final jury, and will politely
accept your evidence, and remain of his own opinion! Joe
Randall, "expert investigator," now is your hour! Drive to
Atlantic Avenue, where the wholesale fish-dealers have their
stores, and find that Italian who shipped the barrel of eels! Pull

off your coat and climb into the attic and search the boxes of records—it will not be so hard now as seven years later, for there are not so many records, and the dust is not so thick! When you find the book of express receipts, showing the barrel of eels consigned to "B. Vanzetti, Plymouth," six days before Christmas, 1919, it will count with the jury—instead of being set aside, unseen by the agate eyes!

XI

The little party turned their car home that night, well content with what they had achieved. Next morning they sat down to a conference with eminent legal authority, and Cornelia offered her testimony, and learned that it was not available, because most of it was hearsay, and anyhow, she had better not take the stand, because she would be questioned concerning Vanzetti's beliefs, and it was not desirable to have the jury know that he was an anarchist. Of course everybody in Plymouth knew it perfectly well, but if it was not introduced in the evidence, the jury would be ordered to disregard it, and would do so—that being the merry fiction of the merry legal game. Could Cornelia testify that Vanzetti was a pacifist, and repudiated violence? Could she testify that he did not believe in the overthrow of the United States government by force? No, she could not testify that, and therefore nothing she could say about Vanzetti's character would count with the jurors. How could they fail to be suspicious of an American woman who confessed to intimate friendship with a dangerous Italian Red?

Furthermore, there was a question whether Vanzetti should be a witness himself. He could not deny his anarchistic opinions, which would so antagonize the jurors that they would find him guilty of anything, regardless of evidence. It was a delicate matter, because Vanzetti was a draft-evader, and the jury would consist of men who had gone to the war, or had sent their sons. Also he was an infidel, and the jury would consist of devout church-goers. There was that letter found on Vanzetti, denouncing a certain Catholic priest as a "pig." The jurymen in Plymouth County were not apt to be Catholics themselves, but they would think that Italians ought to be Catholics, and it would be better to appeal to the district attorney's sense of fair play not to introduce that letter.

Vanzetti was stubborn, and clamorous to be heard in his own defense; but then, he would not stop denying that he had met Boda at the Johnson place the night of the arrest; and how could he expect to get away with that, in face of the testimony the prosecution could offer, if the issue were raised? No, Vanzetti must be made to realize that under the law he was not required to testify, and no conclusion unfavorable to him could be drawn from his failure to testify.

Again the future rose up and shouted! Ten million hands were waved unseen, ten million warnings were voiced unheard! The fates that held Cornelia and Betty at their choice granted no forewarning of the man with the marble smile and the agate eyes, the supersalesman of automobiles who seven years later was to be the final jury in the case. Not once did they hear him repeat his formula, which was to make him seem like a gramophone through the weary months of the future; the formula which would balk the friends of love and justice who traveled from all over the world to appeal to him; the formula which took the place of all evidence and all thought—"Why did not Vanzetti take the stand in his own behalf?"

CHAPTER 9

THE WEB OF FATE

I

PLYMOUTH COURT-HOUSE stands at the head of the square, a large and stately building of red brick, with ivy climbing the walls, and white colonial entrances, and a niche containing a figure of justice, open-eyed. The court-room is bare and white, with a throne of polished wood, and over it a great seal of the "Plymouth Society," with the flags of the United States and the Commonwealth of Massachusetts draped on top. It is all extremely solemn and formal; the bailiff wears a uniform, and carries a "wand," or long stick with which he holds the spectators in awe.

On the morning of the trial of Bartolomeo Vanzetti the room was filled with spectators from Bridgewater, curious to behold the wicked bandit; also a few working-people of foreign birth, Italians and Portuguese of North Plymouth who remembered what Vanzetti had done for them in the strike. The men had put on celluloid collars with gilt studs and no ties, the women wore shawls and aprons; they sat, morning and afternoon, following with strained attention a mysterious procedure in a strange tongue. There were spectators from Boston, but no reporters from there; the case excited only local interest, and was left to local correspondents.

The prisoner was brought in, shackled to a deputy by each wrist; also a steel cage was brought in, and he was locked inside. This in itself was almost equivalent to a conviction— it made him look so alarming to a jury, so much like a wild beast. The district attorney entered—a stocky man of German parentage, florid, blond, good-looking, smartly dressed. Fred Katzmann was his name, a Mason and a "joiner," prominent in the political ring which governed the county. Most political rings in America are financed by the local cor-

porations, and exist to carry out their will; the efficiency of
a public official usually consists in the fact that he knows their
needs and wishes so thoroughly that he does what they want
without having to be told.

In this case Fred Katzmann's course was very easy—to
consult his prejudices. He knew that the Reds were pledged to
destroy American institutions, and therefore it was a patriotic
service to destroy the Reds. Later on he went before the
alumni of his college, assembled for banqueting, and the chairman introduced him as a hero who was going to save the Commonwealth from its secret foes; the banqueters cheered him
tumultuously, and he made a speech accepting the stern duty.
All the district attorneys of the neighboring counties were making such speeches at this time—it was an easy way to be popular,
and to conceal orgies of grafting and blackmailing—what was
soon afterwards to be described, in the charges against one of
the most oratorical, as "malfeasance, misfeasance, and non-
feasance in office."

Fred Katzmann was personally an easy-going man, and cultivated a manner of geniality which made a hit with juries. When
the lawyers for the defense came in, carrying briefcases and
looking important, he greeted them coidially; they were his
friends, and during the procedures he would refer to them as
"my brothers." He would carry on a merry battle of wits with
them, and the moment court was adjourned, he would walk out
side by side with them, and they would sit at lunch and "josh"
each other about the points they had lost or won. It was exactly
like a tennis tournament—except that in tennis they used a
ball, while in this legal game it was a wop.

II

A door in the front of the court-room opened, and there
entered a thin, shrunken old gentleman with a white mustache
and a face like parchment. He wore a black silk robe, and the
moment he appeared the bailiff pounded on the floor with his
wand and shouted, "Court!" and all the lawyers stood up, and
the spectators stood up, and remained standing. The bailiff
drew a breath and shouted, "Hear ye! Hear ye! Hear ye!
All persons having anything to do before the Honorable, the

Justices of the Superior Court, now sitting within and for the County of Plymouth, draw near, give your attention, and you shall be heard! God save the Commonwealth of Massachusetts!" Whereupon the wrinkled old gentleman sat down, and everybody else did the same.

Webster Thayer, judge of the Superior Court of the Commonwealth of Massachusetts, was what the pathologists call a "ticquer"; that is, he blinked with a nervous affliction as he gazed about his domain. His sharp, withered face was a symbol of the old Puritan spirit; his voice, like a steel saw cutting through wood, was an ancestral inheritance, produced by three hundred years of cold and foggy winds. He aspired to exhibit repose, but his fear of so many foreigners in his court-room showed itself by incessant nervous glances. He was obsessed with a phobia on the subject of Reds, and talked about it incessantly, with so much repetition that many persons avoided him, or ruthlessly shut him up.

Cornelia had never heard of "Web" Thayer before, but he was to be the subject of her study for seven years, and before long she knew him completely. During this Plymouth trial he did not know who she was; but during the second trial, that of Sacco and Vanzetti a year later, he had heard about her, and he summoned her three times to his chambers to impress his personality upon her and to justify his ways. So she learned that the basis of his being was an inferiority complex, a sense of the gulf which yawned between him and the great ones of his community, and which he would never cross, even though he won his way to the Supreme Judicial bench. He was a Thayer, but not of the "right" ones; and in Massachusetts it is a special offense to bear an honored name unless you are one of the "right" ones. There are the "right" Cabots—and assuredly they are not those who used to be called Caboto and Kabotinsky, and got permission from a too complaisant court to Americanize themselves. There are "right" Coolidges, and Calvin is not among them, and would not be, though he were president of the United States for half a dozen terms.

"Web" lived in Worcester, which is a city in the wilds of the far west—that is to say, forty miles removed from the cultural influences of the Back Bay. It is a hardware center, the home of hardware men, who hustle and "boost" and make "selling talks." "Web" had gone to Dartmouth, a small college in the hills of New Hampshire, whose graduates are looked down upon by the haughty scions of the Harvard "Gold Coast." "Web" asserted his uneasy personality, and drew attention to himself, something the "blue-bloods" never do, because they do not have to. In this Sacco-Vanzetti affair "Web" would do what the Commonwealth wanted him to do, but he would do it in such a way that the Back Bay would blush for him, and comfort itself by calling it one more sign of the degradation of politics, a consequence of turning over public affairs to the "mob."

He was a man of intense vanity, and played the judicial game as a drama in which he was hero and king. But he could never be sure whether he was successful in the rôle, and the actor would stop in the middle of the play to ask the audience. To the lawyers, or any one else who came to his chambers after the sessions, he would say, "Am I handling this all right?" To the newspaper reporters he would say, "Now, boys, give me a good deal on this." If the reporter happened to be a young and pretty woman, as it did in at least one case, he would employ the arts of gallantry, which are somehow less welcome from an old man with a skin like a mummy's. He would take a seat beside her on the train going to the trial, and smile and ogle, and present a flower to her, and discuss the case. His voice had a penetrating quality, and when the train stopped, every one in the car would hear what he was saying. He must have known the mental discomfort he was causing to his auditor, yet something drove him to go on.

There is an ancient tradition among those who deal with the law that a judge must not discuss a case in public, at least not while it is actually before him. But in handling Sacco and Vanzetti, "Web" Thayer could not keep within these traditional limits. He would talk about the case in a club dining-room, until all the men would leave the table; he would approach a Dartmouth professor on the football field, asking in a loud voice, "Did you see what I did to those anarchistic bastards the other day?" The horror of these words became such in Massachusetts that the Commonwealth had to send its policemen with hickory clubs to crack the skulls of demonstrants who carried the words on a banner. Because there was no way to keep them from being spoken aloud, Boston Common had to be closed to public speakers for the first time in its three hundred years of history.

III

One by one the talesmen took the stand, and were questioned; under the Massachusetts practice, all this questioning was done by the judge, and the defendants' lawyers could only exercise the right of challenge. One by one the jurors were selected: Arthur W. Burgess, shoemaker of the town of Hanson, Henry S. Burgess, caretaker of the town of Wareham, Joseph Frawley, shoe-finisher of the town of Brockton, Charles A. Gale, clerk, of the town of Norwell—so it went, all Anglo-Saxon names. Put none but Americans on guard! Edwin P. Litchfield, shoe-worker of Pembroke, Oliver B. Poole, clerk of Brockton, Alfred M. Shaw, Jr., laborer of Carver, Charles C. Wilbur, tackmaker of Kingston: such little people of the old stock, having failed for one reason or another to become rich, looked with bitter contempt upon the immigrants who came pouring into the country, to beat down wages and make life harder for the "white men" of New England. Far from having any sense of class solidarity, they clung to the American idea that their children would rise and join the leisure class; their attitude to the Italian was that of the poor whites of the south to the Negroes. "All these wops stand together," said one juryman to another, discussing the case at lunch in a restaurant. The remark was overheard, but nothing came of it.

Another juror, Arthur S. Nickerson, a foreman in the Plymouth Cordage Company! Another foreman of that same company had thrown Vanzetti, the agitator, out of their plant, and kept him out four years and more; others had refused him employment, and some one had caused him to be shadowed by detectives for eighteen months after the strike. Now Nickerson was to help decide whether or not Vanzetti should be set at liberty to lead another strike, and deprive the cordage company of another two hundred thousand dollars a year in extra wages! Vanzetti's friends saw with dismay his lawyers permit such a juror to be accepted. They asked themselves, could it be because one of the lawyers was a stockholder in the company, and looking to the company for legal business as well as for dividends? It was permissible to ask.

The assistant district attorney rose, and addressed the jury, telling them what he was going to prove. He told them all that elaborate "theory" about the Coacci house and the bandit-car, which had been stolen a month before the Bridgewater crime, and found in Manley woods abandoned after the South Braintree crime. He brought this car, a Buick, in front of the courthouse, and he told them about Boda, and how he was going to prove that Boda had been driving a Buick car a short while before the crime. He told them about Orciani—despite the fact that they had had to drop Orciani on account of an American alibi. He told them about Sacco, despite the fact that they had had to drop Sacco from this case on account of another American alibi. He built up in the jury's mind an elaborate picture of bandit-gangs, bandit-houses and bandit-cars—and then in the course of the trial he failed to produce a particle of evidence to connect either Sacco, Coacci, Orciani or Boda with any crime, or to connect Coacci's house with any crime, or to connect any one of the five men with the so-called bandit-car. One scrap of testimony—a milkman had seen Boda driving a Buick car a month or two before the crime; or at least he thought it was Boda and he thought it was a Buick. Yet they brought in all this complicated and alarming mass of "theory," not merely at this Plymouth trial, but at the later trial of Sacco and Vanzetti for the South Braintree crime; they showed the bandit-car in both cases, and the bullet-hole in it, and planted the mass of suspicion in the minds of both juries.

IV

Benjamin F. Bowles to the stand: a special officer employed by the shoe-company, and at the same time a member of Mike Stewart's police force in Bridgewater. He had been riding in the seat alongside the driver of the truck, when two bandits, one with a shotgun, the other with a revolver, had rushed out and opened fire. The chauffeur of the paytruck had fainted from fright, and Bowles had seized the steering-wheel and guided the truck with his left hand, while with his right he fired a revolver at the shotgun bandit, until the bandit turned and ran. Later in the trial Bowles took the stand again and changed his testimony, so as to make it fit with the story he had told at the preliminary hearing: he now swore that he had fired, not at the shotgun-bandit, but at the other one, the revolver-bandit. So here was the picture this super-policeman presented to the jury: he had steered a fast-moving truck with his left hand, fired a revolver at a bandit with his right hand, and at the same time used his eyes to study the appearance of a second bandit, so effectively that he could give a detailed description fitting the features, hair, eyes and clothing of Bartolomeo Vanzetti, now sitting in the prisoner's dock before him! At the preliminary hearing Bowles had been "pretty positive" that the shotgun bandit had had a "short and croppy" mustache; but now at the trial he was "positive" that this bandit had had a "bushy" mustache.

Next came a shoe-inspector, Frank Harding, known as "Skip," who had witnessed the crime. He had talked to a reporter of the Boston *Globe,* an hour or two afterwards, and described the bandit as "smooth-shaven." At the preliminary hearing he had described him as having "an overgrown Charlie Chaplin mustache." Now at the trial he identified him as Vanzetti. He had positively identified Orciani as the other bandit; but that fact was not evidence at the trial. Neither was the *Globe* reporter's testimony, for that was not discovered until years later—when it might as well not have been discovered at all. To the Pinkerton detectives "Skip" had described the bandit-car as a Hudson; and he had been an automobile mechanic and knew cars. But now he swore it was a Buick—which happened to be what the "theory" required.

Then came the paymaster, Cox, who had described the shotgun bandit at the preliminary hearing as "short and of slight build." Now he made it agree with Bowles—"five feet eight." But no effort of the district attorney could get him to say that he was sure Vanzetti was the man.

Then came the elderly Georgina Brooks, and with her the age of miracles came back. Mrs. Brooks testified that she had looked out of the window of the Bridgewater railroad depot—she specified which window—and had seen "fire and smoke from a gun." It so happened that between that window and the spot where the firing had occurred, there intervened the full bulk of two two-story houses. The Sacco-Vanzetti defense employed a surveyor to make a map of the scene—but like everything else, it was too late.

Also Mrs. Brooks testified that on her way to the depot, and before the crime, she had inspected the bandit-car and the bandits. She identified Vanzetti as a man she had looked at twice, and who had looked at her "severely." Why she should have turned to look at the car a second time, and been so particular about examining the features of a man sitting casually in an automobile was something Mrs. Brooks could not explain. But she admitted that with one eye she could barely make out the silhouette of objects, and that she had been undergoing treatment for the other eye.

Then young Shaw, a schoolboy who had heard the firing and dodged behind a tree. He had seen the shotgun-bandit run away, at a distance of a hundred and forty-five feet, and said that he could tell the man was a foreigner by the way he ran. "What sort of a foreigner?" and the boy replied, "Either Italian or Russian."

"Does an Italian or a Russian run differently from a Swede or a Norwegian?"

"Yes."

"What is the difference?"

"Unsteady."

Then came Mike Stewart, large, powerful, heavy-lidded. He brought with him his theory—but you may be sure he never mentioned the "detective machine," from which the theory had been born! Neither did he mention the Pinkerton reports, and how they confuted the testimony of "Skip" Harding. "Skip" had taken down the number of the bandit-car, and given a memorandum to Mike, who had unfortunately lost it. Also, unfortunately, there was no number-plate on the car which the police had found in the Manley woods.

They introduced Vanzetti's cap, and a man swore it resembled the cap worn by the shotgun-bandit—although Cox and Mrs. Brooks had sworn to a shotgun-bandit in a soft hat. And that was practically all they had to offer, except for an empty twelve-gauge shotgun shell which they claimed to have picked up at the scene of the shooting. When Vanzetti had been arrested, he had had four shotgun shells in his pocket, and these were put into evidence, but the jury never heard Vanzetti's story of how he came to have them. He had spent the day of his arrest at Sacco's, while the family was packing up for Italy, and these shells, left over from hunting, were picked up on a shelf; Vanzetti had put them into his pocket, saying that he would turn them over to some comrade and get fifty cents for the cause. But that story must not be told to the jury, because Vanzetti would be asked what he mean by the "cause," and he would have to answer that it was the evil cause of anarchism. Nor would it do to put Sacco on the stand, or his wife, because that would bring in the other crime, and the lawyers were maintaining their legal fiction that the jury knew nothing about it— although, of course, every one of them had read about it on the front page of all the papers, and the assistant district attorney had brought Sacco in as a part of the "theory"!

V

Such was the case of the Commonwealth of Massachusetts against Bartolomeo Vanzetti. And now it was the defendant's turn to produce his alibi, and persuade a Yankee jury to believe it. Cornelia and Betty and Joe, watching these proceedings day by day with strained and fearful attention, realized too late how difficult it was going to be. There sat those native sons of New England, lean-faced and stern—elderly men, most of them, because the younger and more active found means to avoid jury duty. Men with such names as Burgess and Gale and Litchfield and Nickerson and Shaw were invited to believe the testimony of Vittorio Papa and Carlo Balboni and Vincenzo Brini and Enrico Bastoni and Teresa Malaguti and Adalaida Bongiovanni and Marguaritta Fiocchi: men with black hair and eyebrows, broad faces and high cheek-bones, uncouth and sinister, clad in ill-fitting cheap store-clothes; women short and stout, with broad mouths and low foreheads, with no collars to their shirt-waists, wearing aprons in front of them and dingy shawls about their shoulders, speaking a foreign jabber which was turned into English by an interpreter who looked as much like a bandit as the others. These were the "Dagoes" who were taking bread out of the mouths of the old stock, swarming into the factory towns, carrying fire-arms, living like pigs, and raising litters of as many little pigs as any farmer ever saw. "These wops all stand together," said one juryman; and all native New England agreed.

Mrs. Mary Fortini, Bart's landlady, told how she had waked him up at six o'clock that morning before Christmas, and how he had gulped down his bread and coffee, and hurried to get out his cart and his eels. Carlo Balboni told how he had come home from his night work, and caused Mrs. Fortini to wake Bart, so that he, Balboni, might be the first customer. John Di Carlo, who kept a shoe-store, testified how Bart had brought him eels while he was cleaning out the store, a little after seven. Each of these witnesses was harrowed by the prosecution, who sought by every legal trick to trip them up in their testimony.

The issue of "radicalism" was not supposed to be brought into the trial; the jury was not supposed to know about it, and in the years that were to follow you would hear judges and editors and governors and college presidents and other eminent persons stoutly maintaining that this issue had not entered the case until the defense had brought it in at the second trial. But behold, here was the suave district attorney, questioning the shoe-store proprietor: "Have you ever discussed government theories over there between you? Have you discussed the question of the poor man and the rich man between you?" And later comes Michael Sassi, a gardener, to the stand, and the prosecutor asks, "Have you heard anything of his political beliefs? Have you heard him make any speeches to your friends in the cordage company?" This questioning led by accident to some character testimony—in spite of the effort to bar such testimony. Said the district attorney, "You have dined many times with Vanzetti, haven't you?"

"With Brini, as his guest, I dined many times: Vanzetti boarded with him and sometimes he was present."

"You used to play cards with the defendant?"

"Vanzetti does not play."

"To smoke, didn't you?"

"I do not smoke."

"How many times have you drank with him?"

"Vanzetti does not drink."

Said Bart, commenting on this evidence: "What a method to find out whether I had been robbing in Bridgewater or delivering fish in Plymouth on the 24th of December, 1919!" Poor

Bart, who had to sit in complete silence, watching all this from inside a cage, sternly rebuked on the one occasion when he dared to interrupt! He had to see the rascalities of the prosecution, and the unconvincing quality of the defense—he who, from first to last, understood the case better than any other person interested in it, even the most famous and most expensive of lawyers! He who could read every motive, understand every character, predict every event, and advise, generally in vain, what should be done—he had to sit and watch everything done wrong, and ruin come down upon him like a slow-grinding glacier.

VI

One by one came Italian witnesses, telling the story of Vanzetti's movements through every hour of that fateful day. Vincenzo Brini had come home from night-work, and got some eels, and chatted with his friend and former boarder. Bastoni, the baker, had refused to rent the horse and wagon; the time was exactly seven-forty-five, because the cordage whistle blew as Bart entered the store, and "that whistle is our bread and butter." And then Beltrando Brini, twelve years and a half old, bright-eyed and eager, speaking very good English, and thoroughly alert to the meaning of this scene. Trando had first been with Bart about seven-thirty, and had been sent home to hunt out his rubbers from the attic. He had rejoined Bart just as the latter left the baker's, and told about his disappointment over the horse and wagon, and how he had talked about it every day thereafter. He told how he and Bart had gone from house to house, up one street and down another, delivering their eels, until two-forty that afternoon. He named the streets and the people, described the houses and told of conversations, every detail that lived in his mind.

And Mr. Katzmann took him and spent two hours trying to trap him; making him tell parts of his story over and over, hoping that it would vary; pretending that Trando had said things he hadn't said; trying to mix him up about the number of hours he had been with Bart—because Trando took out the time he was hunting rubbers and the time he went to lunch, and Mr. Katzmann pretended not to understand this. He asked what did the basket of eels weigh, and could Trando carry it the long route he had described. Trando replied that any one could see, the basket got lighter as he delivered. In the end Katzmann had to give up, and pay Trando the high compliment of calling him such another as Katzmann himself. Turning to the jury he said: "The parents of such an intelligent boy are right to be proud of him, but what he told you from the stand is a lesson learned by heart."

There came a string of Italian housewives, telling how Vanzetti had sold them eels; eight or ten testified, and there were twice as many more, but the lawyers said it would be a mistake, "the jury will be bored with so much eel-talk." If they refused to believe a score of Italian witnesses, would they believe two score or three score? The lawyers insisted that the alibi had been proved. But Bart was not satisfied, he was angry because of the efforts of the prosecution to claim that he had had a "cropped mustache." He pointed to his soft and silky hairs, which could not be got to stand out; there were so few of them, that was why he had always worn his mustaches long; if he had cut them short, there would have been nothing. For eight years he had been going about this town of Plymouth with his walrus mustaches, and everybody knew him; but this jury contained only one Plymouth man, and did not know him. Bart insisted that the truth about his mustache must be proved, and in a passion of indignation he told his lawyers that if they did not do it, he would rise up in court and denounce them for treason to their client.

So at the last moment the Italian "runner" went scurrying to find some of Vanzetti's friends who knew that his mustaches had never been trimmed. Also Cornelia and Betty and Joe and the Brinis went hunting—and strange was that experience, painful that discovery about human nature, in this terror-ridden town of Cordage. Policemen who knew Vanzetti, and had seen him on the street many times a week for eight years, were afraid for their jobs if they testified as to the length of his mustaches! Contractors who had hired him were afraid for their future contracts! Italian barbers were afraid for their little shops, and their little bootlegging on the side!

In the end they found two policemen who gave nervous and halting testimony that Vanzetti had always worn his walrus mustaches. They found an Italian cement contractor, Christofore, who had employed Vanzetti, and found him a good workman, and had always known him with his mustaches. The prosecuting attorney browbeat this witness, who knew no English, asking him about the mustaches of this person and that—among them of Beltrando Brini, aged twelve and a half years! He asked about the proprietor of one of Plymouth's big hotels—what kind of a mustache did this gentleman have, and Christofore described it, a small mustache that he was growing. After the noon recess the gentleman was put upon the stand, and exhibited to the jury a completely smooth-shaven face! What was the use of all this mustache-talk, said the district attorney, when they put a mustache on a man who had never had one?

The only time in her life that Cornelia ever heard Vanzetti swear was when he talked about this dirty trick which had been played upon him. For trick it was—whether the hotel proprietor had got shaved especially for his appearance as a witness, or whether it had just happened, that he had got shaved since the Italians had last met him. This much was certain: Christofore had seen this hotel proprietor with a mustache, and so had Vanzetti and many of his friends. The jury could not know, because, with one exception, they were outsiders. But Katzmann and Judge Thayer had sometimes been known to stay at this man's hotel, and to sit in front of his fire-place in the evening, gossiping with him about what had happened during the day.

VII

Such was the closing scene of this duel of evidence. The jury listened to the genial Mr. Katzmann become suddenly stern and patriotic. "Dagoes stand together!" he exclaimed—and it was easy for them to draw the conclusion that Americans should profit by their example. Then came Judge Thayer, thin-faced, tight-lipped, sharp-voiced, such a great man as these little men of the jury had been taught to reverence. Nothing of the inferiority complex now, nothing of the restless uneasiness, the vulgar craving for attention. It was the great actor now, playing the part which had been his life-study. He knew exactly what instructions to give to these Yankee jurymen, to appeal to

their prejudices without seeming to do so. When students of
the case sought to ascertain what he had said, it was discovered
that the court stenographer's notes had been burned, and that the
copy furnished the defense was strangely lacking in part of the
judge's charge.

The jury retired to deliberate, and carried with them the
four shotgun shells which were alleged to have been found upon
Vanzetti. They had been identified as ordinary hunting shells,
containing bird-shot, which would not be apt to kill a man. But
the jurors decided to investigate further, so they opened them,
and behold, they were filled with buckshot, which would surely
kill a man!

Now there is no point upon which English and American law
is more strict than this, that all evidence in a criminal trial must
be produced in the presence of the defendant. Vanzetti was
entitled to know about those buckshot, and to explain the fact
if he could. Maybe he would have taken the stand, maybe Sacco
would have done so; maybe they might have wished to ask, who
had had the keeping of those shells for the past six months, and
what were the chances of their having got mixed up with other
shells. There were no identifying marks upon them—but Vanzetti never had a chance to point this out. The jury went ahead
and brought in a verdict; and next day one of the jurors happened to meet Judge Thayer in a restaurant, and showed him
several of the buckshot. Judge Thayer knew at once that if this
story leaked out, the whole expensive trial would go for nothing.
He hurried to Katzmann, who came and got the buckshot from
the juror before he left the place. Then Katzmann phoned the
other jurors to come to his office, and warned them, and the
matter was hushed up.

It was half a year later that the facts got out, and then several
of the jurors made affidavits about it. An effort was made to
invalidate the trial on this ground, but the matter was never
argued. If it had been, it would have been argued before Judge
Thayer! Whenever during the next seven years the defense
discovered new evidence, they would make a motion for a new
trial, and under the laws of the august Commonwealth of
Massachusetts, a decision would be handed down by Judge
Thayer! When the defense set up a claim that the judge in the
Sacco-Vanzetti case had shown prejudice, they made a motion,

and it was referred to Judge Thayer, who solemnly listened to arguments, and solemnly handed down a decision to the effect that he had no jurisdiction! Incidentally he solemnly stated that he had no prejudice; and this after he had been going about among his clubmates for several years, saying, "Did you see what I did to those anarchistic bastards?"

The indictment charged "attempting to rob" and "attempting to kill." The judge in his instructions had directed that the second charge should be ignored, because the evidence showed that the bandits had merely sought to intimidate the guards; they could hardly have missed their targets with a shotgun at such close range. But after the jurors had opened the shells and found the buckshot, they decided to ignore the judge's instructions, and brought in a verdict of guilty on both counts. The judge, in an effort to correct this error, took the liberty of ignoring one-half the jury's verdict and sentencing the prisoner to the maximum penalty of fifteen years in state's prison for attempting to rob.

The scene in the court-room when the verdict was brought in was a heart-rending one. For ten days the friends of Vanzetti had sat in a tension of anxiety, and now their grief was not to be restrained. Cornelia bowed her head in her arms and wept, while Betty sat, white-faced and quivering, clutching Joe's hand. The Italian women became hysterical; they screamed and wailed, and the contagion spread from one to another—it was a scene of utter desperation, never anything to equal it. Vanzetti had to stand up and cry to them, "Coraggio! Coraggio!" His guards permitted that much before they shackled his wrists to their own, and led him swiftly out by a side door, and put him into a car and whisked him away to the jail.

Next day when Cornelia and Betty went to see him, for the first time they met an utterly broken man. Again and again he said the words with which he had first greeted them, "My enemy have got me!" He told them what the rest would be—he, the clear-sighted one, the thinker, the analyst of class forces. "I am a convicted. Nick is the friend of a convicted, he is a bandit already, he is a dead man. The jury will say, 'One of them is bad, why should other be better?' " And when Cornelia pledged her word that she would move heaven and earth to have this verdict set aside, he told her, "You will try, Nonna, but never will be succeeded. It is not for bandit I am convicted, it is for anarchista. If men do sooch trick like you see in court, what is use for hoping?"

Then it was that he swore, because of that mustache trick which had been played by the hotel proprietor. At that time he did not know about the buckshot. He did not know about the Pinkerton reports, which had been kept hidden by the prosecution. He did not know about the witnesses who had been rejected by the police because they did not describe the bandits according to the "theory." But he did know about the great cordage company, and the losses he had caused it in the strike; so, when Cornelia talked about decent people who would not stand for that "mustache trick," he laughed a bitter laugh. "You will see, Nonna. They will say, it is for jury to decide. They will say, musta trust jury, musta stand by court."

VIII

They put Vanzetti in an automobile, and with another car full of armed men in front and a third one bringing up the rear, they drove him to Boston and shut him behind the stone walls of the dingy old Charlestown prison—built in 1805, when the population of Massachusetts was one-tenth what it is now. It stands directly across the river from the city, so placed that on certain mornings when the sun rises clear, the shadow of Bunker Hill monument strikes its walls. An odd turn of fate, that this Italian seeker of liberty should have been convicted within sight of Plymouth Rock, and killed on ground over which Paul Revere had ridden.

They weighed him and measured him and scientifically scrutinized him, and dressed him in faded khaki, and put him in a cell containing an iron cot, and a free space eight feet long and one foot, ten inches wide, with light falling from a narrow slit in the ceiling. In that cell he would stay, fifteen and a half hours out of twenty-four, for the next seven years—except for the holidays of another indictment, trial and sentence. Of the remaining hours a day he would spend seven working in a tailor-shop, and forty minutes in a yard, overcrowded, smoky and dusty.

Soon after the beginning of this régime the Catholic chaplain of the prison came to see him. It is a Catholic maxim—therefore a prison maxim—that "once a Catholic, always a Catholic"; and even an alleged atheist is a human being, and may respond to kindness and sympathy. The good Father Murphy talked to him, not about religion, but about general matters; and then, having got on friendly terms, remarked, quite casually, "Tell me, Vanzetti, who drove the car at South Braintree?" Thereupon the alleged atheist rose up with dignity, and asked for the privilege of being alone in his cell, and the consolations of organized, institutionalized and subsidized religion were missing from the remainder of his life.

Instead he sought the consolations of literature. He wrote a long letter, pouring out his soul—and incidentally revealing that he was coming to feel at home in a new language; he no longer had to look up every word.

"I was just thinking what I would to do for past the long days jail: I was saying to myself: Do some work. But what? Write. A gentle motherly figure came to my mind and I rehear the voice: Why don't you write something now? It will be useful to you when you will be free. Just at that time I received your letter.

"Thanks to you from the bottom of my heart for your confidence in my innocence; I am so. I did not spittel a drop of blood, or steal a cent in all my life. A little knowledge of the past; a sorrowful experience of the life itself had gave to me some ideas very different from those of many other uman beings. But I wish to convince my fellow-men that only with virtue and honesty is possible for us to find a little happiness in the world. I preached: I worked. I wished with all my faculties that the social wealth would belong to every umane creatures, so well as it was the fruit of the work of all. But this do not mean robbery for a insurrection.

"The insurrection, the great movements of the soul do not need dollars. It need love, light, spirit of sacrifice, ideas, conscience, instincts. It need more conscience, more hope and more goodness. And all this blassing things can be seeded, awoked, growed up in the heart of man in many ways, but not by robbery and murder for robbery.

"I like you to know that I think to Italy, so speaking. From the universal family, turning to this humble son, I will say that,

as far as my needs, wish and aspirations call, I do not need to
become a bandit. I like the teaching of Tolstoi, Saint Francesco
and Dante. I like the example of Cincinnati and Garibaldi. The
epicurean joi do not like to me. A little roof, a field, a few books
and food is all what I need. I do not care for money, for
leisure, for mondane ambition. And honest, even in this world
of lambs and wolves I can have those things. But my father
has many field, houses, garden. He deal in wine and fruits and
granaries. He wrote to me many times to come back home, and
be a business man. Well, this supposed murderer had answered
to him that my conscience do not permit to me to be a business
man and I will gain my bread by work his field.

"And more: The clearness of mind, the peace of the conscience, the determination and force of will, the intelligence, all,
all what make the man feeling to be a part of the life, force and
intelligence of the universe, will be brake by a crime. I know
that, I see that, I tell that to everybody. Do not violate the law
of nature, if you do not want to be a miserable. I remember: it
was a night without moon, but starry. I sit alone in the darkness, I was sorry, very sorry. With the face in my hands I began
to look at the stars. I feel that my soul want goes away from my
body, and I have had to make an effort to keep it in my chest.
So, I am the son of Nature, and I am so rich that I do not need
any money. And for this they say I am a murderer and will
condemn me to death. Death? It is nothing. Abbominium is
cruel thing.

"Now you advise me to study. Yes, it would be a good thing.
But I do not know enough this language to be able to make any
study through it. I will like to read Longfellow's, Paine's,
Franklin's and Jefferson's works, but I cannot. I would like
to study mathematics, physics, history and science, but I have
not a sufficient elementary school to begin such studies, especially the two first and I cannot study without work, hard
physical work, sunshine and winds; free, blassing wind. There
is no flame without the atmospheric gasses; and no light of
genius in any soul without they communion with Mother
Nature.

"I hope to see you very soon; I will tell you more in the
matter. I will write something, a meditation perhaps and name
it: Waiting for the Hanger. I have lost the confidence in the

justice of man. I mean in what is called so; not of course, of that sentiment which lay in the heart of man, and that no infernal force will be strong enough to soffocate it. Your assistance and the assistance of so many good men and women, had made my cross much more light. I will not forget it.

"I beg your pardon for such a long letter, but I feel so reminiscent to you that hundred pages would not be sufficient to extern my sentiments and feelings. I am sure you will excuse me. Salve.

"Give to all my best regards and wishes, Your
"BARTHOLOMEW VANZETTI."

IX

Cornelia and Betty and Joe were back in Boston, the first two having been hurriedly summoned for the funeral of Great-aunt Priscilla. It is highly inconvenient, belonging to one of these big families; there are so many funerals, weddings and christenings, which it would be unthinkable not to attend.

An extraordinary thing had happened to this aged female Brahmin in the closing months of her life; the bacillus of eccentricity, which lurks in all Boston blue blood, had suddenly flared into activity. Priscilla Quincy Adams Thornwell, spinster, aged eighty-seven, stiff as a ramrod and model of every known or conceivable kind of propriety, had suddenly fallen under the spell of an Episcopal faith-healer, who was traveling about the country insisting that every bishop, even every country parson, could demonstrate the living presence of God, work miracles, and stop the slow dribble of Episcopalians into Christian Science.

Great-aunt Priscilla almost succeeded in arising and taking up her bed and walking, in spite of the complete anchylosis of her spine; she insisted that she would have done it, had it not been that her relatives persisted in reminding her of her great age—a "negative suggestion." She took up the habit of being what she called "instant in prayer," which meant that she was liable to start talking to God at any moment. It was embarrassing to her relatives and friends, because of course no one likes to interrupt a talk with God, and feels something of an interloper even to sit and listen to it. Great-aunt Priscilla summoned her brother, Abner, over whom she had great authority, because he was only eighty-five years old, and tried to persuade him to appeal for a cure of his deafness. But Abner argued that if God had meant him not to be deaf, God wouldn't have made him deaf; and this was a relief to the family, because it frightened them to imagine Abner becoming "instant in prayer," with that deaf man's voice which filled the biggest house in Boston.

And now it was discovered that Priscilla Quincy Adams Thornwell, spinster, had left a letter asserting that the Episcopal service for the burial of the dead was a denial of the faith of Jesus, and specifying that she was to be buried from Trinity Church with the services for Easter Morning! It was a problem for authorities in ecclesiastical etiquette; but to defy a Thornwell was unthinkable, so the rector and his assistants finally decided that One to whom a thousand years were as a day might conceivably accept any day as Easter. There were no lilies on the market, but there were plenty of roses, and the occasion created almost as much excitement as a vaudeville show that was likely to be raided by the police. It was as if everybody were secretly wondering whether the Lord might give some sign of his displeasure at this setting back of the church calendar for three months. But apparently the Lord understood Boston, a city which is governed by the old, and especially the old ladies.

They were all at this service, even though they had to motor a hundred miles from the country. They wore their black dresses and bonnets, some new and shiny, some old and rusty—but never forget that the rustiest might be the richest. To wear a dowdy dress and a mangy fur tippet might mean one who was able to scorn ostentation—just as illiteracy in an English duke means that he is above the laws of grammar. One of these old ladies might dispose of millions upon a whim, and her lightest word was social law. They sat in family pews which had belonged to them since the great brown-stone church was built; beside them the younger generations—sweet-faced ladies, better dressed, and oh, so neat and clean, gazing with rapt faces at a fairy-story setting of white roses and candles and stained-glass-window saints, and a procession of toddlers in white robes, singing in cherubs' voices to the rolling music of four organs in four different corners. How beautiful it all was, and how serene—and how amazing to come to it out of that world of lies and cruelty which Cornelia and Betty had just left!

Look about you at these perfect Anglo-Saxon faces—not a foreign one among them—so elegant and so satisfied! Note the costumes, polished to the last pin, and chosen with impeccable taste—broadcloth and patent leather and spats for the men, veils and laces, silk stockings and delicate scents, flowers and unostentatious jewelry for the ladies! Note the soft, cultivated voices, the gracious manners, rehearsed for centuries! Note the ancient formulas, the ritual established since eternity; the prayers and anthems rising to an Anglo-Saxon God, untainted by His temporary sojourn in a Hebrew womb. Bland saints in all the windows, with golden haloes and bright-colored robes, untainted by contact with the fishing industry. A rector who was the last word in Back Bay fashion, the Harvard manner grafted upon a mediæval ecclesiastic.

While the sweet-faced ladies gazed up at him adoringly, he pronounced a little eulogy upon the virtues of the dear departed, whose faith and funds had nourished the church for two generations and a half. It wasn't customary to make speeches at church funerals; but since this was an Easter Sunday service, a different rule might well apply. The rector referred to the recent new fervors of the deceased, a matter which required tact, because this rector had got his training in days when the theological department of the university was separate from the medical. He made an excursion into the field of modern thought, revealing that he had heard of the science of astronomy and knew that the earth was small; more amazing yet, he gave up the Virgin birth, saying that we did not know just what had happened on that occasion, and perhaps would never know. It sounded like a hint at some scandal in the Holy Family, and would have made a scandal in Episcopal circles in other cities: but not in Boston, where everything is far advanced, and Trinity Church has to compete with King's Chapel, which is Unitarian, and even more intellectual, and if possible more fashionable.

x

The funeral had the effect of bringing Cornelia and Betty back into the family, and they heard the latest gossip. Alice

Winters was still supporting her "little theater," but very un-happy, because her poet, supposed to be storming Parnassus, was getting drunk every night, and neglecting his muse for a brazen, yellow-headed flapper. Clara Scatterbridge was getting stout, and the best reducing experts could not solve her prob-lem; she concealed the dire truth from these advisers, but not from the Argus eyes of the family—that she kept an assort-ment of sweets in her boudoir, and nibbled chocolates and candied fruits all day.

Great-uncle Abner was very melancholy now; he was the last of the old generation, he said, and his time would come soon—which was certainly a negative suggestion! He could no longer remember the chess moves he had made last week, and his son Quincy was losing games on purpose, in order to keep up the old man's spirits. Abner had gone to stay with the Scatterbridges, because he liked to be with the children; each of the younger ones had a donkey to ride, and Abner had one too, and rode at the head of the procession, all over the estate—a most laughable sight. But everybody had to keep a sober face, because if you laughed at anything whatever, the old man would think you were laughing at him, and would take ineradicable offense.

Deborah came to the little apartment to have lunch with her mother and daughter; and presently it transpired that the Argus eyes of the family had observed Betty going about town with a young man by the name of Joseph Jefferson Randall. Who was he? A grandson of the actor? Betty said no, he was one of the Randalls of Pakenham Court House, Virginia, and a nephew of Senator Randall, now ambassador to one of the South Ameri-can countries.

"Don't you think, dear, you had better let your mother meet him?" inquired Deborah, mildly.

"No, Mother, I don't," said the younger generation. "Joe is much less radical than I, but he always says what he thinks, and so he would make you very unhappy."

"Don't you say what you think, my daughter?"

"Practically never, Mother. I bite my tongue off several times every hour."

Deborah said no more, but Betty knew what she would do—and so did Deborah. What are the secret, underground channels of the blue-bloods, by which they find out whatever they wish to know? Do they have indexes and card-files, like the Quaker attorney-general, so that they can telegraph and ascertain who is who, and what are his family scandals? Anyhow, the next time Deborah came to town, she knew that Joe's father was a "drinking man," whose wife had divorced him. Fortunately Deborah hadn't found out that Joe himself was married; but she imagined the worst, because divorces are a matter of heredity, like cancer, she said.

Deborah's hope was to persuade Cornelia and Betty to accompany Betty's older sister to Europe for the rest of the summer—since young Priscilla's wedding had been put off by the death of her great-aunt, whose namesake she was. Failing in that, Deborah's next campaign was to persuade the pair to come out and spend the summer at the Rupert Alvin palace on the North Shore. Deborah was lonely, she said, pathetically; her husband had so many cares just now, owing to the collapse of business. Deborah even went so far as to promise that Cornelia and Betty would be free to believe and say what they pleased, and she would not argue with them—a most remarkable "come-down" for so haughty and stern a lady.

Anything to get Betty away from the companionship of that dangerous young Virginian! To divert her with yachting and tennis and lawn-parties and picnics, in the company of sound and wholesome graduates of the Harvard "Gold Coast," their blood free from the hereditary virus of divorce! But both Cornelia and Betty were obdurate; they were going to stay cooped up in that hot little apartment all July and August, to consult lawyers and organize committees and raise funds for the defense of two anarchist bandits!

XI

The men of the Thornwell family indeed had their hands full that summer. The expected post-war collapse had come—or rather it had been brought about by those who realized that prices had got too high, and that "deflation" was necessary. Naturally, these men wanted to deflate everybody but themselves, and having the power, they did so. The heads of the great banking groups, of whom Rupert Alvin was one of the most careful and conscientious, had devised what they called the "Federal Reserve System," a chain of banks financed by the government and run by the bankers; its function was to enable the great bankers to save themselves in times of panic, by issuing vast sums of new money, and lending it to the big industries, whose stocks and bonds are the mainstay of banking credit. That meant that when a panic came, it was the little fellows and the outsiders who were "deflated," while the big bankers and their friends sat on a rock and waited for the storm to blow over.

Having this power in their hands, Rupert and his associates in the course of that summer of 1920 had their Federal Reserve banks suddenly raise the discount rates in the farming country; the result of which was to force the dumping of the country's farm produce on the market. Prices collapsed to a point where most of the farmers were bankrupt, and in the Northwest there were whole counties with every single farm sold for taxes. Meantime the big industrialists of the East, having bank-credit, were able to hold their products, and close down their plants and wait.

But if Rupert and his Pilgrim National crowd thought they were going to have a happy time riding that storm, they learned a sad lesson. The saying that uneasy lies the head that wears a crown, applies to the kings of modern credit as well as to those of Shakespearean drama. It was as if Rupert were the guardian of a huge honey-pot, and had the job of apportioning its contents to all the flies in New England. They swarmed about him, making a quite terrifying buzzing—and it was a fact that many of them had stings, more or less dangerous, and threatened to use them, and sometimes did. Impossible for a great banker to sleep with all that clamor in his ears! Impossible for any member of his family to sleep—because there were lady-flies as well as gentleman, and they too could buzz and sting!

To drop metaphors, it was a fact that a small group of bankers had to decide, during that panic, which industries of the community were to be saved and which were to go to the wall. And needless to say, in a place like Boston, it was not a question of vulgar material efficiency, it was a question of social status. Who was who, and who was married to whom, and what was the relative blueness of this blood and that? The difference between the attitudes of Boston and New York in this matter are set forth in a story which all financial men delight to tell, about the New York banker who wrote to a Boston friend, saying that he had a position for a capable young man. The Boston banker sent one, with a letter explaining that he was a great-nephew of the late Josiah Quincy Thornwell, a nephew of John Quincy Thornwell and of Rupert Alvin, a cousin of the Cabots, and so on. Whereupon the vulgar New Yorker dismissed the applicant and sent a telegram, reading: "I did not want a young man for breeding purposes, I wanted one for banking."

The emergency now was the most desperate the Boston blue-bloods had faced for a long time. It was no mere play question, like belonging to a Sewing Circle, or getting your daughters into Camp Putnam and the Friday dances, or your sons into the "Porcellian" and the "Alpha Delta Phi." No, it was a question of your very life-blood, that privilege upon which your family existence was based. So you forgot your good manners, and fought as your ancestors had fought, in the days before they had any manners. You threatened and stormed, and raked up ancient, long-buried family skeletons, and made life miserable for a great banker who had for years been suffering from high blood pressure, and had been warned by Morrow, eminent authority upon diseases of the rich.

Rupert became morose under the strain. His pink and purple bulges, which had seemed to be radiating geniality, now took on the aspect of a threatened explosion. He fell to grumbling about human nature. Nobody cared about anything but money; friendship, family pride, honor, all were gone. He would carry his burden of sorrow for days, and suddenly it would become too heavy, and he would dump it in some quite unsuitable place. An elderly widow, a friend of Cornelia's, sought him as adviser about the purchase of bonds, and the great and busy head of the Pilgrim National Bank kept the astonished lady for half an hour while he impressed upon her the solemn duty of guarding her property. "Hold on to it! You have nothing else—absolutely nothing! When it is gone you will discover that nobody respects you, your friends have no use for you. Nothing counts to-day but money!" The widow-lady might have had her feelings hurt, but she understood.that it was impersonal, a revelation of the banker-soul.

But for the most part Rupert kept his pessimistic thoughts to pour out upon his spouse in the privacy of their chamber, after the lights were out, and they lay in the chaste retirement of their twin beds, under brocaded blue silk counterpanes. He would expatiate upon the abnormal greediness of this one and that, and after he had begun to snore, Deborah would lie still and petition the Lord to soften the hearts of the greedy ones, and spare her good and noble husband, who was sacrificing his very life to preserve sound and conservative banking in New England—which meant, of course, banking under the control of the Pilgrim National group.

XII

There are some whose claims were not to be questioned. Unthinkable that any Thornwell should go to the wall, or any one who could claim kinship, even by marriage. Those huge Thornwell Mills had to have many millions of credit, to enable them to store their manufactured products, and turn off their operatives to starve. And of course they got it; you have only to imagine the hysterics that Clara Thornwell Scatterbridge would have had in the boudoir of Deborah Thornwell Alvin, if Rupert had dreamed of refusing! John Quincy Thornwell needed a small fortune, for a shipping deal he had been putting through on the side; and he got it from Rupert's bank. Rupert also needed a fortune, for some of those subsidiary plants which he and Henry Cabot Winters had taken away from Jerry Walker, and had kept all to themselves. Rupert got this money from the Fifth National Bank, of which John Quincy Thornwell was president. So these big fellows shifted millions about from their right-hand pockets to their left-hand pockets, and shrewd lawyers like Henry Cabot Winters were there to tell them exactly how to do it, so they need never worry if some spy told on them, and caused a government bank-examiner to drop in.

They knew that their rivals had spies on them, because they had spies on their rivals. And when these spies would bring in reports of what was going on, Henry Cabot Winters and the other legal spiders would be called in to consider how to meet the rivals' moves. If it was discovered that some little fellow, having less expensive legal talent, had slipped up somewhere, and done something which the law did not allow, then was the time to use your pull with the bank-examiner, whom you had caused to be appointed a few years ago, and whom you were going to make into a bank-president in the course of another year or two—after he had completed the job of putting your rivals out of business.

That was the way the blue-bloods kept the banking industry a strictly blue-blooded affair. The foreigners, and especially the Jews, had got into everything else. For decades they had been boycotted as department-store owners, but now several of the biggest and most successful stores were in the hands of Jews. They had got clothing and wool and leather; they had the theaters, and were breaking into law and medicine—but they were never going to get the banking-business, not if Rupert Alvin and the rest of the "high hats" could prevent it. And they could!

At this time there was a Jewish banker who had broken into the reserve. Simon Swig was his name—which in itself was enough to demonstrate the impropriety of allowing a Jew to become directing head of a bank! He had come into the country as a common immigrant, and now had got hold of the Tremont Trust Company, an honorable institution, and was running it on bargain-day principles—paying five and a half per cent on savings accounts, and advertising the fact, which was unethical, but brought in the business. He was a rascal, so the blue-bloods said, and doubtless it was true, but you had to remember that in high finance rascality is a question of degree. The respectable bankers were breaking any number of laws, but having the banking authorities in their clubs, they were not punished. Neither were they exposed, because they had the newspapers, and their "news bureaus," run by large stout subsidized "experts"— whose expertness lay in making the public believe whatever Rupert Alvin and men of his sort desired.

In the course of that chain of troubles, the state bank-examiners swooped down one morning and tacked a notice on the door of the Tremont Trust Company, to the effect that it was closed and forbidden to do business. And that was all there was to it—the Tremont Trust stayed closed, and it didn't do any business. If it had been a "blue-blood" bank, it would have been "tided over"; instead of which it was turned over to a "blue-blood" receiver, and paid its savings depositors a hundred cents on the dollar—which seemed rather to justify the claim of Simon Swig that it had been sound all along.

XIII

What started the trouble that summer was the problem of Charles Ponzi. An Italian immigrant who had come to America about the same time as Vanzetti, and with even less money in his pocket, Ponzi, too, had washed dishes for a living; but he had not wasted his time dreaming about "joostice"—no, he was the sort of immigrant America wants, he had dreamed of making a million dollars in a week, and he had done it. He discovered a curious situation in international exchange, so he said; it was possible to buy postal coupons in Vienna, and sell them at a higher rate in Switzerland, and thus you could turn a thousand dollars into twenty-five thousand. It made good advertising copy, and was no more false than what the big bankers were telling the public about their Federal Reserve System. Anyhow, Ponzi opened a dingy little office in School Street, quite in the correct Boston tradition—for many of the big New England corporations had dingy little offices in some of those two-hundred-year-old houses in dark and narrow streets which had been laid out by cows.

Charles Ponzi advertised that he would sell you a forty-five-day certificate, which you were free to redeem at any time, but if you would wait till the end of the forty-five days, you would get fifty per cent interest. The tidings spread among the million inhabitants of Boston, and all those persons who cherished the dream of getting rich without working came to buy certificates—which meant that Ponzi had approximately a million customers. Such a mob of people tried to get into his dingy office all at once that the police reserves had to be called out to keep them from being crushed to death. In that suffocating room you saw rich ladies in silks and jewels, newsboys, street peddlers, workingwomen with babies in their arms, scrubwomen clutching in their hands the earnings of half a lifetime on their knees. They all wanted to give it to Ponzi, and he took it, and fulfilled the immigrant's dream by buying himself a palace in the country, with the most expensive custom-built limousine in Boston to bring him to town.

Ponzi was imperiling the savings banks by causing the public to draw out all their money; he was buying into the big trust companies, and in danger of becoming a real banker. Worse yet, he was filling the public mind with unrest, talking recklessly to the newspapers. He kept saying that in making a hundred per cent profit in three months he was merely doing what many big bankers were doing—the difference being that he was giving the public fifty percent, whereas the big bankers gave only five percent. If any one were to say how near to the truth that was, the person would not be believed, so it would be useless to say it.

The bank-examiners and district attorneys got busy, and filled the papers with rumors that Ponzi was about to be arrested. It was difficult to take action because the ex-dishwasher was now worth about twelve million dollars, and actually had five millions cash in Boston banks, and nobody so rich had ever been arrested in New England. Moreover, he had hired a very able lawyer, who was later on disbarred as a "fixer"; he paid that lawyer a million dollars before he got through, and would undoubtedly have got off, had not Rupert and his crowd been so determined to get him out of the way.

As often occurs with financial storms, this one got out of control, and brought down several institutions: the Cosmopolitan Trust, the Prudential Trust, the Fidelity Trust—it was a rollcall of respectability. It so happened that the Commonwealth of Massachusetts had several hundred thousand dollars in these banks, and several counties had as much. The city of Cambridge, the home of Harvard University, just across the river, was stuck for half a million—the greater part having been got by a trick played upon the city treasurer a few months before the crash. All this caused a terrific scandal, and a long train of consequences most distressing to Rupert Alvin and his friends. For the examinations of the banks disclosed that many of the state legislators had been borrowing money without any security, and had used this money to buy stocks in public utilities, while passing a bill to triple their value.

Not so long ago the Pilgrim National crowd had driven the Boston Elevated Railway onto the financial rocks, and taken it over; then, in order to put it back on its feet, they had jammed through the legislature a so-called Public Control bill, whereby the Commonwealth guaranteed dividends to the Elevated stockholders, which made necessary a ten-cent fare. So here was the blue-blooded and high-hatted and in all ways ineffable Rupert Alvin playing Santa Claus and angel to the politicians and legislators of his Commonwealth! The disclosure was half a year in the future, but that only meant the prolonging of Rupert's worry; for of course he knew what was in the records of the banks, and he knew that when the public has lost a lot of money and become furiously angry, it is much harder to keep news out of the papers.

XIV

Another trouble looming, if possible even more serious! Jerry Walker had come back from his nervous breakdown, and had found out some details of the intrigue by which Rupert and Henry Cabot Winters had persuaded the other bankers to join in taking his ten-million-dollar properties. Jerry had consulted lawyers, and made a deal with one of them, a bristling little bull-dog of a man who had taken many a million away from big bankers on previous occasions. Now, under the law, Jerry had a right to put questions to Rupert, as to what Rupert had done to him, and Rupert was compelled to answer, under penalty of being considered to have admitted his guilt! So there would come to the Pilgrim National crowd and their lawyers long letters full of questions, agonizingly direct and to the point; and there would be conferences of great financial and legal personages, and private conferences in Rupert's study late at night, in which Rupert and his brother-in-law would go over what they had done to Jerry, and many times wish they had done it a little differently!

Betty Alvin found out about this, because she ran into Lucile Walker in the lobby of one of the hotels. They had not met since Betty's departure for Europe, more than a year ago; so they rushed into each other's arms, girl fashion, and then adjourned to the tea-room to talk things over. Lucile had solved her financial and other problems in the good old established way; she was now Mrs. Percy G. Townsend, her husband a manufacturer of some kind of electrical equipment. He was young and enthusiastic, and so was his wife, and they were going to work hard and build up a business, and then some day one of the big banking groups would take it over.

Betty told a little about her adventures in Hungary and Russia and Plymouth, Massachusetts; after which there was an embarrassed pause on Lucile's part, and she said, "I suppose you know what Papa is doing?" When Betty said she didn't, Lucile told about the suit that was coming; and when Betty said that she was not taking her father's side in his business fights, Lucile told more of the story. It was going to mean a dreadful lot of publicity for all of them, because those big State Street bankers would be put on the witness stand and questioned about the deals they had made, and how they had divided Mr. Walker's properties. Betty said she had told her mother that she would never touch any of that money; just now she was wrestling with the problem whether she ought to take any money at all from her father. She was able to earn her own living, and wanted to—but also she wanted to give her time to organizing a Sacco-Vanzetti defense, and she couldn't earn a living at that.

Betty went home and told her grandmother; and so when Cornelia happened to meet Henry Cabot Winters, she was able to pose as a woman of the world, in touch with secret news channels. Henry, of course, had no trouble in guessing how she knew, and there developed a curious situation. A couple of years ago he had been indignant at the idea that Jerry Walker might be using Cornelia as a means of getting information from the Thornwells; but now he wanted to use Cornelia to get information as to the plans of Jerry Walker! He went so far as to propose a "swap": if Cornelia would find out all she could from the Walkers, Henry would use his inside connections to help Cornelia's beloved bandits. He would get in touch with the officials, and find out what their plans were, and might even be able to find some way to get those rascals off.

Somehow this tickled Cornelia's funny-bone, and she burst into laughter. "You and Rupert must be badly scared," she said; and after Henry had made sure that she was not going to talk to the Walkers about it, he admitted that they were. It was not that they had done anything wrong—nobody in Boston ever does that—but it was going to be such a mess, to have the letters and telegrams and confidential memoranda of a great banking project spread out in the newspapers.

"Can't you clean out your files?" asked Cornelia, with a twinkle in her eye. He answered that it wasn't so easy as it sounded, because one document referred to the next, and there were copies in a dozen different banks. If you took out very much, your employees were bound to know it, and that exposed you to spying and blackmail. Uneasy lies the head that wears a crown!

XV

Troubles! Troubles! Even in far-off Italy, that summer and fall, people were occupied in making troubles for Rupert Alvin and his associates. The big bankers had filled up their vaults with the gold-embossed and red-sealed financial promises of European governments; and vain was the hope to save themselves by unloading this paper on the public. Because after a bank customer had bought it, he generally came back to leave it as security up to eighty percent of its market value; and how could Rupert refuse to lend money on a bond which he had certified as an investment for widows and orphans? So it had come about that every time a European premier sneezed, Rupert Alvin jumped in his sleep; when the anarchists paraded in Milan or Turin and waved their black flags, Rupert couldn't sleep at all.

That summer the radical labor unions of Italy made their long expected coup—moving in and taking possession of the principal steel and machine plants of the country. But having got in, they didn't know what to do next, because they could not turn a wheel of the plants without coal, and the coal had to come from England or America, in English or American ships, upon English or American credit. Were English or American coal men going to extend credit to Italian anarchists, anarcho-syndicalists, communist-anarchists and left-wing socialists? The coal men of England and America, like all the other big business men of those countries, were going to do what their Rupert Alvins told them; and the Rupert Alvins said thumbs down on Reds. So the Italian workers had to make peace with their masters, and give up the plants; and then it was necessary for the masters to organize a counter-revolutionary government, to break up the labor unions and kill off the leaders. To do that they had to have the machinery of reaction and slaughter—and where else should they come for it but to America?

So it happened that Rupert Alvin, in the midst of all his troubles with Ponzi, and Simon Swig, and the half dozen closed banks, and the threatened Elevated Railway scandal, and the hiding of evidence in the Jerry Walker case, and the unhappiness over Betty and Cornelia—with all this nightmare-load riding his shoulders, Rupert Alvin had to interview agents of the banking and manufacturing interests of Italy, and listen to plans for the coup d'état which was to turn that country into a dictatorship of big capital. No possible way to avoid it—unless all the money that had been loaned to Italy during and since the war was to be lost. The bankers of Boston and New York and Philadelphia and Chicago had to get together and do for Italy what they had already done for Hungary and Roumania and Czechoslovakia and Finland and Esthonia and Latvia and Lithuania—so many miserable little bonded states that it gave a hundred percent American a headache to learn the names.

And meantime Bartolomeo Vanzetti paced his cell, in the space eight feet by one and a half allotted him for pacing. He knew what was happening, because his friends brought him a few facts, and he could reconstruct the rest, with that clear mind which understood social forces. He knew that it meant the ruin of all his hopes, all chance of freedom for the peasants and wage-slaves of Italy for years, perhaps decades. He knew what the American bankers would do; he foretold how, when the time came to float the loan, they would have the newspapers bought and the propaganda ready, and would carry the mass of Italian-Americans into reaction with them. Meantime they had Vanzetti in jail, where he was safe—and they were going to see to it that he stayed!

CHAPTER 10

THE LEGAL SYSTEM

I

On the 11th of September, 1920, the grand jury of Norfolk County brought indictments against Nicola Sacco and Bartolomeo Vanzetti, charging them with the murder of the paymaster and guard at South Braintree in the previous April. This county shared with Plymouth the same district attorney; and Nick and Bart were brought before the same Judge Thayer. They pleaded not guilty, and the trial was set for February. Meantime Bart went back to the tailor-shop at Charlestown, serving his sentence for the Bridgewater crime; while Nick returned to the county jail at Dedham—a very unhappy man, because they gave him nothing whatever to do in this prison, and he nearly went out of his mind.

Meantime a little group in Boston set about organizing what they called the Sacco-Vanzetti Defense Committee. In the beginning it consisted entirely of Italians, the foremost among them being Aldino Felicani, anarchist printer, a tall, ascetic-looking young man, soft-voiced and reserved. He would set up type for the circulars, and translate them into Italian. Others would address envelopes, and visit the meeting-places of radicals in neighboring towns, and circulate subscription lists. So would come a few dollars here and a few dollars there. At the outset there was no office, no secretary, only the volunteer labors of a few comrades.

Joe Randall had finished his book on the "White Terror"; he had lost hope of bringing it up to date, since events happened faster than pen could move. Now he became a volunteer press agent for the committee; he wrote news stories, and made carbon copies, and went about trying to cajole this editor and that into giving a little publicity. With him came another young journalist, Art Shields, a tireless worker; you would see lights burning and hear typewriters clicking in the office until two or

280

three o'clock in the morning. Betty learned to make speeches, and put her youth and beauty and social prestige to work; she would visit labor headquarters and "vamp" the officials, seeking to overcome the bitter prejudice of Irish-Catholic and Yankee labor leaders against a pair of wops who were admitted to be infidels, anarchists and draft-dodgers. Cornelia and Betty would go together to places where they encountered ladies with blue blood ever so slightly tinged with pink. The services the pair had rendered to the suffrage cause—now victorious—gave them prestige, and they could get small checks.

The Sacco-Vanzetti Defense Committee was from the outset a peculiar organization. It consisted largely of a name, and nobody could say just who were its members, or what was their authority. Those Americans who later joined and helped to build it up did so from sympathy with an oppressed group, and they served as a "front"; they were featured in the newspapers, they made speeches, and conferred respectability. But they did not know so much about the case, and naturally they had to defer to the Italians in a crisis.

Among these latter, also, appeared a division; there was an Italian "front": such men as Felicani, the printer, and Felice Guadagni, the journalist whom Cornelia had met when he came down to help in the Plymouth cordage strike; also Rosina Sacco, wife of the prisoner, an alert and intelligent woman, devoted to her husband's cause. These were known; but there were others who stayed in the background, and in a time of crisis would reach out a hand, as it were from behind a curtain, and influence a decision. These were anarchists, intimates of Sacco and Vanzetti, and it was easy enough to understand why they kept hidden; they stood in danger of deportation, and perhaps of being accused of crimes, along with the two in jail. But it made committee functioning difficult, when you never knew what decision would be changed, or by whom, or for what reason. Public statements would be prepared and issued in English, and then translated into Italian, and the discovery would be made that the Italian version was quite different, and even contradictory; yet it would not be known just how this had happened.

There was the element of fear, and of course, the element of suspicion. It was inevitable that the enemy should send spies among the committee—and that these would be persons sufficiently cunning to pose as "good radicals." From first to last the prosecution was fully informed as to everything that went on among the committee, the decisions that were taken as well as the arguments and the quarrels. These spies came and went; and after they were gone, they would joke about how they had collected money for the cause and spent it having a good time in their own fashion. Then you would hear the great ones of Massachusetts, who had employed these spies, solemnly charging that the funds of the committee had been stolen!

II

Among both English and Italian groups there were sharp divisions according to political beliefs. Some insisted that this was a criminal case, and should be handled as such; others thought it was a case of labor persecution, to be featured as an episode in the class struggle. Strange as it might seem, the anarchists for the most part took the former view; they saw clearly that efforts to make anarchist propaganda might not merely bring about a conviction of the two men, but might get their defenders into trouble. But a socialist like Joe Randall was free from such fear, and to him the case was an effort of big business to put two of its dangerous enemies out of the way; he could never write anything about the case that was not disguised propaganda for socialism, and of course he did not like to have his propaganda cut out by non-socialist members of the committee. Young persons like Betty Alvin, who at this stage of her life insisted that she was a communist—such young persons wanted to put in a different kind of propaganda, and their persistence increased as the case grew more conspicuous.

It was a controversy that would never cease, up to the very last hour, and even beyond it—when men and women fought with deadly bitterness over the question of what should be done with the ashes of the victims. You saw the germs of it at the first meeting, when eight or ten ill-assorted enthusiasts fell to discussing what kind of lawyer should be employed for the trial. Should they get a labor man, who would make an appeal to the movement throughout the country? Or should they get a respectable lawyer, who would confer dignity upon the case, and impress the public and the jury in the good old Boston way? Still another possibility, should they look for a criminal expert, with knowledge of the trickeries of a highly technical game? Joe and Betty united for the first plan, Cornelia urged the second, while the Italians divided between the first and third.

A powerful factor in the decision was, of course, the two prisoners, who never wavered for a moment; to them it was a class-war case, they were being persecuted because of their threat to the rich of Massachusetts. To Vanzetti the very idea of respectability was an insult, the idea of legal trickery nearly as bad. All such hopes would prove delusive, and only the labor movement could save them. "Unless a million men can be mobilized for our defense, we are lost!"—so he said in the first days, and so he said in the last.

As for Sacco, he was even more extreme; shut up in his half-dark cell in Dedham jail, he was like a rat in a trap, a creature all of steel springs and fury. He brooded incessantly, and ate his heart out, and never let himself be fooled by a hope. "They have got us, they will kill us," he would say; and whenever his enemies came near him, he would throw his revolutionary convictions into their faces. "Viva l'anarchia!" were his last words, and this summed up his attitude at every stage of the seven years' struggle.

III

Cornelia went downtown to have lunch with Henry Cabot Winters, who knew all the lawyers in town. First he would make the protest which family proprieties required; and then he would betray his secret amusement—being in truth rather proud of his runaway mother-in-law, who was telling the world to go to the devil in the very best "old Boston" manner.

But this time Cornelia missed the usual twinkle in Henry's fine dark eyes. In the first place, the great lawyer was worried by some of the things he had learned that Jerry Walker had learned about him. And in the second place, Henry had been shocked by the Wall Street "bomb explosion." Five days after the indictment of Sacco and Vanzetti a wagonload of explosives had gone off in front of the building of J. P. Morgan and Company in New York, and thirty-three persons had been blown to fragments. The newspapers were certain that this was the work of anarchists, and the Boston *Traveler* had come out with a full-page article, to the effect that the crime had been traced to the Galleani group, a vengeance for the arrest of the bandits, Sacco and Vanzetti.

"Mother, that is a horrible thing!" said Henry; and Cornelia said, yes, it was indeed horrible for a newspaper to prejudge the case of two accused men, and make it impossible for them to get a fair jury in the community. Henry, as a lawyer, must know that such an article would have that effect, and under the very strict laws of Massachusetts was contempt of court.

But Henry did not discuss that aspect of the matter. "I am told," said he, "that the Boston anarchists made no attempt to conceal their glee when they learned of that explosion."

"Why should they?" said Cornelia. "If they had learned that an earthquake had destroyed every building in Wall Street, they would have been still more pleased; but that would not mean they control earthquakes. Their glee expressed their conviction that the practices of Wall Street cause boundless suffering to the workers of America; and in that they are right."

"Now, Mother," said Henry, "let's look at the menu. We don't want to get off on politics."

Cornelia laughed. "I am always entertained to discover the identity of attitude of my Back Bay and my anarchist friends. The anarchists don't want to get off on politics either, they share your faith in direct action."

Henry ordered the lunch; and Cornelia repeated what she had learned from the radical papers, that the explosion had been caused by a load of blasting gelatine, being illegally taken through the city in the daytime; while Henry repeated what he had read in the capitalist papers, that it was an anarchist bomb. He wanted to know, with some irritation, "Do you think that anarchists never use bombs?"

"I have been told they sometimes do."

"Yet you can be certain these two friends of yours never did any such thing?"

"They aren't accused of having done that, Henry."

"I know. But people say—"

"What people, Henry?"

"Well, friends of mine who are in position to know the inside."

"Will you tell me their names?"

"I can't do that."

"Did you ask who gave them the information?"

"No, but—"

"I am interested to watch the process of rumor. People say this and people say that, and always when you try to get something definite, there is nothing. Can you bring me a single fact, Henry—one that you as a first-class lawyer would respect? I am ready to deal with it honestly; and surely it's worth the family's while to keep me from being led into a trap." Cornelia looked her son-in-law in his dark fine eyes, gravely and steadily; and he said all right, he would try to help her.

IV

The waiter brought oysters, since there was an "r" in the month. And after he had set down the crackers and the lemons and the paprika, and made all the necessary flourishes, he went his way, and Henry returned to the dangerous subject of bombs, which haunted the thoughts of all leisure-class Boston in those desperate days. Despite his pretenses of omniscience, Cornelia represented his only direct contact with the anarchist movement.

"You know, Mother, somebody did make bombs—the ones that went through the mail. You can't dispute that."

"No, of course not."

"What do your friends say about those?"

"Vanzetti is quite certain it was a frame-up."

"By whom?"

"Some one of the big detective agencies, which are making millions out of this anti-red agitation."

Henry smiled pityingly. "You accept that?"

"I don't accept it as a fact, because I don't know. I certainly accept it as a possibility."

"Believe me, Mother, you'll have to look for a better alibi. Frame-ups don't happen."

Henry saw the pair of brown eyes fixed upon his dark ones. They were soft, and always kind, but they were persistent, and he had learned that they saw deep. "Be careful, and don't commit yourself too completely. You may need an alibi yourself, my son." And that was hardly fair at the beginning of a luncheon; a poor appetizer for a great lawyer who was going to be a defendant, and get large daily doses of his own medicine. His look clouded, and for a while he was less quick to interrupt.

"Five or six years ago, Henry, I'd have agreed with you about the frame-up; I'd have said it was a device of criminals in trouble, and a sign they were hard-pressed. But now I know that the frame-up is a regular weapon in the class-struggle, just as well understood as, for example, jury-fixing, or the buying of labor leaders. Did you ever have William M. Wood for a client?"

"No, Mother, I have never been that fortunate."

"How rich is he?"

"I don't know; pretty rich—ten or fifteen million, maybe."

"Enough to be one of our leading industrialists, the president of our great woolen corporation. You'd think he was big enough not to frame up conspiracies against his workers, wouldn't you? Do you happen to remember what he did in the Lawrence strike, seven or eight years ago? He couldn't see any other way to break the union, so he had dynamite planted, to be blamed upon the union leaders. He was indicted and tried for it—"

"And acquitted, if I remember correctly."

"Yes, you know what it means for a great mill-owner to be acquitted in his own bailiwick. It is a fact that the men he hired to do the job were convicted; and I leave it for you to suggest that he didn't know what they were doing for him. This much is certain, the story was given out to the newspapers that dynamite had been found by the police in a shoe-box in the union headquarters. The box had been brought there by a detective, and somebody slipped up on the time, and the story was in the Boston *American* before the raid took place and the dynamite was found! That was bad management, at least."

The great lawyer could not help smiling. "I will say that if I had had the matter in charge, it wouldn't have happened that way."

"Well, don't forget that it is a part of American labor history, and graven into the consciousness of all those people you call 'Reds.' So when the great gossip machine starts to grinding, and we hear that 'people say' our friends are guilty, that 'everybody knows it,' and that 'frame-ups don't happen,'—well, Henry, we fall back on the good old tradition of English and American law, that every man is innocent until he is proved guilty. And in the effort to get him a fair trial we go to a lot of trouble—such as inviting ourselves to lunch with our rich and famous sons-in-law, and asking for the names of lawyers who might possibly care about justice!"

V

Henry supplied the names of respectable lawyers, and Cornelia went to interview them, but in vain. Later on, after years of struggle had made a world issue of the case, it would be possible to interest great lawyers in it; but at present there was no man who would burden himself with the defense of two anarchist infidel draft-dodgers accused of murder.

Also Henry named some of the legal tricksters, and Cornelia had curious experiences interviewing these. There was one uniform objection to all these powerful ones, the amount of money necessary to start their powers into action. Some said fifty thousand, some said seventy-five; and this was a stage in the life of the Sacco-Vanzetti Defense Committee when there were discussions as to whether they could afford to rent a post-office box, and whether it would be the part of wisdom to buy a second-hand typewriter.

Later on there would be ladies of wealth and fashion interested in the case, and money would be pouring in from labor groups all over the world; but at this stage, when money would really have counted, the only large sum in sight was what Cornelia could raise on her income and lend to the committee. She had discovered by talking to bankers that she could not raise very much, because her life expectancy at sixty-five was limited. If she had wanted fifty thousand dollars for an orphan asylum, or for a house to live in, or even for a string of pearls to hang about her withered neck, she had three daughters and three sons-in-law, any one of whom would have written her a check, and been glad to get such a hold upon her. But when it was a question of imperiling the Commonwealth by aiding and abetting anarchism, Cornelia did not have to ask for the money, she could hear in advance the polite but firm rebuke.

The problem of a lawyer was settled by the Italians. It happened that Lee Swenson was in New York, recuperating from the labor of saving a bunch of I.W.W. from jail in Kansas, and swearing to himself by all the gods he disbelieved in that never again. But Carlo Tresca came to see him, and Swenson knew Carlo from the Ettor-Giovannitti case. Carlo told the pitiful story of two anarchists in jail in Massachusetts, who had the skids under them, all ready to be slid into the electric chair; he told what a fine fellow Bart was, and how he had all but had tears in his eyes because he missed seeing the Statue of Liberty, and now maybe he would never see it; and about Nick's wife and little boy, and the new baby expected in a month or two. Carlo came again and again, and appealed to Lee Swenson's friendship, until finally he said he would go up to Boston and look things over.

Lee Swenson was of Swedish descent, and came originally from Minnesota. He had been in practically every big criminal case which involved labor during the past fifteen or twenty years. As a cub lawyer he had helped to get evidence for Moyer and Haywood in Idaho; he had helped to defend the McNamaras in Los Angeles and Tom Mooney in San Francisco, and several groups of the I.W.W. in Chicago and the middle west. He stood six feet and a couple of unnecessary inches, and was badly put together; he did not know what to do with his big hands and feet, nor in fact with any part of himself; he liked to sit on his neck, and his feet liked to get up off the floor. He had a thick shock of yellow hair, and when it was not arranged it looked as if one of those western windstorms had hit it, and when it was arranged it appeared to be done with vaseline.

Lee Swenson was too intelligent a man not to know the disturbing effect he produced upon the respectable citizens of New England. Was he really rattled by them, as he pretended, or did he enjoy the effect he produced, somewhere back in the deeps where he kept his laughter until it came rumbling forth like thunder from the mountains? After he had been nosing into the case for a couple of weeks, he asked for a conference with Cornelia, and she invited him to her little apartment to dinner, on an evening when Joe and Betty were scheduled for a hearing before the carpenters' union. Before they went into the dining-room, Lee Swenson sank into Cornelia's one Morris-chair, and then slid most of the way out of it, and said, "Will you be shocked if I cross my legs?"—and did it without waiting for an answer.

"Not at all," said Cornelia, hastily.

"Not even when you discover that I wear woolen socks?"

"I know you are making fun of Boston, Mr. Swenson."

"My God," said he—"I beg your pardon, Mrs. Thornwell, but this is a terrible place for a man that grew up in a sod hut. I realized when we were defending Ettor and Giovannitti in Salem that I didn't fit, but I never had time to go into details, and never happened to meet the right person. But I believe you are it."

"Is that why you wanted to talk with me?"

"No, but you can do it on the side. Tell me how to avoid shocking judges and juries who talk through their noses."

"Do you really want me to tell?"

"I said it."

"Well, why do you wear a broad-brimmed black felt hat such as nobody ever saw in Boston?"

"But it's what I had when I came to town, and I can't afford another."

"Are you really that hard up?"

"Maybe you don't know how it is with a radical lawyer. Imagine a score or two of cases, each like this one. There is two dollars and fourteen cents in the treasury to-night. They offer to pay me a hundred and fifty a week while the case lasts, but you know how it will be, they'll be seventeen weeks behind in their payments at the end of eighteen weeks, and when I get a check, there'll be some emergency next day that I'll pay out of my own pocket. You see, I'm not really going to be a lawyer—that will be merely incidental; I'm going to be organizer, propagandist, press agent and promoter; any money I get, I've first got to raise, and understanding that the committee will begrudge me every cent I take."

"Surely it won't be as bad as that, Mr. Swenson!"

"You are a newcomer, Mrs. Thornwell; but this is my twentieth committee, and believe me, I know them. It won't be their fault, they will be sincere and devoted, most of them; but they will be poor, and narrow-minded—not used to spending money with the magnificent abandon of us privileged persons. They won't see what I need with so much, and when the newspapers and the outside public begin to tell how I have got away with one or two hundred thousand on the sly, they will think maybe it's the truth. I tell you this in advance, because, when it's over, my one chance of getting arrears of salary will be by vamping some of the rich ladies, your friends who will be interested in the case. And then I'll get my new hat."

"Meantime," said Cornelia, hastily, "you can at least get a haircut."

But the other replied, "If I did, the hat would be bigger than ever, with nothing to hold it but my ears."

VI

After they had dined, and were back in the little living-room, in front of the coal grate-fire, the lawyer asked if he might close the door. He drew his chair close to Cornelia, and slid down into it and began: "Mrs. Thornwell, I have been digging into this case, and I am completely baffled, and don't know what to do. The last time I talked with Vanzetti, he told me that you were the one American he would trust. He admires your granddaughter, but he's afraid she would be shocked if I talked straight to her."

"He is mistaken," said Cornelia, smiling in spite of herself. "I am far more easily shocked than Betty. The younger generation is taking life into its own hands."

"Well, if you don't mind, I prefer the old ones. You and I have suffered, and we have a deeper foundation under us. Do you mind if I ask for your confidence?"

"Not at all, Mr. Swenson. I will tell you anything I can. But I fear it won't be much."

"First, all you know about these two boys—everything that will help me to judge them."

"Sacco I hardly know at all. I only met him two or three times prior to the arrest. I have been to see him three times in

Dedham, partly because I wanted to make up my mind about him."

"And what are your conclusions?"

"He is a difficult man to know, under the circumstances. He has a primitive mind, I judge. He does very little thinking; he is satisfied with a formula, that the rich exploit the poor, and are the enemies of the poor, and always have a self-seeking motive in relation to them. And of course I don't fit into that formula. Why should a rich woman, who might have everything she wants, burn up gasoline and tires traveling down to Dedham to visit an anarchist in prison? He is instinctively polite, and affectionate to his friends, I am told. He hasn't given me any hint of a suspicion, but he probably fears that I may be another trap the enemy has set for him. You know, of course, they put a spy in the cell next to him soon after his arrest?"

"Yes, he told me that."

"Also they wanted to get one into his home, to try to board with his wife. I'm told the district attorney had that bright idea. I suppose it is too much to expect those gentry to have delicate sensibilities, but you'd think they might have guessed that a woman who was deprived of her husband, and was expecting another baby in two or three months, would rather have a woman-boarder than a man. Anyhow, somebody found out about it, and naturally the Saccos are very suspicious. So I haven't tried to talk about the case with either of them. When I have seen Nick, I have talked about his garden, and the wonderful tomatoes he used to have—those tomatoes were like so many babies to him. I take him a bunch of chrysanthemums— they let him have flowers, though they won't let Bart have any."

"Oh, surely not!"

"It's a regulation at Charlestown, I suppose that a saw or a knife might be hidden in them; or maybe drugs. I get round it by wearing one flower, and when I ask the guard if I may leave it with Bart, he is ashamed to say no. I am trying to win the hearts of all of them, because it seems to me the jailers are in jail as much as the prisoners."

"We are all in jail, Mrs. Thornwell. Take it from one who has been playing the game twenty years—we are prisoners of the system. I walk about with a chain on my wrist, and at the other end are fastened so many lies that it seems like the population of all seven of Dante's hells. That is a part of what I want to talk to you about."

VII

It took Cornelia a good hour to tell the story of how she had come into the Brini home and what she had seen there. She told about Bart's ideas and dreams, his work and his play and his personal habits. She told about the sick kitten he had refused to have killed, and the rabbits he had brought home in a sack, and kept in pens for several months—until the sorrowful realization was forced upon him that there was no earthly way to keep those creatures from getting out and gnawing the vegetables of his Catholic neighbor, Mrs. O'Dowd. She told about the lost purse he had refused to take from the policeman, and the boots he had let the poor laborer keep, and the lessons in hygiene he had given to the "riformista," Compagno Culla—all those incidents which were destined to become Vanzetti legends, and be repeated whenever his Italian friends mentioned his name.

Also, because a lawyer had a right to the whole truth, she told him about the fights; and how the anarchist youths had come armed to the Galleani meeting, vowing to defend their hero to the death; and how Bart had got a gun and declared that he would never let himself be taken and put through the third degree.

"Now you are getting to what I want," said Swenson. "Do you know whether that gun is the same one that he had on when he was arrested?"

"I believe he gave it away," said Cornelia. "From what I know of him, he wouldn't keep any piece of property as long as four years."

"Well, I can't get them to tell me where they got those guns; at least, I can't get them to tell me the truth. That's why I'm so up against it. They are afraid of me, afraid of everybody."

"They have reason to be cautious. But won't they take Tresca's word for your reliability?"

"I suppose if I could get them both together with Carlo, we could come to an understanding; but as it is, they go on repeating the stories they told to the police; and their friends outside do the same. Orciani has been driving me about, looking for evidence, and I've been appealing to him. Do you know him?"

"Only slightly."

"He has the courage of a man with the mind of a child: a simple Italian peasant, picked up off the countryside and dumped into the maelstrom of America. I have managed to win his affection, and he will talk to me frankly about everything in the world but this case. I point out his contradictions, but it doesn't make any difference. It is a peculiarity of Italian anarchists that I have observed, they can go on insisting that black is white longer than any other human beings I have ever seen. But somehow it has got to be put across to them that they can't go before a Yankee jury with those stories—it will be throwing away their lives."

"What stories, Mr. Swenson?"

"Well, the one about what they did on the night they were arrested. I can't get a single one of those fellows to admit to me that they were in front of the Johnson place that night; yet it's a physical fact that any jury will see—there's a swampy meadow on both sides of the road, and no other way for Sacco and Vanzetti to have got from the place where they admit they got off the street-car to the place where they got on again. If we're going to save them, we've simply got to make a story that a jury will believe."

There was a pause; Lee Swenson got up and went to the door that led into the dining-room, and opened it, to make sure the Negro maid was not listening. Then he came back, and when he spoke again, it was in a lower voice. "Mrs. Thornwell, I know enough about Boston to understand that you will be startled to hear me discuss the 'making' of stories to be presented to a jury."

"You use what I might call an optimistic phrase, Mr. Swenson."

"Every professional man does that when he deals with the shady parts of his job. You may know that when the fashionable ladies go to a surgeon for an abortion, he refers to it as a 'curettage'."

"I have three daughters," said Cornelia, placidly. "But I

thought that in this case, if we are dealing with men who are innocent—"

"You thought we might trust to the truth?"

"I admit I was that naïve."

"Well, Mrs. Thornwell, I can only tell you—in my experience with labor frame-ups in a dozen states, I have always found it necessary to fight the devil with his own fire."

VIII

Cornelia's little round face wore an anxious look, and her soft brown eyes were wide open, staring at the man in front of her. She saw a big, rough-hewn face, marked by small-pox; with a lower jaw which had a way of thrusting itself up, making a deep crease on each side of the mouth. The eyes were set under shaggy yellow brows—in short it was the face of a fighting man, no product of a Back Bay drawing-room.

But somehow Lee Swenson had learned how people felt in drawing-rooms—possibly from Henry James, whom he read incessantly. "You are saying to yourself that I grew up in the wild and woolly west, Mrs. Thornwell, and things are different in Massachusetts. But I assure you it is one system, from Maine to California, when some radical is accused of violence in the class struggle. The authorities are sure the man is guilty, if not of this crime, then of others just as bad, and so to 'make' a case against him is a worthy work. When a class-war trial begins, you will see on the stand police officers who know that it is part of their job to swear to whatever the chief tells them; and maybe an ex-convict, who knows that the prosecution has something on him, and testifies as a condition of getting off; and a prostitute, who carries on her ancient profession at the discretion of the police. In this case there will be workers from that shoe factory, semi-morons, incapable of knowing the difference between right and wrong, but knowing what a reward is, and having rehearsed a lesson until they can say it in their sleep. It will be simple and easy—'Yes, I saw the bandits, I saw them shoot, I am positive these are the men.' These witnesses will sit with Sacco and Vanzetti in front of them, and when they are asked to describe the bandits, they will describe the men in front of them, and what could be more convincing?"

"I attended the Plymouth trial," said Cornelia. "I was shocked by its unfairness, but I hated to believe it was a deliberate frame-up."

Said Lee Swenson: "My knowledge of your Massachusetts procedure was got at the Ettor-Giovannitti trial, seven years ago, as perfect a frame-up as ever came under my eyes. The men were no more guilty of murder than I was; every particle of the testimony was 'made,' and the whole case prepared and the indictments drawn up by lawyers of great corporations. The victims were Italians, I.W.W. leaders, efficient and dangerous—the more so because one of them was a fine poet. And how did we save their lives, Mrs. Thornwell? Was it by trusting to the truth? As a matter of fact, we had seventeen eyewitnesses to the shooting of Anna Lo Pizzo, and they absolutely insisted that it was done by a police officer, and they identified the officer; but because they were all Italians, and there were so many of them, we didn't dare use their story, for fear the jury would think it was a frame-up! That's how far the truth gets you in Massachusetts!"

Lee Swenson waited for Cornelia's comment; but what could she say?

"Some day," continued the lawyer, "I'll tell you the inside of that story—as weird a tangle of plot and counterplot as you could want for a crime-romance. The district attorney was carrying on a political fight against William M. Wood, the head of the woolen trust, and so we were able to get hold of the checks which Wood had paid to have dynamite planted, in a frame-up against the union leaders. With that evidence in hand we practically blackmailed the executives of the woolen mills, and made them take the stand, one after another, and testify that the speeches of the strike leaders had been opposed to violence. I could name several laws of your great Commonwealth we broke in putting that job across—and if we hadn't done it, the world would never have read 'Arrows in the Gale,' by Arturo Giovannitti."

Cornelia sat staring before her, pondering this strange moral dilemma. At last she said, "I have always been taught, Mr. Swenson, that one gets a certain moral backing from telling the truth."

"I know—I also have read Emerson; but how would it work

in our courts of law? Consider Vanzetti's trial in Plymouth. There was an alibi, as good as any one could want. The crime occurred on the day before Christmas, and everybody had something to remember—the eels. Did you accept that alibi?"

"I was absolutely convinced by it. I have been all over North Plymouth with Trando, and he showed me the places; every spot is alive to him with the memory of Bart, whom he adored. The things jump out of the child, in a way that couldn't happen if he had had to learn them. He will interrupt a talk, 'There is one of the houses where I took the eels, and Bart was across the street, and I had to go for change.' He will say, 'Under that tree he dismissed me, and gave me fifty cents for the work.' If you knew those simple, kindly people, Mr. Swenson, you couldn't doubt their story."

"All right—but where does that leave your argument? You trusted to the truth with that Plymouth jury—and it got you nowhere! No, Mrs. Thornwell, we must fight the prosecution with its own weapons. We have to do the reverse of what they have done—convince ourselves that the boys are innocent, and that whatever we do to get them off is a worthy work. And then take a joy in the performance—learn to build a good alibi with the same pleasure that a novelist gets from constructing a detective story, with every detail fitting precisely, and contributing to the final result—an acquittal, and a booming reputation as a lawyer who has never lost a client."

"Is that really what you want me to believe about your profession, Mr. Swenson?"

"In strict confidence, you understand, Mrs. Thornwell!"

"Oh, of course."

"I want you to believe there is no other way to be a successful criminal lawyer in America; I have never heard of any man who has done it, and I do not believe it can be done. That is the game, and you either play it, or you play some other game."

"It sounds as if it would be hard on the nerves."

"This is America, and you know our motto, 'It's a great life if you don't weaken.' You play for high stakes, and every time it is 'doubles or quits,' if you understand the slang of the gambler. Win the big case and you're on top of the heap; lose it, and you're a dead one! That's why it's so foolish of me to take a case like this. There is no way to win except to make a big public splurge; and then, if I don't make good, it is back to the sticks for me. That is the real moral problem that confronts a radical lawyer, Mrs. Thornwell—can he afford to have a heart? Can he feel sorry for some hero-soul like your Bart, who has apparently got into a jam not of his own making? It's a decision I have to make, and naturally it depends very largely upon Bart's friends."

There was a pause. "Just what is it you want me to say, Mr. Swenson?"

"For the present, nothing in particular. That may come later. What I want is for you to know the situation—what a murder trial is, and how it has to be fought—so that later on, when you find out about this detail and that, you won't be horrified and disgusted with me, and draw out and leave me alone with the Italians."

IX

Lee Swenson had said his say, and it was up to Cornelia. She sat with her two hands locked together, and her eyes closed, and only the trembling of the lids to tell what was going on within. When at last she spoke, her voice was weak, and so were her words. "I never had anything like that put up to me in my life, Mr. Swenson."

"I can believe that. Your life has been lived among people who are not accused of crimes. And you have your strict moral code—which doesn't allow for perjury!" Then, seeing a trace of tears in the old lady's eyes, he added quickly, "I fear that I misunderstood you in one way, Mrs. Thornwell—I thought you knew more about your great moral city than apparently you do. You went to consult Larry Shay about this case, didn't you?"

"How did you know that?"

"Well, I have sources of information. How did you come to go to him?"

"My son-in-law, Henry Cabot Winters, named him."

"Why did he name him?"

"He said he would be the best man to get the boys off"

"And what happened when you went to see him?"

"He wanted fifty thousand dollars, and I told him we didn't have it."

"What did he say?"

"Well, he pointed out that it was a capital case, and would mean a lot of hard work."

"What did you understand by that?"

"Wasn't it obvious? It will take a lot of time to prepare the case, and it may be a long trial."

Lee Swenson laughed, one of those polite laughs which he kept inside him, out of consideration for Boston. "You are much too good, my dear Nonna! I think I will call you by Bart's name, if you don't mind, because it is friendly, and at the same time respectful."

"I don't mind," said Cornelia.

"Out west," said the other, "they call me Lee, and they don't wait a whole lifetime, as they do in Boston. But now let me explain about Larry Shay: if he had taken the case, there wasn't going to be any trial."

"How do you mean?"

"I mean that Larry is the official 'fixer' for the political ring which governs Boston and its environs. If you have committed a crime, and got caught, your friends go to him to find out what it will cost to have the case dropped."

"Oh, Mr.—Lee!"

"You, lovely and naïve blue-blood lady, carried to this legal shark a proposition to bribe some of the prosecuting officials of your state, and he made you an offer, and you didn't even know what it was about!"

"Do you really know all that?"

"Everybody knows it that knows about the insides of this town. Worse than that—they 'make' the cases, for the purpose of collecting blackmail. I could tell you quite a number of stories, only they are not fit for a lady's ears—having to do with women and road-houses."

There was a pause, while Cornelia thought hard. "You mean, Lee Swenson, that if I raise fifty thousand dollars and pay it to these politicians, I can have the case against our two boys dropped?"

"I mean exactly that. And there's another moral problem for a blue-blood lady who has lived a sheltered life, and listened to

her husband, the governor, make fine speeches about their noble
Commonwealth!"

X

The telephone rang; Betty calling. She and Joe had had a
successful time at the carpenters' union, had got a twenty-five
dollar contribution. Now Betty was going somewhere else. She
could not explain over the phone, but she would be late, and
Grannie was not to wait up for her. Go to sleep. She hung up,
and Lee Swenson took his departure, saying that he had put
enough burdens upon her mind for one evening. He would
not ask anything definite, she would need time to think matters
over. Cornelia thanked him.

She did not go to sleep, but sat in the Morris chair which
the lawyer had vacated, and moral whirlwinds seized her
thoughts and flung them this way and that. She, Cornelia
Thornwell, widow of the sternest governor that Massachusetts
had had for a century, the most ruthless punisher of law-
breakers and corruptionists—she had sat in this room and listened to a proposition that she should conspire to commit
perjury! Yes, that was it, no use mincing words. She had
heard, and from now on would be accessory before the fact
to whatever might be done! She had not risen and denounced
the proposer and ordered him from her home; no, she had
hesitated—which in itself was guilt—and when he had told
her it was confidential, she had assented, which was double
guilt!

Punishment for Cornelia Thornwell, feminist and suffragist!
Now she knew what the wise men had meant when they told
her that woman's place was the home! Woman's place was the
Sewing Circle, where they made long flannel petticoats which
the poor would not wear! Woman's place was the Parish House
of Trinity Church in the City of Boston, where perfect ladies
gathered to arrange for visitation of the sick and care of
widows and orphans! If a lady insisted on going out into the
harsh and wicked world, this was what she ran into—perjury,
subornation of perjury, conspiracy to commit perjury! Cornelia saw these awful phrases in the headlines of all the newspapers of Boston.

The soul of Bartolomeo Vanzetti came to keep watch with
her, and share her worries. Bart did not sleep soundly in his
prison cell; he lay awake and brooded over the case, and
thought of letters to write, and suggestions to make to friends
and lawyers. So now he came in spirit, and Cornelia asked
him all those questions she would never ask in the flesh. What
did he want her to do? What would best serve his cause, the
"joostice" for which he lived?

She questioned her own soul. What was right, what was
wrong? To stand by the stern moral code of Puritan Boston—
which all of them preached, and some of them practiced? Say
that the law was sacred, and an oath was binding before God,
and it was better for men to die than to break God's law? Easy
to say that, when it concerned yourself; something in you
would take pleasure in dying for a code. But when it was
some other man's life, did you have the right to force your
code upon him?

Vanzetti had proved that he did not subscribe to that code,
because he had told lies to the police. But then, he faced the
same problem as Cornelia; it wasn't for himself that he lied,
but for others. Sometime previously Cornelia had put to him
a very grave question. There appeared to be much more evidence against Sacco than against him, so it might be wise to
demand separate trials, and save at least one of them. But
Bart had turned the idea down without a moment's hesitation.
"Save Nick, he got the wife and kids!" That was his attitude,
from first to last.

Something easy to understand—to lie for a wife and kids!
In contrast with that, Cornelia's ideal seemed far-off, cold and
aloof. In this world truth was a luxury, denied to all but the
fastidious, the ivory-tower personalities, who had no hearts and
no sympathies! Who were good at shutting their eyes and refusing to know uncomfortable facts!

Cornelia thought over Lee Swenson's statement, that her life
had been lived among people who were not accused of crimes.
A careful and lawyer-like phrase! Not those who did not commit crimes, but those who were not accused! Cornelia searched
her memory, and forced herself to face reality. Did her sort of
people really refuse to lie? The case of Jerry Walker leaped
to her mind, because she had just been talking to her son-in-

law about it. Had Rupert and Henry lied to Jerry Walker, in order to get his property away from him? Of course they had! Henry had even lied to Cornelia, and treated it as a matter of course. They had lied to their associates, and their associates were now accusing them of it—so Cornelia had learned from family gossip.

Sooner or later Rupert and Henry were going upon the witness-stand, to be cross-questioned as to what they had done. Were they going to admit their conspiracy to take ten million dollars' worth of property from Jerry Walker? Were they going to say that the law was sacred, and that an oath was binding before God? Of course they were not! What they were going to do was to follow the Lee Swenson formula—sit down with their lawyers and frame up an elaborate story, learn every detail of it by heart, and go upon the witness-stand and lie like troopers—or, in the modern equivalent, like policemen who know that it is part of their job to swear to whatever the chief tells them! Rupert and Henry would do that, and all State Street would know they were doing it, and take it as a good joke, nothing worse.

XI

A world of lies, a world run on the basis of lies, so that when you talked about truth-telling you were a Utopian and a dreamer; worse yet, a traitor to your friends, to your business associates, your family, your class! A fastidious person, an ivory-tower esthete, preferring your own peace of mind to the rights of those who had taken you into their confidence, assuming that you would play the game as everybody else played it, for your profit and comfort as well as their own!

Lies! Lies! It was the autumn of the year 1920, and a great political campaign was at its climax; America had ceased to be a republic, it was an absolute monarchy, its ruler the Prince of Lies! That little man, "Silent Cal," whom Cornelia knew so well as governor of the Commonwealth, was being elected vice-president of the United States by a lie! He who had run away from the police-strike was being rewarded for breaking the police-strike! His backers had managed to suppress the report of the citizens' committee, which had worked so hard to avoid a strike, and had told the whole truth; instead, they had made a nursery-legend, such as the pious Parson Weems had invented about George Washington and the cherry-tree!

And worse yet, look at the man they were making president! Cornelia's mind was a witch's caldron, with the tales Joe Randall brought home; for Joe knew the newspaper men, and picked up the gossip which could not be printed, and used it to spice the meals he ate in the little apartment. Joe's mind had turned rancid, after four months' contact with American morals and American justice; he found his pleasure in believing the most shocking things about the great and noble persons of the land. This Senator Harding, who was to be the next president, had been picked out by the oil-men, who were planning to loot the oil-reserves of the nation; he was handsome and dignified, a magnificent statesman, when you read about him in the capitalist newspapers—but Joe called him an old booze-fighter, a small-town rake, whose idea of entertainment was to sit in his shirt-sleeves and chew tobacco and play poker all night with his cronies, "the Ohio gang." His managers had had to get a newspaper man to write his speeches for him, because, when he was turned loose for himself, he used polysyllables like a Negro preacher, with no idea what they meant.

And worse yet, he traveled round the country with a young girl who was his mistress! He stayed in rooms in various cheap hotels with her, and when the house-detectives ventured to object, he would present them with his card! It was something entirely new in American history, and Joe Randall turned his fancy loose to play with the theme; some day, he said, the American people would build a memorial to this oil-statesman, and when the radicals came into power they would carve an inscription across the front of it, and set it with flaming red rubies: "Nan Britton's Boy!"

XII

A cruel, cruel world! Impossible to live in a place where such wickedness was done! A sudden weariness seized Cornelia, a failing of the heart; it was time for her to quit, to move on and leave the world to a new generation, which had stronger nerves and could face such issues. The runaway grandmother would run back to shelter.

The fire in the grate had burned nearly out, and the room was growing cold, the chill creeping into the bones of the old woman sitting in the chair. She looked at the clock; it was after two in the morning, and suddenly she realized that Betty had not come home. What could the child be doing at that hour?

Lee Swenson had asked her not to tell Betty about these problems. But that was hardly fair. Betty had come to be her mainstay—she realized it all of a sudden. Betty was young, Betty was not afraid, Betty could face any facts there were! To try to hide anything from her would be one more deception, in a world which seemed to be made of nothing else.

There was a sound in the hall, and Cornelia turned her head. A key in the latch, and the door opened. There was Betty, rosy, shining from a walk in the chill night air. "Why, Grannie! You waited up for me! You shouldn't have done that!" She closed the door, and came to Cornelia, brimming over with affection and concern. "You poor dear, you let the fire die down, you are cold!"

Betty herself was warm; the blood flooded her cheeks and throat, it came and went, like northern lights in the winter sky, a lovely thing to watch. Her eyes shone—something must have happened to-night, they were so much alive. Such an eager face, a smile with two rows of white teeth, even and smooth, almost translucent. She wore a soft brown coat, with a neckpiece of fur, matching her hair, her eyes—a picture that people turned to look at on the street. So delicate, so quick and sensitive—and she knew about this wickedness, she could face it and not quail from it, not feel old and chilly, ready to die!

"Grannie dear, what is it? You're worried about something!" She could read Cornelia's mind as if she entered it. "What is bothering you? Has Lee Swenson been telling you something discouraging?" Then quickly, "Don't let him frighten you, my dear! We're going to get those boys off! Is he afraid about them?"

"No, dear—"

"Then what did he say? Tell me, what?"

"We talked about many things, this case and others. It is a terrible world, Betty dear."

"Yes, they frame people; and then sometimes, people have done something, too! It's hard to tell which is which, and your poor dear head is addled with trying to know it all! Is that it?"

"Mr. Swenson didn't want me to talk—"

Betty laughed gayly. "The old rascal! He thinks he's going to keep secrets from Joe and me! I know, it's very dangerous, and we mustn't whisper. But you tell him, I know what's in your head before you do, and he can't run this case without Joe and me. This is a young folk's job, believe me!"

Betty shed her coat, and the little brown bowl of a hat trimmed with fur, and knelt down and put her warm cheek against her grandmother's cold one. "The idea of worrying a nice old Victorian lady with secrets and mysteries! I suppose he told you that government witnesses don't always tell the truth, and defense lawyers sometimes fight the devil with fire. Is that what you're worried over?"

"Where were you so late, dear?" countered Cornelia—the only evasion she could think of in a hurry.

"Never you mind—that's more secrets and mysteries, I'll tell you in the morning. Now you go to bed, before your old bones turn to ice." She led Cornelia into her bedroom, and turned down the covers, and brought her a glass of hot milk, describing her as "seecka kitten," from the days when Cornelia had been worn out with the work in the cordage-plant, and Bart had nursed her so tenderly. When she had drunk the milk, Betty tucked her in like a baby, and kissed her good-night and put out the light, and raised the window, and said, "Now be a good child, and in the morning you shall hear some nice gossip!"

XIII

Bright sunlight, and the Negro maid building the fire, and Cornelia in her dressing-gown in the big chair before the grate, drinking her coffee and nibbling her toast. Betty sat by her in a blue silk kimono, and when she was through eating, took the tray and set it one side, remarking, "So you won't upset it or anything in your excitement." Then she closed the door, and took a seat close to her grandmother, and pushed her bobbed hair back from her forehead, and said, "Now, bless

your old dear heart, get yourself together and don't faint dead
away—Joe and I are married."

Cornelia's hands went limp in her lap. "Married!"

"Yes, dear."

"But Joe has a wife!"

"Yes, that's an old story."

"But then—but—you can't marry a man who is already
married."

"We can, Grannie dear, we arranged it; you see, we married
ourselves."

Something inside Cornelia quit working for a moment—
heart, or lungs, or solar plexus which controlled them both—
and her voice failed her altogether. Betty's voice was steady,
but one of those waves of color flooded her neck and face,
right up to the bobbed brown hair. "You see, Grannie, since
the law won't be sensible, we took matters into our own hands.
Joe's wife is in Reno, but it takes a lot of time, one can't be
sure how long; and it was too silly that we who love each
other should sit around waiting for some politician to give us
permission to live our lives."

There was a pause. Cornelia's voice had not yet come back.

"Let me say right away, Grannie, this isn't any free love
foolishness. You'll be thinking about Mary Wollstonecraft and
all that, but I was only a child then, I was using a lot of romantic words. But now I'm twenty-two, and I'm in love, and
I want my man, and I want him for life, and he knows that—
I've told him that if any other woman tries to take him away,
I'll scratch her eyes out. So you see it's perfectly respectable
and conventional."

"Y-yes," said Cornelia, feebly.

"I have waited—I've been a good six months and more making up my mind I wasn't making any mistake. Now that I'm
sure, I'd be perfectly willing for any judge or clergyman to
say the magic words that would change it from immorality to
the holy bonds of matrimony; but you see how it is, the judge
won't do it for an indefinite time, and the clergyman never will,
because Joe's wife has not committed adultery—at least, she
has, her man is out there with her, but it isn't going to be
legally proved, so the curiosity of the Episcopalian clergymen
will not be satisfied according to canon law. I have looked all

this up in the library, and I'll explain it if you don't know what
I mean."

"No, I understand," said Cornelia—still feebly.

"Well, Grannie dear, in your marrying time no one did his
own thinking, but now the world is changing, so my dear
blessed old chaperon has got to sit down and ask herself this
plain question: Do you think that my love for Joe, or his for
me, would be in any way more sanctified or purified by any
formula that any judge or clergyman could pronounce over us?
Do you really believe that?"

Cornelia had to think.

"Be sure, now."

"No, I guess I don't."

"All right, then. And do you think we'd be apt to be more
true to each other if we had dressed up in party clothes, and
spent several thousand dollars for flowers in Trinity Church,
and had four organs play the Lohengrin wedding march going
in and the Mendelssohn wedding march going out, and had
the rector say a formula which seems absolutely superfluous to
both of us? Do you believe that?"

"No, dear, I suppose I really don't. Only—we always have
done it in our family."

"Most of the time," said Betty. "But this is a special case,
and Joe and I talked it out and decided that it is just too silly
that our love-life should be maimed for we can't tell how long.
We decided that the law is an imposition, and we have taken
the liberty of being our own clergy, that is all."

"Yes, dear. But—suppose you get into trouble?"

"Well, we'll do our best to keep it from happening. We have
taken the best advice. But if there should be an accident, we'll
face the consequences. I promise you I won't have what they
call a 'curettage'—as you remember Aunt Alice did not so long
ago. You didn't know I knew about that, I suppose! And
neither will I have an appendicitis operation, like Cousin Julia.
I wouldn't mind a bit having a baby by the man I love, and
telling the world exactly what I had done and why; only, of
course, the family would die, so if the worst comes to the worst,
you and I and Joe will take another trip to Europe, and stay
there till we can marry. And meantime you must be a good
sensible soul, and tell yourself that Joe and I are married be-

fore God and you, and when he comes in you are to kiss him on both cheeks and welcome him as your grandson-in-law. Because, you see, he's quite embarrassed about it, knowing how eminently respectable you are. Indeed, he's that way himself, coming from Virginia—he's almost as bad as Roger Lowell, and I had to take matters into my own hands, and do all the marrying, so to speak. But now it's done, and I want you to feel comfortable and happy about it, so that we can be comfortable and happy too. The sensible thing is for you to chaperon us, and let us meet here, because it's very disagreeable having to go to third-rate hotels, and besides, it's dangerous, because the politicians in this pious Puritan city are preying on the free lovers—those who happen to be rich and prominent. Joe says they have a regular blackmail ring, they catch some man in a hotel room with a woman, and it costs him anywhere from twenty to two hundred thousand dollars—that is, of course, unless he can show the card of a United States senator and presidential candidate!"

There was a pause. "That's all, Grannie." Then another pause.

"You are putting a heavy responsibility on me, dear."

"One more secret to keep!" Betty stood up, looking like a new-risen sun with laughter and joy and health. "Bless her dear old frightened soul!" She stooped and put a kiss on each of Cornelia's cheeks, and one on her forehead; then, laughing again, "You don't have to carry the burden if it's too heavy. I'll take it all off your blessed shoulders."

"How, dear?"

"Say the word, and I'll move into an apartment with Joe, and write a note to Mother, telling her all about it. What do you say?"

This time there was no pause. Cornelia said instantly, "No! No!"

XIV

"Bring me good choosing book," wrote Bart. "I will get the fundament which I have so long needing." So whenever Cornelia went for a visit, she would take two or three volumes from her little library: Benjamin Franklin's autobiography and

Paine's "Rights of Man," the letters and speeches of Jefferson, Thoreau's "Walden" and Emerson's essays, a life of Garrison and one of John Brown. She thought he ought to know that New England in which he was to fight for his life, and he agreed with her in this. He had the most intense interest in history, and the lives of men who had played a part in it, especially in the cause of liberty and "joostice." He identified himself with these great characters, he lived their lives, finding comments on his case in their words, and vindication in history's verdict upon them. He read every minute that the prison regulations permitted, and at Cornelia's request he would write comments on the margins of the books, and many pages of pencil notes. It was a regular college course in New England culture, and each time they met there was progress to report.

The old Charlestown prison is built in the form of a cross, and in the center is a large airy room, in which the prisoners are permitted to see visitors. Cornelia would come, with her books and her one flower. She would have to wait while he washed his hands and face—because he was shoveling coal now, and wheeling it in a barrow for the prison furnaces; he would apologize for the condition of his clothes, which he could not help. Cornelia had interceded with the warden and got him this job, instead of the work in the tailor shop, which fitted him ill. Outdoor labor was what he had been used to during his ten years in America, and it kept him in physical condition.

He was a model prisoner, except that he would not stand indignities from his keepers. Once when Cornelia came she was told that she could not see him, he was in "solitary" upon bread and water, because he had refused to do his work. There followed sessions with the warden, and it transpired that Bart considered that the guard had addressed him in a way injurious to his dignity. It took tact on Cornelia's part to patch up this situation; for the American prison system does not allow for dignity, and it is not easy to persuade authorities that an anarchist has a soul. But they could understand that it was unwise to exasperate a man who received visits from ladies of high social station, and who might cause a fuss in the newspapers.

Also Cornelia visited Mrs. Sacco, in the village of South Stoughton. The new baby had arrived, a lovely little girl, and

Cornelia and Betty took this news to the prisoner in the county jail at Dedham, and received a warm welcome. Poor Nick required a great deal of cheering, because he was a man who had lived by physical activity, and could not read and study and think like Bart. He had to learn to spend about twenty-two hours a day in a cell, with nothing whatever to do, and he did not want to wait for a trial, he did not want lawyers to fool with his case and waste the money of the anarchist movement—he wanted to be killed and have it over with. Cornelia and Betty would argue with him, in patient half-English and half-Italian, finding ways to appeal to his pride, reminding him of revolutionary heroes who had managed to endure prison. Why not work out a régime for himself—do gymnastics, of both body and soul? Why not study English, so as to do better work for the cause if he got out, and to write his message to the world if he failed?

The next time they came, they would find that he had shaved himself meticulously, and wore one of the flowers they had brought him. He was practicing walking about the cell on his hands, and counting the number of times he could "chin" himself on his cell-door—he had got up to forty-something, which was remarkable for any man. He was proud of that, and when they told him about the lovely eyes of the baby, his spirit bounded as high as previously it had sunk low. Two races comprise the Italian nation: those of the north who are descended from Teutons and Gauls, and are capable of reflection, like Vanzetti; and those of the south, descendants of Greeks and Carthaginians and Moors, brown and excitable people, who live their lives outside, and utter extremes of emotion with many words and gestures. An odd turn of fate that so many of these should have come to Massachusetts, to annoy the stern and forbidding ghosts of Puritans!

xv

Lee Swenson had decided that he would take the case. He said no more to Cornelia, but evidently there had been some understanding with Betty and Joe, for the young couple sat in at long conferences, and covered half the state in Betty's runabout, interviewing witnesses and tracing clews. Cornelia suc-

ceeded in raising five thousand dollars by pledging one-half
her income—which meant that a money-lender was willing to
gamble that she would live more than two years, in spite of
all her worries and labors. She brought in this money, after
which the Sacco-Vanzetti Defense Committee had an office,
and a post-office box, and no less than two second-hand typewriters clicking away on envelopes. There was a pamphlet telling about the case, mailed out to lists of radicals all over the
country. Articles appeared in socialist and labor papers, both
in America and Europe; for Joe and Betty wrote long letters
to Pierre Leon, and he would translate them into French and
publish them in his paper. So the readers of anarchist and
communist and socialist papers all over Europe began to hear
about two Italians who had fallen victims to the White Terror,
in what had once been the sweet land of liberty, but was now
the banking-headquarters of reaction for the whole world.

Also Cornelia's labors among the blue-bloods were not without fruit. Many of these people knew the corruption of their
political parties, and the alliance between the politicians and
the exploiting interests. They had heard of the Ettor-Giovannitti frame-up, and had watched another strike in Lawrence, a
little more than a year ago, with several near-murders committed by thugs in the mill-owners' employ. They had seen
the "Reds" paraded down State Street in chains, and had seen
the government forced to turn most of them loose, having not
even a pretense of evidence against them. So a few well-to-do
persons began to take an interest in the Sacco-Vanzetti case.
This gave an air of prosperity—and brought a new development, highly characteristic of the great Puritan city. One afternoon Lee Swenson called Cornelia on the phone. "How are you
to-day? Nerves fairly strong?"

"What has happened?"—for Cornelia knew his way of teasing her.

"Do you remember the talk we had in your apartment, when
I told you there might be a way to put our boys·on the street?"

"I remember."

"Well, can I drop in for tea and tell you about it? Send the
maid out if you can—it's a time for being alone!"

The lawyer came, and this is what he had to report. Felice
Guadagni, journalist, who was one of the mainstays of the

committee, had had several visits from an Italian woman named De Falco, an interpreter for the district court at Dedham, in Norfolk County. She claimed to come from the district attorney's office, and offered to have the men released at the price of sixty thousand dollars. There had been several conferences, and Felicani, the printer, had met the woman, and when he pleaded poverty, she had offered to get the price reduced to fifty thousand. The sum was to be disguised as a retaining fee for the brother of an official, who was to be hired by the defense. The Commonwealth would then decide that there was not enough evidence against the pair, and they would be turned loose. "So there's your righteous and law-abiding Boston!" said Lee Swenson—and looked at Cornelia with a twinkle in his wild western blue eyes.

"You think it's really genuine, Lee?"

"Lawyers tell me it's a common procedure in other counties. The woman undertakes to give us satisfactory assurances."

"What would they be?"

"She has already given Felicani the names of other cases she claims to have settled in the same way, and we can investigate them. But first we have to decide the question—do we want to buy the boys off, or do we want to trap the rascal politicians and get something on them?"

Said Cornelia: "It seems to me it all depends on whether we are sure our boys are innocent. I believe they are. Do you, Lee?"

He answered:

"Yes, I do. But that is not the only point. Even though innocent, they may be convicted; and the problem is, do they want to risk their lives for some propaganda?"

The lawyer would be allowed to see his clients in the evening, so he said that he would run out to Charlestown and ask Bart about it. "I'll make my guess," he added, "if no ladies are present, he'll say, tell them to go to hell."

CHAPTER 11

THE GRAFT RING

I

QUINCY THORNWELL was dining with his Aunt Cornelia. He called her that, scrupulously, though he was only two years her junior; he had done it, scrupulously, for forty-five years, since he had been a freshman at Harvard, and she had married into the older generation. Every so often he came to dinner, as a mark of respect, and because family solidarity must be maintained, as the last trace of order in a disintegrating world. For the same reason he put on his honorific clothes; a matter of ritual, a symbol of membership in a group which did the right thing always, as a matter of course and without discussion.

Cornelia also did her part. Her dinner-gown was years out of fashion, but that was a sign that she was superior to fashion. Her little apartment was in a tenement, but that did not matter, because everybody knew it was eccentricity, not necessity. Visiting members of the family had brought boxes now and then, quite casually, and almost without mentioning it; so now she had silver, and shining crystal, and old family china, and linen with strawberry designs, lighted by four tall thin tapering candles. There were flowers in the center of the table—sent with Quincy's card. The Negro maid wore a white cap and apron, and had learned how to serve a meal, because Deborah had sent a real servant to give her lessons. No matter how "red" your poor mother may turn in her old age, she must be kept in touch with the decencies of life.

Quincy—continue to pronounce him like a disease of the throat—was dieting under a doctor's orders, and shrinking up rapidly in the process, so that there were more wrinkles in his face every time you met him. He had become almost entirely bald, and with a bright pink scalp. His nose and cheeks were red, with fine little veins of purple—his blue blood showing

312

through, he would say, mockingly. The extraordinary thing was that when he opened his mouth in laughter, which he did frequently, you saw a cavern of exactly the same color; it seemed unhuman, and when you knew him well you realized that it was.

No more canvas-backs, cooked a quick brown on the outside and deep purple inside, according to the fastidious taste of an habitue of the Somerset Club! No more good honest roast beef, not even any more Boston beans, since they too were high protein, and suspected of uric acid! You must have fish for Quincy, and then chicken—white meat, if you please; and no mayonnaise on the salad—the devil of it was it made you talk about food, and started other people telling their diets, and the women with their everlasting reducing. Thence the company got onto the subject of drink, and after that there was nothing but the private life of their bootleggers. Good conversation was dead in Boston.

What Quincy meant by good conversation was gossip about the hundred or two persons he knew, and the thousand or two he knew about. They were always doing queer things, or getting into trouble, and he would tell the tales with comical embellishments, and throw back his head and chuckle. He had been a widower for the greater part of his life, so no woman had felt free to point out to him how queer he looked when he revealed his dental plates. But his mother or some one had taught him very young that it is bad form to laugh, so he had a series of chuckles which became convulsive, and turned his face a deeper red, but never became audible.

He talked about the family. Poor old Father was failing fast; he had to have a man to go about with him. He still insisted on riding a pony along with the Scatterbridge children, so the attendant had to have a pony too—impossible to imagine a more comical spectacle than that family procession, riding all over the estate but never going off it, for fear of automobiles. Impossible to play chess with Father any more, yet it was necessary to pretend to play, to avoid breaking the old man's heart. The universal curse of life, that our ambitions exceed our abilities! Nothing of that sort for Quincy, he had found out what he could do, and confined his wishes to the possible. He might never be heroic, but he would be a lot safer.

James Scatterbridge was one of the unsafe ones. Tried to do

too much with those enormous mills. It seemed there would never be any market for cotton goods again. Rupert and John Quincy—that was Quincy's older brother—were having the devil's own time pulling James through. Both of them were showing the strain of running all the finance of New England. To the devil with it, said Quincy; enough for him if he could watch the beast, and judge the right moment, and step in and slice off a juicy chunk. Rupert and John scolded him because he didn't produce anything; and he chuckled—a fine mess they had produced!

The maid brought in a pitcher of steaming hot water, with a couple of glasses; and Quincy took from his hip-pocket a silver flask, comfortably curved to fit that portion of the anatomy. He understood that he had to "bring his own" when he came to Aunt Cornelia's, because she was engaged in more serious kinds of law-breaking, and could not afford to expose herself to the lesser risks. Quincy mixed himself a mild dose of rum and sugar and water, and Cornelia took a sip, in order to be good company. "My ancestors used to smuggle in molasses to make this stuff," said the old gentleman. "Now the stuff itself is smuggled, and a new aristocracy is emerging, that will dine on spaghetti from gold plate."

So he talked about prohibition! They were bringing it in by the schooner-load, everywhere along the coast, every night that didn't happen to be moonlit or stormy. Yet the prices got higher and higher, and the quality worse and worse. You might get ever so good a bootlegger, and investigate his ancestry, his police record, his church affiliations and all that, and still you couldn't be sure, because the rascal dealers would fool him. They were making synthetic stuff in the cellars of Boston slums, putting it onto boats, unloading it on the shore, and selling it for Canadian Scotch. The "booties" were being held up all along the line, they would pay the police where they started from, and then the police would send a motor-cycle cop after them to hold them up and get some more.

It was a good thing for labor, Quincy admitted; made it possible to get work done on Monday, so for that reason the law would probably stay. But it was mighty demoralizing; graft was spreading so fast, you hardly knew the old New England. Quincy had been talking that day with a politician in a boardroom, watching the course of stocks, and this politician had quoted the value of the pickpocket, burglary, and confidence men concessions of Suffolk and Middlesex counties. "What do you think of that?" said Quincy, and had one of his convulsions of chuckling.

"It makes me think of something I want to ask you," said Cornelia. "I also have connections with the underworld nowadays."

"I know," said Quincy, "those two wops of yours."

"No," said his aunt, "not the wops, but the officials who are prosecuting them. I need a lot of advice, provided it can be confidential."

The old gentleman became instantly serious. "My dear Aunt Cornelia, I gossip about every family in the world but one!"

II

Cornelia set forth her problem. The Italians who were trying to save the lives of Sacco and Vanzetti found no difficulty in believing that the Commonwealth of Massachusetts was corrupt. They knew all the bootleggers—some of them *were* bootleggers —and were used to paying the police. But Cornelia herself found it hard to believe that the woman, Mrs. De Falco, who told them they could buy the freedom of Sacco and Vanzetti for fifty thousand dollars, really knew what she was talking about, and had the power she claimed.

Quincy Thornwell looked thoughtful. "Fifty thousand dollars is a lot of money, Aunt Cornelia, even for our politicians. My advice would be, say forty, and when you come to the real showdown, it will be thirty."

It might have been possible to see a humorous aspect to that reply, but Cornelia was not in a smiling mood. "You mean it is genuine, then?"

Quincy answered, it surprised him a little, coming from Plymouth and Norfolk counties. Suffolk everybody knew about, it was Irish, and the decent people had moved out and let the "micks" have their own way. Suffolk County comprised the city of Boston proper; and years ago, when it had gone Democratic, the old aristocracy of wealth and fashion had begun an exodus, and now lived in suburban towns, where they could run their local governments and spend their own taxes. They regarded Boston as the place where they came to clip their coupons and do their shopping and go to the theater. So long as the politicians refrained from stealing the banks and public buildings, the blue bloods generally let them alone.

"It sounds like regular city hall stuff," continued Quincy. "You know that people refer to the city hall as the 'steal works.' When they arrested those wops, the gang thought they had no friends, and could be sent up without trouble, and it would be a good mark for the police. But now it appears they have money, and money is more than good marks. It seems obvious enough."

"Quincy, do you think a civilization can endure on the basis of corruption like that?"

"No, of course it can't."

"You give up our civilization?"

"I gave it up a generation ago, when I saw we didn't have sense enough to keep the scum of Europe out. We built a nation on the basis of self-government, and we could do it because we had people who were capable of self-government. But when we let ourselves be overrun by hordes of peasants, we signed our own death-warrant. A few of us old fogies protested, but we couldn't stop it, and we gave up. I said to Uncle Josiah, thirty years ago, I wouldn't touch politics again with a ten-foot pole. And Father said the same."

"Josiah insisted we could teach them, Quincy."

"The last thing in the world they want is to learn anything from us. They hate us because we are different, and better, and we know it. All they want is to rob us of everything we have. You saw those wops plundering the shoe companies—and now the Irish step in to plunder the wops. That's the way it goes in the jungle."

"But, Quincy, the government in Norfolk County is Yankee, and so are most of the voters!"

"That's all right, but if you dig into it, you'll find it's the Irish ring, mark my words. Some of the loot will go to Larry Shay, the head fixer for the crime concessions."

Said Cornelia, "I went to see Shay about this case. Henry told me he'd be a good lawyer to try it."

"None better in Massachusetts. What did he say?"

"He wanted fifty thousand dollars."

Quincy had one of his spells of chuckling. "And you didn't notice the coincidence in price! Don't you see, Aunt Cornelia— when you didn't take up Larry's proposition, he tried it on the Italians! He figured that you, being a simple old lady, might really believe the wops to be innocent; but the Italians wouldn't share your touching faith, so they'd talk turkey. If the politicians had been wise, they'd have warned the Italians not to mention the matter to you."

"As a matter of fact, they did," admitted Cornelia. "They tried to keep Lee Swenson out also. The woman has refused to meet him."

"Well, there you are," said Quincy. "He has a bad reputation —he's a labor agitator and a publicity seeker, and they want to deal with criminals. No, Aunt Cornelia, you don't have to worry about it, all you have to do is raise the money. Have you got it in sight?"

"I don't know. Some of the Italians have hinted it might be got."

"Send out the boys and raid another payroll!" said Quincy, with a grin. "Well, I'll tell you, I'm not a millionaire, as you know, and I have to work for my money—even though it seems easy to those who never played the market. But I'll chip in a few thousand to help you out of this trouble. I think the family would put up the whole amount, if they could be sure it would teach you a lesson."

"You mean," said Cornelia, "I would never again believe in the government of Massachusetts?" There was a naughty twinkle in her eye.

But now her worldly-wise old nephew was "talking turkey" himself. "I mean that you'd take a little care of yourself, and quit fooling with anarchists."

"But, Quincy, don't you think it is up to us people of the old stock to set the wops an example? If I sell out, what will be left for them?"

"Don't you really want to get your friends out of trouble?"

"Yes, but I want to get a lot of others out of trouble also. It would be a poor bargain, from our point of view, to save two men from the electric chair and leave millions in slavery."

"Now, Aunt Cornelia, don't start your Bolshevik propaganda.

on me! I know I'm a parasite and a bloodsucker, but every last one of your wops would take my place if he could get it, and I assure you, before he does get it, he's got to fight."

To which Cornelia replied: "If you only knew how much like a Bolshevik you talk, you'd be quite shocked by yourself!"

III

The first serious split in the Sacco-Vanzetti Defense Committee was developing over the problem of the De Falco offer. On the one side was Lee Swenson, backed by Betty and Joe, who were like two bloodhounds held in leash. On the other side were some of the anarchists—those who stayed in the background, and were not seen in headquarters.

Lee Swenson came to Cornelia. "Nonna, we have a marvelous case to fight. I know what I'm talking about, I can make it the most famous labor case in American history, if the committee will only stand behind me, and give me the funds. This De Falco thing is plain blackmail; the police know that Sacco and Vanzetti are innocent of the crime, but they think they've got other things on the group, and expect to trade on our fears. You know how it is with the anarchists, they are liable to be deported—and maybe there are other secrets that break their nerve. Some of them want to settle; they won't say it plainly, but they are blocking my moves."

"But, Lee! Yesterday Bart said to me he'd rather die than be bought out."

"I know; but Bart is in jail, and it's the committee that is paymaster. I have an idea some of them are going ahead with their plans to raise the money and close the deal. If we persist in having our way, they might throw us down and ruin us."

"Oh, surely not that!"

"You are new at the game of intrigue, Nonna. It might even happen by accident—we have got to allow for the spies on our committee. The prosecution will have one, and the Department of Justice will have one, and they probably won't even know each other. If we delay too long and talk too much, we may find ourselves arrested, charged with an effort to bribe the noble-minded authorities."

Joe and Betty had already made a few automobile excursions,

following Mrs. De Falco's car. They had seen it spend a couple of evenings parked near the car of the gentleman who was to be employed for a retaining fee now reduced to forty thousand dollars. On one of these occasions a public official's car had come up, and he had entered the house. Also Lee Swenson had investigated some "references" the woman had offered; that is to say, murder cases and other crimes which had resulted in dismissals and acquittals through her intervention. What Lee found was that when he started to question the lawyers and relatives who had negotiated these settlements, they became ill at ease and refused to talk—which was to be expected under the circumstances.

Also he had an "investigator" looking into Mrs. De Falco herself. She was one of the many who hung around the courts, looking for openings to be of service to lawyers and witnesses. In short, she was a "runner," one of those who intervene between accused persons and lawyers. Ignorant foreigners who have broken the law are badly frightened, and the "runner" is a comforting friend, who helps to steer them in a strange world —and incidentally finds out how much money they have, or how much their friends can raise, so that the lawyer can fix the fee at the maximum, and then "split" with the "runner." Such a person soon learns the tricks of the courts, and profits by many forms of graft. An odd circumstance, that the investigators reported Mrs. De Falco had an improvident husband, and the fruits of her legal labors went to maintain a home for several children. A complicated world to work in!

She persisted in refusing to see Lee Swenson under any circumstances; so Lee sent to New York for his dictograph— the one he had used in breaking up the government witnesses in a frame-up against the I.W.W. in Seattle five years previously. He set it up in the room where Felicani had been meeting Mrs. De Falco, a big barren place in an old tenement house, next door to a print-shop. He got his own stenographer, and another whom he could trust—and whom the jury would have to trust, because she had served with the A.E.F. in France! The trap was set for seven o'clock in the evening, and the De Falco woman came on schedule time and repeated her assurances of what she was able to do, and explained that it was impossible to come any lower in the price. Meantime several persons strolled casually into the room and out again, so as to be able to testify that Felicani and Mrs. De Falco were talking; and the stenographers diligently took down what they got of the conversation. Unfortunately the printer next door, not having been warned of the plot, started up one of his presses, which caused the dictograph to sound like an avalanche in Switzerland!

However, part of the conversation was recorded; and now, what next? Some of the committee insisted upon waiting, they wanted to get money and mark it, and pay it to Mrs. De Falco. But they delayed to act, and Lee Swenson suspected they were playing for time, their real purpose was to raise the full amount and settle the case. He insisted, such a story would not lie quiet more than a day or two; so many persons knew about it, and the moment the authorities got a hint it was a matter of minutes which would act first. Joe Randall, as a newspaper man, backed up Lee in this; everything depended on how the story first reached the public. If the authorities filed a complaint, charging Felicani with an effort to purchase justice, that would be what the world would believe about the Sacco-Vanzetti Defense Committee, regardless of what evidence might later be produced. Trust the capitalist press for that!

So Lee took matters into his own hands, and filed a complaint, charging Mrs. De Falco with soliciting a bribe. It was a matter for which some of the anarchists never forgave either him or Joe. Who were these two, non-anarchists, therefore enemies of anarchism, to come in and play with the lives of two comrades? To involve Sacco and Vanzetti in an effort to use capitalist courts, which they regarded with abhorrence! Was not Mrs. De Falco herself a human being, a victim of the class system? What business had an anarchist giving information against her, and trying to send her to jail? The Italians did not hesitate to charge that Lee Swenson wanted to get the money, instead of the De Falco woman; he wanted a big legal case for himself!

IV

A terrible world to live in! A world full of tangles impossible to unravel, of dangers impossible to foresee! A world in which wild beasts roamed in the darkness, slaying and devouring—no change from the old days of the jungle!

About twenty-four hours after the De Falco story was spread on the front page of all the Boston newspapers—"Reds Charge Bribery Plot to State," and so on—Cornelia's telephone rang, and she heard the voice of her oldest daughter. "Mother, is that you?" The voice was trembling, so that Cornelia's heart started at the first sound. "What has happened?"

"Oh, Mother, the most dreadful thing! I can't tell you over the phone! I will come at once. Be at home!" There was a sob in Deborah's voice, something that was rarely heard. But no chance to ask more—she hung up the receiver.

Half an hour later she came in, breathless from hurrying up the stairs. Her mother had never seen such distress on her face. Mutely she held out a letter, which Cornelia took. It had a canceled special delivery stamp, on an ordinary envelope, such as you buy at the post office, addressed on a typewriter to Mrs. Rupert Alvin at the Commonwealth Avenue address. Cornelia opened it, and found a typewritten sheet of paper, which seemed to burn her eyeballs as she read:

"Call off your daughter and your mother from the aiding and abetting of anarchists, or you and your family will live to regret it. Why do you let your daughter travel about town day and night with a young anarchist with a criminal record? Look up his wife he deserted. Do you want the world to know that your daughter sleeps with him under your mother's protection? We want no Russian free love in Boston. We will expose them in the papers if they do not get out of town, and your other daughter's wedding will be postponed again.

"AMERICAN PATRIOT."

So there was a bagful of cats turned loose, to rampage over the place, and maintain a dreadful clamor. No possibility of counting them—any more than the stream of wild questions flung at Cornelia's gray head. One horror, of course, led the rest: was it true that Betty was living in adulterous relations with a married man, and Cornelia abetting the crime? It was a question difficult to answer without sounding cynical to a pillar of Trinity Church in the City of Boston. Cornelia said, as calmly as she could, that Betty and Joe loved each other truly, and were going to marry as soon as the law permitted, after Joe's wife had got her Reno divorce. Oh, horrible! horrible! Deborah broke down, and hid her face in her hands, because she could not contemplate such depravity in her mother and her daughter. Or would it be more accurate to say, because she thought that she ought not contemplate it? Human motives are complicated, and in the effort to have our own way we sometimes contrive elaborate emotional dramas.

Said Cornelia: "They will be a perfectly respectable married couple as soon as it is over. There are some in our most fashionable society who have done the same thing."

"At least they had the decency to wait till they were divorced!"

"As to that, Deborah, you should ask your cousin Quincy. He dines frequently at Mrs. Jack Gardner's, where I understand they discuss such cases in detail."

Then the other counts of the indictment. "No Deborah, Joe has no 'criminal record,' I assure you."

"But how do you know it?"

"I know it because I know Joe. He is a fine young idealist, whom I love, and was glad to accept in his present rôle."

"An anarchist free-lover!"

"In the first place, he isn't an anarchist, but a socialist, which is the opposite pole of thought. He is much more conservative than Betty, and their honeymoon quarrels are over his efforts to tone her down. You should be grateful to him."

"But what does this letter mean—his 'criminal record'?"

"It is nothing but a coward's attempt to frighten and distress us. Joe was connected with the American legation in Russia, and he saw President Wilson begin his private war on the Russian people, which was nothing but wholesale murder for the benefit of the British Tories. Joe said what he thought about it, and he may have actually done something to try to stop it. If he has a 'criminal record,' that is it, I am sure."

"And his wife—she is really going to get a divorce?"

"She is planning to remarry."

Deborah made a face of disgust. Ugh, such a world! it seemed to say. It did not improve the long lean features, so much like those of Josiah, which Cornelia had come to know too well.

She waited until the ugly moment was past, and then said, very gently: "There are two great improprieties, Deborah—one is love without marriage, and the other is marriage without love. The latter was my portion, and I assure you, if Betty had to choose one or the other, I am glad it was the other. I did not will this situation, and if they had asked my advice, I would have told them to wait. But they settled it for themselves, and it was a condition and not a theory that confronted me. Betty offered to tell you, but I could see no good in distressing you."

V

They argued the ethics of free love versus purchased love for a while; until Deborah's practical mind got to work at its customary task of telling other people what to do. "We must not have a scandal—now that· Priscilla's wedding invitations have been sent out! We must think up some reason for Betty to go to Europe at once, and stay until the man can marry her."

"I fear you will not be able to arrange that, Deborah. Betty is wrapped up in this case of Sacco and Vanzetti, and the trial is coming in the spring. She and Joe are working over it day and night, and surely, when a young couple are busy and happy, it is not the part of wisdom to break them up."

"But this, Mother! This!" Deborah held the letter in her trembling hand. "How can we face this horrible thing?"

"It is an effort to break our nerve, and it must not succeed."

"But what can we do—if they expose us?"

"How *can* they expose us? Betty lives here, and Joe visits here occasionally, but never unless I am in the apartment. Are they going to break into my home to look for evidence against my granddaughter?"

"Betty must come back and stay with her parents at once!"

"Betty is a grown woman, responsible for her own life. I think you will have to let her make her own decisions, and face her own enemies."

They argued back and forth, and in the process Cornelia's mind became more clear. "I am quite certain nothing will happen, Deborah, except the writing of more letters. The police have spies in the office of our committee, and they pick up bits of gossip, but they don't really know anything. Surely we can

stand upon our family dignity, and ignore anonymous slan-
derers! You and I and Joe and Betty are the only ones who
know the facts, and we are not going to tell any one else—
except, of course, Rupert."

Poor Rupert! He was almost worried to death, his wife broke
out. That dreadful man Jerry Walker was bringing a suit and
charging all sorts of outrageous things; and some of Rupert's
associates were quarreling with him for having got them into
the mess. They had entirely forgotten how glad they were to
get their share of the profits. And then this business about the
Boston Elevated—had Cornelia been told about that?

"Not much, except what has been in the papers."

"Well, they are going to make all the members of the legislature testify as to their stock investments, and they are looking
up the loans they got from some of the banks. They will call it
bribery, of course, but it was nothing in the world except that
Rupert was trying to save the Elevated from bankruptcy, and
the stockholders from ruin, and those vicious politicians were
holding him up, refusing to grant any increase in fares. They
wouldn't vote until they got money to buy Elevated stocks. You
can't imagine what the politicians are!"

"My child, I know exactly what they are—they are trying
to send two of my friends to the electric chair, unless we will
raise forty thousand dollars to buy them off. Betty and Joe
and I have been having to make that decision in the last few
days, and I think the reason you got this letter is because we
refused to pay."

Deborah sat staring before her, her tall forehead wrinkled in
thought. Her surrender was not indicated by throwing up her
hands, but merely by beginning to talk sensibly. "Mother, I
ought to meet that young man."

"Of course you ought—that is, provided you will behave
yourself, and understand that he is your son-in-law."

"Is he—does he look like a gentleman?"

"He comes from an old Virginia family, and they think they
are quite as good as we are—in fact, I understand they sometimes make fun of us, saying that we talk through our noses."

"I suppose I'll have to tell Rupert," said Deborah. "He might
get one of these letters, too. I'll tell him to-night, and we'll
make some arrangement—I don't know just what. I suppose this

—what is his name, Randall—ought to be invited to dinner."

"Thank you, my dear, that is certainly sensible."

"Well, if they are going to be married, we have to try to make it seem decent. I don't want people to say that Betty married a man she picked up off the street."

"No, it is not at all like that. You can tell people they met at the first session of the Third International in Moscow."

VI

Priscilla Quincy Adams Thornwell had been a sufficient time in her grave for it to be proper for her grand-niece, Priscilla Thornwell Alvin, to be united to the young mountain of copper. So there was another of those stately ceremonials which mark the coming and going of the generations, and advertise their social importance. Out of this union there would proceed many copper hills and branch banks, bearing the sacred names of Thornwell and Quincy and Adams and Shaw and Cabot, shuffled into new combinations. Engraved invitations were sent to all members of the clans, and the hot-houses of the florists were emptied, and Trinity Church became a mid-winter bower, and the four organs played the Lohengrin march coming and the Mendelssohn march going, and there was a procession of two little "flower-girls," and six young ladies with faces rigid and intense with the effort of keeping in step under the eyes of so many relatives. They wore drooping hats and carried large bouquets of roses, as white as the driven snow before it has been driven through the bituminous smoke of Boston. This symbolized the undoubted purity of the bride, and nowhere in the consecrated spaces of the brown-stone edifice was there a single red rose of adultery.

Except in the hearts of the supposed-to-be-happy parents of the bride, haunted by the cruel secret of their younger daughter's shame. Rupert and Deborah were in the grip of a terror such as had never before attended a Thornwell wedding-service. Their imaginations played with a string of horrors, which might be perpetrated by a writer of devilish anonymous letters. After all, what limit could you set to the perversity of such a creature? A bomb in the church—say in the vestibule, where it would not kill any one, but would make a scandal heard round the world!

Or perhaps what was called a "stink-bomb," that would drive everybody from the edifice! Or foul whispers by an old gipsy woman, or poison-leaflets distributed in the pews—it had happened once in Boston history. There was a moment when the hearts of Rupert and Deborah jumped into their throats—when the rector pronounced the bold challenge: "If any man can show just cause, why they may not lawfully be joined together, let him now speak, or else hereafter for ever hold his peace!"

A dreadful silence, during which Rupert and Deborah heard a voice shout out that the younger sister of the bride was living in adultery, and therefore the family was not "eligible." But no one else heard a sound, and the ceremony was completed; six immaculate ushers from Harvard marched out with the six bridesmaids, and the little flower girls carried the bride's train. The bride and groom were whisked away to the Alvin home, where an elaborate breakfast was served to the family and intimate friends. The bride, now attired in traveling costume, was kissed on both cheeks by relatives male and female—her pure white forehead was stained by the red lips of adultery, and she did not know it! Yes, Betty hugged and kissed her good old sister several times, and wished her all the respectable luck which so respectable a young lady was bound to have; and if there were tears in Betty's eyes, they were not tears of shame, because Betty was lost to shame, and only her poor mother had to blush for her, and weep for the dreadful hidden secret—and tremble, because the danger was not yet over—there might be poison-leaflets thrown into the departing bridal-car, in place of the rice and old shoes which Boston society had abandoned as undignified.

But again the fears proved baseless, and the young couple departed in blissful certainty that everything had happened exactly as it had always happened, and as it ought to happen—one and the same thing in Boston. They took the train to New York, and from there to Palm Beach, where they stopped at the most expensive hotel, and dressed themselves three times a day in the proper summer costumes, and innumerable attendants rushed this way and that to anticipate their needs, and no one embarrassed them by a smile or hint that they were suspected of not being entirely accustomed to the intimacies of holy matrimony.

So, in secrecy and retirement, a young creature who was to
bear a string of honored names began his career; and the conscientious young progenitors had nothing in the world to worry
about except the inescapable problem which dogs the footsteps
of Boston blue-bloods en voyage—whom is it safe to know and
whom not? If people hail from Seattle or Oshkosh, it may be
rather amusing to talk to them, because they will not presume
to expect to know you at home; but if they come from New
England, then you have to speculate anxiously as to who they
are, and wish you had Mother or Aunt Alice to advise you.
Can they be the "right" Cabots? Do any of the "real" Lowells
come from New Hampshire? Are the Adamses of Scituate the
ones who are cousins of the Adamses of Concord, or can they
be those dreadful people that were divorced some years ago?
Better to walk the esplanade in solemn dignity by yourself, than
take the risk of making such a serious misstep!

VII

An odd experience for Cornelia and Betty—to take part in
this orgy of hand-shaking and kissing—to be dipped, as it were,
into an ocean of propriety and perfume, to be transported to a
fairy-land of white veils and roses, frock-coats and silk hats and
kid gloves, crystal and silver and pearl and diamond wedding-
presents—and then to step into a motor-car and be carried along
the Back Bay and across the river, and find themselves within
the gates of an ancient stone dungeon, stained dark by factory
smoke, with steel bars on the windows and steel doors clanging,
and faces of grim command, and faces of lowering hate, faces
brutalized and degraded, marked by disease, fear, cruelty—a
thousand evils which poverty, ignorance and neglect inflict upon
the tormented human race. Church doctrine teaches that between
heaven and hell there is an abyss across which none may travel;
but Cornelia and her granddaughter crossed it at least once, and
sometimes two or three times a week; they went back and forth
between celestial and infernal regions, associating freely with
both angels and devils—and finding them not so different one
from the other as their fears and hates caused them to believe!
Bart came, with the coal-dust hastily washed from his face
and hands, but not from his neck and wrists. He greeted them

with his smile of joy, and asked to sit near the window, in the sunshine, so rare in his life. He saw the white roses they were wearing, and learned that they were bridal roses; he traveled in fancy to the River Magra, where weddings meant fiddles and dancing and wine, in addition to flowers and white veils. Such lovely country, such happy people—if it were not for landlord, for padrone, for wicked go-vérnment, taking boys away from home to make soldier, to make cruel war!

They talked about the case, and Bart with tact and gentleness strove to convey to his dear friends the unhappiness which was tormenting him. Never had he thought it could happen that he would be the means of sending any human being to prison, a place of wickedness and suffering like this. "Is something should not be attempting, Nonna, it is not according with filosofia anarchica. Mrs. De Falco is criminal, yes, but is poor victim, is ignorant, is not blam-èd for what she do. It is principle for me—it is wrong ever to call law, to punish wit' judge and sooch thing."

"But, Bart, you told Lee you would leave it to his judgment."

"I know, I have shame for that. I am stranger, poor man, have not mooch knowledge. I think, friend have bring lawyer, he is educate, he onderstand, he try hard for helping—how can I make contraddizione? But then come Italian friend, they say, 'What is this, Vanzett', you are anarchista, you make woman be arrest? You have deny principle of whole living?' And I say, 'It is true, I have done wrong, I would better be convict of any crime in world!' "

"Well, Bart"—it was Betty speaking—"you should have an anarchist lawyer."

"Is not many soocha t'ing, Betty, is hard for be. Should not have no lawyer. Anarchista should stand in court, should say, 'Is wicked place, is wicked sistema. You have power, you have victim in hand, you can crush him, but you cannot crush his soul, his doctrine it live, will spread to whole umane kind.' "

"Then you really don't want to be saved, Bart?"

"I want for anarchismo be sav-èd."

"Joe has gone to Maine, to try to get the record of one of the witnesses for the prosecution, that we have heard has been convicted of crime. Now, if we find it is so, do you want us to use the fact? It will hurt the man's feelings, no doubt."

Vanzetti sat with brow furrowed in thought. "I not know. I have said always, it is good for speak truth. I think anarchista can speak what is truth."

"Yet you might be the cause of the man's being sent to jail again. It might turn out he is wanted by the police for something else."

Time was needed to answer that! It was a complicated world, and often it would happen that Vanzetti would agree to the proposals of Betty and Joe and Lee Swenson, and then think it over, or hear the protests of his comrades, and decide that it was not according to "filosofia anarchica." All he could say now, having brooded over the problem of Mrs. De Falco through long hours in his cell, was that he did not want her sent to jail, not even to save his life. Anyhow, he was sure the move against her would not help his cause; rather it would embitter the go-vérnment, it would make them redouble their efforts for a conviction. It was difficult to explain this in a foreign language, but Bart's idea was that the authorities would consider Lee Swenson was not playing the game. The law, from the point of view of a politician in power, was an opportunity for graft, and the most dangerous person in the world was not the bandit, but the man who threatened the graft system.

"He is not so mooch fraid for bandit, he know plenty bandit, is us-èd him, do plenty business with him. It is big bandit put up money for election him. But man what expose, man what tell newspaper, tell people, he is real nemico—what you say, enemy, he is one you musta keell. I think he keell me for teach Lee Swenson he cannot break graft in Massachusett."

"I am sorry if we have made things worse, Bart." It was Cornelia speaking, and her words brought tears into the prisoner's eyes. He laid his hand upon her arm, and begged her pardon for his bad way of saying things, it was hard to express these complicated ideas. He was not afraid to die, and whatever happened, they must not grieve. He was a poor, unknown man, he had talked for years unheeded; to be executed for his beliefs was perhaps the one way he could make them known. But he wanted to die with a clean conscience—not having caused a mother of several children to be sent to jail, for trying to get her pitiful share of that loot which the rich and powerful ones of the community tried to keep for their own.

VIII

Lee Swenson had obtained a postponement of the Sacco-Vanzetti case until the month of June, to give him time to prepare. The law of the Puritans, otherwise stern and parsimonious, would be prodigal only of delay. Sacco would sit in his cell in Dedham—when he grew bored with standing on his head or walking on his hands—and wonder by what malicious turn of fate it had happened that he who despised the law was tangled in a legal net, denied even the boon of swift, uncomplicated death. Now and then there would be papers he would have to sign on his own behalf; invariably he would refuse to sign them, and there would begin a campaign of diplomacy.

Visits from his wife, carrying the newly born infant, surely a reason to make a fight for freedom! Visits from committees of this "gruppo" and that, bringing messages and resolutions, a newspaper article, a cablegram from Italy. You could never tell what odd circumstance might turn the trick with Sacco: a bouquet of flowers, a chat about what was to be planted in the garden this spring, or questions as to what would be blooming in Torremaggiore at this time of year—and suddenly the hard shell of anarchistic principle would melt, and the tormented man would smile, and stretch out his hand for the paper, saying, "Is crazy t'ing, but you say it, I sign heem."

Meantime typewriters were clicking, and circulars and pamphlets going out, and a scrapbook filling with clippings about the case. Throughout labor and radical circles in America the names of Sacco and Vanzetti were becoming known as the latest victims of the "frame-up" system. Money was coming in, and several investigators were at work, and the busy brain of Lee Swenson was spinning counterplots like a nest of caterpillars in a pine tree. Under the law of the Commonwealth he had the right to a list of the witnesses to be used by the prosecution; and part of his preparation of the case was interviews with these persons, and efforts to get their stories from them, to break them down, to delve into their past and find out anything that would discredit them, or frighten them, or cause them to swing over to the other side.

Under this system, a legal case became a miniature war, a contest of sappers and miners, of spies and counterspies; some witnesses would sell out more than once, and change their stories back and forth—one statement to the Pinkerton detectives, a different one to the friends of the defense, yet another to the district attorney, another to the lawyers of the defense—and which one finally got to the jury was a matter of price, or else of psychology. Some witnesses wanted money, and then more money; but there were others who had a secret spring of loyalty or prejudice, which, if you could touch it, might turn the trick for a few days or forever. One would do anything to help a buddy who had been in France, the next would do anything to oblige the Pope of Rome; one wanted to electrocute all Italians because he had been knifed by one in a street fight twenty years ago; another abhorred Yankees because a school-teacher had beaten him as a child.

A singular education for a daughter of the blue-bloods, to help in a job like this! An education which would surely not have won the approval of her theocratic forefathers, nor yet of the plutocratic trustees who supervised the curriculum of Radcliffe! But at least you could say it was an education based upon fundamentals, and getting to original sources. What was present-day New England actually like? What did its people really do and think and feel? What was its working governmental system, as distinguished from the one written on paper, and taught in schools, and glorified in Fourth of July orations and newspaper editorials? Surely these were matters worth knowing about, even if you did not get a sheepskin diploma, and three Greek letters on a key, and two Latin words at the end of your name!

Elizabeth Thornwell Alvin took two different trains and traveled into the Pocono Mountains of Pennsylvania, and was bumped for ten or fifteen miles in a buggy over country roads deep with the soft mud of early spring, and in a ramshackle farmhouse, with the paint peeled off and the fence palings molded and rotten, she met a girl who had been working in the Rice and Hutchins shoe factory in South Braintree on the afternoon when the bandits had opened fire on the paymaster and the guard. This girl had a feeble chin and prematurely decayed teeth, and a baby due to make its entrance into a world of torment in a very few days. For some reason she got it into her weak head that Betty was there in the interest of the district attorney's office, and she immediately became hysterical, bursting into tears and shrieking that she was in no condition to come to a trial, and could not be forced to testify; anyhow, she knew nothing, because when the shooting had started, she had hidden under a bench.

Betty soothed her, assuring her there was no wish to force her to do anything; so presently the girl calmed down and became communicative. Too bad she could not go, because two of her former shopmates were getting good pay to testify against those wops, and they sure ought to be run out of the country, coming in and taking honest people's jobs away, and fighting and all that, and it sure was up to we Americans to stand together against them. Later, by deft questioning, Betty drew from this patriotic young person the information that her mother had been an Irish peasant and her father a French peasant. A triumph of "americanization," and the speeding up processes of a machine age! Betty's ancestors, who had been tinners and carpenters and indentured servants, had taken three hundred years to acquire their superiority to the new immigrant workers; but here was a shoe factory girl who had managed it in one-tenth of the time!

IX

The case of Mrs. De Falco was set for trial in a Boston police court, and Betty and Joe turned their energies to this—digging into the records of public officials, and running down clews of graft. Shudders ran up and down the spines of persons high in political power, and rage seethed in their hearts against blue-blood intruders who were not content with the security which wealth and prominence conferred, but turned traitor to their own privileges, and attacked the bases of law and order. What did these high-hatted snobs want, anyhow? What was the matter with them that they could not be content with public officials who protected them, keeping them safe against bombers and blackmailers and burglars and pickpockets and a thousand such predatory creatures; making everything so comfortable, that they might be born, and grow up, and live long, and go to pieces like the one-horse shay, of old age and decrepitude, without ever knowing a moment of danger or making a real effort in their lives?

The politicians and police might laugh at the blue-bloods, but they respected and feared them, because of very real powers they still held; not merely finance, utilities and the choicest real estate, but solidarity, knowledge, culture—the latter a far-off, mysterious thing, but awe-inspiring, like the power of a voodoo magician, who can cause your right arm to wither and fall off; or anyhow, he says he can, and how shall you be certain about it? The lower orders, having captured the city, were afraid of their captives, and dared not make use of their power; they stood, fierce-eyed barbarians, at the doors of the temples, and watched the priests, clad in frock coats and high hats, performing mysterious offices, impossible to comprehend or imitate. In the end the barbarians capitulated, and sent their sons to study in the temples, and become as much like the conquered caste as they could!

Politicians and police were used to many kinds of eccentricities on the part of rich persons. Those who had enormous powers and no duties necessarily had to work off steam. They dressed themselves in pink coats, and rode to hounds and broke their necks; they raced motor cars at high speeds, and learned to save themselves behind the steering-post when they crashed; they flew in airplanes and landed on top of houses; they built submarines and got stuck at the bottom of the sea; they worked in chemical laboratories and asphyxiated themselves, or invented explosives and blew themselves up; they went yachting to the North Pole to hunt walruses, or to the equator to collect baby chimpanzees for a psychological laboratory.

Hardly a millionaire estate without something weird and mysterious upon it: the largest collection of old pewter in the world, or a single-tax enclave, or an herbarium with Brazilian butterflies, or a laboratory for the investigation of ghosts, or a mausoleum prepared in advance of death, or a fireproof and bombproof shelter for safety against mobs! And now and then a more sinister case—a clergyman with a fondness for choir-boys, or an aged sybarite who must have fifteen-year-old virgins shivering in his arms; a young lady of fashion who frequented the "black and tan" cafés disguised as a man, or who taught the sex-lore of the Orient to her female intimates!

The police were used to all this. They even got used to the idea that now and then a rich eccentric would turn against his own and commit class-suicide. They knew that in the home of a dead poet in Cambridge, a shrine to which pilgrims traveled from all over America, the poet's grandson was upstairs entertaining syndicalists and communists, and figuring the easiest way to overthrow the capitalist system. That was treason, but it was treason to the rich, and the rich were the ones to deal with it. What worried the politicians and police was when these young fools took to hounding the politicians and police. That was the treason that really mattered, that was a stab in the back, and the most dangerous activity one could pursue in America.

And here was Betty Alvin quite blandly going to it, heedless of all warnings. So came a string of developments, distressing to a blue-blood family. Anonymous letters, more abusive and more widely scattered; telephone calls, with sinister voices pronouncing dooms; visits to Rupert from his banking associates, who talked about alarming rumors they had heard; a call from the Republican boss with whom Rupert did business, and who asked him if he didn't have troubles enough! So again Betty was summoned to her father's home, and went through the worst scene yet; she lost her serenity, and shed many tears, but she would not go abroad, nor give up either her lover or her anarchists. Again she was disinherited and disowned—whether in words, or actually upon paper, she had no way to know.

A heavy strain upon Rupert, and a strange freak of fate! Or could it be that there actually was some intelligence overseeing the universe, and that Betty's revolt was a punishment visited upon a great banker who had left undone those things he ought to have done, and had done those things he ought not to have done? Rupert could not escape this idea, because he had been brought up in Trinity Church in the City of Boston, and had heard it—not exactly preached, but skirted on the edge of, every Sunday morning for fifty years. He would have liked to ask his rector, or some other clergyman: could there be a God perverse enough to object to Rupert's having taken the feltplants of Jerry Walker, which Rupert could finance and Jerry couldn't? Could any God have wanted him to let the Boston Elevated stay on the rocks and be pounded to pieces? Could any God be so silly as the fanatics and agitators who denounced

Rupert for having loaned money to legislators—when it was perfectly obvious that it was not Rupert who had elected these legislators, and that lending them money was the only way to get a raise of fares and make the stock of the Elevated worth anything? No, God was not going to punish the president of the Pilgrim National Bank for having protected the people who had trusted their fortunes to him! But then, how could God be letting Rupert's lovely young daughter be seduced by anarchist free love, and exposed to the furies of scandal, at such a trying moment of her father's life?

X

One by one the members of the family received "poison pen" letters. Clara Thornwell Scatterbridge came to her mother, incredulous of the scandal, because her maternal soul had never desired an impropriety. Alice Thornwell Winters came, elegant and precious, regarding her virtue as a hard-won possession, deserving of commensurate rewards. No use expecting others to live up to one's own standards—"though I do think, Mother, Betty is beginning rather young. I must say I am aghast at this new generation, they don't even trouble to apologize for their indiscretions. And I don't know what to make of you, Mother— I thought you believed in the old standards. I heard that these radicals practiced free love, but somehow I didn't think of it in relation to my own mother."

"Well, Alice," said Cornelia, "you must consider my life. I was faithful to the old standards, I lived my life without love, and where did it get me?"

The carefully cultivated features of Alice Thornwell Winters wore a puzzled look. Alice prided herself upon being sensitive to all ethical and esthetic values—they were the same thing, she always insisted—beauty was truth and beauty was goodness— but of course beauty must be recognized by a discriminating intelligence—it was something that could not be explained—it was a gift, very rare, but Alice had it. "Really, Mother, how can you feel that you have had such a hard life? Your children love you, and your grandchildren would, if they saw more of you. Josiah was saying to me only yesterday it was hard to understand why you found so much in Italian anarchists, and so little in your own people."

"Well, my dear, perhaps I know the Harvard values too well, and have got bored with them. Tell Josiah to come to dinner, and tell me what new things he has learned and accomplished. That is, unless you are afraid to expose him to my free love ideas."

That was a nasty stroke of a cat's claws, and the sensitive Alice winced. For everybody in the family had heard about the "wild oats" of "Young Josiah," only son of Alice and Henry—known as "Josie" to his boyhood playmates, and as "Si" to the members of "Porcellian" and of "Alpha Delta Phi." Alice allowed for him, because he was a man, and that was the way men did, apparently; they got over it in time, and settled down. But nowadays the girls were doing it, too, and how would there be any esthetic standards, if the women did not maintain them? That was what shocked Alice in the episode of Betty and Joe— it was so unesthetic, to come to the apartment where Betty's grandmother lived! To which Cornelia answered that she had never been to a roadhouse, and could not judge, but it might be, of course, that some of them were fixed up esthetically. Look out for the cat's claws of this gentle-seeming old woman!

Alice went away, and Josiah Thornwell Winters called up, and made an appointment to dine with his grandmother, and tell her what he had learned and accomplished as a Harvard senior. But when he came, he did not mention the subject—because meantime the current of his thoughts had been diverted. The grandson and namesake of the stern old governor had fallen the newest victim to the calamities which were raining upon his conspicuous family.

Cornelia happened to drop in at the office of the defense committee, and Lee Swenson gave her the first news of the event. "I don't like to repeat gossip, Nonna, but my guess is, your latest family trouble is a result of what you and Betty are doing, so you need to know about it."

"What do you mean, Lee?"

"There's a story all over town—last night the political gangs were roaring drunk in their bootleg-joints, and when they had a round of drinks, they would say, 'Have one on Young Josiah!' "

"What has he done?"

"Well, they caught him in a hotel room with a woman. Undoubtedly she lured him there—it's a regular system they have. They took a flashlight photograph of him, and Henry Cabot Winters paid seventy-five thousand dollars to kill the story."

Cornelia, the "Red," was supposed to be lacking in shame; but now she looked down, instead of at her friend. "Can it really be true, Lee?"

"It is what is being told. You can find out, of course."

"They can do that kind of thing in Boston, and not be punished?"

"It's the punishers who are doing it, Nonna. It's a blackmail ring, and the district attorneys get a share of the loot. There is an aged millionaire in this town—perhaps you know him—old man Barbour?"

"I have met him."

"Well, they got him in the same kind of jam, and soaked him to the tune of three hundred and eighty-six thousand. You can hardly believe that, but I got the amount from one of his lawyers. And then young Searles—he inherited a fortune from his uncle, I think it was, and the gang got him in an apartment with a couple of girls and cleaned him out. Over in Woburn they got a bunch of moving-picture people in a roadhouse for a wild party, and it cost those celebrities a hundred and five thousand."

"One might expect it of people like that," said Cornelia. "But it is something new for the Thornwells, unless I am mistaken. I'm glad that my Josiah is not here to see what has become of his name."

XI

So it was that when Josiah Thornwell Winters came to dinner two or three days afterwards, his grandmother did not chat about the polite nothings of the Harvard curriculum and of "Porcellian" and "Alpha Delta Phi." Throwing aside those reticences which are supposed to be the crown of womanhood, she talked in plain language about unspeakable things— "man to man," as she put it. And "Young Josiah," who had never dreamed of such a thing from an old lady, turned pink to the roots of his hair and looked as if he wanted to grab his hat and run; but after a while he got used to it, and found it a relief to talk about realities. He had come very close to shooting his head off, and neither the horrified grief of his pure mother, nor the withering scorn of his successful father had been of the slightest use to him.

He was twenty-two years old, and at the age of seventeen he had sprung up to the Thornwell height of six feet and more, but had never filled out his lean figure. His shoulders were stooped and his complexion pale, and his fingers yellow with nicotine; but he had the most elegant Harvard drawl, and a complete equipment of skepticism and boredom, applied to matters about which he knew nothing, as well as to those about which Harvard had taught him everything. His manner was "right," his clothing had the proper shade of carelessness, and his apartment on the "Gold Coast" contained shelves of exquisite smut, beginning with Petronius and ending with James Branch Cabell, in numbered editions at from fifteen to fifty dollars a volume.

But now all that solemn pose of maturity had fallen like a cheap actor's cloak, and Cornelia confronted a raw, weedy youth with vicious habits and a sick sense of shame. "I'm a rotter," he said, "but I could tell you things to show you it wasn't entirely my fault. The Pater gave me the razz—he all but told me I'd oblige him if I'd eat a chunk of cyanide—and I said nothing. But you must know, Grandmother, he hasn't been any saint."

"I know he keeps a woman," said Cornelia, grimly.

"More than that. There's a tradition on the crew—you know, after he was graduated, the Pater coached the crew for a couple of years—and he told the fellows they would have to go with prostitutes, or they'd lose their virility. That made the church crowd hot, and they got rid of him, but the story stayed on, and a lot of the fellows think he was right. Now, of course, the Pater says I've gone too far, but then, who is to do the measuring? It was my hard luck that I knew too much about both my father and my mother. Do you want me to talk about Mother?"

"I want you to tell me the truth."

"Well, Mother has wonderful emotions, but she's a little

short on brains, and I rarely got anything useful from her. When I was about fifteen, I heard a terrible quarrel between her and the Pater, they told each other all the dirt they knew. I was behind a curtain, and had to stay there, because I was ashamed to let them know I'd heard the beginning. You know Mother's way, she has platonic thrills, but she doesn't go the limit, so that makes it all right. The Pater had got a story on her—her friends were talking about how she had traveled to New York with one of her poets, and had lain in his arms all night in the sleeping-car berth, but not parted with her virtue; that was her remarkable spirituality, and the fellow was supposed to enjoy it, too. The Pater called her some rotten names, and then she told what she knew about him, and that was my introduction to the subject of love. It wasn't exactly helpful, was it?"

Cornelia accepted the plea.

"Well, when I was sixteen, I was visiting a fellow from St. Mark's. It was a place on the North Shore, and he had an aunt—one of these up-to-date ladies who had divorced one husband and was getting rid of another, and her lover was in Europe, and she was bored. She came from New York, and they are ahead of us—but not more than a year or two, I have found —perhaps because they get the new shows a season earlier. Anyhow, this was good family, a country club crowd, no end of money, and it seemed all right. She came to my room at night—all fixed up, very beautiful and sweet-smelling, and what chance did a kid stand against a proposition like that? She stayed around a while, and taught me a lot—until her lover came back from Europe, and then we said good-by. But it was only a week before a young widow took me on. You can't imagine how it is, Grandmother—I know it wasn't that way in your time. The women know what they want, and they just go to it."

"Are they trying to marry you?"

"Not often. Some have husbands, but they've been reading Freud, and have got the idea that all their troubles are repressions. And the young girls are worse."

"All of them, Josiah?"

"No, of course not—there are plenty of girls like Priscilla and Betty—I suppose they are straight. What happened to me was, I got a reputation, so I drew the wild ones. I was supposed to be a lady-killer. I don't imagine I'm abnormally attractive, but family counts for a lot, and Harvard, of course—the high-hat stuff. Anyhow, I assure you I never had to do any seducing, and I never made any promises I didn't keep. I've spent a lot of money, but always in respectable ways, I mean entertainments and presents and so on. I never got stuck for blackmail but this once."

Cornelia smiled. "You remember Æsop's fable," she said, "about the lioness who had only one cub, but that one was a lion."

XII

Young Josiah skirted around the cage of this "lion" for quite a while. It didn't seem really decent to tell such "dirt" to one's grandmother. But Cornelia pinned him down. "I have other grandchildren coming along, and I need to know about my city."

"Well, it's a rotten hole," said the youth. "I think this blackmail business is a result of the fact that Bostonians have to pretend to be so much better than they can be. Or maybe it's the Irish, bringing us Yankees off our high horses."

"Who was the woman?"

"She belongs to what is known as 'Larry Shay's stable'—not a very elegant name, but you say you want to know Boston. She looked like a society girl, and I really thought she was."

"Where did you meet her?"

"I had seen her around Harvard Square for a week or two, and I thought she lived in the neighborhood—a neglected young wife or something. She can't be over nineteen; she was dressed up to the minute, and looked like springtime. I suppose she was watching me, finding out about my habits. Anyhow, she passed me now and then, and always looked willing, but not too eager. This time I was sitting in my car, waiting for a fellow, and she came along smiling, and naturally I was smiling, and she walked up and said, 'You are Josiah Winters, aren't you?' She said, 'I know your cousin, Betty Alvin, but I'm not a "Red" like her, so don't be afraid of me.' She had got posted about Betty, and of course I thought Betty knew lots of people that the rest of the family wouldn't know. I laughed, and asked her if she'd

like to ride, and she got in, and we rode all over, and I kissed
her a few times, and she said she had never done anything like
this before, and paid me a lot of compliments, but she wouldn't
go to a roadhouse, and when we came back to town we had
supper, and a little champagne, and—the upshot of it was, she
knew a hotel where a girl-friend of hers lived, and she wouldn't
be afraid to go there. So we went to a room; and about ten
minutes after we got in, somebody put his shoulder to the door,
and there were half a dozen men, and one of them held a
camera, and another set off a flashlight, and they said they were
county detectives, and I was under arrest, and the picture
would be in the Boston 'Telegram' the next afternoon. The girl
went into hysterics—she was a good actress, I must say—or
maybe she liked me and was sorry—I'm fool enough to wonder, because she was so young. But there it was, and the Pater
pungled up seventy-five thousand bucks, and took it out by
telling me what he really thought of me. It took quite a while,
and went into details."

Cornelia was moved to say, "You must allow for the financial
strain."

"No, it is what he really thinks; he's been cherishing it up
for a long time. He is disappointed in me, I'm a weakling, and
he needs a strong man for his successor. He might stop and
think, what has there been in my life to develop strength—
assuming I had the possibility? When the Pater got through
Harvard he had to pitch in and fight his own way; but I never
had to, it was no good trying to fool myself with the idea that
I was anything but a millionaire's son. Of course Mother's
spoiling me was from affection, but that didn't change the result. I have enough of the Pater's brains to understand what
happened. I never had to do anything but call somebody else.
If the car was out of order, tell the chauffeur; if I wanted a
bunch of flowers, tell the gardener. So many servants to wait
on one kid; so many courtiers, to make you think you're the
top of the heap—so why should you climb any higher? And
then the women come, and after that, it is impossible to break
through. I don't mean merely sex—I mean all the things they
want to do—tea-parties and dances and motoring and yachting.
Honest truth, Grandmother, except for things like this blackmail, there's nothing to choose between the fashionable girls

and the ones you pick up; they want to do the same things, and the only difference is where you go, and how much it costs. The one thing none of them will let you do is any serious work."

There was more to this revealing story, and Cornelia listened to it all and asked many questions. "I ought to have known these things many years ago," she said. "I might have helped you a great deal."

"Yes, of course. Nobody talks straight to us fellows. Mother doesn't know much that is real, and the Pater has been so busy making money—too busy to think what good it will do anybody. He must be pretty sick, because I show so few signs of solving the problem for him."

"Wouldn't you like to come and see me now and then? Perhaps Betty and I could bring you in touch with people who are doing worth-while things."

"Well, Grandmother, of course, I'll meet anybody you say, but I don't see much hope in that crowd of yours. The way it looks to me, you and Betty have got a little money, and family position, and they are using you for what you are worth."

"Yes, my boy," said Cornelia, gently, "but what I thought was, you might forget those Harvard ideas. I will take you to Charlestown prison and introduce you to one of my wops, who has never had either money or family position, and no education except what he picked up after washing dishes fourteen hours a day. He cannot express himself in English very well, yet he has managed to impress me as a very great man. It is possible he might impress you also, and make you realize what it means to men who lose the money that you get."

"I don't understand just what you mean by that," said Young Josiah from Harvard.

XIII

The trial of Mrs. De Falco came up in a Boston police court, and Cornelia extended her knowledge of the "blackmail ring" and its power. A long-haired Swede from the West had come into Massachusetts to tell them how to run their system of justice; a "Red" and an enemy of society, who would not play the game as other lawyers played it, but tried to throw sticks into the machinery! Well, they would show him—and they did.

The magistrate was an Irish-Catholic, an ardent patriot, and these were the days of most bitter prejudice against anarchists, atheists and wops. The lawyer representing the defendant was an aggressive and loud-mouthed Jew, and the way he and the judge collaborated was a prophecy of an immortal drama of the emotions called "Abie's Irish Rose." When Felicani, and Lopez, a Spanish anarchist, explained their conscientious objections to taking an oath, the devout Hebrew gentleman went after them hammer and tongs, and the devout Catholic gentleman beamed with delight. After that, it ceased to be the trial of an alleged bribe-seeker, and became the trial of two self-confessed free-thinkers. The judge actually ordered Lopez under arrest, and it took a lot of persuading to change his mind.

The two stenographers took the stand, and the fact that one of them had served with the A.E.F. in France did not help them in the least. Did they know the voice of Mrs. De Falco? If not, how could they be sure that the voice they had heard over the dictaphone was the voice of Mrs. De Falco? To be sure, others had seen Mrs. De Falco talking in the room; but maybe these others were lying, maybe somebody had staged a performance to fool the stenographers and make them think they were listening to Mrs. De Falco, when in reality they were listening to some other Italian woman making a bribe proposition! Who could set a limit to the rascalities that atheists and anarchists might contrive, in order to discredit the legal system of the great Commonwealth of Massachusetts?

And then Mrs. De Falco herself, an alert and capable young woman, whose wits had been sharpened by years of battle for life in the police courts. She sturdily denied every charge; and especially she denied any trace of connection between herself and any officials. The high officials of Norfolk and Plymouth counties were upright and honorable gentlemen, and never had made any proposition to let criminals escape for a money consideration, and never had the employment of a relative as counsel for accused criminals had anything to do with subsequent dismissal of proceedings against such criminals. That was, of course, the real issue being tried in this police court; to find the Italian woman guilty meant to find the great Commonwealth of Massachusetts guilty, and how could a patriotic judge do that? When the testimony about the officials began to come in, the judge ordered everybody out of the court-room except the witness and the counsel.

The defendant was acquitted; and Lee Swenson, feeling very blue, went off by himself, and sat down at a luncheon table in a restaurant—when who should come in but the aggressive and loud-mouthed Jewish lawyer! He was feeling good, naturally, and joined his victim at the table, and "kidded" him a bit, after the fashion of lawyers—and incidentally talked about the case, as one sensible man to another. Mrs. De Falco had hung around the courts for so many years, she of course knew both the high official and his brother, and she had tried to capitalize her knowledge and get some money out of the Sacco-Vanzetti defense. She knew the details of other court cases, enough to be able to make it appear that she was able to "swing" deals; she had gone to meeting-places with officials, to talk about other matters—knowing that she would be followed by the defense, who would thus conclude that she had a "pull."

Maybe so, said Lee; but it seemed to him a little strange that a lawyer should be saying such things about his client, and making so elaborate a defense of two other persons who were not his clients! Could it be that any of the officials were paying for this legal victory? The lawyer denied it, and Lee smiled his patient Swedish smile. Of course, you could never be sure; it might be that it had all happened as the other said; sometimes truth really was stranger than fiction. It might be that the officials had happened in while Mrs. De Falco was there, purely as a coincidence; or again, it might be that all of them had met there to say their prayers.

The judge had been of that opinion, and the case was history. The one thing Lee Swenson had accomplished—he realized it, now that it was too late—was to exacerbate the prosecution, to give to all officials having anything to do with the Sacco-Vanzetti case a reason for bitter and personal animus. The name of Lee Swenson became a byword to all politicians and officials; the Sacco-Vanzetti Defense Committee became a nest of active and dangerous foes, and the task of sending two wops to the electric chair became one with the defense of every criminal-in-office in the entire community. Which was exactly as Vanzetti, lying through those endless hours in his prison cell, had figured out and predicted. Always it happened, sooner or later, that everything turned out as Vanzetti had figured out and predicted!

CHAPTER 12

SHADOWS BEFORE

I

SPRINGTIME in New England! Not all the giant factories with belching smoke, not all the dingy tenements, billboards, hot-dog stands and filling stations could conceal the fact that something magical was happening to the land. Even to prisoners in jail, there was a difference in the air which crept through the corridors. Just as boys know when to fly kites, with no outsider to remind them—so Nick Sacco knew it was time for the garden to be spaded, and when you went to see him, he would ask who was going to do it, and what was to be planted. It was good form to insist that he would be out in time to weed the garden, and to eat the first tomatoes.

Vanzetti, who spent fifteen and a half hours in a cell with only a slit in the top for light, and worked in a yard blackened with coal dust and smoke of near-by factories—even he knew that it was spring. You took a bunch of mayflowers when you went to see him, and the guard could not refuse to let you give him one. A pitiful thing, a frail blossom, but—"flower in the crannied wall"—it was a symbol, it meant a whole springtime; it meant those beautiful woods about Plymouth, and the walks which Bart had taken with Nonna and the children. "How happy we been, Nonna! We not know what happiness we have, till we los-èd him!"

He would talk about the things they had done and seen; it was all alive in his memory, it came like a vision, shining with a light that never was in any springtime. He fed his soul upon such memories, lying through the long hours in his cage. Friendship, kindness, beauty—he had had these "blassings" in his life; not a full share—but then, he had observed that people who had a full share did not appreciate so much their "blassings." "Plenty people go in sunshine, they not think. But I got

346

little time for seeing, I make notice!" He would move nearer to the window.

Betty had occasion to go to Plymouth, and she brought back Beltrando Brini in her car with her. Another kind of spring-time, a musical talent putting forth buds! The little boy came to the prison, and after Cornelia had interceded with the warden, he was brought into the big reception room, and unlimbered his fiddle and tuned it up. Bart sat watching every move, bursting with pride, as if he were the child's mother. Trando was scared, of course, for he was only thirteen and a half, and this was a terrible place, slouchy brown figures gliding here and there, watchers with hard faces and eyes. But he tucked the fiddle under his chin, and quavering notes stole on the air—"When you and I were young, Maggie"—the tune which Bart had heard him struggling to play, back in those happy days at home!

He had learned other tunes now—"Old Black Joe," and "Home, Sweet Home." He could almost play Drdla's "Sere-nade"—he would try it, if Bart would excuse mistakes; Bart sat with tears running down his cheeks, no use trying to hide them. The convicts stole to the doors of their cells and strained their ears; even the hard-faced keepers listened, and were re-minded suddenly that they, too, were in jail, victims of the hatreds they themselves engendered. All the prison drew to-gether, realizing its shame; the steel bars were melted—and the harder and tougher moods which had made the steel. Oh, man, how strange a fate—to make jails for yourself, and be led out by a little child with a magic wand—and then find yourself afraid, and obliged to run back and shut yourself in! A clock struck, and visitors must leave, and magic cease.

II

Such holidays of the spirit were rare in the life of Cornelia and Betty these days. For the most part their talk was about harsh reality. The trial loomed near, a portentous event, a battle of armies; no longer a mere matter of two wops accused of crime, but a contest over the good name and dignity of the august Commonwealth. A lawyer had come from the wild west and opened an office and started a propaganda campaign, slandering the good name of Massachusetts all over the world. He was raising tens of thousands of dollars—no one could say how much, but they guessed high, and every dollar was a separate outrage and insult; a refusal to play the game according to the rules.

Lee Swenson knew the danger into which he had put his clients by the De Falco procedure, and this thought was a goad which gave him no rest. He was a cyclone of energy; writing circulars, or suggesting ideas for others to write; printing appeals, getting lists for mailing, writing to this person and that, to get information, to pull wires for publicity, money, or support; interviewing witnesses, hunting up new ones, probing this or that detail of their lives. He would come out to dine with Cornelia, and sit in her big Morris chair by the window, and fan himself and sigh with exhaustion; but in a few minutes he would be telling about a new idea, and before long something else would pop into his head, and out would come his notebook, and what was supposed to be a memorandum might turn into a new set of campaign plans.

Another lawyer had come, a friend of Swenson's from the west; Fred Moore, an Irishman, but a radical, and Swenson's aide in many a fight. Also there were two more journalists on the staff, John Nicholas Beffel and Eugene Lyons, devoted young fellows, passionately convinced of the justice of the cause, and writing newspaper and magazine stuff that went all over the world. As an investigator, there was Bob Reid, a Boston constable, gray old veteran who had been through the Ettor-Giovannitti case with Swenson, and could follow the trail of the authorities like an Indian hunter. If there was anything about Massachusetts police practice too dreadful for Cornelia to believe, all she had to do was to ask this man, and he would cauterize her doubts.

And then another figure, still more alarming to a lady who had lived a sheltered life; a figure out of the underworld, furtive-eyed, silent—a man whom Swenson or Moore usually saw alone, and with whom they made mysterious appointments. Lee, it appeared, was going to try the "stool pigeon" methods of the authorities. Somebody had actually committed the South Braintree crime, he insisted, and the Bridgewater one, too; the way to nail down the prosecution was to find the guilty men.

A rumor had come to Lee that in a city not far away from Boston there was a gang of real bandits who were driving an automobile which they called, jeeringly, "Sacco's car." Now the lawyers were spending money to trail this gang, and Cornelia began to hear whispers of dread names. Lee Swenson saw himself playing the "lead" in a fifth act, in which the prosecution would be confronted with the real evidence, so overwhelming that truth would be vindicated and justice done.

Lee was much of a boy, in spite of his forty years, and he managed to communicate this excitement to Betty and Joe and Cornelia. But he found it impossible to get the Italians of the committee to share his idea; as in the De Falco case, it was contrary to "filosofia anarchica." When you argued about it, you would meet shrugs of the shoulders; let the cops do their own dirty work. "We no raise money for sooch job." When you declared that here might be real bandits, there would be a still higher shrug of the shoulders, a wider sweep of the hands. "What if they did? Is poor feller, musta live. Is victim of wicked sistema, what right I got for punish?"

And when you took the question to Bart and Nick, you met exactly the same response. They would not be saved at the expense of any other human being; they would not compromise their principles, even to prove their innocence. The business of anarchists was to end the system of exploitation, after which crime would cease of itself. If you could live according to these principles, all right, then live; if you could not, then it was up to you to die. Such stubbornness was embarrassing to persons of Yankee upbringing, who believed in adjusting means to ends, and took "law and order" seriously. Also embarrassing to a lawyer, who had spent twenty years training himself to play a certain game, and now was expected to play it and not play it at the same time!

III

Day by day, as the work continued, the intricacies of the case developed. The list of witnesses for the prosecution numbered more than fifty, those for the defense close to one hundred. There were not investigators enough to run down all the clews, there were not cells enough in the human brain to hold all the details. The crime had occurred in mid-afternoon, on a busy street, and there were many witnesses, each one a separate problem; the more you dug into him or her, the more extra problems you would discover—husbands, wives, sweethearts, children, employers—to say nothing of policemen and investigators and prosecuting officials who had been there before you! The witnesses were mostly persons of low social station, the neglected poor of America. To probe into their lives, to uncover their family skeletons, their vices and secret shames, their greeds and fears and vanities and hates—it seemed to Cornelia there was nothing so horrible being done in all the world. Except, perhaps, the work which a large force of Americans, guided by sentimentality and superstition, were now performing in France; digging up the dead bodies of soldier boys who had been slain in battle, and had been rotting underground for three years.

Take the soul of Lola Andrews. Cornelia lived with the soul of Lola Andrews for months, walked, talked, ate, slept, dined or fasted with Lola Andrews; because Betty took Lola for her task, consecrating her youth and beauty, her social charm, her faith, hope and charity, to the task of trying to persuade Lola to tell the truth. Naturally Betty, being new at the practice of psychopathology, not very well informed as to the diagnosis and treatment of hysteria, paranoia, hyperesthesia and all abnormalities, would bring her problems to Grannie, and the two would hold long consultations, and Cornelia would visit the famous Dr. Morrow and ask his advice.

Lola Andrews had begun life in the wilderness of Maine, as the hapless child of an Italian man and a Yankee farmer's daughter. Her mother died, her father disappeared, and she grew up, slim and small, black of eyes and hair, a kind of woodland sprite, used to the sneers of the world. At the age of seventeen, when she was married, her hair was such a mat of filth and vermin that her husband had been compelled to take her to a barber and have her head shaved close. This husband was a soldier returned from the Philippines; after a child was born, Lola began running out to dances, and he left her. During years of misery she made the discovery that by screaming and crying she could get people to pay attention to her; so she became an hysteric, and at any time during the investigation, if anything happened that Lola didn't like, up would go her hands and forth would come a shriek. After which, she would calm down, and talk quite reasonably about her own interests.

At the time of the South Braintree crime Lola had been taking care of an elderly man who was bedridden, in the hope that he would leave her a part of his property at his death. Meantime, since he gave her nothing, she scrubbed floors, she went out and did washing—and of course was preyed upon. The police of the town knew about her life, yet in this case they would be willing to make use of her.

It was Lola's story that she had been walking down the street, four hours prior to the crime, and had twice passed what she thought was the bandit car. It was a great weakness of the prosecution that the crime had taken place at such speed, there had been only a minute or so for observation; but here was Lola, who had stopped and chatted with the bandits. One of the two men standing by the car was yellow-haired—and when Joe Randall heard this part of the story he said, "Look out, Lee Swenson, they are after you!" The other man had been under the car, doing something to the works, and this was the one Lola had made a special point to observe, and was willing to describe in any way that seemed most to the advantage of Lola.

So here was a problem in applied psychology; to explore the dark caverns of this tortured soul, to know more about her than she knew about herself, so that you could pull the strings and manipulate her to the ends of "joostice." But alas, it was easier to dream than to accomplish; the science of psychopathology is still in its infancy, and the few months' time allowed was insufficient to bring it to maturity. Lola would have moods of frankness; she was nearing forty now, her charms were gone, she was a poor wreck, and this was her chance to get what was coming to her; the world was a place of "dog eat dog," and why should she worry about a pair of wops who would never worry about her? Why should she worry about what she had said at preliminary hearings, or to newspaper reporters, or investigators, or any of the other people who had pestered her? All she had to do was deny it, and the district attorney would protect her, and the jury would believe her.

There was a secret spring by which the soul of Lola might be moved, but alas, the defense did not find it until after the trial.

The fates so willed it, that everything that was really significant in the Sacco-Vanzetti case was not found until after the trial. Lola's son was living up in Maine, under another name, and in the effort to keep his esteem, she would make sacrifices—for a few days. When confronted with this son, and his reminder of other cases where she had "staged a show," Lola broke down and admitted that she had lied, and that her identification had been "framed." She made affidavit to this in the presence of her son and several reliable witnesses. But under police pressure, she took it all back, and made another affidavit, with a lurid tale about how the defense had intimidated her. Subsequently she took that back also.

Such was Lola Andrews, who sat in the witness chair at the trial, and identified Sacco as the "dark-complexioned man" who had been under the car, and identified the car as the bandit car because, "when I heard of the shooting I somehow associated the man I saw at the car." And when the defense started to question her about her past life, she suddenly threw her much-tried fainting stunt, and Judge Thayer hastened to adjourn court. When she was asked the cause of her excitement, she said it was because she had recognized in the court-room a man who had assaulted her in a toilet in Quincy! And Judge Thayer, who had no more training in psychopathology than Cornelia and Betty, ordered all the doors of the court-room closed, while the officers attempted to catch the man whom Lola had recognized. Never had she had so much attention, never had she been such a heroine!

Along with this problem came Mrs. Campbell, the elderly woman who had been with Lola on the day of the crime, and had gone into the shoe factory with her to seek a job. It took fancy detective work to locate Mrs. Campbell, because she was not listed by the prosecution; when she was found, the reason was apparent—she completely wiped Lola out. The man they had spoken to was not the man under the car at all, but a man in khaki clothes standing near the factory; neither of them had spoken to any man who was working on an automobile. An investigator for the government had come to Mrs. Campbell, and hearing her story, had assured her there was no need for her to come to Dedham to testify, what she knew was of no importance, and it would cost too much money to bring her.

It would have added ten or twenty dollars to the seventy thousand which the great Commonwealth was spending to put two wops out of the way.

A topsy-turvy world, a lunatic's dream of a world, impossible to believe in, even when you saw it with your eyes and heard it with your ears! What could you make of a world in which you studied Lola Andrews for months, and came to know every quirk of her fantastic soul; in which you saw her exposed and discredited by witness after witness—even a policeman and a newspaper reporter to whom she had admitted that she did not see the faces of the men she thought were the bandits; and then, in the face of all this, you saw the Honorable Fred Katzmann, district attorney of Norfolk County, stand up to address the jury, and solemnly declare: "I have been in this office, gentlemen, for now more than eleven years. I cannot recall in that too long service for the Commonwealth that ever before I have laid eye or given ear to so convincing a witness as Lola Andrews!"

IV

And then Carlos Goodridge! This man, the manager of a small music store, had happened to be in a pool-room near the scene of the crime. There were four other men in the room, and none of them had got a glimpse of the bandits, and to these others Goodridge had admitted that he could not identify the bandits. "If I have got to say who the man was, I can't say." But seven months later Goodridge and his wife were in court, charged with stealing several hundred dollars of money and goods from the music store. It so happened that Sacco was there at the same time, pleading to some motion, and Goodridge saw his opportunity, and told the authorities that he recognized Sacco and could identify him as one of the South Braintree bandits. Could a deal have been made? Impossible to say; but the case was "placed on file"—that is to say, Goodridge did not have to serve the sentence for his crime, but took the witness stand and swore to the guilt of another man.

And here was Lee Swenson, insisting to Cornelia and Betty and Joe that the prosecution would be able to "get away" with that! Judge Thayer would find some trick of the law to bar all testimony to the effect that Goodridge had a sentence hanging over him; he would send the jurors from the room while the matter was argued, so they would never know they were listening to a criminal. Lee insisted that the only hope would be to "get something else" on that fellow! Lee's instinct, what he called his "smell for crime," told him that Goodridge had been in jail. But where? And how to prove it?

It was a matter to which the lawyer hung on with bulldog grip; they must follow this clew and that, they must get more investigators, spend more money. But they had only a few weeks, and the right clew came too late! After the trial they knew all about Carlos Goodridge—his real name was Erastus Corning Whitney, which in itself meant that he had committed perjury when he testified against Sacco. He had served terms in Elmira Reformatory and in Auburn State Prison, New York, and was now wanted in that state for grand larceny. He had had a number of wives, and Swenson collected a string of affidavits from these ladies, setting forth his habits of marrying under various names, of stealing everything in sight, and of lying freely. One added that he had been attacked by Italians whom he had cheated of their belongings, and had borne a grudge against Italians ever since.

Too late! Too late! The curse that lay upon the Sacco-Vanzetti case, that everything came too late! When the only thing you could do was to make another motion before Webster Thayer, and have that just and upright judge respond, "Motion denied!" Lee Swenson and one of his men tracked "Goodridge" to the little village of Vassalboro, Maine, and confronted him with his record, and he held out his wrists for the handcuffs. Later they had him arrested, but—strange solidarity of the rulers of America—New York State did not want him now, could not be persuaded to take him! When once a criminal has obliged the police in any part of the country, he has become a member of the gang, and is immune.

And stranger yet, the august judiciary will rally to his defense, and not permit him to be slandered by having his criminal record exposed! Webster Thayer, a Daniel come to judgment, would hand down his decision on the motion for a new trial, rebuking the defense for its pursuit of Goodridge, and saying that he had done right to resist a lawyer's efforts to intimidate him. "Motion denied!"

V

Too late! Too late! Several times, in the midst of investigations for South Braintree, they turned up evidence concerning the earlier case. Evidence which would have saved poor Bart, if only it could have been got to the jury! New witnesses —Yankee witnesses—who had seen the Bridgewater shooting, and declared that the bandits did not look like Vanzetti! Witnesses who had stated this to the police, and been told to go home and keep quiet! Now this case was legally dead; Vanzetti's friends could not even have the poor pleasure of bringing the new evidence to the attention of Judge Thayer. No matter what happened at the coming trial, Bart would stay in Charlestown prison fourteen more years—save in the unlikely event that Massachusetts might elect a governor with a heart.

So now Cornelia heard those ghostly voices which on past occasions had shouted to her in vain! If only she had waited until that family which was away from home had come back! If only she had turned up this street instead of that! And of course these vain regrets brought terrors for the future; Cornelia and her friends began to hear, far off and faint, the ghostly voices warning them about the new case. They were like enchanted people in an old-time legend, living halfway between two worlds, holding communion with both. Lee Swenson, sitting in Cornelia's big chair, with his chin in his hand and his heavy brows knitted in thought, became some medieval magician, wrestling with spirits and demons he challenged, but could not command.

> *Creature of Flame, thou shalt not daunt me!*
> *'Tis I! 'Tis Faust! Thy peer I vaunt me!*

Many things this new Faustus demanded of the "busy spirit that ranges round the world." Find the man with a bullet hole in his overcoat! Again and again this clew turned up; there had been a man by the name of Roy Gould, who had been fired upon by the bandits, and the bullet had pierced his coat. But nobody knew this man's address. Manifestly, the police would not have overlooked such a witness; and the fact that he was not listed by them made it sure that he had failed to identify Sacco and Vanzetti. Presently it was learned that he was a salesman of shaving paste; some one reported that he was in the habit of selling his wares to crowds at circuses and fairs, so it was a question of getting a list of all the circuses in New England!

Like all others, this mystery was solved too late. The man turned up, several months after the trial. The bandit car had passed within five or ten feet of him, and the bandit who was supposed to be Sacco had fired at him, and he said it could not possibly be Sacco. He would go down into history as the "Gould motion"; one of nine different appeals for a new trial, which would compel Judge Thayer to repeat nine times his celebrated formula, "Motion denied."

Also the witnesses who were to refute Louis Pelzer, a shoe cutter and dullard who had been in the Rice and Hutchins factory when the shots were fired, and had run to the window, and then dropped down out of sight. He had really seen nothing and had so stated to many persons; but the prosecution was to get hold of him, and drill him for a star witness. Deep in the soul of this Jewish boy was a reverence for authority, the buried memories of a hundred pogroms, when his ancestors had cowered in ghetto tenements and seen whole families brained before their eyes. When a blue uniform appeared in the room, when a prosecuting official frowned upon him, something inside Louis Pelzer gave way.

So he was going to say that one of the bandits was the "dead image" of Sacco; he would learn this phrase, and repeat it as often as desired. And where were the witnesses to break him? Three of them, fellow-workers, would be found by the defense; but the most important of them would be found too late. Four months after the trial, Louis was to make an affidavit, declaring that his testimony was false, the words "dead image" had been put into his mouth by the district attorney. Six months after that, he was to take it all back, and be safe with the police again!

But most loudly the ghostly voices shouted about the Pinkerton reports. The operative "H.H." had been on the scene immediately after the crime, and his reports wiped out the most important of all the witnesses of the prosecution, Mary Splaine. Not merely had she identified other men, but she had told stories to the Pinkerton operative which in themselves discredited her. And all this was known to the prosecution—but not a hint of it to the defense! Most amazing circumstance of all— that detective was going to attend the trial, and take the stand and testify against a defense witness! Henry Hellyer, the "operative H.H.," came to the court-room where Mary Splaine swore away the life of Sacco, knowing what she had told him, and what he had written and turned in to his employers! The mockery of it—the devilishness of it—that prosecuting authorities would play such a trick! And the ghostly voices would shout into the ears of Cornelia and Betty and Joe, and no one of them would hear a sound! Lee Swenson might sit with his chin in his hand, and bend his brows and torture his wits all night—but the "busy spirit that ranges round the world" could never be conjured to give him a hint of that secret!

VI

There was a fatality hanging over Cornelia. She had seen it coming—no way to stop it, yet she had pushed the thought away and refused to face it. But now the trial was only a week off, and there could be no more evasion. Lee Swenson telephoned, asking if he might come to dinner that evening; he wanted to be alone with her, he said—and she knew the time had come.

Lee looked very tired; there were deep lines about his mouth, and deep shadows under his eyes, and he hardly tasted his very good dinner. For a while Cornelia managed to divert him— asking for the news. A curious development in the case, ready-made for a detective romance: from a scrubwoman whom he had befriended, Lee had learned that detectives had hired the janitor of his tumble-down office building to deliver the contents of his trash-basket every night! He knew that they had their minds fixed upon the sixteen thousand dollars which they thought Sacco had buried; so the lawyer would divert his tired mind by drawing maps of buried treasure! He made a plot of Sacco's garden: sixteen feet north from the southwest corner, twenty-two feet east—then dig! The next time Cornelia went to Stoughton, she must find out if anybody had done so!

Dinner was over, and the maid dismissed, and the doors closed; the clouds came back to the lawyer's face. "Nonna," he said, "we are going to lose these boys!"

"Oh, Lee!" Cornelia's voice almost failed her.

"They have got us sewed up in a strait-jacket."

"Why do you think that?"

"Do you realize what lies ahead of this trial? We start on the day after Memorial Day, and then comes the anniversary of Belleau Wood, and then Bunker Hill Day, and before we get through it will be the Fourth of July! And all these dead soldier boys they are bringing home, all the weeping and praying and dedicating our lives to our country!"

"What has that got to do with it?"

"You ask me seriously? This is going to be the great peacetime service for heroes to render to the nation; a defense of our heritage against foreign anarchy and Bolshevism. And what have we got? Very few Yankee witnesses! A string of wops—worse than at Vanzetti's trial!"

The lawyer began to count on his fingers—the scores of witnesses he had been able to find. On the day of the South Braintree crime, Bart had been selling fish, and digging clams and bait in Plymouth, and had met few Yankees. He had stopped and chatted with one Yankee fisherman—but the jury would say this fellow had got mixed up on the date. Bart had bought some cloth from a Yiddish peddler, of whom Katzmann would make a monkey. For the rest, they would have to depend upon Alfonsina and Lefevre Brini, and Antonio Carbone and Angelo Giadabone—hardly the sort of names to impress a Yankee jury!

As for Nick, he had been in Boston that day, but talked to only one American he could remember. He had had lunch with Guadagni at Boni's restaurant, and later there had been two other Italians present; he had paid some money to an Italian grocer, and then gone to the consulate, to get his passport—but the man who waited on him there had gone back to Italy, and all they had was a deposition, not very convincing to a jury.

So much for the alibis. And then for the identifications; what perversity of fate that so many of them depended upon wops!

Why did it have to be that Goodridge had been working for an Italian at the time of the crime, and that his former employer was also an Italian? And the men in the pool-room, to whom Goodridge had declared that he could not recognize the bandits! Such names as Magazu, Arrigoni, Mangoni, D'Amato! And then a bunch of men who had been working on a trench in the street when the bandit car passed; a whole gang who would testify that they had seen the bandits in the car, and that none of them resembled Sacco or Vanzetti. But what good would it do? "It's just no use to put on a string of Italians, Nonna—three are better than thirty, because you bore the jury and get them cross. Fred Katzmann will make some playful remark—'What is this, a Columbus Day parade?'—and after that the jury will never stop smiling."

There was a long silence. "Remember, Nonna, this means death for both of them. There is no middle ground."

"I know it, Lee."

"And if we don't win the verdict, don't fool yourself about the future. Remember, so long as Web Thayer lives, he stays the boss of this case; the supreme court of Massachusetts has seldom reversed a verdict in a capital case—only two or three times in its entire history. So it's now or never."

"I know, Lee." Cornelia's voice was faint.

Again a silence. The lawyer's somber look was fixed upon her, and she could not meet it.

"Do you really want to save those boys, Nonna?"

"Of course I do!"

"Then why don't you do it? Why not testify for them?"

"You told me you couldn't use character witnesses."

"I don't mean that sort of witness, Nonna. I mean, why don't you let me fix you up a story, about how you went down to Plymouth on April fifteenth of last year, and spent the day with the Brinis, and had lunch with Bart, and later walked on the beach and saw him digging clams? That's the way to win this case, Nonna; it will end right there—a knockout!"

VII

What was it—some instinct buried deep in Cornelia Thornwell, something in the very fiber of her being, that made it necessary for her to be shocked by these words—even though the idea had been haunting her mind for months? Nothing really new that Lee Swenson could say to her—yet she had to let him say it, and act as if she had never thought of it! "Oh, Lee, I couldn't do it!"

"Why couldn't you? Did you really never tell a lie?"

"Never one like that!"

"Little ones, Nonna, for little occasions. But this is a big occasion! This is life or death!"

Again a pause. When the lawyer resumed, his voice was grim, and he dropped the playful nickname. "I am not going to try to put pressure on you, Mrs. Thornwell, as I have on other witnesses in my life; for after all, it is your case—Bart is your friend, far more than he is mine, and why should I want to save him more than you?"

"Don't put it that way, Lee!"

"But that is the way to put it! You have your friends, and you have your principles, and you must weigh them, and decide which you value more. We all have to make such choices— Bart made one, you remember, he lied for his friends. Those lies he told in the police-station were to save Boda and Orciani from sharing the fate of Salsedo. He will tell a different story on the witness stand, and whether it is the truth or not—judge for yourself!"

Another pause. "What is it, Mrs. Thornwell? Have you religious scruples about an oath? Do you believe God will blast you to eternity if you save these boys from the electric chair?"

"No, it isn't that."

"Is it patriotism? Do you think it will help your country to let a bunch of crooks kill a pair of idealists, as a means of frightening the others?"

"No, not that."

"Then it's just a matter of good form? It's that you are a lady, and such things are not done!"

"No, not that, either. As a matter of fact, they are done all the time. My sons-in-law are lying in business, and they will lie on the stand to back each other up."

"Exactly!" And to himself Lee Swenson thought, "She has been debating it with herself!" Aloud he said, "What is it, Mrs. Thornwell?"

"It is just—I wouldn't know how to do it!"

"But if that is all that troubles you, here's a thoroughly qualified expert to take charge. Put yourself in my hands, as if it were a surgical operation, and I'll guarantee we'll have Nick on the street before the Fourth of July, and we'll start a move to get Bart pardoned!"

"But Lee, how could I do such a thing?"

"If you mean it as a technical question, nothing more simple: you take the stand and swear that you were in Plymouth that day, and you recite the details of some other day when you were actually there. It can all be worked out, very easily. You were in the habit of going there off and on, nobody can dispute that. You remember the date, because of something that happened the day before or the day after. Perhaps there was a concert you had just been to, or there was to be one, and you had to leave in order to attend it. We can go back and find a public event to tie to; or perhaps you have a diary, or some letters."

"But suppose I did something in Boston on that day?"

"There'll be a way to get round it. You understand that, according to your story, you only had to remember back three weeks. As soon as you heard Bart was arrested, you naturally looked back, and realized that you had been with him the day of the crime. But anybody who is going to refute you has got to begin now, and remember back a year—which isn't apt to happen. If they have documentary evidence, like a letter—well, the trial will be over a day or two after you testify. There might be a scandal among your friends, but nothing serious, and anyhow, the boys will be free—you understand that when a jury has acquitted them, they can't ever be tried for South Braintree again."

VIII

Lee kept his promise not to put pressure on her. What he did was to go over the case, telling what each government witness would testify, and just how that testimony had been "made." As a piece of prophecy it was a miracle, but Lee claimed no occult powers. With bitterness he said, "If I want to know what the other side is doing, I figure what I would do myself."

He had talked with some of these witnesses; others, who had refused to talk to him, had become the subject of "reports." So he knew their motives, and how they would be controlled. When there had been need of "rough stuff," the police had done it. The more subtle work had been done by college-bred gentlemen of the district attorney's office, who had learned to manufacture in weaker minds like Mary Splaine and Frances Devlin what the psychologists term a "false memory." They would take these women to the jail again and again and show them Sacco and Vanzetti; they would present pictures of Sacco and Vanzetti, insisting that these were the bandits, these were the men whom the women had seen in the bandit car; until in the women's minds the prison memories and the photograph memories became superposed upon the bandit memories, so completely merged with them that they could no longer be separated.

There were a thousand tricks that successful prosecuting officials knew. They stood in with the political ring, they could promise favors—contracts and business, a job for a man who needed it, immunity from trouble with the police. "I am a friend of Mr. Jones, in the district attorney's office"—such a statement would tear up an auto tag, or suppress a liquor charge any day. "It is what we call power," said Lee Swenson, "and those who hold it know how to use it."

Like Virgil, leading Dante through successive stages of the infernal regions, Lee Swenson conducted the widow of Governor Thornwell into the interior of the Boston "ring." He knew the way, because in the Ettor-Giovannitti case he had had these forces to deal with, and other lawyers associated with the case had "put him wise." Indeed, the factional quarrels in the political gang had been such that one side had betrayed the other, and Lee had seen documents that would have entitled leading statesmen to spend the rest of their days in Charlestown prison. When you had listened to his stories for an hour or two, you understood Lola Andrews' statement that it was "dog eat dog"; you forgot the Emersonian notion of making truth count in Boston!

Cornelia, probing her own soul, confessed to a certain snobbery in her attitude toward perjury. It was a thing she associated with foreigners accused of crime, and with Irish politicians.

The City Hall belonged to the Irish, so it was called the "steal works"; but the State House with its golden dome was run by gentlemen, and was a sacred spot. Now, however, Lee Swenson declared there was ten times as much graft in the State House —the only difference was that it was legalized; such things as fixing up laws to enable great corporations to plunder the public. There under the golden dome you would encounter a blue-blood banker who wanted his attorney made into a supreme court judge, so that the banker would be safe forever after; or a state bank commissioner who wanted to become president of a bank; a great lawyer who wanted to use his inside knowledge of politics to plunder the clients of banks; a financier who was lending money to legislators, who were passing bills to multiply the value of his public utility holdings.

Cornelia understood all these references; Lee Swenson was attacking the Thornwell family, undermining its claims to moral superiority. He was pointing to scandals in which her family was involved—some that were in the public prints, others that were whispered in the gossip of the clubs. And she knew it was all true; she knew that Rupert Alvin and Henry Cabot Winters and John Quincy Thornwell were busy right now framing up their perjury in the Jerry Walker case. When an I.W.W. lawyer hinted this possibility, she did not rebuke him. She did not even protect her family dignity when he mentioned that her son-in-law had begun his legal career as counsel for the Boston streets railways, which meant that he had done most kinds of dirty work known to the legal profession.

"Believe me, Nonna, I can tell you," said the man from the wild west. "I began with the Great Northern Railroad, and spent my time gyping poor workers out of damages. I was paid five hundred a month, very nice for a young fellow, and I had the way clear before me, right up to the top, maybe a seat on the supreme court bench—that is how you get there. But it made me sick; I couldn't forget the faces of the men I had robbed, and their pitiful wives and children. I just couldn't look at myself in the mirror. So I threw up the job, and went in to try to help the workers; and what I saw—well, I have a simple formula, Nonna, I don't care what a man has done in the labor cause, he can never be so guilty as those who take dividends of his sweat and blood."

Said Cornelia: "Henry has talked to me a lot about the Sacco-Vanzetti case, trying to drag me out of it. The next time he broaches it, I'll ask him about some of these matters."

At which the lawyer smiled. "Well, get it straight. Don't ask if he pays bribes to witnesses; don't ask if he 'frames' them. Everything is done very carefully and decorously, in the office of a great Boston lawyer. When a witness comes in he doesn't see the chief, he sees a young subordinate. The witness says, 'I saw the man and he was wearing a blue hat.' The young lawyer interrupts him, 'Oh, surely you are mistaken, we have information that the man was wearing a red hat. Think it over and see if you weren't mistaken.' He sends the witness away, and next day the witness comes back, and meets another subordinate, and says, 'I saw this man and he was wearing a red hat.' 'That is right,' says the young lawyer. 'And he was walking,' says the witness, 'rather slowly.' 'Oh, surely you are mistaken,' says the lawyer, 'we understand he was running at top speed. Think it over and see if you don't realize that that is how it was.' So the witness goes away, and next time he comes he meets a third subordinate, and he says, 'I saw this man, and he had a red hat on, and he was running very, very fast'—and so on, until he knows exactly what happened. So then he meets the chief, and tells the chief what he saw, and the chief says, 'That is a very good witness, a dependable person.' When he presents the witness to the jury, he assures the jury this is a dependable person, and no one can possibly say the great and famous lawyer ever did a dishonorable action."

IX

"Lee, I just *couldn't* do it!"—those were Cornelia's parting words. He answered, "Think about it,"—knowing well that she would think about nothing else. Cowardice, weakness, false pride—she was willing to call it any bad name, but there was something in her that stopped dead when she tried to think of going upon the witness stand and swearing to a made-up story. How could truth ever exist in the world, if somebody did not stand by it?

Vanzetti came, as usual, to keep the midnight watch with her. "I am poor wop," said he. "But what you say if it was a

Thornwell?" Cornelia's fancy played with that theme. She saw her daughter Alice, in one of those ferocious quarrels which had marked the early stages of her marital disharmony; with jealousy gnawing her heart, Alice bought a revolver and shot Henry, and so was on trial, in danger of the electric chair. But no, it was absurd, the electric chair was not for Thornwells, there could be no such issue; they would adjudge Alice insane, and put her in a sanitarium, take a year or two to "cure" her, and then let her loose. But suppose, for the sake of argument, Alice was in danger, and Cornelia had to take the witness stand. If she told the truth her daughter would be executed, and if she lied her daughter would go free. Which would she do?

Right was right, and wrong was wrong, people said, and it sounded simple. But when you met a concrete case, you discovered that you could not live by formulas. To refuse to do a lesser wrong, and thereby do a greater—was that moral? On the other hand, if you said that the end justified the means, where would you stop? Every man would be a law to himself, and there would be chaos instead of order. There must be rules, something men could count on. But the moment you said that, you had a system, with high judges sitting on top, sentencing men to death for the convenience of the Boston aristocracy. Cornelia remembered Mr. Emerson, who had said that a good citizen must not obey the laws too well.

The cruelty of the dilemma lay here, that what was supposed to be justice was really class-greed. Bart and Nick were not going to be tried because they had held up a payroll; they were going to be tried because they were dangerous leaders of social revolt. That would be the real motive power behind prosecutor, judge and jury; that would be the thought in the minds of every one of them, at every stage of the trial. The rest would be pretense, a cloak of propriety. And that was the real lie—the real perjury: Fred Katzmann's genial smile, veiling a sneer; Web Thayer's cold dignity, with a wink now and then to the jury. When Cornelia remembered what she had seen in the Plymouth court-room, it seemed to her that God would surely forgive any lies that served to thwart such knavery!

So she swung back and forth, from one point of view to the other, never satisfied with either. Lee Swenson said no more, but from that day his presence was a question. Bart's

picture on the mantel-piece was a challenge—what was friendship worth, it seemed to demand. You were not asked to give
your life for your friend, but only your ethical code; your
exclusiveness, your idea that you were something special, apart
from the harsh, rough world—in short that you were "Boston"!

From first to last Betty never spoke about the matter; and
that was surprising to Cornelia—it had the effect of putting
her off by herself, as if in a museum, or a mausoleum. Betty
and Joe were bound to have talked about the matter; everybody
on the committee must have thought of it. "Mrs. Thornwell
could save our boys, if she would!" To that Betty would make
reply, "No use to put anything like that up to Grannie, she
belongs to the old generation." Cornelia wondered, would the
new generation take the liberty of lying when it pleased? The
issue did not arise, because Betty and Joe had been in Europe,
and could hardly invent a special trip back, in order to be with
Bart on the day of the South Braintree crime!

X

If Cornelia could not face the thought of perjury, neither
could she face the other alternative. When she thought of the
electric chair, and Bart and Nick strapped into it—no, no, it was
too horrible, it simply *could* not happen! So each skirmish in
this war of conscience served to start Cornelia into new activity.
In spite of aching back she would write more letters, in spite
of tired limbs she would set forth to a committee meeting, or to
speak to a group of women, to assault the ears of the heedless
and drag them away from a bridge party to a murder trial.

She had the idea now that she could help the cause by persuading a group of ladies of good family to go to Dedham and
watch the proceedings. They would move to the town for a
month, and invade the court-room in a phalanx, and sit like the
"tricoteuses" of the French revolution, doing fancy work! They
might frighten "Web" Thayer into a semblance of impartiality,
and possibly even restrain Fred Katzmann's crude wit at the
expense of wops. The courts were supposed to be immune to
outside influences, but Cornelia knew her Boston too well for
that.

In one way or another, several ladies of social standing had become interested in the case. There was Mrs. Lois Rantoul, who was a Lowell, than which nothing could be more impressive in a court-room. And Mrs. Jessica Henderson, well-to-do —though she had hurt her social position by getting arrested, along with Cornelia and Betty, the day President Wilson had been welcomed to Boston. Mrs. Henderson and her daughter Wilma had spent the night in that old Joy Street police station, and had fed their blood to the vermin—a modern form of initiation into a sisterhood of social justice.

And then Mrs. Evans, still earlier on the ground. Elizabeth Glendower Evans was the widow of a young lawyer who had died before he had ever had a case. She had become a charity worker, through youth and middle age. Now she was gray-haired—and what a relief to Cornelia to have some one else who was elderly and respectable, to help bear the brunt of criticism! Mrs. Evans had got her social awakening during the Lawrence strike of two years ago; she had gone, with others, to see fair play, and instead had seen an unresisting striker felled to earth by three husky policemen, and shoved into a patrol wagon like a dead log. Next morning she saw the man, with head cut and plastered, arraigned for assault, and she arose and told the court what she had seen. Said His Honor: "Your testimony would be important if the police were under accusation"—and thereupon he sentenced all the strikers. Mrs. Evans spoke again, saying, "I go bail for all these prisoners," —which was very picturesque, and made a front-page story in the papers.

"Old Boston" again, you see! She was a stockholder in the Lawrence mills, which made it still more picturesque, and shocking to the mill masters. To go to strike headquarters, and say to I.W.W. leaders, wops and dagoes and guinneys and such riffraff, "I don't know whether the wages you ask are reasonable, but I do know that you are persecuted by the authorities, and denied the legal rights to which you are entitled, and to that extent I am with you"—to say that was to become, in the columns of the press, leader of the revolution and commander-in-chief of the picket line.

Now Mrs. Evans was interested in the Sacco-Vanzetti defense, and was going to the trial at Dedham, to watch Web Thayer and Fred Katzmann, and be horrified like everybody else. And maybe her testimony would have been important, if Thayer and Katzmann had been on trial. But that time had not come, and would not come for five or six years.

XI

Captain John Quincy Thornwell, Jr., Cornelia's grand-nephew, oldest son of the president of the Fifth National Bank of Boston, had been an officer in Battery A, the fashionable militia organization, in which the young blue-bloods dashed about expensively. Tall, golden-haired, haughty, he had looked so "fetching" in his fancy uniform that he had fetched a wife who would some day own ten per cent of the electric light industry of New England. "Captain John" was a director in his father's bank, a builder of airplanes, and of anything else which had to do with killing—so sure of his own superiority he was.

Never would Cornelia forget the day when he and his unit had departed for France. She had gone with the heartbroken young wife to see them off; a dreadful experience—all the Boston blue-bloods there in their expensive limousines, many of them stuck in a swampy field alongside the Ipswich River, caught by a sudden deluge of rain, and an ear-splitting thunderstorm; all social influence, all family connections set at nought by the irreverent elements—it was quite like being at war—blue-bloods actually struck by lightning and killed! And these refined and delicately nurtured young Harvard men, dressed in water-soaked khaki plastered with mud, standing at attention for the "Star-Spangled Banner"; then struggling with exasperated horses, to get very real and bloodthirsty cannon dragged out of mudholes!

"Captain John" had ridden off, like many others, forever; in the desperate fighting in the Argonne Forest he had disappeared from human ken. But in the process of digging up the remains of American soldiers in France there was found a seal ring with one of the bodies, and this ring was sent to Boston, and mentioned in the papers, and "Captain John's" mother went to inspect and identify it. So now the family had a corpse in an air-tight coffin, over which to be publicly sentimental for the glory of their country. A famous sculptor was designing a monument, and meantime there were to be parades and muffled drums and prayers and salutes—and one of the street intersections most frequented by the wealth and fashion of Boston was to be christened "John Quincy Thornwell Junior Square." All over the city and in the suburban towns they were doing this; so that future generations of tourists would walk down Jones Street, looking for the corner of Jones and Smith, and would be perplexed to discover that there was no such place, but that a quite ordinary crossing with a drugstore, an undertaking parlor, a grocery and a delicatessen shop, was known as "Michael Callahan O'Grady Square."

These ceremonies were to take place on May 29th, two days before the opening of the Sacco-Vanzetti trial at Dedham; and the event was the subject of a vehement discussion between the great-aunt of the hero, and his cousin, Elizabeth Thornwell Alvin. Unthinkable that any relative should fail to attend this ceremony! Cornelia was going, because she was always hoping to keep peace with the family; but Betty declared that she preferred to attend a circus, in a last effort to trace the man with the bullet hole in his overcoat! When Cornelia argued that "John did give his life for his country," the new generation answered, "Don't talk like a legionnaire! He gave his life for Father's bonds. I didn't want them and I'm not going to get them, so I can't see that I owe any reverence to my military cousin."

"He is dead, Betty—"

"Exactly, and we aren't helping him by parading behind his corpse. We are doing it for our own glory, and especially for the young fellows—so that when Father wants them to protect his bonds again, they'll think they are being glorious. It is vicious propaganda for militarism, and if you who call yourself a pacifist do anything to help it along—it will simply mean that you're old and tired, Grannie dear!"

XII

Was it accident, or was it the playful malice of fate, that Memorial Day fell on a Monday, so that the patriots had two whole days, preceding the trial of Sacco and Vanzetti, to rouse the population against the Reds? On that Sunday and Monday it was estimated that at least two hundred thousand Bostonians, one-fifth of the whole population, took part in ceremonies. The governor and the mayor were busy all day long, making speeches at breakfasts, luncheons and banquets, with parades in between, and dedications and unveilings. Senators and congressmen, councilmen and district attorneys took a double holiday from stealing, and delivered eloquent praise of the flag, and denunciations of its foes, the vicious and malicious "radicals." There was high mass in hundreds of Catholic churches, with parades of the Knights of Columbus, and speeches by the biggest and most successful rascals in Massachusetts. There were memorial services in Forest Hills Cemetery, with nine hundred veterans of the Grand Army of the Republic decorating graves. There were religious services in Fenway Park, with veterans. of three wars forming in Copley Square, and loud-speakers installed so that huge throngs might hear. The Park Street Church unveiled a tablet, with names of the members who had given their lives in the World War. The Elks paraded, and had a bugler sounding taps. The oldest veterans, too feeble even to put wreaths on graves, were taken in launches, to strew flowers on the bay in honor of the unknown dead.

All over the Commonwealth the same thing went on; no community too small to have its heroes and its memories. Flag poles were set up and monuments unveiled. Quincy, the largest city in Norfolk County, from which the Sacco-Vanzetti jury was to be drawn, dedicated three squares to its dead. One man had been killed in the Spanish War, another in an uprising in the Philippines; many years they had spent in the land of the shades without distinction, but now they were called up—on the day before two anarchist bandits went to trial! The first Quincy boy killed in the Civil War was resurrected for honors—sixty years he had been forgotten! In Bridgewater, scene of the crime for which Vanzetti was in prison, the remains of a World War veteran brought back from France were buried with solemn ceremonials; in Braintree, scene of the second crime, another body was buried, with the whole population in attendance—a parade, and speeches by officials, with the selectmen and other great persons standing by with bared heads. Another in Quincy, another in Weymouth—with banners furled, and muffled drums, and soldiers firing a salute over the grave.

A storm of patriotic fervor, a torrent of eloquence, in support of America, and in denunciation of her foes; hundreds of thousands of patient people, standing reverently in the spring sunshine; millions of the same kind reading about it in editions of a dozen great newspapers; and only one circumstance to mar the perfection of the double holiday—the fact that the papers were obliged to print details of several scandals then in the midst of exploding with a frightful stink. The attorney general of the Commonwealth had just filed charges against the district attorney of Middlesex County, just across the river from Boston, charging him with having blackmailed a group of leading moving picture producers of something over a hundred thousand dollars, the price of immunity for a "Nero's Circus" which they had held in a roadhouse. The papers were full of lurid details about naked girls dancing the highland fling; they said that several leading politicians and criminal lawyers of Boston had shared in the loot.

Also the state bank commissioner was digging into the matter of the bribery of legislators revealed by the recent bank failures; and it was an embarrassing fact that many patriotic orators of this double holiday had been sharing in such graft. The public did not know it, but the orators knew it, so they pounded the rostrum, and waved their arms until their faces grew purple and the sweat dissolved the starch in their collars; the loud-speakers bellowed, and the parks and public places, the churches and temples and banquet halls resounded with sentiments of seraphic idealism, voiced by persons whose social functions were those of hogs in a trough.

XIII

It was not so bad at the ceremony which Cornelia attended; because that was Thornwell, and you may be sure the clan saw to it that no person tainted with scandal did any orating at John Quincy Thornwell Junior Square. The clan knew—for were they not the paymasters? The mayor of the city happened to be a blue-blood that year—a rare interval of respectability. And if the chief magistrate of the Commonwealth was to go directly from the governor's chair to the vice-presidency of one of Rupert's banks, and soon after having appointed two of Rupert's very good friends to the supreme judicial bench—

well, that was a scandal of such colossal proportions that it became respectable. Men could not face the implications of it, so it was not discussed, except by a few insiders, and members of the rival banking group, who knew what Rupert was after.

A grand stand had been built, and flags and bunting made the consecrated square into a child's dream of peppermint candy. Lines of ropes and policemen kept the throngs back; and there came "Captain John's" own Battery A, khaki-clad, with rumble of guns and tramp of horses, and fluttering of pennants, red field, with figures in yellow. And the infantry, known as the "Cadets," in long blue trousers with yellow stripes. There came a hundred Grand Army veterans, pitiful old boys in every stage of decrepitude, carrying their tattered battle flags, and wearing their faded blue uniforms, covered with medals and decorations. There came khaki-clad veterans of American Legion posts, and the Boy Cadets, their faces newly washed and shining. There came automobiles full of great personages in braided broadcloth suits and shiny top hats, and ladies in costly chiffons and new spring bonnets.

A beautiful show; with rolling of drums and blowing of bugles, and standing up and sitting down again, and baring heads and bowing them, while the rector of Trinity Church in the City of Boston offered an invocation to the God of Battles, and His Son, the Prince of Peace. War and Peace were thus mixed up in the ceremony, so that nobody could tell at any moment which was which. The orators declared that the way to insure peace was to prepare for war; upon which program the nations had just led themselves into the greatest war to end war in all history, and now were spending several times as much money to prepare for an even greater war to end war.

It would be safe to say that in that vast throng of cheering and singing and reverently listening people, these traitor-thoughts found lodgment in only one head, that of the little old lady who sat in the front row, among the highest of the high-up dignitaries. She, the widow of a former governor, a Thornwell, and the great-aunt of the hero, could not have been denied her proper place without making a scandal, and emphasizing the dreadful rumors that she had been seduced by the enemy within our gates, and turned into a friend of bomb throwers and bandits. So nice to look upon, with her hair now almost white, and her little round face much wrinkled, but still jolly, and her new spring costume selected and presented by her daughter Alice of impeccable taste; so gentle in manner, so quiet and lady-like—it was impossible to believe what everybody knew about her, that she was actually going down to Dedham the next day, and face all the uproar and notoriety, and lend her sanction to the defense of desperate anarchists on trial for their lives.

She watched with tears in her eyes, while her great-grand-niece, the little daughter of the dead hero, came forward to draw the veil from the bronze tablet. The bugles blew, and the audience rose and bared its head, and the bands started to play "America," and everybody sang—a sublime moment. The lovely young widow of the hero had to hide her face in her hands, and even the stolid James Scatterbridge and the cynical Henry Cabot Winters and the stately Rupert Alvin were not ashamed to be moved. Cornelia's tears were right and proper, and she kept her traitor-thoughts to herself. No one guessed that she was weeping for other heroes who were still to die. For the little boys in their khaki uniforms, lifting their shining faces to the orators and the beautiful waving flags! For the mothers who brought them there, to be consecrated and pledged to future slaughters! For the great humble masses who packed the streets, in every direction, and stood bareheaded and trusting, gazing up to the great ones, and believing every word the loud-speakers told them!

A sharp division in that audience, between the many who believed, and the few who knew. To the former the name America, and its symbol, the flag, meant liberty and justice for all mankind; while to the few it meant private property in land, machinery and credit, and the exploitation of labor based thereon. By means of this system, the knowing ones had brought the lesser nations and weaker peoples into debt to them; so America and the flag meant battleships and guns and airplanes and poison gas to collect this tribute to all eternity. That was the reason these busy gentlemen took two days off from business, and built stands and tacked up decorations, and set up loud-speakers to carry the words of politicians and priests and preachers to crowds in the public squares. That was why you heard no patriotic address which failed to mention the "enemy within our gates," the vicious and criminal "Reds" who refused to love America and appreciate her ideals, but wanted to over-throw the greatest government in the world, and repudiate all the debts, and nationalize all the women, and make America a vassal of what the orators called the "Bolshevikis," or some-times, like Judge Webster Thayer, the "arnychists."

The photographs in the following section, with the exception of the South Braintree holdup scene, were all taken from 1920 to 1927, when Sacco and Vanzetti were arrested and their case was being tried.
In addition to captions, most of the photographs are accompanied by quotes from the novel and page references for these quotes.

Plate 2.
This photograph, taken in 1960, shows the location along Pearl Street, South Braintree, where the shoe factory paymaster and his guard were slain in the payroll holdup that began the Sacco-Vanzetti case.

"... the paymaster of the Slater and Morrill company took the pay-money, about $16,000... from the office to the factory, a distance of a couple of blocks."
Page 222

Plate 3.
Frederick G. Katzmann, attorney of Norfolk County

"The district attorney ... a stocky man of German parentage, florid, blond, good-looking, smartly dressed. Fred Katzmann was his name, a Mason and a 'joiner,' prominent in the political ring which governed the county."
Page 247

United Press International

United Press International

Plate 4.
Judge Webster Thayer

*"His sharp, withered face was a symbol of the
old Puritan spirit; his voice, like a steel saw
cutting through wood, was an ancestral inheritance, produced by three hundred years of cold
and foggy winds."*
Page 249

Plate 5.
Jurors leaving Dedham Courthouse for noon lunch after the eighth had been picked (1921)

"... such little people of the old stock, having failed for one reason or another to become rich, looked with bitter contempt upon the immigrants who came pouring into the country, to beat down wages and make life harder for the 'white men' of New England."
Page 251

Plate 6.
Fred H. Moore, First Counsel for Sacco and Vanzetti (1927)

"Another lawyer had come, a friend of Swenson's from the west; Fred Moore, an Irishman, but a radical, and Swenson's aide in many a fight."
Page 348

Plate 7.
**Vanzetti (left) and Sacco (right) in prisoners'
cage, Norfolk County Courthouse, talk with
Mrs. Sacco (1923).**

*"The prisoners sat in their steel cage... trying
to understand the complex procedure in a
strange tongue: Bart with his heavy drooping
mustaches, his melancholy face now deeply
lined; Nick, restless-eyed, impatient; both of
them pale with a year away from sunshine."*
Page 381

Plate 8.
Nicola Sacco (1920)

Plate 9.
Mrs. Nicola Sacco (1921)

"Poor little woman ... her face, usually bright and eager, was worn and lined. She would sit all day, silent and rigid, trying to understand long words in a language that was still partly alien to her."
Page 399

Plate 10.
Sacco and Vanzetti handcuffed, being led to court

"Four times each day the prisoners made their march down the middle of the street, accompanied by military escort."
Page 403

Plate 11.
Guards outside the courthouse during the trial

"Back to Dedham courthouse with its high white dome, with a ring of port-holes like an ocean liner ...."
Page 408

Plate 12.
William G. Thompson (left) counsel for Sacco and Vanzetti, and Herbert Ehrmann, associate counsel, leaving the State House in Boston after making a plea for their clients (1927)

"A man in his early sixties, with iron-gray hair and ruddy skin, six feet tall and broad shouldered, dry and humorous, smoking a pipe and looking like a Yankee farmer, Thompson proved to be the boss of which the case had been in need. He became convinced that the machinery of justice was being used for persecution, and turned into a crusader in defense of his clients."
Page 514

Plate 13.
Celestino F. Madeiros

"*Celestino F. Madeiros was a young Portuguese, member of a gang which had robbed a band in Wrentham and killed the cashier. He was in Dedham jail while his appeal was being heard, and his conscience troubled him, he said, when Sacco's wife came to the prison with the baby. On November 18th, 1925, he scribbled on a piece of paper: 'I hear by confess to being in the South Braintree shoe company crime, and Sacco and Vanzetti was not in said crime.'*"
Page 520

Plate 14.
Bartolomeo Vanzetti

Plate 15.
Sacco (center right) and Vanzetti (center left) before entering the courthouse on the day of the sentencing, April 9, 1927

"After sentence had been passed, no other judge of the Superior Court could take jurisdiction, and 'Web' would be the undisputed master. On April 9th, four days after the Supreme Court's decision, he had the two 'Bolsheviki' brought to Dedham court-house ...."
Page 533

Plate 16.
**Governor Alvan T. Fuller
at his desk in the State House**

*"This supersalesman of automobiles was as
cold as marble; utterly selfish, and lacking not
merely in the finer feelings, but even in the
common every-day kindness, of which politicians often have too much. No friend, no
matter how intimate, ever got a discount on a
car. In politics he granted no quarter; he gave
the punishment and took none. In business he
was the modern slave-driver with a fountain-
pen instead of a whip."*
Page 542

Plate 17.
**Sacco (right) and Vanzetti (center) with a
guard**

*"The law specified that ten days prior to the
date of execution condemned men should be
moved to the death cells in Charlestown prison
.... the sheriff and his deputies entered the
cells of the two men in Dedham jail, and
ordered them to dress. No reasons given, no
time allowed to pack their books and papers;
they were shackled, and taken out into the
darkness to a waiting automobile."*
Page 573

Plate 18.
Arthur D. Hill (1928)

*"They ... went to the old stock and retained
Mr. Arthur Dehon Hill. Silver hair and rosy
cheeks and a manner of complete assurance ...
He was so correct that he dared to make jokes
about it."*
Page 621

Plate 19.
Michael Musmanno (second from right) speaking to newsmen after he filed a motion for a new trial at the Dedham Courthouse and an application for a writ of habeas corpus to stay the execution of Sacco and Vanzetti

"Elias Field was helping, and also Michael Angelo Musmanno, a young lawyer who had been sent on from Pittsburgh by some Italian societies. A naive and warm-hearted person, Catholic and conservative, he had fallen in love with an anarchist infidel and an anarchist atheist, and was bewildered by the hatred which unloving Boston felt for his clients."
Page 621

Boston Globe Library

Plate 20.
Demonstration for Sacco and Vanzetti in Boston, March, 1925

"Those who believed in picketing and street demonstrations proceeded to organize and send out a call for martyrs."
Page 623

Boston Globe Library

Plate 21.
**Sacco-Vanzetti sympathizers arrested
August 10, 1927. Katherine Anne Porter is
fourth from left.**

*"One thing all sympathizers could do, and
that was to get arrested."*
Page 632

Plate 22.

Death march of sympathizers in front of the State House in Boston (1927)

"On Tuesday afternoon some thirty paraders made their appearance in front of the State House, each wearing a placard with a Sacco-Vanzetti argument upon it .... They walked in silence, keeping in motion, paying no attention to any one ...."
Page 632

On sign: **If They Are Not Innocent** Why Are You Afraid of A New Trial?

Plate 23.
Demonstrators outside the State House in Boston, August 22, 1927

"A great crowd in front of the State House, more picketing having been announced. Policemen so plentiful, they could have touched hands all the way along the front of the great building."
Page 662

Plate 24.
**Arrested for picketing: Edna St. Vincent
Millay (left); Lola Ridge (right)**

*"There were well-known names among them.
Edna St. Vincent Millay .... Loveliest of
women poets, she would find this a devastating experience; life would not seem the same
after a rendezvous with murder."*
Page 693

United Press International

Plate 25.
**Mrs. Rosina Sacco (right) and Miss Luigia
Vanzetti leaving after a final visit to
Charlestown State Prison death house,
August, 1927**

United Press International

Plate 26.
While searchlights made the scene almost as light as day, more than 200 state and city police guarded the walls of the Massachusetts State Prison at Charlestown as Sacco and Vanzetti were put to death.

Plate 27.
Demonstration in Union Square, New York City, August 22, 1927

"In every great capital of the world there were mass meetings and protests ...."
Page 745

United Press International

Plate 28.
Demonstrators in Union Square, New York City (1927)

Plate 29.
**Funeral hearses of Sacco and Vanzetti
leave Massachusetts State Prison in
Charlestown following the execution.**

Boston Globe Library

Plate 30.
Mourners follow in the wake of the hearses.

"Sunday the day of the funeral. The crowds ... made all movement difficult; they were so great that people were pushed through plate glass windows, and when these crashed there was a panic, because the crowd thought the police had started shooting."
Page 749

Plate 31.
Funeral procession in Boston, August 29, 1927

"It was an Italian funeral, with great floral wreaths borne by mourners, and the undertaker marching in a Prince Albert coat and top hat, in spite of a drizzling rain. State police — the 'Cossacks' — rode ahead and alongside the hearses, to see that the procession followed the prescribed route. In the rear followed several open cars full of flowers ...."
Page 749

Plate 32.
**Mourners with floral wreaths on the day
of the funeral**

CHAPTER 13

TRIAL BY JURY

I

"Court!" shouted the bailiff, and pounded on the floor with his "wand." It was the court-room at Dedham, in Norfolk County, instead of Plymouth, so it was a different bailiff, but he looked exactly like the other, and so did his wand and uniform. There entered the same thin, shrunken old gentleman with white mustache and face like parchment, wearing the same voluminous black silk robe. The lawyers and spectators rose with the same show of reverence, and the bailiff pounded the floor again and repeated the ancient formula: "Hear ye! Hear ye! All persons having anything to do before the Honorable, the Justices of the Superior Court, now sitting within and for the County of Norfolk, draw near, give your attention, and you shall be heard! God save the Commonwealth of Massachusetts!"

Also there was the same district attorney, Fred Katzmann, blond hair and bursting red face, round, pulpy and smooth-shaven, his plump figure and manner of elaborate cordiality to his equals and Prussian sternness to his inferiors. There were three assistants; one of them was a "ticquer," like Judge Thayer, and presently they were to put on a witness who was a "ticquer," and there would be three of them in solemn confrontation, all blinking away, but not keeping time. There was Lee Swenson, his lanky western figure outtowering the rest, his face haggard from long nights of work, his black clothes hanging loose about his frame—but he had made the concession to Massachusetts sentiment of getting his hair cut. There was Fred Moore, from California, alert and aggressive; and the McAnarneys, associate counsel, two Irish Catholic brothers, retained in a vain hope of contributing respectability to anarchist wops accused of murder.

375

The court-room was crowded: a great number of "veniremen," to be questioned as possible jurors, and many spectators, more than could find seats. The newspapers had been full of the case, the desperate character of the criminals, the radical agitation concerning them, the precautions taken by the government to protect the court. The judge and the district attorney had a bodyguard day and night. Picked men from several police departments of Norfolk County were on duty; fifteen armed men scattered about the court-room, and three more at each door. Male spectators were searched thoroughly as they entered the court-room, and women had their handbags opened. An atmosphere of tension, almost of war.

Vanzetti was brought by armed guards in an automobile from Charlestown Prison, "where he is serving a sentence of from twelve to fifteen years for the Bridgewater hold-up"—so said the papers, and the veniremen read it and talked about it; when they became jurors, they were assumed to be ignorant of Vanzetti's previous conviction, and all persons who respected the legal system of the Commonwealth would solemnly pretend to accept this fiction. Almost in the center of the court-room was the steel "cage," shaped like a piano box with fancy grillwork, open in front, a psychological device for overcoming the legal presumption that a wop is innocent until he is proved guilty. The jurors gaze at him locked in throughout the trial, and by the time they are ready to vote they know him as a creature who belongs in a cage. Near the jury box was a tall standard, with an American flag.

A stir in the audience; the bandits were coming! A side door of the court-room opened, and there entered several policemen and then a guard with a handcuff on his wrist, and then a wop made safe with the other handcuff on his wrist, and another handcuff on his other wrist, and another wop chained to that; this second wop with a handcuff on his other wrist, and another guard chained to that: in short, four men chained together, the two on the outside being guards and the two on the inside being alleged bandits; all four symbolizing the fundamental human fact, that slavery enslaves masters as well as servants. It was glorious spring sunshine outside, and here were some hundreds of people who might have been walking in the woods, picking mayflowers, or sitting on the beach engaged in high philosophic discourse; but they were crowded in between four white-washed walls, breathing foul air and shortening their lives, fastened to their seats by manacles of hate, fear and greed.

A few others, held by love and a sense of justice! "Society matrons and college girls," as the newspapers described them, they sat in silence, watching the procedure, sometimes pretending to be busy with their "fancy work"; doing their refined best to be unaware of being the cynosure of all eyes. These were the "Red sympathizers," or "pinks," as patriotic orators derisively called them: women who left homes of luxury to come and meddle with the course of justice, lending encouragement to bomb throwers and assassins, and making things harder for brave officials. Their presence was a continual irritant to the police, who would have liked to lock such troublemakers up, along with their anarchist pets.

And yet, mixed with this anger was awe; for some of these were "blue-bloods," the wonderful, almost supernatural beings whose names appeared in the society columns of the papers. To Judge Thayer they represented everything in the world to which he aspired, and every now and then he would steal a glance at Mrs. Lois Rantoul—who was a Lowell—or at Mrs. Cornelia Thornwell or Mrs. Elizabeth Glendower Evans, as if to see what they were thinking about him; presently his curiosity would get the better of him, and he would invite one of them to his chambers, and try to convince her that she was mistaken in believing these desperate anarchists to be innocent. He, the judge on the bench, would do that; and little by little the news of it would spread among lawyers and judges up in Boston, who were under the necessity of pretending to hold the dogma of judicial infallibility.

II

Between "Web" Thayer and Lee Swenson there existed an antagonism of temperament, which showed itself the very first hour. In order to practice in Massachusetts the lawyer should have complied with some formality. He had not known this, and now Judge Thayer proposed to bar him from the case. There were hasty conferences among the "blue-blood" ladies, and they kept the telephone wires to Boston busy; with the result that next morning when Lee Swenson renewed his application for judicial courtesy, there were several leading lawyers of the city lined up in a row behind him. Too bad these great ones could not have stayed all through the trial, and restrained "Web" Thayer from making their community a byword throughout the world!

The veniremen, fresh from two days of patriotic celebrations, sat under the shadow of the flag and heard the black-robed old gentleman explain to them what patriotic celebrations are for. "You must remember the American soldier had other duties that he would rather have performed than those that resulted in his giving up his life on the battlefields of France, but he, with undaunted courage and patriotic devotion that brought honor and glory to humanity and the world rendered the service and made the supreme sacrifice. So I call upon you to render this service here with the same spirit of patriotism, courage and devotion to duty as was exhibited by our soldier boys across the seas."

Such was the mood in which the men of Norfolk County approached this trial. These were the wops who had sent bombs through the mail two years ago—so it was whispered—and the Wall Street explosion had been revenge for their arrest. Now, whoever voted them guilty would never sleep safe in bed. Wives had hysterics at home, and husbands promised to "lie out of it" at any cost; so, one after another, they took the stand and swore to a disbelief in capital punishment, or to an invincible conviction regarding the case. After three days a panel of five hundred veniremen had been exhausted, and still five jurors were lacking. Such a thing had never been known in the history of the county, and newspapers made "streamer heads" out of the desperate dangerousness of the situation.

It happened that on the night of June 3rd, Representative Samuel Wragg was being made the worshipful grand master of the Masonic Lodge of the town of Needham. Fred Katzmann, the district attorney, was a Mason, and the slain paymaster of the shoe company had also been a Mason. His worshipful brothers would not shrink from their duty to his memory. The father of Representative Wragg, a deputy sheriff, appeared without warning at the ceremony, and notified the members of the lodge to appear in court next morning. That surely seemed to violate the law, which specifies that in such an emergency special veniremen shall be summoned "from among the bystanders." But Judge Thayer overruled the objections of the defense—just as he overruled Lee Swenson's efforts to question the veniremen.

One of the jurors selected over the protest of the defense was Walter Ripley, an old man who had been chief of police of the city of Quincy. For many years Ripley had watched juries file in and out of court-rooms, but never had he seen one stand and salute the flag. But now, when he was made foreman of the jury, he set a new precedent for the Commonwealth; every time he entered the jury box, he faced the flag and solemnly saluted it. That was his way of "telling the world." These anarchists—the male population of New England made an obscene word out of it—were trying to "tear down the flag," and he was going to show them. On his way to court he had met an old friend in the railroad station, and said that he was going to act as a juror in the trial of two "guinneys." "Damn them, they ought to hang anyway!" said Ripley, according to the affidavit made by his friend several months later.

III

Joe Randall was attending the trial as a newspaperman, representing some labor papers. Also there was John Nicholas Beffel, representing the Federated Press. These two mixed with the other reporters, and sat at lunch with them in the Dedham Inn, and so got all the "inside dope." This was irritating to Judge Thayer, who naturally assumed that all the newspapermen were on his side, and was accustomed to join them at lunch in their private dining room, and tell them what he wanted to have published. It happened that the Italian Government had sent a representative to attend the trial, to make sure that two Italian citizens received fair play; this gentleman, the Marquis Ferrante, naturally did not understand that there could be such a thing as a "radical" newspaperman, so he talked freely to Beffel, and gave him a carefully worded statement, intended as a broad hint to Judge Thayer. "The Italian authorities are deeply interested in the case of Sacco and

Vanzetti, and this trial will be closely followed by them. They have complete confidence that the trial will be conducted solely as a criminal proceeding, without reference to the political or social beliefs of any one involved."

Beffel made carbon copies of this statement, and gave it to the other men. The judge came in, and after he had finished his lunch and was ready to leave, one of the reporters handed him a copy of the statement. He read it, and did not fail to get its hidden meaning. His face flushed, and with a gesture of anger he said, "Why, that fellow came clear out to my home in Worcester and assured me that the Italian Government had no interest in this case!"

The reporters, seeing that he was in a mood for talk, gathered round. One of them spoke of Fred Moore, with whom the judge had been arguing all morning over the selection of jurors. The old man's face showed that there was still life in it; his yellow parchment skin became suffused with blood. "What do you suppose that fellow wanted me to ask those veniremen? 'Are you a member of a labor union? Are you opposed to union labor? Are you a member of a secret society?' "

"Web" went on, his conversation turning into a stump speech, as it always did, in a dining room or a railroad train, on a football field or a golf green, whenever he could get an audience. "Did you ever see a case in which so many leaflets have been broadcast saying that people couldn't get a fair trial in the State of Massachusetts?" He looked at Joe Randall, for he knew that Joe was the wicked author of these leaflets. His voice rose high and shrill, and his hands shook as he waved them. John Nicholas Beffel, annoyed at the turn of events, stepped closer and said, "I wish to inform you, Judge Thayer, that the statement of the Marquis Ferrante was given out at his express request. He asked me to copy it and give it to the other newspapermen." But the old man brushed him aside and as he went out, shook his fist, exclaiming to the group of men: "You wait till I give my charge to the jury. I'll show 'em!"

The reporters stood, dumbfounded. A judge, actually then sitting on the case, going back to court in that mood, to deal with men on trial for their lives! Manifestly, it was a "big story," and if the newspapermen could have had their way, unhampered by owners, it would have taken the front page of every newspaper in Massachusetts. But newspapermen do not have their way; they do have owners, and have to practice what is known as "taking policy." The representative of the Associated Press, Jack Harding, advanced the classic formula of his organization, that the matter was "controversial," and therefore not to be handled. "Controversial," in the sense of the Associated Press, means anything detrimental to the ruling class of America. It is manifest that members of this class, being all in office or high station of some sort, can speak, and have their utterances count as news of an important and dignified character. It is when their enemies attack them that the "controversy" begins.

The other reporters from the capitalist papers agreed to hush up the incident. Beffel and Joe Randall might break step if they wanted to; but they could only publish the story in a few labor and socialist papers, where it would count for nothing; and they would get themselves barred from the private dining room, and from the precious "inside dope." The defense counsel agreed that nothing could be done; but of course the story went up to Boston, and caused several lawyers and judges of the city to say that "Web" had gone mad, and that something ought to be done about it—only, alas, nothing could be done, because all the judges, and even the court employees of Massachusetts are appointed for life, and if you were to try to impeach "Web" in the midst of this case, you might just as well turn the Commonwealth over to the Reds and be done with it.

IV

The prisoners sat in their steel cage, gazing about with anxious eyes, trying to understand the complex procedure in a strange tongue: Bart with his heavy drooping mustaches, his melancholy face now deeply lined; Nick, restless-eyed, impatient; both of them pale with a year away from sunshine. They were neatly shaved, brushed and washed, dressed in new suits, with black silk ties and clean collars—doing their best to look like Americans, to impress an American jury. They gazed at the elderly stern-faced men who were to decide their fate: not one foreigner among them, all English names, old Yankee ancestry. Every one on that jury had had a son or near relative in France—and those relatives who were not dead or crippled had been marching in the patriotic celebrations of the last few days.

Assistant District Attorney Williams arose and made a speech to the jury, telling what his side intended to prove. Once more Cornelia listened to that story about a bandit gang, about Boda and Orciani and Coacci, the bandit house and the little shed behind it, the Buick car with the bullet hole in the side, the little Overland car in which the bandits had escaped, after they had "thrown away" the Buick car in the Manley woods. The jury would be taken downstairs to inspect the Buick; they would be taken on a tour, Judge Thayer accompanying, to see the shack and the shed. Cornelia had heard all this at Plymouth, and had seen the prosecution fail to produce any evidence whatever. She had not yet learned about Mike Stewart and his "theory," derived from the "detective machine"; the whole procedure seemed to her a lunatic's dream, and she watched in a daze to see what would happen in the course of this second trial.

Exactly the same thing happened as at Plymouth; no evidence appeared. The farce became so apparent that even Judge Thayer could not stand for it. As to Boda he said, late in the trial: "But he is not connected in any way with the murder. Anybody else driving a Buick car, if it was a seven-passenger car, would stand almost in the same relationship. . . . But there is not one identifying feature." He forced the prosecution to admit that "Neither Orciani nor Boda was in South Braintree at the time of the murder and there was no concert of action between them and Sacco and Vanzetti as to the murder." He ordered that "all evidence obtained by the jury on the view at the Coacci barn or shed be entirely disregarded." But of course it wasn't disregarded, and the prosecution knew what it had fixed in the jury's mind. Even after the district attorney had expressly admitted that Orciani was not one of the murderers, he brought him up before the jury as a dark and sinister mystery, challenging the defense to explain why they had not put him on the stand.

Physicians described the wounds of the dead men; and then came the identification witnesses. Lewis L. Wade, a shoe worker, had thought in the Brockton police station that Sacco was one of the bandits; but now he said he was not sure. It was a blow to the police, and as Wade left the stand, one of the officers called him a "piker," and another muttered, "We are not through with you yet." A few weeks later Wade lost his job—after seventeen years' service with the shoe company. Two others who testified for the defense met the same fate. Not all the dangers were on one side!

There came Mary Splaine, bookkeeper of the shoe company, who had run to the window and looked out. Mary was one of the victims of that process of suggestion which prosecuting officials understand well. She had looked at Sacco so many times that she saw him as the bandit; she sat and looked at him once more and described him in minute detail, height, weight, square shoulders, high forehead, hair brushed back and between two and two and a half inches long; "dark hair, dark eyebrows, thin cheeks and clean-shaven face of a peculiar greenish-white." No one could have asked a better identification —until you considered the opportunity which Mary had had to see the bandit. Then you realized that she was claiming a physical impossibility. She was in a second-story window, eighty feet from the car, and she saw the bandit for the length of time it took the car to travel thirty-five feet at eighteen miles per hour—one or two seconds, amid the wildest excitement and shooting.

The defense confronted Mary with the record of what she had said at the preliminary hearing, after three different examinations of Sacco, "I do not think my opportunity afforded me the right to say he is the man." Now, surprised and confused, she said, "That is not true. I never said it." Having a day to think it over, and to be warned that stenographer's notes are not to be so easily waved aside, she took the stand and corrected her testimony, admitting that she had said what was in the record, but claiming that she had changed upon "reflection."

The defense tried desperately to break Mary Splaine; but she was one of those covered by the tragic phrase, too late! For her they needed the Pinkerton reports—the evidence of the operative Henry Hellyer, who was in court, and whose knowledge was in possession of the prosecution. He and Captain

Proctor, of the state police—another witness, also in court—
had shown Mary Splaine a photograph of a criminal called
"Tony the Wop," and Mary had positively identified him as
one of the bandits; so the police had set out to get him—
and learned that he had been in jail at the time of the crime!
Also Mary Splaine had told Hellyer a long story about two men
in the factory who had plotted and carried out the banditry.
Mary gave their names, and Hellyer made "discreet inquiries"
of the owner of the factory, who said the accusation was baseless; the superintendent told him to pay no attention to Mary
Splaine, "because she is one of the most irresponsible persons
he ever came in contact with." So read the report of "H.H.,"
hidden from the defense until five or six years later.

V

Next came Louis Pelzer, not bright, son of two mutes: the
Jewish boy, haunted by the memory of pogroms, and in terror
of the police. He had peered out through a window, and amid
flying bullets had written down the number of the bandit car,
and made note of the bandit so exactly that he could describe
even the pin in his collar. The defense lawyers took this pitiful
creature in hand, and soon had him mopping the sweat from
his forehead. It became evident that he could not understand
simple questions, and tangled himself in lie after lie. Yes, he
had lied to Robert Reid, investigator for the defense; he had
said he did not see anything, because he did not want to be a
witness. The defense put on three fellow-workmen of Pelzer's,
two of whom testified that instead of putting up the window to
look, he had dived under a bench when he heard the shooting.
The third testified, "I heard him say that he did not see anybody." The district attorney did the best he could in defending Pelzer to the jury. "He was frank enough here, gentlemen, to own that he had twice falsified before to both sides,
and he gave you his reason. . . . He is big enough and manly
enough now to tell you of his prior falsehoods and his reasons
for them."

And then the Lola Andrews circus. Three days of the expensive time of the Superior Court of the Commonwealth of
Massachusetts was given up to Lola. She told her tale of how,

four hours prior to the crime, she had seen two men with a car drawn up by the curb, and how she had talked to them, and the one under the car was Sacco. When the defense began to go into the details of her past life, she fainted impressively, and Judge Thayer ordered the court-room barricaded, so that when Lola was restored, she might pick out the man who had assaulted her in a toilet in a Quincy rooming-house. But that man was apparently an adept in the occult lore of the Hindoos, and possessed the power to dematerialize his body and disappear through the walls of court-rooms; the police could not catch him—but Lola won time to think, and also she won the jury, and Judge Thayer to keep the defense from asking her bad questions. When Fred Moore spoke of her testimony as "hopelessly confusing," the judge gave him a stern rebuke. "That is an unfair criticism of any witness."

When the defense had its chance, it put on Mrs. Julia Campbell, who had accompanied Lola on that visit to the shoe factory to look for a job, and testified that Lola had spoken to no man in or near an automobile. A policeman and a reporter testified that she had told them she had not seen the bandits. Harry Kurlansky, a small shopkeeper of Quincy, had talked with her on his doorstep and heard her tell how the police were hounding her to testify against Sacco and Vanzetti. " 'The government took me down and they want me to recognize those men,' she says, 'and I don't know a thing about them. I have never seen them and I can't recognize them.' "

That testimony looked so bad for Lola, it was one of the times when Judge Thayer felt it necessary to jump to the rescue. He began to cross-question the witness: why hadn't he set to work as a good citizen to find out who it was that was trying to make Lola give false testimony? Such an obvious thing for a small shopkeeper, a foreigner in a New England town, to tackle the police and the district attorney's office, and make them stop framing a witness! Said the judge, "Did you attempt to find out who this person was who represented the government who was trying to get her to take and to state that which was false?" Naturally Kurlansky was taken aback by such a question, and could only say, "Well, it didn't come into my mind. I wasn't sure, you know. It didn't—" The judge pinned him down, as to why he didn't think of it, why he didn't do it—thus leaving him completely discredited before patriotic jurors, who gave all their spare time to supervising the work of police chiefs and district attorneys.

VI

Presiding over a murder trial is a complicated and exacting business. Common sense and humanity have nothing to do with the procedure; it is a matter of rules and decisions, millions of intricate and subtle details, the interwoven and organized history of the trials which have been held in New England for three hundred years, and in Old England for twice as long. All this you have to have at your finger-tips, for each decision must be rendered immediately, you cannot take it under advisement and look up the precedents overnight. Your reputation depends upon your decisions being such that the highest court, reviewing your work, will sustain you. The strain is incessant, and may last for many weeks; the rules allow ten days' rest to a judge after each ordeal.

"Web" Thayer had been playing this game for many years, and knew all the tricks; including the one of favoring his own side while seeming to be impartial. His spoken words would go into the record, to be studied by the higher judges; but his manner would not go in—so the art was to keep his words fair, and do the damage otherwise. Every time Swenson or Moore would make an objection, "Web" would turn and look at him over his spectacles with a kind of ironical curiosity. "What is this that has come out of the wild west to teach us how to conduct a court in Massachusetts?" Then his eyes would turn to the jury, and give half a wink; with a bored drawl, he would say, "Objection overruled," and jury and court officials would be all one grin.

Within its narrow limits the judge's mind was quick and cunning. He was instantly on the alert to spoil any advantage his enemies were gaining, and ingenious to find reasons to interrupt, to block questions, to bar out evidence and confuse witnesses. Frequently he sat with some of the prosecutors in public places, and he always knew what the prosecutor was aiming at, and if he missed a point, would prompt him. Once, realizing that he had gone too far, he apologized blandly: "I

am always telling the district attorney what to say." The naïve
court reporter put that into the record!

And later came the incident of the cap which had been picked
up at the scene of the crime, and which the prosecution sought
to identify as Sacco's. It was too small for him, but the jury
would overlook that. When the son of Sacco's employer was
on the stand, Judge Thayer tried to get him to say that this cap
resembled Sacco's. Naturally, when a man runs a factory with
many workers, he can't remember the details of all the caps
they wear; young Kelley was embarrassed, not liking to displease a great judge, but he had to say, "I can't answer it when
I don't know right down in my heart that that is the cap."
"Web" was determined to get something more damaging than
that; and at the same time he tried to fix it so that his questions
would seem to be coming from Assistant District Attorney
Williams. Said the judge, "I would like to ask the witness one
question: whether—" then he turned to Mr. Williams: "I wish
you would ask him, rather."

The defense lawyers tried to break up this game, but "Web"
stuck to it: "I would rather it came from Mr. Williams. Will
you put that question?" The somewhat slow Mr. Williams—
"Web" came to hate him bitterly for this and other faults—
asked the witness whether the cap was "alike in appearance
to the cap worn by Sacco." The witness replied, "In color only,"
which would seem clear enough; but "Web" refused to be
defeated. Said he, "That is not responsive to the question"—
meaning, of course, that it wasn't what he wanted. He went on,
telling the witness what to say: "In its general appearance it is
the same." Those words came from the just and upright judge,
and the witness would have had to be very rude indeed to contradict them. "Yes, sir," he said. When the defense objected
to this singular method of "framing" evidence in open court,
the judge made it all right by directing the court reporter to
falsify the record. "You may put the question so it comes from
counsel rather than from the Court." Mr. Williams then obediently put the question, and the witness obediently answered
again. But the court reporter, whether from stupidity or malice,
failed to take the judge's instructions, and copied out the whole
dialogue, and there it stands in cold print, to be handed down
to the scorn and fury of all future times.

And this partisanship and cunning combined with the cheapest vanity and craving for display! The photographers were constantly making pictures of Judge Thayer, and he was never too busy to pose for them. On the front page of the papers you saw Judge Thayer sitting on the bench with a legal tome open before him; Judge Thayer with a palm leaf fan standing in front of the court-house; the twelve gentlemen of the jury being entertained by a victrola, with Judge Thayer in the center of the picture.

And then, sitting in his chambers, spitting on the floor, and talking about the case with Tom, Dick and Harry; with court officials, interpreters, policemen, newspaper reporters, photographers—incredible as it might seem, even with ladies of social prominence who were there as friends of Sacco and Vanzetti. So furious was his hatred against these "anarchistic bastards," he was not content to send them to the electric chair, but must throw mud at them on their journey. To Cornelia Thornwell it seemed that the poor old man had literally gone out of his mind; so also it seemed to dignified "blue-bloods" when she told them what was happening. But what could be done about it? The Commonwealth makes the proud boast that no judge has ever been impeached. Were they going to break that record, tarnish that scutcheon, for the sake of two Italians who were anarchists, infidels and draft-dodgers, even if they were not bandits and murderers?

VII

Carlos E. Goodridge to the stand: the man who had managed to exchange a jail sentence of several years for aid in sending Sacco to the electric chair. Judge Thayer knew all about that situation; and just as Swenson had predicted, he refused to permit any questions to be asked of Goodridge, to reveal the fact that he had pleaded guilty to larceny in Massachusetts. Moreover, the judge called the lawyers to the bench while he was discussing the matter, so that the jury might have no hint that they were listening to the testimony of a crook. Thayer would not even permit the discussion to get into the record, and when he saw the court reporter starting to take down his words he exclaimed, "Get the hell out of here!" So the proprieties were preserved, and the glib and plausible Goodridge took the stand, and told the trusting jury how he had run out of the pool-room, and seen the bandit car go by, close to the curb, and how a bandit "poked a gun over towards" him, and this man was Sacco and nobody else.

The defense was hog-tied and helpless. Concerning the rest of Goodridge's record, the fact that his very name was an act of perjury, they had no evidence. The court-room rang with the cries of the several fine women whom Erastus Corning Whitney had married and betrayed, of the owners of horses he had stolen, of others whom his glib tongue had swindled; but the fates which held Sacco and Vanzetti at their choice allowed no sound to be heard. When later these sounds had been duly transcribed upon legal paper, and sworn to before notaries, and laid before Judge Thayer in the form of a motion for a new trial, that Daniel come to judgment would repeat his deadly formula: "Motion denied!" When the matter was carried before the Supreme Judicial Court, that august body would apply its vast learning to the problem, and decide, first, that the failure to let the jury know of Goodridge's record was not ground for reversal, and second, that the discovery of new facts about Goodridge was not basis for a new trial. "Decision sustained."

Blocked and thwarted at every turn! Police officers took the stand to tell how witnesses had identified Sacco and Vanzetti in the Brockton police station immediately after their arrest; but when the defense tried to ask them about witnesses who had refused to identify, "Web" Thayer held up his mighty hand and cut him short. No witness could be asked about what any other witness might have said! By this device the defense would be kept from using the trial proceedings to fish for evidence. The bare idea that they should try to do it was so preposterous that both the judge and the jury burst out laughing.

Again the voices shrieked. Roy Gould, the salesman of shaving paste, the man with the bullet hole in his overcoat, who had been within ten feet of the bandits, and would swear that Sacco was not the man! Mrs. Kelly and Mrs. Kennedy, the only persons who had had an extended view of the driver of the car, and whose written statements that he was not Vanzetti were in the hands of the district attorney! All those witnesses who had been taken to the police station by Henry Hellyer and Captain Proctor, and had identified photographs of other bandits, but had refused to identify Sacco and Vanzetti—in spite of the posing, and pulling down of caps over the eyes, and pretending to aim pistols! So many voices crying warnings, filling the court-room with their clamor—in vain!

VIII

In the papers Cornelia read news of great concern to her family; the demurrer to the suit of Jerry Walker had been overruled; the last bar was down, the tremendous case was to be tried out before a jury. "Fifteen Million Dollar Conspiracy Charge!" said the newspapers. To Cornelia it meant a family agony; all three of her sons-in-law, two of her nephews-in-law, two or three cousins, were going to have to take the witness stand, and be questioned for weeks and months as to the details of their business procedures. Jerry Walker's lawyers had not minced words in setting forth what they expected to prove: the great bankers, headed by Rupert Alvin and Henry Cabot Winters, had "entered into a secret combination and conspiracy to carry into effect by their combined power and influence, by duress of the plaintiff, by fraudulent concealments, false representations and by wrongful, illegal and fraudulent means which are hereinafter stated with certainty and particularity, to deprive the plaintiff of his shares in the above-named companies." The "yellow" newspapers smacked their lips over the promised feast, while the dignified ones put the news away in the financial columns, as if to say that these abusive words were used in a technical sense, and did not mean what the ordinary reader would suppose.

Already families had been broken up over this issue, and wives were not speaking to one another. Mrs. John Quincy Thornwell, wife of the president of the Fifth National Bank, was telling everybody that Rupert Alvin had drawn her husband into the mess without his knowledge. Mrs. Rupert Alvin, wife of the president of the Pilgrim National, was outraged because her sister, Mrs. Henry Cabot Winters, was taking the affair with flippancy, having said to her intimates that it would be an excellent thing if some of these gentlemen were sent to

jail, so that their wives would know where they were! Slanders
and recriminations—bitter feuds starting—a whole kettle of
Back Bay codfish!

In the Sacco-Vanzetti trial one of the lawyers fell ill, and
Judge Thayer put off the trial over the week-end. Cornelia
was planning to write a lot of letters and raise some money
which was badly needed; but Deborah telephoned from her
place at the North Shore, her mother must meet her in Boston
at once, something about Alice, very serious. Cornelia assumed
it was more of the Jerry Walker quarrel. "You know, Deborah,
I consider the Walkers as my friends, and I am not going to
have anything—"

But Deborah broke in: "It has nothing to do with that,
Mother. It is something personal, something desperate—I can't
give you any hint over the telephone. Come to the house at
once."

So Betty drove her grandmother to Boston. Betty had work
to do at defense headquarters. She was going to get out a rush
circular about events at the trial, and she wasn't going to let
Joe have anything to do with it. Under the very strict laws
of Massachusetts, Judge Thayer had the right to call it contempt of court, and if he tried to, the defendant was going to
be a young lady with the very bluest blood in New England;
old "Judge Fury," as Betty had taken to calling him, would get
a sure enough front-page story if he tried it! Joe was going
to stay in Dedham and write newspaper and magazine articles,
which would be published outside the state, and so beyond
"Judge Fury's" reach.

"I know what you'll find," said the young lady Bolshevik—
"another of Aunt Alice's geniuses gone wrong. I hear she's
going wrong with him." And so it proved. Alice had got the
love of art and the art of love mixed up. A chaotic Bohemian
pianist had cast temperamental glances at her, and she proposed to accompany him to Europe, and had notified Henry that
she expected to get a divorce. "And right now!" cried Deborah—"while Rupert and Henry are driven nearly to death
with this Jerry Walker affair, and the Elevated Railway business, too—and Betty, and you—Mother, we simply cannot have
another scandal now!"

So the family phalanx must gather about the frantic woman,

and guard her with their spears, and frighten away "that impossible man," as Deborah called him. Cornelia, the mother, and only woman member of the old generation, must take most of the burden. She must face her second daughter's hysterics yet again—she had lost count of the times, it had been more than twenty years of melodrama; first frantic jealousy of Henry, then bitter hate, then indifference, with various stages of romantic thrills for this, that and the other great or some-day-to-be-great poet or painter or musician. This time was the most terrible of all; this time all bars were down, all reserves thrown away—it was most decidedly not "Boston," not to be believed.

For twenty years Alice had sought something, and the women and the men of the family had formed the phalanx about her, and held her captive. "Now look at me!" she cried. "I am an old woman! My skin will soon be parchment, and my chance is nearly gone!"

"Your chance at what?" asked Cornelia, quietly.

"Love!" cried the other, with unaccustomed clarity.

The mother felt a sudden uprush of pity. "Does love depend on complexion?"

"What else?" cried Alice, wildly. "And look at me!"

Cornelia looked, and realized. It was true that her vain and beautiful daughter was showing her years; no longer the wild rose complexion, the girlish charm, the serenity and security of young matronhood. Alice's skin was getting dry, there were lines that no beauty doctor could take away, those fatal tight strings under the chin which nothing can hide. Deborah's neck had been like that for years, she had worn a black velvet band about it. But such a device would make Alice "look a fright"— she grabbed up a ribbon and wound it into a halter, to show her mother what she would be like!

She loved Franz Cezak! He was not a "strolling Bohemian," as Deborah had basely insinuated; he was no common musician at all, but the younger son of a great family, who had been received as a house guest in Back Bay homes. Alice loved him, and she didn't love Boston, and she was going to be happy!

Would she really be happy? asked the mother, and began the brutal task of undermining poor Alice's castle in Bohemia. Did this love-artist know that she had very little money in her own right, and that it is not the custom for American husbands to subsidize the art-romances of their wives? Was it true that the man was some years younger than Alice, and if so, did art-lovers behave like other men in the matter of women's age? Was Alice expecting to come back to Boston, the morning after her nuit d'amour?

Clara Scatterbridge, the youngest daughter, came in; having all the future of her many sons and daughters, coming one by one to marriageable age, to weep and plead for. Rupert Alvin came, leaving all his cares of state. He had put into action the machinery which the ruling classes have established for the quick and efficient collection of scandal; just as he could tell his mother-in-law all the gossip of the "Italian colony" concerning the anarchist "gruppo" of East Boston, so he could tell his sister-in-law about a Bohemian pianist, who had an art-love in every concert town. He had been knocked down and almost killed by a well-known cricket player of Philadelphia, and in Paris he had run away from a duel with the exiled Russian Prince Dolgorovitch, "or whatever it is," said Rupert, with Anglo-Saxon contempt for a name with such termination.

And then young Josiah Thornwell Winters, Alice's only son, who was to get his "sheepskin" from Harvard in a few days. Young Josiah's own behavior didn't give him much standing in court, he admitted, but he was promising to settle down and make a man of himself, and it would certainly be easier if he had a mother in blameless Boston, rather than following a pianist about Bohemia. The rest of the family withdrew while this intimate episode in the drama was played out.

IX

Cornelia went to see the husband, and found that Henry was taking a most un-Bostonian attitude. "Mother," he said, "it seems to me Alice had better have it out, and see whether there's anything in this romance business for her. You, as a Bolshevik, ought not be shocked by that."

"Mine has been a revolt with a purpose," said Cornelia; "and if Alice has a purpose I don't know what it is."

"Well, I have said for years that Alice ought to have a divorce. If she had a husband, she might settle down—"

"But this man won't be a husband, Henry!"

"I know; but something has got to pull her loose from the family. I haven't said it to them, because after all, it's a Thornwell affair. But it's been plain to me, ever since I realized that I wasn't the man for Alice. The misery has been because the family couldn't make up its mind to face a divorce; they'd rather have a fit of hysterics once a month for twenty years. I don't want to talk about Alice, for she's your flesh and blood—"

"Go on, Henry, say what you think. I've got to understand you all."

"Well, Mother, fundamentally it's that Alice hasn't got any brains. Why didn't you teach her some of your sense of fun?"

"You forget, Henry, I didn't do the teaching. The house was full of Josiah's sisters and aunts, who knew what ought to be done always. I waited too long before I fought."

"Yes, Mother, we've all made mistakes. I ought to have given more time to my son. I left him to his mother, while I made the money, and now I've got too much money, and no wife, and a son who has the structure and constitution of a marshmallow. That's my reward for hard work—not much reason for going to the office in the morning, is there?"

"I know, Henry, you've talked like that before; but you go to the office in the morning, and go on doing what you did the day before. We're all of us like so many ants—we do what the others do. Because I have tried to think for myself, you decide I am cracked in the head."

"No, Mother, not at all!" Henry's gallantry came to the rescue. "I really have a great admiration—you should hear me boasting about you in the clubs—nobody can sport such an exciting mother-in-law! Truly, you're the talk of the town—they tell me you have assumed the moral leadership of all the Bolsheviks at the trial."

"They tell you something very foolish, like all the other tales about the Sacco-Vanzetti defense. What became of the evidence you promised to get me, Henry? Have you forgotten it?"

"No, Mother—"

"You didn't find it so easy as you thought?"

"Not that; but fifteen million dollars is a lot of money, and Rupert is terrified as to what he has to admit in the Jerry

Walker case. Also he's had to take charge of the Bar Association—the job they are planning, to oust our district attorney. I suppose you've heard about that?"

"No, Henry, I've been out of touch with the criminal world of late." She laughed, and he laughed, too—they always had a good time. If only Alice had had her mother's ability to laugh!

"It's a long story, I'll tell you about it some day. When the blackmail ring got after the Thornwell family, Rupert insisted that we had to put them out of business; he's a sterner moralist than I, you know. We started work through the Bar Association—you are reading about this Mishawum Manor case, of course."

"Did you and Rupert start that?"

"The episode happened four years ago. Didn't it strike you as peculiar that it should be taken up now?"

"To tell the truth, I've been too busy to think about it."

"Well, so has the public! The fact is, I got detectives and got the story for Rupert."

"Why did you start in Middlesex County?"

"Well, you see, the district attorney there happens to be an American, and we thought it would be good policy to show impartiality. After we have put Tufts out, nobody can kick if we come over here to Suffolk and tackle Joe Pelletier!"

"I see!" said Cornelia. She knew that she was being admitted to the inside of Boston public life—the center of the center and hub of the hub! "Joe" Pelletier, district attorney of Suffolk County, comprising Boston proper, was a leading Catholic orator and hero, National Advocate of the Knights of Columbus, knighted by the Pope for his services to the holy cause. Incidentally he was one of the tools of the "blackmail ring," and may have got a share of that seventy-five thousand dollars which Henry had "pungled up" to pay for the flashlight picture of his son in the hotel room with a woman. So now the Thornwells were out to "get him"!

It was one more crisis in the unending struggle between the blue-blood and the Irish-Catholic elements of the city. Cornelia had watched it all her life, so she did not have to ask many questions. "It seems unfortunate," she commented, "that Rupert has to be mixed up in this Elevated scandal right now."

"But that is part of the fight," said Henry; he explained

that Joe Pelletier had taken up the scandal and was threatening prosecutions, as a means of frightening Rupert and the rest of the Pilgrim National crowd. Something like half the patriotic legislators of Massachusetts had been borrowing money from the banks, and speculating in Elevated stocks, before they passed the bill which boosted these stocks on the market; and now Pelletier was trying to fasten it on Rupert. It was a question which would "beat the other to it." "Make your bets!" said Henry Cabot Winters.

"Your smile is a sufficient betting tip!" replied his mother-in-law; and he said yes, it was coming out all right, only Rupert was the worrying temperament, and getting worse. The doctors tried to get him to stop, but they hadn't chosen a very helpful way. They took x-ray pictures of his veins and showed how they looked like white ribbons, which meant deposits of lime and other minerals; they had given the poor fellow such a list of things he mustn't eat that when he dined out he picked around in his plate like a chicken. His rosy and purple bulges would soon be turned into hollows.

X

Alice's castle in Bohemia collapsed. Did one of the Thornwell men convey to the tempestuous genius the information that the Thornwell ladies had no money of their own? Anyhow, the celebrated artist discovered a series of concert engagements in California, and wrote Alice a letter of great wisdom and sympathy. The tormented woman died a score of soul-deaths, and retired to a fashionable sanatorium to try a rest cure with "stuffing." A little later she would be trying a fasting-cure, and after that a diet of grapes exclusively, and then she would be paying thirty dollars an hour to have her troubles listened to by a psychoanalyst.

Meantime Cornelia had hurried back to Dedham, where the trial had reopened, regardless of Thornwell family troubles. Again she sat all day on a hard bench in the court-room, and wrote memoranda in a notebook, and in the evening conferred with the lawyers and the committee and the journalists until late at night. Each afternoon, after court, she went by special favor of the sheriff, to say a few words to Bart, and hear his

advice about the procedure, and comfort him with affection.
The prosecution had come now to the identification of
Vanzetti as one of the bandits. They put on the stand a man
named Levangie, gateman at the railroad tracks across which
the bandit car had passed immediately after the shooting. This
old man told how a train was coming when the car drove up,
and he started to put down the gates, but the bandits forced
him at the point of a revolver to raise them and let the car
cross ahead of the train. He identified Vanzetti as the driver
of the car.

When the defense had its turn it put on a locomotive fireman,
not a Red but an Irishman, who testified that three-quarters of
an hour after the shooting he talked with Levangie, who said
that he did not see the bandits, all he saw was the gun, and he
"ducked into the shanty." Three other witnesses gave the same
testimony. As it happened, Levangie had told one of the defense
lawyers that he could not identify the bandits, and first he
admitted having said this; later he contradicted himself, and
said he did not remember any such interview. He was a loose-
jointed fellow, shifty of eye, and did not seem at all abashed
when he was caught in false statements; rather he took the
whole affair as a joke.

It became a joke to all the world, when the district attorney
came to discuss Levangie's testimony in his address to the jury.
Mr. Katzmann was in a dilemma, because the gateman had
identified Vanzetti as the driver of the car, whereas Mr. Katzmann's other witnesses agreed upon the driver as young, small,
light-haired and sickly looking. The district attorney managed
very ingeniously to repudiate Levangie while at the same time
asking the jury to accept him. The gateman thought he had
seen Vanzetti driving the car, but really he had seen him in
the rear seat!

That was all the real evidence they had. But to cover the
weakness, they put on some more that looked like evidence. A
man named Dolbeare, who thought he had seen Vanzetti in an
auto full of foreigners in South Braintree, some five hours
before the crime. He had seen a car going past him, and what
had attracted his attention was one man leaning forward talking to another, and that it was a "tough-looking bunch." He
did not know Vanzetti, had never seen him before, and never

saw him again until after the arrest. He admitted that carloads of workmen drove through the town all the time, on the
way to the shipyards. He could not identify any other man in
the car, nor give a single detail about any one; all he could
do was to identify Vanzetti as one man who had been in that car.

And then a man who claimed to have seen Vanzetti on a train
the morning of the crime, coming from Plymouth to East Braintree. This man was completely refuted by the conductor and
three ticket-agents—no ticket had been sold for such a journey.
Also the prosecution put on another crossing-tender, who had
noted a car at his crossing, near the Manley Woods, an hour
after the crime, and thought it was Vanzetti in the front seat of
the car. And that was all the identification! That was the main
part of the evidence upon which the august Commonwealth of
Massachusetts proposed to send a man to the electric chair!

When Cornelia examined her notes, and questioned others
in her party, to see if her memory was playing her false, she
was appalled by the thing she saw happening before her eyes.
They were actually attempting to convict Bart of murder without one real item of identification; solely upon such facts as
that he had been with Sacco the night of the arrest, and had a
gun and cartridges, and had told lies to the police about himself and his doings! So farcical was the identification of Bart,
and so completely were the identifications of Nick shot to pieces
in the course of time, that three years later Judge Thayer found
himself backed against the wall, and forced to admit that "these
verdicts did not rest, in my judgment, upon the testimony of
the eye-witnesses." This news would certainly have surprised
the gentlemen of the jury, who had spent a week or two listening to these eye-witnesses, and had been solemnly assured by
the district attorney himself that never in his eleven years of
office had he "laid eye or given ear to so convincing a witness as
Lola Andrews!"

XI

Almost three weeks it took the Commonwealth of Massachusetts to present its case against the two anarchist wops.
Thirty times the prisoners emerged from the county jail—at a
quarter to nine every morning except Sunday, and again at a
quarter to two every afternoon except Saturday and Sunday—

and marched from the jail to the court-house: chained to a deputy on each side, with ten or twelve policemen marching in front, and as many in the rear. They always walked in the street, not on the sidewalk, for greater safety against surprise attack. Small boys would gather to stare, and the deputies would command, "Stand back!" It was their only chance to justify the expense to the county.

Seated in the cage, side by side, the prisoners would gaze straight before them. They could not see the spectators, nor was any one permitted to speak to them, except their lawyers. After a time the stern guards learned to make an exception of Mrs. Sacco, who would go to the cage and chat with her husband until court opened. Poor little woman, she had to bring a nursing baby with her, and her face, usually bright and eager, was worn and lined. She would sit all day, silent and rigid, trying to understand long words in a language that was still partly alien to her.

Her husband also would try, and the more he understood, the hotter became his revolutionary fury. Several times he and his companion boiled over—impossible to sit in silence while lies were told and rascality committed under the forms of law. When the policeman who had arrested them swore that Bart had several times started to reach for his gun, Bart cried out, "You are a liar!" A terrible breach of decorum—the guards seized him and shoved him into his seat, commanding, "Shut up!" When Lola Andrews was in the midst of her identification, Sacco rose in his seat and cried, "Am I the man? Take a good look! I am myself!" Again a great shock, and a sensational story for the papers. Nick's picture took the front page.

Later, when the defense was having its innings, there were more scenes. The interpreter provided by the court was an Italian by the name of Rossi; he belonged to the Norfolk County "ring," and was a friend of Mrs. DeFalco's, and of Judge Thayer's—he had a child named Webster Thayer Rossi, and he used to drive the judge up to the University Club in Boston; if the judge did not discuss the case with him on the way, it was the only chance "Web" ever lost.

Either this Rossi did not know how to interpret correctly, or he did not wish to; at a critical point in the testimony of Alfonsina Brini, he misstated in English what she had said in

Italian. Bart knew enough to catch the error, and insisted upon calling attention to it, and would not let the guards silence him. Again and again he saw these errors, and to Cornelia, when she came to see him in the jail, he insisted, "That fellow is a crook!" Over and over he said it, "He is a crook! Crook!" Cornelia thought it was Bart's prejudice against everybody in power; but it was another of those things that were to be proved too late. Before five years had passed, Rossi was to get a two year jail sentence for trying to sell his influence with judges.

Such misfortune appeared to dog the patriots who were prosecuting Sacco and Vanzetti; so many of them got into trouble with their own laws—but always after the verdict, when it was too late to count! There was an agent of the Department of Justice, named Shaughnessey, who had had the job of watching Red meetings and had supplied a mass of information concerning Sacco and Vanzetti. This ardent patriot stole a carload of hogs—a rather difficult object to get away with, one would think. Later he got twelve years for a holdup. But when in the course of later appeals, the defense had occasion to suggest the possibility of improper conduct by Department of Justice agents, "Web" Thayer was outraged by this, and delivered a stern rebuke.

XII

And then Captain Proctor, head of the state police. The Proctor story was so atrocious, that naïve old ladies like Cornelia Thornwell thought it would only have to become known in order to split the community wide open. But in fact, it hardly made a ripple. Massachusetts was so used to official knavery that it had lost the power to react, even with surprise.

Captain Proctor had been in the police service of the Commonwealth some thirty-six years, and was an old hand at the "frame-up"; among other jobs, he had "made" the Ettor and Giovannitti case. When Sacco and Vanzetti were arrested, he was called in by Mike Stewart, and interviewed all the witnesses, and tried to help out Mike's "theory." But in the end he told Mike, "You've got the wrong men," and withdrew from the case.

But still, gang loyalty held him, and when Fred Katzmann called on him to identify the so-called "mortal bullet," which had been extracted from the body of the dead guard, he came. This bullet was the crucial issue in the whole case; it was what tied Sacco and Vanzetti to the case, because the other five bullets found in the dead bodies were of such a size and make that they could not have come through either Sacco's pistol or Vanzetti's. The prosecution claimed that the "mortal bullet" had been fired from Sacco's pistol, and could have been fired from no other pistol. They put on an "expert" who swore to that; and then they put on Proctor, who backed up the "expert."

At least, that is what everybody thought he did, and the trial was concluded on that basis; the prosecution laid the utmost emphasis upon it, because Captain Proctor had qualified at great length as an authority upon bullets and revolvers, who had been studying the matter for twenty years, and had been a witness in more than a hundred capital cases. Said Katzmann, in his closing argument to the jury, "You might disregard all the identification testimony, and base your verdict on the testimony of these experts." And Judge Thayer put the weight of his judicial authority behind that; he explained to the jury what the testimony meant, that "it was Sacco's pistol that fired the bullet that caused the death of Berardelli. To this effect the Commonwealth introduced the testimony of two witnesses, Messrs. Proctor and Van Amburgh."

Nothing could be more positive; and so the matter went to the jury; so it stood in the minds of all students of the case for two years. But then Captain Proctor was near death, and his conscience troubled him; two men whom he believed to be innocent stood in the shadow of the electric chair, because of a conspiracy into which he had entered with the prosecution, to misrepresent his testimony to the jury. So he made an affidavit in which he set forth what had happened. Repeatedly he had been asked by the prosecutors to testify that the particular mortal bullet had been fired through the particular pistol belonging to Sacco. He had made many tests and measurements in the effort to convince himself that this was so, but he could not get the proof, and refused to give such testimony. "The district attorney desired to ask me that question, but I had repeatedly told him that if he did I should be obliged to answer in the negative." At the trial the questioning had been done by the assistant district attorney, later to become a learned judge. His question had been framed very carefully, and Proctor's answer no less carefully: "My opinion is that it is consistent with being fired by that pistol."

A verbal trick, you see; the witness meant that the mortal bullet *might* have been fired through that pistol; but the district attorney represented to the jury that his words meant something entirely different—that it *must* have been fired through that pistol, and could not have been fired through any other pistol in the world. That was how Judge Thayer passed it on to the jury in his charge; and in after years, with the printed words of his charge before him—preserved immutably, to be handed down to the scorn and fury of all future times—the embittered old man rendered a decision in which he ingeniously twisted the defense contentions concerning the meaning of the Proctor affidavit and the answering affidavits of Katzmann and his assistants, which really did not answer at all.

It was "Web's" way, shown in almost every decision he rendered. You would state something in plain words, as explicitly as the language permitted; you would wait patiently, a year or two, while the old gentleman had an appendicitis operation and an attack of pneumonia; and finally he would hand down a decision in which he accused you of having said many things you had never thought of. He would set up a whole regiment of straw-men, and in a valiant duel chop off their heads; he would fill pages in the stately law-books with refutations of arguments which had never been heard anywhere save in his own hate-tormented head. And then at the very end, sitting upon his throne with the whole world for an audience, he would solemnly declare: "With reference to the question of prejudice, there is not any now and there never was any."

CHAPTER 14

JUDGE FURY

I

FOUR times each day the prisoners made their march down the middle of the street, accompanied by military escort. Four times each day the jury made a march, from their hotel to the court-house, at noon to a restaurant and back, then to the hotel in the evening: twelve "good men and true," with court officers preceding and following, the aged foreman toddling at their head—he was to die within three months. It was a heavy strain upon old men, to sit for six hours a day in a crowded court-room, in suffocating midsummer heat. The judge mercifully said they might take off their coats, but their Puritan consciences required most of them to be uncomfortable.

Seven weeks their semi-imprisonment lasted; the bored victims got to know one another too well, and when they were tired of playing cards they sought refuge in the daily newspaper. They were not allowed to read about their own case—the sheriff cut it all out of the papers; but they read about a court up in Boston, where Charles Ponzi was being punished for having made five million dollars without permission of the Federal Reserve Board. The financial wizard's digestion had been wrecked by the ordeal of law, so the papers explained, and he had to be taken out to a restaurant each day, to get his diet of little neck clams and cream of tomato soup.

And then the story of Mishawum Manor, where the emperors of the moving picture world had been entertained by naked young ladies dancing the highland fling! Who could have invented more delicious material for the beguiling of bored jurymen? The Hearst newspaper put it on the front page each day: the romantic life story of "Brownie" Kennedy, the "madame" of this roadhouse; the number of husbands she had deserted, the millionaires she had plundered and ruined; details about the "champagne and chicken supper," the hugging and the dancing, and how the guests had disappeared to the rooms upstairs, so that at one time there was nobody to eat the chicken or drink the champagne. Later they were reassembled, much in déshabille, and the young ladies—names, addresses and prices all given— were flinging their very highlandest, when a flashlight went off and a photograph was taken of the scene. Most of the guests were too drunk to know what this meant; when they woke up next afternoon, they paid a thousand dollars for "entertainment and breakage," and thought that would be the end of it—just as if they had been at home in Hollywood.

But no, this was a pious Puritan community; and presently the emperors of moving pictures were receiving letters informing them that several of the young ladies who had been hired for the party had husbands, and these husbands were threatening suits for the desecration of their wives; furthermore, some indignant moralist had carried the story to the district attorney of Middlesex County, and that official was greatly shocked. Middlesex is sacred territory, because it contains the city of Cambridge, home of Harvard, the center of the center and hub of the hub. It would take no less than half a million dollars to wipe out the stain which these Hebrew and Babylonian emperors had put upon New England culture.

After much dickering, and threats and counterthreats, the dispute was settled by the payment of a hundred and five thousand dollars, which, according to the newspapers, had been divided among the chiefs of the political "ring," including the Middlesex district attorney—no Irish-Catholic "mick," but a blue-blood of registered pedigree, a gentleman with two hobbies, Red-baiting and college athletics. Only a year ago he had led a spectacular raid against "Red headquarters" in Cambridge, with a patrol wagon, cops, reporters and camera men, and had confiscated a load of literature. He was engaged in umpiring the Yale-Princeton football game, when the newspaper reporters came to inform him that the Supreme Judicial Court had removed him from office. Being a good sport, he went on with the game.

Middlesex County lies immediately to the north of Norfolk, and at its nearest point is only four or five miles from Dedham; so it might occur to some jurymen to wonder, could this corruption have crossed the border, and affected those in charge of the present trial? The authorities deemed it wise to provide automobiles, with bailiffs for chauffeurs, to keep the jury entertained. On holidays the twelve good men and true were escorted to the beach to picnic, and Sundays they went to church in the morning, and in the afternoon they motored to witness some of the patriotism rampant in the community.

On Sunday, twelve days after the trial started, the bodies of three dead soldiers, dug out of the ground in France, were buried in the city of Brockton, in Plymouth County, and the whole town turned out for the ceremonies. On the same day at Whitman, in the same county, two bodies were buried. On the following Sunday another one at Hingham, in Norfolk County. The day before that was the anniversary of the Battle of Belleau Wood, celebrated by veterans all over both counties; the day before that was a great New England holiday, Bunker Hill Day, celebrated in every town. On June 25th, just as the defense was getting under way, the sacred Plymouth Rock was restored to place with a new shrine over it, and there was a great celebration in Vanzetti's old home, reported in all newspapers and read about by all jurors. A week later five thousand veterans of the "Yankee Division" assembled in Plymouth, and held their exercises over the Fourth of July, the great American patriotic holiday. On that day the town of Quincy, in Norfolk County, witnessed the greatest parade of veterans in its history; the whole countryside echoed with the sounds of firecrackers and bells and military exhortations. "Never shall America forget the brave boys who died for her!"—so said the orators.

II

And then the college commencements! There are a score of colleges and universities in Massachusetts, to say nothing of two hundred and forty-nine high schools; and all of them celebrated their exercises while the Sacco-Vanzetti trial was in progress. All had eminent persons to deliver orations, and few were the orators who did not refer to the enemy within our midst, and the need for good citizens to stand together. These exhortations would be quoted in the next day's newspapers, and read by the twelve good men and true in their legal quarantine.

Cornelia took a day off and went up to the Harvard exercises.

Impossible to refuse, for it was the crisis of the effort to hold
Alice in line, and this was an occasion that would never come
again, the graduation of her only son; the public appearance of
Alice with Henry, and with all the family about her, would set
forth their solidarity to the world, and repudiate malicious
gossip. Such was the requirement of propriety. The three sisters
might quarrel ever so bitterly among themselves, but the world
must see them side by side, going through the formalities with
dignity.

So now Clara spent the night in the Winters home in Boston,
to keep Alice from taking poison or running away. Deborah
came early in the morning, and the two of them worked with
moral exhortations, and cups of strong coffee, and an expert
hairdresser, to get their distracted sister into shape for exhibi-
tion. Clara rode in the car with Alice and Henry, to relieve
them of the necessity of talking—Clara could always tell a
thousand stories about the progress of her brood.

Deborah sent her car early in the morning to bring her
mother; and there they were, three middle-aged ladies and one
old one, dressed with the restrained and dignified but none the
less expensive elegance of the Brahmins; Henry in tall silk hat
and frock coat, braided trousers and spats; Quincy Thornwell,
gentleman of leisure, escorting Priscilla Alvin Shaw, returned
from her honeymoon in Florida. They took their appointed
places in Sander's Theater, bowing right and left, greeting
their friends, exchanging compliments with the nearest. All the
conventions were satisfied.

The academic procession moved through the "Yard"; all the
dignitaries in their gorgeous-colored silk hoods and gowns, led
by the university marshal, and followed by thirteen hundred
graduates-to-be, all in caps and gowns. It was a special occasion,
because Harvard was making an innovation; for the first time
in its two hundred and eighty-five years, women were to be
awarded regular Harvard degrees—not just Radcliffe degrees
signed by President Lowell. There were thirty-six of these
intruding females, but they were not permitted to leave the
sacred yard with the men, they had to join the procession near
Lawrence Hall.

In Sander's Theater the sheriff of the county called the
meeting to order; the dean of the divinity school offered a

prayer, three graduates delivered orations, and the Governor of the Commonwealth made a speech. A curious moment for Cornelia Thornwell, with ghosts walking upon the platform, in costumes much out of style. How many years since she had sat up there, and heard Josiah's stern dry voice? The fashion in speeches had not changed a particle; they still talked about the responsibility of educated men for citizenship; they still rebuked disturbers of the public thought. Said Governor Cox: "We ought to stop complaining about the wrongs other men are doing until we are sure each one of us is doing his part honorably and well."

President Lowell arose to confer the degrees; an old gentleman with a brown mustache and full red cheeks and proper coldness of manner. He belonged to the inner circle of the sacred caste, enjoying an income of not far from a million dollars a year from the family cotton mills and real estate. He had been a lawyer on a small scale, when the great financial interests of Boston had selected him to take charge of their university. Under his direction there had been established a Graduate School of Business Administration, to put a gloss of culture upon the crudities of commercialism; the institution had grown with such speed that it was turning matters about, and taking a lot of the gloss off Harvard.

There was a slow procession of thirteen hundred young men in black gowns and mortar-boards, walking across a stage, putting out a hand and taking a roll of sheepskin; listening to a little speech, if it happened to be a "cum laude," with an extra sentence if it happened to be a "magna cum laude," and several sentences if it happened to be a "summa cum laude." It seemed symbolical of New England hypocrisy that these were not real diplomas, but merely blanks; next day the graduates had to go rooting in tubs, in the basement of the theater, to get their own!

The only thrill in the ceremony is when one of the young men happens to be known to you; then you make a decorous little noise with the palms of your hands—the relic of enthusiasm among the blue-bloods. Cornelia looked at the young faces, grave and pale, mostly, but still clean and alive. She looked at the sheriffs and mayors and politicians and lawyers and bankers —masks of cynicism, hardness and dullness. What evil power presided over the lives of men, to work this transformation from youth to age?

It came the turn of Josiah Thornwell Winters; and Cornelia hoped that not many of these graduates were hiding a tragedy like his. She had heard from Quincy Thornwell the end of the story: the woman from "Larry Shay's stable," who had succeeded in making Young Josiah think she was only nineteen, and innocent, was in reality twenty-five, a victim of drugs, and also of a disease. This latter she had passed on to her victim, so now he was paying several visits a week to leading specialists, and his pale set face as he walked across the platform was due to the fact that walking hurt him. But all over Sander's Theater, members of the audience nudged one another, whispering, "The grandson of Governor Thornwell—the tall one." They thought about his blue blood, and mothers with marriageable daughters pondered ways to meet him.

There was an elaborate banquet at the close of these ceremonies; and also a series of class banquets, at which the "old boys" got together and listened to patriotism and jokes. At one of these revelries the orator was that courageous patriot, District Attorney Frederick G. Katzmann, of Norfolk and Plymouth counties. The chairman introduced him as one who had set out to rid Massachusetts of the Reds, and the orator accepted the stern duty, and talked about the Sacco-Vanzetti case, and what he was going to do to those anarchists. Tumultuous applause from the assembled banqueters, and toasts from their hip-pocket flasks, and singing of "Fair Harvard" and "He's a Jolly Good Fellow!"

III

Back to Dedham courthouse with its high white dome, with a ring of port-holes like an ocean liner; the jury making its daily marches, and the foreman saluting the flag; the manacled prisoners parading down the middle of the street with their military escort; the guards keeping watch, searching the spectators, even the handbags of the ladies; the newspapers reporting sensations.

The defense was having its innings. Frank Burke, a man in his fifties, formerly sealer of weights and measures for the city of Brockton, and now giving demonstrations of glass-blowing, had been on the street in South Braintree, where the bandit car crossed the railroad tracks. The car had passed within ten feet of him, and the bandit in the right front seat had leaned out and snapped a gun at him—it had failed to explode. The man supposed to be Sacco had been in the right rear seat, and Burke got a good look at him and described him, a flat, full face, with broad heavy jowl—no resemblance to Sacco. There had been so much patriotism in the trial that Burke thought a little would be welcome from him, so he tried it, and there resulted a curious dialogue between him and the district attorney:

"What was the color of the gun you saw?"

"Blue."

"You have seen them, haven't you?"

"Yes, my boy brought one home from the war."

"Did you think I asked about your boy bringing one home?"

"No, but you were asking me about automatics, and I told you when I seen one."

"You thought you would tuck that in, did you?"

"I am not attempting to tuck anything in, Mr. Katzmann."

"Did you do it inadvertently?"

"Yes, sir, I am trying—"

"And have all your answers made heretofore that have not been called for been done inadvertently? I want you to tell the truth."

Five laborers took the stand, men who had been digging an excavation, and had witnessed the murder. These men all swore that neither Sacco nor Vanzetti were in the bandit car; but they were Italians and Spaniards, having to talk through interpreters, and it was easy for Katzmann to discredit them. One laborer estimated that he was forty or fifty feet from the shooting; Katzmann very cunningly got him to answer a complicated question—that he was as sure of the distance as he was that the bandits had not been Sacco and Vanzetti. Then he measured the distance on the map, and said it was ninety-five feet; and that finished Pedro Iscorla. In his closing speech Katzmann attacked all these laborers as cowards, because they had stood by with picks and shovels and failed to attack bandits who were shooting guns.

Two gun experts testified for the defense. Experts always balance one another—if you have as much money as the other side. One was a champion pistol shot and department head in a cartridge company; the other was superintendent of the testing department of the Colt Automatic Pistol Company, which had made Sacco's gun, and he should have known more about it than Captain Proctor, who had found himself on the witness stand vainly trying to take the weapon apart. Both the defense experts testified that the "mortal bullet" could not have come from Sacco's gun; nor did they, like Proctor, take back their testimony later on.

Witnesses appeared to counter the testimony of the gateman Levangie, and say how he had told them he did not see the bandits. The same for Goodridge, the ex-convict; four men swore that he had made statements contradicting his present testimony. Too bad these poolroom gentlemen were not named Jones, Smith, Brown and Robinson, instead of Magazu, Arrigoni, Manganio and D'Amato!

And then the witnesses to answer "Fainting Lola": her friend, Mrs. Campbell, a white-haired old woman who broke down and wept because she did not like to call Lola such a liar; the policeman and the reporter to whom Lola had admitted that she could not identify the bandits; and then Kurlansky, the storekeeper, who got his rebuke from Judge Thayer for having failed to tackle the police and prosecuting authorities of Norfolk County, all by his valiant self!

And then poor Joseph Rosen, the Jewish peddler of cloth, who had sold Vanzetti a piece of suiting at a great bargain because it had a hole in it. He had gone with Vanzetti to show the goods to Mrs. Brini, and they had had a long talk. Three weeks later he had read of Vanzetti's arrest for banditry, and had seen his picture and recognized him, and realized that it was the day he had sold the cloth. He told his story to the jury, and Katzmann provided a four-hour circus for bored jurymen by kidding Rosen's Yiddisher dialect, and asking where he had been on a certain day a year ago, and where he had been three weeks ago. Poor Rosen tried to protest that if he had a little time he could remember some of that; which of course Katzmann and the jury took to mean that he could have the lawyers' help in remembering it.

As a matter of fact it would have been easy for the prosecution to have verified Rosen's story if it had cared to, for he said he had sold cloth to many persons in Plymouth that day, including the wife of the chief of police. But it was as Lee Swenson had told Cornelia—hardly any use at all to put on foreign witnesses; the jury took it for granted that their stories were "built," and whether they were all "built," or only a few of them "built," made no difference in the result. Of course no jury would ever dream that the cultured gentlemen who represented the Commonwealth would do such a thing as tell a witness what to say! Never in a thousand years could they be made to realize that of the five identification witnesses upon whom the case against Sacco rested, one was a many times convicted crook, one a hysterical prostitute, one a half-wit, one a disordered fantast, and one a feeble victim of police pressure; all five of them persons who had made statements identifying other men as the bandits, or else saying that they could not identify any one. And all this known to the prosecution, and some of it to the judge on the bench—so that the procedure represented a conspiracy between the district attorney and the judge, to deceive the jury, to hide the essential facts from them, and persuade them that white was black.

IV

The great day of the trial: Bartolomeo Vanzetti taking the stand in his own defense! He looked neat and proper in his new black suit, clean white collar and little black silk tie. He had grown bald about the temples during his long confinement, but he still had his heavy droopy mustache; his earnest, deeply lined face was that of a student and thinker.

They took him out of the "cage" to give his testimony, and stood him in the prisoner's dock, with a little low railing before him, where for hours he answered the questions of his lawyers. His manner was quiet and courteous, and his command of English remarkable; he had profited by his year of study to drop most of his Italian peculiarities, and the newspapers commented upon his education, so that Cornelia was proud of her pupil. Only once did he let himself be goaded by Katzmann into a flash of "redness"; when he had occasion to refer to the place where some of his friends lived, working on the railroad near Springfield: "Yes, in a shanty, you know, the little house where the Italian live and work like a beast, the Italian workingman in this country."

He told the jury the story of his life: his childhood in Italy, his slavery to a pastry cook, the breakdown of his health, the death of his mother. He told about coming to America, his work in the great rich club in New York City—he no longer called it a "clooba"—and then in the smart restaurant; his work in the brickyard, the stone quarry, on the railroad, the Worcester reservoir—near the home of Judge Thayer; then in a wire mill, then for the Plymouth Cordage Company. He told about his going to Mexico, because he did not believe in war; he had learned by now that he had not been liable to the draft, and he mentioned it, but apparently without result.

He told about his fish-selling business—and the defense counsel showed his license to dig clams, and the receipts for his fish. All the morning of the South Braintree crime he had been selling fish in Plymouth—in Cherry Street, Standish Avenue, Cherry Court, Suosso's Lane, Castle Street. A little after the noon hour he had met Rosen, and bought from him the piece of suiting with a hole in it; Vanzetti still had the cloth, and it was introduced in evidence. He had taken Rosen to Mrs. Brini, because she worked in a woolen mill, and was a judge of cloth. In the afternoon he had left his cart in the yard of Melvin Corl, the fisherman, and had gone down to the shore, where Corl was painting a boat, and at the actual moment of the South Braintree murders he had been chatting with Corl. The owner of the boat-yard, Gessi, had come along during the talk, and another man, Holmes. Later Bart had dug clams and bait, and had gone home and had his supper at six o'clock, and had spent the evening in Plymouth.

He told about his doings from that April fifteenth to the day of his arrest three weeks later. He had gone to the club in East Boston, and had been asked to go to New York to see about Salsedo and Elia. But there Katzmann and Thayer stopped him; it was the intention of the district attorney to argue that the defendants had no reason to be afraid on the night of their arrest, and to tell lies to the police. Katzmann wanted to argue that the worst that anarchists had to fear was getting a free trip to Italy; that as Sacco was going anyhow, the claim of fear was obviously silly. The entire ruling class of Massachusetts was going to maintain that argument for six years; so the jury must be kept from realizing that sixty-seven hours prior to the arrest of Sacco and Vanzetti, their friend and comrade Salsedo had jumped, or had been thrown to his death from the fourteenth story of the Park Row Building in New York! The defense came back to it, again and again, but they were blocked here and blocked there, and the real meaning of the matter was never made clear to the jury.

It was the aim of the prosecution, not so much to refute the testimony of Vanzetti, as to rouse the prejudices of the jurors against him; to fill them with emotions of hatred and fear, so that they would be incapable of thinking; to make them see an anarchist infidel draft dodger as a depraved wretch, deserving to die many deaths. When the time came for cross-examination, Mr. Katzmann's first question had nothing to do with the problem whether Vanzetti had sat in a bandit car and pointed a shotgun out of the rear window; it had to do with the problem whether the jury was going to find him guilty, regardless of whether he had sat in the bandit car or not. Said Mr. Katzmann: "So you left Plymouth, Mr. Vanzetti, in May, 1917, to dodge the draft, did you?"

Mr. Katzmann of course knew perfectly well that Vanzetti had not been liable to the draft; but he went on to rub in the sneer, with that mock indignation acquired in the course of eleven years' service for the Commonwealth: "When this country was at war, you ran away, so you would not have to fight as a soldier?" The district attorney was not interested to question Vanzetti about the South Braintree crime, and try to prove that he was there; the district attorney was not interested in trying to break Vanzetti's alibi; he was only interested to prove that Vanzetti had lied to the police, and that he was unpatriotic.

He took up the prisoner's effort to organize a meeting, and the pitiful circular he had drafted: "You were going to advise in a public meeting men who had gone to war? Are you that man?" "Yes, sir," answered Bart, quietly, "I am that man, not the man you want me, but I am that man." The newspapers made much of this scene; it was what their readers were hungry for. "A tensely dramatic moment," said the Boston *Traveler*, and described how the prosecutor "thundered." Said the *American,* "The district attorney's voice was vibrant with emotion. It thrilled the spectators."

v

But it was during the cross-examination of Sacco that the great official's vibrations did their heaviest thundering, and the spectators, and readers of newspapers, got their choicest thrills. Nicola Sacco had a poor command of English, and had to call for the aid of the interpreter-crook; also he had poor command of his emotions, and could be jeered at and goaded, provoked into saying things that would ruin him. The district attorney asked him seventeen hundred questions; and more about patriotism than about anything else. Said Mr. Katzmann: "Did you leave this country in May, 1917?"

Said Sacco: "I can't answer in one word."

"Please answer my questions, Mr. Sacco"—"in thundering voice," the newspapers said. "One week before the day of the first draft in May, 1917, did you leave this country?" There followed a long dialogue, a scene which made Cornelia think of a deer in the forest, when a wolverine or lynx or other fierce creature drops upon him from a tree, and chews into his neck as he runs. That is a common event in nature; but in this case appeared a phenomenon unknown to zoology—another animal running alongside the fleeing deer, to keep any one from interfering with the neck-chewing process. This creature went by the name of a webthayer.

"Did you say yesterday you love a free country?"

"Yes, sir."

"Did you love this country in the month of May, 1917?"

"I did not say,—I don't want to say I did not love this country."

"Did you love this country in that month of 1917?"

"If you can, Mr. Katzmann, if you give me that,—I could explain—"

"Do you understand that question?"

"Yes."

"Then will you please answer it?"

"I can't answer in one word."

"You can't say whether you loved the United States of America one week before the day you enlisted for the first draft?"

"I can't say in one word, Mr. Katzmann."

"Did you love this country in the last week of May, 1917?"

"That is pretty hard for me to say in one word, Mr. Katzmann."

"There are two words you can use, Mr. Sacco, yes or no. Which one is it?"

"Yes."

"And in order to show your love for this United States of America when she was about to call upon you to become a soldier you ran away to Mexico."

That question was, obviously enough, not intended to elicit any information of use to the jury; that question was, purely and simply, a sneer. And Katzmann hammered and hammered upon it; eleven separate times he repeated the word "love." First, did Sacco run away for love of his country? Then, did he run away for love of his wife? "Would it be your idea of showing your love for your wife that when she needed you, you ran away from her?"

Said Sacco: "I did not run away from her."

Said Sacco's lawyer: "I object."

But the webthayer said: "He may answer,"—and added, with his usual cunning: "Simply on the question of credibility, that is all."

So the wolverine or lynx went on with the neck-chewing. "Would it be your idea of love for your wife that you were to run from her when she needed you?"

Said Mr. McAnarney: "Pardon me. I ask for an exception on that."

The webthayer excluded the question; but obligingly indicated to the neck-chewer how he might go on. "He had not admitted he ran away."

So, of course, the torture was resumed. "Then I will ask you, didn't you run away from Milford so as to avoid being a soldier for the United States?"

"I did not run away."

"You mean you walked away?"

"Yes."

"You don't understand me when I say 'run away,' do you?"

"That is vulgar."

"That is vulgar?"

"You can say a little intelligent, Mr. Katzmann."

"Don't you think going away from your country is a vulgar thing to do when she needs you?"

"I don't believe in war."

"You don't believe in war?"

"No, sir."

"Do you think it is a cowardly thing to do what you did?"

"No, sir."

"Do you think it is a brave thing to do what you did?"

"Yes, sir."

"Do you think it would be a brave thing to go away from your own wife?"

"No."

"When she needed you?"

"No."

VI

The prosecutor kept at the wife question until he had got all the hate out of it he could, and then he took up the sneer that "wops" come to America to make money. "Is it because,— is your love for the United States of America commensurate with the amount of money you can get in this country per week?"

"Better conditions, yes."

"Better country to make money, isn't it?"

"Yes."

"Is your love for this country measured by the amount of money you can earn here?"

"I never loved money."

This went on, until the defense broke in again. Said Mr. Jeremiah McAnarney: "No, if your Honor please. And I might state now I want my objection to go to this whole line of interrogation."

Said the webthayer: "I think you opened it up."

Said the lawyer, very humbly: "No, if your Honor please, I think I have not."

Said the webthayer: "I think you have,"—and went on to give an argument which for prejudice-carrying capacity exceeded anything the fertile mind of the district attorney had been able to conceive. It was the contention of the defendants that on the night of their arrest they had been going with Boda and Orciani to visit some of the anarchist comrades, and collect the dangerous literature from their homes, and hide it until the storm of persecution had blown over. And now here was the webthayer, elaborating an even more complicated sneer than the one about love of country and of wife. Said he: "It seems to me you have. Are you going to claim much of all the collection of the literature and the books was really in the interest of the United States as well as these people and therefore it has opened up the credibility of the defendant when he claims that all that work was done really for the interest of the United States in getting his literature out of the way?"

Said Mr. McAnarney: "That claim is not presented in anything tantamount to the language just used by the Court, and in view of the record as it stands at this time I object to this line of inquiry."

There followed upon this a phenomenon never observed in any forest; the wolverine or lynx desisting from his neck-chewing, and letting the webthayer take his place on the victim's back! The webthayer liked his mockery so well that he repeated it five separate times, in detail, and several other times by implication. "Are you going to claim that what the defendant did was in the interest of the United States?" And each time with a broader wink at the jury, a broader grin from the jury in response. When the defense lawyer objected, "Your Honor please, I now object to your Honor's statement as prejudicial to the rights of the defendants and ask that the statement be withdrawn from the jury"—then instantly the webthayer was on the alert to protect the record and make everything look all right. "There is no prejudicial remark made that I know of, and none were intended. I simply asked you, sir, as to whether you propose to offer evidence as to what you said to me."

After which he went on to repeat the sneer and rub it in; and closed, as usual, by telling the wolverine or lynx how to get back to the neck-chewing: "I will let you inquire further as to what he meant by the expression." So, of course, Katzmann took the hint, and went on, exactly as if there had been no interruption: "What did you mean when you said yesterday you loved a free country?"

Poor Nick! He was a talkative, eager young fellow, a propagandist; and for fourteen months and two days they had had him behind steel bars. He had boiled, he had seethed, he had all but exploded. And now suddenly he saw a hope! "Give me a chance to explain," he pleaded; and the cunning prosecutor said: "I am asking you to explain now." Actually, the great Mr. Katzmann asked him to explain! The great Judge Thayer said it would be all right for him to explain! The jury, the spectators, everybody was ready to listen—while he told what he thought about America, about Italy, about liberty, about the workers and their rights, the rich and the poor, good food and vegetables, schools, free speech, Debs, the capitalist class, Harvard College, D. Rockefeller, Morgan, working people, war, socialism, Abraham Lincoln, Abe Jefferson, the Irish, the Germans, the French, governments, devilment and robbery—everything! Perhaps he could not convert them, but at least he could make them understand him!

Forgive him if his stump-speech is long—he has all the conclusions of a lifetime to state! Forgive him if it is jumbled—he has no time to arrange it, he does not know at what moment they may shut him off again and lock him up for another fourteen months! Forgive him if it is incoherent—he is groping desperately for words in a strange tongue, stammering, halting, starting again, tripping himself up with his excitement, the intensity of his convictions. And meantime the bland prosecutor stands silent, smiling—why should he trouble to work, when his victim will hang himself with his own rope? The judge is content, for he knows it will look well in the record—the defendant has had a chance to express himself, no possible claim that he was misrepresented. Most content of all are the jurymen—because they have power to punish a wop who is insulting and defiling all their most sacred Yankee prejudices.

Said Nicola Sacco, in defense of his life:

"When I was in Italy, a boy, I was a Republican, so I always thinking Republican has more chance to manage education, develop, to build some day his family, to raise the child and education, if you could. But that was my opinion; so when I came to this country I saw there was not what I was thinking before, but there was all the difference, because I been working in Italy not so hard as I been work in this country. I could live free there just as well. Work in the same condition but not so hard, about seven or eight hours a day, better food. I mean genuine. Of course, over here is good food, because it is bigger country, to any those who got money to spend, not for the working and laboring class, and in Italy is more opportunity to laborer to eat vegetable, more fresh, and I came in this country. When I been started work here very hard and been work thirteen years, hard worker, I could not been afford much a family the way I did have the idea before. I could not put any money in the bank; I could no push my boy some to go to school and other things. I teach over here men who is with me. The free idea gives any man a chance to profess his own idea, not the supreme idea, not to give any person, not to be like Spain in position, yes, about twenty centuries ago, but to give a chance to print and education, literature, free speech, that I see it was all wrong. I could see the best men, intelligent, education, they been arrested and sent to prison and died in prison for years and years without getting them out, and Debs, one of the great men in his country, he is in prison, still away in prison, because he is a Socialist. He wanted the laboring class to have better conditions and better living, more education, give a push his son if he could have a chance some day, but they put him in prison. Why? Because the capitalist class, they know, they are against that, because the capitalist class, they don't want our child to go to high school or college or Harvard College. There would be no chance, there would not be no,—they don't want the working class educationed; they want the working class to be a low all the times, be underfoot, and not to be up with the head. So, sometimes, you see, the Rockefellers, Morgans, they give fifty,—I mean they give five hundred thousand dollars to Harvard College, they give a million dollars for another school. Every day say, 'Well, D. Rockefeller is a great man, the best man in the country.' I want to ask him who is going to Harvard College? What benefit the working class they will get by those million dollars they give by Rockefeller, D. Rockefellers. They won't get, the poor class, they won't have no chance to go to Harvard College because men who is getting $21 a week or $30 a week, I don't care if he gets $80 a week, if he gets a family of five children he can't live and send his child and go to Harvard College if he wants to eat everything nature will give him. If he wants to eat like a cow, and that is the best thing but I want men to live like men. I like men to get everything that nature will give best, because they belong,—we are not the friend of any other place, but we are belong to nations. So that is why my idea has been changed. So that is why I love people who labor and work and see better conditions every day develop, makes no more war. We no want fight by the gun, and we don't want to destroy young men. The mother been suffering for building the young man. Some day need a little more bread, so when the time the mother get some bread or profit out of that boy, the Rockefellers, Morgans, and· some of the peoples, high class, they send to war. Why? What is war? The war is not shoots like Abraham Lincoln's and Abe Jefferson, to fight for the free country, for the better education to give chance to any other peoples, not the white people but the black and the others, because they believe and know they are mens like the rest, but they are war for the great millionaire. No war for the civilization of men. They are war for business, million dollars come on the side. What right we have to kill each other? I been work for the Irish. I have been working with the German fellow, with the French, many other peoples. I love them people just as I could love my wife, and my people for that did receive me. Why should I go kill them men? What he done to me? He never done anything, so I don't believe in no war. I want to destroy those guns. All I can say, the Government put the literature, give us educations. I remember in Italy, a long time ago, about sixty years ago, I should say, yes, about sixty years ago, the Government they could not control very much those two,—devilment went on, and robbery, so one of the government in the cabinet he says, 'If you want to destroy those devilments, if you want to take off all those criminals, you ought to give a chance to Socialist literature, education of people, emancipation. That is why I destroy governments, boys.' That is why my idea I love Socialists. That is why I like people who want education and living, building, who is good, just as much as they could. That is all."

VIII

July 7th was the date of this oration. Three days previously all patriots had celebrated the Declaration of Independence, with its opening assertion that "all men are created equal." If the author of that document, "Abe Jefferson," could have been present in the Dedham court-house, he would have been able to understand the blundering protest of an uneducated foreigner, chained for life to an edge-trimming machine in a shoe-factory. But not so this jury, not this judge nor this prosecuting attorney! To them it was treason; and the moment the orator ceased, the wolverine or lynx was on his neck again. "And that is why you love the United States of America? She is back more than twenty centuries like Spain, is she?"

Worse yet, the presumptuous wop had dared to insult Harvard College! The district attorney waited until after lunch, to refresh himself and gather his energies to deal with such insolence. "Did you say in substance you could not send your boy to Harvard? Don't you know Harvard educates more boys of poor people free than any other university in the United States of America?"

The defense lawyers objected, but were overruled, and poor Sacco had to answer. If he had been an authority on educational statistics, his answer would have been that Harvard was educating free something over one hundred students, while the University of Wisconsin had educated free in that year five thousand, eight hundred and ninety-five, and the University of California had educated free eleven thousand, three hundred and forty.

But alas, poor Nick was not an authority on educational statistics, and could only say that he didn't know; thereby confessing to a more serious crime than first degree murder. Said the outraged Mr. Katzmann: "So without the light of knowledge on that subject, you are condemning even Harvard University, are you, as being a place for rich men?"

More argument, more interruptions; the defense lawyers protesting, Judge Thayer overruling them—he and Katzmann like two skillful basket-ball players, keeping the ball in play between them and working it down the field to the goal. "Did you intend to condemn Harvard College?" (Objection overruled.) "Were you ready to say none but the rich could go there without knowing about offering scholarships?" (Objection overruled.) "Does your boy go to the public schools? Are there any schools in the town you come from in Italy that compare with the school your boy goes to?" (Objection.) And then, free nursing in the town of Stoughton! The number of children in the schools of Boston, and what did Sacco know about it! Said Mr. McAnarney: "I object to that answer. I object to the question and the answer." Said Judge Thayer: "The question may stand, and the answer also."

To Cornelia Thornwell, watching this scene, listening to these interminable wrangles, this was not a real procedure in a court; this was some kind of crazy dream, a world of cross-questions and crooked answers, another Alice in Wonderland. Yes, that was it—Cornelia was in the home of the White Rabbit and the March Hare, the Mock Turtle and the Queen of Hearts! "He's murdering the time! Off with his head!" A world where things changed their form suddenly, where they grew enormously big and terrifying and then shrunk to littleness, so that you had to laugh at them! A world in which a blond and genial gentleman with bursting red pulpy face turned suddenly into a wolverine or lynx, chewing a deer's neck—and then into a basketball player, romping down a field with a judge! Anything but a responsible public official, conducting a judicial procedure involving human life!

> I'll be judge, I'll be jury,
> Said cunning old Fury;
> I'll try the whole cause and condemn you to death!

They got onto the question of the literature which Sacco and Vanzetti claimed they had been intending to gather up. "Books relating to anarchy, were they not?" "Not all of them." "How many of them?" "Well all together. We are Socialists, democratic, any other socialistic information, Socialists, Syndicalists, Anarchists, any paper." They discussed for a while what had been intended with the literature, whether it was to be destroyed or only hidden for a while. Sacco admitted it was to be hidden. "Certainly, because they are educational for book, educational." Said the prosecutor: "An education in anarchy, wasn't it?" Said the witness: "Why, certainly. Anarchistic is not criminals." This greatly incensed the district attorney. "I did not ask you if they are criminals or not. Nor are you to pass upon that, sir." What a light this threw upon his purpose! And upon the argument which Cornelia was to hear in future years from the whole of official Massachusetts—that the purpose of·this cross-examination had been to prove that Sacco and Vanzetti had not been genuine "Reds," but were merely making a pretense at it!

On and on, with no end in sight. Presently the wolverine or lynx was back at his neck-chewing—though you would think his victim must by now be bled to death. "And you are a man who tells this jury that the United States of America is a disappointment to you?" Again an objection of the defense, and the webthayer telling the wolverine or lynx how to proceed. The judge pointed out that Katzmann had made the mistake of "assuming" that Sacco was the man. So of course Katzmann took the hint, and framed it as a question; *was* Sacco the man? The lawyers again objected, and the judge overruled, and the lawyers asked an exception, and then the victim couldn't understand the phrase, "passed judgment upon the United States of America," and it had to be explained to him: "Well, tell us about how disappointed you were, and what you did not find and what you expected to find. Are you that man?" Yes, Sacco admitted, he was the man; and the jury was greatly enlightened.

IX

The ordeal was over at last, and a court official came to Cornelia Thornwell, saying that His Honor would like to see her in his chambers. Another interview with the judge—the third during the trial! It was intolerable to him that members of the aristocracy which he reverenced should be sitting there in court day by day disapproving of the procedure; he must argue with them, he must explain and defend himself, he must bring the great ones to appreciate his services. He meant it for a compliment to them; but unfortunately he paid the same compliment to newspaper reporters and photographers, and other persons whom the aristocracy does not recognize.

He had taken off his black silk robe and hung it on a hook, and was now a quite ordinary little old man, small, narrow-shouldered, with white hair and a feeble chin and bloodless complexion. He rose from his chair and bowed her to a seat, and she saw that his hands were trembling, and his blinking worse than usual—he was a tired old man, who had been through a severe ordeal and was wrought up and suffering. He was fussy in his manner, over-cordial and lacking in repose; he repeated himself, saying the same words several times: "Now, Mrs. Thornwell, you see, you see! You see what I told you about those men!"

"How do you mean, Judge Thayer?"

"You heard the testimony that fellow Sacco gave? You see he admits it, he admits the worst—they are arnychists, of the most desperate character—they say it, defiantly—they defy the court and all society!"

"But, Judge Thayer, I have always known they were anarchists. I don't understand they are on trial for anarchism."

"No, but it shows their character, their ideas. They have no respect for the law—they are men who would commit crimes."

"But I heard Sacco's employer testify that he was a good workman, that he had not been absent from his machine but one day in a long time—he was trusted with the keys to the factory—he had been a night-watchman—"

"Oh, but Mrs. Thornwell, you should hear what Kelley says outside!"

"What do you mean, what Kelley says?"

"I cannot tell you his words, they are not fit for a lady's ears; the substance of it is that Kelley is afraid to tell the truth about what he thinks of Sacco."

"Judge Thayer, you appal me!"

"How do you mean, madame?"

"You are going outside the testimony of the case, considering gossip that people bring you, things that the witnesses are unwilling to say under oath!"

"I am dealing with people who are terrorized. You cannot imagine the condition in this community, the time we have had getting men to come forward and testify at all. Think of the situation, Mrs. Thornwell—what it means, where it was necessary to summon nearly seven hundred veniremen in order to get a jury!"

"And so you think that our legal system has broken down, and you throw it overboard! I have read that men were executed upon the gossip of spies in Turkey under the sultans, and in Russia under the tsars, but I did not know we had come to that in Massachusetts."

The old man's face showed that he had blood in him after all. He held up a shaking hand to stop her. "Mrs. Thornwell, it is a grave impropriety for you to address such words to a judge who is presiding over a trial!"

Cornelia rose. "You well know that I did not seek this meeting, Judge Thayer. If it is your idea that you are free to say what you please in condemnation of these men, and that impropriety begins when you hear what you do not wish to hear, then I would advise you to confine your talks to your social inferiors, for I have not been brought up to carry on conversation on that basis."

The pitiful old man had risen, trembling so that he had to hold onto the back of the chair to sustain himself. His voice became shrill—it was like a thin strip of steel. "Mrs. Thornwell, I deeply regret having to say such a thing to you, but it amounts to contempt of court, what you have said to a judge while he is sitting upon a case."

"I will leave your chambers," said Cornelia, haughtily, "and trust that you will refrain from troubling me with further invitations. But I will not fail to tell you what is the opinion of every disinterested person in the court-room—that the scenes witnessed to-day constitute a travesty upon justice, the worst I have ever heard of in my life!"

She started to the door. But even then the old man could not give up. He came hurrying behind her, stretching out a hand that seemed to be palsied. "Mrs. Thornwell! I warn you! You are letting yourself be deceived! You are being used by unscrupulous persons! We are surrounded by criminals, by desperate and embittered enemies of our institutions! You owe it to your ancestry and your heritage to stand behind us—we are trying to protect the community—a public service—patriotic

duty—a   desperate   danger—arnychists—assassination—conspiracy—" they were snatches of words that Cornelia heard,
while she was going down the corridor, not yet out of sound
of the shrill metallic voice.

                                        X

Frank P. Sibley was a star reporter of the Boston *Globe,*
covering this trial in a special effort to be fair. The *Globe* aims
to be what is known as a "family newspaper," and has become
one of the wealthiest in America upon a policy of publishing the
name of everybody in Eastern Massachusetts not less than twice
every year. It gives pages of local gossip from every town and
village: "For the Friday evening meeting of the Ladies' Aid
Society of the Methodist Episcopal Church a delicious walnut
cake was provided by Mrs. Amanda Lubb, who is visiting her
niece, Mrs. Peter Bobbs of Scrugham Corners," and so on.
Sibley, who contributed to a column of sentimental comment
signed "Uncle Dudley," was an old-fashioned Bostonian, having
notions of honor and dignity now going out of fashion. He was
covering this murder trial as a high civic duty, signing his daily
articles, and taking them very seriously.

And here he saw the judge on the bench, forcing himself upon
newspapermen, insisting upon talking about the case with them,
such an impropriety as had never been heard of. Judge Thayer
joining reporters walking back to the court-house from lunch,
asking them what they thought of his conduct of the case;
telling them of other murder trials he had conducted, and of
compliments he had received from justices of the Supreme
Judicial Court of the Commonwealth for his skillful handling
and exact rulings! Sibley could not tell such things in his paper,
for that was not what several hundred thousand families of
Eastern Massachusetts wanted to read with their morning cod-
fish balls. But he thought it his duty to write a letter to the
attorney-general of the Commonwealth—to which that blue-
blood gentleman thought it his duty to make no reply!

Did a rumor come to Judge Thayer? Or was there something
in the attitude of the newspapermen which conveyed, even to
his obtuse mind, that he was not "making a hit"? Anyhow, he
was anxious; and now in that private dining-room of the Ded-

ham Inn where the reporters lunched and discussed their stories, comparing notes so as to protect one another from error, they were surprised to have the judge come up to them without warning and announce: "I think I am entitled to have a statement published in the Boston papers that this trial is being conducted in a fair and impartial manner."

Naturally, the group of men at the table were taken aback. Even a newspaper reporter must respect somebody, and who should it be if not the learned judge of the Superior Court, presiding at a trial which involved the attendance of some two hundred persons, and was costing the county of Norfolk some two thousand dollars per day?

Thayer turned to the star reporter of the *Globe*. "Sibley, you're the oldest. What do you think? Is this trial being fairly and impartially conducted?" And Sibley had to think in a hurry. "Your Honor, I have never seen anything like it." His Honor stood and pondered that compliment. Some little bird must have whispered to him that it would be better to take it at face value; he turned on his heel and walked out of the room.

And now came the cross-questioning of Sacco, with the judge on the bench delivering his elaborate sneer at the defense: "Are you going to claim that your client, in collecting this literature, was acting in the interest of the United States?" The question revealed such an obvious effort to distort Sacco's meaning, and expose him to the prejudice and hatred of the jury, that Sibley quoted the sentence in his story; with the result that during the recess he found himself summoned into the judge's chambers. His Honor took him to task for having quoted such a sentence; no such question had been asked, and the judge had verified it by getting the transcript of his remarks. He presented to Sibley a typewritten record, upon which the question did not appear.

Sibley, of course, was embarrassed, and said that he had written the sentence down as he heard it; he could only assume that his hearing had played him false. He was about to ask if the judge wished him to publish a retraction, when the bailiff entered, announcing that the jury had arrived. The judge entered court, and so did Sibley. Next day, when the actual record of the case was available, the reporter consulted it, and found that it showed Judge Thayer's question, in the exact words quoted in the *Globe!* Five times the old man had asked

that question explicitly, and several times more by implication;
but now he had got frightened, and in an effort to cheat the
public and hide the truth, he had gone to the extreme of preparing a doctored version of the record, and trying to palm it
off on a reporter!

XI

The funds of the defense had run out. A collection was taken
among the sympathizers at the trial, and six hundred dollars
raised; but that was not enough. Cornelia wrote letters and
sent telegrams; then, in one of those moods of mischief which
had always been incomprehensible to the Thornwells, she called
up her daughter, Deborah, at the North Shore place. "Deborah,
there is some trouble, very serious—something I must see you
about at once. No, I can't talk about it over the telephone, you
must come here to Dedham." She used, as nearly as she could
remember, the words by which Deborah had summoned her to
Boston. The daughter, of course, thought instantly of Betty and
Joe, having always this scandal hanging over her head.

It was a drive of two or three hours, and she arrived about
lunch-time. Her mother was waiting at the Dedham Inn, and
there was Betty, looking very lovely, though pale and tired—no
visible trace of a scandal. But there was a trace of tears in the
child's eyes—one does not so easily sever family ties—even during the class struggle! "What is it?" asked Deborah, of her
mother.

Cornelia replied that they couldn't talk about it here. "Wait
until the afternoon session is over."

"You mean of the court?"

"Yes, my child, I cannot miss this afternoon, there is to be
some important testimony. You come with me."

"To a murder-trial, Mother!"

"Surely, if I can stand a murder-trial, my daughter can!"

Mrs. Rupert Alvin had never done such a thing in her life.
She regarded courts as vulgar places, and attending them as evidence of sensation-seeking. She might get her name into the
papers; she looked around for reporters, in the same spirit as
her ancestors in this neighborhood had looked for wild Indians
with tomahawks. She met some of the ladies, old and young, who

were aiding the defense, and managed to find something wrong, either socially or sartorially, with every one of them—though she kept her thoughts to herself. "Mother, is there anything wrong about Betty?" she whispered. Cornelia said no, it wasn't that.

They sat in the court-room: Deborah straight as a ramrod, motionless for three hours. Her manner said, Do not assume that I have any interest in this, or that I give it my sanction. She heard Guadagni, journalist and lecturer, telling the story of his lunch with Sacco in Boston on the day of the South Braintree crime. The murders had been committed at a little after three; and from one to two, or later, Guadagni had been chatting with Sacco, discussing the banquet being given by a group of Italians, in honor of the editor of the Boston *Transcript*, who had been decorated by the King of Italy in recognition of his services in getting America into the war. The affair took place that same day—which was how Guadagni fixed the date; Fred Katzmann strove in vain to make him admit that it might have been some other day.

"You know, Mother," said Deborah, when it was over, "those Italians don't think anything at all of telling lies to help one another out of trouble."

"Yes, my dear, I know," said Cornelia. "It's just like the men of our own family, sitting up nights fixing their stories for the Jerry Walker case."

And when they were outside again, apart from the crowd, and the danger of reporters, "Well, what do you think of our boys, Deborah?"

"You mean those two prisoners? Mother, I don't see how you can force yourself to tolerate such people! Dark, sinister-looking—"

"Most Italians are dark; but that doesn't make them murderers."

Deborah shuddered. "I feel the hate in them—something frightful! Those set, intent faces—"

"My child, they are intent upon the question of whether they are going to the electric chair. It seems really important to them."

XII

They went to Cornelia's room in the hotel, and she lay down to rest. Deborah sat up straight. "Now, Mother, what is it?"

So Cornelia told her: "My dear, I have to pain you, I must sell my jewels."

"Mother! What do you mean?"

"The defense has run out of funds, and I am not going to let those boys lose the chance for their lives. I must have some cash, and there is nothing I can think of but to sell my jewels."

"But Mother, how dreadful!" Deborah was shocked into incoherence. The family heirlooms—they were priceless—treasures with spiritual associations—surely the children had some rights!

"You miss the point, my child," interrupted Cornelia. "I want to sell them to *you.*"

Deborah said, "Oh!" She looked at her mother—no trace of a smile on the little round face, no twinkle in the soft brown eyes! Deborah said, "Oh!" again, and began to realize that this was another manifestation of that sense of humor which her father had found so untimely. A bit of maternal whimsy had brought a big limousine rolling its stately way from the North Shore to Dedham!

Cornelia proceeded with entire gravity. "Of course I know that some day you will have these jewels, you and Clara and Alice. But meantime, I have to have money for this case. You know Queen Isabella sold her jewels to finance Christopher Columbus—at least, the legend says so. I want to sell mine in a still worthier cause, and I offer you a third share."

"How much money do you have to have, Mother?"

"Five thousand dollars. I have no idea what those jewels are worth—it must be thirty or forty thousand—"

"We are not going to give up our family jewels, Mother, you know that, so don't be foolish. If the money was for you, none of us would hesitate a moment; but it seems so dreadful to us to have you throwing everything away on these anarchists— men who hate our country—"

"Now, my daughter, let us not go into that. I am making you a strictly business proposition. I offer to sell you one-third of my jewels for five thousand dollars. I will give you a formal receipt, and go to the bank and get them the first day I am in town."

"You know I don't care about that, Mother." Deborah sat, gazing in front of her for a minute. It was clear that she was in a trap, no way out. So with no more ado she went to her handbag, took out her checkbook and fountain-pen, sat at the desk, and created five thousand dollars.

She possessed the power to do that magical thing; she did it frequently—at the board-meetings of orphan-asylums, in homes for the halt and the deaf and the blind, in vestry-rooms and parish-houses of Episcopal churches. The fact that she had such power, and was willing to exercise it, caused a kind of halo of glory to exist about her; it affected the souls of charity workers and superintendents of institutions, of curates and clergymen, so that a trembling seized them when the great Mrs. Alvin swept into the room, their knees went weak under them and almost gave way. Deborah knew of this, and while she pretended to be unaware of it, the pretense was highly artificial; in reality this sense of power was what she lived for and by, and she watched the persons with whom she dealt, and expected them to pay her exactly the right tribute of deference and excitement, and if any one of them failed, then Deborah was incensed against that person—though she always found some other reason for it, the person was too talkative, self-assertive, overdressed or underdressed, anything that wasn't "Boston."

Betty, shrewd little minx, had learned to analyze these manifestations: a fascinating study in psychology, a mingling of worldly glory with Christian humility, a checker-board pattern, black and white, in a woman's soul. To be proud of your money and what you did with your money was the very acme of vulgarity, it was the thing which marked you as the wife of a "lumberman," or a "Pittsburgh millionaire." So you were never proud of your money, you were proud of your lack of pride, of the distance which an assured breeding put between you and your money. You associated yourself with the poor and lowly, because that was your Christian duty; and if the poor and lowly looked up to you, it was because of your Christian virtue, and not because you had the power to turn them out to starve and freeze. If they were really refined and worthy poor, they understood this, and so everything was upon a high plane; it was

God who had appointed all things, and assigned to each his station and form of conduct, and each did what God wished, and felt the emotions which God inspired. Such was the collective soul of Trinity Church in the City of Boston.

XIII

Other witnesses testified to the alibi of Sacco, supporting Guadagni. Dentamore, a bank department manager, had joined them in Boni's restaurant, and taken part in the talk about the banquet which the Italians were giving to the editor of the Boston *Transcript*. A Boston grocer testified that Sacco had paid him a bill on that day; he had his notebook, with the payment entered. Also there was a deposition of a clerk in the consulate, now in Italy, telling how Sacco had applied for a passport on that day; Eugene Lyons had gone to Italy to get that evidence.

There was more alibi testimony for Vanzetti. His friend Alfonsina Brini took the stand and told how he had sold her fish that morning, and brought Rosen to sell her cloth that afternoon. The district attorney was so angry in his cross-questioning that he made her cry; it seemed to him unpardonable that she should have made an alibi for Bart on two separate days, for two separate crimes; he would not realize that Bart had been practically a member of the Brini family, ever since his coming to Plymouth nine years back, and that all the Brinis saw him every day. The district attorney made Mrs. Brini stand up while he read into the record a stipulation to the effect that she had testified to an alibi for Vanzetti on another occasion. The jury was not supposed to know anything about the Plymouth trial and conviction, but of course they did know all about it, and smiled to one another while this statement was read. The lawyer fellows were trying to tie red tape over their eyes, but they would not be blinded!

Another legal hocus-pocus: in order to avoid having the Plymouth conviction brought into evidence, the defense had had to agree not to introduce character witnesses for either defendant. Now the prosecution came forward with a demand that the jury be instructed to disregard all evidence as to the good character of either defendant. So Cornelia Thornwell heard one of those voices which had cried to her in vain in Plymouth county-jail: not the voice of a ghost, but of the far-seeing Vanzetti! The very trick he had explained to her—his enemies had made a convict of him, and now were using his conviction to cast a cloud over both him and Nick, to send them to their deaths. Mr. Katzmann put on his sternest manner and read to the jury the stipulation:

"The Commonwealth assents to the request of both the defendants that all evidence heretofore offered in the course of this trial to the effect that one or both of said defendants bore the reputation of being peaceful and law-abiding citizens, be stricken from the record of this trial, and that such evidence heretofore offered be entirely disregarded by the jury so that the result of striking same from the record there is no evidence before the jury that either or both of said defendants bore the reputation of being a peaceful and law-abiding citizen."

All in vain the years that Nicola Sacco had worked for the Three-K Shoe Company, earning from forty to sixty dollars a week as expert edge-trimmer, with extra pay as night-watchman for long periods! All in vain those annual gardens full of ripe red tomatoes, and the surplus given to Mr. Kelley, the boss! All in vain the ten dollars a week Rosina had put by, till they had fifteen hundred in the savings-bank, with the record of deposits to show that it had been got by labor, not by hold-ups! All in vain the hard toil which Bartolomeo Vanzetti had performed for the owning class of New England, in stone-quarries and brickyards, on railroads and reservoirs! In vain his years as fish-peddler, the friendship of hundreds of Italian housewives, of little Italian children, so that when they heard of his dreadful fate, they wept and wrung their hands, and would never cease to talk about him all the days of their lives! In vain his plea, "Save Nick, he got the wife and kids!" Again the lawyers made their demands for separate trials, but Judge Thayer stood firm to save the funds of Norfolk County. Ten thousand dollars a week for seven weeks was all two wops were worth!

XIV

A bell rang in the soul of Cornelia Thornwell: last call for witnesses! She knew what was coming, and was not surprised

when Lee Swenson asked her to have lunch with him; nor when
he got a table apart from others, and looked about to make sure
there was no listener. "Well, Nonna, what do you think of our
chances?"

"I don't know what to think, Lee. I have no experience. You
must tell me."

"Well, I think that speech of Sacco's finished us."

"Oh, Lee!" Something went weak inside Cornelia, and she
lost interest in lunch. She sat, staring before her, while the
lawyer went on, lowering his voice.

"One last chance, Nonna. Do you really want to save those
boys? In two hours I can fix you a story; you go on the stand
and tell it, and it'll cinch the case. You can't imagine how easy
it will be—Katzmann won't dare be rough with you—if he did,
I could rip him to pieces with this jury. They'll have no time
to investigate; they can't take more than a day with their rebuttal witnesses, and that is the end—the case is closed, and
anything that comes out afterwards is a joke."

"Lee—don't ask me! Don't ask me!" That was all she could
say; he saw the pain in her face, and dropped it. "All right, I
won't worry you."

But she could not drop it; she had to argue with him about
the case. "Lee, how can they convict men on such evidence? I
have kept a record: thirty-one witnesses have said Vanzetti
was not the man; twelve others, put on by the prosecution, ought
to have known him for the bandit if he really was, and they
didn't." She went on, clamoring her protest. Not one of the
witnesses who identified Bart or Nick had ever known them before, or claimed to have seen them before; in every case it was
a question of remembering strangers; and to American eyes
half the Italians in the world looked like Sacco!

"Yes, Nonna," said Lee, patiently.

"And the least time afterwards was three weeks—everybody
had three weeks to forget what the bandits looked like! Some,
like Goodridge and Pelzer, had nearly a year!"

"It's the jury you have to convince, Nonna—not me!"

"But you must make that clear to them, Lee!"

"I'll do so, never fear. But I can't deny that they are anarchists; I can't deny that our principal witnesses are Italians.
Those are the fatal facts."

They sat, with the food on their plates growing cold; something that had happened to them many times. Life or death was in the balance. Should Lee Swenson, in his speech to the jury, stress the lack of evidence against Vanzetti? If he did so, he might get Vanzetti off. But if Lee knew anything about this Yankee jury, they would "soak" Nick all the harder; and Bart had positively forbidden it to be done. Once again he commanded, "Save Nick, he got the wife and kids!"

They groped in the dark, and beat bare hands against stone walls; they heard in imagination those warning voices which were to haunt the rest of their lives. If only they had known this, if only they had done that! They went back to the courtroom, and the case for the defense was closed. And next day the prosecution put on its rebuttal witnesses—one of them Henry Hellyer, the Pinkerton operative "H. H."! He came to discredit one of the defense witnesses, and the bland Katzmann questioned him, serenely sure about those secrets, locked in his head, which would have blown the case of the prosecution higher than a kite. Actually, Hellyer had in his hand the reports he had turned in on his investigations; when he was uncertain, he said, "I can find out"—and he examined his notes, right there before everybody. And the defense had no idea what was in the notes, no suspicion of the chance they were losing! The bland Katzmann turned the witness over to Mr. McAnarney, and that gentleman said, "No questions, if your honor please." The voices of all the future, shouting into the ears of the defense, were heard by no one. Not a single "hunch," not a dream, not a spirit-voice or a telepathic message!

XV

Next morning Lee Swenson and Fred Moore pleaded the case of the defense, and then the bland prosecutor rose to close the arguments. He had four hours in which to apply those arts he had learned during eleven years' service to the Commonwealth; four hours in which the minds of these twelve good Yankees and true belonged to him, to mold and shape as he would.

For seven weeks they had listened to testimony, most of it dull and soporific, obscurely related to the main issue. Lawyers had wrangled, using long technical terms beyond the grasp of uneducated men. The total amount of testimony was thirty-five hundred typewritten pages, more than a million words. To study them, and analyze their meaning and relationships, to digest them and evaluate them, would occupy a brilliant legal mind several months; and here were two real estate men, two machinists, a grocer, a mason, a stock-keeper, a clothing salesman, a mill-operative, a shoemaker, a last-maker and a farmer. They could not assimilate the evidence, and they would not have either time or opportunity to try. They must make some sort of guess; and one who understood their prejudices could determine what that guess would be.

The wops and most of their lawyers were "furriners"; but the genial and friendly prosecutor was their county official, whom they had elected. For purposes of this trial he called himself "the Commonwealth," and in that guise he could say pompous and magnificent things without sounding foolish. He was honest, and he was conscientious—he told them so himself, in grave and weighty words:

"Gentlemen, there is some responsibility upon the Commonwealth. There is some responsibility upon a prosecutor who produces witnesses whose evidence tends to prove murder. He may think well. He should think long, and he should always have his intelligence and his conscience with him before he puts the stamp of approval of the Commonwealth of Massachusetts upon him as a credible witness before he takes the stand seeking to prove the guilt of men and if proven will result in their death."

From the point of view of prosody that statement could have been improved: but the jurors knew what it meant. This was Fred Katzmann, the prominent and successful, and he would tell them what to think. For example, about Lola Andrews— a distracted, hysterical female, who had stultified herself several times in Mr. Katzmann's presence. Now he told the jury what to think about her: "I have been in this office, gentlemen, for now more than eleven years. I cannot recall in that too long service for the Commonwealth that ever before I have laid eye or given ear to so convincing a witness as Lola Andrews." Concerning Pelzer he told them that the witness had twice falsified, but was "big and manly enough now to tell you of his prior falsehoods and his reasons for them." (The reasons were cowardice.) Concerning Levangie, who had identified Vanzetti as driver of the bandit car, he asked the jury to believe that Levangie had seen Vanzetti in the càr, but thought he had seen him driving when he wasn't!

And then the amazing incident of the cap. There were two caps in evidence—one which had been picked up at the scene of the crime, and the other which had belonged to Sacco, and which the police had taken from his home, after he had been arrested. This latter cap Nick had not seen for fourteen months. While he was on the stand it was suddenly held up, and he was asked if it was his.

Of course the poor fellow did not know what to think; the prosecutor might be playing some trick upon him, getting him to recognize a cap which was not his cap, and then accusing him of lying. All he could say was, "It looks like my cap," and again, "I think it is my cap, yes." Badgered about it, and told to put it on, he finally was brought to say, "I don't know. That cap looks too dirty to me. . . It look like, but it is probably dirt —probably dirty after"—meaning that it was dirty after the police had kept it for a year and shown it about.

That was what Nick said; and now behold the outraged Mr. Katzmann, storming before the jury: "But that is not all, gentlemen. He has falsified to you before your very faces . . . he would not admit, gentlemen, that the cap was his!" Fred Moore interrupted, on behalf of the defense, declaring that this was not a fair account of what was in the record. But Judge Thayer failed to make the facts clear to the jury, and Katzmann went right ahead: "Why, gentlemen, deny the ownership of that cap?"

And then the Proctor incident; a long, detailed argument to the jury, to the effect that two experts had testified that the "mortal bullet," taken from the body of Berardelli, had come from Sacco's revolver. Said Katzmann: "You might disregard all the identification testimony, and base your verdict on the testimony of these experts." And all the time Katzmann knowing that he had framed a trick question, to which Captain Proctor could answer yes, and fool the jury as to what he really believed. Two years later, when Proctor made affidavit to this trick, both Katzmann and his assistant, Williams, made answering affidavits—and they were trick answers, seeming to deny Proctor's statements, but in reality not denying the essential one!

From half past two in the afternoon until seven in the evening a court-room packed solid with human beings listened to the district attorney deal with witness after witness in that spirit. The Supreme Judicial Court of the Commonwealth of Massachusetts has never specifically declared that a prosecuting attorney must be fair; and Katzmann's successor, five years later, would be cynically flippant on the subject. When it was pointed out how Katzmann had concealed the witnesses Kelly and Kennedy from the defense, because they said that Vanzetti was not in the bandit car, Katzmann's successor would argue before Judge Thayer, as one lawyer to another lawyer: "I wonder if Mr. Thompson has not an exaggerated and too ethical notion of the functions of a district attorney."

But nothing like that now! To this jury Mr. Katzmann was the lover of truth, the noble-minded, upright friend of justice. Also he was the patriot; when he came to the end of a four-and-a-half-hour tirade, exhausted, dripping with perspiration in the heat of a crowded court-room, he remembered that the prisoners were wops, while the jurymen were Yankees. His final words were a call to local solidarity:

"Gentlemen of the jury, do your duty. Do it like men. *Stand together, you men of Norfolk!*"

XVI

Next day was Bastille Day in France, and a new Bastille was built in America. "Web" Thayer mounted his throne and delivered his charge to the jury. The throne was banked round with flowers, gifts from admirers of law and order; and "Web's" discourse began in a lofty and emotional strain, as if affected by the intoxicating perfumes. "The Commonwealth of Massachusetts called upon you to render a most important service. Although you knew that such service would be arduous, painful and tiresome, yet you, like the true soldier, responded to that call in the spirit of supreme American loyalty. There is no better word in the English language than 'loyalty'." Thus again he related the trial with the dead bodies brought back from France, and the patriotic exercises going on all over the country.

In the copy he gave out to the newspapers he added the sentence: "Keep courage, gentlemen, in your deliberations, such as was typified by the American soldier boy as he fought and gave up his life upon the battlefields of France."

The judge was supposed to be guiding the jury through the mazes of technicalities, explaining the law, what they were to decide and what not. He took two hours for his oration, and used more than half of it in legal generalities and moral exhortations. He talked about God and country, state and fellow-men, and the highest and noblest type of true American citizenship "than which there is no grander in the entire world." He talked about the pure waters of the government, "the grandest and noblest in the civilized world," and he talked about "the day that little band of Pilgrims landed at Plymouth Rock." He used up so much time in that way that when he came to the mass of identification testimony, he could deal with it only briefly and in abstract terms. To the alibi testimony of the two defendants he gave only a couple of paragraphs, and without mentioning any witness specifically.

But he found time for an elaborate discussion of "motive" in connection with crime. In great detail and at great length he explained that the motive in the South Braintree crime was robbery—something never disputed by the defense, and therefore needless to mention. The question was, not. if the South Braintree murderers had committed murder, but whether Sacco and Vanzetti had been at South Braintree. When the judge proceeded to deal with the wrong issue, it was plain enough that he was throwing dust into the jury's eyes.

And then the "consciousness of guilt," upon which Thayer was to hammer during the next six years of the case! He had deliberately obscured this issue, by blocking the testimony about Salsedo and Elia; and now he proceeded to give more than one-fifth of his time to explaining to the jury what might have been in the minds of two men who lied to the police when they were arrested. The judge who had not mentioned a single alibi witness now found time to deal, point by point, and in great detail, with the testimony of the arresting police officers, and of Mr. and Mrs. Johnson, to whose place Boda and Orciani, Sacco and Vanzetti, had come on the night of the arrest. His charge called up the most dark and sinister images. "If a person is willing to use a deadly weapon such as a revolver upon an arresting officer in order to gain his liberty, what would you naturally expect would be the quality of the crime of which such person would be consciously guilty?"

And then the testimony about the bullet. Did the judge know about the catch in Captain Proctor's testimony? Solemnly and definitely he told the jury that the captain of the State Police had testified: "It was his (Sacco's) pistol that fired the bullet that caused the death of Berardelli." Two years later Web Thayer would be twisting and turning and wriggling like one of Vanzetti's Christmas eels, to make people think he was denying that he had said that to the jury; but there were his words, and they were false, and they sealed the fate of the two anarchist wops. Had not the great Mr. Katzmann told them, only the afternoon before: "You might disregard all the identification testimony, and base your verdict on the testimony of these experts." To exhausted and bewildered jurymen, looking for a life-line, this was something to hang onto; and they grabbed it. Headed by their flag-saluting foreman, who had said, "Damn them, they ought to hang anyhow!" the twelve good Yankees and true retired to the jury room to deliberate.

XVII

A hot summer afternoon; the jury locked in its room upstairs in the court-house; the prisoners back in their cells in the jail; the judge in his chambers; the lawyers, the court officials, the reporters sitting about the grounds, under the heavy shade trees —the two sides, prosecution and defense, keeping rigidly apart, a miniature war.

Cornelia went to her room in the hotel. She could not sit up; but then she could not lie down; she would get up and pace about, doing odd things, aimlessly. Impossible to read, impossible to think consecutively; if any one spoke, you started; if the telephone rang, you went faint. No one had eaten; the very thought of food made your stomach uneasy. Betty would sit by the bedside and try to comfort her grandmother; she would start to talk about something, and then realize that she was not being heard; they would look, and discover fear in the other's eyes.

How long did juries usually take? Anywhere from an hour to two or three days, said those who had experience. The longer they took, the better, from the point of view of the defendants; so you must not be impatient! But there ought to be some way provided by which the mind could be put to sleep through such an ordeal. But then, no one could say for how long the sleep should be!

"Betty, don't you suppose we ought to see Bart?"

"Nonsense, Grannie dear," said the girl. "You wouldn't know what to say to him, any more than you know what to say to me. Let me teach you the Russian alphabet."

At six o'clock they went out, and strolled toward the courthouse. The jury room was dark—Judge Thayer had ordered the twelve taken to supper. Swenson and Moore were sitting on the grass—in their shirt sleeves, something shocking to the proprieties of this staid New England town. Workingmen might do such a thing, but never gentlemen—unless they came from the wild and woolly west; it was almost enough to convict their clients. They put on their coats and stood up when they saw the ladies coming; they discussed the rumors, which had begun to fly—how the jury looked, what a court officer had been heard to whisper. Lee held Cornelia's arm. "Keep a stiff upper lip, Nonna! There are many legal tricks—this isn't the end!" "Oh, Lee! then you think—" "I don't think—I wait! But prepare for anything."

The jury was back again from supper. The lights were shining in the upstairs room, the shades down. Now and then a shadow moved across. Irresistibly your fancy was drawn to that room; impossible to be in any other place, to think of any other thing. The twelve good Yankees and true would be arguing; now and then they would take a ballot; they would question the ones who disagreed, find out what was troubling them, argue again, cite this detail and that, seeking to change the doubters—but which way? Surely in all that group there must be some who could think—some who could realize the hazardous nature of the evidence—the almost complete lack of proof concerning Bart! But no, Mr. Katzmann had told them that the reason the defense had concentrated its arguments on Sacco was because they considered the case of Vanzetti hopeless! He had said—

"What were you saying, Lee?" The lawyer had made a remark about the swallows; they didn't have that kind in the west. Yes, he was trying to help her, to distract her mind! It was kind of him; he was one of the kindest of men. She said: "Do they fly all night, Lee? Or does the judge order them to bed?" And she did not know that he smiled.

XVIII

It was five minutes to eight o'clock. Suddenly one of the little groups in front of the court-house began to melt and flow into the building. One, and then another. People were going inside! Then loungers about the square began to notice it, people in the corner drug-store; like magic the word spread— the jury was ready! One of the guards condescended to tell the lawyers—the sheriff had telephoned to bring the prisoners over. It took about ten minutes to fetch them; and in that time the court-room was crowded, and half the town of Dedham thronged outside. The doors were locked, the armed policemen guarding them.

The prisoners in their cage; Vanzetti tense, anxious, his brows knitted; Sacco pale, almost green. A deep silence; then came the jury filing in. One glance was enough; every man had his eyes fixed on the floor. Lee Swenson made a gesture of despair. Cornelia saw it; and caught Betty by the arm.

The jury was polled; they answered faintly to their names. Said the judge to the clerk, "You will please take the verdict." Said the clerk, "Gentlemen of the jury, have you agreed upon a verdict?" Said the foreman, "We have."

The jurors rose; the prisoners rose; they stood facing one another. "Nicola Sacco!" said the clerk, "hold up your right hand. What say you, Mr. Foreman, is the prisoner at the bar guilty or not guilty?"

"Guilty," said the flag-saluting foreman. "Damn them, they ought to hang anyhow," added a voice from within him; but the clerk did not hear that.

"Of murder?" said the clerk.

"Yes."

"Murder in the first degree?"

"Yes."

"On two indictments?"

"Yes."

There was a pause.

"Bartolomeo Vanzetti, hold up your right hand. What say you, Mr. Foreman, is the prisoner at the bar guilty or not guilty?"

"Guilty."

"Of murder?"

"Yes."

"Murder in the first degree?"

"Yes."

"On two indictments?"

"Yes."

A look of incredulity was on the face of Vanzetti. He could not realize that this had happened to him. He stood with his hand still in the air, like a statue. The dead, expressionless face of the old judge was gray. "Gentlemen of the jury, as I did this morning, I again offer you thanks for the services you have rendered. You may now go to your homes, from which you have been absent for nearly seven weeks. We will now adjourn."

The bailiff began his familiar formula: "Hear ye! Hear ye!" But now Sacco realized what had been done to him; he shouted above the bailiff: "Sono innocente!" And then to the jurors, who were filing from the court-room, "Two innocent men! You kill two innocent men!"

Mrs. Sacco had been close behind the cage. At her husband's cry she leaped to her feet and rushed to him, and flung her arms about his neck. "You bet your life!" she cried—the only way she knew of being emphatic in this strange tongue. "Oh, Nick! They kill my man!" Her shrieks rang through the room—a terrible moment; women began to weep.

Sacco stood, caressing his wife, trying to comfort her; Vanzetti still like a statue—not a sound from him. But Rosina's shrieks rose louder and louder; she fought away the lawyers who tried to disengage her hands; she was a wild thing, possessed of more than human strength; she thought they were going to take Nick away and electrocute him that night, and the lawyers tried to explain to her the refinements of American law—the appeals and technicalities, the infinitudes of red tape, the millions of words to be printed and the hundreds of thousands of dollars to be spent. But she only shrieked the louder, "They kill my man! I got two children—what I do?"

Until at last the stern policemen pulled her hands away, and forced her back, and formed a ring with Rosina outside. Quickly they locked the handcuffs upon the prisoners—an old story to the police, American efficiency. Snappy orders, "All ready! March!" Through the door they went, guards outside closing about them, twenty-five men in a solid bunch, guns ready. "Stand back! Out of the way there! Forward, march!" The sheriff's men flung a line across the street, holding the curious onlookers, while down the street into the twilight went prisoners and escort, tramp, tramp, tramp! Anarchists, who do not believe in organization, learn a lesson from the grimly efficient Commonwealth!

CHAPTER 15.

THE WHISPERING GALLERY

I

SACCO and Vanzetti were back in their cells: the former in jail in Dedham while his appeals were heard, the latter in Charlestown State Prison, working at his old sentence of fifteen years for the Bridgewater crime. Nick, as usual, had nothing to do all day—a cruel form of punishment; it required tact and sympathy on the part of visitors to persuade him that it was worthwhile to stand on his head and walk on his hands, as a means of not going mad. Bart was now making license plates for automobiles: the one industry which the Commonwealth had been able to save from the grasp of private capital, and which therefore could be used to keep state convicts from wholesale madness. It was not happy work, for it involved the touch and smell of acids, which gradually undermined Vanzetti's health, and made more difficulty for those who lived with him in sympathy.

A black hour for the world, testing the souls of idealists. Famine in Russia; the notorious inefficiency of communist bureaucracy had caused the rains to stop falling—so it was reported by correspondents and explained by editorial writers of capitalist newspapers. Throughout Europe the White Terror enthroned; in Italy banded assassins in the pay of banks and industrialists, murdering the leaders and rooting out every trace of social protest, turning the country over to that ultimate product of natural selection, the beast with the brains of an engineer. Sacco and Vanzetti sat in their cells, and read of these events, and stretched out their hands to the future, whose children they were.

Each in his own way, they would learn to make their appeal to that future. Bartolomeo Vanzetti, dish-washer, ditch-digger and fish-peddler, would learn to write; he would labor all day

445

at a stubborn and hostile language, and conquer it, and shape it to his ends. He, whose schooling had ceased at the age of thirteen, would make himself a master of letters; he who had never seen the inside of a college building, would write such prose as no living graduate of Harvard had ever achieved; he who was to die as a common criminal, would defend his faith in words of elemental eloquence, outranking anything produced by an American since Lincoln's second inaugural.

It would take long practice. Locked up alone in his cell, Bart would write letters: letters to his lawyers, to members of the committee and friends of the defense; letters to strangers who wrote to him, letters to his anarchist comrades of Mexico, France, Russia. The rules of the institution allowed only two letters a month, but they did not prevent Bart's handing a packet of manuscript to his lawyer.

At first his efforts would be crude; he would be looking up long words in the dictionary, and stringing them together, a kind of Babu English. He would use Italian words literally translated, producing novel effects. He would concoct strange polysyllables, apparently of his own imagining; you would start to smile, until it occurred to you that it might be a new kind of poetry. To Cornelia he wrote: "Even if we will be killed at once by the carnefice, or little by little by the confinement, you remain to hold light the banner of the human vindications, and to accomplished redemption."

And again: "Do not desperate, comrade, of the cruelty of the human events. Out of every little doctrine all too small and inadequate, out of every party, petty and inefficient for the great problems of the human justice and freedom—will ripen the historical nemesy and the inevitable palingenesy."

He began translating passages from Italian books into English, things which interested him, and which he wanted Cornelia to understand; he would take her criticisms and study them, and then try again—a correspondence course in composition, having the added excitement of a race with the executioner. He wrote:

"I was very beneficiated by your last visit and English-lesson. In a letter received to-night, one Friend tells me that my English is not perfect. I am still laughing for such a pious euphension. Why do not say horrible? Nevertheless, I can made a better translation than the one in argument. I did it as I did for an experiment, to prove if an almost letterally translation is intelligible. I show it to some friends, asking them if they understand it. The answer was 'yes,' while it should have been 'no,' that I might have remade the work with much profit and better result.

"Of course, as the writing is beautiful in its original, and as I labored very much at the dictionary, so I was thinking to have accomplished something worth, and the disillution was, as almost all disillatin, rather cruel. But when a poor one is surrounded by many great difficulties, the small ones appear always a joke to him, and after your visit I found myself in the best of the mood—that is, I was decided to do in the future as much more good than the much bad I did in the past. I analized attentively the original—it is almost impossible intellectual pleasure—which for hours has made me forget myself, the cell, and the other sorrowy things."

II

Cornelia's contribution to the defense was to be a pamphlet telling the story of the case, and summarizing the evidence of the two trials. The procedures that she had watched with horror in Plymouth and Dedham she would now set down in black and white, so that her friends could take them home and study them. In the apartment on the north side of Beacon Hill sat the little old lady all day, her shoulders stooped over a volume of typewritten testimony, and sheafs of pencil-notes scattered over the vacant places in the room.

Betty and Joe came to help, and they sorted and classified and compared, and argued over this detail and that: identification testimony relating to Sacco, relating to Vanzetti, relating to both and to neither; alibi testimony, and refutation thereof; testimony relating to Sacco's cap and to Vanzetti's pistol—where was it Bart had said he had never fired the gun with which he had been arrested? Where was it that Katzmann asked him his reason for concealing the price he had paid for the gun? Betty would search, and Joe would search, and they filled note-books with lists of cross-references. The half-dozen thick volumes of typewritten testimony began to show signs of wear, and had to be bound more tightly. Precious objects they were, having cost the defense two or three thousand dollars of hard-begged money.

Cornelia was finding that as she grew older she wanted less and less sleep. Life was becoming more precious as its supply ran out, and nature was trying to save every moment. She would awaken at three or four o'clock in the morning, and the details of the pamphlet would come swarming into her mind, she would wonder about this point and that, and presently decide she might as well get up and go to work. So Betty would find her working by electric light, having failed to notice the coming of day. Betty would scold, and try to put her to bed again. Betty would threaten to get up early too, and Cornelia would have to scold. The pamphlet grew to the size of a book, and would have become an encyclopedia if they had let it. Then began the painful process of cutting down and summarizing; and every time they left out a point, it seemed that the life of Bart and Nick hung upon the decision.

Lee Swenson was retiring from the case: he had done his best, he said, and failed, now let some one else have a try. There were tears in the eyes of both when he said good-by to Cornelia. They promised they would never forget each other—little danger of the promise being broken! "Don't worry about the past, Nonna," said Lee; "you did your best." She didn't know what to answer; she didn't know what to think about the questions that haunted her. What would have happened if she had done what Lee wanted? Would she have done it, if she had foreseen the present situation? And what was going to become of a country in which the law was a cheat, and dreamers of justice its predestined victims?

Fred Moore was taking over the case; a lawyer less hated by the authorities, it was hoped—though this proved a delusion. He was younger than Swenson, an Irishman and a fighter, wrapped up in the labor cause; a strange combination of emotional temperament and keen analytical brain; a man who suffered deeply—as all men did who took up the cause of the underdog in America. He, like Swenson, had witnessed dreadful things, and told Cornelia stories of savagery and corruption that made her shudder.

It was Moore's task to prepare the appeal to the Supreme

Judicial Court from the various rulings of Judge Thayer at the Dedham trial. To this end there must be drawn up what was known as a "bill of exceptions" in the case: that is to say, a list of the objections which the defense had made to the judge's rulings, together with the testimony concerned. It amounted to a summary of the case, giving the essentials which the higher court would need; and it was necessary that the defense, the prosecution and the judge should agree to every word. The three parties had to sit day by day at a table, with a copy of the testimony before them, marking the passages to be recopied, and phrasing summaries of the rest. A long, slow job, for which Judge Thayer had allowed from the middle of July to the first of November.

Thayer, Moore and an assistant district attorney did the work. Thayer disliked Moore, but in the course of time he came to hate the assistant district attorney, and to like Moore by comparison, so he chose Moore to talk to about the case. A curious episode: one hot summer afternoon, the assistant district attorney had left the room, and the old judge looked up over the piles of papers and wiped the perspiration from his forehead, and shook his head sorrowfully. "Moore, there are mountains of perjury on both sides of this case!"

"Maybe so, Judge," said the lawyer. "But your side has the most."

The old man did not bother to resent this way of putting it. "I know," he said, "you think those fellows are innocent!"

"I do, Judge."

"Well, I *know* they are guilty."

"How do you know it?"

"Never mind how—but I know." It was the formula of ruling-class Massachusetts, which for six years they would repeat; not in print, not for the public, but in the smoking-rooms of the clubs, in homes or offices, wherever one tried to pin them down and get the facts. "Never mind how—but I know!"

III

It was going to cost eighteen thousand dollars to print the "bill of exceptions"—two elaborate volumes; to say nothing of lawyers' fees, and office expenses, and the cost of raising the money. You got lists of names—members of radical organizations, subscribers to liberal papers, contributors to charity organizations, members of women's clubs—anybody who might have either a heart or a conscience; you got typists and had envelopes addressed, and prepared a begging circular and mailed it, and then with the money that came in you got more lists and more typists and more circulars—it was the wheel of life.

But the returns did not come fast enough. The case was lagging, threatening to die. The men were in jail, and they stayed there, and the public wanted to go to sleep and forget them—the usual way. Look at Mooney and Billings out in California, exclaimed the young radicals—men whom everybody knew to be innocent, yet they stayed in prison, forgotten—several years already, and it would be many, many more. The friends of the defense were not content to have lawyers pore over the testimony and appeal to a court without a heart; they wanted to dramatize the case, to find new evidence, to break down the witnesses of the government, above all to catch the real criminals, who had done the murders. They wanted to have mass-meetings in the cities, to have the story of this Massachusetts "frame-up" told to labor audiences. Naturally, it occurred to them, what an impression if a lady of Mrs. Thornwell's respectability and prestige would take the platform! They wanted Cornelia to go to New York and address a meeting; and when she realized that there was no other way to get the indispensable money, she consented.

So then, more distress among the Thornwell clan. They had thought the limit was reached when the head of their family defended "anarchy" at home; but to go outside the Commonwealth, and attack its courts among strangers—that was really treason. Deborah came and protested with all her dignity; when that was in vain, Alice quit her "rest-cure," and threatened to go completely insane; when this too failed, there was a family conference, fully as agitated as those of war-time. Great-uncle Abner insisted upon being brought. Because it was no longer possible to make him hear a word, they had to write out the proceedings for him; and every now and then he would punctuate the debate with his booming formula: "Lock her up!"

They turned the matter over to Henry Cabot Winters, because of his sense of humor, which they did not understand or like, but which they knew was the only hope. Rupert would put the information department of the Pilgrim National Bank at Henry's service, and would himself call upon the representative of the Federal secret service in Boston. Henry would see the district attorney, and all together they would make a real effort, and pull the poor distracted old soul out of this mess.

Henry went to the telephone and called up Cornelia, who was not supposed to know about this conspiracy, but could guess. When she heard that her son-in-law wanted to be invited to dinner about a week from now, she laughed. "Are you going to bring that information you have been promising?"

"If it isn't too late, Mother. I know, I have neglected you—but I've been so frightfully busy! Now we've got another extension on the Jerry Walker case, so I have a little breathing space. If it's not too late, I really would like to take a week off and see what I can find out about your friends and their problem."

"That's very good of you, Henry; but you know we have no way to pay for such distinguished legal services."

"You pay with your company, Mother. We are growing some dewberries on our place that are as long as your thumb, and I will send you a supply in the morning, and you can have them made into a short cake or a cobbler or whatever you fancy; and I'll bring a bottle of Madeira—the real thing, because I am the only person that knows the combination to the vault!"

IV

Cornelia did her own shopping. She got a live and lively lobster, done up in a strong paper bag, with two holes in it so that he might breathe; like a condemned man, he must be kept alive till the moment of his execution. She got a small chicken, and some green peas, and a head of lettuce, and climbed the hill with them in a little basket, smiling to herself—it was old, *old* "Boston"! The Negro maid was a-flutter, and Cornelia was a-flutter—treating Henry as if he were royalty. The remarkable dewberries had been brought by the chauffeur, each wrapped separately in tissue paper, to keep it from a bruise; they now reposed in whipped cream and sugar, on top of a thin flaky cake.

Exactly at the moment of seven-thirty came the great lawyer, dressed as if he were the principal orator at a banquet of the bar association. Treating Cornelia as if she were royalty; and yet smiling at himself, and at her—it was a game you played, and you did not take it too seriously, yet you must take it seriously enough; it was a way to make life worth living, to save yourself from beastliness, cruelty, and despair—the latter, especially, always reaching after you. Cornelia did everything a perfect hostess must do, and thinking to herself, "I have not escaped from the family! I never will escape from the family!"

Henry liked a good dinner, just enough to make it worth while to fix it for him, yet not enough to be gross. He praised everything, purposely while the maid was in the room, so that she stood, transfigured into a double row of shining white teeth. It was picturesque to have a mother-in-law who lived in a tenement; it was elegant to know that she was just as completely a lady, and served just as good a dinner, as if she were on the other side of Beacon Hill. All this stayed in the background of your thoughts, and upheld you in the hours when you thought about your hysterical wife, and your son who had the constitution and structure of a marshmallow, and your money-making, which brought you law-suits and scandals.

They sipped the real Madeira, and gossiped about amusing aspects of family life. Quincy Thornwell, incorrigible bachelor, had been smitten by the widow of a banker, killed in the war; would she have him, and what would they do with her three children, and what about the family, the new cousins and "in-laws" that would be added to the Thornwell clan? Andrew Alvin had been thrown from his polo-pony and got a broken shoulder; a man in his forties, Andrew's one idea of happiness was to ride a horse as crazy as himself; they had made him master of the hunt in one of the suburban towns, where the smart set dressed themselves in pink coats and shiny leather boots, and rode at daybreak on autumn mornings to the music of horns, and paid enormous bills for damages to farmers' crops. A certain fast-riding young lady was "setting her cap" at Andrew; her father had made many millions out of war-contracts, and now they were trying to "break in" upon the blue-bloods. Would Andrew condescend or wouldn't he? It was typical blue-blood conversation.

V

With Madeira warming his stomach and the smoke of a cigar warming his head, Henry Cabot Winters sat by the open window, the sound of children shouting in the street below helping to make privacy for conversation. "Well, Mother, I have been making a few inquiries about those adopted sons of yours. I've brought some documents." He pointed to a leather brief-case, stuffed to capacity, which lay upon the sofa.

"Well, Henry, what did you find?"

"They had a cache of dynamite, and on the night of the arrest they were getting Boda's car to move the stuff to a safer place."

"How did you learn that, Henry?" Cornelia tried to keep her tone playful.

"Needless to say, men who make and plant bombs to destroy their enemies do not invite me to their meetings. I have no first-hand knowledge of the fact—"

"Let's cut short the preliminaries, Henry. You have been talking to the police, and that is what their under-cover agents have brought them. Did they tell you that Rosina Sacco once had her husband in court for failure to support her?"

"No."

"That's another of the stories they are circulating; I can tell you a dozen, if you're interested. They say the fifty dollars poor Bart sent to Tresca to help pay Salsedo's lawyer was part of the loot of the South Braintree crime. But I happened to know that Bart had saved up about four hundred dollars out of his fish business. Tell me, do your police friends know what became of the sixteen or seventeen thousand dollars those bandits got?"

"They tell me it went to Italy, Mother."

"I see! When they started out, they were sure it was in Coacci's trunk. When they didn't find it there, they decided it was buried in Sacco's garden. Now, they say it went to Italy. Have they given you any real evidence about it?"

"No, Mother."

"Well, then, the situation is this: all the resources of state and Federal secret service have been used, and they have never been able to find that the group or any individual connected with the group has had any unusual amount of money, or has spent much money for anything; they have not one trace of a clew. Poor little Boda, whom they call a payroll bandit, had a car that was in hospital all winter—"

"That wasn't the car he drove, Mother."

"Can you prove that he drove any other car?"

"There is reason for believing it."

"Well, it wasn't a good enough reason to be put before a jury. Web Thayer threw Boda out of the case—but now you bring him back! I knew him well, a friendly little fellow, a salesman of macaroni—"

"Is that what he told you, Mother? He was a salesman of whisky."

"Really? Well, that explains one mystery in the case—why Mike Stewart couldn't find any of Boda's macaroni customers! That was why Mike became suspicious. But now we have a perfectly respectable explanation—surely you, Henry, cannot blame Boda, since you buy whisky!"

"Not Boda's kind, Mother!"

"Well, you haven't come to argue about prohibition, so let me see what you've got in your brief-case."

VI

There was a reading lamp on the table beside Henry Cabot Winters, and it threw strong shadows on his fine dark features and thin, sensitive hands. Cornelia noticed that the hands trembled as they drew out the documents. Was it the toll the competitive game was taking from the great lawyer? Or was it that he cared so especially about rescuing his mother-in-law from a career of crime? Cornelia watched with curiosity what came out of the brief-case: quantities of typewritten stuff bound together, reports and correspondence. Henry would no doubt be able to get access to secret service records; or Rupert would get them for him. Would it be ethical to ask him for answers to some of the problems which had been tormenting the defense?

Cornelia saw some red-bound pamphlets, then a red-bound

book. "Is that some of the literature Vanzetti had? Or some they got at Sacco's house?"

"They didn't get much at Sacco's, Mother; somebody had burned most of it. I am told the defense lawyers wanted some, and all they could find was a four-volume technical work on the chemistry of explosives. Is that so?"

"You have come to bring me things, Henry, not to get them."

"Yes, but you ought to meet me half way. You don't really *want* to be fooled, do you?"

"Not in the least, Henry. I want all the real knowledge I can get."

"Let me ask you, did you ever sit down and think seriously and honestly whether it might be possible that these men had connections with the fighting crowd?"

"Are you talking about bombs now—or about banditry?"

"Let us begin with bombs."

"I have lain awake many a night debating it with myself. About Sacco I have to say that I don't know; I never knew him well enough—and of course I can't find out now; one does not talk about such things to him or to his friends. But I really knew Bart, and I try to imagine him committing an action that would destroy human life. He would have done it in a moment of rage against social injustice; he talked violently, and he would have fought the police on the picket-line, I am sure, and killed them. But to prepare in cold blood to blow a man up with a bomb—I try to imagine it, and it simply cannot be done—it is not my Bart any longer. I never knew a man who had more tenderness and pity."

Said Henry, searching among the papers, "I have a curious document, a letter from Vera Figner, the Russian terrorist, in her own handwriting; I can't read it, of course, but there's a translation attached. She is telling about her days in the Schluesselburg Fortress, and how she walked with another girl prisoner in the courtyard, and noticed that this girl would turn aside now and then from the path. When Vera Figner asked her why, the answer was that she could not bear to step on the bugs and other creatures in the path. Is that your Bart?"

"It might be." Cornelia smiled.

"Yet this girl had blown up human beings with bombs, and

had done other acts of desperate cruelty. She did them for the
cause."

"Yes—and I have to remember that Bart had seen just as
dreadful evidence of class tyranny in America as that girl had
seen in Russia. So I say: 'It might have been. I cannot be sure.'
But you know, Henry, I lived in a crowded little place with
him for over a year, and I never heard—"

"Your hearing was handicapped by the fact that you didn't
understand his language, Mother."

"That it true. I learned to understand simple things, but not
political discussions, of course."

"Did you read his literature?"

"No, only what he translated to me."

"In other words, what he considered proper for you to know
—the sentimental and idealistic part. Did you ever see a book
called 'Faccia à Faccia col Nemico'—that is to say, 'Face to
Face with the Enemy'?" And Henry held up a thick book,
bound in red paper covers.

VII

The little room in the apartment on the north side of Beacon
Hill vanished, taking with it two years and a half of tragic history. Bart was a free man, selling fish in Plymouth, and Cornelia and Betty were paying him a visit, a few days before
Betty's sailing for Europe. There came two Italians with a
motorcycle and a side-car, Coacci and Orciani, bringing a heavy
package which Bart showed to Cornelia, with a twinkle in his
dark eyes, saying that it was a bomb. He opened it, and showed
her what he called "mental dinnameet." "I take heem queek, I
get him distriboot, never let polissman get heem, giammai!"

"Yes, Henry," said Cornelia, "I have seen that book."

"Bart's group were the publishers of it, were they not?"

"Yes."

"But you never read it?"

"No, Mr. Katzmann!"

"Mr. Katzmann is relieved to hear you say so. It is a dreadful book, Mother."

"I know that it contains the life-stories of various anarchist
martyrs. They were fighting for liberty in Europe, Henry—"

"Yes, if you insist—for liberty of a sort. But the point to get clear is, they were fighting with bombs and the assassin's dagger. Without exception, they were men who did such terrorist acts; and all of them were idealists—many of them men of fine personal morality—who wouldn't eat meat, or would step aside to avoid killing a bug. They correspond in every way to your boys—with the single exception that they admitted their guilt, and boasted of it."

"A considerable difference, Henry."

"Not when you consider the special circumstances. There is no hope for a revolution in America, but there is hope in Italy —or there was two years ago; so America is the place where money is collected, and Italy the place where it is spent."

"You are talking about banditry again, now?"

"I am talking about both; for they are mixed up together in this book. I felt sure you hadn't read it, so I had some translating done; a few passages that are crucial I took the trouble to verify myself, looking up word after word in the dictionary, so that I could assure you I wasn't being fooled by the police."

"That was very patient of you, Henry." She saw the deep anxiety on the face of her son-in-law, and understood that he had come to wrestle with the powers of darkness for her soul.

"Here, for example, is a passage from the introduction. It tells us that these martyrs are worthy of emulation, and that we must not let the world's disapproval influence or frighten us. Listen:

" 'To the latest critics of anarchism Ravachol appears a detestable degenerate; Caserio an epileptic or a paranoiac; Bresci a desperate self-destroyer. . . . But to the modern free people the enormous importance of individual acts of revolt remains unchallenged as a promise and a symptom. . . . Such acts are the thousand year stones of the great revolution; the first abrupt, short-lived sparks which the ashes of indifference easily cover and preserve, to be revived stronger than ever by, and added to, the great fire of freedom.'

"Now, Mother, why do men write and print and circulate words like that, unless they mean what they say? Read the book, and you discover that Ravachol was a bandit-anarchist; he made a business of robbing the rich and giving the money to the poor. He was scrupulous about it, never keeping a penny for himself."

"I never knew Ravachol, Henry, but I do know Bart and Nick, and the idea does not fit them—it is unthinkable." And she added: "I am arguing against violence on both sides, Henry; and neither will pay attention to me. Which side do you think ought to begin—those who have everything they want in life, or those who suffer misery and outrage?"

VIII

Henry Cabot Winters was not interested in pacifism; he was turning over the pages of the red-bound book. He got up and came over and laid it on the arm of the Morris chair in which his mother-in-law sat. "Look at that!" he said. "A diagram of one of the bombs used by the assassins. Is that strictly historical information? Or is it literary? Don't you think it possible that the men who printed that picture might have had in mind that bombs could still be made that way? There are nearly five hundred pages of such stuff, Mother."

"My guess about the matter would be this, Henry: that Vanzetti was the despair of his group—he could not follow along. He would have been torn between rage and pity—just as I am."

"Here is 'Fight for Your Lives.' Here is the leaflet, 'Plain Words'—an outrageous thing, widely circulated. I am told, Mother, that when Swenson and Moore went over Vanzetti's anarchist books to get some exhibits for the jury, they had to reject many because they were too violent. They ventured to use others, only because the jury couldn't read them. Maybe you know if that is true."

"Maybe I do, and maybe I don't, Henry."

"Don't worry, Mother. This is a family matter."

"Go ahead and tell me what you know."

"I know that those fellows were up to some devilment the night they were arrested. They told a tangle of lies to the police—"

"You must know what had happened to Salsedo and Elia, Henry."

"Yes, and it was a good reason for lying that night. But why go on lying for a year afterwards, when they knew what they were arrested for, and knew their lies had all been nailed down? Why go on lying to their own lawyers? I am told that Swenson and Moore couldn't get the truth out of them at any time—and we don't have to rely on police spies for that, Mother, it is in the record. Were you there the day Tom McAnarney cross-examined the couple—what were their names?— Sacco and Vanzetti came to their house the night of the arrest."

"The Johnsons. Yes, I heard that."

"Well, the cross-examination aimed to show that the Johnsons weren't sure about recognizing the men. In other words, Sacco and Vanzetti were going to deny they were there, and only after the trial started did they decide on the other story— that they had been hiding anarchist literature. I am told that the men's own lawyers know they were hiding dynamite—the men have admitted it."

"All I can tell you, Henry, is this—if it's true, the lawyers haven't told me."

"They wouldn't. But here's another story—that Lee Swenson tried every way he knew to get you to make an alibi for Vanzetti; he didn't give up until the very last day of the trial. Is that true?"

"I told you I wasn't going to answer questions, Henry."

The other smiled. "That is answer enough, Mother. But don't worry—nobody is going to get anything out of me. And don't imagine I am being shocked—I know the game of criminal law."

Said Cornelia, "I have heard that some of our blue-blood lawyers have been known to frame testimony."

"Yes, Mother, I have done it, more than once—when I was good and sure the other fellow was doing it. I am not after Lee Swenson—I am just trying to convince you that those two adopted sons of yours are not sentimental pacifists and saints."

"I never thought that of them, Henry."

"Well, it's what your literature is telling the public. You are collecting money on that basis, from persons who wouldn't give it on any other."

"I am telling the public I believe the men to be innocent of the crime of which they have been convicted; that I attended both trials, and consider them travesties of justice. That is all I can tell, because it is all I know."

"Not quite all, Mother—if you will pardon me for reminding you. Will you tell the public what doctrine these men taught? Will you say they circulated books calling for bombings, and giving diagrams of bombs?"

IX

There was a long silence. At last Cornelia said: "The public is ignorant. It believes that men who had anything to do with dynamiting would be apt to engage in banditry, and ought to be executed anyhow. To admit the possibility of dynamite means death. But surely, Henry, a lawyer can distinguish. Also you can see that it is impossible for me to establish a negative—to prove the men's innocence. It is not enough for you to show a possibility—even of dynamite! You must bring real proof."

Henry smiled. But then, noting a tear on the old woman's cheek, his tone became gentler. "You don't like to hear that your anarchist friend may have deceived you, Mother?"

"No, my son, not that at all. I know Vanzetti so much better than you could imagine—it is as if he were sitting in this room, listening to the conversation, and explaining matters to me. When I face the idea that he may have associated with terrorists, then I think, not that he deceived me—of course he would have had to deceive me, for his friends' sake, if not for his own. What I think is, how he must have suffered—more even than I guessed!"

"The persons who were blown up with bombs also suffered, Mother."

"Yes, I know, and that is what the world thinks of, inevitably. The bombs were aimed at members of our class, and they were highly inconvenient. But you see, I have been trying to understand both sides; to find out, not merely how bombs are made, but how bomb-makers are made. While you hear dynamite exploding, I hear policemen's clubs falling on strikers' heads. Don't forget, I was on the picket-line, and heard that sound, I saw such crimes committed, I said to myself: 'Never again will I blame these workers for anything they do!' I said 'anything,' Henry—and now I don't forget that I said it."

"I know, Mother—"

"You don't know! You haven't the remotest idea! You cannot dream what it feels like to be down there in the social pit, stamped upon by the hob-nailed boots of policemen, and the iron-shod hoofs of horses! To have clubs splitting your skull, or beating your flesh black and blue! Remember, I saw Vanzetti carry a half-conscious man off the picket-line, I sat by while he bathed the broken head, I saw him weeping, I heard him babbling like a child, incoherent, hysterical, with mingled grief and rage. He has that temperament, he suffers more than either you or I do—he cares—that is the difference, he really cares! You and I care whether we have our dinner in proper style, whether the Madeira is real or not, whether the lobster was alive or not, whether the chicken is the right age and the salad dressing sufficiently solid, whether we have got on the right costume and the right tie, whether we hold our knives and forks the right way, whether we make a sufficient display of worldly cynicism, whether we are sufficiently skeptical about all enthusiasms, sufficiently dead to faith, hope and charity—"

"Now, Mother!"

"I know, you bring me facts, Henry—take a few in return! I could go over our conversation point by point, every remark we made about other people and about life, and that would be it. Last week it was Quincy sitting there, and he told me all the latest from Mrs. Jack's sickroom; they came to ask for a contribution to the Charitable Eye and Ear Infirmary of Boston, and she said, 'I didn't know there was a charitable eye or ear in Boston.' That is our wit, Henry, the tone of our world. We are raising our young people on it—and then wonder why they are going to the devil!"

"You are setting me a large problem now, Mother."

"No problem at all! We are living off the labor of these wops whom we despise, and hold in order with clubs and bayonets. Think of it, Henry—that man whose head I saw split open was getting nine dollars a week to keep a family on, and his crime was that he was asking twelve. We women were getting six dollars a week, and our crime was that we were asking eight— and Vanzetti's crime was helping us! There was the greatest and richest cordage concern in the country—their net profits that year were nearly three million dollars! Think of the families we know who are living off those profits, doing nothing else, unless they choose! Think of the imbecilities—one collecting butterflies and one collecting pottery, several getting drunk, one doing charity—God save his soul, he is running a mission for newsboys just down the street here, and keeps it in a place over a pool-room, a hangout for pickpockets and pimps, where every now and then they hold a prizefight! But if you talk to cordage stockholders about going among their working-people and living with them, becoming real leaders and guides and friends, spending the surplus product upon a system of training in self-government, so that industry may become democratic without revolution and violence—if you should talk about that, they would say you had very bad taste, and stop inviting you to their dinner-parties!"

X

The little white-haired old lady had got up from her chair during this stump-speech. She was walking about, and had made several gestures—a consequence of having been so much among the wops. The poor soul was bound to be humiliated, having the truth pointed out to her; she would have to excuse herself, and blame somebody else—it was human nature. Henry Cabot Winters understood psychology, and sat patiently, waiting for the storm to blow over.

Cornelia began telling the story of Sacco, as Sacco had told it to her. He had been in the Milford foundry strike, and had been knocked down on the picket-line, and then thrown into jail. The police had followed their usual tactics of knocking down wholesale, for the purpose of breaking the courage of the workers; it was all that anybody in New England knew or thought about industry, it was the "American plan"—so said the widow of the late Governor Thornwell, pouring out her bitterness. "And remember, Henry, while you are bringing your indictment against these wops, they learned their anarchism right here in New England. Nick was a perfectly ignorant working-boy when he came, and Bart was a religious dreamer, slightly touched with utopianism. If they became militants and terrorists, we taught it to them!"

"They learned it in a foreign language, Mother; and certainly they followed foreign models."

"That is true enough. But men don't act upon what they read

in books, they act upon the realities of their daily lives. The principal fact in Bart's life for the past few years has been the war. The capitalist system was trying to put him into a uniform and send him out to kill his fellow-workers; and he was resisting with all his power. To abolish the slaughter of workingmen for the profit of masters—that has been his leading thought, ever since I have been his friend."

"Does he expect to stop war by blowing people up with bombs?"

"Militant anarchists do; they think that if enough workers would resist, forcibly, to the death—if enough of them were willing to be martyrs—the capitalist class would lose its pleasure in exploitation. Whether that is right or wrong is another question—but that is what the militant anarchist thinks. And watching the thing as I have done, it seems that you men who are running our country want to prove him right, because you shut off every avenue of redress and hope. You corrupt politics, so that it is a piece of rusty junk instead of a running machine. You make the law into a net of red tape, in which the worker is tied hand and foot. You make the newspapers a mess of falsehood and sensation. Your colleges are busy turning young men into quick climbers. Your churches have no time for social justice—they are turning prayer-wheels and saying magic words—"

"In short, Mother, there is nothing left but dynamite!" There was a touch of acid in the great lawyer's tone; it was getting to be a very long stump-speech.

"There are two things for the rebel, Henry; one is to die suffering, and the other is to die fighting. I try to persuade them that the former is more effective in the long run, but I can't always get them to see it. Sometimes I imagine there is a pleading look in Bart's eyes, as if he would like to tell me that he wishes he had taken my advice."

"Yes, I know," said Henry, "we are familiar with the fact that men are militants until they get caught, and pacifists afterwards. It is the purpose of jails to effect that transformation."

XI

This duel of moral forces continued until the arrival of Betty and Joe, who had been to a theater, and then walked home.

Betty had been told that her uncle was coming, and she had had
no trouble in guessing what for. When she and Joe entered the
living-room, and saw the little white-haired old lady in the Morris chair, looking so anxious and strained, and the great lawyer
completely surrounded by an array of documents, it seemed to
Betty that the combat was one-sided. "Well, Grannie dear, has
he succeeded in convincing you that our boys are bandits? Or
is it dynamiters they are, Uncle Henry?"

"Henry," said Cornelia, "these young persons are so clever
I cannot keep anything to myself."

Said Betty, "The efforts of my family to keep me in the
nursery at the age of twenty-three are mysteriously unsuccess-
ful! I suppose Father and Uncle Henry have been interviewing
the police, and getting all the dirt on Bart and Nick. Let me
tell you some, Uncle Henry—I understand that Captain Proctor interviewed all the witnesses, and told Mike Stewart he had
got the wrong men, and wouldn't have any more to do with the
case. Is that true?"

"I haven't talked with Proctor," said the lawyer.

"Well, you could help us so much, if you only would, Uncle
Henry. I'm told that Chief Gallivan of South Braintree says
the whole thing was a frame-up. Make him talk! Make Katzmann give us the address of Roy Gould, the man who got a
bullet through his overcoat. And those witnesses that Mike
Stewart had at the Brockton police station—surely our good
uncle who loves us ought to get their names!"

The "good uncle" continued to wear the genial smile which
was part of his stock in trade as man of the world. He was
interested in the phenomenon known as the "new generation."
He looked at this vision in pale blue chiffon, with a little basket
of blue straw turned upside down on her hair cut like a boy's;
her cheeks shining from a long walk, apparently without the
artificial aids which were coming to be the fashion, even among
the blue-bloods. An amazing thing that a girl with such charms,
who might have gone anywhere, should be devoting herself
exclusively to Bolsheviks!

Said Betty, as fast as her thoughts: "Grannie, you look
tired; you have been worrying! Is it because the police say the
money went to Italy, to make an anarchist revolution? Or have

they found out how Bart and Nick were hiding dynamite the night they were arrested?"

"You seem to be well informed, my dear niece," said the lawyer.

"Some day, Uncle Henry, after our boys are on the street—or in their graves, whichever it is—I'll tell you what I know about the Sacco-Vanzetti case, and you'll think you are listening to the memoirs of Mata Hari, the international spy. Your dear niece has become the super-sleuth of the social revolution—if the movie people knew what I have, Hollywood would be a deserted village, and studios would rise on the shores of the Back Bay. It is my job, when the police send a new spy, to get him alone and remind him that he is an Italian, and get him to tell me what he has told the police. Do you know how they found the maps of Sacco's buried treasure in Lee Swenson's trash-basket, and had three men digging in Mr. Kelly's garden one whole night?"

Henry Cabot Winters still wore his smile; but it was not in his voice as he said, "My niece does not seem to be much horrified at the idea of blowing people up with bombs."

"Uncle Henry, to be blown up with a bomb seems to me a nice clean experience, compared with things I saw in Europe, caused by the greed of elderly statesmen whose shirt-fronts were entirely covered with ribbons and decorations."

"So then, because statesmen blundered—"

"Blundering had no part in it, Uncle Henry—they knew exactly what they wanted, and they took it. It is the organized greed called patriotism that I'm talking about. And while I'm sick of all kinds of killing, it is the men who kill for greed that I am out to get. Those who kill for a cause, no matter how mistaken—those who risk their lives for the good of the workers—seem to me to shine with a bright light in comparison."

"That halo extends to bandits, my dear niece?"

"I will answer you, Uncle Henry, that small bandits break the law and are punished, while big bandits make the law and go free."

Cornelia thought that conversation had gone far enough. She knew exactly what Betty had in her mind—the Jerry Walker case. In a minute more, the child would be referring to it! "Betty dear, if you love me—"

"Love you, Grannie? I love you enough to let you think your own thoughts and live your own life, which is more than anybody else will do for you. I love you so much that I will suppress my combative impulses, and show respect to my elders. Uncle Henry, you want to know if I think Sacco and Vanzetti ever did a job of banditry. If I knew, I would tell you; but of course nobody really knows, except the men who did the job. The spies who bring tales to the police are earning their livings by pretending to know what they only guess, and the evidence they bring is not fit to hang a dog on. I can only estimate the chances. I have tried with all my might to picture Bart and Nick committing such a crime, and I cannot do it—the idea is preposterous and unthinkable. And this much I really do know—this I would die for—they never were proved ¡ guilty, and their trials were a shameful and wicked farce. Now, is that a respectful answer, Grannie?"

"Yes, dear—"

"All right; and if it won't be presuming, you look very tired, and I think we ought to adjourn and talk about something cheerful. May I tell them the news, Joe?"

Joe Randall, who realized that he did not have even the status of an "in-law" in this family, had retired to a corner of the room and lighted a cigarette. "It's all right with me," he said.

"Well, Joe has a telegram advising him that the divorce decree has been made final, so to-morrow we are going to be married, and the shadow of the great scandal will be lifted from the family, and we shall no longer get poison-pen letters in our mail, and Joe won't have to go off to his own place when he brings me home from the theater, for fear one of my relatives will be shocked by the sight of him staying here."

Henry Cabot Winters rose with his most courtly manner. "Permit me to be excused, and not inconvenience you!"

"No, no, Uncle Henry, it's an old story to us, we have been a scandal for so long that we shall miss it. At least I shall—Joe will be relieved, because at heart he is an old-fashioned Virginia gentleman—look at him blushing!"

Yes, Joe was blushing! It made him cross as the devil that Betty insisted upon placarding their love affairs before the family. He knew why she did it, of course—she was determined not to be ashamed of what she was doing—she would not let them put her on the defensive—her love was just as true as if it had been blessed by a clergyman. But all the same, no man likes to be made to blush!

Henry Cabot Winters behaved with the extrème of gallantry. "Permit me to offer my congratulations," he said, and held out his hand to the bridegroom. The family solidarity was going to be preserved, in spite of everything!

Cornelia had her Bolshevik granddaughter in her arms, and was weeping on her shoulder in orthodox family fashion. Betty too had tears shining in her eyes—a reaction from the strain they had just been under. Women, who have been but a short time emancipated, do not defy and insult the mighty males of their clan without terrific inner disturbances. They wouldn't admit it, of course; they would pretend they were crying over the end of a trial marriage! "There, there, Grannie!" said the trial bride. "Our scandal is over, and it wasn't half as bad as you imagined. Joe and I have had all our domestic quarrels in advance, so we can have the fun of a wedding without any of the grief."

XII

The marriage of Elizabeth Thornwell Alvin to Joseph Jefferson Randall did not take place in Trinity Church in the City of Boston, and there were no little flower-girls strewing roses in the aisles, nor bridesmaids with large drooping hats, companioned by stern-faced ushers from Harvard. Not all the influence of the Thornwells could have persuaded the rector of Trinity to marry a man who had allowed his former wife to divorce him without that scandal which Episcopal Church ordinances require; neither would the rebel Betty have consented to be made into what she called a "holy show."

The event took place in what was known as the "Community Church," a gathering place of eccentric persons who worshiped the ideal of brotherhood embodied in the personality of "Comrade Jesus." As this ancient Hebrew agitator had been born in a stable, his followers had purchased an old garage on Beacon Hill, and made it over with whitewash and lively red and blue paint, with stairs going up the side, and a gallery running all the way round, leading to offices from which spiritual dynamite was mailed out to the indignant respectability of the Back Bay. The pastor was a new style Christian with a sense of humor, willing to marry a young couple whose scandals did not conform to canon law.

So, on a warm afternoon of early autumn there appeared several automobiles in front of Number 6 Byron Street, and there entered Betty and Joe and Cornelia, with half a dozen other rebels old and young, and as many wide-awake and observant young men, who came to make certain that a member of their profession did not marry the daughter of the most powerful banker in town without a proper front page send-off. Some of them carried black boxes, and the "Red" bride and groom were lined up with the "Pink" pastor in the center, and there was a clicking of shutters, and a cry of "Once more, please!" A distressing scene to relatives of the bride, who had come in a vain effort to confer respectability upon the occasion.

An extraordinary moment for the Community Church: the president of the Pilgrim National Bank and his wife in attendance, dressed exactly as if for a real wedding, and holding themselves sternly erect, unaware of the existence of newspaper photographers. Also the older sister of the bride, Mrs. Priscilla Alvin Shaw, descending carefully from her motor car, clad in the voluminous garment known as a "maternity gown." Also Aunt Clara Scatterbridge—without even having been invited, but determined to do her part to maintain family solidarity, and hush the voice of scandal. This wedding, while unorthodox and unesthetic, was legal; so the horrible black shadow would be lifted from the Thornwells! No more poison-pen letters, no more whispers in Back Bay drawing-rooms! The escutcheon would be wiped clean—and the family was so relieved, it would accept any kind of performance, in any kind of made-over garage.

The bridegroom being a newspaper man, his colleagues would be loyal to him; those who happened to know that he had had a former wife, would not mention it. They would "play up" the note of social drama—the press agent of the Sacco-Vanzetti Defense marrying into the sacred Brahmin caste! The young couple were going to spend their honeymoon in a factory, getting first-hand information as to the lives of the workers; the daughter of the most powerful banker in Boston had actually got a job in a paper-box factory, at a little less than two dollars a day, and promised to live on it for a year!

When the reporters actually got upon the scene, and witnessed the big shiny limousine of the Alvins, with a chauffeur in uniform, and an equipage equally costly for the bride's sister, and yet another for an aunt—only then did they realize the explosive power of the story. This wasn't merely a local story, this was an "A.P. story"! The reporter for the Hearst paper had an inspiration: it was a "sociological marriage"! A Hearst reporter would not hesitate to tackle Jehovah himself, if he could get into heaven; so he walked up to the great banker and asked him for a comment upon his daughter's honeymoon. The haughty Rupert looked straight over the young ruffian's head—he was tall enough to do that. But alas, the mother of the bride, being less trained in the wiles of "Hearst men," committed the mistake of opening her mouth. "Mr. Alvin makes it a rule not to be quoted in newspapers." The reporter, seizing his golden opportunity, explained, "I just wanted to know, Mrs. Alvin, if your husband agrees with his daughter's ideas on social questions." The great lady replied, haughtily, "My husband does not agree with *any* of his daughter's ideas!" So, of course, the whole town had a hilarious laugh next morning.

In fact, the story "took" so well that the word went forth to follow it up. The reporters tracked the bride to the paper-box factory, and took pictures of her at work. They tracked her to the little apartment where the "sociological honeymoon" was to be passed, and published her in a fifty-cent apron, frying her first supper of bacon and eggs; they gave the price of all the ingredients, and a schedule of the "sociological budget." They interviewed the ardent young lady propagandist on every subject with which her father could fail to agree: trial marriages, love and freedom, birth control, social justice, the banking system, capital and labor, the Lucy Stone League. Nor did they fail to call up the palace on the North Shore, and ask if Mrs. Alvin would come to the phone, and hear a summary of her daughter's opinions, and say whether her husband would agree with them!

One of the McAnarney brothers, attorneys for the defense, got into conversation with old Mr. Ripley, the flag-saluting foreman of the jury, and was told, quite casually, how this foreman had had revolver cartridges, similar to the ones which had been found upon Sacco, and how Ripley had marked them, and taken them into the jury room and shown them to some of the jurors, comparing them with the exhibits of the prosecution. A thrill of excitement ran through the Sacco-Vanzetti defense; here, as in the Plymouth trial, was evidence improperly introduced, never seen by the defense. As fate willed it, Ripley died before his testimony could be taken. But the jurors were interviewed, and several swore that they had seen the cartridges; also Ripley's widow had seen them.

It was the first of a series of motions for a new trial, which were to entertain the friends of the defense for a period of six years. The "Ripley motion," and then the "Daley motion"—Daley being the friend of Ripley's, who told of the conversation at the railroad station, when Ripley said that he was on the way to report for jury duty in the case of a couple of "guinneys" accused of banditry, and, "Damn them, they ought to hang anyhow."

And then a letter from Frank Burke, the exhibitor of glass-blowing, telling how he had run into Roy Gould, the salesman of shaving-paste. The mystery of the man with the bullet-hole through his overcoat solved at last! Gould had been up in Nova Scotia all this time; now he was in Portland, Maine; and Fred Moore jumped onto a train, and the friends of the defense got the greatest thrill yet. For it was just as they had been told—Gould had been within five or ten feet of the bandit who was supposed to be Sacco, and this bandit had fired at him and pierced his overcoat. Gould came to Dedham jail and looked at Sacco, and said that he had never seen him before, and that he bore no resemblance to the bandit.

So the Boston papers broke into headlines, "New Evidence in Sacco Case," and hope sprang to life in every heart. Surely there would be a new trial now! Surely it would not be possible to execute a man, when it was known that evidence of such importance had been deliberately withheld from the jury!

For that was what had happened—the salesman of shaving-paste had given his name to a police officer, and this officer made affidavit that he had turned it in to both the local and the state police. Captain Proctor had had it!

To ardent young radicals that seemed a scandal of major proportions, and they proceeded to send out press items and to print leaflets and mail circulars—only to discover that nobody was interested except ardent young radicals. The great Commonwealth was content to leave the matter to what it called "the orderly processes of law"—which meant precisely this and nothing else: that affidavits would be typed out and sworn to, and submitted in a motion to Judge Thayer, who would take a year to study over them, and would then produce one of his famous decisions, in which the defense position would be misrepresented, and arguments of the defense would be met by answers to other arguments which the defense had never thought of!

In this case the old judge's decision was such as to cause people to wonder whether his hatred had not driven him insane. He gave his reason for denying the motion in the following words: "The affiant (Gould) never saw Sacco, according to his affidavit, from April 15th, 1920, the day of the murder, until November 10, 1921, when he went to Dedham jail at the request of Mr. Moore. In other words, the affiant must have carried a correct mental photograph in his mind of Sacco for practically eighteen months, when he only had a glance in which to take this photograph on the day of the murder." "Web" Thayer actually wrote those words, and read them from the bench, and caused them to be printed in the law-books—along with the affidavit of Gould, which stated in the plainest possible words, not merely that Gould had not seen Sacco on April 15th, 1920, but that Gould had never seen Sacco in his life until the occasion when he saw him in Dedham jail, eighteen months after the crime, and three months after the conviction!

XIV

And then the "Pelzer motion." Louis Pelzer was the bewildered Jewish shoe-worker, who had made such a spectacle of himself on the witness-stand, claiming to identify Sacco upon

seeing him many months after the crime, and at the same time
admitting under cross-examination that he had lied to an investigator for the defense. Now Pelzer made an affidavit to the
effect that his identification of Sacco was false, and that the
words, "his dead image," had been put into his mouth by the assistant district attorney, Mr. Harold Williams, whom the august
Commonwealth was soon to make into a superior court judge.

And then the "Goodridge motion." Here was the star witness
of the prosecution, whose criminal record had been kept from
the jury by the perfect team-work of those expert basketball
players, Messrs. Katzmann and Thayer. Now the defense got
onto the trail of the several-times-convicted crook, and obtained all his record, the jail sentences, the numerous wives,
and the warrant for horse-stealing in New York State, which
would have meant a long sentence, as a third conviction. Fred
Moore and another man ran their quarry down in the little
town of Vassalboro, Maine, and saw his wrists held out for
the handcuffs. Moore was naïve enough to be surprised that
the authorities did not want this crook any more—neither in
Maine, nor in New York, nor in Massachusetts could the machinery of exact and impartial justice be prodded into action.
Moore, being an Irishman, and emotional, was emphatic with
his victim, and brought down upon his head a stern rebuke
from the just and upright Mr. Justice Thayer for his method of
procedure. Which was all that came of the "Goodridge motion"!

And then the "Andrews motion." The son of "Fainting
Lola" was discovered, also living among the "Mainiacs." He
consented to come to meet his mother, who was working as a
waitress. He reminded her of various emotional dramas in
which she had played a rôle; with the result that Lola had
more hysterics, and broke down and admitted that her testimony against Sacco had been "framed." In the presence of two
well-known labor leaders she signed an affidavit, declaring that
her reason for swearing Sacco's life away was that "the Commonwealth was in possession of facts relative to the private
life of the affiant which the affiant was not desirous of having
brought out on the witness stand," and that by threats based
on that knowledge she was "coerced and intimidated." She
named the four men who had done this; one was Mike Stewart, inventor of the "theory," another was Brouillard, a police

officer, the third was Mr. Harold Williams, soon to be a judge, and the fourth was District Attorney Frederick G. Katzmann. Another thrill ran through the little band of defenders. For Lola Andrews had been the other star witness of the prosecution—it was she of whom Katzmann had said with such intense solemnity to the jury, "I cannot recall that ever before I have laid eye or given ear to so convincing a witness as Lola Andrews." Even the capitalist newspapers were moved to protest now; the Boston *American* declared that either Lola was crazy, "or else some one in the district attorney's office at that time ought to be arrested and tried for attempted murder." Upon reading that, the police authorities of the august Commonwealth got busy—not to arrest themselves for attempted murder, but to compel Lola and Louis to sign new affidavits, declaring that their previous affidavits were false, and had been obtained by threats from the defense lawyers.

xv

The Great Novelist who makes up history was desirous of making a perfect melodrama, and also a perfect demonstration of class justice, out of the Sacco-Vanzetti case. To that end it was necessary to provide an answer to the question: what would happen in the pious Puritan Commonwealth of Massachusetts if a rich man were to commit a murder? While Sacco and Vanzetti were in jail, awaiting trial, a poor devil of a Swede by the name of Johnson, having a wife and two young children, but no job, and no food in the house, and no coal in the month of January, went into some woods on a private estate, with a saw and wheelbarrow, for the purpose of gathering dead wood, which was lying in profusion on the ground. The aged owner of this estate was a Cunningham, a name of great honor in the fashionable town of Milton; and in the pride of his name and great possessions he took a rifle and shot the unarmed Swede. He fired without aiming; the victim had just got over a fence, escaping. The killer was arrested and brought to Dedham jail, and spent eight days in a cell near Sacco, and then was politely bailed out.

Cornelia, in her thinking about Massachusetts justice, had imagined a rich person committing murder, and had guessed

that such a person would be declared insane. But the case of
Commonwealth *vs.* Cunningham showed her that she had expected too much from the law. The blue-blood families keep
their insane members hidden away in remote wings of old mansions, and do not permit the stigma to be put upon them in
public proceedings. For thirteen months the killer of John Johnson did not even have to make a plea. At last he was brought to
trial in Dedham Court House, where Sacco and Vanzetti had
faced the jury. Public feeling had cooled off; and no evidence
was produced to prove that he was either an anarchist, an infidel, or a draft dodger. So the stern Mr. Katzmann became gracious and mild; the crime was called "justifiable homicide," and
the killer was acquitted.

Also it was necessary to the perfection of the Sacco-Vanzetti
melodrama that the victims should have continual evidence of
the venality of their persecutors. The Great Novelist arranged
it that three more times during the next six years emissaries
should come to the defense, pointing out the folly of spending
so much money upon lawyers' fees and circulars, when the
small sum of fifty thousand dollars, slipped to the right lawyers, would set their two friends "on the street." And lest the
young radicals should be unable to believe that these emissaries
really possessed the power they claimed, the Great Novelist
caused what was known as the "Coakley-Pelletier scandal" to
break into continuous explosion, after the fashion of Chinese
firecrackers strung on a line all the way along a city street.
For months the newspapers were filled with picturesque details about the crimes and sexual misadventures of Boston millionaires, and the prices they had paid to politicians and officials.

Dan Coakley was a Democratic lawyer, who had run the city
of Cambridge for some twenty years: a lively personality who
had begun life as a street-car conductor and had given up his
job when the company installed machines to register fares. He
had his license as a conductor, signed by the superintendent of
the company, with the words scrawled across it: "Discharged
for neglect of duty." It had amused Dan to frame this document, and hang it in his law office, while he was preparing damage suits which cost the company hundreds of thousands of
dollars. Needless to say, he was an ardent patriot; he had paid

the expenses of the Massachusetts delegation to the Democratic convention in San Francisco, so that they might vote for the Quaker attorney-general, who was so heroically smashing the Reds. For years, if you wanted to get out of trouble in either Middlesex or Suffolk County, the password was, "See Coakley."

The district attorney of Suffolk County, which includes the city of Boston, was "Joe" Pelletier. (All Massachusetts statesmen go by their pet names, unless they have a great deal of money.) "Joe" likewise was an ardent patriot, and never lost a chance to deliver an oration for God, country, and the pope. He was National Advocate for the Knights of Columbus, which is the political auxiliary of the Catholic Church; he had been knighted by the pope; and it was his job to drop charges against wealthy criminals, after they had paid proper retaining fees to the proper lawyers.

This had been going on for so many years, under the protection of the flag and the crucifix, that the ring had got bold, and had taken to "framing" cases against victims. That was all right when it was a couple of anarchist "wops," but it was a different matter when it meant sending women to lure rich blue-bloods into bed, and have detectives smash in the doors and take photographs of them. The "ring" had a regularly paid staff of women, and three apartments in the Back Bay. In one case they had gone so far as to have the woman hidden in a closet, unknown to the victim, and in this way they had got an enormous sum from a terrified old railroad president—an Adams, and a "right" one! In another case they had collected forty thousand dollars from a man on his deathbed.

XVI

It was after the trapping of Josiah Thornwell Winters that the blue-bloods decided to smash this "ring." Councils were held in the Union Club, and a citizen who had no scandals was found—the head of the Watch and Ward Society—and persuaded to the dangerous job. Godfrey L. Cabot was his name, and before he got through, it was a well-known name to the readers of Boston newspapers. For of course the ring knew what he was doing before he knew it himself, and was setting

traps for him after a fashion too fantastic for anything but
reality. Mr. Cabot got a dictaphone in Coakley's office, and
hired a spy to hire himself to Coakley and arrange to bribe
Pelletier. But presently the spy was arrested, and Godfrey L.
Cabot was indicted for hiring a man to offer bribes. The climax
of hilarity came when it was revealed that it was Dan who had
hired the spy, to get himself hired by Godfrey to come and
hire Dan to bribe Joe!

Impossible to imagine more melodrama than this scandal
provided for the readers of Boston newspapers through the
better part of a year! Underworld ladies trapped into telling
their stories, with stenographers hidden behind screens; elderly
blue-bloods "railroaded" into lunatic asylums for their money;
hotel proprietors forced to part with their property for a small
part of its value; the "badger game" and the "shakedown,"
the "girl with the dimpled nose," a "visiting actress," "the
Egyptian mystic, Omar Kaldah"! Hardly a day without a new
millionaire in the pillory, or a "scion of wealth" relieved of his
patrimony! A series of sensational trials, with witnesses
"grilled" and "broken" by great lawyers who "thundered" and
"stormed." United States Senator "Jim" Reed, endowed with
the voice of a bull, defending his Democratic colleague, "Joe":

"Does this diabolical persecution spring from religious prejudice? Is that the thing which inspires Cabot and his crew; that
makes them gather witnesses from the four quarters of the
earth; that gives protection to the criminal and the near-crim-
inal? I do not know, but this I boldly say, that I have never
seen such digging in the catacombs of the past, such raking of
the dust of time, such malicious ingenuity, such fixed determination as we have witnessed."

And then the attorney-general, answering the bull-voiced
senator, and describing the "national advocate" of the Knights
of Columbus in metaphors taken from classical oratory:

"The sword of justice was placed in his hands and he made
of it a highwayman's club. He used the scales of justice to
weigh the price of corrupt favors. He has bartered the powers
of his great office to the highest bidder. For personal ends he
has protected the criminal and oppressed the innocent. He has
so far forgotten his honor and his oath that he has brought
reproach upon the fair name of the Commonwealth, has al-

lowed her mantle to be dragged in the mire, has debauched his high office for his own selfish ends, and like Esau of old, has sold his birthright for a mess of pottage." No wonder the life of the attorney-general was threatened, and guards had to protect his home!

Also Dan Coakley was indicted and tried. The blue-bloods employed no less than thirty-six detectives to guard the jury; when Dan was acquitted, the blue-bloods wished they had hired more of them. However, Dan was disbarred from practice; and "Joe" Pelletier, National Advocate for the Knights of Columbus and hero of all Catholic patriots, was removed from office and disbarred. But not until he had gone up and down the county telling what he knew about his enemies. He announced himself as candidate for mayor—Democratic Catholic "Joe," friend of the common man, persecuted by holier-than-thou exploiters and wholesale bribe-givers. The common man thought that sounded very good; to him the victims of the blackmail ring were millionaire degenerates, preying upon his daughters; and since the law could not get them, let Joe take their money, and give part of it to the church, to be expended for orphan asylums and altar cloths!

But what a shudder in blue-blood circles, when this man who knew all secrets got up on the stump and started reciting names, places and dates. Stopping not at the most exalted offices! When he discussed the Supreme Judicial Court, he said things of interest to the friends of Sacco and Vanzetti, who were making such expensive appeals to the supreme judicial virtue of that great tribunal:

"Go up some day and watch the justices of the Supreme Judicial Court file down to the Union Club. Whom do they eat with? The capital interests, the corporation lawyers for the street railway cases, the gas cases, the light cases. These are the men that break bread with them. That may not mean anything to you. If so, bless you for your innocence! I confess to being more suspicious by nature."

Thus people's friend "Joe," soon to be tried by that same tribunal!

CHAPTER 16

THE LAW'S DELAY

I

JUDGE WEBSTER THAYER was considering the various motions for a new trial, and Bartolomeo Vanzetti was manufacturing automobile license plates in Charlestown State Prison; in his free time toiling at the task of becoming a master of English prose. He wrote an elaborate pamphlet on the Plymouth case, the importance of which, as a preliminary step to the frame-up, he alone had realized. Then his "Story of a Proletarian Life," an autobiographical sketch, written in Italian, and later translated into English with the help of friends. To Cornelia he wrote, "I have received many praises for it. I must look out to not be spoiled."

There is a story of old-time New England, how the rebel Thoreau refused to pay taxes to a government which captured fugitive slaves. He was put into jail, and his friend Emerson came to see him, somewhat shocked. "Henry, why are you here?" The answer was, "Waldo, why are you *not* here?" This anecdote was recalled by an author who came to visit Vanzetti in his cell at this time, and wrote about the case: "Now, as formerly, Massachusetts has its finest soul in jail." To this Vanzetti replied:

"I understand and appreciate the reasons by which you were adviced to exalt me far above my little merit. If there is a little of goodness in me—I am glad of it—but really I do not deserve your praises (as they are). I think there are some prisoners within these very four walls which exile me from society, which are much better than I . . . Humble I wrote for the humble who must conquire the world to peace and freedom; and I try to make plaine humble but ignored truths."

He studied incessantly, and criticized what he read. "Last evening I read a chapter of the 'psicology' (by William James). I perceive at once to deal with a really great one. He speak

478

with simplicity as Reclu and others did. I will learn a good deal from this lecture. I feel the fever of knowledge in me."

He studied the problems of his own revolutionary movement, and contributed to the anarchist press. "Actually I am overloaded of works. To-day, at noon, instead of eat my dinner I have finished the translation—from English into Italian of a quite long article. Beside that I intend to write the last letter upon 'Syndicates and Syndicalism.' I have wrote a historical, theoretic treaty on the subject. I wrote it in epistolary form. They were published—many congratulations came to me —at last the syndacalist replied to me with an article that is a misery."

He grew still more ambitious; he would write a novel! It was to be a story of an immigrant laborer: as he phrased it, "a story that really happened and has me as a spectator." "Events and Victims" was the title he chose, and he labored at it incessantly. He was not satisfied with translations made by friends, and rewrote a great part of it in his own English, patiently groping his way through the labyrinth of strange idioms. When the long labor was finished, he wrote:

"I realize, by proof, how hard the literary test is. I have no illusions. I wrote more for exercise than for anything else, and I perceived to have gained something through it by improving my capacity. The fact told had happened. As for the ideas, they are sincere. But the write was spoiled when it happened that an egg, believed cooked, smashed in my pocket outsetting thus my whole nervous system."

II

Poor old Bart! Lovable, queer, slyly humorous fanatic, keeping his sense of whimsey, the same in a prison cell as Cornelia had known it in the Brini household, and during long walks on the beach and in the woods of Plymouth! He appreciated the troubles of his friends, who were not great writers themselves, trying to help one who was excessively ambitious. To Mrs. Evans he wrote:

"A few years ago, a good divvol of comrade, felt to have something to say and wrote it down in an article that he sent to the weekly for publication. In the enclosed letter he said to the edictor: 'I have put down the words: please put down for me the commas and the periods.' To make that written presentable, the poor edictor almost lost his reason and he wrote to the writer: 'Next time, if you wish your article to be pubbliced, just put down the commas and the periods that I will put down the words for you.' "

And then the problem of keeping alive, while spending fifteen and one-half hours per day in a prison cell! Bart's friends gave him advice, and he himself took much thought. He read the edicts of an American specialist in omniscience, and commented:

"Mr. A. Brisbane always trouble me. Several month ago I read in a book of physical culture, that to sit down is an unhealthy habit and that the more one stand the better he feel. I like to feel well and consequently I took the advice. But to-day Mr. A. Brisbane tell me that the more we lay down the better it is. So I do not know now what I have to do for my good health. Till now I used to read on my feet, more often leaning like an elephant against the wall; from now I will maibe sit down. Of course, the best way to prevent diseases and troubles to a man is kill him while he feel well. Accept, please, my regards and thanks."

And always with his passionate love of the outdoors, and everything to be found there. In the summer-time Cornelia went to visit friends in the country, near the paper-box factory where Betty and Joe were working. Because the strain of her long labors was telling upon her, she took to outdoor work, and wrote much about her adventures. Bart replied:

"I am still smiling—to not say laughing. Yes, I would be very amused to see you work in your garden, for I alway laugh in observing the women at a manual work. When I wish to smile—I have only to think at a woman choping wood. I have take the ax out from the hands of some dozen of them, and cut the wood.

"But here we are! You know how to make an asparogus bed! I do not know to do it, and I have thought many time of it, for I like asparogus, and I intend if the possibility should come to cultivate them. Now I know by whom to be taught; and would it be possible, you would know what a worker I am, and what a garden I will plant and work out under your advice joined to some of my critersims. You would also know what a lighted heart the rough Bartolomeo has. In spite of all, I often feel yet as a child. I like to sing, to play and to foolish. But indeed, the water is rough now. Maibe, thanks to all the good ones among whom you are prominent, we will reach the shore someday."

III

More discoveries of evidence, and more appeals to Judge Thayer. The defense got an expert on arms, and he studied the so-called "mortal bullet" under a high-powered microscope, and submitted a series of charts with very expensive photographs, proving that this bullet could not possibly have come through the Sacco pistol. To that the answer of the Commonwealth was easy; they too had money, and could employ experts. There were more long affidavits, full of technical terms and mathematical formulas. From first to last there were only two things a layman could be sure of; that every statement by every expert would be flatly contradicted by another statement of another expert; and that "Web" Thayer would believe the experts of his own side, and overlook those of the defense.

These charts and affidavits constituted what was known as the "Hamilton motion." Then came the "Proctor motion": an amazing story, exploding like a bombshell among the friends of the cause. A new lawyer had become active in the defense, William G. Thompson, and it happened that he had had some dealings with Captain Proctor of the state police. He went to Proctor and pleaded with him, and worked upon his conscience, with the result that the old man blurted out the whole story of his part in the "frame-up." Thompson begged him to come and tell it to Judge Thayer, and Proctor said he would—provided the judge invited him. The lawyer went to Thayer in a fine fervor, thinking that the judge would be concerned about the truth, and be glad to see it prevail. But to his dismay he discovered that Thayer did not want to talk with Proctor. "We will try this proposition on affidavits," he insisted.

So Proctor told his story, how the district attorney and his assistant had framed a question to Proctor in such a way that the jury would think he meant one thing, when in reality he meant another. And then came the answering affidavits of Katzmann and Williams, another illustration of the subtle art of betrayal—these answers were framed in such a way as to seem to deny the Proctor charge, but in reality to leave the central point untouched, and by implication to admit it!

The too-ardent young radicals imagined that this story would "blow things wide open." But they found that what seemed a bombshell to them was a small firecracker to the rest of Massachusetts. This was the Harding-Coolidge era; "Nan Britton's boy" was president of the United States, and the "Ohio gang" were the rulers of the nation. The oil men had finished looting the oil reserves of the navy, and the Veterans' Bureau, supposed to take care of the victims of the great war, had stolen some hundreds of millions; all along the line, the password of government was "loot," and the power of the secret service and the attorney-general's office was used to threaten and intimidate those who disturbed the looters. In such a world it was hard indeed to get publicity for injustice done to a pair of wops; and after you had got it, the response of the public was that of the flag-saluting jury-foreman: "Damn them, they ought to hang anyhow!"

Boston was different. Boston had blue-bloods, Boston was pious, proper, and proud. But the payrolls for city work were padded with the names of many imaginary laborers; twenty policemen were accused of breaking into stores, holding wine parties in warehouses, and robbing prisoners. The state police were confiscating liquor, and selling it again, or giving it to their politician friends, who found it agreeable. The formula, "It just came off the boat," was changed to read, "It just came from the State House." By stages of graft you could mount, higher and higher, until you found yourself dealing in millions, and associating with the great bankers, who had loaned money to state legislators without security; these legislators had bought Elevated Railway stock, and had then voted a bill guaranteeing dividends, thus causing twenty-five million dollars worth of stock to jump from twenty-five to ninety. Rupert Alvin and his Pilgrim National crowd had not even had the inconvenience of being indicted for that crime; one rebel legislator, Thomas A. Niland, one opponent of graft among politicians, had hired a sandwich-man and set him to picket the

Court House with a sign, reading: "Mr. District Attorney, indict the bribe givers and bribe takers of the Boston Elevated."

IV

The Jerry Walker case came to trial. More than five years after his properties had been taken from him, the manufacturer of felt got a chance to tell his troubles to a jury, and the public to see what happened to big bandits in the august Commonwealth of Massachusetts. The case was tried in Dedham Court House with the round white dome and portholes like an ocean liner; and it was destined to be appealed to the Supreme Judicial Court, and finally decided within four weeks of the Sacco-Vanzetti case.

The Jerry Walker trial lasted from the beginning of November, 1923, to the end of November, 1924; the longest law-battle ever known in the history of the Commonwealth. During that period of time Cornelia Thornwell heard about little else when she was in touch with her family. Two of her sons-in-law, two nephews-in-law, and two cousins-in-law were involved, and the families ate, slept, walked, rode and prayed with the case for the whole thirteen months. It was not merely that fifteen millions of dollars were at stake, but the family honor, and the safety of the country's banking system; for if Jerry Walker won his case, all the business men who had lost their properties to bankers would set up similar claims. What would be the fun in banking, if you were confined to the interest on your funds, and could not use your control of credit to get possession of industry?

Cornelia was making it a rule to visit Sacco once or twice a month in Dedham jail, and she would stop at the court-house and watch the great duel of law. No guards with rifles on the steps, no gruff policemen to search your hand-bag, no steel cage for the defendants! No; for these were not the little bandits who break the law, these were the big bandits who make the law. Everything quiet and dignified, in the Harvard manner. With the exception of poor Jerry Walker himself, everybody was Harvard—the real reason poor Jerry had lost out.

Polished gentlemen, with soft voices and slow drawls, dressed with elegance, and always immaculate, regardless of weather and possible weaknesses of the flesh, arguing fine points of law, and presenting mountains of documents and miles of figures to a bewildered jury. You would not have guessed that there was anything very special or thrilling in process—unless you knew the sacred names, and realized that here were the bluest of blue-bloods, the center of the center and hub of the hub. These men who sat on hard benches listening, who took the witness-stand to testify for days and sometimes weeks, were the inner ring of those who held the financial and industrial power of New England for their own. There were times when, if you had sat with an adding machine, and tabulated the wealth owned by men in the court-room, it would have amounted to several hundred million dollars; if you had counted the wealth of other persons which they controlled, and used to sway markets and support credit for their own advantage, it would have totaled billions.

The trial would occupy a hundred and eighty-seven days of actual hearings; more than two thousand exceptions would be taken to the judge's rulings, to be submitted to the higher court; the testimony would be close to six million words, and the cost of the procedure to the County of Norfolk would be more than two hundred thousand dollars. Out of its great generosity of heart, the legislature went so far as to pass a special measure, providing for the payment of nine dollars a day to the jurymen in this case—and the bill was made retroactive! It was in the public interest that these wholesale bandits should fight out their fights in a court-room, instead of hiring private armies and settling it on the streets. When the issue had been decided, these two facts would stand out: first, that Harvard blue-bloods had the money; and second, that their fellow-members of the Union Club had permitted them to keep it.

v

To Cornelia Thornwell the really significant thing was this: that so many concerned with the defense of the case were lying. The great bankers were hiding what they had done to Jerry Walker, and their great lawyers were sitting down with them, day after day and night after night, framing what they were going to say. For five years Cornelia had known that they would do this; it was so well understood in the family that nobody was equal to the task of attempting to fool her. There were fifteen millions of dollars at stake; and the driving power of this sum was so colossal that it swept every barrier before it, and truth, honor, dignity, justice, law, country, God and religion went out like the contents of a chicken-ranch when a dam bursts at the head of a valley.

Privately these bankers were quarreling bitterly among themselves as Cornelia knew; the wives were cutting one another at bridge-parties, and families were riven pro tem. But on the witness-stand every man stood by the ship, and obeyed the orders of the captain, Rupert Alvin. Cornelia got a new understanding of her oldest son-in-law. He had always seemed to her a semi-comic figure, with his face and neck of pink and purple bulges; humorless, naïve in spite of his heavy pomposity, and pathetic while being hen-pecked by a Thornwell lady whose family was older and greater than his. But now Cornelia observed him as a man among men, and realized what are the qualities of a successful bandit-leader.

They might be summed up in a single word, dependability; the gang must know that the leader will always be there, and will never change; that he will be the incarnation of solid, heavy, earnest greed, an irresistible and incessant push for large sums of other people's money. Also, the gang must know that the leader will give them individually a greater share than any other leader of equal greed-power. A quality of Rupert's that came out in the trial—he was a veritable mountain of righteous respectability. He had only wanted a small share of the loot for himself, and it had been necessary for his associates to insist that he should have a large share. Said Quincy Thornwell, gossiping with his Aunt Cornelia during the course of the revelations, "You always have to insist that Rupert takes a large share. And you always do it. If you don't, you are not in on the next big deal."

Now here he was on the witness-stand, telling the story of his relationships with Jerry Walker; the president of the Pilgrim National Bank, who had promised poor Jerry a three-million-dollar loan at twenty-seven per cent interest, and had "strung him along" for months, having the plans all made, the syndicate of bankers formed, and Henry Cabot Winters sup-

posed to be getting the agreements ready—when as a matter
of fact Rupert had ordered that no agreements be got ready,
having no purpose but to have poor Jerry in a "jam" when his
"paper" came to maturity.

For more than a week Rupert was cross-questioned by Jerry's
little bull-dog of a lawyer, and he was most gentlemanly and
aristocratic about his lying. He had reduced it to a formula,
suitable to his simple mind; he could remember ten thousand
details which were to his advantage, and he did remember
them, promptly and exactly; but whenever there was any detail which would have been to his disadvantage, then he had
forgotten about it. And that was all; it was charmingly easy
—he had only to say, "I do not remember." The cross-
examiner might phrase the question in a score of different
ways, he might make any number of approaches to it, but he
could never get anything from the imperturbable Rupert except, "I do not remember." It amused the lawyers of Jerry
Walker to go over the record, and count up the number of
matters about which Rupert's memory had thus been adjusted
to his interests; he had managed to forget one hundred and
seventy-three different things.

Only once a bad slip! Early during the negotiations with
Jerry Walker he had put the blame on Henry Cabot Winters,
and had said to Jerry, "Henry has had his teeth in this thing
once"—meaning in Jerry's felt-business. That was a terrible
admission, and Rupert made it elaborately, and in great detail,
before his lawyers managed to interrupt, and convey to him
that it wouldn't do. The great banker then took the liberty of
consulting his counsel; after the consultation, he retracted his
admission, and denied that he had ever said any such thing
to the plaintiff. A distressing moment; for there sat the reporters of half a dozen newspapers, their pencils plying busily,
and the whole of State Street and the Union and Somerset Clubs
waiting to read the story that afternoon.

Then, the ordeal being over for Rupert, he went back to
Boston, and attended an assemblage of some men's organization connected with his Episcopal Church. Some evil person
proposed that the organization should take a stand upon the
question of social justice, and Rupert got up and moved that
the resolution be tabled, and made a powerful and impressive

speech, in which he declared that the purpose of the Episcopal Church was "spirituality," and that it should not be lured into controversies over mundane affairs. The Boston newspapers all reported the discourse, and were strong for "spirituality."

VI

Mr. Justice Thayer was rendering his decisions upon the various motions for a new trial. The "Ripley motion," the "Daley motion," the "Pelzer motion," the "Andrews motion," the "Goodridge motion"—he denied them all; and he was judge, and the sole judge. He decided that his own conduct had been proper, he decided that the new evidence was not such as to warrant a new trial.

The one thing his victims got out of these decisions was a holiday every time. The law required that the defendants should be present at all stages of the proceedings; and so a miniature army would be called out to move Nicola Sacco from Dedham Jail to Dedham Court-house, and Bartolomeo Vanzetti would leave his cell for a whole day, and become the delighted center of an automobile parade. He wrote Cornelia about it, beginning with his breakfast, "a cup of coffee, three slices of bread, two frankforts and mashed potatoes, all as cold as ice cream could be." Later when it was proposed to publish this narrative, Bart was distressed, and insisted upon its being made plain that he had made this remark playfully, because of course the prison authorities could not prepare hot food out of hours.

"After such a breakfast, an official took me in the 'Guard Room.' The little chauffeur, an old officer, and the bravest one were waiting for me. I was chained with the last one, and all four left the room and went down to the street where the automobile was ready. Six or seven officers stood at the door, with their right hand near the back pocket, ready to protect me from any attack. One must be most ungrateful man of the world for not feeling quite reconoscent."

And then his love of nature, the joy of escaping from darkness into sunshine and open air:

"So we enter now into a Park the name of which I already forget, but the beauty of it, I will never forget anymore. If

I were poet and know the meter, I would write a song of it in third rhyme. (Italian, terza rima). I am not a poet, but neither so profane to disturbing such splendor with my poor ink. The concerned officer point to me a big brick building, saying 'It is the Fine Arts Museum.' He point many other buildings saying that they are almost all a private schools. I was, then regretting to have only a pair of eyes, able to look in one direction alone. I observe everything, the trees, the bushes, the grass, the rocks, and the brook along the way on which I was raptured. The drops of dew look like pearls; the sky reflects himself in the waters of the brook, and let one think that it is bottomless."

VII

Nicola Sacco had been for more than three years a victim of the law's delay. He had spent all but an hour or two each day in a cell with nothing to do, and the strain of it was affecting his mind. He could not understand why persons who espoused his cause should look for justice to one old man who hated him and was determined to have his life. He could not understand why this one old man should need years to decide matters about which his mind was made up in advance. He could not understand why the money of the anarchist movement should be wasted upon futilities. Brooding thus, he became morose, like a dog chained up; he suspected every one who came near him, he would not sign any more legal papers; presently he would not write letters, nor leave his cell, nor speak to any one.

Cornelia would travel to Dedham to test her social prestige upon the "chief officer," as he was called, to obtain some amelioration of the harsh prison régime. The chief officer was large, stout, superannuated, and Cornelia, seeking to win his favor, had to listen to long discourses concerning his diet; he was centered upon "reducing," and talked about it in more intimate detail than even Clara Thornwell Scatterbridge. He would keep an old lady standing while he enumerated the pounds he had managed to take off by this method and that; and the next time she came, he would forget what he had told her, and tell it again. "Would you believe that I used to weigh two hundred and sixty?"

This man who could not keep from eating too much would take a tin plate of cold food, with two slices of bread on top—a narrow plate, made especially to go between the bars of a cell—and if the prisoner in the cage complained of monotony and failed to eat the food, the chief officer would discourse for another hour to his visitors: these men were worth nothing, the more you did for them the less grateful they were. When Cornelia went away, he would grumble to the other officers about rich women who came "butting in on prisons," spoiling the inmates, insisting on new things that nobody had ever heard of before. "Gosh, if that old hen would mind her own business!"

Some friends of this old gentleman insisted to Cornelia that he was well-meaning, and trying to do his duty as he saw it. But to her he seemed the embodiment of that mountainous, colossal, insensitive stupidity which was in authority throughout the world—which indeed seemed to be the very nature of authority. Several years ago there had been a legislative investigation of county institutions, and a severe arraignment of conditions; but the county graft-rings had been able to block every move, and nothing had been done.

Sacco was more of a problem than the average prisoner. He could not work in the plant which made shoes for the prisoners, because he was such a swift worker, he cleaned up everything in sight; moreover, another prisoner had attacked him, hating him as a "Red" and an atheist. He could not work in the carpenter shop, because he was a "murderer," not to be trusted with tools. Kitchen work was barred for the same reason. In short, there was nothing for him but twenty-two hours a day in a cell; so he became frantic, and at half-past one o'clock in the morning leaped from his cot and began to pound his head against a chair, in an effort to dash out his brains. He succeeded in cutting four gashes in his scalp, which a surgeon had to sew up. Then Nick declared what he called a "hungry strike," and for thirty-three days he did not touch food.

The chief officer was not allowed to do anything about it—so he understood the law; if a wop didn't want to eat, nobody had a right to make him eat. It was good anarchist doctrine, and Cornelia discovered that many members of the defense committee agreed with it. The Italians were convinced that there was no hope of saving Nick from the chair, and according to their philosophy, a man had a right to end his life if he wanted to. If he did so, the agony would be over, and the cause would have a good martyr.

There was a hearing due on one of the motions for a new trial; one of those interminable farces that occurred every month or two, whenever a motion was made, a new affidavit submitted, an argument heard. Every such time the miniature army would go into action, and the two wops would be brought in and locked in the cage; Judge Thayer would enter with a rustle of black silk robes, and the bailiff would pound with his wand and repeat his formula, beginning, "Hear ye! Hear ye!" The judge would sit down, and have another chance to pour out his withering contempt upon the prisoners and their counsel.

But during the "hungry strike," the sheriff refused to take the responsibility of moving Sacco from the jail to the court-house. What was to be done? Fred Moore had an office assigned to him, across the hall from the court-room; and there was a terrible scene—the lawyer maintaining his intention of going before the judge with a motion to determine Sacco's sanity, and the anarchists arguing, denouncing, threatening, clamoring for the prisoner's right to decide his own fate, without the intervention of aliens, enemies, traitors and spies. The uproar became so great that the judge sent the bailiff to command order. In the end Moore went ahead and made the motion, with Cornelia standing behind him. For this neither of them was ever forgiven.

VIII

Examinations were made, and the prisoner adjudged insane, and committed to the Boston Psychopathic Hospital—where they made short work of his anarchistic right to commit suicide. They strapped him into a chair and put a rubber tube up into his nose and down into his gullet, and poured in some milk. It is a hideously painful experience, and rather than undergo it again, Nick agreed to eat. After that he was committed to the Bridgewater Hospital for the Criminal Insane, where they were kind to him; the doctors would listen while he set forth his principles, and would agree that they were beautiful principles—as indeed they were. Very soon Nick was strong again, and a "good fellow," eager and sociable. Outdoor work was given to him, and he did it gladly.

So now he was "cured," and must go back to Dedham. But the physicians refused to certify him unless he was to have occupation; so the chief officer was induced to modify his time-honored régime. Nick was to do basket-weaving, and three times a week a volunteer teacher was to come and give him lessons. This was Mrs. Bang, a Danish lady, who taught manual training to blue-blood children in private schools; she must guard the dark secret, that she came three afternoons a week to visit an anarchist atheist draft-dodger convicted of banditry and murder.

Mrs. Bang was one more problem in Sacco's life. Why should a person who was able to wear good clothes and drive about in an automobile, take six long journeys a week, through a New England winter, to teach anything to a prisoner without pay? It did not fit into the class-war theory. But Mrs. Bang won his confidence—it was easier, because she was a foreigner. Strange to say, she found that Nick loved America, and wanted to live here. His wife talked about going back to Italy, but he insisted that the children had a better chance in the new world. Page Mr. Katzmann!

Nick made bags from twine, decorated with beads; he made an elaborate tray of reeds, with flowers and butterflies. He developed a wish to learn English, the better to take his lessons. So came letters, to Mrs. Evans, to Mrs. Henderson, to Cornelia: letters in home-made spelling, but otherwise clear and direct. For example, when Cornelia made a present of clothing to his family:

"I remember a years ago on our love day when I bought the first lovely blue suit for my dear Rosina and that dear remembrance still remains in my heart. That was the first day nineteen twelve in Milford, Mass., the celebration day of the five martyrs of Chicago, that in the mind of the humanity oppressed never will be forget. So in morning May first nineteen twelve I dress up with my new blue suit and I went over to see my dear Rosina and I asked her father if he won't let Rosina come with me in the city town to buy something and he said yes. So in afternoon about one o'clock we both us went in city town, and we went in a big store and we bought a brown hat, a white underdress, a blue suit, one pair brown stock, one pair brown shoes, and after she was all dress up, I wish you could see Rosina, how nice she looked, while now the sufferings of to-day had make her look like an old woman. But I never was ambitious to buy her diamonds and so-so, but I always bought everything that could be natural and usefull.

"Just now I am sitting alone always, but with me, in my soul, in my heart, in my mind, are all immense legion of the noble and generous friends and comrades. Here I say I'm sitting writing to you these few lines; the sunlight it shines on my face and for a brief time it is a relief to my soul, and it brighten my mind by looking at the clear blue sky and the beautiful mother of nature. . . . I will live for humanity and for the solidarity and for the fraternity and for gratitude to all the friends and comrades who have worked for Sacco and Vanzetti; and I will live for freedom and for justice that is the justice of all of us."

IX

From scenes in Dedham jail Cornelia would walk a few blocks to Dedham court-house, and watch the male members of her family engaged in wholesale respectable perjury. She saw Henry Cabot Winters, who had spent his life harrowing other persons, and now for the first time was toad instead of harrow. Every trace of the familiar ease and charm was gone from Henry's manner; he was exactly like any other witness telling lies and getting caught; the perspiration appeared upon his forehead, and had to be mopped away repeatedly. Under solemn oath he had declared that on a certain date he had had no interest whatever in the concerns of Jerry Walker; and then Jerry's lawyer produced the charge-accounts of Henry's office, in which the great man and his subordinates kept a record of the expenditure of their valuable time. On those pages Henry was set down as having given a thousand dollars' worth to the Jerry Walker matter, and then five thousand more—it meant several days! He had even gone so far as to open a separate account for time given to the felt-business; he was starting to take it over, at a time when the owner was resting serene in the promises of Rupert and the other bankers, that he was to have three million dollars' credit to handle his war-contracts!

Jerry Walker's lawyers produced the accounts of all his concerns, and showed how prosperous they had been. They showed the complicated series of moves whereby Henry Cabot Winters had made it impossible for Jerry to get a dollar out of any of them. The lawyer had started fake bankruptcy proceedings against one enterprise; he had secretly purchased some of Jerry's notes, and caused other persons to start lawsuits, to place attachments and obtain injunctions. And now here he was on the witness-stand, squirming and wincing, obliged either to admit that he had done these things, or else to be proved a perjurer.

On another day Cornelia heard the cross-examination of a great banker from New York, president of one of the dozen institutions which control the financial life of America. This gentleman had held several hundred thousand dollars' worth of Jerry's notes, and had turned them over to Rupert and Henry, to be used in clubbing Jerry to his knees. He had sat down with the lawyers and learned an elaborate mass of perjury, and felt very uncomfortable while telling it to Jerry's lawyer, because that lawyer happened to know him well. The lawyer asked a simple question, about which he knew the banker was going to lie; and he fixed his stern gaze upon his victim, a sort of hypnotic stare. Something happened to the witness, he "lost his head," as the saying is; all that elaborate structure of falsehood which he had learned went suddenly out of his mind, he couldn't remember the beginning or the end of it.

A dead silence in the court-room, a long, long silence, apparently endless. The witness sat with the lawyer staring into his eyes, like a rabbit fascinated by a snake. At last the judge had to intervene: "Are you conscious at all of any mental agitation just now, so that you would like to leave the stand for a time and compose your mind? I think we have been waiting nearly fifteen minutes for your answer to that question. Are you sensible of a desire to leave the stand for a while? If you are you may do so."

But the great banker could not think what to say, even to that. The Court had to repeat and urge. "You might answer that question. I ask you if you desire to leave the stand for a time and collect your thoughts on this subject?"

Finally the witness found his voice: "I would like to, to be perfectly sure on this."

Upon which the proceedings of the Superior Court of the Commonwealth of Massachusetts, now sitting within and for the County of Norfolk, came to a halt. The great Wall Street banker left the chair, and sat apart in the court-room, while everybody else, including the judge and the jury, did nothing but wait. An amazing, an incredible scene. Whispers of the spectators now and then, but mostly dead silence, so as not to interrupt the mental labors of the man of millions, supposed to be trying to recall whether he had had a certain conference with a certain man on a certain day—but in reality trying to bring back to mind the elaborate structure of falsehood which his lawyers had worked out for him.

For almost an hour that extraordinary pause continued; and all the while there were ghosts in the court-room, calling to Cornelia Thornwell. The ghosts of Nicola Sacco, being harrowed by District Attorney Katzmann! Nick being accused of the crime of having slandered Harvard College! Cornelia imagined him asking for an hour's time to dig up from his subconscious mind the statistics, that Harvard educated free something over one hundred students every year, while the University of Wisconsin educated five thousand, eight hundred and ninety-five! She imagined Nick asking for an hour's time to recollect whether he was "that man" who had dared to criticize America, after running away to Mexico! She imagined him sitting for an hour trying to recall what his lawyers had told him he had been doing on the night of his arrest! Picturing such things, Cornelia had an impulse to laugh out loud; which would have been a shocking breach of decorum—the Superior Court of the Commonwealth of Massachusetts, now sitting within and for the County of Norfolk, would never have recovered from it. But no, Cornelia had been for forty years the mistress of a blue-blood household, and she sat, perfectly rigid, keeping her excitement inside.

X

Dark days for the Sacco-Vanzetti defense, that year of 1924, with first Nick in the insane asylum, and then Bart. Funds had run out entirely; Fred Moore was a lawyer without an office; there was no committee, no program, no action—nothing but two wops in torment, and a promise of some legal decisions in an indefinite future. Judge Thayer was having an attack of pneumonia, and then of appendicitis; but refusing to die and let some other judge deal with the case. He would keep the half-crazed victims in their cells, until he could have the glory and the thrill of summoning them to court again, and with his cold metallic voice like a thin strip of steel cutting into their souls.

Betty and Joe had finished their year in the paper-box factory in a blaze of excitement. They had organized the workers, and been discharged for their activities; whereupon the workers had declared a strike, and stayed out nearly a month, and got soundly walloped by police and bosses. Betty had had her turn on the picket-line, and as a result had changed her philosophy; she was all for solidarity, and opposed to every label —socialist, communist, anarchist, or what not—which split the workers and wasted their energies. She would go to Charlestown to visit Bart, and they would get into an excited controversy, and Bart would write treatises to controvert her heresy. He would forget his own deadly peril, in his anxiety to save Betty from a false theory.

That was characteristic of all the Boston anarchists—they were strong on theory, and weak on actuality. It was that which made the defense so difficult; when a new move was to be made, they had to be persuaded, and it was a job that took until the small hours of the morning, and then had to be done all over again. No anarchist committee meeting ever ended, because somebody had a right to say something more; no decision could be taken, and if it was, it wasn't binding. If you didn't like it, you said nothing, but went off and worked against it. If anybody said that wasn't fair, you shrugged your shoulders and said: "Shoo—er, why not? Ain't I got right for say what I please? No, I no got to say it in committee, I say it when I want say it. If you not like it, you got right say so—any time, any place."

In other words a committee of anarchists was a contradiction in terms; it was not a committee, but a number of impermeable and unassimilable units, and anybody who ever did anything was sure to be regarded as a dictator or meddler. Fred Moore was sleeping on a canvas cot in the committee-headquarters, and living on pancakes, because he had turned in his last salary-check to pay the printer; yet, if you brought up a new plan to raise funds, you would be sure to hear that it was contrary to "filosofia anarchica." If, nevertheless, you insisted upon action, you would be told, "All right, do it, if you want, you got right." But if you insisted that the sanction of the committee was necessary before the action could be effective, you would hear, "No, we don't give no sanction, if you want do it, you do it for self."

Even at times when money was on hand, it was almost impossible to get them to pay it out. Money was contrary to "filosofia anarchica," it was an instrument and a symbol of graft. What did people need so much for? What right did they have to it? In one desperate pinch, Cornelia sent an organizer to New York, to address meetings and appeal to the radical labor unions, especially the Jewish clothing-workers. This man sent back a couple of thousand dollars; but he had to come back to Boston in order to get his weekly pay-check to keep him going.

Fred Moore's idea was to spend money to get more; it was the American way. When he learned that there was a convict in Atlanta penitentiary who might tell something about the real bandits, he wanted to get on the train and rush down there; he did not want to spend a night arguing with the committee, and miss his train as a result. When he wanted to send a man to Italy to hunt for Coacci or Boda, or to trail a suspected bandit to Texas or the Argentine, Moore would have to threaten to drop the case; it would be the only way to get a check signed.

Such were the sufferings of lawyers in contact with anarchists: and equally real and anguished were the sufferings of anarchists in contact with lawyers! To rebels and "libertarians" the lawyer was the incarnation of repression and enslavement; he was a spider who spun webs of tradition about the limbs of humanity. Everything he did was waste, his very language was an insult, and the expense he incurred meant a bleeding to death of the radical movement. Let the martyrs die, and spend the money upon "literature," said the fanatics. But the lawyer would point out that the money would not come for "literature," it came to keep the martyrs alive, and he was the sole possessor of the secret lore whereby that might be accomplished.

As individuals, you would find many of these Italian anarchists simple and lovable, sometimes charming; in their naïveté a relief from New England stiffness and solemnity. You must be patient with their fanaticism, realizing that it was the excess of a virtue; they represented the principle of variation, without which human life would be that of the ants and bees. When you found them most exasperating—when you felt like taking the whole of "filosofia anarchica" and dumping it into the Back Bay—then you must remind yourself that great scientists had held and taught this creed, Kropotkin and the Reclus brothers; great poets, such as Shelley and Emerson; moral teachers, such as Tolstoi and Thoreau, George Fox and William Penn, Jesus and Buddha. Not all these had called themselves by the name anarchist, but all had stood for the principle, the supremacy of the individual conscience over social compulsion. If the movement produced more dangerous lunatics than it did prophets and saints, that was the price which humanity had to pay in the search for higher types of being.

XI

Dark days for idealists and dreamers of "joostice"! Fascist reaction enthroned in Italy, and reaching out to control America; organizing the Italians into murder-bands, to break up Socialist meetings in American cities, and obtain the deportation of Italian radicals, to be shot at home. In such activities they would have the coöperation of American police, and of Federal secret service; Mussolini was the new hero of our bankers and college-students, generally voted the greatest man in the world.

It was a presidential election year, and Senator LaFollette, who had exposed the oil-thieves, was a Bolshevik and betrayer of his country, while "Cautious Cal" was the strong silent statesman, who had made more speeches than any other man ever in the White House. In their frenzy of reaction the big business men even set out to smash the proposed constitutional amendment prohibiting child-labor, and keep several millions of little ones in mills and mines, instead of going to school. There was a ferocious campaign in Massachusetts, an explosion of all the forces of bigotry and avarice. The little group of workers for the Sacco-Vanzetti defense lived in the midst of that uproar, like travelers in an African jungle who hear the beating of tom-toms and see the glare of fires upon which human flesh is being roasted.

Cal Coolidge's political and financial boss was a great lord of cotton-mills in New England, soon to be made a United States senator. He it was who led this campaign, and rallied the business men and bankers, the newspaper editors and college professors, the bootleggers, the criminals, and the hierarchy of the Catholic Church. This latter organization, kept generously by the business interests, had invested its funds in choice real estate, and become one of the wealthiest corporations in the Commonwealth. Now was the time for it to pay its debt, and suffer the little children to come unto the mill-masters.

The head of this religious machine was Cardinal O'Connell, jovially referred to by the newspaper men as "Big Bill," and by his enemies as "the papal bull"; a huge hippopotamus of a man, weighing over three hundred pounds, and like Clara Thornwell Scatterbridge and the chief officer of Dedham Jail, devoting his attention to the problem of "reducing." It happened that Cornelia had spent her summers near the prelate's summer residence, and seen him daily, taking his constitutional, a picturesque figure in a scarlet cloak, against a background of azure river. To his intimates he was a genial and convivial soul —not troubled by the eighteenth amendment, but having access to the best stores of conviviality. He was an organist and a judge of pictures, a generous buyer of old masters and rare books; a Renaissance prince of the church, building a white stone palace out on Commonwealth Avenue. The Jews had built themselves a Temple Israel nearby, a plain concrete structure, and the Irish-Catholic conductors of street-cars, answering the questions of tourists, would point their thumb contemptuously and say, "That? Sure, that's Cardinal O'Connell's garage."

Cornelia went to see him, a little later on, escorted by her nephew Quincy. She pleaded with the great man to say a word for mercy to Sacco and Vanzetti; but he was cautious and preferred to talk about Japanese art and Buddhist philosophy. Quincy sat, a much-amused spectator; being a wit and diner-out, he knew the great man, and had brought his Bolshevik aunt to tea by way of a prank. Going and coming, Quincy told stories about the Cardinal, who had begun life as an Irish "mick" in "the Patch," as the slums of Lowell were known. He was much too intelligent a man to believe the mythology he taught; but he held that it was what the masses needed to keep them obedient. He owned many blocks of stock in cotton-mills, and was a reactionist now, but in his young days had been a modernist, and highly indignant because some of his writings had been put on the Index.

There were many Catholics among the millionaire industrialists and bankers of Massachusetts, and the Cardinal would invite them to dinner; they would come with stars on their bosoms and garters on their legs, and would be in heaven. The great prelate could ask them for a million or two any day, and buy the best sites for orphan asylums and seminaries and church colleges and what not. In this way he had spent fifty million dollars in ten years. So now when these mill-owners and bankers wanted the people of Massachusetts to vote their children into wage-slavery, "Big Bill" was the boy to do their job.

Four Sundays during the month of October, 1924, he made every priest in the diocese stand before the high altar at high mass, and read aloud a diatribe, based upon the lies circulated by the manufacturers' agents, representing the Children's Bureau at Washington as a device of Moscow for the undermining of the American home. Mrs. Florence Kelley, leading social worker, and champion of the child-labor amendment, had once been the wife of a Russian. Thirty-two years previously, she had divorced this man, and had received from the courts the right to resume her father's name of Kelley; she had been a "Kelley" for sixty out of her sixty-eight years of life. But now the opponents of the child-labor amendment placarded her from Maine to California as Mrs. Wischnewetzky, Bolshevik agent! By methods such as this, they induced the people of Massachusetts to vote down the amendment by two to one, and the little children of the Commonwealth were saved for God and Senator Butler.

XII

In November, 1924, after a year, Judge Thayer handed down his decision on the Proctor motion for a new trial. This motion was the main reliance of the defense lawyers; they could not imagine how the confession of one of the state's leading witnesses that he had "framed" his evidence in collusion with the prosecutors, could fail to be ground for a new trial. But "Web" would show them! He would crowd all his arts into one document—twisting and wriggling, evading issues; misrepresenting everything the defense lawyers had claimed about the Proctor confession.

The issue was very simple, but "Web" wound it up in thousands of words, and to make plain all his tricks would require thousands more. He said that the questions asked of Captain Proctor were clear, and must have been perfectly understood by him; which would have been a good joke, if it had been meant as such. Of course they were understood by Proctor, and no one had ever suggested that they were not. What Proctor had confessed was that the questions had been contrived for the purpose of being obscure to the jury: which was certainly an entirely different matter.

Next "Web" asked whether the questions were "unfair or improper." Of course they were not. What had been "unfair and improper" was that the witness and the district attorney had framed the questions in such a way that the jury would think they meant what they didn't mean; also that the judge had represented to the jury that they meant what they didn't mean.

The question which had been "framed" had to do with whether Proctor, as an expert on fire-arms, believed that the "mortal bullet" had come through Sacco's pistol and none other. And it really made you wonder if you were dealing with an insane man when the judge went on from point to point, asking over and over again why Proctor hadn't said plainly what he meant; as if Proctor had tried to make matters plain, and failed—when the whole point of the confession was that he had deliberately made matters obscure!

But "cunning old Fury" was not insane; he knew what he was doing, and went ahead, twisting every contention out of shape, misrepresenting the plain meaning of the plainest English words. He charged the defense lawyers with having claimed that Proctor "honestly believed that the mortal bullet was not fired through the Sacco pistol." But Proctor had not said that, and the defense had not said that he had said it.

Funniest joke of all—"Web" said that the answers of the district attorney and his assistant to the Proctor confession were "clear and convincing." To employ the slang of Pierre Leon, you could "bet your shoes" they were! They were clear and convincing of the fact that Katzmann and Williams knew that Proctor's confession was true, and had not dared to deny it while Proctor was alive. They had carefully evaded the main point; and the judge now carefully followed suit; relying, of course, upon the fact that nobody would have the text of the answers, nor the patience to disentangle the sophistry in them.

Having performed this intellectual feat, "Web" was proud of it, and went out, as usual, to boast. He thought he had earned a holiday, so he went to Dartmouth, his college, to attend one of the football games. On the field he saw Professor James P. Richardson, and came up to him, demanding in a loud voice: "Did you see what I did to those anarchistic bastards the other day? I guess that will hold them for a while. Let them go to the supreme court now and see what they can get out of them!" There was more to the discourse, and the professor stood, upon pins and needles, as the saying is, because it seemed to him an unimaginable impropriety, and he knew that others were listening. He got away as quickly as he could.

It was "Web's" way. He was engaged upon a crusade, to destroy the Reds in Massachusetts; and he did not understand how others could fail to be interested in his exploits. He would punish his friends, his club-mates and associates with long tirades, until they would be bored and ask him to quit. A group of lawyers who lunched in the club at Worcester, would turn their shoulders to him and talk about other matters. The old man would sit mumbling to himself: "They don't understand! They don't realize! The Vandals are at our gates, and are going to destroy us!"

XIII

This failure of the "Proctor motion" was the finishing blow for Vanzetti. Impossible to hope after that! Impossible to go on enduring the indignities of prison. Bart decided that his friends and the whole movement were being betrayed. Also he took up the notion that his ill health was due to slow poisons given to him in his food. He too declared a "hungry-strike," and about Christmas-time of the year 1924 was certified to the Bridgewater asylum. The Sunday after he was taken away, the prison chaplain preached a sermon to his flock, pointing out the danger of departing from the holy faith. Look at poor Vanzetti, who had lost his mind, a hopeless wreck! It was the same Father Murphy who had said, "Tell me, Vanzetti, who drove the car at South Braintree?"

To the psychiatrists at Bridgewater this prisoner represented a well-known type; a victim of what they called "delusions of grandeur," or the "messianic complex." He had the notion that the future would be interested in him and his sayings and doings; that books would be written about his case, and translated into many languages, and read by millions of people. He lived his life and endured his sufferings in the presence of future generations, who would reverse Judge Thayer's verdict upon him, as they had reversed other verdicts upon agitators and rebels—John Brown and Giordano Bruno and John Huss, Galileo and Socrates and Jesus. Furthermore, he had the fixed idea that he could learn to write English, and accumulated quantities of manuscript, which he thought would convert others to his cause.

In order to pacify him, it was necessary to pretend to agree with him, and then one could have quite interesting talks. He was a man of surprising culture, considering that he had been a laborer all his life; he was reflective, shrewd, even humorous at times. He did not make friends easily, preferring to sit aloof; but when a physician said that he believed in "joostice," the prisoner would be eager to explain his brand of it, and would sit for hours, telling Dr. Stearns with the utmost seriousness how a society might be run without government or forcible repression.

These specialists in human mentality were not asked their

opinion as to the probable guilt of this convicted bandit, but they could not help having ideas on the subject. They reported Vanzetti as of the intellectual, not the motor type; awkward, not active. They said that if he committed an assault, it would be, not with intent to kill, but to show feeling. They pictured a man with his excess of emotion and imagination, attempting to commit a hold-up; it was their judgment that his heart would beat violently, his knees would shake, he would hear a noise behind him, and whirl about and shoot blindly, or throw away the gun in a panic—a "brainstorm," as it was known to the writers and readers of crime-news. The psychiatrists furthermore reported that the professional bandits and hold-up men in the prisons jeered at the idea that Sacco and Vanzetti could have done that South Braintree job; they were offended in their dignity by the suggestion that a couple of bunglers and novices could have got away with anything so competent and swift.

XIV

The jury brought in its verdict in the Jerry Walker case; a terrible blow to the Thornwell men—saying, in effect, that they had perjured themselves upon the witness-stand. The jury found that Jerry Walker was entitled to damages equal to the market value of his properties at the time they were taken from him, plus the interest; a trifle over ten and one-half millions of dollars. It was the biggest verdict ever brought in the Commonwealth, and men talked about it in the clubs for weeks.

The decision was announced a week before Christmas, and completely spoiled that gracious season in the Thornwell, Winters, Alvin, and Scatterbridge homes. Rupert took to his bed with a severe "coryza"—since it would not do for a great banker to have a common cold. He entertained his wife and visiting ladies of the family with terrible pictures of the collapse of Boston banking, consequent upon the custom of allowing decisions concerning millions of dollars to rest in the hands of men who could not have financed a peanut-stand. According to Rupert, all the bankers in Boston would immediately be sued for all the money they had made in the last ten years—which was a commentary on the city's banking-system from a leading authority.

Rupert's expensive lawyers would be put to work at once to appeal the case; and even while he was scolding and pessimizing, and snuffling and sneezing and snorting and blowing with the coryza, Rupert's mental dynamo was driving away at new plans. The details of the appeal would be left to the lawyers, while Rupert would concentrate on the judges. He had suggested the appointment of two or three members of the Supreme Judicial Court, and hoped he could count upon them. He began figuring over the others: their families and connections, social and financial. Whose men ·were they, and what obligations were they under?

Presently Rupert would be sending for good gossips, such as Quincy Thornwell, who could help him pick up information. If any of these judges had close relatives who were lawyers, it might be a good idea to retain these. If they had intimate friends who could talk to them, methods must be worked out to approach these friends—in a strictly high-minded and proper way, of course—pointing out to them the dreadful state of uncertainty in which the financial affairs of Massachusetts were left by this unprecedented jury decision. How could big bandits stay in business, if, after they had held a pistol to the victim's head and got him to sign a document excusing them for the robbery, the police should be allowed to step in and say that the document didn't count?

It would take more than two years for the Full Court of the Supreme Judicial Court to weigh and decide this mighty issue; so Rupert had plenty of time to continue his intrigue. He would not have to buy any members of the higher court; he trusted that nobody had been appointed who was not the sort of person to respect great bankers and appreciate their difficulties as the invisible rulers of America. It was an unwritten custom that as soon as a man was appointed to this court he was also made a member of the very old and exclusive Union Club; so Rupert and his associates would meet the justices at luncheon every day when the court was in session; and while they would not be so crude as to refer to the case, they could talk about business stability and the sanctity of contracts; they could arrange for others to do the same, the big and weighty men to whom the justices had had to come, to beg for the favor of appointment. At the time when Rupert knew the

Full Court was giving its time to the case, he would bring it about that great bankers from New York would happen to ride up in the elevator with the justices and happen to remark in clear tones that all business in New England was held up, waiting to find out if the courts were going to permit credit to be undermined and contracts repudiated.

xv

Yet, with all this power in his hands, Rupert was nervous; he could not help worrying, to the great damage of the calcified veins in his ankles and legs. His brother-in-law tried in vain to keep him cheerful: Henry Cabot Winters, who had worked out for himself a wonderful scheme, whereby he was going to snap his fingers at all courts and their decisions. Henry was going to make over his property to his sister, and then go into bankruptcy!

Ordinarily this service is performed for business men by their wives; but Henry was afraid of Alice. Not that she would keep his money—no Thornwell would ever be a thief; but she might have a brainstorm, and decide that it was for the good of his soul for the money to be turned over to an occultist society. Just now the mad streak in the Thornwells was manifesting itself in Alice's determination to be a lady "chela." She was bringing bowls of rice and fresh straw for bedding to a real "shri," who was at one with Brahma, and must not be spoken to. Every day Alice put on a snow-white robe and stood in front of a black screen in a pitch-dark room, in order that her aura might be studied, and her soul-troubles diagnosed thereby.

But Henry had a sister, Agatha Winters, who was pure "New England," unmarried and unchanging. He went to see her in the village where she lived in the family homestead, devoting herself to church work. He explained his troubles; wicked men had conspired to ruin him, and if they succeeded, obviously he would no longer be able to contribute to his sister's support, and she would no longer be able to give her time to the Lord. So Agatha knew that it was the Lord's purpose for her to aid Henry against his enemies. She had learned from the Old Testament that the Lord aided His own against others, and that He was not too scrupulous as to the means.

So Henry put five hundred thousand dollars' worth of liberty bonds into Agatha's name, and had them sold and converted into a bank-draft payable to her. She endorsed it, and Henry sold her some of his property for it. He then bought more liberty bonds, and had them sold in Agatha's name, and put the money into another bank-draft, for which Agatha bought another half-million dollars' worth of his property. This procedure was continued until Agatha was the registered legal owner of every bond and share of stock and piece of real estate which Henry owned, including everything which he had got from Jerry Walker; including even the automobile he drove, the yacht on which he spent his week-ends, the five-gaited snow-white Arabian stallion which he rode, and the apartment-house in which he kept his mistress, a charming and popular concert-singer.

So the great lawyer could go into court and swear that he did not own a dollar in the world; and Agatha would be able to produce canceled vouchers, showing the actual payment of cash to the full market value of every piece of property she had acquired. Hidden away in a safe-deposit box to which Henry alone had the key there was a will, executed by Agatha in Henry's favor; and a deed, selling back to Henry for the sum of one dollar and other good and valuable considerations, all the property which Henry had sold to Agatha. This latter document was blank as to date; thus Henry had everything fixed so that, the day the Supreme Judicial Court upheld the Jerry Walker verdict, he could file a petition in bankruptcy, and wipe out his share of the claims forever. After which, he would take back his property again, and laugh in the face of his enemies!

XVI

The Thornwell generations came and went. Great-uncle Abner had a paralytic stroke, which intercepted the nerves in his legs. No longer did he ride about "Hillview" on a pony, but sat in a wheel-chair and stormed and fussed when his attendants delayed to bring his meals. He still had his deaf man's voice, but could not hear a sound; you wrote your ideas on a pad for him to read. You did not have to write very much, because he was interested in his own ideas, and content if you would sit and nod and smile. Every time he found anything in his *Evening Transcript* damaging to the reputation of a "Red," he would cut it out and mark it, and mail it to Cornelia with injurious comments.

To make up for the loss of Abner's legs, Betty's older sister, Priscilla, brought four of them, eagerly kicking, into the world. The first time it was a boy, and his name at once became Alvin Thornwell Shaw, quite a load for two tiny red legs to kick under. Since his father was a mighty mountain of copper, it pleased his Aunt Betty to refer to him as the young copper hill; and when the second heir arrived and proved to be a niece, Betty took to calling her the little branch bank. Betty herself was not going to provide her mother and father with any grandchildren—at least not for a while. Betty talked defiantly about the wicked practice known as "birth control," and said that this was not a fit world into which to bring babies. What was the use of raising boys for the military men to take away from you and kill? What was the use of raising either boys or girls when their grandparents would insist upon leaving them millions of dollars, thereby turning them into parasites and deadheads?

Family propriety compelled the inviting of Cornelia to act as godparent to both the copper hill and the branch bank; but each time she modestly declined, not feeling equal to the responsibility of training either Thornwells or Shaws. But she attended the baptisms, which were in Trinity Church on a weekday afternoon, with many relatives and some invited friends. The font had been made beautiful with flowers, and there was a hymn sung by those present, and the precious infant slept soundly, wearing the embroidered christening robe, two yards long, which had been made for Great-great-great-grandfather Thornwell, the sea-captain, and used at the baptisms of his infant descendants ever since. When the splashing of cold water woke the victim up, it let out a yell of indignation, which was a good sign, the old ladies said, because it let the devil out; the old men chuckled, and commented—a powerful voice, like Abner Thornwell's and Josiah's—it was the old stock!

There were two godfathers and one godmother for the boy, and the second time one godfather and two godmothers for the girl. Each time these sponsors in baptism did promise and

vow three things in the infant's name; of which the first was
that it would "renounce the devil and all his works, the vain
pomp and glory of the world, with all the covetous desires of
the same." Cornelia Thornwell looked about her: here was the
elder Shaw, grandfather of this infant, who sat tight upon a
huge store of treasure, and some twelve years ago, when his
wage-slaves in the Mesaba Range had dared to revolt, had sent
in thugs and gunmen to slug and murder them, exactly as if
it had been at home in Massachusetts. And here was Rupert
Alvin, who had taken away ten million dollars from Jerry
Walker, and now was trying to undermine the highest court
of his Commonwealth in order to keep it. The covetous desires of the world!

And then the "vain pomp and glory." Here were stately
male personages in striped trousers and cutaway coats, or
braided black broadcloth, the very stick-pins in their ties having
ritual significance; here were ladies, who had made a life-study
of the art of demonstrating their millions and tens of millions
without appearing to do so. Here was a temple built with hands,
having single windows which had cost thousands of dollars,
and nothing within sight of it that was not luxurious. Outside
were shining limousines, and liveried chauffeurs waiting. At
the Alvin mansion there was a collation, and heads of finance
and fashion would eat cake and drink punch, and gossip about
everything that was expensive and therefore important. At the
Shaw mansion they were preparing a dinner-dance for next
week, that would be the most costly affair of the season; they
would furnish the newspapers with every detail of a great
family advertisement, and eagerly read every word next morning. The vain pomp and glory of the world!

And all this in the name of Comrade Jesus! A strange, strange
prank of time! Cornelia came out from the famous brown-
stone temple, erected to the glory of the proletarian martyr,
and walked past the statue of Phillips Brooks, which graced one
side of it. A figure of the Son of Man, stepping out of the
side of the building and laying his hand upon the shoulder of
the great Bishop of the Blue-bloods. Bishop Brooks had been
quite a radical in his day, and the wits of the city were wont
to say that the hand of Jesus was an admonitory hand, and that

Jesus was saying, "Be careful, old man, remember what they did to me, and I didn't say half what you are saying!"

From this ceremony Cornelia went to visit Vanzetti, who had been certified back to Charlestown, and was shoveling coal again. She was moved to tell him where she had been, and what she had seen, and her thoughts on the subject. "I have been wondering, Bart, if they should make a martyr out of you, will people be committing crimes and hypocrisies in your name a couple of thousand years from now?"

It was an idea the prisoner took seriously; the thought of martyrdom having become the mainspring of his lonely life. "Nonna," said he "if they make me martyr, I fix it, I write message it cannot be mistake. If anybody say Vanzett', it mean joostice, it mean freedom—it cannot mean nothing but!"

XVII

It was Boston, pious, proper, and proud. The *Telegram* was publishing onslaughts upon Sacco and Vanzetti, calling for their blood because they were "atheists." One day the staid bankers and brokers of State Street, proceeding about their business in front of the Old State House, scene of the Boston Massacre, were astonished by the spectacle of the publisher of the *Telegram* rolling in the gutter, pummeling and being pummeled by the Honorable James Michael Curley, until recently mayor of the city. Next day the two champions were issuing statements in the newspapers, each claiming to have done the more successful pummeling. The day after that the publisher was publishing a cartoon of the ex-mayor, showing him in prison stripes—he having "done" a few months many years back. And then the ex-mayor was sending the publisher to jail for criminal libel: all this in Boston, pious, proper, and proud, thirsting for the blood of "atheists"!

CHAPTER 17

THE MILLS OF THE LAW

I

BETTY ALVIN was now twenty-six years of age; old enough to know better, as her family and friends insisted, but she continued to give her time to the stirring up of social discontent. She and Joe had taken up the task of founding a labor college in Boston, to teach the workers to think for themselves, instead of for the stockholders and the bankers. Joe was teaching a class, two evenings a week, the history of European labor movements, and writing a book on the subject. Betty, learned young lady, was expounding "labor theory"; trying to adhere to a policy of working-class solidarity, and being perpetually pulled and hauled between socialists and communists. However, they would all excuse her, on the basis of her "bourgeois upbringing." In the daytime she inspected accounts and paid bills; or, when this was not possible, sallied forth to raise money. She would visit the offices of Irish-Catholic labor leaders, and do her best to persuade them that it was really in the interest of unions for idle-rich girls to meddle in their affairs, and teach them complicated theories with long foreign names.

Hard-fisted individuals these, having fought their way in a world of realities—which included Democratic and Republican politicians seeking votes and promising favors; also agents of employers making presents of boxes of cigars, and willing to lose unlimited sums at poker. "Parlor pinks," who mixed in the affairs of such gentry would learn a lot of things not in the Radcliffe curriculum; they would have a hard time deciding which leaders to educate and which to kill off. For the sake of Sacco and Vanzetti in the shadow of the electric chair it was necessary to be patient and tactful; to appeal to class solidarity, and to human feelings not entirely atrophied. Thus you might get a chance to present your case before some labor

510

body, and have anywhere from twenty-five to a hundred dollars voted to the defense.

Betty had now been for more than three years the lawful and duly certified wife of Joseph Jefferson Randall—even though she insisted upon belonging to the "Lucy Stoners," and remaining "Betty Alvin," not even "Mrs." Was it a part of the same eccentricity, that she refused to do her duty by her family, and pass on to the ages those excellences of which the family was so conscious? Did these modern young wives repudiate babies altogether, and, if so, what substitute had they to propose? Deborah never failed to make such inquiries when she met her daughter.

Now Betty came to Cornelia: "Grannie, I guess it's my turn."

"How do you mean, dear?"

"Well, there's a saying that accidents will happen in the best regulated families, and it seems that the Lord is on the side of the Thornwell clan." Such was the fashion of speech of these modern, hard-boiled young women; they would not permit themselves any of the traditional thrills of their sex, which they called being "soppy." When they referred to matters ordinarily considered "delicate," they seemingly went out of their way to find the most offensive language, with which the ears of their chaste grandmothers had never in a whole lifetime been assailed. In Betty this reaction was especially violent, as a result of having been brought up in Boston, and hearing somebody say "Hush!" several times every day. She persisted in going about telling all her friends, both men and women, the medical facts about herself; refusing to put on garments ingeniously contrived for the hiding of her shameful condition, going to her labor college and teaching classes at a time when she was a scandal on the street.

She even told two "wops" about it, when she went to see them in jail. They, being peasants, took it as a matter of course; they were used to babies, as to all other kinds of young animals. Betty would even permit Vanzetti to be "soppy"—he being in jail, and having a hard time to keep his sanity. Poor devil, he needed something young and new and sweet and healthy and happy to occupy his thoughts, so when Betty went to see him, she told him how it felt when the unborn baby kicked. It might have been one old "nonna" gossiping with another old "nonna," scrubbing clothes on the banks of the River Magra.

In due course the infant phenomenon arrived. It was a boy, and his name had been determined several months before he was born—Rupert Alvin Thornwell Randall; it would be worth millions to him some day, in spite of his mother's protests. The war that was to last all his lifetime began in the first weeks; for of course his name wouldn't be his name, until it had been conferred upon him in Trinity Church; and here were his mother and father declaring that he wasn't going to be baptized! The family brought Betty to admit that it wouldn't do any harm; if they chose to dress him up in an old linen robe two yards long and sprinkle cold water on his head, she would not interfere, but certainly they must not expect her or Joe to waste time on such foolishness. Neither must they get the idea that this particular grandchild was going to be permitted to visit them, and be waited upon by servants and demoralized by the uses of luxury. Rupert Alvin Thornwell Randall was going to live among working people, and grow up to be of some use in the world. The grandparents did not argue that; they would have the baptism first, and save the little one's soul. The other issues could be fought out later!

II

Cornelia was continuing to devote her life to the Sacco-Vanzetti case. She would get herself invited to gatherings of ladies, and tell them the cruel story, and when they said they were "so sorry," she would ask just how sorry, and explain that sorrow was measured in figures on a bank-check. She would help the defense committee to organize entertainments and benefit performances—which, alas, sometimes cost more than they brought in. She would visit headquarters, and try to keep things moving, to reconcile the endless clashings of personalities. Always there was something needing to be done, and one could not do it, or even urge it, without antagonizing somebody. What Vanzetti called "umane beings" had not yet evolved to a stage where they could merge their personalities and coöperate; they had to waste the greater part of their energies in friction. Cornelia would be so discouraged that she would give up, and tell them to do what they pleased; but then they would do nothing—and meantime there were Bart and Nick on the way to execution!

The antagonism between Fred Moore and some members of the committee had waxed with the years. It was impossible for anarchists to get along with any lawyer; it was especially hard with this one, who was hell-bent upon discovering the real criminals, and insisted upon spending defense funds in tracing clews, chasing off to Atlanta penitentiary or to Texas, sending some one to Italy or to South America to run down a story. Moore would either have his way or quit; and in the end his enemies made his position impossible, by undermining the faith of his clients in him. He received a letter from Sacco, signed, "Your implacable enemy, now and forever"; so the lawyer realized that the days of his usefulness were over. "I have failed," he said to Cornelia; "and it's a game where nothing succeeds but success."

There was an interregnum, with no lawyer, no anything else —except two prisoners on the way to the electric chair. Finally the committee was reorganized; some Italians withdrew, some Americans were taken on, and overtures were made to William G. Thompson to take charge of the new motions and appeals. He knew how much trouble it would mean, and set his fee at a figure which he meant to be prohibitive, twenty-five thousand dollars. There was a problem for Cornelia and Betty and Joe!

It was solved by a curious turn of events, hardly possible in any part of the world except Boston. A young man by the name of Charles Garland, while a student at Harvard, had known Jack Reed, and become troubled in his conscience. Now Reed had given his life to the Russian revolution, and was buried under the Kremlin walls; while his friend Garland fell heir to a million dollars. His conscience not permitting him to accept it, he turned it over to a committee, to be expended for the benefit of labor. So there was the "Garland fund"; and in this emergency it was persuaded to lend twenty thousand dollars to the Sacco-Vanzetti defense, and William G. Thompson was put in charge of the case.

A man in his early sixties, with iron-gray hair and ruddy skin, six feet tall and broad shouldered, dry and humorous, smoking a pipe and looking like a Yankee farmer, Thompson proved to be the boss of which the case had been in need. He became convinced that the machinery of justice was being used for persecution, and turned into a crusader in defense of his clients. Before he got through, the fee he had charged did not cover his office overhead; yet his enemies accused him of having profited unduly, and tried to have the Bar Association proceed against him for the offense of defending anarchists.

He had his strict ideas of propriety. This was a law-case, and was to be tried in the courts, and everything which savored of "propaganda" must be rigidly avoided. Which brought him, of course, into conflict with active friends of the cause. To Joe and Betty, propaganda was the essence of the defense; it was propaganda which had made possible the appeals and kept the two men alive; it was propaganda which brought in money to pay lawyers. Vanzetti's opinion was summed up in his formula, "Unless a million men can be mobilized in our defense, we are lost." He wanted the money spent, not for legal proceedings, but for speakers among the labor unions. But Thompson forced the canceling of a mass-meeting in Boston, by threatening to withdraw from the case if it was held.

Mary Donovan was now recording secretary of the committee without pay: an Irish-Catholic girl who had gone to college and joined the Socialist party, and been formally excommunicated by her bishop. She had a position as state factory inspector—but did not retain it very long after she took up the Sacco-Vanzetti defense. It was supposed to be a civil service position, but the politicians did not let that trouble them. They brought charges against her and proved that she had worked for the defense during several hours when she was supposed to be working for the Commonwealth. She offered to show that others in her department had done private work on public pay for weeks at a time; but that kind of evidence was not wanted.

Another recruit, Gardner Jackson, Amherst man, a newspaper reporter, very conscientious—the "Y.M.C.A. type," as an enemy described him; passionately convinced of the innocence of the prisoners, and being drawn in more and more deeply, until finally he was giving all his time without pay. But he was not a "radical," and did not want any movement to use the case for its own ends; therefore socialists, and more especially communists, quarreled with him. These disputes went on until the very end—and afterwards, when the different groups fought over the corpses of the victims. Said Mary Donovan, white-faced with anguish, "These bodies belong to us! Can't they even go to their graves in peace?" But the communists thought that the bodies belonged to the international revolutionary movement, and should be used to waken the masses to class-consciousness.

III

But those horrors lay in the future, and the Master of Events led men to them blindfolded. Neither radicals nor conservatives might lift a corner of the veil, to see what lay beyond it. They could imagine, and fear—and shrink back, unable to face what they feared. They would clench their hands and set their teeth and redouble their efforts to stave off the inevitable.

The mills of the law were grinding. One by one they ground up the motions for a new trial: the Ripley motion, the Daley, the Pelzer, the Andrews, the Gould, the Goodridge, the Hamilton, the Proctor motions. Judge Webster Thayer denied them one by one, and they became the basis of appeals to the Supreme Judicial Court, and to the public for funds to defray the bills of official printers. Defendants' Bill of Exceptions, Defendants' Amended Bill of Exceptions, Defendants' Consolidated Bill of Exceptions; and the various Defendants' Briefs and Defendants' Supplementary Briefs—legal arguments addressed to the higher powers, pointing out the innumerable ways in which Judge Thayer had broken or overlooked the rules of the game.

When you read these, you could not see how "Web" had a leg to stand on; how any court could sustain the mass of evasions and falsehoods which he called his decisions. But apparently he had no worries about this; he was proclaiming his security to all and sundry. "Let them take it to the Supreme Court and see how far they'll get!" He knew that if the court reversed him on grounds of prejudice, it would be equivalent to declaring him unfit for office. The chief justice came from Thayer's home town of Worcester, where they are very clannish, being looked down upon by Boston. Long before the trial, at a public dinner to Thayer, this chief justice, Rugg, had made a speech paying tribute to Thayer, and telling how helpful Thayer had been to Rugg when Rugg was beginning law practice.

In January of 1926, three days were set for hearings before this august tribunal, and Cornelia visited the Court House in Boston, a dingy gray old building crowded into Pemberton Square—which in her girlhood had been a lovely little park, surrounded by fine old red brick mansions of the best families. The Supreme Court room was upstairs, simple, bare and gloomy as a tomb; Cornelia sat and watched a row of seven elderly gentlemen in black silk robes at their work of adjudging life or death. William G. Thompson was called upon to argue, and the little group of friends thrilled and exulted. But, alas, such thrills were not contagious, they did not affect the elderly gentlemen behind the high raised desks. They sat, like black-clad mummies; and in the course of the long argument, Cornelia observed one of them with head sunk forward and shoulders collapsed, perfectly peaceful. Poor old man, he was nearly eighty, but still needed the job.

The average age of these ultimate arbiters was sixty-eight, and increasing every year; several were ill a good part of the time, so that it was a rare event to see a full bench in session. That threw a double labor on the few who were capable. But there was no way to get rid of the old ones, for the greater their age, the less chance that they would think of a new idea; and what the owners of property wanted was to have all things legal and governmental stay as they were. If owners of property wanted anything, they could buy it; they did not have to call elderly black-clad mummies to their aid.

The Chief Justice, Rugg, sat in the center; oddly enough, he was the only young one, being fifty-four, handsome, alert, bland and smiling while he crushed counsel with his rulings. He had been an efficient county prosecutor, and an ardent reactionary, and this was his reward. As a trustee of Clark University, in his home town of Worcester, he was the ardent

supporter of an academic clown who was turning a really distinguished graduate school into a laughing-stock of all scholars.
Also he was a trustee of Amherst, and there had helped to oust
one of the half dozen liberal college presidents in America.

Cornelia sat, her eyes roaming from one to another of the
faces. She knew the names, she knew the family gossip, and
would put this bit and that together. This one had been appointed by the governor who, after his term, became a vice-
president of a great Boston bank; that other one the same.
The family was venturing to hope that they were "safe" for a
reversal of the Jerry Walker verdict. One was a Catholic, a
former city solicitor; in matters concerning anarchism he would
be tempted to stand by God and Cardinal O'Connell. One
mumbled when he spoke, but Cornelia hoped his mind was still
alert; also that he had not been affected by his acquaintance
with Senator Crane, the respectable corruptionist who had collected the campaign funds of the rich. William Murray Crane,
first governor and then United States Senator, had run Massachusetts politics in the interest of his own property and that of
his friends. Had he made the mistake of overlooking the highest
and most powerful of the courts?

Their enemies had not overlooked them; the men who
answered corruption and class-arrogance with hate and blind
destruction. During the days of the bomb-scares, somebody
had planted a large one in a toilet in the court-house, close
to the chambers where the august justices met. That was not
merely a crime, it was an impropriety; and these old men would
have been superhuman if they had not wanted to get hold of
an anarchist, and teach a lesson to the others. The actual makers and planters of the bombs they could not punish, for these
had changed their names and got away to Italy or South America—so the Department of Justice agents declared; but in
Sacco and Vanzetti they had two who were at least friends and
sympathizers.

On May 12th, 1926, the justices handed down their voluminous decision, in which they passed upon the Dedham trial
and the exceptions thereto, and all the earlier motions for a
new trial. Twenty-two thousand words of legal technicalities—
fifty-six separate propositions which amounted to this: that
Judge Thayer had been right in everything he had done, and

that none of his discretionary rulings betrayed irrationality or corruption—something the defense had never claimed. To admit what the defense really claimed—that the judge had revealed a thoroughly prejudiced mind—would have meant to declare him unfit to hold his position; and that they would not do. From now on it would be the law of Massachusetts that a judge who desired to use his enormous discretionary power against accused persons might do so without fear of being reversed.

The plain truth was this : in other cases, where it seemed to the Supreme Judicial Court that prejudice had been displayed in a trial, they found a way to spare the feelings of the erring judge —finding some technical ground on which to order a new trial. Never had there been more prejudice, never more errors, than in this case ; but for some reason known only to them, the elderly justices declined to employ their usual device.

IV

A frightful blow for the defense; wiping out all the concealments of Katzmann, the bitter prejudice of Thayer, the confession of Proctor, the criminal career of Goodridge, the wobblings of Pelzer and Lola Andrews, the testimony of Gould —all legally dead forever! Shocking were the things which you might hear about the Supreme Judicial Court of Massachusetts from anarchists, and the aiders and abettors of anarchism, and their dupes like Cornelia Thornwell! She even got into a violent fuss with her son-in-law, Rupert Alvin—at least it was violent on Rupert's part; Cornelia could not help laughing—it seemed to her the funniest thing that had yet come out of the case. Actually, the president of the Pilgrim National Bank declared his admiration for the great integrity of the Supreme Judicial Court of Massachusetts! And after all his efforts to tempt the court from virtue! "Really, my son," said Cornelia, "there ought to be certain allowance for a sense of humor, even between a man and his mother-in-law! How long can you look at me with a straight face, knowing what you know that I know about our judges?"

Rupert tried to be sarcastic. "How can I tell what you think you know, since you have been associating exclusively with Reds?"

"No, my son, that won't help you! What I know is not from Reds but from bankers. You forget that for many years I was privileged to sit in a room while a great leader of Boston finance discussed his private affairs with his father-in-law. I never paid attention to the details—I wish now that I had—but I assure you I noted the atmosphere, and sometimes I left the room because it was so unpleasant."

"I defy you, Mother, ever to say that I have hinted at corruption in our judges!"

"If by corruption you mean selling their decisions for cash, as has happened in California and other states not so far away, I will grant that I have no evidence; but if you mean favoring our wealthy and powerful, if you mean protecting our ruling group in everything they do, then I say that the judges of our virtuous Commonwealth were appointed for that purpose and none other, and that their lives and records were gone over with a fine-tooth comb, before any one of them ever got started toward appointment. I have heard you scold a hundred times about the low quality of our political life, and the character of men who rise to high office in it."

"Yes, Mother, but never the courts!"

"There is an old question which you hear asked in church, Rupert: do men gather figs from thistles? You know how many times we have heard of judges going with cap in hand to beg favor from some political boss—either Murray Crane, or the Democrat in charge. How many of our judges can you name who are really legal scholars, publicists, economists or statesmen? They are products of the spoils system—retired politicians, ex-district attorneys or city solicitors—tools of the big corporations, put there as reward for services. Most of them have spent a life-time protecting public service and accident insurance companies, upholding laws against labor, upholding vested privilege in every form. How many of them have been in your pay, Rupert, before they went on the bench?"

She waited; and then remarked with a smile, "You could count faster if you wanted to. I know of a judge who was counsel for a great banker fearing indictment for perjury—and I know that he got that banker off through a district attorney who was afterwards disbarred for malfeasance in office."

Rupert showed a desire to withdraw from this unprofitable discussion; and his mother-in-law smiled.

"It was only in the most high-minded way, Rupert, I know! Our bankers name men who have been in their pay, and then it is the fiction that they forget gratitude! The public is expected to believe that men who have been truckling and time-serving politicians become spotless and noble-minded the moment they put on a black silk robe! But you know, and I know, that you are hoping for the Supreme Judicial Court to hand you Jerry Walker's money. And you know that they are killing my two boys for threatening property rights in New England."

V

The old evidence was wiped out, but new appeared to take its place and keep the case alive. First, the defense discovered Mrs. Kelly and Mrs. Kennedy, the two women who had looked out of a window on the bandit car, and had a perfect view of the one supposed to be Sacco. They had made to Fred Katzmann statements to the effect that Sacco was not the man, and Katzmann had kept this evidence from the defense for five years. Thompson now demanded the reports, but Katzmann's successor, Ranney, was mysteriously unable to find them. This was the time for Ranney to appear before Thayer and deliver his cynical pronouncement: "I wonder if Mr. Thompson has not an exaggerated and too ethical notion of the functions of a district attorney!"

Then the Madeiros confession. Celestino F. Madeiros was a young Portuguese, member of a gang which had robbed a bank in Wrentham and killed the cashier. He was in Dedham jail while his appeal was being heard, and his conscience troubled him, he said, when Sacco's wife came to the prison with the baby. On November 18th, 1925, he scribbled on a piece of paper: "I hear by confess to being in the South Braintree shoe company crime, and Sacco and Vanzetti was not in said crime." He handed the paper to a trusty, who gave it to Nick.

A long investigation began. Madeiros told a detailed story of the South Braintree crime, but refusing to name any of his associates. However, a skilled lawyer knows how to get the facts out of a man, and the job was attributed to a group of freight-car thieves and hold-up men of Providence, known as the "Morelli gang." Several of them were in jail, and their records were traced; Cornelia now studied the career of such persons as Bibba Barone, Steve the Pole, Gyp the Blood. Also she listened to more wrangling in the committee, because the anarchists resisted the efforts to pin the crime on the Morellis or anybody else. "What for we play polissman for state Massachusetts?"

But Thompson went ahead, and collected a mass of affidavits to be submitted in a motion for a new trial: which went the usual round, and served the purpose of keeping Sacco and Vanzetti alive for another year. Motion filed May, 1926; hearing before Judge Thayer, September; decision and appeal, October; argument before the Supreme Judicial Court, February, 1927; decision April, 1927; all very solemn and very expensive, with ancient legal phrases and complicated rules, making certain that no layman could be his own lawyer. Bart would watch the game, and joke with Cornelia; he was glad to be kept alive, of course—he could speak more words for the cause; but at the same time he begrudged the money, which might better have been spent for literature. Bartolomeo Vanzetti, the anarchist wop, had become fond of William G. Thompson, the blue-blood lawyer, who was a learned and a great-hearted man. "But he is very naïve," said Bart, gently; "he believe in the Supreme Court."

The prisoner went on to explain. "It must be that way with a lawyer; he think he have to get his what you call them, precedents, right. He think if he can show how it was done before, then he has won. It is like chess—you ever play chess, Nonna?"

"My brother-in-law used to be a champion."

"Well, you make move, you say 'check' and you have won. It is a game. But this is not a game, this is war. You say 'check,' and your enemy he knock the figures off the board, he throw them in your face." As time passed, and the courts did this to the great lawyer, over and over again, Bart would remind Cornelia, and add, patiently, "I think some time they foolish Mr. Thompson."

VI

Then came the confessions of Letherman and Weyand—two agents of the Department of Justice, whose consciences had begun to trouble them. They had got out of the secret service now, the war upon the Reds being less active. They made affidavits, telling of the part which Federal agents had played in getting the conviction of Sacco and Vanzetti. They said, in substance, that the Department had felt sure that Sacco and Vanzetti were not guilty of the South Braintree crime, but that, since they were dangerous anarchists, it was desired to get them out of the way. The Department had turned over to the district attorney's office a mass of evidence, in return for an agreement on the part of the district attorney to help the Department get information. There was much correspondence in the files of the Department in Boston which would show what had been done.

So the energies of the defense were turned to getting hold of these files. Thompson made application to the United States Attorney General, Cal Coolidge's village lawyer from Vermont; a strong, silent protégé of a strong, silent statesman—and never more silent than now! Thompson did not get the files, and neither did anybody else get them. The attorney-general made no affidavit, and neither did any of his subordinates, and there was not a squeak from Fred Katzmann or Harold Williams, now a judge!

The motion for a new trial was argued before Judge Thayer in September of 1926. A great sight was William G. Thompson that day, for his moral sense was stirred, and he talked like an old-style prophet. He paid his regards to Fred Katzmann:

"Just think of what it means, if your Honor please! Think of what it means!

"Mr. Katzmann knew and knows to-day whether Fred Weyand and Lawrence Letherman told the truth. That truth is a truth of vital importance. Think what they say! The files of the Boston office are full of correspondence with Mr. Katzmann and of documents showing the closest coöperation between the Federal Agents and the District Attorney—not Stewart—the District Attorney in the preparation of this case.

Every Federal agent who knew anything about it believed these men to be innocent of murder. 'Every one of us believed they ought to be deported. They were anarchists, they did not believe in organized government or private property.'

"Oh, how those words will ring around this world, 'private property'! Think what is going to be said about it! The man who does not believe in private property in America may be killed whether he is guilty or not. That is going to be said from one end of the world to the other if this thing is allowed to go through. Can we afford it? I do not care how high an opinion your Honor has of Mr. Katzmann. It may be he was misled. Far be it from me to make any further or other attack on Mr. Katzmann than simply what the facts warrant. He has remained silent in the face of those accusations. Nothing that I can say is more eloquent than that silence. I desire to say nothing in addition to that silence."

VII

So much for the district attorney; and then Thompson turned his attention to the village lawyer from Vermont, the strong, silent protégé of a strong, silent statesman. Said he:

"And what do you say of the refusal to produce those papers? Take all the circumstances, sir. . . . We have got a telegram from New York, but we cannot get the papers in those Boston files. What inference does your Honor tell the jury may fairly be drawn against a man if he is an humble man who is in the possession of relevant evidence and refuses to produce it? Do you tell them that it is going to help him or that it is going to hurt him?

"Is there anything so exalted in the office of the Attorney General of the United States that the inference that you draw against any other men who hold back documentary evidence should not be drawn in this case? I am not talking about him personally, of course; I am talking about him in his official capacity. Personally, I have no doubt he is an admirable citizen. But there is some reason of strong policy why those papers are not produced here. What can that reason be? What can it be? Are you going to say because Sacco and Vanzetti are Italians, because they are poor folks, because they are aliens, because they have no constitutional rights we will let Mr. Sargent hold back what might set them free?"

And then Thompson turned upon Katzmann's successor, Ranney, who had argued that the "secrets" of the Department of Justice were sacred and must be protected! Said Thompson:

"What are these secrets which they admit? They have then admitted secrets, have they? There are secrets, are there? I thought there were from the fact that it was not denied or contradicted. And I will say to your Honor that a government which has come to value its own secrets more than it does the lives of its citizens has become a tyranny, whether you call it a republic, a monarchy, or anything else. Secrets! Secrets! And he says you should abstain from touching this verdict of your jury because it is so sacred. Would they not have liked to know something about the secrets? The case is admitted by that inadvertent concession. There are then secrets to be admitted. . . .

"Mr. Ranney says that I have argued that all these Federal agents ought to be in jail. I was not so bold as to make that suggestion, if your Honor please. All I ventured to call your Honor's attention to was the fact that one of them already was in jail, namely, our friend, Shaughnessey, sentenced for twelve years for highway robbery, a man who was then investigating Sacco and Vanzetti, and going around with a badge of the United States on him as his authority so to do. I do not suggest what ought to be done to these agents. I do say, as a citizen, that it is a shame that Weiss, a man capable of making the suggestions that he made, and doing the things that he did in this case, should still be wearing the uniform of the United States and boldly operating around this town, and not even taking the trouble to come in here and deny these charges."

VIII

All that got under "Web" Thayer's skin most frightfully; you had only to watch his gray withered face and trembling hands while he listened. It made him so furious that he took only five weeks to write his decision—instead of the year he had been requiring hitherto! There were persons who believed that the reason for the Sacco-Vanzetti conviction had been ill-mannered I.W.W. lawyers from the wild and woolly west; but here was a respectable lawyer, one of the leaders of the Boston bar; and here was "Web" raging at him, with elaborate and complicated sneers such as "Web" loved, and which exhibited his learning, not merely in the legal field, but in the medical. Said "Web":

"Since the trial before the jury of these cases, a new type of disease would seem to have developed. It might be called 'lego-psychic neurosis' or 'hysteria' which means: 'a belief in the existence of something which in fact and truth has no such existence.' . . . This disease would seem to have reached a very dangerous condition, from the argument of counsel, upon the present motion, when he charges Mr. Sargent, Attorney-General of the United States and his subordinates, and subordinates of Former-Attorney-General of the United States Mr. Palmer and Mr. Katzmann and the District Attorney of Norfolk County, with being in a conspiracy to send these two defendants to the electric chair, not because they are murderers but because they are radicals. . . . This would seem to be a very low estimate of the District Attorney and his assistants. The physician, ordinarily, in diagnosing a disease, seeks to ascertain the length of time the symptoms have existed, with a view of ascertaining how deep-seated the disease is and whether it is curable or not. In these cases, from all the developed symptoms, the Court is rather of the opinion that the disease is absolutely without cure."

But the most amazing thing in that amazing decision was what the learned judge had to say about the issue of "radicalism," and the part it had played in the trial. Defending himself, with his back to the wall, "Web" cited some dialogue which he said had passed between Katzmann and Sacco. But you searched in the transcript of the testimony for that passage, and couldn't find it. You would go back and search some more —you must have skipped a page, it must be there somewhere. You would get others to search—until finally it had become certain that "Web's" citation was invented! So much progress "Judge Fury" had made since the days of the Dedham trial, when his utmost daring had been to present Frank Sibley with a page from the transcript with a passage cut out. But now he concocted passages, and inserted them in his decisions, in quotation marks, to be printed in the law-books, and handed down to the scorn and fury of all future times! Said Mr. Justice Thayer, in his rôle of fiction-writer:

"Mr. Sacco said that he feared punishment, that he was afraid of deportation, that he did not want to go back to Italy, that he had told all these falsehoods because of his fear. Mr. Katzmann, in his cross-examination, brought out all these facts and then he asked this question: 'Mr. Sacco, you say you feared deportation and that is why you told all these lies and why you did what you did?' and Mr. Sacco said 'Yes.' Then came the next question: 'Mr. Sacco, at the very time when you were telling these lies, you had already secured a passport for Italy on which you, your wife, and two children were to sail two days after the night of your arrest?' and the answer was 'Yes.'"—Not a word of that in the record!

IX

Incidents such as this furnished propaganda for the radical and labor press. No need of comment—they were their own comment. The story spread, in wider and wider circles. Pierre Leon, in Paris, would publish in his paper everything that was sent to him, and it would be taken up by socialist and communist agencies, and translated into a dozen languages, and made the subject of editorials and protest meetings all over the world.

The little group in Boston, laboring in obscurity and despair, had accomplished more than they knew. Their propaganda had influenced many thousands whose names they would never know. In part it was the natural drama of the case, the contrasts and thrills supplied by the Great Novelist; in part it was the personality of Vanzetti. Joe Randall had been right when he said, at that first meeting in Plymouth Jail: "The police have given us a good martyr." For five years Bart had been tried in the fire, and he had stood the test; it would be hard to say how any man could have stood it better. Outside, in times of excitement, he had been fanatical and violent; but now those faults were remedied by prison bars; now he was of necessity the student and thinker. He met persons of the cultivated class, and learned that they, too, were concerned about "joostice." Without weakening in the cause of his beloved proletariat, he came to understand that goodness is not a matter of class, and that love can break down as many barriers as greed can set up.

He was gentle, he was wise, and he was dignified. The humiliations of prison life had failed to affect him; he had conquered his jailers. A few days after his arrest, Mike Stewart, bluff and burly, had patted him on the back and called him "Bertie"; but now the guards understood that he was a superior man, and before his death the life of the prison had come to revolve about him. He sat for many hours a day in his cell, writing letters; and the least of these bore the stamp of his personality. He had a style now—both in English and Italian. To a friend he wrote:

"I have been told that the Italian is one of the most beautiful of languages: to me it is: it is my mother's language: it is the angelic language to me. Yet all languages are beautiful when they voice the beautiful, the good and the true. Your words are harmonious and sweet to me as friendship's voice is —they are music, the vibration of life."

Always thinking of others; with that natural courtesy which springs from a kind heart. To a rancher's wife on the Pacific coast he wrote:

"By the solidarity of the workers, friends, and comrades I always have money to enable me to buy some food and fruits, cheese, etc., when the institution food does not agree with me. I am satisfied with what I' have. Very often I think while eating of some starved human creatures and I feel a little ashamed though I have always done my part to assure a piece of bread to each mouth. So please do not be excessively troubled for me. Good sentiments and friendly words are most necessary to me—and you are very most prodigal."

So he said; but in truth he needed more than sentiments and words; he needed the bosom of that Mother Nature whom he loved with a passion both filial and romantic. When he heard that Cornelia was visiting Plymouth, he wrote to her: "Oh! that sea, that sky, those freed and full of life winds of Cape Cod! Maybe I will never see, never breathe, never be at one with them again!" He poured out the anguish of his

effort to know and to achieve—in spite of terrifying handicaps:
"Exactly talking, I am not busy in writing but in trying
to write. For, the prison's spell is telling its story also on me,
and how so! It seems to be increasing my understanding and
diminishing my power of expression. In fact . . . it is . . . an
experience all right! but an experience that undermines the life,
straight to its sources and centers so that as long as consciousness and memory are not yet weaken, you can realized something . . . but, as to express oneself at one's best one has to
be at one's best while after such experience one is not any
longer at his best! he can not any longer express himself at the
best of his power. These are the reasons why I am busy in
trying to write and writting very little at all. Oftentimes I
manouvired hard to write down what I wish; then, reaching it
I perceive that it does not says what I mean and I torn the
writting in many little pieces.

"The crux of this inner drama is not only about expression
. . . it is that I doubt my own thoughts, my opinions, my
feeling, my sentiments, believes and ideas. I am sure of nothing, I know nothing. When I think of a thing and try to understand it, I see that in the time in the space and in the
matter that thing is, both before and after, related to so many
other things that I, following its relations, both backward
and forward, see it disappear in the ocean of the unknown
and myself lost in it. It is easy to create a universal sistem,
to human minds; that is why we are blessed by so many of
universal sistems while no one know what a bed-buck is."

X

Cornelia would visit Charlestown and discuss these high
metaphysical problems with Bart, and then she would go to
tea-parties and dinners in the Back Bay, and tell her blue-
blood friends about this philosophical fish-peddler, and now
and then persuade one to call upon him. So gradually the class-
lines were broken down in Boston, and strange things happened—things which could not have been duplicated anywhere
else in the world. For example, the Madeiros reprieve, and the
way it was engineered!

The Madeiros motion for a new trial, turned down by Thayer,

was in process of appeal to the Supreme Court. But meantime, the mills of the law were threatening to grind up the principal witness! Madeiros was scheduled to be executed for the Wrentham bank murder, and if he were to die, what would be left of the "Madeiros motion"? The Governor of the Commonwealth was asked to postpone the execution, and he refused to act. By what means could his hard heart be moved?

Cornelia went to call upon a certain venerable lady, one of the oldest inhabitants of Beacon Hill, tremendously looked up to, even though she took no part in politics or practical affairs. Hardly anything in her home less than a hundred years old—except the occupant, who was ninety-something, and regarded Cornelia Thornwell as one of the young matrons. A shrine of respectability, with a little wizened female deity in a faded black silk dress, to whom Cornelia told her troubles—the losing struggle she was waging with politicians and bankers and business men who thought they were protecting society and upholding order when they took a chance on killing innocent men. See what was happening to a fine, upright lawyer like William G. Thompson, who was being abused up and down for daring to defend two anarchists!

The old, old lady listened, and then said, "My dear, the trouble is, these persons don't know Boston history. Tell them what John Adams and the first Josiah Quincy did."

"What is that?"

"You don't know history either! When the British soldiers were indicted for murder after the Boston massacre, John Adams and Josiah Quincy defended them, to be sure they had a fair trial."

"Did that really happen?" exclaimed Cornelia.

"Yes, indeed, my dear, you can look it up in the books. If you want to make any headway in Boston, why don't you really find out about us?"

It happened that at this time a New York newspaper had sent its labor editor to study the Madeiros case. This man had come with the usual prejudices, but convinced himself against his will that Sacco and Vanzetti were innocent. He wanted to do something to help, and Cornelia told him of this colonial precedent. Seeing the chance, he took it to one of the most bitter reactionaries in Boston, a man whom Cornelia herself would never have approached, for she knew that he had put up, out of his private purse, more than half a million dollars for the war upon the "Reds."

This powerful person, who had been demanding a quick death for Sacco and Vanzetti, was confronted with that sacred precedent, and felt himself rebuked. Had John Adams and the first Josiah Quincy really done such a thing? If it was true, he would do no less! He would write or call upon the Governor, and ask for a reprieve of the Madeiros sentence! He did so; and the result was, the reprieve was granted, and Sacco and Vanzetti got another six months in which to make their impression upon the world!

XI

Seven years had passed since the felt plants of Jerry Walker had been taken from him by Henry Cabot Winters and Rupert Alvin and the rest of the "Pilgrim National crowd." Two years had passed since the jury had brought in that tremendous verdict of ten and one-half million dollars in Mr. Walker's favor. In the course of seven years the new owners had made more than that amount of money out of the properties; but still Mr. Walker had not got a penny. The case had been appealed to the Supreme Judicial Court, and at last, in the fall of 1926, the seven old gentlemen in black silk robes were ready to hear the argument. A great event in the legal world of Boston: the highest priced lawyers in the city pitted against one another, for the highest stakes in history. You might be sure that none of the elderly judges would fall asleep this time! They listened day after day, while more than two thousand "exceptions" were explained and debated before them; the mere brief of the plaintiff filled three printed volumes.

The wrangling over, the seven judges took their seven heads full of arguments, and the printed briefs and the huge "bill of exceptions," to meditate and discuss among themselves. Three or four months they would need to make up their minds; but—a dreadful circumstance, almost blasphemy to mention —Rupert and Henry thought that they foresaw the outcome! In strictest secrecy the word went the rounds of the family; no need to worry, everything was going to be all right!

And so it proved. On the ninth of March, 1927, the black-clad justices spoke the final word on the Jerry Walker case: declaring that the verdict of the jury had been an error, and that the trial judge should have directed a verdict for the banker-bandits. From this time forth all banker-bandits who desired to put pistols to the heads of businessmen need only have to take the precaution to make the businessmen sign a paper forgiving them for the action.

An amazing decision for a court which was forbidden to deal with the facts, and claimed that it never did so! The release which Jerry Walker had been induced to sign, at the time that he had parted with his properties, had been an obvious part of the conspiracy; he had signed it in ignorance of what had been done to him, and one consideration of the release had been his parting with more of his property. So the jury had decided; but now the august justices stepped in and declared that this was not so; the conspiracy had been over before the release was signed, and "no fraud or duress entered into the execution of the release." In order to say this, they had to do exactly what "Web" Thayer had done so many times in the Sacco-Vanzetti case; that is, to shut their eyes to a mass of testimony which stood in the record. When it came to sparing the rich or condemning the poor, all judges appeared to be alike.

A great relief to the masters of the Boston banking-ring. No longer need they fear having to part with most of their wealth acquired during the last few years! They patted the old boys of the court on the back at lunch-time in the Union Club, and told them that they were true friends of sound and conservative business. All right to talk about the case now; neither would there be any harm if you offered to take a son or a favorite nephew into the bank at a generous salary. In time of peace prepare for war!

Jerry Walker's legal bull-dog was raising a howl, and talking about appealing to the United States Supreme Court; but that was all rubbish, said Henry Cabot Winters—the Federal courts would never take jurisdiction. He went about among his friends and took his share of the back-patting. The great bankers and lawyers who had made faces at him now began to make smiles. Since they were to keep the money, they would manage to forgive him for having forced it upon them. John Quincy Thornwell was in Paris at the time of the decision, and Henry sent him a cablegram which was the talk of Boston clubs and drawing-rooms for many a day thereafter. "Tout est suavé sauf l'honneur," said Henry. Since the World War all Boston blue-bloods know French—or they have secretaries who help them pretend to. The humorless president of the Fifth National Bank of Boston would find somebody to translate and explain those shining words: "All is saved but honor!" Goethe made the remark that every bon mot of his had cost a purse of gold; but Mr. Jerry Walker operated upon the modern scale, with splendor suited to the masters of mechanized production; he had paid ten and one-half million dollars for that bon mot of the Back Bay!

XII

Property was safe, so now there was time to think about life. The seven black-robed old gentlemen got to work on the Madeiros motion in the Sacco-Vanzetti case—the last chance for a new trial. They had been stung by world-wide criticism of the law's delay, and wanted to get the matter over, so that Massachusetts might have peace again. The motion had been argued in February, and on April 5th came the unbelievable opinion: Judge Thayer's decision, like all his other decisions in the case, had been "in his own discretion," and it was to stand! All lawyers commented upon the amazing contrast with the Jerry Walker decision, less than one month earlier. When it was a question of safeguarding the lives of workingmen, the Supreme Judicial Court held itself powerless to deal with the facts, and could only pass on the judge's interpretation of law. "Finding no error, the verdicts are to stand." But when it was a question of protecting the property of bankers, the court had not hesitated to set aside the verdict, and to declare that the jury had been unjustified in drawing the conclusions it had seen fit to draw.

The decision was written by Justice Wait, who had begun his public career as an alderman of the city of Boston—an occupation which leaves a man in no ignorance as to the relationship between business and politics, and the power of big

money in American affairs. Immediately after the decision
was made public, his home was put under guard, and the homes
of all the other judges, district attorney and officials. Judge
Thayer's home had been guarded for the past nine months, and
a husky detective followed him everywhere he went.

It was "Web's" hour of triumph, and he made the most of
it. His cries of exultation echoed through the dining-rooms of
Worcester and Boston clubs. He would button-hole acquaint-
ances on the golf-links, and boast of his perfect knowledge of
legal precedents. "I told them they couldn't put it over on
me! I wasn't going to be intimidated by anybody or anything!
I told those damned fools they couldn't hoodwink me! I represent the integrity of the courts of Massachusetts, and I shall
see that the integrity is maintained! I taught a lesson to that
long-haired arnychist from California! Yes, and I'll teach a
lesson to the people who are raising money and slandering the
courts of this Commonwealth!"

A prominent member of the Worcester Country Club came
out to his car and told his family and friends how he had
just been one of a group of men to whom "Web" had been
holding forth, referring to Sacco and Vanzetti as "those bastards down there," as "Bolsheviki," and saying that he would
"get them good and proper"; that he would "show them and
get those guys hanged. No Bolsheviki can intimidate Web
Thayer!" In one of the clubs of Boston a horrified whisper
went the rounds—a United States senator had said to the
steward in the dining-room: "If you let Judge Thayer come
to my table again, I'll have you fired." The "blue-bloods" shook
their heads and said it was a consequence of the low type of
men who were being appointed to the bench. But even so, the
courts must be upheld!

"Web" and the district attorney, who knew all tricks of
the law, were quick as a tiger in their next spring. No other
appeals were on file; and if "Web" sentenced the men, he
would clinch the case. After sentence had been passed, no
other judge of the Superior Court could take jurisdiction, and
"Web" would be the undisputed master. On April 9th, four
days after the Supreme Court's decision, he had the two "Bolsheviki" brought to Dedham court-house, with the round white
dome and portholes like an ocean liner, and had them locked

safe in their cage—the same from which they had gazed at him six years ago through a period of seven weeks. With rustling black robes he emerged from his chamber, and took his seat upon his throne: a frail old man, more withered than ever; badly scared, yet clinging desperately to his dignity in this great hour of triumph. Lawyers and spectators looking up to him, a score or two of armed men protecting him—inside the court-room with automatic revolvers on their hips, outside on the steps with rifles in hand. "I represent the integrity of the courts of Massachusetts!"

XIII

"Nicola Sacco, stand up," said the clerk of the court; and Nick rose, pale and haggard, dressed in his best black go-to-court suit.

"Nicola Sacco, have you anything to say why sentence of death should not be passed upon you?"

Poor Nick, he knew many reasons, which he wanted to shout to all the world. But his friends had advised him that he could produce no impression in a Yankee court-room, because of his blundering English. He had made up his mind to let Bart speak for him; but standing before that gray old man who had tortured him for six years; seeing the row of newspaper men, with eager pencils poised, ready to flash his words to the farthest ends of the earth—such a temptation was too much for a propagandist soul. Nineteen years Nicola Sacco had been in America, driven, humiliated, repressed; and here for the second time in his life America was ready to listen. He spoke; and the court reporter and the newspaper men kindly straightened out his dialect, and the world read:

"Yes, sir. I am not an orator. It is not very familiar with me the English language, and as I know, as my friend has told me, my comrade Vanzetti will speak more long, so I thought to give him the chance.

"I never knew, never heard, even read in history anything so cruel as this Court. After seven years' prosecuting they still consider us guilty. And these gentle people here are arrayed with us in this Court to-day.

"I know the sentence will be between two classes, the op-

pressed class and the rich class, and there will be always collision between one and the other. We fraternize the people with
the books, with the literature. You persecute the people, tyran-
nize them and kill them. We try the education of people always.
You try to put a path between us and some other nationality
that hates each other. That is why I am here to-day on this
bench, for having been of the oppressed class. Well, you are
the oppressor.

"You know it, Judge Thayer—you know all my life, you
know why I have been here, and after seven years that you
have been persecuting me and my poor wife, and you still
to-day sentence us to death. I would like to tell all my life,
but what is the use?"

It was no use whatever, and so Nicola Sacco sat down.

XIV

"Bartolomeo Vanzetti, stand up," said the clerk of the court;
and the other figure in the cage stood up: thin, worn, and
partly bald, but with the droopy mustache as big as ever; a
large, loose figure in a neat black suit with a little black silk
tie.

"Bartolomeo Vanzetti, have you anything to say why sentence of death should not be passed upon you?"

"Yes," said Bart, quietly.

And now he would reap the reward of those years of hard
work in his lonely cell; of his practice writing letters, and
treatises on syndicalism, and an autobiography, and a novel,
and a translation of Proudhon, and even a poem about a
nightingale! Bart would be able to find words; with hesitation
now and then, but not too much; with mispronunciation enough
to be picturesque, but not enough to be offensive. Quietly,
firmly, he spoke, as one who has meditated long upon his
ideas; as one who was addressing posterity, rather than the
casual few in a court-room. Posterity, hear him!

"What I say is that I am innocent, not only of the Braintree crime, but also of the Bridgewater crime. That I am not
only innocent of these two crimes, but in all my life I have
never stolen and I have never killed and I have never spilled
blood. That is what I want to say. And it is not all. Not only

am I innocent of these two crimes, not only in all my life I have never stolen, never killed, never spilled blood, but I have struggled all my life, since I began to reason, to eliminate crime from the earth.

"Everybody that knows these two arms knows very well that I did not need to go into the streets and kill a man or try to take money. I can live by my two hands and live well. But besides that, I can live even without work with my hands for other people. I have had plenty of chance to live independently and to live what the world conceives to be a higher life than to gain our bread with the sweat of our brow.

"My father in Italy is in a good condition. I could have come back in Italy and he would have welcomed me every time with open arms. Even if I come back there with not a cent in my pocket, my father could have give me a position, not to work but to make business, or to oversee upon the land that he owns. . . . But I have refused myself of what are considered the commodity and glories of life, the prides of a life of a good position, because in my consideration it is not right to exploit man. I have refused to go in business because I understand that business is a speculation on profit upon certain people that must depend upon the business man, and I do not consider that that is right and therefore I refuse to do that.

"Now, I should say that I am not only innocent of all these things, not only have I never committed a real crime in my life—though some sins but not crimes—not only have I struggled all my life to eliminate crimes, the crimes that the official law and the moral law condemns, but also the crime that the moral law and the official law sanction and sanctify,—the exploitation and the oppression of the man by the man, and if there is a reason why I am here as a guilty man, if there is a reason why you in a few minutes can doom me, it is this reason and none else. . . .

"We have proved that there could not have been another judge on the face of the earth more prejudiced, more cruel and more hostile than you have been against us. We have proven that. Still they refuse the new trial. We know, and you know in your heart, that you have been against us from the very beginning, before you see us. Before you see us you already know that we were radicals, that we were underdogs, that we were the enemy of the institutions that you can believe in good faith in their goodness—I don't want to discuss that —and that it was easy at the time of the first trial to get a verdict of guilty.

"We know that you have spoken yourself, and have spoke your hostility against us, and your despisement against us with friends of yours on the train, at the University Club of Boston, at the Golf club of Worcester. I am sure that if the people who know all what you say against us have the civil courage to take the stand, maybe Your Honor—I am sorry to say this because you are an old man, and I have an old father —but maybe you would be beside us in good justice at this time. . . .

"We believe more now than ever that war is wrong, and we are against war more now than ever, and I am glad to be on the doomed scaffold if I can say to mankind, 'Look out; you are in a catacomb of the flower of mankind. For what? All that they say to you, all that they have promised to you —it was a lie, it was an illusion, it was a cheat, it was a fraud, it was a crime. They promised you liberty. Where is liberty? They promised you prosperity. Where is prosperity? They have promised you elevation. Where is the elevation?'

"From the day that I went in Charlestown, the misfortunate, the population of Charlestown, has doubled in number. Where is the moral good that the war has given to the world? Where is the spiritual progress that we have achieved from the war? Where are the security of life, the security of the things that we possess for our necessity? Where is the respect for human life? Where are the respect and the admiration for the good characteristics and the good of the human nature? Never before the war as now have there been so many crimes, so much corruption, so much degeneration as there is now.

"This is what I say: I would not wish to a dog or to a snake, to the most low and misfortunate creature of the earth —I would not wish to any of them what I have had to suffer for things that I am not guilty of. I am suffering because I am a radical and indeed I am a radical; I have suffered because I was an Italian, and indeed I am an Italian; I have suffered more for my family and for my beloved than for myself; but I am so convinced to be right that you can only kill me once but if you could execute me two times, and if I could be reborn two other times, I would live again to do what I have done already.

"I have finished. Thank you."

XV

It was "Web" Thayer's turn. He, too, rose to speak. As it turned out, he rose to apologize; to plead that it was not his fault. A singular fact, which Vanzetti had noted about the legal machinery of the august Commonwealth—he had commented upon it to Cornelia—that everybody put the responsibility on somebody else! The arresting policemen had said it was not their fault, they had been obeying the orders of their superiors. The jailers one and all said the same thing. The chief officer of the jail had said that the higher powers would not permit this and that. Members of the jury had said that they had had to follow the instructions of the learned judge. And now here was the learned judge—at the very crisis of events—putting the blame upon the jury! The Supreme Judicial Court had said that the trial judge had had the final say as to the facts. And now here was the trial judge putting the responsibility upon the Supreme Judicial Court!

Could it be that even "Web," the insensitive, had been awed by the majesty of Vanzetti's words? Could it be that "Web," the vainglorious, was assailed by a doubt about himself? Be that as it may, the braggart was gone from his manner, and his voice was no longer a thin strip of steel, but trembling and mumbling. He said:

"Under the law of Massachusetts, the jury says whether a defendant is guilty or innocent. The Court has absolutely nothing to do with that question. The law of Massachusetts provides that a judge cannot deal in any way with the facts. As far as he can go under our law is to state the evidence.

"During the trial many exceptions were taken. Those exceptions were taken to the Supreme Judicial Court. That Court, after examining the entire record, after examining all the exceptions—that Court in its final words said, 'The verdicts of the jury should stand; exceptions overruled.' That being true there is only one thing that this Court can do. It is not a matter of discretion. It is a matter of statutory requirement, and that being true there is only one duty that now devolves upon this Court, and that is to pronounce the sentence.

"It is considered and ordered by the Court that you, Nicola Sacco, suffer the punishment of death by the passage of a current of electricity through your body within the week beginning on Sunday, the tenth day of July, in the Year of our Lord One Thousand Nine Hundred and Twenty-seven. This is the sentence of the law.

"It is considered and ordered by the Court that you, Bartolomeo Vanzetti . . ."

Here Vanzetti broke in: "Wait a minute, please, Your Honor. May I speak a minute with my lawyer, Mr. Thompson?"

Said Thompson: "I do not know what he has to say."

Said Judge Thayer: "I think I should pronounce the sentence . . . Bartolomeo Vanzetti, suffer the punishment of death . . ."

But here came Nick, with one of his wild cries: "You know I am innocent. Those are the same words I pronounced six years ago. You condemn two innocent men."

But the mumbling voice went on, in the solemn legal formula: ". . . by the passage of a current of electricity through your body within the week beginning on Sunday, the tenth day of July, in the year of our Lord, One Thousand Nine Hundred and Twenty-seven. This is the sentence of the law." It was customary for the judge to add, "And may God have mercy on your souls." But for some reason Judge Thayer omitted this part of the formula.

CHAPTER 18

I

CORNELIA THORNWELL would wake up in the middle of the night, trembling, in a cold sweat. They were going to murder Bart and Nick! Impossible to fool herself any longer; they did actually intend to do it!

For hours she would lie, evolving plans; going over in her mind the names of persons she knew who might be capable of a concern for either justice or mercy. She would turn on the light by her bedside and make notes of things to be done during the day. Betty and Joe, who now lived in the next apartment, would come in at daylight and find her writing letters. Impossible to rest!

There being no more hope from the courts, the energies of the defense were turned to the Governor of the Commonwealth, who had the power to pardon, or to commute the sentences to life-imprisonment. Legally, his power was subject to the consent of his "council," a sort of state cabinet; but then, he had power over this "council," being what was known as a "strong" man, accustomed to having his own way.

Alvan Tufts Fuller was his name, and he had begun life as a trick bicycle-rider and racer. He went into the bicycle-repair business, and prospered, and when the bicycle gave way to the automobile, he stayed on the top of the wave, and obtained the agency for the Packard car in New England, and also in Pennsylvania, and of the Cadillac car in New England. Upon every machine sold in these territories he received twenty per cent of the purchase price. Since the Packard limousine was a five thousand dollar car, it amounted to a great sum, in the neighborhood of two million dollars a year. "Allie" Fuller, trick bicycle-rider, was now the richest man in New England; authorities differed as to whether his fortune

540

was twenty millions or forty, but as a rule they guessed the higher sum.

He had begun his political career as a "Roosevelt Progressive," but that thin veneer had worn off quickly. He had been elected to Congress for two terms, but had been too busy to attend the sessions—except when it was necessary to make a speech denouncing the "Reds." He had served four years as lieutenant-governor, and had earned the enmity of the Thornwell clan by insisting upon an exposure of Rupert Alvin's purchase of the legislature in connection with the Elevated Railway bill. Fuller played the rôle of an "independent" in politics, stern and incorruptible; he made a grand gesture of refusing to take his salary—thereby obtaining advertisement worth many times the amount. He wanted the legislators and officials to have the same scorn for small sums of money; if they had possessed an income of two millions a year, they would doubtless have obliged him. As it was, they took their salaries of fifteen hundred dollars, and eked them out by means of tips from the lobbyists who swarmed to the State House, or the hotel-rooms nearby.

The system of universal graft which is American government was going on, and Fuller knew that it was going on. Once in a while some "reformer" or "crank" or "sore-head" would force an exposure, whereupon the lieutenant-governor would leap up and make a fuss in the papers, and the public would know that they had an honest public servant. The statements he made got him into trouble; the Speaker of the House sued him for slander and won a verdict—only to have it upset by the Supreme Court. But Fuller got the advertising. and on the basis of it became Chief Executive of the Commonwealth—the great master of millions condescending to play the game of democratic politics. The procedure consisted of going about shaking hands with grimy workingmen who thought he was still the bicycle repairer of thirty years ago. Hale and hearty, full of animal magnetism, with a rough exterior and a "golden heart," he kept the admiration of the "plain people." To the starving strikers of Fall River he began a campaign speech, "I am not a politician"—and they believed him. "I am no orator," he would say—and doubtless meant it, not knowing that this was a device explained in every treatise on oratory.

A typical specimen of the "strong man" in American affairs; a competent executive, a driver of other men, but utterly devoid of ideas, and incapable of thinking except in current tags. He had known all his life what he wanted, and had gone after it and got it. To a salesman of Packard automobiles, the human race is sharply divided into two parts: those who have the money to buy Packard automobiles, and those who have not. To the former, "Allie" Fuller would come forward smiling and voluble, his mentality concentrated upon flattery and "service." To that far greater number whose costume and manners make clear that they have not the price of a Packard car and never will have it, the attitude is one of indifference, except just prior to election day.

This supersalesman of automobiles was as cold as marble; utterly selfish, and lacking not merely in the finer feelings, but even in the common every-day kindness, of which politicians often have too much. No friend, no matter how intimate, ever got a discount on a car. In politics he granted no quarter; he gave the punishment and took none. In business he was the modern slave-driver with a fountain-pen instead of a whip. When, after the war, the workers in his repair and body-factory came to him, pleading humbly that on account of the increase in the cost of living they could not get along on a wage of twenty-five dollars a week, he gave them a brutal refusal. There was a strike, which was embarrassing to an ambitious politician in later years. But no diminution of that two million dollar a year income!

Such is the way by which "strong" men build up fortunes; and then they sit on the heap, regarding with instant instinctive hostility any one who suggests that there is any other ideal in life, or any other duty. And now such a man was called upon to decide the issue of life or death for Nicola Sacco, who had stood up in court and said: "I know the sentence will be between two classes, the oppressed class and the rich class, and there will be always collision between one and the other." He was to decide the issue of life or death for Bartolomeo Vanzetti, who had stood up in the same court and said: "I have refused myself of what are considered the commodity and glories of life, the prides of a life of a good position, because in my consideration it is not right to exploit man."

II

The Madeiros confession, the Letherman and Weyand confessions, Judge Thayer's decision, with its tone of raving— all these had brought a new element into the Sacco-Vanzetti case. So-called "decent" people—that is, people who had money, but nevertheless believed in fair play—were shocked by a too-obvious demonstration of class justice. One by one the few daily newspapers in America which profess a trace of liberalism were persuaded to investigate the case, and one by one they took up the campaign for a new trial.

The Springfield *Republican,* the only liberal daily in New England, pleaded the cause. The Boston *Herald* published an editorial, which won the Pulitzer prize for the best newspaper editorial of 1926. "As months have merged into years, and the great debate over the case has continued, our doubts have solidified slowly into convictions, and reluctantly we have found ourselves compelled to reverse our original judgment." That gave a terrible shock to Boston conservatism; for substantial persons who didn't read the *Globe* in the morning read the *Herald,* and such an editorial interfered with the digestion of cod-fish balls. A friend of Governor Fuller's met him on his way to the State House that morning and said, "Have you seen that the *Herald* has come out for a new trial for those wops?" Said His Excellency, "What? Has the *Herald* fallen for that bunk?"

Now had come the death sentence; and all those energies of protest which had been centered upon the courts were turned upon the Chief Executive. "Write to Governor Fuller! Wire to Governor Fuller!" said the bulletins and appeals of the defense committee. The State House was inundated by a flood of mail. It came, literally by the bushel-basket full, several times every day. The best brains of the world, the finest and most sensitive spirits, laid aside their work and composed appeals, of a sort which they imagined might stir the conscience and influence the judgment of the chief executive of a great Commonwealth. They spent money upon telegrams and cablegrams, they wrote letters for which a collector of autographs would have paid large sums of money; and what became of the product of their efforts?

The defense committee received a letter addressed to the Governor, signed by a dozen or more labor members of the British Parliament, asking him to do what he could to bring about a new trial. Gardner Jackson, Amherst graduate and a presentable person, was selected to deliver the document, and he took the precaution to take along the State House reporter for the Boston *Globe,* to introduce him.

His Excellency was not in, and they met his efficient private secretary. To him Jackson handed the letter from the members of Parliament, and the secretary took one glance at it, and burst out: "Oh, those God-damn crooks! Do you think we pay any attention to this stuff? It comes in here by the barrelful and we immediately chuck it into the fire." Then he turned upon the reporter, demanding, "What do you mean by bringing this fellow up here on a matter like this? First thing you know, those God-damn wops will be getting out and coming to live near you in Brookline. How would you like that?" It was a witticism, and the secretary laughed loudly, and threw the letter back at Gardner Jackson.

Such was the agent through whose hands would pass everything which came to the Governor on the case. When documents of great urgency were entrusted to him, and it was discovered several days later that the Governor had never seen nor heard of them, the defense committee would be infuriated, and would blame the secretary for failure of their hopes. But Joe Randall would laugh—he was furnishing labor papers with news on the case, and was up at the State House at all hours of the day and night, meeting the other reporters and hearing the gossip. "Don't fool yourself, Nonna!" said he—cynical young "Red." "The secretary forgets what Fuller doesn't want to have remembered. He is paid two salaries to serve as the goat, and have us blame him instead of his boss!"

Alas for blue-blood ladies, who left the refinements of an exclusive home, and mixed themselves in the public affairs of capitalist society! Cornelia Thornwell was now seventy-two years of age, and her hair was snow-white, and her step no longer firm—she had to be helped upstairs now and then.

And here she was, forced to measure her wits against a super-salesman of automobiles and his entourage. Startling were the tales which Joe Randall brought home about the goings on of the "State House gang." Down underneath the beautiful golden dome there was a cellar, stocked with liquors confiscated by the state police; and the heads of this "gang" were presenting the stuff or selling it to all and sundry, including the state legislators. Still more dreadful, to the mind of an old-fashioned lady, some of this crowd were using the state police boat, the *Lotus,* for what the newspaper slang termed "orgies"— drunken parties with women. All the reporters knew about it —but the friends of Sacco and Vanzetti had to wait until nine months after the wops were in their graves, before a disgruntled employee at the State House spilled the Boston beans to some prying clergymen, and an investigation was forced.

III

Cornelia Thornwell belonged to the little group of those who have a right to know. Therefore she went to her son-in-law, Henry Cabot Winters, and asked him to find out for her the Chief Executive's real attitude toward the Sacco-Vanzetti case, and what he intended to do. It was only a month after the Jerry Walker victory, and Henry was his old genial self again, pleased to have a call from his Bolshevik mother-in-law. He reported his relations with the Governor to be fairly good; he had not joined with Rupert in his row—the canny Rupert had warned him not to, for in the game of politics you can never tell at what hour your deadly enemy may become your best friend.

The great lawyer would go up to the State House, and not merely find out, but put in a word for some form of executive clemency, as a matter of political tactics. So much Cornelia had been able to accomplish by twelve years of radical propaganda in her family! She was deeply grateful, and went home and prepared a fine dinner for her son-in-law, with ribs of spring lamb, and new potatoes and green peas, and strawberries from Georgia.

But alas, the news which Henry brought completely spoiled the dinner for them both! Cornelia hardly ate a mouthful, and

Henry made a poor pretense. "I'm sorry, Mother," he said, "but you've got to steel yourself to the worst. There is no chance of saving your two boys."

Cornelia went white, and her soft brown eyes were wide with horror. "Henry, why?"

"Well, the police have got to Fuller, and he's heard all the worst about your anarchists. I don't think there's any power in the world that can change his opinion."

"What has he heard, Henry?"

"All the things I've told you before: that they were dynamiters, and were hiding dynamite on the night of their arrest."

"But, Henry, they weren't even accused of that!"

"I know—not publicly; but it's the real reason they were prosecuted, and the reason they were convicted, and Fuller has got it fixed in his mind. 'Bad actors,' he calls them."

"Then he's going to execute men for one crime, because he's heard rumors they committed another!"

"As a matter of fact, Mother, he is equally convinced they were bandits, too. He's been told that the money went to Italy, to make a revolution there. They've even told him rumors about having found maps in Lee Swenson's trash-basket, showing where the treasure was buried."

"My God, Henry! That was a joke!"

"I know, so you told me—but it was a poor time for joking. The police are using everything they have. It seems there's a woman in Milton who told Mike Stewart that Vanzetti made the bomb that blew up Judge Hayden's house."

"Henry, that is the talk of lunatics!"

"No, Mother, it's the talk of the police, and the Governor regards himself as the head of the force, and he stands by it. They have told him that two of the crowd blew themselves up with a bomb they were making in Bellingham—the Galleani formulas didn't work right."

"You keep talking about bombs, Henry."

"I'm telling you what was told me. Fuller says that both your boys were regular terrorists, and had a criminal record. He insists that Vanzetti was a convicted bandit before he came to trial at Dedham. He has got it into his head that Vanzetti was arrested, indicted, tried and convicted of the Bridgewater crime, and then arrested, indicted, tried and convicted of the

South Braintree crime. It didn't happen that way, did it?"
"Of course not, Henry! They arrested them for both crimes.
They decided to convict Bart for Bridgewater, as a means of
making things look blacker for Nick."
"Well, that's what I thought, and I tried to get it across to
Fuller, but he didn't take kindly to it. He doesn't like to have
his mind changed."
"Henry, you appall me! You mean he is actually as ignorant
of the case as that?"
"I don't know so much about the case myself, Mother, but
I was able to note half a dozen mistakes he made; and you're
going to have a hard time changing him, because stubbornness
is his leading quality. He makes a virtue of it, because he can't
think, and knows it, and resents having to try. That's what
you're up against, and you might as well know it at the outset—no use fooling yourself. Go and see him, and make sure,
if you want to."
"Will he see me?"
"He says he'll see everybody—that's going to be his grand-
stand play. You understand, he's a politician, and has to play
the game. He will pretend to be open-minded—but I'm telling
you what's in the back of his head, and what will be his final
decision."

IV

Cornelia discussed the soul of this Governor, and a possible
way to move it. No use in public propaganda, mass-meetings
and petitions; he regarded them with contempt. Could he be
reached by social pressure, the snobbery of the automobile
dealer, who sold high-priced cars to high-priced customers?
Henry answered that Fuller himself didn't appear to care for
the social game; but doubtless his family would be glad to
be received. The only sign of an interest in culture on Fuller's
part was that he went abroad and purchased paintings. He
didn't really know about painting, and would not have dared
to buy the work of Americans, for fear of playing the fool.
But "old masters" were standard, as safe as corner real estate
on Tremont Street; so he would pay a quarter of a million
dollars for a Van Dyke, and put it in his drawing-room, and

that would make a great stir in the papers. But it hadn't had any effect socially, as Cornelia knew; to the inner circle of Boston exclusiveness, Fuller was His Excellency during office hours, but at tea-time and in the evening he was a dealer in motor-cars.

"Too bad that Alice is so spiritualized," said Henry. "She might give them a dinner." Alice, he added, was now receiving the ministrations of a Yogi "master," being subjected to the most esoteric rite of healing, which consisted of blowing into her ear.

Cornelia got out her address-book, which had secret marks, indicating degrees of responsiveness to subversive propaganda. She and her son-in-law compiled a list, and laid out a program upon which blue-bloods should be asked to concentrate—to persuade the Governor to appoint some sort of commission to investigate the case, and give it an informal new trial. If, as Henry believed, the supersalesman himself was hopeless, the strategy was to get him committed to an arrangement whereby the final decision would rest with more open-minded persons.

The little old lady had an inspiration: instead of appealing directly to the Governor, they would concentrate their energies upon Bishop Lawrence of the Episcopal Church, blood-brother to all blue-bloods, and official delegate of the Prince of Peace on earth. Persuade the Bishop to appeal to the Governor for an impartial commission! To make a thorough job of it, why not determine the commission in advance, and make certain of getting competent and high-minded persons? Why not? agreed Henry; so they proceeded to discuss names. Cornelia worked herself up to a pitch of excitement. "Couldn't we ask him to appoint Mr. Lowell?" She meant President Lowell of Harvard University. The blue-blood ladies, while paying full homage to this great personality, do not grant him his title, as in the case of the Bishop; by this means they indicate the fact that the intellectual life, while important, is a merely human affair, while the spiritual life is from God.

"He wouldn't take the responsibility," said Henry, "but of course it would settle the matter if he did. Fuller wouldn't dare go against Lowell and the Bishop."

So it came about that at the office of Mr. John F. Moors, of the firm of Moors and Cabot, investment bankers, there assembled one afternoon a group of socially and intellectually significant persons: half a dozen Harvard professors, and the wives of several others; Episcopal clergymen of Boston and Concord; and such persons as Mrs. Thornwell, Mrs. Evans and Mrs. Winslow, with Mary Donovan and Gardner Jackson to represent the committee. They met for the purpose of working out a method of approaching the Bishop of the Blue-bloods, and asking him to bring it about that the University-president of the Blue-bloods should be invited to conduct a blue-blood trial of Sacco and Vanzetti, and thus save the good name of the Commonwealth of Massachusetts before the civilized world.

A curious gathering: soft-voiced, gentle, noble-minded, but not entirely efficient persons, meeting in dead secrecy, with their fingers upon their lips, in this melodramatic neighborhood of State Street; a group of kindly conspirators, babes in the woods surrounded by ravenous wolves—in the form of newspaper reporters who would gobble up their respectability with half a dozen snaps of their slavering jaws. So careful they must be, to make exactly the right approach to the ineffable Bishop; putting on felt-slippers and walking on tiptoes! Not saying anything extreme to him! Not declaring that the men were innocent, but merely that they had not been proved guilty to impartial minds! Sparks began to fly from the eyes of Mary Donovan, Irish ex-Catholic Joan of Arc of the labor movement. A curious contrast between self-contained and decorous ladies of the Back Bay, and this fiery Celtic girl, plain of garb, severe of countenance, making no secret of her bitter scorn for liberals and their ritual.

Silence! Secrecy! Hush, not a word! Even the widow of Governor Thornwell had lost caste, because she had had her name in the newspapers! No one who had been in the newspapers must approach the Bishop, nor even be named to the Bishop—for fear the timid episcopal soul might seek refuge in the recesses of the episcopal hole and refuse to emerge. The members of the Sacco-Vanzetti committee were "untouchables," and merely to have it known that they desired a certain procedure would be sufficient to render it episcopally impossible. All were warned to silence, the meeting dispersed—and in an hour or two the newspapermen had the whole story on the front page, each after its own fashion. The Hearst man explained the social stratifications, referring to the Sacco-Vanzetti committee as the "low minds," the Moors group as the "middle minds," and the Bishop Lawrence group as the "high minds"!

V

Mr. Thompson had presented an appeal for clemency from Vanzetti, and an explanation that Sacco refused to make any appeal, but ought to have it granted just the same. It was, perhaps, the most singular document ever submitted to an automobile salesman in the history of the industry. Bartolomeo Vanzetti had insisted upon writing it himself, with only verbal revision by his lawyer. He took it as an occasion to explain his doctrines and beliefs to the world:

"Our ideas are not new. In one form or another they have influenced human thought in the western world, and therefore history, for at least two thousand years. Among their modern champions are men such as William Godwin, Shelley, Carlo Pisacane, Proudhon, Reclus, Kropotkin, Bakunin, Tolstoi (in a sense), Flammarion, Malatesta, Galleani, and in your country Tucker, and other great intellects and hearts. The great philosopher Ernest Renan said that Christ was a 'political anarchist.' "

And this to a pious Baptist, who told the newspaper reporters that his real preference in life would be to run a Baptist Sunday-school! A Mason, an Elk, an Odd Fellow and a Knight of Pythias—his idea of literature the *Saturday Evening Post!* Said Vanzetti:

"Our counsel has warned us that what we have to say may deepen the prejudice against us; but we are foremostly concerned to save what no human power except ourselves can deprive us of, our faith and our dignity, since we have already been deprived of almost all of what men can deprive men."

The Governor announced that he would consider evidence from both sides; and so it was a question of repeating all over again the Dedham, and later the Plymouth trial. But under what singular circumstances! Mr. Thompson, the lawyer for the petitioners, was not allowed to make any opening statement, to say what he expected to prove; he was allowed to bring his own witnesses, but not to hear the witnesses of the other side, nor even to know who they were. Sacco and Vanzetti lay in their cells, and men came to the Governor's private office and whispered rumors about them, and their attorney learned about it from gossip in the newspapers! Betty Alvin came home from her brief session in the executive chambers and revised the "Alice in Wonderland" verses to fit this new situation:

> I'll be judge, I'll be jury,
> Said *stupid* old Fury;
> I'll try the whole cause and condemn you to death!

Quite literally, this supersalesman of automobiles was judge, jury, and prosecuting attorney; and so ignorant of psychology that he really thought he could fill all three rôles; so ignorant of law that he really thought it was a trial he was conducting, and would be accepted as such by the world. Or rather, if you could believe the sarcastic young lady Bolshevik, he thought that he was so rich and great that he didn't give a damn what the world thought. In that point of view he had the support of the whole prosperous mob, which gloried in defying the opinion of mankind.

The State House swarmed with reporters. Every Boston paper had several men on the story, and the press associations and New York papers had their own representatives. But those who saw the Governor were cautioned not to talk, and all but the friends of the defense obeyed. The only news was what the Governor's office gave out every day, and mostly it was disguised propaganda. The private secretary had not been quite accurate when he said that they "immediately" chucked the mail into the fire. They first went over it, and extracted letters which were violent in demanding death for the two wops, and these were mimeographed and handed to the newspapermen. So the world read the weighty sentiments of Mrs. J. E. Damon of Brockton, who attached a small American flag to her letter, to make sure it would not be overlooked:

"I feel very sure that you will stand firm for 'law and order.' ... Foreign people will not respect our Government unless we uphold our Judges and Supreme Court. What is this country coming to if radical elements are allowed to do as they see fit?"

Also the sentiments of a representative of Comrade Jesus, the "political anarchist": the Reverend Floyd W. Johnson of the First Presbyterian Church of Central City, Nebraska, who appealed to the Governor of Massachusetts to "let these propagandists of un-American policies know that there is not enough money in Russia to buy even one district court in America." A curious item for members of the defense committee, who at that late hour were being visited by the relative of an important judicial personage, and informed that it would still be possible to work out an "arrangement"! By the payment of only fifty thousand dollars—from Russia or any other place— everything could be settled amicably. Vanzetti—since he was admitted to be innocent—would be pardoned; while Sacco— who might possibly be guilty—would be judged insane, and held until the excitement had died down!

VI

It was a war going on for the possession of public opinion; a day and night campaign, with forays and sallies, rumors and alarms, plots and counter-plots. The big guns thundered from the rear, and independent sharp-shooters crept forth to do sniping. "Hundred percent American" and "Pro Bono Publico" wrote letters to the *Transcript,* and the defense committee changed its "Bulletin" from a monthly to a fortnightly, and filled many columns with letters from friends of social justice all over the world.

Prof. Felix Frankfurter, one of the liberals of the Harvard Law School, published an article in the *Atlantic Monthly,* the Back Bay's palladium of culture, reviewing the case and exposing the manifold errors of Judge Thayer. To Boston conservatism that was a frightful scandal, and something had to be done at once. A champion was found, a tremendous personage by the name of Wigmore, with so many titles and honors that it took two and seven-eighths inches in "Who's Who" to recite them: a graduate of Harvard and of the Harvard Law School, Past President of the American Institute of

Criminal Law and Criminology, Past President of the American Association of University Professors, Commanding Member of the Staff of the Judge Advocate-General of the United States Army with the rank of Major, Member of the United States Section of the Inter-American High Commission, Chevalier of the Legion of Honor of France, Member of the League of Nations Committee on Intellectual Coöperation, and Dean of the Law School of Northwestern University—a Methodist institution lifted to worldly magnificence by Judge Gary of the Steel Trust.

This two hundred and forty centimeter gun went into action from its emplacement a thousand miles away. Dean Wigmore wrote a broadside, starting with two columns on the front page of the *Transcript,* and expanding into seven half-columns on the next page. He gave Felix Frankfurter one of those wiggings which professors exist to receive and deans exist to administer. With annihilating wit he referred to him, all through the two columns and the seven half-columns, as "the plausible pundit"; he accused him of having made "errors and misstatements which if discovered in a brief of counsel submitted in a case would qualify him for proceedings for disbarment."

Alas for poor Dean Bigwig! He had got his citations from Thayer, or from some friend of Thayer's; and never could it have entered his bewigged head that a judge of the Superior Court of the august Commonwealth of Massachusetts would practice the device of falsifying a legal record, quoting statements incorrectly, and even making up passages which he said were in the record, but which were not in the record! If such procedures "would qualify a lawyer for proceedings for disbarment," what would they do to a judge of the Superior Court? Apparently they would qualify him for the enthusiastic support of all the courts and most of the newspapers of his Commonwealth, as well as of the Dean of the Law School of the University of Judge Gary. They would qualify him a few months later to have the banqueting alumni of Dartmouth College stand up and cheer themselves hoarse for a five full minutes by the watches of newspaper reporters.

Defending himself in his last decision, Judge Thayer had boasted that the Supreme Judicial Court had "approved" the verdict of the Dedham jury. Felix Frankfurter had pointed out that this was not true. All that the higher court could do was to "affirm" the verdict, which in the technical language of lawyers is an entirely different matter. The dean now elaborately denied that Thayer had used the word "approved," and he accused Frankfurter of libeling Thayer. "It is a libel on the worthy trial judge, in that it charges him with knowing falsity in an official statement."

Touching indeed the faith of poor Dean Wigmore in his "worthy trial judge" a thousand miles away! Had this "worthy trial judge" failed to furnish him with the full text of the decision? Or had the dean been in such a hurry to burst into the *Transcript* that he hadn't stopped to examine the document for himself? All that Felix Frankfurter had to do in his reply was to refer the worthy dean to the sentence in Judge Thayer's opinion, as printed in the Amended Bill of Exceptions over Judge Thayer's signature, attested by the Clerk for the Superior Court of Norfolk County, pages 366 and 367, where the word "approved" was plainly to be read. So there was Dean Wigless, in the distressing position of having furnished the rope to hang his friend, Judge Thayer, for "knowing falsity in an official statement"!

And then the questions and answers about Sacco's dialogue with Katzmann, which Judge Thayer had invented and inserted into his decision! The dean had accepted this bogus passage, and put it into his letter to the *Transcript,* and the *Transcript* had solemnly published it. Now, said Frankfurter, "a careful search of the record of Sacco's cross-examination discloses no such questions and answers as Dean Wigmore quotes. Will he not be good enough to give me a reference to the page of the record?" Needless to say, Dean Baldhead would not be that good! He would fail to mention the matter again; and the Back Bay's hatred of Felix Frankfurter, Viennese Jew, became so intense that they started a tale of his having been hired by the defense to write the *Atlantic Monthly* article; they raised his price several thousand dollars a day, until they had got it up to the colossal sum of one hundred and forty thousand dollars! Such was opinion in that part of Boston which Vanzetti described as "the golden rabble."

VII

Rumors! Rumors! The State House was converted from a bootleggers' joint to a poison gas factory. Every day new witnesses went to see the Governor, and there was a new crop of stories as to what they had told him, and what he had asked them. The Governor wants to know why Vanzetti didn't take the stand at the Plymouth trial! The Governor has heard that Mrs. Brini got all the Plymouth witnesses together in her home and told them what to say! The Governor has learned that the *Springfield Republican* got twenty thousand dollars from the defense committee for its editorial on the case! And all these rumors were not rumors, they were for practical purposes the truth; the Governor heard them, and the Governor believed them. Surrounded as he was by men who took bribes, how could he conceive that anybody would work for nothing? Some one was causing state detectives to follow the witnesses for the defense, and these detectives would come back with notebooks full of formulas for the poison-gas factory under the golden dome.

Sometime previously the defense had got hold of the reports of the Pinkerton detectives on the South Braintree crime. An amazing revelation to Cornelia and Betty and Joe: those voices which had been shouting to them in the days before the trial, when they had been seeking witnesses, and failing to find them! The ghosts which had shrieked in Dedham courtroom, unheard by mortal ear! The secrets which had been in the head of Henry Hellyer on the witness-stand—the very notes he had held in his hand! Now Cornelia and Betty and Joe might go with this "Operative H.H.," immediately after the South Braintree crime, to interview Mary Splaine, the star identification witness; that marvelous-eyed young woman who had looked out of a factory window in the midst of shooting, and at a distance of eighty feet, in a period of one or two seconds, had noted the minutest physical details of Sacco, including a "good-sized left hand," which he assuredly never had, and "complexion of a peculiar greenish-white," which he had after being kept in Dedham jail for a year, but never while he was growing tomatoes in Mr. Kelley's garden!

Here in these reports you saw Mary Splaine in the company of Henry Hellyer, Mike Stewart and Captain Proctor, inspecting the photographs of criminals, and making a positive identification of Antonio Parmisano, or "Tony the Wop," as the bandit who had played the part which was later attributed to Sacco. Captain Proctor set out to get "Tony the Wop," and discovered that he had been in jail on the day of the crime—the one really safe place for wops in Massachusetts! And meantime Mary had told to "H.H." a detailed and circumstantial tale about two men in the shoe-factory who had plotted and committed the crime; she gave the names of the men, and recited a story which covered the affairs of the shoe-factory for some eighteen years. Six days after the arrest of Sacco and Vanzetti, the detective was entering his report as follows:

"As opportunities occurred I made discreet inquiries about Mr. X, who Miss Splaine accused of having been implicated in the murder and robbery. My inquiries show that there is absolutely no ground for Miss Splaine's accusation and that Mr. X enjoys Mr. Slater's confidence." (Mr. Slater was the owner.) "To-day I took the matter up with Mr. Frayer" (the superintendent). "He ridiculed the idea of Mr. X being implicated and further states that no serious attention must be attached to Mary Splaine's stories, because she is one of the most irresponsible persons he ever came in contact with."

And then, a little glimpse into the soul of an "operative," representing a great national detective agency and looking for bandits. He knows that the police have got Sacco and Vanzetti and are planning to put the crime onto them; and he reports how he questioned a laborer who was digging a trench, close to the scene of the crime. He reports this laborer as having had a very good chance to get a good look, and adds, "Some one who can speak Italian ought to interview this man, as if he went on the stand to-day he would say that Sacco and Vanzetti were not the men."

VIII

Witness after witness went to interview Governor Fuller and returned to defense headquarters, reporting that the super-salesman had got his mind centered on the Bridgewater crime.

So Mr. Thompson did some inquiring and pulled some wires, and managed to get from the lawyer of the shoe company the reports on that earlier crime, made by the same "Operative H.H.," and another man, "J.J.H." Here again the evidence wiped out practically everything the government had proved. On the day of the crime all four of the leading witnesses had described both the car and the bandits differently from the way they later described them at the trial.

These Bridgewater reports seemed of especial importance, because they destroyed the witness "Skip" Harding, who saw the Bridgewater crime, and at the trial identified Vanzetti as the shotgun bandit. Here in the Pinkerton reports was "Skip," talking with the police a few hours after the crime, and that certainty which he had displayed upon the witness-stand was wholly lacking. "I did not get much of a look at his face, but think he was a Pole," he said; and eight or nine days later he again referred to the faces of the bandits, saying that he "did not see them on the day of the hold-up." The car he described as a "black Hudson six," and gave the registration number; as an automobile mechanic, he knew cars. The police decided to prove that it was a Buick. When Harding testified at the trial, he testified that it was a Buick.

Every one of the other principal witnesses was discredited in the same way. The witness Bowles, for example, had described the shotgun bandit as having "red cheeks," "slim face," and "a closely cropped mustache," which surely did not fit Vanzetti. So the defense lawyers felt that they had won their case, and Mr. Thompson prepared an elaborate letter to the Governor, thirty-three typewritten pages. The reports and the letter were taken to the State House and delivered to the Governor's secretary, and everybody waited, on tiptoe with excitement, for some word of the result. A week or two later one of the friends of the defense, arguing with the Governor, happened to remark, "That is disproved in the Pinkerton reports." Said the Governor, "Pinkerton reports? What are they?" "Those reports which were turned over to you," replied the amazed visitor. "I haven't seen any such thing," declared the Governor, and turned to his secretary. "What's this about Pinkerton reports?" "Oh," said the secretary indifferently, "something about a cropped mustache!"

IX

Beltrando Brini was in his nineteenth year, a slender, dark-eyed youth, preparing to enter college, and earning his living by teaching the violin to Italian children in Plymouth. He still went now and then to play for Bart in prison; also he was in demand to play at meetings for the defense. He could play fine music, but the number most effective was "Old Black Joe," because it was the tune which Bart had helped to teach him as a little boy. Trando would tell the story of that ill-fated day-before-Christmas morning, when he had helped to peddle the eels in North Plymouth; he would tell what Vanzetti's teachings and example had meant to him, all through his early life; after which he would play Bart's favorite song, "When you and I were young, Maggie," and tears would run down the faces of women in the audience.

Now Trando went to see the supersalesman of automobiles, and told the story to him; but no tears appeared upon those ruddy, rounded cheeks. It seemed that the great man had worked out a new theory for himself; he pictured Bartolomeo Vanzetti attempting the Bridgewater crime at a quarter to eight that winter morning, and then driving twenty miles or more to North Plymouth, and starting in to sell eels with Trando for an alibi. In vain did Trando insist that he and his father and his mother and Bart's landlady and many other persons had seen Bart from the moment he woke, at six o'clock that morning, long before daylight; in vain did Trando tell about Bart sending him to hunt for his rubbers. Apparently the Governor thought that Bart had gone to Bridgewater and attempted the hold-up while Trando was rummaging in the attic for his rubbers!

And then Mrs. Brini, the gentle and kindly, who shed tears every time she thought of her former boarder, and insisted, over and over: "He is good man! He is good man!" The Governor confronted her with the proposition that she had gathered all the witnesses at her home and taught them what to say. In vain she explained the origin of that tale—that the lawyer had been too lazy to go and interview the witnesses, but had told her to have them come to her home, and he would meet them there to consult about the case.

And then Joseph Rosen, the Jewish peddler of cloth. The defense had to advertise for him in the *Jewish Daily Forward*. One day came a telegram from Buffalo, he had heard about the case and would come. Having learned more English in the course of the last six years, Rosen could take care of himself. When he was ushered into the executive chambers and the Governor started to question him about where he had been six weeks ago, and could he remember what he had done on March seventeenth last, "What's this?" said Rosen. "More of that Katzmann stuff?" He had not forgiven the district attorney for trying to make a fool of him before the jury.

X

And then one of the editors of the Boston *Transcript*. The age of miracles had come; an editor of the sacred *Transcript* had been persuaded to investigate the case, and had become convinced that the men were innocent! He was so conscientious about it, his employers were impressed, and generously let him do it on their time: they would pay for the getting of material, even though they would not publish it! Now this conservative and indubitably respectable gentleman proceeded to the Governor's office, with a brief-case full of documents and charts. He went prepared to point out to the chief executive of his Commonwealth the flaws in the government's case; and he had what he later described to his friends as the most preposterous hour of his life. For the Governor didn't want to have any flaws pointed out to him, and when the editor insisted, his recourse was to interrupt with rude and brutal ejaculations, and to snort through his nose.

But the editor went on, insisting, because it was a matter of justice, and the New England conscience is that way. There was the matter of the discrepancy of the trains, upon which the editor had done enough research work and calculation to have earned him a degree at the Massachusetts Institute of Technology. Practically the only proof the government had against Vanzetti in the South Braintree crime was the identification of Levangie, gate-tender at the railroad crossing, plus the identification of another crossing-tender, who thought Vanzetti had pointed a gun at him and made him raise his gates, while the bandit-car was fleeing with the loot. This latter crossing was on the way to the Manley Woods, where, according to the "theory," the bandits had "thrown away" the Buick car, not far from the Coacci house.

This made what the jury had accepted as a story; but now came the editor, showing that each of these two crossing-tenders had specified a certain train, and the time of these trains was a matter of record, and they didn't fit. The Governor thought that possibly one train or the other had not been on time; but the editor answered that there were such things as "train-sheets." He had the greatest difficulty in the world convincing his Governor that a railroad has records showing the hour at which every train passed every station, even as far as six years back. As a matter of fact, the sheets of those trains had been produced on the stand at the trial, and the district attorney might have found the truth if he had wanted it.

A singular interview! The Governor would profess complete mastery of matters concerning which it was evident that he knew very little, and when he was corrected, would fly into a rage and demand, "What right have you to question me?" The too-conscientious editor could not make his arguments clear, because the Governor did not know the elementary facts upon which the arguments rested; nor could he explain these elementary facts, because that would offend the great man's dignity. He came out from the interview to report that the situation was hopeless from the point of view of the defense. He realized, of course, the political game that was going on: the "grand-stand play," in current slang. The Governor would have the whole world marveling at his patience and open-mindedness, while in reality he was impatient of argument, and his mind was closed.

XI

Bitter struggles in the rooms of the defense committee on Hanover street, where radicals and conservatives fought over the question of how to meet this desperate situation! Controversies lasting until the small hours of the morning, and then not settled! Feuds between respectable persons who wanted to follow the guidance of respectable lawyers, and young socialists and communists who wanted to make mass appeals, and have parades on the streets, and threats of a general strike! The young radicals organized a protest meeting in Symphony Hall, to tell Boston the facts which the Governor knew and was hiding; but then came Thompson and Frankfurter, and forced the calling off of that meeting, by threatening to withdraw from the case. Joe Randall and his wife would labor all night to prepare hair-raising stories for the newspapers; but when the reporters came to Thompson, he would wave them away with a phrase, "Nothing for the papers to-day." It was easy to understand his point of view. There was no worse charge to be brought against a lawyer by respectable Boston than that he was "trying his case in the newspapers"; and Thompson clung to his belief that somehow it was going to be possible to persuade respectable Boston to grant justice to his clients.

A brilliant idea came to Betty—to collect the testimony of persons with whom Judge Thayer had discussed Sacco and Vanzetti during the past six years! To present respectable Boston with the profanity, vulgarity and hatred which old Judge Fury had poured out in the presence of everybody, from senators to club waiters! This idea was presented to the lawyers, and at first they were horrified; but as time passed, and the Governor's bias became clear, they worked out a way to make it into a legal procedure. They would appeal to the Governor on the ground of Thayer's prejudice; if that did not succeed, they would make a further move in the courts on that basis, with a possible appeal to the Supreme Court of the United States on a writ of certiorari.

So began a still hunt among those who knew but did not admire the "worthy trial judge." There were many such persons in high station; but would they consent to violate the reticences which protect social life? Appeals to their consciences were made, and a few yielded: George U. Crocker, a former city treasurer, and member of the University Club, where Judge Thayer had lived during the Dedham trial; Mrs. Lois Rantoul, who was a Lowell; Robert Benchley, one of the editors of *Life;* Elizabeth Bernkopf, a newspaper correspondent; John Nicholas Beffel; and Prof. Richardson, of Dartmouth College, to whom the judge had said, "Did you see what I did to those anarchistic bastards yesterday?" What "Web" had really said was "arnychistic bastards," but there was no use trying to get that across to the public; nobody would believe it, and anyhow, all persons who handled the story— reporters and compositors and copy-readers—would decide that it was an error, and do their duty. Prof. Richardson said he thought that "Web" had also said "sons-of-bitches"; but of course there was no way to get that printed in a moral community.

A picturesque little drama over the getting of the signature of Frank P. Sibley, star reporter of that premier family-paper, the Boston *Globe*! "Sib," as he was known to his colleagues, was a much beloved and slightly picturesque figure, known to everybody on the streets of Boston—six feet tall and wearing a Windsor tie, as near to a "Bohemian" as could survive in that frigid atmosphere. He had been the correspondent of the *Globe* at the Dedham trial, and had heard many expressions of prejudice by Thayer. He had agreed to sign an affidavit, and it was got ready; but then he discovered that he couldn't sign it, his managing editor wouldn't let him! In fact, "Sib" had come to agree with his managing editor —it was necessary for a newspaper reporter to be impartial. Just like a judge!

A serious disappointment to the defense, for Sibley was an experienced man, who had been covering major court cases in New England for some twenty years; moreover, he didn't have to rely upon his memory of Thayer's conduct, he had written a letter about it to the attorney-general of the Commonwealth. There was a conference of Joe Randall and Gardner Jackson and others who knew the newspaper game, and there came a tip from one of the editors of the *Globe* as to how the issue might be forced. Let the *Globe* hear the threat of public exposure of the fact that it was refusing to let one of its reporters sign an affidavit in the interest of justice. Mild blackmail, in short!

William G. Thompson was consulted, and proposed to submit the Sibley affidavit to the Governor as his own affidavit, and have Sibley called before the Governor—which would, of course, open up the story. Armed with that dire threat, Gardner Jackson went to see the managing editor of the *Globe,* under whom he had worked for seven years, and they had their first quarrel in that long period. The managing editor said that they were playing an unfair trick upon his paper, that it was a dirty thing to do, and so on. He would not give any decision; but that same afternoon Frank Sibley came to Thompson's office and affixed his signature!

XII

The supersalesman of automobiles had announced that he would not appoint any commission; the law did not permit him to delegate his authority, but required him to make the decision himself. But Cornelia and her blue-blood friends went on with their quiet intrigue, and one day there appeared in the papers a letter signed by the Bishop of the Blue-bloods and four of his flock, appealing to the Governor for an advisory commission. Just as Cornelia had foretold, it was impossible for a mere automobile dealer to withstand such pressure; he changed his mind. As a great man in public life, he of course did not announce that he had changed his mind; he merely announced that he was going to do what he had previously announced he was not going to do.

More intrigue, to induce him to name the right commission! Dignified established persons, wholly without taint of contact with anarchism, atheism or draft-dodging, called upon the Governor, or wrote letters, pointing out to him that there was one eminent citizen who would be trusted by all right-minded persons in New England to give a just and impartial opinion regarding the guilt of the two accused men—and that was "Mr. Lowell"! It was the "middle minds" who were inspiring this intrigue; Cornelia, partly of her own impulse, partly led by her friends, had come to center her hopes upon the august President of Harvard University. "Radical" friends, including her granddaughter and her grandson-in-law, laughed at her for believing that Mr. Lowell would prove himself more free from prejudice than any other millionaire. But they had nothing in particular against him, and nobody to prefer, among those whom the Governor would consider. "So let dear old Grannie go ahead," said Betty; "it keeps her hoping."

Grannie went ahead, and in due course an announcement

came from the State House; the Governor had appointed a commission consisting of A. Lawrence Lowell, President of Harvard University, Robert Grant, retired judge of the Probate Court, and Samuel W. Stratton, President of the Massachusetts Institute of Technology. A vast and unanimous sigh of relief went up from the Back Bay. At last the terrible problem would be settled, and settled right! It would be dealt with by gentlemen, instead of by vulgarians and political tricksters, corrupted officials and police agents! A new atmosphere would be brought into the case, and the world would see that Massachusetts brains and breeding still counted for righteousness and dignity! Two of the three members of the commission were registered blue-bloods; the third, though he came from the west, had been adopted and placed in charge of the great school which, next to Harvard, was Boston's pride, the place where the technicians of her giant industries got their exact and efficient training.

XIII

Vanzetti was now in Dedham jail, and Cornelia made a trip to carry him the good news. Needless to say, he did not know the President of Harvard University, but if Nonna said that he was a good and great man, Bart was willing to believe it. But she must not forget that it was hard for a rich man to rise above the ideas of his class. Was Mr. Lowell a very rich man? When the prisoner learned that he owned huge cotton-mills, and enjoyed an income of close to a million dollars a year from the ill-paid labor of wage-slaves, the prisoner said, "He must be a very great man if he do joostice to anarchistas."

Bart preferred to converse about Proudhon's "Peace and War," which he was translating. Here was his idea of a great man. They discussed the formula, "Property is theft"; and Bart showed a letter to the Vanguard Press, to which he was sending the manuscript of the translation. "By gosh, don't loss it!" was his injunction.

Also he had been doing more work upon his novel, "Events and Victims." It was in reality a very short novelette: the story of an immigrant worker in America; but alas, no magazine would publish such material! Bart thought that if some one would send a copy to Russia, it might be published there —or possibly made into a moving picture. In America, of course, they wanted moving pictures about the rich, or in praise of riches. Bart had put a passage about the "movies" into his novel, and he read it now to his friend.

A curious circumstance: in nine or ten weeks he was to die, in the midst of terrific public clamor; and the chiefs of the moving picture industry would hold a meeting and resolve that the name of Vanzetti was to be forever barred from the screen, and that all pictures which had been taken of the case should be immediately destroyed. They, the propaganda chiefs of capitalism, knew who their enemies were, and no mistake about it. Said Bartolomeo Vanzetti, speaking to the suppressors of his fame:

"I went out and walked towards the theater, hoping to see Johnny whom I knew to be passionately fond of moving picture shows. That night they were showing a screen version, a fragment of one of those romances which distort truth and realities; falsify history; provoke, cultivate and embellish all the morbid emotions, confusions, ignorances, prejudices and horrors; and, purposely and skillfully pervert the hearts and, still more, the minds. The characters of these morbid melodramas are always of two opposite types, one very good, the other very bad. The good ones are the good folks who are always good, always do good, are always right, and in the end always triumph. The others are always bad folk, who are always wrong, always do evil and finally pay the penalty. Just the reverse of life!

"Thus meditating, I reached the theater. Of course it was, as usual, crowded to the doors. The common people, being all heart, with little brain and less knowledge, are passionately interested in such senseless stories, and not a scene escapes them. They develop a wild and unreasoning affection for the unreal characters of the unreally good, whose hatreds and loves, risks and triumphs they share, and fervid hatred for and resentment against the unreal characters of the unreally bad gang. They lose their heads, weep, sigh, laugh, smile, fear, hope and throb, and, forgetting their cross of infamy, leave the theater more stupid than when they entered it."

The Advisory Commission could not get to work until after
the college commencements were over. But meantime the secret
hearings before the Governor went on, and in the offices of
the defense committee several typewriters clicked all day and
most of the night, and sacks full of letters, leaflets, and pamphlets went out. The barriers set up by the capitalist press
were broken down; even the great news agencies had to spread
the world's protest. The flood of letters rose higher in the
Governor's office, and while the secretary still boasted of the
promptness with which he burned them, they did not fail to
produce an effect—especially when reinforced by the explosion
of bombs in front of United States embassies in Europe, and
the crashing of window-glass in Argentina.

Cornelia wrote letters, and carried on long telephone conversations, and traveled about visiting businessmen and bankers
in their offices, and wealthy ladies in their homes on Beacon
Hill and Commonwealth Avenue. For the most part they
listened with the patience which her age and station demanded;
they promised to study the case, and often did so. Now
and then they told her that while they appreciated her sincerity, they knew that she was being imposed upon by scoun-
drels, and that it would be wiser if she did not force them to
discuss the matter.

Cornelia knew what to expect; she had watched Boston for
a couple of generations, and read of it still earlier. In any moral
issue, officialdom had always been on the side of reaction,
and the broadcloth mob had supported it—even to the extent
of putting a rope about the waist of William Lloyd Garrison
and dragging him through the streets. But always there had
been a small minority of choice spirits who had come out in
opposition, and made the glory of the city's history. Among
these had been the oldest names and the bluest blood; and so
it was now. There appeared an open letter addressed to Governor Fuller, asking a list of pertinent questions, and the
signers of that letter included the best that Massachusetts had
to show in every form of culture. Nor did these people stop
with writing letters; they wrote their names upon checks, and
gave time and thought to the case—everything that civilized

human beings could do to make headway against brutal power. The Thornwell family offered a miniature of the whole Back Bay. Cornelia crusading, and her granddaughter Betty ready to turn into a militant, and get her head broken by the police; while on the other hand the aged Abner Thornwell, oldest member and nominal head of the family, was sitting paralyzed in his wheel-chair, boiling like a steel crucible about to explode. Great-uncle Abner—so he was always referred to, because of the children—resembled his sister-in-law Cornelia in one thing, that he could not think or talk about anything but Sacco and Vanzetti; his conversation, a monologue on account of his complete deafness, resembled a verse-form with a refrain—"Burn them! Burn them!"

Abner insisted upon writing bloodthirsty letters to the Governor and to the newspapers. This would have been a scandal, because everybody knew of Cornelia's part in the case; and since she had taken it up first, family etiquette declared it to be hers. So the Scatterbridge family, with whom the old man resided, entered into an elaborate conspiracy to suppress his letters; secretaries, chauffeurs and attendants, butlers, footmen and maids—everybody had to be warned to bring the old gentleman's letters to Mr. James instead of mailing them! In the end the victim found out about that, and worked himself into such a fury that the family was afraid he would die on the spot. He had to be allowed to mail a letter to the Governor, and to have an acknowledgment, as his rank and station required; James having sent his secretary to explain the circumstances and see that the letter was not given to the press.

XV

Between these two extremes the other members of the family were distributed here and there. Henry Cabot Winters had become quite sympathetic toward his "Bolshevik mother-in-law"; he gave it as his legal opinion that she had come out of her seven years' struggle with unexpected glory. Regardless of whether her wops were innocent or guilty—and Henry said he had no opinion—she had proved to all the world that they had not had a fair trial. Who could have foreseen that luck would oblige her with such incidents as the making of bogus citations by "Web" Thayer, and the annihilation of poor "Dean Wigless" in the columns of the *Transcript*? Manifestly, the judicial system of Massachusetts had slipped up. While the great lawyer would not do anything about it, nor even say anything about it, he would furnish his mother-in-law with first-class legal advice free of charge.

Also Quincy Thornwell had been impressed by the interest taken in the case by men of standing in the financial world, such as John F. Moors, who was a member of the "Fincom," or Financial Commission—a device of the blue-blood bankers to watch the politicians, and keep them from stealing too large a percentage of the public funds. When Mr. Moors publicly said there was something wrong, Quincy stopped arguing with his aunt, and took to toddling round on his withered legs, a faithful messenger-boy, bringing gossip from the dinner-tables of the rich.

Mrs. Jack Gardner had left Fenway Court for palaces and mansions above; but other hostesses had taken her place, and Quincy would bring home the funny stories which smart society liked to tell about the supersalesman of automobiles, and his old paintings and other efforts at culture. He had proposed to appoint Harry Garfield, president of Williams College, to the Lowell commission, but Mrs. So-and-so had insisted that it wouldn't do, because Harry's grandfather had been assassinated by an anarchist. It had really been his father, said Quincy; but the State House wasn't very strong on history. Cornelia added that the assassin had not been an anarchist, but a plain lunatic, which was different, whether the Governor would admit it or not.

"As a matter of fact," said Quincy, "on that basis the Governor would himself be barred from deciding, because somebody murdered *his* grandfather."

Cornelia took that bit of history home with her, and mentioned it to the sarcastic Betty, who retorted: "Somebody murdered him too late!" Cornelia shuddered, and said "Hush!"—looking about for a spy. The thing of which she lived in hourly terror was that some lunatic might kill somebody connected with the government—in which case it would be all over with Sacco and Vanzetti, and perhaps with the defense committee as well!

Another person who had been startled by developments in the case was Betty's mother. Impossible that Deborah should not be shaken by the letter from Bishop Lawrence, whose prize parishioner she was—he came to a state dinner at her home once every year. Yes, Deborah said, her mother had had ground for the protest; but now her troubles were all over, Mr. Lowell had the matter in charge, and would see that it was straightened out.

There was quite a tug of war in the Alvin family, for Rupert said thumbs down on all anarchists. But of course he wouldn't dare to say so publicly, in defiance of his mother-in-law and his wife. What the great banker did was to keep out of the uproar, by pleading temporary retirement on account of ill-health. His doctors had insisted that he should find a "hobby," something else to be interested in but other people's money. So he was taking up church architecture, designing with his own hands a miniature English abbey, and having it built as a private chapel on his North Shore estate. It was costing a hundred and fifty thousand dollars, but was really an economy, so the great banker explained; it would be a church for his friends and servants on the estate, thus saving gasoline and tires, and later on it would be a mausoleum.

XVI

And then the Scatterbridge family. Clara had raised her brood, who were in schools and colleges, and asking questions; therefore the mother was trying to understand public affairs, but finding them extremely complicated. She accepted the pamphlets her mother gave her, but the trouble was, she fell asleep so easily. As that was bad for her "reducing," she found it better to go to bridge parties. When Cornelia told her a sad story about the wife of a shoe-worker, whose marriage had been a sort of death in life for seven years, Clara would be deeply touched, and would write a check to help feed and clothe the Sacco children. Then, in course of their talk, Cornelia would learn that Clara had just given a check to a patriotic lady who had called on her, representing a society which was seeking to compel all foreigners to be good, by having them registered and finger-printed by the police. This society was sending out literature demanding death for Sacco and Vanzetti; so Clara's money was at work on both sides!

But no such conflict in the case of Clara's husband. James Scatterbridge was one of the stern ones, upon whom Cornelia could make no impression whatever. The sarcastic Betty explained it by what she called "economic interpretation." A great lawyer like Uncle Henry had to keep his mind open, because he could never tell which side might hire him; a banker like Father didn't have to worry, because no matter whose money was stolen, it always came back to the bank; but an industrialist like Uncle James was a slave-driver with a whip, and if he didn't hold it tight there would be no money for anybody.

James Scatterbridge would keep Abner's stuff out of the papers, because family dignity required it; but he would go about among the lords of cottons and woolens and shoes and hardware and transportation, and voice his conviction that this was the great test of our institutions, and if we didn't teach a lesson to the forces of disorder, the government might as well abdicate once for all. James had a voice that was like his annual product of a hundred million yards of cotton sheeting being ripped all at once by a giant hand; and just now was a great moment in his life, because he had been invited to address some important gathering of his fellows. He had set his best advertising man to writing a speech for him to learn, and Cornelia heard him rehearsing it in the library, in the presence of his adoring wife and several indigent female relatives: denouncing the rumors that the cotton industry was going to be lost to New England, and likewise the rumors that the *"boot*nshoe" industry was going to be lost.

James pronounced this latter as one word, with the accent on the first syllable; and he said it several times—"I say that the *boot*nshoe industry shall *not* leave New England!" It was a kind of incantation, which became effective when you said it loud enough and often enough. Quincy Thornwell explained to Cornelia that the old families who owned the cotton mills and shoe factories insisted on having all the money in dividends, and left nothing to keep the plants up. James hadn't put a new machine into his mills in thirty years—so of course he was being undermined by Jews who got capital in New

York and cheap labor in the Carolinas, and had no fear of blue-blood bankers conspiring to put them out of business because they were not graduates of Harvard and members of the Union Club!

XVII

Nemesis was waiting for James Scatterbridge, with such a tragedy as she prepares for powerful, aggressive, absolutely certain men. His sons were growing up; the oldest, James junior, was a member of the Harvard class of '27, and Cornelia failed to attend the graduation, because of the anguish and suspense of the Sacco-Vanzetti case. The second son, Josiah Thornwell Scatterbridge, was a sophomore at Harvard, and called on the phone, saying that he wanted to see his grandmother; so Cornelia invited him to lunch.

She hardly knew these children of Clara and James; to her they were still the nursery mob that scratched rare old furniture and smeared chocolate caramels on brocaded upholstery. They were growing up into individuals, but she had not had time for them. Now came "James's Josiah"—such was his awkward designation—a shy, yellow-haired youth with staring blue eyes—and revealed the amazing thing that had happened. "Grandmother, I went to a meeting of the Liberal Club in college, and heard a man tell something about your case. It sounds to me pretty rotten, and I don't think the family ought to leave you to do all the work. I thought I'd ask you to give me something to read, so that I can answer what people say."

So there was punishment for a powerful, aggressive, absolutely certain manufacturer of one hundred million yards of cotton sheeting per annum! He had a son who was sensitive and open-minded, and was going to disgrace him before the world! "James's Josiah" took the handful of pamphlets from his grandmother, and he did not fall asleep over them, but read them in a day, and told his brothers and sisters what was in them, and there were family rows, and word came to the father, who summoned the renegade to his office.

There was a stormy scene, in the course of which the son was absolutely forbidden to believe certain things which he could not help believing. He explained how he could not help it—thus administering to his father a subtle form of annoyance, which no enemy could have made worse. There was a "bust-up" between father and son; and when Clara heard about it, there was a near "bust-up" between husband and wife. For Clara took the boy's side; he had a right to think for himself, and should most certainly not be put to work in the mills by way of punishment. Maybe Clara's mother was right; there was a lot of rottenness in politics, and it was time that women began to make their votes count. So there was the Scatter-bridge family, in the same turmoil over the Sacco-Vanzetti case as all the rest of Massachusetts!

CHAPTER 19

ACADEMIC AUTOCRACY

I

WHILE presidents of great colleges delivered baccalaureate sermons and partook of graduation banquets, the two wops waited in jail, with the grim sentence hanging over their heads —to "suffer the punishment of death by the passage of a current of electricity through your body within the week beginning Sunday, the tenth of July, in the year of our Lord, One Thousand Nine Hundred and Twenty-seven." A singular perversity in the Governor of a great Commonwealth, a reluctance to grant even the smallest concession to hated defenders of hated wops: he would not say whether that sentence was to be postponed, but would leave the whole world to speculate for a month, and to imagine the execution. Said the defense committee in its June bulletin: "Torture of the body practiced in the Middle Ages is nothing compared with the torture of the mind and heart upon these two innocent men and their families and friends."

The law specified that ten days prior to the date of execution condemned men should be moved to the death cells in Charlestown prison. Since there had been no reprieve, this law applied to Sacco and Vanzetti. The authorities of Norfolk County were anxious to get rid of them, on account of the expense; and so upon the first minute of the first day of July, the sheriff and his deputies entered the cells of the two men in Dedham jail, and ordered them to dress. No reasons given, no time allowed to pack their books and papers; they were shackled, and taken out into the darkness to a waiting automobile. With a dozen armed men riding behind and before, they were taken to Boston, through the sleeping city, and lodged in the "death cells."

No one told them what this procedure meant, and they took it to mean immediate execution. Vanzetti's first action upon his arrival was to start writing a farewell letter to the com-

573

rades. From now on they would live in solitude, close to the electric chair. Their friends cried out in horror—foolish sentimentalists, who had not yet brought themselves to face the thought of that electric chair! But the ruling class of Massachusetts knew what it meant to do, and went ahead. Not until after the move to the death cells did the Governor condescend to postpone the date of execution for a month.

The Lowell Commission held its first session on the last day of June. They met in the Governor's Council chamber in the State House; a large room, done in white, high-studded, Doric style, with rich mahogany furniture, and soft velvet carpets. The desks are arranged in a circle, one continuous desk, with swivel chairs; overhead, a heavy chandelier, in which the history of New England's technical progress had been recorded: first whale oil, then coal oil, then kerosene, then gas, and now electricity.

The first meeting of the Commission was "to determine procedure," the papers said. The first procedure determined was secrecy, and it was very determined; not merely were spectators and newspaper reporters to be excluded, but witnesses and lawyers had to agree not to discuss on the outside what they said on the inside. A bitter disappointment for the defense committee, whose one hope was the education of public opinion. "It is very bad," said Vanzetti. "It means they kill us."

On the fifth of July the Commission began to hear witnesses, and the friends of the defense received more shocks. The Constitution of the United States provides that every man accused of crime shall "be confronted with the witnesses against him." But these important gentlemen were going to examine witnesses, while Sacco and Vanzetti stayed in Charlestown prison, ignorant of what was going on. Furthermore, the Commission reserved the right to exclude defense counsel from the room whenever they saw fit, and to limit cross-examination as they saw fit. When the rules of legal procedure suited the convenience of the three important gentlemen, they would apply, and when the rules were inconvenient, they would be set aside.

Joe Randall, reporting developments for labor papers in New York, was one of the crowd which haunted the State House corridors and besieged the doors of the executive chambers. So he heard gossip not meant for "radical" ears; and after the third day he came to the apartment on the north side of Beacon Hill, and sat down by Cornelia and took her hand and said, "Grannie, I'm sorry—you've got to brace yourself for another blow."

Cornelia winced; her lips trembled, in spite of her best efforts. Poor old lady, she had had more than her share of blows. The young reporter's heart ached for the pitiful shrunken figure in the big Morris chair. "What is it, Joe?"

"Your dolly is stuffed with sawdust, Grannie."

"How do you mean?"

"I mean, your great Mr. Lowell is just another 'Web' Thayer."

"Oh, no!"

"Take my word for it, and get ready for the worst. The newspaper fellows fool the public, because that is what they are paid for, but they don't as a rule let themselves be fooled. This Commission consists of Thayer, Katzmann, and Fuller all over again—with a little touch of Rugg and Wait and the rest of the supreme court judges, for dignity. They know that the men are guilty, and their purpose is to find evidence to justify the verdict. Mark my words, Grannie, before they get through they'll do everything that Thayer has done, even to misquoting testimony and falsifying the record. Only one difference—Mr. Lowell will see to it that they have better manners."

"You are too optimistic," said the sarcastic Betty.

II

If it took Cornelia two weeks to realize that these predictions were right, it was only because she could not bring herself to admit the plain meaning of events. Witnesses emerged from that "star chamber," and kept their promise not to talk to reporters; but they talked to their friends, including the defense committee. So came pictures of three elderly grayheads, impatient, bored and irritated—partly on account of the weather, for it was stifling summer heat, but more especially by witnesses trying to get them to believe what they considered a wicked tangle of perjuries and deceptions.

Fuller was a politician, and used to making pretenses; but

none of the three commissioners had ever been anything but an autocrat, and it was impossible for them to conceal their annoyance at the efforts of men and women to persuade them that notorious dynamiters and bandits were anything else. Lowell had already made the pronouncement that Sacco and Vanzetti were not really anarchists—that was just a camouflage their friends had invented for them! And what Lowell said became the truth, for his two colleagues regarded him as on the whole the greatest man in Massachusetts, and therefore in the world.

Betty turned out to be right on the subject of his manners. He could be courtesy incarnate when he wished to; but this was not one of the times. He interrupted the defense lawyers, and badgered them like schoolboys. The fact that William G. Thompson had been a trial lawyer for thirty-six years did not save him; nor the fact that he had been a federal prosecutor, nor the fact that he had been a Harvard lecturer. Said Lowell, "I don't know whether you are trying to reach the truth or not. I assume, of course, that you are." Said Thompson: "I am not going to put any question to this witness or to any other witness in the case unless it is assumed by the Commission that I am here *not* to deceive the Commission. There has been a good deal of imputation and it is very painful to me."

A. Lawrence Lowell was an international and constitutional lawyer, but so far as concerned criminal trials he was a complete novice; yet he would show William G. Thompson how to handle witnesses, and did so. He took charge of the procedure, as he had done with everything all his life. He had a tremendous notion of his own powers, and was not there to have anybody tell him anything. His purpose was to protect the institutions of New England, now under attack by vicious radicals. The impulse to support those in authority was as automatic in this university president, as ever it had been in any of his stern forbears who had carried a hickory staff at divine worship, and cracked the knuckles of the inattentive and the polls of the somnolent. (Judge Grant often nodded at these hearings, but that may have been a device, of course.)

When "Web" Thayer made his appearance at the doors of the executive chambers, to render an accounting of his stewardship, every other person was immediately ushered out, and no one but his three fellow club-members asked him any questions, or heard his answers. Did he say why he had misquoted the Sacco-Vanzetti record in his decisions, or how he had come to invent and to cite bogus testimony? Did he admit that he had referred to his victims as "anarchistic bastards"? Did he admit that he had called them "sons-of-bitches"? The record of the hearings was silent on the subject.

When Fred G. Katzmann appeared, and Thompson tried to cross-question him, and pin him down as to some of his actions which the defense lawyer thought were not quite up to standard, even for district attorneys—then it was the business of the Commission to protect this former official. They had promised him that he would only be detained one hour, and he was impatient to get away. Exactly like Rupert Alvin, he suffered from failures of memory whenever he was in a tight corner. The defense lawyers tried to get something definite on the business of Mike Boda. The police had had Boda on April 20th, only sixteen days before they had arrested Sacco and Vanzetti; yet they made a mystery out of Boda. Was it not true that he was a very small man? And did any witness at the trial describe a small bandit? Katzmann would not be trapped. "Are you asking to test my memory? Look at the record." It so happened that at this very hour, in a room immediately adjoining, the Governor was demanding of one of his visitors: "If Vanzetti was a good man, why did he associate with Boda?"

III

Too late, as usual, the friends of the defense began to acquire information concerning the members of this Commission. Robert Grant was one of the bitterest Italian-haters in New England. He had put it into a book, virtually labeling them a race of pickpockets. To a librarian in Washington he had expressed his violent opinion that Sacco and Vanzetti ought to be killed. To John F. Moors and Professor Morison of Harvard he had expressed disapproval of any one taking issue with the verdict at the trial, or with the subsequent decisions. Yet he considered that there was nothing in the way of his acting as an impartial arbitrator!

"Bob" Grant had begun life as a popular novelist in the genteel New England style. The rising plutocracy of America had resorted to his works to learn the circumstances under which toothpicks should not be used, and similar lessons in the conduct of a good life. He had been awarded a small-salaried position as probate judge, where he had displayed an unusual talent for sarcasm, and an air of being much too good for mundane affairs. He was now seventy-five years of age, and was retired from service on the bench, which left him free to pass judgment upon Italians. A frail, pathetic, querulous, old man, he sat in the stifling heat of midsummer, suffering greatly, sometimes closing his eyes—but that does not always mean that a judge is not paying heed. Judge Grant heeded with an air of boredom, of extreme suspicion, and discourtesy of a kind which does not come naturally, but has to be cultivated as a fine art. When he ventured an opinion, it was of an infantile nature. "Why, Mr. Thompson, you find everybody wrong! You say harsh things about Mr. Katzmann, who seems to be an estimable gentleman!"

The elderly judge's attitude was curiously revealed in the matter of Mr. George U. Crocker, formerly treasurer of the City of Boston, who told about the behavior of Judge Thayer. Mr. Crocker had never been introduced to Thayer, but had had the judge's acquaintance forced upon him in the University Club; Thayer had come to his table at breakfast, uninvited, and sat down and compelled Crocker to hear him scold and denounce the "arnychists," and read passages from his decisions: "There, I guess that will hold them!" Finally Mr. Crocker had instructed the head-waiter not to permit Judge Thayer to join him at table. When Mr. Crocker told the Commission about this, Judge Grant inquired, "Mr. Crocker, do I understand that you are repeating what was said to you at a social club by a fellow member of that club?" In other words, the secrets of a gentleman's club were more sacred than the lives of two wops!

President Stratton, of "M.I.T.," as it was known, was the youngest of the Commission, being only sixty-eight. He came from Illinois—a great handicap in Boston, which considers Worcester the far west. He was a physicist, and had risen by competence in science—including the science of knowing the rich and what they wanted. Four years ago he had been taken into the sacred circle of the Back Bay, and now he would have needed tremendous moral courage to oppose a domineering person like President Lowell. A capable administrator but with no reflective capacity, his social opinions had been indicated by his banning a speaker against militarism from the Y. M. C. A. of his great institute.

IV

A. Lawrence Lowell had been born to that apex of greatness in Boston, which permits the fortunate one to be eccentric. He rode about Cambridge in an elderly high motor-car painted a brilliant Harvard crimson, and decorated with as much polished brass-work as a yacht. He carried his papers in an old green bag, and wore a coat-skirt which he switched as he walked; Heywood Broun, who had seen his figure in the Harvard "yard," wrote that he "ambled sedately to a hanging." He had a face of cold virtue, and from all persons less important than himself he exacted the most rigid conformance to propriety. He was wholly lacking in enthusiasms, and appeals to him to recognize the beauty of anarchist character froze on the speaker's tongue. He cultivated both in writing and in speaking a style which for dullness could not be exceeded in the college world. A stiff legal mind, made wholly out of precedents, he had facility and self-esteem, and could be extremely genial when he wanted something, such as an endowment. On the other hand, if a common person said or did anything out of the ordinary, he would reveal a remarkable talent for ungraciousness.

Injustice did not exist in the world; it was a delusion contrived by cunning agitators, and they were not going to fool the mighty mind of the President of Harvard University. A characteristic moment early during the hearing, when the witness Pierce, a shoe-worker who had refused to identify Sacco as the bandit, told how he had lost his job at the factory for this refusal; he was "fired," and one of the convicting jurymen had taken his place. Also another witness had lost his position for refusing to identify. "What does this tend to prove?" demanded the irritable Judge Grant. The answer of the lawyers

was, "It proves duress." Said Lowell, with contempt which
took in lawyers, witnesses, and his own colleague: "Oh, don't
you see, they claim this was all nothing but a frame-up."

Infallibility was his prerogative upon three different counts:
as a millionaire, as a college president, and as a Lowell. There
was a popular quatrain about the city of Boston, as "the home
of the bean and the cod, where the Lowells speak only to
Cabots, and the Cabots speak only to God." Never for an
instant did it occur to this great man to doubt that he could
wade into a mass of complications and determine the truth
in a month. With complete insouciance he would make statements of fact about crime and criminals, which experts knew
to be nonsense. "This cannot be so" . . . "they do not do that"
. . . and so on.

V

The fallibilities of academic autocracy were strikingly revealed in the reception accorded to an eccentric lady who was
sent over by Governor Fuller to tell her story to the Commission. Let "Tootsie Toodles" be her name—it was no less
melodious. The newspapers had called her a "mystery witness," but she was no mystery to the defense—on the contrary,
an open volume, ancient and much handled. She was, according
to Lowell's euphemistic phrase, "not unimpeachable in conduct"; also she was an hysterical fantast. Prior to the Dedham
trial, she had come to the defense lawyer, and told an elaborate story, offering to repeat it on the witness-stand. But
there was some dispute about the price, and she went to the
prosecution and offered to tell a story for them. She went
back and forth between the two sides, until she had ruined
herself with both—they realized that she was mentally irresponsible.

Ranney, the assistant district attorney representing the government at the Lowell hearings, knew all this, and admitted
the woman's "not unimpeachable" record. He grinned at the
scene; when the three old gentlemen were not watching, he
made motions of wheels going round in his head—a school-
boy sign for an insane person. There came a former employer
of Tootsie, Mr. Jackson, and the commission asked him, "What
of her mentality?" The answer was, "She's twelve ounces to

the pound." President Lowell of Harvard inquired, "What does that mean?" and the witness replied, "She's not all there." The great educator enlarged his vocabulary considerably before he got through with this adventure—it was a sort of slumming expedition for him. They brought in the former chief of police of South Braintree, who said that he had known Tootsie since she was born, and she was "what you'd call a nut." But he was mistaken; Mr. Lowell would never have called any person or anything by a word of one syllable.

The three important gentlemen, looking for any sort of evidence to save the good name of their Commonwealth, received Tootsie—it would not be proper to say with open arms, considering her "not unimpeachable conduct"—but with that polished and perfected elegance which blue-blood gentlemen display to all ladies when they meet them socially. When Tootsie stood up, they all stood up, and bowed—it was like a court reception, or a Harvard commencement.

Her story was that she had known Sacco in the year 1908, when they had both worked in the Rice and Hutchins shoe-factory—he was a "laster," she said. She had seen him on the street in South Braintree on April 15th, 1920, a few hours before the crime, standing near the alleged bandit car. She heard a man whom she declared to be Vanzetti say to him, "Hurry up and finish this job. I have to be back in Providence at three o'clock and dig clams."

There were slight errors in this story. It wasn't Providence to which Vanzetti had to get back; they don't dig clams in Providence, so it must have been Plymouth. Also it was a slip about Sacco having been a "laster" in the Rice and Hutchins factory in 1908, for in April of that year he had landed in America, a lad of seventeen who had never seen a shoe-factory. He had gone to work carrying water to laborers in Hopedale, and it wasn't until four years later, after his marriage, that he had learned shoe-work.

All this, of course, was known to Thompson, and he set out to establish it. His first question was: "What time did you say that Sacco first worked in the Rice and Hutchins factory, what year?"

And Tootsie, who knew what he was driving at, started up

and began to scream. "What is the idea of my coming up and talking with you when I come in here to-day to have my character overhauled? Has my character got anything to do with what I saw and what I heard?"

Said Lowell, majestically: "You will oblige the Committee by answering questions. We won't allow your character to be assailed."

Said Tootsie, louder yet—so loud that for the first time the newspaper reporters could attend the sessions through the tightly closed doors: "My character is just as good as yours, or Sacco's or Vanzetti's, or any of that gang that you have got down there and what they do. I will not allow my character to be overhauled."

Said Lowell: "Nobody is overhauling your character."

Said Ranney, the assistant district attorney: "Answer that question."

So Tootsie replied: "1908." She added: "If I am wrong I will say I am wrong." Even the members of the Commission smiled at this. But their appreciation of it was superficial; they could hardly be expected to realize that Tootsie, entirely by accident, had provided the best summing up of the Boston Brahmins to be found in the literature of the world. If I am wrong I will say that I am wrong! But don't *you* dare to say it!

For an hour Thompson read passages from Tootsie's earlier statement, inconsistent with the story she was now telling; and always her answer was that the stenographer was crooked and had written the wrong answers. She became more and more excited, and screamed louder and louder, until Lowell stopped the proceedings, and Judge Grant, greatly agitated, toddled across the room, exclaiming, "I will get her a glass of ice-water." He trembled so that he poured a part of it down her neck.

Ranney came out of the room disgusted, and told the reporters that Tootsie was "so loud" and "so unreliable" that Katzmann had refused to use her, for fear she would "break up the case." So the reporters for once had an "inside" story. They published it, to the annoyance of the Commission, and also of Tootsie. She read, and set out forthwith for the office of the Boston *Post,* a perfectly respectable capitalist newspaper, strongly Catholic. She interviewed a reporter, and told him that the stories were all wrong, that she believed Sacco and Vanzetti to be quite innocent of the crime of which they had been convicted. The person she had seen in South Braintree was the brother of a friend of hers, who happened to look like Sacco. The *Post* published this correction; and the defense produced the *Post* report before the Commission, to prove what had happened.

The lawyers for the defense naturally took it for granted that the absurdity of the whole affair was obvious. But when the report of the Commission appeared, they discovered to their consternation that the three elderly gallants had accepted Tootsie Toodles as one of their reasons for sending Sacco and Vanzetti to the electric chair! Said the greatest man in Massachusetts, and therefore in the world:

"The woman is eccentric, not unimpeachable in conduct; but the Committee believe that in this case her testimony was well worth consideration."

VI

Two things the three elderly gentlemen desired ardently to do: one, to prove that the defense at the Dedham trial had hired perjury; the other to break the alibi of Sacco in Boston on the day of the South Braintree crime. Everything which they did upon their own initiative was directed to these two ends; and it was only while this was going on that they failed to be impatient and bored. They had laid down the program that they would themselves summon no witnesses except the members of the jury, and Messrs. Katzmann and Thayer. But in the midst of the proceedings they suddenly forgot this rule, and without warning to the defense lawyers summoned to the State House two Italians, Bosco and Guadagni, who had testified at the Dedham trial that Sacco had had lunch with them on the day of the crime.

The Italians were asked to repeat their story, which owed its certainty as to date to the fact that it was the day of a banquet given to Williams, editor of the *Transcript*. Guadagni, a socialist, had been rebuked by Sacco and the others for proposing to attend an affair in honor of a militarist. Guadagni was the orator whom Cornelia had met during the Plymouth Cordage strike, a friend of Vanzetti's from the beginning, and original organizer of the defense committee; he had become one of the editors of an Italian daily paper, *La Notizia*. A ruddy-cheeked little man with sharply-pointed black beard and mustaches, speaking English with an accent, he told the three great gentlemen of the Governor's Commission what he remembered; and then to his astonishment he became the object of a persistent attack by the President of Harvard University, who thought he had the Italian trapped in a fraud. Ten days previously Lowell had consulted the files of the Boston *Transcript*, and found that there had been no banquet to Williams on April 15th; he had consulted the files of the *Gazzetta del Massachusetts*, an Italian weekly, and both papers agreed that the banquet to Williams had been on May 13th. Williams, now in Washington, had been consulted, and agreed that that was correct.

An unhappy moment for the two lawyers, Thompson and Ehrmann, representing the Sacco-Vanzetti defense in its later stages. They had had nothing to do with the Dedham trial, and if there had been any "framing" of witnesses, they did not know it. They had received no warning in this matter of Bosco and Guadagni, and so, of course, they were helpless. "Might there not possibly have been two banquets?" suggested Thompson; but Lowell waved that inept suggestion aside with a peculiar little gesture of the hand, a series of quick motions, characteristic of him. "Do not disturb the operations of this mighty brain," it seemed to say. Aloud he replied, "No, no, no, it cannot be. I have investigated the matter." The lawyer, greatly distressed, turned against his own witnesses, saying that Mr. Lowell was a man of honor, and the witnesses should admit the whole truth.

A trying situation for two humble self-educated strangers, there in the stately executive chambers under the golden dome. Said Guadagni: "If I am not crazy, there was banquet on fifteenth April. If I not tell truth I go jail." He insisted that he would find a record of it, and Lowell waved him aside with a gesture of disgust; all these wops were alike, there was no truth in them. "Very well," said he. "Bring the record to-

morrow morning if you find it." And the pair went crestfallen
away.

VII

But next morning early they turned up at the law office of
William G. Thompson, staggering under the weight of an enormous tome, the bound volume of Guadagni's daily paper, *La
Notizia,* for the year 1920. They laid it on the lawyer's desk,
open to the issue of April 16th, and translated word by word
a half column account of the banquet to Williams on the previous day. The dinner had been a humble one, and the report
said, "A more formal dinner will be given." The two lawyers,
who had been sunk in the depths of despair, now suddenly
felt like schoolboys. "This saves the men!" exclaimed Thompson. "This is our case right here!"

The two middle-weight Italians, assisted by Gardner Jackson, lugged the huge tome to the State House with the golden
dome, and sat all morning outside the tightly shut white doors.
It happened to be the two-hour session with Tootsie Toodles,
and they listened to the comedy, and shared the hilarity of the
newspaper reporters. When Tootsie rushed out, screaming, they
were ushered in, and the tome was spread out on the council
table, and Guadagni offered to translate it for Lowell—thereby
giving offense, and being informed that the president of Harvard University read Italian fluently. There was a long silence
while the three gentlemen read, more or less fluently; and
finally the President of Harvard University turned from the
reading and shook hands with the two Italians. "Gentlemen, I
was under an impression which I find was mistaken. I
apologize."

A stirring scene: the greatest man in Massachusetts, and
therefore in the whole world, apologizing to two wops! What
more could two wops want? Or two lawyers? Thompson advanced the idea that the Commission should make some acknowledgment of the fact that the alibi had been established.
Trying to make something out of the incident for Sacco and
Vanzetti! But the great academic brain saw the ruse. That
would come in due time; that was an affair for deliberation.
Lowell did go so far as to say that he would give to the

Governor an adequate account of the evidence produced. But for the rest—no publicity! More quick little waves of the imperious right hand. He reminded them sternly that they were under pledge not to report anything about what happened at these sessions.

Silence! Never so long as time endures must the populace know that the University President of the Blue-bloods has been humiliated!

Some time later the defense got their copy of the stenographic record of what had taken place, and they discovered thirty-two pages of the attempt of Lowell to break down the testimony of Bosco and Guadagni, but not a single line about the apology he had been compelled to make! No reference to the dialogue that took place, nor to the argument of defense counsel! There was a brief parenthetic note to the effect that Bosco and Guadagni had brought in the files of *La Notizia,* but not a word to show that the alibi testimony had thereby been restored to credibility!

So was Joe Randall justified of his statement to Cornelia Thornwell, "Your dolly is stuffed with sawdust!" Of his prophecy that the haughtiest and most righteous blue-blood gentlemen would "doctor the record," exactly as "Web" Thayer, the vulgarian, had done! When Cornelia heard that story, and got the full significance of it, she went away to her own room, and sank down upon the bed and sobbed. It became a sort of prayer: "Oh, God, let me die! Take me away! I am a fool, and all my people are fools!"

VIII

In the meantime, through this hot month of July, Governor Fuller was continuing the hearings in his own chamber in the same State House. "I feel myself obligated to hear anybody they send"—so he declared; and several times each week he motored up from his summer-home, escorted by two police cars. The witnesses would file through his rooms, and then go away in silence; a régime of secrecy modified by rumors and whispers. If the witness was one who had testified at either trial, the reporters would look up the previous testimony, and say that the witness had told that same story to the Governor.

If the witness had said anything new that was injurious to Sacco or Vanzetti, the reporters could get it in a round-about way. Otherwise they would call it a "mystery witness."

Each day the Governor's impatience grew, and the pretense of impartiality wore thinner. Ladies of refinement who had attended the Dedham trial had the disagreeable experience of talking with a man who made perfectly evident his belief that they were lying. Witnesses who had one definite thing to tell would be challenged to tell some other thing, and humiliated because they could not do it. Robert Benchley, one of the editors of *Life,* came from New York to make statements about the ravings of Judge Thayer at the golf-club of Worcester; to his surprise he was challenged to point out one passage in the entire record indicating that the trial had not been a fair one. Since Benchley had never seen the record, he was "stumped", like everyone who interviewed the Governor. But he took the Governor's advice and studied the record; and then he took the trouble to write the Governor a letter, pointing out many passages indicating unfairness. Like everyone else who did this, he got no response.

Still stranger the experience of John J. Richards, lawyer of Providence, Rhode Island, who had been United States marshal during the war, and had arrested the Morelli gang, and had them all sent to prison. He received a telegram requesting him to call on the Governor of Massachusetts, and he came, at his own expense. He was asked, abruptly, "What do you know about the Sacco-Vanzetti case?" He replied, "I know nothing." Said Fuller, triumphantly, "I thought so!" Richards naturally wondered why he had been invited, and suggested that possibly it might be because of what he knew about the Morellis and Madeiros. Said the Governor sharply, "That matter is closed. The Madeiros confession is an invention." Then he proceeded to cross-question his visitor: "Are you in the employ of the Defense Committee?" Said Richards, much startled, "I am not. I know nothing of such a committee."

Here was a former officer of the law, explaining what he believed was the truth; and the supersalesman received him as a suspected criminal. "What do you know about the South Braintree crime? Why did you wait six years to come around and tell about it? Have you ever been in South Braintree?

How did they get you in on this Madeiros thing?" And so on.

Mr. Richards came out from under the golden dome in something of a daze, and went to Ehrmann's office. Rosina Sacco happened to be there—tormented little woman, drawn and haggard, with her daughter Inez, six years old, born after her father's arrest. Richards listened pityingly while she voiced her hopes in the Governor; afterwards he said to the lawyer, "You might as well shut up shop. Those men are as good as dead now. Fuller has no intention whatever of considering the evidence on their behalf."

IX

An author had written from California to the Governor, pleading with him to go and meet the two alleged bandits, and judge their characters. It was the author's idea that no one could encounter the soul of Bartolomeo Vanzetti and consider him a bandit. But the owner of the Packard Motor Car Company of New England would show the author a new line in souls. One morning the Governor left the State House, and stepped into his car with police-officers, and sped away without warning to Charlestown Prison.

Bart and Nick, as the sentences now stood, were to be executed on August 10th, and were both in strict confinement; the little walk across the prison yard which the prisoners got out of this interview was their first glimpse of daylight for nearly a month. Both of the men were on a "hungry strike"; they were going to starve themselves to death, as protest against the secrecy of the Governor's hearings. But modern labor and suffrage agitation has established in the minds of wardens and jailers the fact that human beings do not die of starvation for a long time. Bart, on his seventh day of a fast, was able to walk cheerfully across the prison yard to the warden's office.

The Governor and the wop sat down together—no other witness. But later on, of course, Bart told his friends about it. The Governor had a question firmly fixed in his head, and which he used as a means of "stumping" witnesses: "Why did not Vanzetti take the stand at the Plymouth trial?" He now asked this question of Vanzetti. Since the answer involved the whole story of Vanzetti's radical beliefs, and his relations to lawyers of Catholic and capitalist mentality, he was still answering at the end of an hour.

The Governor had to leave then, because Lindbergh had come to Boston. The Governor was due at a reception, but he promised to come back and hear the rest of Vanzetti's answer. He made his escape through the warden's home, running quickly to avoid the picture-snapping newspapermen. They reported that he seemed greatly flustered; he knocked off his straw hat while jumping into his car. Could it be that a rabid anarchist had said something to offend the sensibilities of the owner of the Packard Motor Car Company of New England? A picturesque story, of which the newspapers would have made much more, if there had not been the flying colonel, and also a million dollar prize fight to be featured the next morning!

The great man came again, and talked with Vanzetti for two hours. Like all salesmen, he had learned to be agreeable; he wore his fixed professional smile, and shook hands with Bart at least ten times, so Bart declared. That a man could "smile and smile and be a villain still" was a thing not dreamed of in the philosophy of Bartolomeo Vanzetti, and he poured out his heart, and explained his ideas—he took the matter so seriously that he wrote a long letter adding things he had overlooked. Bart told his lawyers he was sure the Governor would not execute a man to whom he had behaved with such great courtesy. And the lawyers also found the Governor's manner encouraging. Said His Excellency, genially, "I wanted to tell Vanzetti to eat!" And again, "Isn't Vanzetti an attractive man!"—it might have been a schoolgirl instead of a supersalesman.

His Excellency also summoned Sacco to the warden's office, and tried to have a conversation; but this did not come off so well. Sacco was polite, but not to be taken in by supersalesmanship. The conversation, relieved of Italian dialect, ran somewhat as follows:

"Sacco, I want to have a talk with you."

"There is nothing for me to say."

"But I want your version of this matter."

"I have not asked for a pardon."

"But I would like to hear your story."

"What is the use? You have your tendencies, and you could not see mine."

"What do you mean?"

"I mean that I am a poor man and you are a rich man, and we have nothing in common."

"But I was a poor man once. I worked in a rubber shop at seven-fifty a week."

"Yes, but now you are a millionaire, and your money thinks for you. I have nothing to say."

So the interview ended. Sacco was very gentle about it, and afterwards he became a trifle remorseful. He said, "I didn't treat him right. He outdid me in courtesy. But I wanted him to know the truth. He won't see it the right way, and why should I let him fool himself?" Sacco was the man with a formula; and for once the formula happened to fit.

Also the Governor summoned Madeiros to the warden's office; and here was the supersalesman handling a different line of goods. Madeiros had taken the burden of the South Braintree crime upon himself, and thereby put the ruling class of Massachusetts in an uncomfortable position. Naturally, they would pay a price to get out of it. Said the Governor—if the story of a prison employee may be credited:

"Madeiros, I understand that you are sore because you didn't get a square deal from the government."

"Yes, sir, that is so."

"The district attorney double-crossed you, I understand."

"Yes, sir, he did."

"Well, if that is so, I might do something for you. Of course, there is nothing in this South Braintree story of yours."

"What I told about South Braintree is the truth."

"Oh! In that case I won't do anything for you. You are guilty of two murders!"

x

On the 25th of July the Lowell Commission heard arguments of counsel. For five hours William G. Thompson analyzed every aspect of the case, and if his speech could have been listened to by the thinking people of America, it would have saved the lives of his clients. But the speech was heard only by three elderly autocrats, one of whom had a tendency to appear to be dozing, while another had great respect for what the third was thinking. We may imagine the third thinking as follows: "You are an able lawyer, and are performing an intellectual feat, but I do not need you to tell me what to think."

Not all the evidence in the Sacco-Vanzetti case had been discovered; the defense would keep on finding it, up to within a few hours of the execution. But most of it was now available, and it seemed as if the Great Novelist who makes up history had been concerned to take every item of evidence produced by the prosecution at the Dedham trial, and wipe it out by a later discovery. Even to that cap picked up at the scene of the crime, which the district attorney had striven so hard to fit onto Sacco's head, and which "Web" Thayer had striven so unjudicially to force a witness to identify as Sacco's!

The main point about this cap had been that it had holes in the lining, and the "theory" was that the holes had been due to Sacco's habit of hanging the cap on a nail in the factory. There had been a great amount of testimony on this point, and Katzmann had made the most of it in his speech to the jury. In his later arguments before Thayer he had gone so far as to say: "that alone was enough to warrant the conviction of the defendant Sacco." The issue had been carried to the Supreme Judicial Court, and made the subject of a special ruling; after which Judge Thayer had made both cap and ruling the subject of special emphasis. In rejecting the last bill of exceptions, he had summed up the proposition as follows:

"In the lining of that cap there were nail-holes, which the Commonwealth claimed were made by the nail upon which this cap had been hung. Now the Supreme Judicial Court has said, in the decision of these cases, that that evidence was competent, because it tended to prove that that cap belonged to Sacco; and if the jury should find such to be the fact, then Sacco was present at the time of the shooting."

Such had been the word of Supreme Justice on the matter of a ragged and dirty "pepper-and-salt" colored cap with earlaps! A man's life had depended upon it, and depended upon it still! And now, before the Lowell Commission came ex-Chief of Police Gallivan of South Braintree, telling the true story, never before revealed. The cap had been handed to him by the shoe company superintendent, and the chief had carried it under the seat of his automobile for at least ten days, possibly twice as long; he had made the holes in the lining, while looking for some mark of identification; then he had passed the cap on to police officer Scott; and neither Gallivan nor Scott had been put upon the witness-stand, to tell the jury how those holes had come to be!

Why Chief Gallivan had been passed by as a witness for the prosecution was obvious enough—he was too plain-spoken a man. To the Lowell Commission he summed up the Dedham trial in one pungent formula; and if the three old gentlemen had thrown out the whole record, and confined themselves to Gallivan's one formula, they would have earned the thanks of posterity. Said the Chief: "The Government would put on a witness and then the defense would rush in to offset it, and I guess Katzmann was just as wise; he would dig up one to offset him. The case appeared to be to see who could get the biggest crowd. In other words, to see who could tell the biggest lies."

XI

Also the matter of Vanzetti's revolver, which was supposed to have belonged to Berardelli, the slain paymaster. According to the "theory," Berardelli had dropped it, and Sacco had picked it up, carried it off, and given it to Vanzetti. There was no evidence that Berardelli had had his revolver with him at the time of the shooting—he had taken it to a repair place, and there was no record to show he had got it back. No one had seen him with a revolver at the time of the crime. The sole basis of the "theory" was that Vanzetti's revolver happened to be of the same make as the one Berardelli had owned. The prosecution had put on the stand an expert from the factory, who had been a former federal agent, and had led the jury to believe that he thought the two revolvers were identical. But now, before the Lowell Commission, he admitted that he had felt prejudice at the trial, and that his testimony had been misconstrued. Said the witness Lincoln Wadsworth:

"But I have felt that I had created the impression that there was a possibility that that was the pistol. Well, that is just a possibility. . . . There is just the one possibility in the number of pistols a factory of that kind happens to make. There was no distinguishing number so that you could tell that that was the pistol."

The witness went on to tell about his interviews with the assistant district attorney, and how the latter had failed to be interested in having the truth made clear:

"But Mr. Williams did not seem to want to have that at all, so that I just let be on it. And then in the court-room I felt sure I would have a chance to say the same thing that I have said here, but when the time came to be cross-examined I simply was not, that was all, and I went down on the records, as I thought, and still think, that while not a direct statement that that was the pistol, it might lead to the impression that that was the pistol." And then, summing up the whole matter: "There are thousands of times more chances that it was not than that it was."

So it went, with detail after detail; impossible to find a single one that stood the test of time! Every one of the prosecution's "star" witnesses was ruined. Mary Splaine had told Henry Hellyer twice that she did not see the faces of the bandits, and the detective had written it down at the time—for use of the shoe company and the insurance company, and their allies, the police and the district attorney. Goodridge was a horse thief, his very name a perjury; he had sent two men to the electric chair to escape a jail-sentence, and the district attorney and the judge had refused to allow this to be brought before the jury. Pelzer had told many persons that he did not see the bandits; so had "Fainting Lola" Andrews. Both of them had made affidavits to this effect—and then taken them back, so that you might believe them either way, or neither.

Not one rag of evidence to cover the naked prejudice of three elderly autocrats! The collapse became so complete that it was a matter for jesting; there was even a haberdasher, to visit the prison and measure the left hand of Sacco! Mary Splaine had based her identification of the bandit upon his "good-sized left hand"—seen at a distance of eighty feet for a period of one or two seconds. Now came the haberdasher, testifying that Sacco's left hand was smaller than normal. Governor Fuller's way of meeting that detail was to take Mary Splaine out on the street and invite her to describe a man in an automobile at the proper distance. But, alas, he did this in front of the State House with the golden dome, and there was not any cobbler-shop to cut off Mary's view at the end of one or two seconds; nor was Mary up in the second story, looking down amid the wild excitement of a bandit raid, in imminent peril of shots.

There had been a million words of the Dedham trial testimony, and few persons had ever digested it all; Cornelia Thornwell, who had been studying it for six years, knew how hard was the task. Certainly the Dedham jury had not done it, much as they might assure the Governor and his commission that they had given a fair trial. Certainly the Governor had not digested it, for when you referred to witnesses by name, Mary Splaine and Lola Andrews were about the only ones he could remember. Certainly the three old gentlemen had not done so, for they made pitiful slips and asked helpless questions. But now came a great lawyer, William G. Thompson, having sat up nights with those volumes for several years, and presenting to the Commission a summary of their contents.

For example, a study of Sacco's sartorial career in South Braintree on the 15th of April, 1920, as presented by the government witnesses. At half-past eleven Lola Andrews had talked with him lying under an automobile, wearing a dark suit. Five minutes later, a hesitating witness thought he had seen him in front of a drug-store, dressed "respectably." Less than an hour later, according to another uncertain witness, he was smoking a cigarette in the depot, wearing dark "ordinary wearing apparel" and a soft black hat. When he actually shot Berardelli, he had changed into dark green pants and a brown army shirt, according to Pelzer. A few seconds later, he passed within Mary Splaine's vision, having changed to a gray woolen shirt, and wearing no hat or coat at all; but having lost a cap at the scene of the murder, although he had made his first appearance in a soft felt hat. A few yards further on, Sacco had resumed his dark suit—if one could believe the witness Goodridge.

There were many thousand words like that in Thompson's argument; and who could dispute the lawyer's final statement, that Sacco and Vanzetti had "never had the kind of trial required by English tradition and by American constitutional law as a prerequisite to taking away their lives"?

XII

Anguish in the hearts of all friends of the defense; they knew that the decision was going against them—even while they would not admit it to themselves. Pitiful the plight of hard-working and law-abiding lawyers, who had made all the proper moves, and won the chess-game a dozen times over—and now their opponents would dump the board and throw the chessmen into their faces! While Vanzetti sat in his cell and wrote memories of his mother, and Sacco composed a farewell letter to his son, men and women whose hearts were too tender for this grim world thought up frantic new schemes to move public opinion, and raced about like ants in a nest which has been stepped on.

Jessica Henderson motored Cornelia Thornwell to New Haven, where lived Mrs. Berardelli, the widow of the slain guard. With them went Musmanno, and a Mrs. Florence, who had testified at the Dedham trial, that Mrs. Berardelli had said to her that the hold-up would never have succeeded if her husband had had his gun with him. (It was the gun Vanzetti was supposed to have picked up after the murder.)

The group now appealed to the woman's sympathies, and she agreed that it would not help either her dead husband or his widow and orphans to take the lives of two men who might possibly be innocent. She consented to send a telegram to the Governor, appealing for clemency. "Write it now," said Mrs. Florence; but the woman said for Mrs. Florence to write it, she would be satisfied with whatever they sent. So Mrs. Florence and the party drove to the nearest railroad depot, and wrote a message and sent it, and it made a front-page story in the newspapers next morning.

But it took the enemy only a few hours to counter that move. They came to the woman and frightened her, and the Boston newspapers carried a story to the effect that the telegram had been sent, not by Mrs. Berardelli, but by an unknown woman from a railroad depot. The ladies made another trip to New Haven—but only to discover that Mrs. Berardelli wouldn't "have anything more to do with it." Returning to Boston, the ladies called upon the Associated Press representative, explaining the circumstances, and asking him to correct the error.

The response of the Associated Press was to put on the wires all over the country the statement that Mrs. Berardelli declared she had never seen the telegram which had been sent in her name. It happened to be strictly the fact; but it wasn't quite the truth!

Edward Holton James was a New Englander of the old sort; he lived in Concord, just across the field from the home of Emerson, which possibly had affected his mind. He was a nephew of Henry James, the novelist who wrote like a philosopher, and of William James, the philosopher who wrote like a novelist. His wife was a Cushing, and wealthy, so he had everything that a citizen of Concord could have to make him respectable; but it didn't keep him out of jail.

Mr. James had spotted certain flaws in the "theory." He had noted the fact that the so-called "bandit-car" with the bullet-hole through the door had been in the hands of the police for hours before any of the numerous examinations had revealed the conspicuous bullet-hole; also he had measured the "Coacci shed," and proved that you couldn't drive two cars into it, as the "theory" required. Now he went down to South Braintree to reproduce the events of the hold-up, and prove that some of the witnesses could not have seen what they claimed. But the selectmen of South Braintree were not going to let the streets of their town be used for Bolshevik propaganda if they knew it, and they arrested Mr. James, in spite of both his ancestry and his money.

And then a little later Beltrando Brini had a bright idea: if the story he had told at the Plymouth trial was fiction, then he was a perjurer. He had told the story to the Governor, and had not been believed; so he drafted a letter to the Governor, asking to be arrested, and he took it about among the other alibi witnesses, and fourteen of them signed it, including Bosco and Guadagni, the two editors. Trando delivered it at the State House, and when no policeman came for him, he went back, with his mother and half a dozen of the other witnesses. It was near the end of the case, and the corridors were crowded with detectives and secret service men, with swarms of reporters—a sensational scene. The Governor was not in, said the secretary; and took the youth off into a room by himself for a "grilling." Who had sent him, and what was this scheme for publicity? "This hurts you more than it helps." And when Trando undertook to explain, "Don't try to make a stump speech; the place for that is the Common."

Said Trando, "I tried to speak on the Common yesterday, and I was stopped."

"Don't try to be a hero!" sneered the secretary. Heroes were not wanted at the State House, and Trando could not get arrested. Too bad he did not know about the room full of booze in the cellar! If he had told about that, he might have got his desire. As it was, he went away with tears in his eyes, his mother sobbing on his arm.

XIII

And yet there were moments of hope. Impossible to believe that a great business man and statesman could be such a hypocrite! Members of the defense committee came to see him, having heard the wild rumors, started from the State House, as to the millions that had been raised and expended for bribes. They offered to put their records at the disposal of the Governor; they had raised some $325,000 in seven years, and had vouchers for it all—bundles and bales of them stacked in a closet. Gardner Jackson and Mary Donovan had worked for nearly two years without a cent. The Governor was surprised to hear it—he had been given to understand that they got fifty percent of every thing they raised. Little Joe Moro, the secretary, had worked for thirty dollars a week, and the only other wages paid in the office were for typists. The Governor was cordial, he seemed to like Joe immensely, shook hands with him several times—he was a good fellow, and everything was all right, don't worry!

But that was in the privacy of his office, the tricks of a supersalesman; molasses catches more flies than vinegar. Publicly the Governor said nothing, and the rumors continued to fly. Professor Frankfurter had got fifteen thousand dollars from the New York *World* for writing an editorial; he had got one hundred and fifty thousand from the committee for writing the *Atlantic Monthly* article. The very dignified editor of the Springfield *Republican* was accused of having received twenty thousand dollars from the committee for one famous editorial. The "State House crowd" lived in such an atmosphere of cash payment that they could not imagine how gentlemen felt about such matters.

Also they lived in an atmosphere of terror. It seemed as if there were as many detectives as real workers under the golden dome. Assuredly, there were more spies than there were friends of the defense; one of them put on a Windsor tie and got himself regularly arrested with the pickets. Every one who had anything to do with the case was shadowed; servants would be offered money for the contents of trash-baskets. All officials having to do with the case, the Supreme Court judges and later on even the jurors, had guards on their homes day and night, and wives trembled every time their husbands went outdoors.

There was fear; and there were newspapers printing headlines and selling editions, making every bomb-scare into a gold mine. Relatives of the Johnson family, the garage people who had testified against Sacco and Vanzetti, had had their rear porch blown up while they were in bed. That made a newspaper story, and helped to damn Sacco and Vanzetti. The police decided that it was a bootleggers' quarrel; but that fact was not revealed—the bootleggers being such liberal paymasters of the police. A threatening letter was mailed to one of the witnesses, and this turned out to be a prank of some boys; the newspapers published the letter on the front page, and never published the true story. Such is journalism, which lives upon sensation, and prints its enormous editions with blood instead of ink.

XIV

The Lowell Commission had finished its hearings and retired into privacy to deliberate. But meanwhile the Governor went on hearing witnesses. They streamed through his office, as many as thirty in one day; all sorts of persons who claimed to have information about the case. Many came secretly, and went away, their names known only to him; they whispered into his ear, and he was supposed to sort out truth from rumor. A hundred times over, in conversations and arguments, he would show that he could not do it, that he had, in fact, no idea of the difference. "Why, I heard it right here in this room!" he would say; and that proved it true.

On the other hand, impossible to satisfy him with any evidence that proved what he did not want to believe! He had got his mind fixed on the Bridgewater conviction, which would prove Vanzetti an habitual criminal. You pointed to Vanzetti's eighteen alibi witnesses, all decent working people, and the Governor would find it suspicious that they talked so much about eels. "But where is the express receipt showing that he got the eels?" The case seemed to hang on that, so the defense set out to look for express records in Plymouth. They discovered that the records, nearly eight years old, had been destroyed. Incidentally, they discovered that a state detective had already made an investigation, and ascertained that they had been destroyed.

They decided they would outwit him, even so. They would look for the receipts of fish-dealers who had sold the eels. Herbert B. Ehrmann, junior counsel, went to consult Vanzetti in Charlestown prison. It was hard for him to remember—he had been accustomed to buy fish from several dealers in Boston. The lawyer went according to his vague description, with Felicani for translator; they hunted at the "fish-pier" in South Boston, but found no one who remembered selling to Vanzetti. Joe Randall got another Italian—two gangs searching. At last, after visiting seven Italian fish-dealers on Atlantic Avenue, the "Guinney market," they found one who said that "B. Vanzetti of Plymouth" had been a customer of his. Had he any records? For a year or two, yes—but seven years, eight years—no, no, giammai! He had changed his partnership in the meantime.

But they argued—could they make a search? The life of two compatriots might depend on it! Yes, there were old papers up in the loft. So up they go, among dust and cobwebs, with an electric flashlight. Old boxes of papers, in bad Italian script— sheafs of loose ledger leaves, but the earliest date is January, 1920. "For God's sake, haven't you got any before that?"

The Italian has got interested—it is a story! "There's an old case, maybe stuff in that." A big box shoved under the rafters, tightly nailed up. "Must have a hammer to open it." Stacks and stacks of old papers: and among them blocks of American Express Company receipts, signed by the expressman, day by day as he called for shipments. And the dates—here are some for 1919—and here is December, 1919! And in the middle of the block, one reading: "B. Vanzetti, Plymouth, one barrel eels!"

Hurrah! We have it! We have them licked! The date is December 20th, which was a Saturday, the very date Bart claimed the eels had been shipped, to be sure to reach him on Tuesday, and got ready for selling the next day! And they are live eels, so the dealer says, you can tell that by the weight of the barrel! Dead eels would be heavier!

Young fellows dancing in a dusty loft! Our wops are saved! They go back to the office with shining eyes. They go to the Governor's office. "We have found the evidence the Governor asked for." This to the private secretary—the Governor himself is busy. "Indeed?" says the secretary. No shining in those hard eyes! "When are you going to stop bringing evidence?"

They will not trust the precious papers to him, but insist upon seeing Wiggin, the Governor's counsel. Then they go away, and wait—and nothing happens; the next time they see the Governor, they mention the matter, and he says, "What does that prove? What evidence is there that Vanzetti ever received the shipment? I understand that the eels were never claimed; they were frozen in the depot."

Says Joe Randall, gnashing his teeth: "It is like that fairy-story we used to enjoy when we were children—how the little tailor wooed the king's daughter. 'Go slay me the dragon,' says the king—so the hero goes and slays the dragon, and comes back, but he doesn't get the king's daughter. 'Go slay me the three giants,' says the king—so he goes and slays the three giants, and comes back, but he doesn't get the king's daughter. 'Go slay me the man-killing boar,' says the king—and the longer the story, the more fun it is."

XV

The supersalesman had evolved a regular set of formulas, by which he challenged the witnesses who came to him. Of Italians he would ask: "Are you an anarchist? Are you a friend of Sacco or Vanzetti? Are you a member of the committee? Have you any friends on the committee? Who sent you here?" To be "sent" was a sinister thing, a sign of an elaborate conspiracy in operation.

For Americans the procedure was more subtle. The first question was: "Have you read the record?" If you answered "No," then you were disqualified. The Governor had read the record, so he said. If you answered, "Yes," the question would be, "Where did you get it?"—for the defense had only two transcripts of the full testimony, and two or three copies of the "bill of exceptions," usually called "the record." If you were able to convince him that you had had access to any of these, he would say, "Have you interviewed the witnesses?" And of course that would "stump" you; how could any one interview the witnesses, when the lawyers for the defense couldn't even get the Governor's secretary to give them the names and addresses of the witnesses? You would answer, "No," and the Governor would reply, "Well, I know about this case, and you don't."

All that mass of complications—a million words of printed testimony, and many times that much spoken into one human ear—and he really thought he could carry it all! Serene, even jaunty, he would come into his office, wearing his automatic smile, and greeting the reporters, "Good morning, boys, a fine day!" He did not ask for help, and gave no thanks when it was offered. Hjalmar Branting, a lawyer from Sweden, son of the prime minister, came over to study the case, and devoted a month to it, becoming certain that the men were innocent. He was granted an hour, and the Governor spent five minutes talking about Sacco and Vanzetti, and the rest talking about the market for automobiles in Sweden. A thrifty supersalesman, making hay even while the thunder rolled and the lightning split the sky!

The floods of mail poured in. Trucks came, bringing masses of petitions; some thirty packages, registered, from France, representing three million signatures, patiently collected at workingmen's meetings. They were burned in the basement furnaces, at night, when the heat would not be troublesome. Messenger boys brought telegrams by the bundle; they were sorted out, one kind for the newspapers, the other for the fires. Said the private secretary: "Everybody wants those wops executed, except people who don't know how to spell their names." He gave out the letter of the Reverend Llewellyn E. Darling, of Grace Evangelical Church of Everett, reporting that a vote had been taken among his Sunday congregation, and it was unanimous in demanding that the convicted men should die. "We believe," wrote this Darling Reverend, "that the source of the petitions · for their release is un-American and would eventually destroy the government of the United States." Comrade Jesus, on his golden throne above, rose up and gave three cheers for the Red, White, and Blue.

XVI

Cornelia had put off visiting the State House; she would see what happened to others, and judge the best way of proceeding. Now she asked Henry Cabot Winters to arrange an interview; and he offered to go along—a notice to a politician that she was still a member of a great family, in spite of all her vagaries. The supersalesman would be polite to her, but also he would be grim, for she was a dangerous woman. He held her to blame for a great part of the publicity which this case had obtained; he had visions of her spending secretly the Thornwell millions in an effort to get her own perverse way.

Cornelia had never met him; he had been a name to her so far. Now she sat in his chamber and studied those eyes, so cold, expressionless—a curious thing, they made you think literally of agates. His face was round, his head partly bald, his costume immaculate, his smile as it were dead. He sat with his back to the window, so that in the matter of vision he had the advantage over his visitors. A large mahogany desk; a green blotter, with a few papers, a fancy bronze ink-stand, and a little state flag on a standard for patriotism. A large room, done in white, with large white doors and heavy carpet and a fireplace never used. "I guess you have seen all this many times, Mrs. Thornwell," he said, respectfully.

Yes, Cornelia had seen it. "When I was a little girl, the old home of John Hancock stood out there in front." So they talked "Boston," and perhaps she would have done better if she had talked nothing else; her social prestige was really the only thing that stood any chance. In a chair at one side sat Mr. Joseph Wiggin, the Governor's private counsel, a Harvard man and a blue-blood, smiling and quizzical; he would have conspired with her in that kind of enterprise, if she had put it up to him in the right, "old Boston" way. To charm an automobile salesman and persuade him to make a concession as a matter of social favor, the right of an aristocratic old lady to have her feelings spared!

Cornelia set out to tell about Vanzetti, and how well she knew him, and what a fine man he was. The Governor listened, but soon tired of it. "I haven't the time to deal with backgrounds and psychology, Mrs. Thornwell." She tried to show him what backgrounds and psychology meant. "Consider Nick. They tell us he went out and stole sixteen thousand dollars, and then came back to his shoe factory and earned thirty-seven dollars and eighty cents!" But she was rousing his male combativeness. "They had to go on working in the factory," he argued. "They couldn't have afforded to change their habits."

Cornelia was studying the bland face and the strange expressionless eyes. What sort of man was this? What motives would sway him? A business man, of a simple type, used to facing simple problems, like those of price; the proper rental for a building, or wages for an employee, easy to decide; a man of action, not a thinker. Now he had to weigh the souls of idealists, he had to estimate social forces—and they were completely beyond his comprehension. "I am a plain man, Mrs. Thornwell, not an intellectual." She had started to tell him about Bart's studies, the books she had seen him mastering by patient toil in the night; but she realized that this was an affront to a merchant of motor-cars who had been studying markets and prices. Neither would it do any good to praise the unselfish motives of the two social rebels. That, too, would give offense to the man of money. "These men who don't believe in private property must be depraved," he had said.

She told him about the two trials, and what she had learned about the various prosecution witnesses. The Governor praised these latter; "clear-eyed," was his word. Said the old lady, "Their eyes may be clear from the outside looking in, but assuredly they were not clear from the inside looking out." She told the long story of the prevarications and waverings of these witnesses, as proved by the records of the preliminary hearings, and by the Pinkerton reports. The Governor knew of these reports now, but he did not know what was in them, and was puzzled by details. He did not even know the names of some witnesses. She spoke of Behrsin, and the Governor said, "Cursin, who is Cursin?"

But everything polite, according to good form; he heard her to the end, giving few signs of impatience. "I will give careful consideration to what you tell me, Mrs. Thornwell. I have great respect for your sincerity, and thank you for coming to see me." Bows and smiles all round, a pleasant hour—and utterly, utterly futile.

"The case is completely indigestible to him, he can't hold it in his mind." Such was the judgment of Henry Cabot Winters, legal expert, as he walked with his mother-in-law down the long marble corridors. "You have to know a great deal about it in order to know anything, and Fuller doesn't know anything."

"What will he do, Henry?"

"He'll take somebody's word for it. He'll think he is deciding, but his mind will make itself up without his realizing it. That's the way he's gone through life—landing on his feet like a cat. What I'm afraid is, he has landed already, and facing the wrong way." As he said this, the great lawyer put his arm under the old lady's, and held her steady as they walked towards his car. "It comes to this, Mother—what I said to Rupert last night: you can make a chauffeur out of a governor, but you can't make a governor out of a chauffeur!"

CHAPTER 20

THE DECISION

I

On July twenty-ninth it was announced that the decision would be given out on the third of August. That was a Wednesday, the day the Governor's council met; and this fact might have significance, because, if he were going to grant clemency, the council would have to assent. Shreds of evidence like that caused hope to rise in the balance. Rumors would come, one way or the other; the Governor had said this, he had asked that.

Joe Randall never wavered in his pessimism. "Fuller has no idea but death; he never has had it for an instant, and he never will." But some of the other newspaper men thought differently; said one: "You can't tell me that a man so happy would send two human beings to the chair!" Others had talked with members of the council, who told, in confidence, of definite statements the Governor had made. The New York *Times* correspondent sent his paper a detailed story to the effect that the Governor meant to postpone the execution, and ask the legislature to pass a special act providing for a new trial. The New York *World* had the same story; the *Herald Tribune* followed.

On the day before August third a peculiar development. Calvin Coolidge, President of the United States, was spending his summer vacation in the Rockies, catching trout with worms, and having himself photographed in ten-gallon hats and other moving picture appurtenances. He received the newspaper "boys" on his front porch and handed them a typewritten slip of paper reading, "I do not choose to run for President in nineteen twenty-eight." This economical sentence caused a thrill in the bosoms of great numbers of public men; and enemies of Alvan T. Fuller imagined that it decided the fate

605

of Sacco and Vanzetti. Careful newspapers like the New York *Times* and *World* do not often let themselves be fooled as in this case—so these suspicious ones argued; something must have changed the mind of the supersalesman on the night of the second of August, causing him to give up the idea of clemency. Could it have been a vision of himself, following the footsteps of "Cautious Cal" up the political ladder; sweeping the next Republican convention in a storm of enthusiasm for another hero who had "crushed the Reds"?

Whether there was any truth in this wild guess, none could say, except Fuller himself. But this much is certain, he desperately wanted that nomination; and it is interesting to note what happened in the following year, when the Republican convention assembled. The name of Alvan T. Fuller was put before the little group of rich men's agents who meet in a hotel room and determine nominations for president and vice-president. The Governor's friends set forth the heroic deed that he had done, and the storm of fervor which this deed would rouse in the bosoms of all patriots. But the politicians of 1928 remarked coldly that this was not 1920. "The Republican party cannot afford to debate the Sacco-Vanzetti case from now until the end of the campaign!" There was not a single vote for the supersalesman; and so furious was he in his disappointment that he refused to let ex-Governor Cox of Massachusetts have the nomination in his place. To Senator Butler, over the long-distance telephone wire, he said: "It will be Fuller or nobody!"

II

August third, the day of the decision. The State House press room and Governor's office were not big enough to hold the mob of reporters, and for the first time in Massachusetts history the legislative chamber was turned over to their use, and the press gallery equipped with telegraph wires. More than eighty men, like hunting-dogs held in leash, leaping and barking. The whole outside world was clamoring for every detail having to do with that scene.

The interest in the case had grown, until it was like nothing in history; great newspapers in New York, which had given several inches to the conviction of the men, were now giving pages to the struggle for a new trial.

Somehow the working classes of all nations had come to know about this case, and had made it their own. They were listening to fiery orators, taking part in parades, throwing bricks through American window glass, setting off bombs in front of embassies and legations. To the ruling class element of Massachusetts this was a proof of the worst they had been told about world Bolshevism; it was a diabolical conspiracy against the good name of the Commonwealth, and to meet it these righteous persons summoned the spirits of their Puritan ancestors, who had withstood persecution and torture at the hands of royal despots and their priestly monitors. The louder the clamor on behalf of the anarchists, the less chance that it would be heeded—so said the stiff-necked ones.

The Governor had not come to his office; rumor had it that he was working on his decision in an unnamed hotel. Over at the Sacco-Vanzetti headquarters in Hanover street, a couple of rooms in a dingy office building with time-worn floors, there were reporters and photographers, bootleggers and poets, Italian laborers and Harvard professors, seated on boxes, bundles of papers, tables and rickety chairs, waiting, waiting. On the walls were posters in many languages, calling for mass-meetings to save Sacco and Vanzetti; one in French, signed by cabinet ministers, referring to "Calvary," which would have pleased Bart; one in German, saying "Justice is dead"; one from Mexico, saying "Freedom and Justice." Bart was right —his name had come to have a meaning!

Cornelia Thornwell stayed in her apartment, and friends came in to keep the watch with her and divert her mind. But no one could talk about anything but the decision. Now and then the phone would ring, and her heart would jump so that it hurt; when it proved to be more delay, she would sink back in her chair, feeling faint. Creighton Hill, a young newspaper-man who was heart and soul for the defense, came in to cheer her; the afternoon papers were full of hints of a reprieve; everybody was hopeful. Judge Webster Thayer was in Ogunquit, Maine, and at the Cliff Country Club that morning had made 18 holes in 84.

Waiting, waiting. Evening, and still the Governor had not

come to his office. Crowds gathered at the State House, and were driven back. The decision would be late, said the secretary. Betty, who was at headquarters, phoned to her grandmother—for the tenth time, trying to brace the tortured soul to meet the coming shock. "Joe says the brute is holding up the decision so that we won't be able to get in any answer to-night. He wants the front page of the morning papers to himself!"

So it proved. At twenty minutes past eleven at night, the last moment when it would be possible to put the text of the decision into the main editions of the big newspapers, and when there was no longer a chance that any friend of the defense could prepare a reply, or find any distracted reporter able to listen to one—at that moment the Governor's secretary appeared with a stack of envelopes, each containing seven mimeographed sheets. The reporters grabbed them, and tore them open as they ran. The word "Die" went by telegraph and cable to five continents, and in a few minutes there were "extras" on the streets in big cities, with streamer headlines across the front page: "Sacco and Vanzetti Doomed to Die"—"Sacco and Vanzetti Must Die, Says Fuller"—"Sacco and Vanzetti Guilty, and Will Die."

III

Wonderful, wonderful was the judicial system of the Commonwealth of Massachusetts, as portrayed in those seven mimeographed sheets! Throughout all this complicated and difficult case it had functioned without one single slip. The judge had been upright and impartial, the jury had been conscientious and fair, the witnesses—for the Commonwealth—had been clear-eyed and unafraid, the Supreme Judicial Court had been infallible. And now came the supersalesman of automobiles, and with his eagle eye he surveyed the procedure, seeking a flaw. Patiently he had studied every word of the record, the later appeals and decisions; he had interviewed jurors and witnesses, and made sure that everything was perfect; now he mounted the rostrum and told the civilized world about it, putting the final seal of completion upon the performance.

One after another he took some aspect of the case, and after mentioning the criticisms of it, disposed of them in one or two majestic and final sentences. First, the jury. "I find that the jurors were thoroughly honest men . . . I can see no warrant for the assertion that the jury trial was unfair." The fact that the elderly flag-saluting foreman of the jury had said, on his way to duty, "Damn them, they ought to hang them anyway!" —that was a detail so trivial that an enthusiastic supersalesman did not bother to report it.

And then "Web" Thayer. "Affidavits have been presented claiming that the judge was prejudiced. I see no evidence of prejudice in his conduct of the trial." The eagle eye had inspected those passages in the record where "Web" had connived at the job of hiding from the jury the fact that Goodridge was an admitted thief; that had been fair. The eagle eye had seen "Web" butting in to discredit the witness Kurlansky, the shop-keeper who had failed to stop the district attorney and police from "framing" the testimony of Lola Andrews; that had been fair. "Web" had permitted the district attorney to browbeat Sacco for not knowing what was not true about Harvard College; that had been fair. "Web" had sneered seven times at the defense lawyers for claiming something which they hadn't claimed; that, too, had been fair. He had let the district attorney tell the jury that Proctor had testified something that Proctor had in fact refused to testify, and that the district attorney knew he had refused to testify; that likewise had been fair. "Web" himself had told the jury the same thing; and that had been fairest of all.

And then the appeals for a new trial, based upon new evidence that had been found: evidence of the foreman's prejudice and misconduct, of Goodridge's criminal career and perjury upon the witness-stand; the retractions of Lola Andrews and Louis Pelzer; the confession of the head of the State Police that he had conspired with the district attorney's office to misrepresent his testimony to the jury; the new evidence of Gould, Kelly and Kennedy, deliberately withheld from the defense. Said the supersalesman: "I have examined all of these motions and read the affidavits in support of them to see whether they presented any valid reason for granting the men a new trial. I am convinced that they do not."

And the judge's handling of these appeals and motions—

that, too, had been complete and marvelous perfection! Everything that he had done—including his lying about the affidavits, and saying that they said what they didn't say; his misrepresentation of Supreme Court decisions, his misquoting of testimony, his making up of passages which he said were in the testimony, but which were not in the testimony—all that had been perfect, and "Web's" motives in doing these things had been as pure as the driven snow in Boston. Said the supersalesman: "I am further convinced that the presiding judge gave no evidence of bias in denying them all and refusing a new trial."

The supersalesman pronounced Vanzetti guilty of the Bridgewater crime, and stressed the fact that he had failed to take the stand in his own behalf—although it was the perfect law of the perfect Commonwealth that he didn't have to take the stand if he didn't want to, and that his failure to do so was not to be used against him. The supersalesman was so sure that the men were guilty that he was not content to say it once, he said it twice about Sacco and three times about Vanzetti; he was so sure the trial was fair that he said it five times—and added for good measure: "The proceedings were without a flaw." He put in an eloquent description of the South Braintree crime, with emphasis upon its brutality, which made fine melodrama for the newspapers; and then he wound up in a blaze of glory, putting himself in the center of the picture, with jury and witnesses about him. "I am proud to be associated in this public service with clear-eyed witnesses, unafraid to tell the truth, and with jurors who discharged their obligations in accordance with their convictions and their oaths."

IV

Ten or a dozen persons crowded into the little living-room of the apartment adjoining Cornelia's, where lived Betty and Joe. The seven mimeographed pages had been read aloud, and passages read over again, and marked with exclamation points and question marks. Hours passed while the clamor and excitement continued. Nobody thought of sleep; impossible ever to sleep in the world again—let sleep be banished from Boston, as punishment for this atrocity! The language of some of the younger men and women was unfit for the older ones to hear; but the older ones realized that this was a special occasion, like nothing in Boston history. The air of the room became gray with tobacco smoke, and the eighteenth amendment to the Constitution was broken, along with the laws against blasphemy and sedition; for some radicals could not stand the strain of this ordeal, any more than could the conservatives, without help from Italian bootleggers.

Joe was at his typewriter, banging away, with a green shade over his eyes; preparing a story to be put on the wires for the early editions of afternoon papers. He was making copies for other newspaper men, hoping they would get this point and that. Now and then the company would interrupt him—to make sure he had got some other point. Over at defense headquarters was another indignation meeting, and there was telephoning, back and forth, exchanging ideas and information. Quotations had to be looked up in the record, and falsehoods nailed down.

How they hated the supersalesman of automobiles—and how they raged at the trick he had played upon them, whereby millions, yes, tens of millions of people would read that statement at their breakfast tables and on their way to work—and would not get the answer of the committee until hours later, and then only in fragmentary form, or not at all! The fingers of men and women trembled as they pointed out passages of especial treachery.

Cornelia Thornwell, old-fashioned and hopelessly out of date, had notions about the dignity and honor of the office which the great Josiah Quincy Thornwell had once filled. It seemed to her that a Governor of the Commonwealth, mounting the rostrum and addressing the civilized world on an issue involving the lives of two human beings—that such a Governor ought at least to tell the truth. "Wouldn't you think he'd leave out errors that can be proved by the record?"

Said Betty, "I'd expect him to lie like Satan."

They would fall upon the seven mimeographed sheets again. Look at this! Look at that! Look at what he put in about Madeiros! "I give no weight to the Madeiros confession. It is popularly supposed he confessed to committing this crime." What did the man mean by that sentence? He didn't explain it—he went on to state his reasons for distrusting Madeiros, but not a word about what was "popularly supposed"! The words could only mean that the popular impression was mistaken, Madeiros had not "confessed to committing this crime." Every reader would get that meaning, and no other meaning. The actual words written by Madeiros had been: "I hear by confess to being in the South Braintree shoe company crime and Sacco and Vanzetti was not in said crime."

Then, an even shrewder trick—a little masterpiece of treachery, as cunningly contrived as the Proctor evasion, and Katzmann's bogus answer to it, and "Web" Thayer's obfuscations of both! The supersalesman summed up Sacco's alibi—that he "claimed to have been at the Italian consulate in Boston on that date but the only confirmation of this claim is the memory of a former employee of the consulate who made a deposition in Italy," etc. Study that sentence, all forgers, traducers and betrayers of all future time, and learn how to smile and be a villain still! The art of falsifying while seeming to tell the truth has never been carried to a higher stage—not in any form of supersalesmanship yet devised in the great empire of superproduction, or taught in the Graduate School of Business Administration of Harvard University.

Strictly and literally, it was the truth that Sacco had produced only one witness to testify that he had been "at the Italian Consulate in Boston on that date." But Sacco had produced five other witnesses who testified that he had been *in Boston* on that date! Affe, the grocer, had testified that Sacco had paid him a bill, and Affe had produced on the stand a notebook with a memorandum of the payment, showing the date. Bosco and Guadagni, the editors, had testified to lunching with Sacco in Boni's restaurant on that day, and Dentamaro, department manager of a bank, and Williams, an advertising agent, had testified to joining the group and chatting. Still more to the point, several of these witnesses had testified that Sacco, in the course of the talk, had told them the purpose for which he was in Boston, to visit the consulate and get his passports! Oh, treachery and double-dealing beyond all imagining—first, the Lowell commission hushing Bosco and Guadagni to silence, and doctoring the record of the proceedings in order to keep the story from the public; and then the mighty supersalesman, stepping onto the rostrum and addressing the whole civilized world, telling it that Bosco and Guadagni did not exist!

V

Cornelia lay in bed, a reaction from the long strain. The Negro maid brought her coffee and toast, but she could not eat; she lay like one dead. It was all over for her; she had done all she could, struggled all she could—so she told herself. The young people might go on, Joe might write newspaper stories, trying to rouse a heedless public; Betty might organize mass meetings and speeches on the Common, but the runaway grandmother's race was run.

She had to lie there and bring herself to face the thought of the electric chair. Through all these seven dreadful years, she had refused to face it—a game of self-deception; but Bart and Nick had been right all along—they had known that the thought must be faced, and they had done it. They had the will, and the philosophy; they had been able to talk about it and joke. Now Cornelia must do the same thing. Remember what somebody had told her—it does not hurt, because the current destroys the brain before there is time for a sensation. And when it is over, it is really over; other persons may worry for you, but you don't worry for yourself. Also, you are a martyr, you have accomplished something for the cause you love.

That was what she must manage to realize. Persuade herself that there was a new generation coming, that would care where this one was indifferent; that would count it as something important that two wops had denied themselves happiness so that justice might be born into the world! Think about those young persons of the future; lie here and shut your eyes, and let them come into your presence and speak to you; feel their gentle hands upon your forehead, bidding you to rest, your tense nerves to relax and your heart to stop pounding.

Cornelia lay wrestling thus; and into her mind came drifting words of comfort. "Now we are not a failure. This is our career and our triumph." Vanzetti speaking; where had she heard him say those words? On a chair by her bedside was a scrap-book, full of letters, manuscripts, clippings. She was moved to sit up and turn the pages; here it was. Shortly after Judge Thayer had sentenced the two men to die, Cornelia had persuaded a reporter for the North American Newspaper Alliance to go to Dedham with her, and see what kind of men these alleged bandits were. Now, reading the interview, Cornelia recalled every detail of the scene; the prisoners coming down from their tier of cells, getting a glimpse of sunshine in the central hall, and lighting up with it—Nick, with his "kid's" grin, Bart with his mature and gentle smile. The reporter, Phil D. Stong, a big fellow, rather blond German face, well-fed and well-groomed—on an expense account, as he told Cornelia, with a laugh; tender-hearted, with the sentimentality of his race—and struck dumb by the discovery of two men of this transparent sincerity and fine idealism in the shadow of the electric chair, face to face with their last enemy and not afraid of him. He had listened, while the victims did the talking; then he had gone away and tried to make a picture of the scene for the readers of a chain of newspapers.

"Both men expect to die. They say so, and the conviction is written in grave, serene characters on Vanzetti's face. Tears touch the young man 'Nick's' eyes for a moment, brightly, but his voice is steady. He is married to a sweet-faced little Italian woman. They have two children.

"In a moment, Nick, with his smooth pompadour, and his boy's face, is laughing with the deputy sheriff in argument about prison fare.

"Vanzetti regards one kindly, but appraisingly. A ferocious mustache covers an expressive, smiling mouth. The stamp of thought is in every feature; the marks of the man whom strong intelligence has made an anchorite."

And then a glimpse of prison life:

"Up from the shops comes a file of gray men, arms folded, faces expressionless—a rhythm of steps and faces.

" 'They been working.' Sacco's fingers move nervously. 'God, when I cannot work I almost go crazy. My fingers used to be busy. I beg, I argue—give me something to do—I shovel coal, anything. At last, they give me brick to clean—after three years. You see me now? I gain a pound a day for thirty days.' The deputy sheriff nods confirmation.

" 'First they give me basket to weave, like children. Better than nothing, but not much. Then I sit alone—seven years— thousands of days—and all for say man's nature can be perfect—day after day—nothing do—breathe, eat, sit up, lie down —because I think man innerly noble—not beast—'

"Vanzetti interrupts his companion gently. He knows the two visitors believe in the enforced regulations which restrain fallible humanity.

" 'We're capitalists,' he says smiling, and pointing to the line of workers. (Men under sentence of death are given no work.) 'We have home, we eat, don't do no work. We're non-producers—live off other man's work. When libertarians make speech, they calling Nick and me names.'

"Sacco gurgles with amusement. The deputy sheriff appears significantly. Suddenly one realizes that these men are to die in a straight wooden chair, just as the world begins its summer holidays.

"Nick and Vanzetti see the new expression and understand. They smile, gravely, sympathetically, as men smile at a child's troubles.

" 'If it had not been for these thing,' says Vanzetti, 'I might have live out my life, talking at street corners to scorning men. I might have die, unmarked, unknown, a failure. Now we are not a failure. This is our career and our triumph. Never in our full life can we hope to do such work for tolerance, for joostice, for man's onderstanding of man, as now we do by an accident.

" 'Our words—our lives—our pains—nothing! The taking of our lives—lives of a good shoemaker and a poor fish-peddler— all! That last moment belong to us—that agony is our triumph!'

"Not declaimed, just said simply."

VI

There were tears in Cornelia's eyes as she finished. "Oh, beautiful! Beautiful!" And when Joe came in, later in the day, she showed him the clipping. "Those are marvelous words —those two paragraphs at the end. I wonder if you couldn't quote them again, and get people to read them."

Joe said that he would try it. In order to give a touch of drama, he put a headline: "Vanzetti to his Judges." The two paragraphs were taken up and reproduced in labor papers, and became, as it were, a spiritual testament of Vanzetti, an untheological prayer which his friends carried about with them, and read while he was dying, and afterwards. Because of the title, people assumed that the words had been a part of a speech in court; but this was not so, they were spoken, quite simply and casually, to a newspaper reporter, the every-day stuff of Vanzetti's mind.

History records that those who heard the Gettysburg address of Abraham Lincoln were ill pleased by it. They found it brief and inadequate, and gave all their praise to the flowery discourse of the great Edward Everett of Boston. But the future seldom chooses words which are flowery; it chooses those which have been wrung from the human heart in moments of great suffering, and which convey a gleam of spiritual illumination. When such words have been spoken, we discover what Paul meant when he wrote, "this mortal shall put on immortality." School children learn them by heart, and libraries are written to interpret them; they are graven upon marble and cast in bronze; armies carry them on banners, temples arise to glorify them, and civilizations are built in their image.

Pass on, Bartolomeo Vanzetti, your work is done! You have fought the good fight, you have finished the race! Fear not the executioner, nor yet the raging slanderer—they are powerless to harm you, for you have carried out your life-purposes—including that incidental one of becoming a great master of English prose! You have spoken the noblest words heard in America in the two generations since Abraham Lincoln died! You have achieved what is called the "grand manner," so rare in literature! That simplicity whereby men become as little children, and enter into the kingdom of heaven; that dignity which causes the critics to bow their haughty heads; that tenderness which touches the heart, that rapture which fires it, that sublimity which brings men to their knees!

In short, old Bart, you have brought the Commonwealth of Massachusetts back into the literary world again! After many years, New England has another great writer—for a short while only, until it has sent two thousand volts of electricity through his brain! What an odd freak of history, that this great one should be a despised wop! That, after all the millions spent upon education, he should not be a graduate of a college, nor even of a high school! That he should not even be able to spell correctly, nor to pronounce correctly, the language of which he is to be the glory!

What a satire upon great endowments, the huge masses of steel and stone, the deans and professors of this and that long-winded subject! As a result of their labors, there are a million persons in the Commonwealth of Massachusetts who understand the correct use of past participles, and would not say, "I might have live"; yet there is not a single one of these millions who can speak a sentence that stands a chance of living! There are ten thousand graduates of Harvard College, every one of whom knows better than to say "onderstand" or "joostice"; yet there is only a handful who understand justice, and not one who will die for it!

VII

The fears of the defense, that they could not get their answer before the public, proved to be groundless. In truth, no answer was needed—the weaknesses of the Governor's statement were so apparent. Impossible to take the lives of two men upon the basis of such an argument! There was a cry of dismay, so shrill that it penetrated even to the sanctum of supersalesmanship. A sudden panic among the "State House gang"; something must be done, and done quickly. The academic autocrats were summoned to the defense of their Governor, and three days later there appeared what was called the "report" of Lowell, Grant, and Stratton to the Governor.

It was much longer than the earlier document, and in its heavy style bore the marks of having been composed by President Lowell. It was argumentative where Fuller's had been assertive; it was fumbling where his had been jaunty. The feebleness and confusion of its arguments suggested the operation of aged minds. To disinterested persons, the most striking fact was that the report could be judged without knowing anything about the case. The elderly gentlemen had managed to make their ineffectiveness evident in almost every paragraph.

Suppose, for example, that you picked up your morning paper, and read what the Commission had to say about the evidence of Roy Gould, the man who had got a bullet hole through his overcoat. "He certainly had an unusually good position to observe the men in the car, but on the other hand his evidence is merely cumulative." What would you make out of that? Assuming that you knew the meaning of the word "cumulative," why was evidence less valid because it was that? Wasn't it the nature of good evidence to be cumulative, and didn't you try to make it as cumulative as possible? Try some other word in that sentence: "his evidence is merely convincing" or, "his evidence is merely conclusive"!

Then that amazing and incredible sentence, in which the three elderly Brahmins summed up their meditations on the subject of one of their victims: "On the whole, we are of the opinion that Vanzetti was guilty of murder beyond reasonable doubt." What did the three elderly Brahmins mean by a man's being guilty "on the whole"? Or by their being of the opinion "on the whole"? Did they mean that there was some part of them which was not of the opinion? Or did they mean that there was some part of Vanzetti which was not guilty? On the Saturday when this report was given out, the New York *Times* made an effort to elucidate this question; and the New York *Times* is an important newspaper, whose queries are apt to be heeded, even by blue-blood college presidents. But apparently the Commission on the whole had decided on the whole that it would be safer on the whole to take no chances on the whole. The New York *Times* recorded that "efforts to reach members of the committee to clear up the exact meaning of 'on the whole' were unavailing."

But imagine the scorn and fury of young radicals—reading that sentence, and not waiting to have the exact meaning cleared up! Said Mistress Betty, now become ferocious: "Is he going to execute Bart on the whole, or is he going to execute him completely?" She pictured the august President of Harvard University appearing before the Judgment Throne, and being informed that he was to be sent to hell on the whole, and roasted for eternity on the whole!

VIII

The three elderly blue-bloods had had a comparatively simple task laid out for them; they had been asked to decide whether

Sacco and Vanzetti had had a fair trial. Was it owing to their age, or to their inexperience with criminal matters, or to their overwhelming prejudice, that they had been unable to stick to their task, but must keep confusing it with the question whether Sacco and Vanzetti were guilty? The latter they could not possibly determine; they had neither the time, nor the facilities, nor the training, nor the temperament. But their self-assurance was such that they attempted it; with the result that they fell to guessing, like everybody else, and they were so naïve as to reveal this to a horrified world.

Thus, in declining to accept the story of Madeiros, they remarked: "If he were tried, his own confession, if wholly believed, would not be sufficient for a verdict of murder in the first degree." Just what was the significance of that? Were the old gentlemen suggesting that two birds in the hand were better than one in the bush? And then, their extraordinary statement, that the evidence of Gould was "balanced" by that of Tootsie Toodles! Joe Randall said that such "balancing" ought to be exhibited on the vaudeville stage.

The handling of the Proctor confession had come to be a test of the honesty of official persons in Massachusetts; and it proved that each new person would find some new method of dodging the truth. The three elderly blue-bloods showed themselves fully as cunning as their predecessors. Said they: "Counsel for the defendants claim that the form of the question and the answer was devised to mislead the jury." That was a fact; and it was an instance of how to lie while stating a fact. Counsel "claimed" it; but why put the burden of the "claim" onto counsel, when counsel were merely restating the confession of Proctor? And then to go on and say: "But it must be assumed that the jury understood the meaning of plain English words." These learned Boston gentlemen claiming that Proctor had used "plain English words," when Proctor himself had stated that he had used obscure English words, and for the purpose of confusing the jury! Let the common sense of mankind judge whether a jury of mechanics and working people would find no obscurity in the statement that the mortal bullet was *consistent with* having been fired by the Sacco pistol! And when both the district attorney and the judge had pretended to misunderstand it, and had told them that it meant what it did not mean!

And then to be nasty, and hint that their own high police official, who had served them faithfully for forty years, and now was dead and unable to defend himself, had made his confession because the district attorney had refused to pay him five hundred dollars for his expert testimony!

To Cornelia Thornwell this report meant the end of all things; her joy in life was gone. For prejudice and trickery on the part of a motor-car salesman she could make snobbish allowances; but in the case of A. Lawrence Lowell no such recourse was available, he was her kind of person, the best she had to offer. For years she had gone to commencements, and listened to his ponderous wisdom, and thought he was a great man; and here in a test she discovered that he had listened to all the gossip, and swallowed the whole "theory"!

She knew what would happen, if she went out among her friends to argue against this report. The friends would gaze at her in dismay. "But, my dear, *Mr. Lowell* says they are guilty!" If she persisted, the friends would add, "But my dear, Mr. Lowell *investigated* the case! He gave more than half his vacation to it!" Those who knew her well, including the members of the family, would say, "But Mother, you *wanted* Mr. Lowell, and now you won't abide by what he says!"

Impossible to make headway against such a tide! In New York men could read that report, and judge it for what it was, a revelation of the mental breakdown of a once-great civilization; but in Boston hardly any one could judge it, Mr. Lowell did the thinking of half the city. He was a god, and had descended from his throne, and devoted his mighty intellect to the affairs of two obscure wops; now for these wops and their supporters to refuse to accept his verdict was not merely blasphemy, it was ingratitude and impertinence.

IX

William G. Thompson withdrew from the case. One more lawyer had failed; one more lawyer had made enemies, and thought it would help Sacco and Vanzetti if he took himself out of the way. But each time it was made clear that the cause of the hatred was Sacco and Vanzetti, no one else; the new lawyer, whoever he might be, would be as much hated as the old one.

They took Cornelia's advice, and went to the old stock, and retained Mr. Arthur Dehon Hill. Silver hair and rosy cheeks and a manner of complete assurance, he should have been Arthur Beacon Hill, according to Joe Randall. He was so correct that he dared to make jokes about it. Real "Old Boston," he thought that every criminal, even an anarchist, was entitled to a fair trial, and to have a lawyer do the best for him that the legal game allowed. But to his surprise he discovered that a great many persons, even lawyers, were strongly disapproving of his conduct in defending these enemies of society.

He started work on Saturday, the sixth of August; and on the night of Wednesday, the tenth, his clients were due to die: rather a short time-limit for the mastering of a complicated case! He began with an appeal to the Governor to extend the time; and the Governor replied by silence. He filed notice of an appeal to Judge Thayer for a new trial, on the basis of newly discovered evidence, and also—delightful inspiration! —on the ground that Sacco and Vanzetti had not had a fair trial, because the trial judge had been prejudiced! Judge Thayer agreed to give up making golf-scores in Ogunquit, Maine, and appear in Dedham Court House on Monday morning, to judge whether Judge Thayer had been prejudiced against Sacco and Vanzetti!

Also Mr. Hill started an appeal before Justice Sanderson of the Supreme Judicial Court, to try to get another motion before the full bench of that Court. Some jumping about for one lawyer, especially when all the courts closed at noon on Saturday. Elias Field was helping, and also Michael Angelo Musmanno, a young lawyer who had been sent on from Pittsburgh by some Italian societies. A naïve and warm-hearted person, Catholic and conservative, he had fallen in love with an anarchist infidel and an anarchist atheist, and was bewildered by the hatred which unloving Boston felt for his clients. A hectic three weeks the young lawyer spent chasing about New England and Canada, in motor cars, and now and then in airplanes, hunting supreme court judges on vacation.

Other lawyers giving advice, some of them secretly. One

was Henry Cabot Winters—hush, not a word! He would call Cornelia on the phone. "Mother, I don't want to get mixed up in this, but you'd better tell those fellows not to overlook saving all their exceptions as basis of a writ of certiorari to the Federal courts; and tell Hill not to let 'Web' get a single point on him—challenge his right to hear a word, or decide any issue, on the basis that it is a prejudiced decision. And when you go to a Federal judge, don't overlook Moore v. Dempsey 261 U.S. 86." Cornelia would have to say, "Wait! Wait! Let me get that down!" She had been wrestling with the powers that ruled her Commonwealth for seven years, but she had not yet learned to have a pencil and pad at the telephone.

Also professors of the Harvard Law School helping—and no secret about that, but on the contrary, picturesque scandals for the Hearst newspapers! A war between the law school and rest of the university, between Frankfurter and Lowell! Lowell had been disapproving of Jews as professors, ever since eight years ago, when another of them, Laski, had made a speech to the wives of striking policemen, while Lowell was preparing to lend the students of his university for strike-breakers. Now here was Frankfurter defending two anarchists in a book, while Lowell was sentencing the incendiary pair to death.

A pretty fight, difficult to keep within the limits of academic propriety! Not so long ago, the great Lowell had dealt a strong punch to the Jewish jaw, in the shape of a program to limit the percentage of such students allowed in Harvard; he proposed to do it openly, instead of secretly, as the custom was. He gave his reasons—among them that one hundred per cent of the books stolen from the university library were stolen by Jews. When this statement was investigated, the evidence turned out to be that one Jewish student had one library book which he had forgotten.

And now here were the Harvard alumni, rallying to the aid of their blue-blood president, by refusing to contribute to the law school endowment, so long as Felix Frankfurter remained a professor; they were making a regular campaign out of this. Among those who had publicly joined it was Mr. Ranney, the new assistant district attorney from Norfolk County, who had been opposing the Sacco-Vanzetti defense before the Governor;

also that blandly smiling blue-blood lawyer, Mr. Joseph Wiggin, who had been the Governor's private counsel, present at all hearings. "You see what kind of advice Fuller is getting!" said Henry Cabot Winters.

x

Disputes at headquarters of the Sacco-Vanzetti committee; factions clashing, radicals jeering at conservatives. "Now you see! You obeyed your respectable lawyers! You were good, and didn't make any noise, you trusted to legal precedents— and where have you got? If you had listened to us, if you had spent the money to make an appeal to labor, we could have had a general strike now, and the boys would have been saved!" But even now the conservatives wouldn't agree. Mrs. Evans thought it necessary to bow to the Governor's decision; while the communists wanted to make a mass appeal for a strike all over the country. Impossible to decide on a single move; and meantime the clock was ticking away the minutes and hours of the victims' lives!

Those who believed in picketing and street demonstrations proceeded to organize and send out a call for martyrs. On Sunday afternoon there were to be mass meetings on the Common; the socialists and the communists each had a "tree," and as usual, they announced rival meetings. Superintendent of Police Michael J. Crowley announced that he would attend both. For the first time in Boston history the entire police force of twenty-two hundred men were on what was known as "twenty-four hour duty." All vacations were canceled, extra men were brought from other cities, the firemen were sworn in as deputies, the state constabulary were ready with armored cars, riot guns, searchlights and gas bombs. Said the sharp-tongued Betty, "The Commonwealth has told ten thousand lies, and each lie must have a club and a gun to protect it!"

Between Boston Common and the park known as the Public Gardens there extends a wide esplanade, half a mile long, lined with old elm trees; since as far back in history as the oldest citizen's great-grandfather could remember, this had been the temple of Boston's free speech. The trees were numbered, and every Sunday afternoon the advocates of anything would have a tree assigned to them, where they might set up a soap box and stand thereon, and say what they pleased to all who cared to listen—with only such interference as came from the voices of the orators under the other trees.

But now the government of Massachusetts had officially endorsed ten thousand lies, and staked its official existence upon them; the one thing it could not stand was to have these lies exposed to the general gaze. Under the socialist tree were women carrying banners, containing the sentence once spoken by the just and upright and utterly unprejudiced Mr. Justice Thayer. He was to speak again from the bench to-morrow morning, and tell all the world how just and upright and utterly unprejudiced he was. Now here was a banner: "Did you see what I did to those anarchistic ——? Judge Thayer." The makers of the banner had left the bad word blank, but that did not improve matters, because there is no limit to what the human imagination may insert in a blank. People might imagine the worst of all possible expressions, so bad that it had never been printed in any newspaper. If they did imagine that, they would be right; and so it was necessary for the Commonwealth to resort to clubs and bullets.

XI

Alfred Baker Lewis, devoted young secretary of the Socialist Party, was denouncing the Governor's decision, when Michael J. Crowley came pushing his way through the crowd, demanding to see his permit. Burly Irish-Catholic Mike, known as "Mickey the Gunman" to the striking policemen, and called even worse names by the booksellers of Boston, whose boss and master he was. For among the many duties of a superintendent of police in that pious city is to supervise the books which the literati may purchase. In the course of the past two years Mike had barred some seventy of the leading novels of the day, practically everything which an intelligent man or woman would want to read.

And so to-day; the public would be forbidden to hear every word that could interest an intelligent citizen. The Salvation Army would go on banging its drum, and the Holy Rollers would continue their contortions; but protest against legalized murder would be met with clubs, and if necessary with bullets.

"Let me see your permit," commanded the superintendent of police; and when the orator produced it, Mike announced, "This permit is canceled and the meeting is forbidden." When the young socialist attempted to protest, "You are not going to argue this case in public," said the majestic Mike—just that and no more; he said it several times, so that every citizen of Boston might feel the full weight of the civic insult. "You are not going to argue this case in public!" Only in the council chamber at the State House, before elderly academic autocrats who would doctor the record when they got through, and keep the public from knowing what blunders they had made!

"This meeting will disperse!" shouted Mike, to the sixteen thousand persons crowded round him; and the blue-clad "cops" began their onslaught—"for every lie a club or a bullet!"

"Come over to our tree! We have a permit!" shouted the communists; so the crowd swarmed over there and Mike came also, and repeated his performance, confiscating another permit. But the communist was not so obedient as the socialist—he went on trying to speak, and was hauled off the soap box and surrounded by policemen, and dragged off to the waiting patrol-wagon. Three other persons they arrested—one of them Edward Holton James, of Concord, nephew of the novelist who wrote like a psychologist and of the psychologist who wrote like a novelist.

A persistent person, Mr. James; perhaps it came from living in Ralph Waldo Emerson's back-yard. He had stood up in Germany, during the war, and said what he thought about the Kaiser. The Germans, not understanding Concord, had decided that he must be insane, so they had shipped him into Holland; whereupon he had promptly got himself smuggled back in a load of merchandise, and stood up again and said what he thought about the Kaiser, and spent three years in a fortress for it.

Now he was so naïve as to think that he owned a share of the Common, and had a right to speak there, and to refuse to be dragged off. He resisted being dragged, and went so far as to slap one of the officers—with the flat of his hand. They taught him his lesson, regardless of his blue-blood and his money; when the "cop" got him alone in the cell he gave him one on the side of the jaw, and Mr. James "passed out," as the saying is, and when he came to he had a cracked jawbone, to keep him quiet for a while.

XII

Arthur Dehon Hill arguing before Judge Thayer in Dedham Court-house, with the round white dome and portholes like an ocean liner. Silver hair and rosy cheeks, his manner of subtle banter now replaced by burning indignation, that a judge with such a record as Web's, and knowing in his heart such prejudice as Web's, should be insisting upon deciding a motion involving two human lives. The lawyer invited the judge to consider how he would feel if the followers of Lenin had seized the government of Massachusetts, and were trying him according to the precedents he had set! He told Web to his face that he had been unfit to try the case from the beginning; he cited in open court what the Lowell commission had said about him—that in talking about the case off the bench he had committed "a grave breach of official decorum." Could any man hear such words about himself, and not be affected by them? Web's answer was that the chief justice of the Superior Court had instructed him to cut short his vacation and hear this motion. "And I am here," said Web, in a low voice. His face was gray, his hands trembling, his eyes blinking fast. His court-house was well guarded that day.

New evidence had been discovered. A young fellow by the name of Candido di Bona had been standing on the street in South Braintree when the bandit-car went by, and now made affidavit that neither Sacco nor Vanzetti was in that car. This evidence was what the Lowell Commission would have called "merely cumulative"; there were already thirty-one persons who had made such statements, either at the trial or in later affidavits, and Web Thayer knew of them all, and intended to pay no more heed to the thirty-second than he had paid to the thirty-first. He thought that he no longer had jurisdiction; that after sentence had been passed, no judge of the Superior Court could entertain any motion. To this the lawyer argued vehemently that nothing could deprive accused men of an elemental right. "I believe that if there is new and important evidence, the courts have the power to consider it, even after sentence has been pronounced—even down to the time the men are strapped in the electric chair. I do not believe the laws intended the courts to regard these men as legally dead as soon as sentence was pronounced."

Arthur K. Reading, Attorney General of the Commonwealth of Massachusetts, had been instructed by the Governor to follow Mr. Hill in his peregrinations among the courts and make certain that he didn't get anything. Handsome, genial, and a good fellow, Mr. Reading was a bitter foe of all Reds, and the aiders and abettors of Reds. Said he: "I have just heard the most preposterous argument that I have ever heard from an able lawyer." He expressed his horror at "this attack on the court for which I have the highest regard." He proclaimed that, "Ours is a government of laws." Such reverence for laws and courts this noble gentleman had—and even while he was orating, his pockets were stuffed full of money, collected from various organizations which had been warned by Arthur K. Reading as counsel that they were in danger of prosecution by Arthur K. Reading as attorney general!

The "Decimo Club" was an ingenious organization which sold memberships to persons who hoped to get rich quickly; but the only ones who did get rich were the promoters of the club, and their legal counsel. A couple of months ago they had secretly handed a check for twenty-five thousand dollars to Mr. Reading, and immediately thereafter he had given to the newspaper reporters an interview telling them that the Decimo Club was all right. He had performed similar "legal services" for the "L.A.W.," an automobile stock-selling scheme with curiously involved features. Altogether he had collected about ninety thousand dollars in such "fees," and within ten months of the time that he had demanded the life of Sacco and Vanzetti, he was to be formally indicted by the House of Representatives and driven from his high office in disgrace —the first time that had happened in the history of the Commonwealth. So nemesis waits for Red-hunters!

XIII

In the meantime Cornelia Thornwell had got into action again—impossible to rest. Pleading with the Governor to grant a respite—but the Governor would not give a hint of his intentions. Calling up friends and relatives, nagging at them to "do something"—when they had no idea what to do. "Henry, do you suppose Fuller can really intend to let those boys die while proceedings are pending before the courts?"

"I'm afraid he does, Mother"—this over the telephone.

"But what can be in his mind?"

"Well, Mother, it is costing a lot of money to keep this thing going. Think of the military expenses! And then, it's bad advertising; every day it keeps up, things look worse for Fuller and Lowell, and naturally they want it over with."

"Do they think they can stop it by a murder?"

"I'm afraid they do, Mother—and what's more, I'm afraid they are right. You can't keep the case alive when the men are dead."

"Henry, you *must* do something for me!"

"But what can I do? I have no pull with Fuller, I don't even drive a Packard car." The great lawyer thought for a bit, and added: "Why don't you try a little social pressure? Get Deborah or Alice or both of them to give him and his lady a dinner-party? I'll come, if it will do any good."

Learn how the world is governed, Cornelia—now in your seventy-third year of life! Once upon a time people did things like this to you, and you were too gentle and trusting, too much of a "lady" to know it, or to believe it when it was pointed out to you. But now do it yourself! Seek out the weak spot in the armor of a motor-car salesman who has forty million dollars, but no "social position," and has a Catholic wife, a cruel handicap in Massachusetts! Get busy at the telephone, and put it up to your daughters, as hard as you know how— if they have one particle of love for you in their hearts, if ever they had a particle of love in their hearts, to spare you this dreadful anguish!

True it is that the motor-car salesman has made public attacks on Rupert Alvin, calling him an arch-corruptionist and things like that; but that is just politics, and social life is another thing altogether. The motor-car salesman will doubtless know what is being done to him; he is a business man, and does not give something for nothing, nor expect to get something for nothing. To be received in one of the greatest homes

in New England, to put his feet under the table with haughty
and unapproachable Brahmins—that counts for nothing to him
personally, or so he pretends, being "bull-headed" and defiant;
but he has a wife, and children growing up to the age of marriage, and what the women and children clamor for cannot
be overlooked by the most self-satisfied of self-made millionaires.

Cornelia had her way. Ladies do in Boston, when they are
persistent, and when they are old. The formal invitation was
written by Deborah Alvin, addressed to Mr. and Mrs. Fuller,
and delivered by a chauffeur at the Governor's summer home,
at Rye Beach in New Hampshire. A couple of hours later an
automobile arrived at the North Shore palace of the Rupert
Alvins, with a formally written acceptance. Deborah got busy,
and invited half a dozen members of the family, and intimate
friends who could be taken into the secret. Clara Thornwell
Scatterbridge came—another stage in her feminist revolt! Alice
Thornwell Winters came, dressed in pale lavender, the color
which harmonized with her aura; having lost a great deal
of weight on a humming-bird diet, she had taken up a new
rôle, and was a picture of delicate and spiritualized melancholy.

The Governor and his lady arrived, in the very latest model
of Packard limousine, custom-built, preceded by a car full of
alert-looking men with bulging hip-pockets, and followed by
another carload. Several posted themselves at the front door,
others walked round and round the house and peered into
bushes and under porches. One, who looked and acted like a
guest, wandered about the downstairs rooms all through the
meal; the Commonwealth was taking no chances—especially
in a home where the mother-in-law was one of the most notorious Reds. These precautions lent an extra thrill to the meal,
but good form required that no one should know anything
about them.

The supersalesman sat at the right of his hostess; on the
other side was Alice, and the matter-of-fact and rosy gentleman had never encountered anything so much like heaven. She
told him about his aura, which was news to him; Deborah told
him about her orphan asylum, and Rupert told about his chapel,
and how a bishop from England had praised the design of the
apse. Never a word about the distressing news which was on

the front pages of all the papers! "Cura nulla medicabilis arte" may have been all right for a poet two thousand years ago, but the social arts of "old Boston" had mastered all human weakness.

Except that at the end of a delightful evening Deborah led her distinguished guest to one side, and burdened him for a moment with the story of how her old mother was suffering so that they feared for her life; would she be presuming if she asked the Governor to reprieve the two wretched men for a couple of weeks, until the hope of court action could be tried out? The supersalesman replied with all the caution of a skilled politician. It would not do for him to say outright, because the final decision rested with his Council. But privately, and in strictest confidence, he would assure Mrs. Alvin of his best endeavors, and she might convey that information to her mother under a seal of secrecy. When the ordeal was over, and Cornelia was free to tell the story to Betty and Joe, she commented upon the way the world is governed. Said Betty: "Don't you know, Grannie, the real cause of the world war— that King Edward of England was not sufficiently polite to his nephew, Emperor William of Germany?"

XIV

On Monday evening Judge Webster Thayer handed down a decision, to the effect that he had no jurisdiction to entertain any motion in the Sacco-Vanzetti case. By this ruling he claimed to have avoided passing upon his own prejudice; but at the same time he said, in open court, "I had no prejudice." He said it many times.

On Tuesday morning he gave another decision, refusing the request for a revocation and stay of sentence. He gave this out from his home in Worcester, where two police officers watched by day and two by night, and one followed behind the judge when he went walking with his dog. In the toilet of a subway station in New York, a bomb had exploded, wrecking the station and seriously injuring two persons. The friends of law and order were certain that the friends of Sacco and Vanzetti had set this bomb; while the friends of Sacco and Vanzetti were equally certain that their worst enemies had done it. In the State House in Boston a package had been found in one of the elevators; after listening for clockwork inside, and hearing nothing, the police had opened it with many precautions, and found two pounds of chocolate.

Justice Sanderson of the Supreme Judicial Court declared that he had no power to grant a motion for a new trial; it was a problem how to bring the matter before the Full Court. Federal Judge Anderson declined to intervene—in spite of "Moore v. Dempsey, 261 U.S. 86." In fact he thought that decision worked the other way. A difficult matter to make a science out of the law, when no one could determine what it meant, and there were no angels to administer it! Justice Oliver Wendell Holmes of the United States Supreme Court said that he had no authority, but pointed out that they were at liberty to try some judge of the circuit court; however, the judges of the circuit court advised trying the supreme court. It was as Bart had noted long ago—everybody put the problem off on somebody else!

Hill and Field and Musmanno went racing about from one court to another, and from one summer resort to another— wherever a judge might be intercepted. Behind them chased Attorney General Reading, his pockets full of money from the Decimo Club and the "L.A.W."; and behind him one or more carloads of reporters, liberally provided with funds by large-scale purveyors of sensation. Hill made another appeal to the Governor for a stay; and the Governor announced that he would not grant the request. That was Tuesday afternoon, and the execution was set for Wednesday midnight.

"What does that mean, Deborah?"—it was Cornelia phoning to her daughter, tormented with anxiety.

"I don't know, Mother. I only know what he told me. He may have his reasons. We ought not to talk about it over the telephone." So there was nothing to do but wait, and guess at the tortuous motives of a supersalesman of automobiles, whose heart was set upon moving to the White House.

Betty and Joe were absorbed in frantic efforts to awaken public opinion. The respectable lawyers were out of favor now, and it was permitted to make "propaganda." The committee had issued a call for a hundred thousand persons to come to Boston and voice the protest of America against judicial murder. About two hundred came. For the most part they only added to the confusion, because there was no one to organize them or put them to work. No two had the same idea of what should be done; and when they came to the committee, they found exactly the same state of disagreement.

Many of the group from New York, especially the liberals and the lawyers, thought that the crucial issue was the Department of Justice files. They started a clamor: "Open the files!" Several newspapers took it up. But this program met with strong opposition from the Italian anarchists. Could there be things in these files which Italian anarchists did not want to see upon the front pages of newspapers? The liberals got so far as to induce the Department of Justice to say that the files would be turned over to Governor Fuller or to President Lowell, if either would ask for them; but these worthies took exactly the same attitude as the anarchists, and for exactly the same reason. There were more things in the class struggle than were dreamed of in the philosophy of amiable liberals.

XV

One thing all sympathizers could do, and that was to get arrested. Over at socialist headquarters in Essex Street was a little group which had a program, and an organization to carry it out. A group of students came there, and placards and sandwich signs were made, calling upon Governor Fuller for justice. Young men and women sallied forth—and as they emerged from the building, a squad of police fell upon them, and took away the signs and tore them to pieces. So the job had to be done all over; the signs were prepared secretly, and would-be paraders came one by one to the place of demonstration, hiding their signs until they were on the picket-line.

On Tuesday afternoon some thirty paraders made their appearance in front of the State House, each wearing a placard with a Sacco-Vanzetti argument upon it. For a while the police let them alone, and contented themselves with keeping the crowd on the other side of the street. On the Beacon Street front of the State House there is an iron picket-fence, which curves in towards the main entrance, making a large half moon; so there was a comfortable space for paraders, and a chance for their sentiments to be legible. They walked in silence, keeping in motion, paying no attention to any one: a form of demonstration which had first been used on Broadway, New York, during the Colorado coal strike, and had been taken up by the Boston suffragists at the time of President Wilson's visit, when Cornelia and Betty and Mrs. Henderson and her daughter had gone to jail. The city had passed a special ordinance to meet that form of insurrection; it provided against "sauntering and loitering," and the suffrage women had called it "loitering for liberty."

Too bad that so many of the demonstrators were foreigners, especially Russians and Jews, who were disliked in Boston. Such names as Berkowitch and Borofsky, Dalevitch and Hurwitz, Timchuck and Suchuck and Shklar did not produce a good effect when read aloud over morning codfish-balls and coffee. But when you call for martyrs you cannot be fastidious, and your recruits will probably come from the martyr races—especially the Jews, who discovered the idea. So Berkowitch and Borofsky, Dalevitch and Hurwitz, Timchuck and Suchuck and Shklar, male and female, walked up and down in front of the high stone building with the golden dome, their faces pale and set with determination. With them walked Alfred Baker Lewis representing the socialists, and Harry J. Canter and Bertram Wolfe representing the communists, and Grace Hutchins representing Beacon Hill and the Back Bay.

State House guards lined the picket-fence, and square-jawed, hard-faced "plainclothesmen" slipped in and out among the crowd. The statue of Daniel Webster surveyed the scene impassively; also the tall equestrian figure of General Hooker, green with verdigris, and white with the droppings of birds on top of his head. From the windows above, the State House gang looked down, and cursed, or cracked their jokes; the bootleggers and friends of bootleggers, the sellers of public privileges, the boon companions of large scale plunderers, who had millions to spend for immunity.

Over on the other side of Beacon Street was the Shaw monument, glorifying a young Harvard aristocrat who had given his life to raise Negro slaves to manhood. Here walked "cops" with clubs in their hands and guns on their hips, wondering how long it would be before they were turned loose on the "Bolshevikis"; also members of the American Legion, stirring up the crowd, crying their hatred of the "goddam Reds." Few of the spectators needed any incitement; their heads were stuffed with the contents of newspapers, and they were sure the "Guinneys" were guilty, and should have been "burned" long ago.

At four o'clock in the afternoon the number of the paraders had grown to a hundred and twenty-five, and the police decided that it had gone far enough. Captain McDevitt appeared and read the riot act. Under the law the "saunterers and loiterers" had seven minutes in which to disperse. When they continued marching, the police surrounded thirty-nine of them, and loaded them into patrol-wagons, and carted them to the old Joy Street police station, followed by a crowd shouting, "Beat them up! Hang them!" That was just words, of course; Massachusetts is a law-abiding Commonwealth, fitting completely into the formula of Lenin which Betty Alvin was so fond of quoting: "The state is a monopoly of violence."

XVI

The monopolists of violence were making their preparations for such a show of their commodity as no city in America had ever witnessed in time of peace. The old Charlestown prison was turned into an arsenal; a cupola-crowned, octagon-shaped building of hand-cut stone, with red-brick wings covered with ivy, its walls now had dozens of machine guns mounted on top, and stores of ammunition, and sixteen searchlights playing at night. Eight hundred policemen, carrying riot guns with bayonets, took possession of the streets approaching the prison, and roped them off, stopping all traffic over Prison Point Bridge, and on Rutherford Avenue, a main thoroughfare, for half a mile. They were posted on all the house-tops surrounding the prison. In front of the gates were a hundred mounted Boston troopers, and a hundred of the state constabulary riding the streets. Firemen were on hand with high pressure hoses to repel mobs, and there was a plentiful store of tear and gas bombs, gas masks and bullet-proof vests.

All day Wednesday the eight hundred and eighty-one inmates of the prison went their usual round, with arms folded and lips shut. They were not supposed·to know what was going on; but rumor spreads in penitentiaries, as fast as anywhere else. All the prisoners knew that the death-sentence was to be carried out at midnight, unless the courts or the Governor intervened. They knew that eighteen Western Union wires had been run into the officers' club of the prison, and that reporters were swarming there to send out the news of the execution. At nine o'clock the prison lights winked out one by one; but nobody went to sleep.

In the death-house, in three narrow cells side by side, were the condemned men; Sacco and Vanzetti and Madeiros, the Portuguese who had managed to hitch his fate onto theirs. Sacco was on the fourth week of a "hungry strike," and Vanzetti was also fasting; they were haggard and wasted, gray and grim. No one was permitted to see them, except their lawyers and relatives. Vanzetti had a sister on her way from Italy; if he were executed according to schedule she would not see him alive. The mother and sister of Madeiros had come for a visit; also Rosina Sacco, who spent her time trying to persuade her husband to sign some papers for the lawyers. But he was more stubborn than ever before. "They have had me nailed to the cross for seven years. Why should I keep it up?" Rosina broke down and had to be carried away.

The newspapermen noted that Sacco and Vanzetti did not behave like other condemned criminals; they did not chat with their keepers, nor sit and play cards with them, shoving the cards under the barred doors of the cells. They preferred to brood, staring at a little square patch of sunlight which fell from the roof upon the floor, the only reminder of the outside world. At night, when the searchlights played upon the death-house, they saw nothing, nor did they hear the sound of horses' hoofs. They were permitted to have their books and papers; despite the fact that Vanzetti had written a statement in which he had called Governor Fuller a "murderer." They wrote farewell letters to the world: still cherishing the "messianic delusion," the idea that posterity would be interested in their sufferings.

XVII

All that day the lawyers rushed about, and the Governor was busy with his advisers. His Council was in session, also the seven ex-attorney-generals of the Commonwealth, invited to advise him as to the law on the matter of a respite. On the street outside, several squads of pickets were being dragged off to jail, with more or less violence. Those who had been arrested the day before were being denied their hearings in police-court, and condemned to pay fines without argument. Some refused, and went to jail; others paid, and came out to join the "death march" again.

Marvelous copy for the newspapers, which printed everybody's guesses as to what was going to happen; every detail about the police preparations, and diagrams of the death-house, and photographs of the electric chair, and of the executioner —a gentleman who made a specialty of sending two thousand volts of electricity into living human bodies; he came from New York, it appeared, and was paid by the piece. For this job he was to get seven hundred and fifty dollars, and shocking as the statement may sound, he was overcharging the great Commonwealth. The people of Massachusetts, having elected their best business man to attend to their affairs, surely had a right to expect the discounts customary to the trade; but here was New York State getting its killings done by the same killer for only one hundred and fifty per!

Young Musmanno went to see his clients, to get another paper signed. They were glad to have some one to remind them that human affection still survived in a world given up to business. Sacco refused to sign, as usual; Vanzetti signed, hoping it would help both of them. He was reading the Beards on "The Rise of American Civilization"—at the same time that he watched its fall. He was not going to be able to finish these large, expensive volumes, so he wanted to give them to the young lawyer as a token of regard. But Musmanno couldn't bear to take them, because it would be admitting that Vanzetti was to die that night. They had quite an argument about it; and several times Sacco would break in with his realist humor: "Take the books, Musmanno! Take the books!"

Musmanno did not take the books, but sped away to make

another plea to the Governor. The prisoners began to sing; there was no law to prevent that, they sang every international song they knew, in Italian and in English.

> Arise, ye prisoners of starvation!
> Arise, ye wretched of the earth!
> For justice thunders condemnation;
> A newer world's in birth!

The rest of the prison heard no sound; but the searchlights flashed into their cells and kept them awake, and cries would run down the tiers of cells—hundreds of men shouting over and over: "Let them out! Let them out!" There was no one to interfere with them, for the guards, many of them, broke down and sobbed.

A singular adventure of Dorothy Parker, young poet from New York, sophisticated and ironical, but not liking official murder. She knew a newspaper reporter, and he got drunk, and volunteered to take her into the prison with him. He got her past the police-lines, and then went to get another drink, and never appeared again. So there was Dorothy, wandering about, patting the noses of state troopers' horses, surveying the lines of guns, and testing Massachusetts prison discipline after bed-time. She sat with the reporters, and gathered the news, and then went to the telephone and called up Sacco-Vanzetti defense headquarters, and was overheard by a horrified deputy-warden—a spy of the enemy inside the defenses! A lovely story for bored reporters, smoking cigarettes and playing cards in the officers' club, and begging for the tiniest item of news to put on the wires—starting with the mystic letters, "SV," and ending with the promise: "Will be add."

What was the supersalesman doing? Said Betty, "It is his idea of drama, to make publicity for himself!" But in this she was blinded by her hatred of the man. The plain truth was, he had decided to have the execution that night, and get it over with. But some of his advisers said it was impossible, with matters as they stood before the courts. Arthur Hill was arguing—a three hour argument before the Council. Up to the last half hour the issue hung in the balance, and swayed, now this way and now that.

Every preparation for death was made; the canvas cover was off the electric chair, and the current tested—the three victims listening to the sounds. They were dressed in their death-clothes—shirts with short sleeves and trousers with short legs, leaving room for the electrodes. But at ten-twenty the warden came to the reporters, his face wreathed in smiles, announcing that he had been notified by the Governor, the execution was "off" for that night. Wild excitement, and some joy, for the burly warden did not like his job the least bit. The reporters flashed the word "reprieve" to the farthest ends of the earth; but five minutes later the warden came in again, his face a blank—terribly sorry, he had further word from the Governor, the execution was "on" again, and was to take place at midnight.

The official witnesses who had been selected, and the one reporter, the Associated Press man, who had been favored above all other reporters, made ready to enter the death-house. But again the warden burst in, at twenty-seven minutes past eleven, almost in a state of collapse—he had had another talk with the Governor, and the execution was "off" for the next twelve days. The reporters leaped to the telegraph-keys—having before their minds a terrible calamity. There are newspapers in the big cities which make a practice of printing descriptions of things which haven't happened, but are due to happen according to schedule; there would be New York papers having on their presses the news that the men were dead. Suppose some of these copies were to get onto the streets!

The "false execution"—such was the name by which the friends of the defense came to know that dreadful evening. They had sat in defense headquarters, and in a church behind the State House which had been mercifully opened to them, and waited for news, and pictured the worst. Rosina Sacco had sat for three hours holding a watch in her hand; when at last the news of the reprieve came in, she collapsed, and had to be carried to the home of friends. In the little apartment on the north side of Beacon Hill, Cornelia Thornwell was at the telephone, dizzy, but able to hear the voice of Deborah: "I told you, Mother! You should have believed me—he would not dare to disregard us."

CHAPTER 21

DAYS OF GRACE

I

SACCO and Vanzetti, brought up from Dedham jail on the first day of July, had been put into the death cells. When the Governor granted the first reprieve of thirty days, to allow the Lowell Commission to work, they had been moved back to what was called the Cherry Hill section of the prison. On the first of August, it being ten days to the new date of execution, they went back into the death cells. Now, the Governor having granted twelve days more, the rules required another return to the Cherry Hill section. "Oh, this is wearisome!" exclaimed Sacco. "This moving!"

He was on the twenty-sixth day of a fast, and barely able to totter. But he would not be assisted; no, he would take care of himself. A slow, feeble procession, the guards at his side ready to catch him if he fell. Vanzetti walked behind; having broken his fast, he had a little strength. Out into the open sunshine in the prison yard; a glimpse of the flower-beds along the walk, of blue sky overhead, white clouds, and gray and white gulls wheeling; the sounds of freight cars being shunted in the Boston and Maine yards, on the other side of the prison walls. A few steps to be climbed; wait, let him alone, Nick would do it by himself. At last he was lying on his cot in the new cell; tortured, distracted—when his wife and son came to see him they found his mind wandering. He was in what is known as a "blind" cell, having a solid wooden door in front of the barred iron door, and a peep-hole through which the keepers could look in.

Vanzetti also was in such a cell, and had fits of frenzied protest against the long drawn out and senseless agony. He talked aloud at night, and disturbed the other prisoners. His words being mostly in Italian, the guards and reporters said they

639

were "incoherent." He shouted about "the machine, the machine!"—which they took to mean the electric chair; not understanding the social system which is crushing human hopes throughout the world, grinding up the souls and minds of millions. Vanzetti was told that his cries were keeping other men awake, and that if he kept it up, he would be put in the padded cell, known as the "Blue Room." At this he became furious, and dragged his cot and wooden bureau in front of the door of his cell, and warned the guards that they would not get him out alive.

Cornelia heard that news, and came to the prison early in the morning. They had refused her admission to the death-cells —only relatives and attorneys were allowed there, a strict rule. Now they told her that Vanzetti was "dangerous," but she laughed at them; Bart had never been dangerous to those who used the methods and the language of love. She told them that she could tame this wild man for them, and without padded cells or strait-jackets. Since they dreaded a scandal very much, they gave way and took her through the prison yard, and into the corridor of "blind" cells.

Poor Bart—a dreadful change from the early days in that prison, when he had been so eager to see her, yet made her wait while he washed the coal dust from his face and hands! And always carefully shaved, clear-eyed, and with his unconscious natural dignity. Now he lay in a dark hole, feeble and wasted, his hair falling out, his teeth decaying, a gray and wasted specter. He started up when he heard her gentle voice, but then had to sink back on the cot, for he grew dizzy if he got up suddenly.

Cornelia asked the guard to let him come out into the corridor and sit with her. She knew that he would be gentle. The prisoner answered that of course he would; but he was not fit to be seen. She promised not to look at him, and so he came, and she looked into his eyes, and smiled and began to talk. She had been to Plymouth a few days ago, to interview a witness for Musmanno; she had seen the Brinis, and had much news about the family. They had moved to a place on Cherry Court, and the baby was grown up. A hundred items of gossip—even the latest reports from Vincenzo's garden, and the explosion which had occurred in his home-made wine!

And then news about that most precious of young creatures, Rupert Alvin Thornwell Randall—a mouthful of names. He was a sturdy one; two years old now, toddling and talking at a great rate; spending the summer at his grandmother's country place on the North Shore, while his mother gave her time to the Sacco-Vanzetti defense. Betty had been so determined that this infant should grow up in a proletarian environment—but alas, it was midsummer, and hot in a little apartment, and out there on the North Shore were cool, refreshing breezes; so the grandparents had the precious one, completely surrounded by a battalion of servants, and all the demoralizing uses of luxury. Betty had to choose between saving one infant and saving the world—a dilemma frequently encountered by reformers. Cornelia told Bart a little about the family duel, which had been going on for two years; now the great banker and his wife had got their way. Bart said they always would, so long as they were able to control the things which other persons needed.

Vanzetti had been writing off and on, in spite of handicaps. He had a statement which he wanted Cornelia to revise; she might assure the warden that there was nothing in it like calling the Governor a "murderer," which had made such a terrible scandal throughout all Massachusetts. He wanted to give her a lot of his manuscripts to keep—but she didn't want to take them, because that would be admitting that he was going to die! In the course of their talk he developed signs of timidity, and said he had written something that he had wanted to show to her, but he was afraid maybe it wasn't very good; it was a poem—a poem about a nightingale! Cornelia reassured him—it wouldn't need to be very good in order for her to be interested in it. He drew it from the lot of papers, and read it to her: this "dangerous" one, sitting in the corridor of the "blind" cells, with a lynx-eyed guard watching every move and listening to every word. The poem began:

When in the course of endless cosmic changes,
Upon the close of winter dark and drear
From far away, benignant, crowned with roses,
We see the lovely, longed-for spring appear. . . .

Cornelia had to tell the poet that such emotions had been expressed before; nevertheless, there were tears to her eyes over the effort of a wop in prison to describe a nightingale in Italy! Springtime in Villafalletto—the fruit trees in blossom and the vegetables thriving—and the poet behind bars, condemned to death! Was it because of her aching pity for the doomed idealist, or was there really beauty and pathos in the closing lines?

Thus in my garden, in bright morning's glow,
I saw thee in an April long ago.

II

Twelve days of grace had been granted to the defense. Twelve days in which to educate the world! Twelve days for lawyers to compose more briefs, packed full of legal formulas and imposing citations; to hop into automobiles or airplanes, and go hunting for judges, and argue, plead, insist—there could not be a total failure of law, when new evidence had been discovered, proving that innocent men were about to be executed. The judges would listen politely and patiently; but in all that long list, from the lowest to the highest, not one would think about anything but precedent, not one would act upon a basis of mercy or justice, political wisdom or ordinary common sense.

"Unless a million men can be mobilized in our defense, we are lost!" Such had been Vanzetti's statement, two or three years ago. It had taken the United States government a year to mobilize a million men, and the Sacco-Vanzetti committee now set out to do it in twelve days. They drafted appeals and sent long telegrams—a great sum in tolls each day. Mass meetings were held in hundreds of American cities and towns, and in all the capitals of the world; the newspapers were full of reports of riots and strikes. But such events only stiffened the backs of the State House crowd; this was "Bolshevism," and the answer to it was several thousand rifles with bayonets, and a plentiful supply of gas bombs and machine guns.

The one thing the State House crowd really feared was a general strike. That was the weapon which had saved the lives of Ettor and Giovannitti, and which might have saved Sacco and Vanzetti. The police were on the alert day and night for the first move towards it. Two Jews, officers of the cap makers' union, started a movement for a strike among the clothing workers of Boston, and were arrested and framed on a bombing charge. The police hadn't the slightest thing on them, and confessed it with a laugh when they released them—after the execution. There were spies everywhere, bringing word, hour by hour, of what was going on in all the centers of sedition. The ruling classes waited for the least little sign of violence, the least departure from the rôle of martyrdom—so odious and exasperating to those who believe in gold and steel.

The "highbrow" sympathizers labored to mobilize liberal opinion. They organized emergency groups and drafted appeals to the Governor, and collected signatures from leaders of every form of intellectual and artistic activity. It was a simple matter to get such persons to voice their horror at the idea of executing men after seven years on the rack, and when there were so many reasons for doubting their guilt. The trouble was that after the signatures were collected, there was nothing to do with them—except to take them to the State House, and turn them over to a man who read the *Saturday Evening Post,* and to whom a list of leaders of international thought was of less significance than a list of the delegates to an "ad-men's" convention.

This salesman of motor cars posed as being completely impartial, and delighted to assure his visitors, "I don't know what an anarchist is, I don't pay any attention to that sort of stuff." But right in the midst of these pretenses some researcher in Washington dug up his hate-speeches—the only ones of any consequence he had made during his four years' service in Congress. He had been an ardent advocate of the exclusion of Victor Berger, the socialist congressman, and with hot anger had called for "the crucifixion of disloyalty, the nailing of sedition to the cross of free government, where the whole brood of anarchists, bolsheviks, I.W.W.'s and revolutionaries may see and read a solemn warning." He had talked about the "red scum," and the "agents of the red flag," and had denounced opposition to preparedness as "a devilish scheme of undermining the morale of the people." These tirades had been delivered just before a thousand men and women were dragged from their homes and thrown into Boston jails.

III

Not since the days of the Civil War had there been such a test of the consciences of men and women in Boston. Strange things happened, unexpected workings of the spirit. To Cornelia Thornwell in her little apartment came the second son of James Scatterbridge, known as "James's Josiah," and sat in a chair and fixed his pale blue, earnest eyes upon her, and in a timid, half-apologetic voice began, "Grandmother, it seems to me as if I ought to do something to help."

"There is plenty to be done," said the old lady.

"I decided I ought to contribute some money, so I went to defense headquarters yesterday evening. I had made up my mind to give half my vacation allowance. But while I was there three Italian laborers came in; you could see they had just come from the day's work, their shoes were covered with mortar, and the backs of their hands had big knotted veins on them. They brought more than fifty dollars which they had collected on the job. I couldn't understand what they said, but I watched their faces, and I realized it was money which their wives and children must need, so I got ashamed of myself. I think we all have too easy a time. I gave every cent I had, and now I don't know what I'll do."

"Lots of college boys go to work in vacation time, Josiah, and sometimes they learn more than in classes."

"I know, Grandmother, and that's what I'll do; but first it seemed to me that I oughtn't to let you and Betty and Joe carry the brunt of all this. Betty says she's going to get arrested next Sunday, and it seems to me I ought to go, too. What do you think?"

Another family problem! Cornelia declined to solve it; she said that in matters of conscience, every person has to act for himself. "It will make your father very angry, of course."

"I know; he's terrible when he gets excited about the Reds. But I don't think it's quite the same as being a Red, to say that men ought not to be executed when there is so much doubt of their guilt. But I can't get Father to see that at all.

You'll be shocked, I know, but he said they ought to be executed, anyhow."

"I've heard many people say that, Josiah; it is almost a respectable opinion in Boston. A member of the Governor's Council has voiced it, I am told."

"We're having a funny time at home right now," continued the youth. "Have you heard about Great-uncle Abner? He is determined to break into the *Transcript* with a letter about the case, and Father has promised Uncle Henry that he won't let him—out of respect for you, of course."

"I know," said Cornelia. "It is very kind of them."

"Father is provoked with you, but he won't have any scandal, and he has been having all the servants bring Great-uncle Abner's letters to him, instead of posting them. Great-uncle Abner found out about it, and there was a terrible row, you could hear him shouting all over the house: 'Am I in jail or am I not in jail? Answer me that? Have I been legally committed? If not, take me out of here, and let me die a free man!' He just wouldn't give up, and Father had to pacify him, for fear he'd have another stroke. What Father did—you won't believe it—he promised to send the letter to the *Transcript*, and he had a printer take the editorial page from an early edition, and reproduce it complete, with the page on the other side also—but with Great-uncle Abner's letter in it. It was quite wonderful—it would have fooled anybody. They put it in the evening edition and brought it to the old gentleman, and he was as pleased as punch—read it about twenty times, and some of his old friends were let in on the secret, and came to see him and patted him on the back and said it was a great letter and ought to settle the case with the Governor. It said there ought to be a Bolshevik hanging from each tree on the Common, and they ought not to have any trials. It said that American institutions must be saved from rape at the hands of Russian gold and Italian dynamite. It was almost as bad as some of the letters that really get published!"

IV

The case worked also upon the consciences of persons who were cursed with artistic temperaments. Such unfortunates read the letters of Vanzetti and recognized a brother in distress. He who had made himself a master of English prose spoke to all other writers, now as in times to come. They gathered from far and near, anxious that a great soul and a prophet should be recognized before he was dead.

There came Arturo Giovannitti, compatriot and fellow-victim of the "frame-up" system: one of those whom Captain Proctor had set out to "get," in the days of Proctor's prime, before his consceince began to trouble him. For more than a year Giovannitti had lain in Salem jail, and had written a haunting poem, "The Walker."

> One-two-three-four: four paces and the wall;
> One-two-three-four: four paces and the iron gate.

Now he walked a somewhat longer road in front of the State House with the golden dome; measured, not by paces, but by minutes—one-two-three-four-five-six-seven. He went to the Common, temple of free speech with elm-tree limbs for arches. "Fellow-workers," he began—being an I.W.W., that was his formula. "Break it up!" shouted "Mickey the Gunman." "You've said enough!" But the poet protested: "I haven't said anything yet! Wait till I finish before you arrest any one." "You're talking against the courts!" was the answer of the superintendent of police. "You're not allowed to talk against the courts!" The mounted troopers drove their reluctant horses into the crowd. "Break it up! Move along there!"

John Dos Passos came, playwright and novelist, genial, gentle, and bold as a young bull buffalo. A graduate of Harvard, he came to save the honor of his alma mater. "You have put your name and indirectly the name of the university to an infamous document"—so he wrote to President Lowell; and then, since no Boston paper would publish his letter, he went out on the picket-line and exposed his head to the policemen's clubs, and his skin to the vermin in the old Joy Street police-station.

"Fair Harvard, thy sons to thy jubilee throng!" There thronged George L. Teeple, of the class of '97, and got himself arrested with the other pickets, and read a statement in court, paying fifteen dollars extra for the privilege, because the judge remarked that there might be an excuse for ignorant foreigners, but there was very little excuse for a Harvard man to violate the law.

Also Powers Hapgood, nephew of Norman and of Hutchins. His was not the sort of head the Boston police were used to breaking. He had completed four years' work at Harvard in three; he had "made" the Dickey and the Hasty Pudding Club, the varsity track squad and the Harvard "Crimson." He had been in the service abroad, and was one of the few undergraduates honored by election to the Harvard Memorial Society. He was one of those young Americans in whom readers of fiction refuse to believe; "unreal and made to order," they say, of a college youth who travels over the country working in coal mines, and becoming a leader of the left wing miners. Now he came to express his opinion of President Lowell, and the opinion was such that official Boston shut it up in the Psychopathic Hospital.

Heywood Broun was carrying on the same fight in New York, as "colyumist" of the *World,* at a salary of four hundred and fifty dollars a week. Broun had been "flunked out" of Harvard in his youth, and this may have made him feel disrespectful. "From now on," he wrote, "will the institution of learning at Cambridge which we once called Harvard be known as Hangman's House?" The *World* published that, but refused to publish the next articles, so the "colyumnist" went on a "permanent strike," which made an enormous sensation among the literati. An extraordinary thing, the way the case "got" the intelligentsia, even that portion which prides itself most upon being hard-boiled and immune to social emotions.

v

Also there came alumni of the University of Hard Knocks. Those foreign names which pleased the readers of Boston newspapers so little belonged to clothing-workers who had given up their jobs, and spent their savings to come and jeopardize their skulls; to sailors from the port, to iron-workers, barbers, bakers and waiters; also to poets and writers who had educated themselves, and thus could understand the soul of Vanzetti. There came Michael Gold, a young Jew from the slums of New York, who had been a newspaper reporter in Boston when not yet out of his teens, and had been one of that group of anarchist sympathizers whom Cornelia had seen, eleven years ago, accompanying Galleani to the Plymouth cordage strike.

Mike was now a playwright and editor of the *New Masses,* but resented being classified as an "intellectual," and wanted to remain a worker; so he dressed in khaki, which gave a shock to Boston. He wandered about, fascinated by the spectacle of a city gone mad with fear. He listened to the conversation of sleek clerks and stock-brokers of State Street, ex-football players of Harvard who wished they might have a chance to tackle the "Reds." He listened to taxi-drivers and soda-jerkers, who knew what they had read in a capitalist newspaper, or learned from others who had read it in some other capitalist newspaper. On the afternoon of the "false execution" he joined the "death march" in front of the State House, and the same two iron-handed cops who grabbed Dorothy Parker the poet grabbed Mike Gold the playwright, and hauled them away to the oddly-named Joy Street police station. "Hang them! Hang the anarchists!" cried the straw-hatted mob; and Mike, who had written a life of John Brown, saw the ghost of William Lloyd Garrison going down the street with a rope about his waist, followed by the "mob in broadcloth," crying "Hang him! Hang the abolitionist!"

Those Boston merchants of a hundred years ago had been, some of them, the "bootleggers" of their day; smuggling "black ivory" from Africa, Negro slaves whose labor would be turned into molasses in Louisiana. The molasses would be brought to New England and made into rum, and the rum would go back to Africa, to make drunk the savage chiefs whose war-victims would compose the next bootleg cargo. Now the great-great-grandsons of those old merchants bore the same names, and looked so much like their ancestors that when they came up for election to the Somerset Club, the directors thought they were voting for the ancestors. These great-great-grandsons had imported hundreds of thousands of white niggers from the Mediterranean and Baltic lands, to operate their steam and electric machines, and had built a colossal system for the exploiting of this new slave labor. These new masters considered themselves civilized, and were willing to install "welfare work," and have their wives "do charity." But at the same time they looked upon these foreign hordes with mingled contempt and fear, and dreaded the day when they might refuse obedience. To suggest this to them was the worst crime that could be committed in modern New England; the "black abolitionists" of 1831 had been replaced, as objects of ruling class hatred, by the "red scum" of 1927.

So it was that Boston was under what amounted to martial law, and there were more detectives watching strangers than there were strangers. Any one who wore a beard, or had a dark face, was liable to be halted on the street and ordered to give an account of himself. A messenger carrying a box of seidlitz powders had to stop for a chemical analysis. Helen Black and Ann Washington Craton—a descendant of the father of her country—were arrested and taken to the police station and cross-questioned for hours; the reason assigned being that they "looked like New Yorkers." Six Italians arrived in an automobile, and two of them needed a shave, so they were held on a bombing charge.

Joe Randall, of course, was a marked man; the fact that he wrote articles for newspapers and posed as a reporter only made him worse than the other "Bolsheviks." Detectives followed him everywhere, in restaurants, in drug stores when he bought an ice cream soda, in barber shops when he got a shave. He made trouble for them by insisting upon talking with them, which was destructive of morale and against the ethics of "shadowing." New "dicks" were substituted, but Joe said you could always recognize them by their blank and stupid faces; there was no other occupation by which such low-grade persons could manage to be well-dressed and well-fed.

Impossible to imagine anything more grotesque than the activities of these anthropoid mentalities, trying to deal with a world of which they had no gleam of understanding. Some of the things they did were beyond the absurdities of musical comedy. Heywood Broun's wife, Ruth Hale, came to Boston at the height of the tragedy. Two sleuths of the city spent the night in a Ford car, keeping watch on Hanover street, opposite defense headquarters, and in the morning a newspaper man asked them what they had been doing, and the answer was, "We had a straight tip on a bomb-plot, and we were watching for the bombers." "Who are they?" asked the reporter. The reply was, "Two women from New York, Ruth Hale and Dorothy Parker."

VI'

On Thursday, the eleventh, Justice Sanderson of the Supreme Judicial Court allowed a bill of exceptions from his ruling to go to the Full Court. Also Web Thayer was persuaded, for the sake of appearance, to permit exceptions to his rulings to be carried up. So there were two more hopes for salvation from the courts; Massachusetts was going to lean over backwards in respecting the legal rights of two convicted wops. Chief Justice Rugg was ill, and Crosby was in Europe; Sanderson was barred from considering his own ruling, so there were Braley, Wait, Carroll, and Pierce, with Braley, oldest member, presiding. He issued a summons for a special sitting on the following Tuesday, to listen to arguments of counsel.

Hope once more in the hearts of all believers in law and order. Surely the ruling group was coming to its senses; it had realized the frightful blunder it was making, and had chosen a dignified way to back down! Patience now, and keep cool, and don't do anything to excite public feeling, and make it harder for the learned justices! Stop the wild talk, and keep the New York radicals off the streets and out of the newspapers! Above all, no disorders on the Common, nor in front of the State House! So argued the "respectables."

Was there really a chance? Or was it merely that those in charge of affairs wanted it to seem that way? Quincy Thornwell came to his Aunt Cornelia, bringing rumors: the Governor had talked with So-and-so, and had said this and that. More important yet, Mr. Lowell was showing signs of weakening; he was defending himself, for the first time in his long life. One of the "middle minds" had been to see him, and he had argued until two o'clock in the morning, trying to justify his decision; he had been so anxious about it that he had followed his visitor downstairs in his pajamas, and out into the garden, flashing a torchlight into the bushes to make sure there were no bombers hiding. Quincy Thornwell chuckled over the picture: assuredly the strangest sight ever witnessed by the chaste nymphs who haunt the shades of the classic elms of Harvard!

And then the learned justices of the Supreme Judicial Court, actually giving signs of humanity! Justice Wait had made a speech, defending the action of the court; and now here was the wife of another one, the presiding justice, Braley, telephoning to Mrs. Jessica Henderson; a Leach of Bridgewater she was, a highly respected person, and twice she called up to say: "Don't worry, my dear, everything is coming out all right, I assure you. They are not going to let them be executed, they will find some way out. The judge does not believe in capital punishment." What could have been the meaning of that? Could it be that these old boys were fooling their own wives, in the effort to cheer them up and keep peace in the family? Or were they using the wives to lull the defense, and damp the dangerous agitation during the critical days? Impossible to guess.

VII

In the Sacco-Vanzetti committee the never-ceasing struggle between those who wanted to be judicious and those who wanted to make propaganda. Lawyers and college professors telephoning in, or calling to make personal pleas: "Remember this is Boston, and keep the New York nuts out of the limelight!" But the "New York nuts" had something to say about that, and so had the Boston newspapers. The visitors came hiking, wearing oil-cloth placards over their shoulders, getting cursed and nearly mobbed in each respectable town they passed through. They came in sport-cars, with bootleg bottles in their baggage. Girls came in pants, and men with no hats or neckties. One brought a portable typewriter, ready for work, and when he found no room in headquarters, he set himself up on the curbstone outside the Hotel Bellevue, and started writing letters for Sacco and Vanzetti. The newspapers, of course, got pictures of him at once. Also they eagerly interviewed a young man who announced his intention of marching to Dedham jail to rescue Sacco and Vanzetti, and was disconcerted to learn that his campaign maps were out of date.

Such were the surface aspects of the invasion, easy to see and to record. But there was another aspect, not so obvious to Boston newspapermen, nor so diverting to their readers. The soul of the demonstration, a common feeling which animated all the participants, men and women, old and young, rich and poor, educated and ignorant: a sense of black despair, of agonizing littleness in the face of a colossal evil; an impotent rage, a hatred, bitter as gall, rolling up in their minds, for this whole great city of greed masked by bigotry—smug and polite and treacherous, cultured and correct and deadly.

Very few of these agitators were professionals; not many of them had any training, any party to guide and support them. They came as individuals, hesitating and confused. They didn't like to do what they were doing; the women, and many of the men, felt like Lady Godiva riding through the town naked—worse even than she, because they had no certainty of accomplishing anything; perhaps they were making fools of themselves to no purpose at all.

They came because American labor would not come. Vanzetti had called for a million workers, and the million workers answered, "What the hell?" Most of them were content for Vanzetti to die—so that American prosperity might live; they were ready to make that sacrifice to Moloch, precisely as the mothers and fathers of Carthage were ready to put their infants into the red-hot iron arms of the god, so that Carthage might live. So, instead of the million workers, came one or two hundred poets, painters, dreamers and lovers of beauty, Greenwich Villagers, bums, bohemians—whatever names Boston, the correct and murderous, might choose to call them. A pitiful little group, throwing themselves against the iron battlements of American capitalism, with its machine-guns and poison gas bombs, its police in the front rank and army and navy in reserve.

And for every dreamer who came, there were thousands who stayed at home, chained by poverty, or a greater share of timidity; waiting, waiting, with a ghastly sense of uncertainty, feeling themselves more effectively imprisoned than Sacco and Vanzetti. Writing letters, but not knowing if they were read; sending telegrams—like shooting arrows into the dark! Unable to get any real news—a few bare events each day in the papers, but no opinions, no guidance, no light. The radio grinding out its eternal silly thumping of drums and whining of saxophones— this greatest story in modern American history not worth a moment's attention!

VIII

Sunday was coming, and what was the committee going to do? Was there to be another meeting on the Common, or should they oblige the lawyers and wait? Agonized arguments, turning into bitter quarrels. "When did you come into this case?" the old-timers would jeer; and to that the answer was obvious: "A fine mess you made of it!" The communists would rage at the members of the committee: "Do you think you own Sacco and Vanzetti? What do you want—to put their ashes in an urn and set it on your parlor mantel?"

Some were determined to speak on the Common, committee or no committee, police or no police. The Socialist Labor Party had a permit not yet confiscated, and the Sacco-Vanzetti defenders would use that; so it was announced, and the would-be martyrs prepared placards on canvas, which could be folded up and hidden under the clothing. Betty and Joe refused to tell the family what they were going to do; so here came Deborah in all her majesty, mixing with the "mob" on the Common, walking about unable to keep her hands quiet, so agitated she was. When it came to a test, she really did love her daughter, in spite of so many bitter words spoken during eleven years of wrangling. After all, it was "Boston"; conscience was conscience, and when you followed yours, you commanded respect from others who followed theirs. When the little group of white-faced men and women marched into the midst of armed ruffians, Deborah's emotions were those which had been felt by patrician Roman matrons, when their Christian children walked into the arena among the lions.

Police Judge Zottoli, an Italian anxious to prove his respectability, had announced that for those arrested in future "the sky would be the limit." But evidently among those in authority there must have been some wiser heads. The police had orders to disperse all gatherings, to allow no speeches, but to do as little arresting as possible; no more martyrs—and especially no well-dressed ones! A curious experience for young ladies who lived on Beacon Street, within sight of this greensward; they were made to leap out of the way of mounted troopers, they had their placards taken away, and their arms squeezed black and blue— but always the last word was, "Move on! Keep moving!" Were these the traffic officers who had been helping them across street-crossings, and knew them? Or were they detectives who had been keeping watch over the wedding presents in fashionable homes?

The Socialist Labor Party changed its mind at the last moment, and refused to allow the use of its permit. So the would-be speakers were all outlaws. They brought soap-boxes—and the "cops" took them away and broke them up. For Joe Randall two young martyrs upon a sudden impulse got down and made a soap-box of their backs; on this precarious pedestal Joe stood, and began: "Fellow-citizens of Massachusetts, we are here to assert the fundamental principles of free speech"—and that was all, for there were three husky "dicks" who had been following Joe about the field, and grabbed him by the arms and pulled him from his platform and led him away.

Joe had made one concession to his anxious grandmother-in-law, he would not resist and get his head broken; he went quietly—and only when he was out on Beacon Street did he discover the scurvy trick which had been played upon him. The three huskies gave him a shove and said, "Move along now, young fellow, and keep moving." "What do you mean, am I not under arrest?" "Move along, buddy, what do you want to get into trouble for?" When he tried to force his way back, they held him. They would not fight him, they would merely block his way, and see that he didn't get to the Common. Later on, when Joe learned that the same thing had happened to "James's Josiah," he realized that it could not have been an accident; some member of an all-powerful family had called in a detective agency, and paid a fancy price to keep his relatives out of jail, and his family name out of the papers!

It was Powers Hapgood who made the real fight that Sunday before the last; Powers, with a young Italian sewing-machine repairer named Cosimo Carvotta, who got inspired by Powers' eloquence, and insisted on rescuing him from the entire police force of the City of Boston. Cosimo had upon him a pocket-knife containing a small screw-driver, an inch long, used upon sewing-machines; he did not try to use it, but they found it in his pocket at the police station, and it was enough to constitute a "dirk," and make a startling story in the papers.

As for Powers, he had a highly honorific arrest, performed by Superintendent Crowley and a captain and a sergeant and other majesties. "I insist on the right of free speech! The people must save Sacco and Vanzetti! We must not allow our comrades to be murdered! Don't forget, Comrades—keep it up— save the men!"—thus the member of the Dickey and the Hasty Pudding Club and the Harvard Memorial Society, being dragged away to the police-box at the corner of Charles and Beacon streets. "Mickey the Gunman" himself pulled the hook which summoned the patrol-wagon, and within five minutes there were a hundred officers at the spot, and a squadron of mounted men to drive back the crowd.

IX

The special sitting of the Supreme Judicial Court was set for Tuesday the sixteenth at ten o'clock. Six hours before that came a dreadful event; some one put dynamite on the front porch of the home of one of the Sacco-Vanzetti jurors, in East Milton, and blew out the front of the house. Once more the authorities were certain that this had been the work of friends of Sacco and Vanzetti; whereas the friends of Sacco and Vanzetti were equally certain that it was the work of their worst enemies. They called attention to the peculiar placing of the dynamite, to make a loud noise and not hurt any one; they called attention to its exact timing—when it would do the utmost possible harm and least possible good to the defense.

The mystery was never solved; but the Governor took occasion to write a letter to the juror, denouncing those who were trying to "coerce the courts," and at the same time assuring the victim that the cost of repairing his home would be paid by the Commonwealth. A singular impulse of generosity from an official who just recently had vetoed a bill providing for compensation to state employees who had been injured in the performance of their duties!

With the crash of this bomb echoing in their ears, the four

black-robed justices assembled. The courthouse, and Pemberton Square around it, presented a scene of war. Benches were placed for barriers in front of courtroom doors, and Cornelia had to exhibit the contents of her handbag before she entered the room. She noticed that detectives assigned the little group of "Reds" to special seats, and then stood near them. Most of the crowd did not get in at all.

There sat in a row, behind a long raised desk, the four white-haired old gentlemen who held the lives of Sacco and Vanzetti in their hands. Henry King Braley, former city solicitor and mayor of Fall River, now seventy-seven years of age; Edward Peter Pierce, recently tried for misconduct, and convicted of very bad taste, seventy-five years of age; James Bernard Carroll, former city solicitor of Springfield, seventy-one years of age; and William Cushing Wait, former city alderman of Boston, sixty-seven years of age. Braley was a fellow-alumnus of Thayer's, Pierce and Wait were fellow-alumni of Katzmann's, while Carroll was a graduate of Holy Cross, which made him a fellow-alumnus of St. Peter. They told their fellow-alumni Arthur Hill and Arthur Reading, that they might have all the time needed; and then they sat, like four black-and-white images, motionless and impassive, while Mr. Hill recited the list of the high crimes of their fellow-alumni, Thayer and, indirectly, Katzmann.

Mr. Hill spared nothing of the story of "Web's" prejudice and the manifold proofs thereof. Also he asked a hearing for the new evidence—of which more was coming in every day. He called it "monstrous" to maintain that there was any stage in the process of taking men's lives when it ceased to be possible to present newly discovered evidence to establish their innocence. "It is the bench and bar of Massachusetts that is on trial," he declared. "It is our entire system of criminal law." He might have added "our entire system of criminal capitalism," but his vision did not extend that far, and very surely he could not have made it clear to four members of the Union Club of Boston.

Then came the genial Mr. Reading, with pockets stuffed with the money of the Decimo Club and the "L.A.W." He asserted his solemn faith that Judge Thayer had been just and unprejudiced; nor was he in the least afraid of being "monstrous" in reciting the law which specified that after sentence had been pronounced by the trial judge, no motion for a new trial could be entertained, no matter what the new evidence might be. The four old gentlemen mumbled a few questions to the lawyers, impossible for the spectators to hear; and then they gathered up their books and papers, and the session was adjourned. The friends of Sacco and Vanzetti went home, to continue that process of waiting in which they had become so expert in the course of seven years, three months, and eleven days.

X

But they did not have to wait very long this time. Massachusetts took pride in paying no heed to "outside clamor," but here was a different situation—a military expense of great sums every day, and enormous losses to retail trade. It was a time for sleepy old gentlemen to wake up and earn their keep. On Tuesday the hearing, on Friday the decision—an unprecedented procedure!

The document was written by Justice Braley, that oldest gentleman whose wife had more than once telephoned to Jessica Henderson, assuring her that everything was all right, no need to worry, the judge did not believe in capital punishment. Now the judge spoke for himself. With the other three judges concurring, he said that the legal system of the great Commonwealth was infallible, and the fact that it contravened decency, humanity, and common sense was of no significance. A long decision, highly technical, bristling with citations; the heart of it in one dreadful sentence: "A motion for a new trial in capital cases comes too late if made after sentence has been pronounced." Such is the law of the Brahmins and the Blue-bloods, which altereth not! "The exceptions are overruled."

Horror among so-called "liberals," those of Boston, as well as those who had come from outside! They had staked all their hopes upon the courts; they had pleaded, argued, practically forced the defense committee to obey, to let them handle it, to put their trust in the processes of law. And here suddenly was the ghastly fact revealed in all its nakedness—there was no law! There was only the class struggle! Exactly as Bartolomeo

Vanzetti had been saying for twelve years, ever since Cornelia had first met him: there was a propertied class, and there was a laboring class, and between them there was a war!

And now a battle under way, and the lines drawn, and deserters hated and punished—if necessary, killed! The immense, rich, eager, nervous, implacable young Empire was smashing a revolt of its slaves, crucifying its resisting gladiators by the roadside for a warning to all the rest! This legal decision was a searchlight, flashing suddenly upon that bloody deed! The Sacco-Vanzetti case was no longer the casual venality of a few local politicians, no longer the accidental malice of one elderly legal despot; the Sacco-Vanzetti case was capitalist government, the same in America as everywhere else in the world—the will of a predatory class!

Once before America had been like that, when the slave power had ruled it, and in those old days New England had had one poet with the gift of ecstasy and prophetic rage. A fugitive slave was sent back from Massachusetts, and Whittier, the Quaker abolitionist, pictured Liberty marching handcuffed down the street—

> *And Law, an unloosed maniac, strong,*
> *Blood-drunken, through the blackness trod,*
> *Hoarse-shouting in the ear of God*
> *The blasphemy of wrong. . . .*

> *"Mother of Freedom, wise and brave,*
> *Rise awful in thy strength," I said;*
> *Ah me! I spake but to the dead;*
> *I stood upon her grave!*

XI

A dreadful ordeal for the whole prison had been that "hungry strike" of Sacco's. They didn't want him to die that way—it was against the rules, and an impropriety; also they were sorry for him, and for his wife and child. They argued and pleaded; the wife and child argued and pleaded, but Nick was obdurate; he would not eat. Neither would he sign any papers for capitalist courts or governors; he would not ask for mercy or for pardon—he was an innocent man, and would die protesting it.

On the thirty-first day of the fast he became so weak that the prison doctor decided to act. He brought some hot beef broth to the cell, and reminded Nick how very painful it was to be fed by a tube through the nose. He went so far as to take hold of Nick's nose, and say that he was going to pour the broth down his throat. So Nick gave up, and drank. They had all their strength, and he had little of his.

Then came young Musmanno, devoted slave of the case, broken-hearted, and shrinking from the job he had to do. They took him first to the cell of Nick, who was eating something. Said the young lawyer: "You are a brave man, aren't you, Nick?"

It was the correct psychology; Nick said, quietly, "Yes, I think I am."

"Well then, I must tell you that the Full Court has turned down our appeal."

"I expected it," said Nick, quietly. "What are they there for?" He did not wince; but he pushed his bowls and dishes aside and forgot them. "Sure," he said, "they have us, they will kill us. We will die like men." Then he said, "I will write a letter to Dante. You will come for that, Musmanno, I want the bimbo to have it when he gets older, and will be able to think about it." "Bimbo" is an Italian endearment for a boy; and Musmanno said he would come without fail.

He went to Vanzetti, the man of emotions, of words rather than of actions. When Bart heard the news, his eyes opened wide like saucers, and he sat staring before him, as if he were in a dream. He got up, and began pacing his cell wildly, shouting in Italian. "There is nobody more innocent in all this world!" He would not take it as a matter of course that a man should die; he was a propagandist, and had reason to live. "A million men! A million men!" he cried. He began to demand that a microphone be brought to his cell, so that he might speak to the workers of the world. Musmanno had to say that both these propositions were equally impossible. All they could do was to make more appeals before more judges. He was leaving for Washington that night, to file an application before the United States Supreme Court.

The young lawyer came back late in the afternoon, but found

that Nick had not been able to work upon the letter to his son.
They had moved him back into the death cells for the third time.
"Oh, this is wearisome!" He lay, very weak, his mind unsteady.
He could only say, "I can't understand it. They will kill us?"
Vanzetti was sunk in melancholy, and would say nothing except,
"My sister! My sister!"

Luigia Vanzetti landed in New York that day; a quiet, thin,
sad-faced little woman in a faded brown traveling cloak, coming
second class, her name kept off the passenger list of the great
liner. A strange fate to have befallen a simple woman of an
Italian village; in Paris she had been set to march at the head
of a huge parade of workers. Now, bewildered by throngs coming to greet her, and by urgent young newspapermen of this
strange land of hustle and sensation, she clutched a gold medal-
lion of the Madonna in her hand; relying upon this ancient
magic to save her unhappy brother, whom she had not seen for
nineteen years. She hoped to convert him, she said; "I will ask
him to see a priest, and return to the faith of his childhood, of
those happy days before he left us." Felicani and Rosina Sacco
had come to meet her, and persuaded her to soft-pedal that
aspect of her mission. As it turned out, she was no more able
to save her brother's soul than she was to save his life.

XII

Henry Cabot Winters had to postpone important legal conferences, worth at least a thousand dollars a day to him, to
come and comfort his distracted mother-in-law; to argue with
her, explain to her—or just listen to her. "Yes, I know, Mother,
it seems very wrong that new evidence cannot be considered;
my judgment is, the Supreme Court won't stand by that ruling
very long—they'll reverse it, or the law will be changed. But
this time they must have it. You see, this Sacco-Vanzetti evidence is not real evidence to them—it's just more wops telling
the same old lies, and every one is tired of it."

"Too tired to consider the good of our courts, Henry!"

"It's just the other way to them, Mother—they think they
are standing by the courts. You must realize the dilemma; how
can they throw Web down?"

"It would seem to me that Web has thrown them down."

"Web has been a vulgarian, of course. But after all, what he said is what everybody thinks; and he's been game, you have to admit that—he had a nasty job, and he stuck to it like a little soldier. For seven years he's risked being shot or dynamited every hour of his life; and now, to repudiate him—it can't be thought of."

"Couldn't they find some other ground to grant a new trial?"

"It's all very well to talk about new trials as a matter of propaganda; but if you mean it seriously, stop and think. With this agitation and uproar—how could there be a trial? You couldn't get a jury in a hundred years. Look at what happened to those people in East Milton! Think of the witnesses—appearing and testifying, with dynamite exploding all around them!"

"We wouldn't need dynamite for those witnesses, Henry; with what we know about them to-day, there isn't one who would dare take the stand."

"All right, grant that is true—where does it leave us? It comes to this, the Commonwealth has had two Reds within a few minutes of the electric chair, and now has to admit that it has no real evidence, the whole thing blows up. We might just as well hand our courts over to the Bolsheviks and be done with it. We'd never be able to convict another one."

"So, Henry, you are going to send two innocent men to death, because it would be embarrassing to admit a blunder!"

The lawyer smiled patiently. "Don't get to believing your rhetoric, and putting it off on me, Mother! You asked me what is in the minds of the Supreme Court, and I am telling you. When I talk to lawyers about it, and bring them to admit that maybe the evidence is weak, that is the argument they end up with—the courts must be sustained."

"A brand new idea of justice, Henry!"

The other smiled again. "On the contrary, an idea as old as courts themselves." He cited the pronouncement of some fine old Tory judge to a too-urgent plaintiff: "It were better that you be ruined, than that the law be changed for the likes of you!" Henry was no legal scholar; but because he lived in Boston, it was necessary for him to possess some handy learning, for public purposes. He told his mother-in-law that this pungent saying went back even farther; it was in Law-French, which is a barbarous combination of old Norman-French with bastard Latin. He wrote it out, in an effort to divert the poor soul's mind for a few moments. "Que est ceo a nous? Il est mieulx qu'il soit tout defait, que la ley soit chaunge pur luy."

XIII

Cornelia insisted that she had to see the Governor once more, to plead with him for mercy. Even granting the worst, these men had been on the rack for seven years, and surely that was punishment! Henry said that would not get her very far; Fuller was a Roman senator, he believed in a life for a life. He had not pardoned a single man during his two terms as governor, and he had shortened only one sentence. But Cornelia, being a very old lady, was entitled under the Boston law to have her way; so Henry called up and made an appointment for her the next morning, and promised to come take her.

A great crowd in front of the State House, more picketing having been announced. Policemen so plentiful, they could have touched hands all the way along the front of the great building. Much scrutiny of those who came into the building—but Cornelia and Henry being obviously of the ruling caste, the guards took one glance and passed them on. Crowds of people in the corridors outside the executive chambers, reporters hungry as a shoal of fish; but etiquette of course forbade the old lady and her escort to talk to them. They were escorted into an inner office to wait.

The Governor's time was given up entirely to the hearing of pleas. People came in groups, every sort—lawyers, clergymen, social workers, labor leaders, writers—he saw them, and took pleasure in puttng to each lot his string of "posers": Did you attend the trials? Have you read the record? Have you talked with the witnesses? Then what do you know about the case? When they set out to tell what they knew, he would not always listen. Said Arthur Garfield Hays, attorney from New York: "I wish to talk to you about the Department of Justice files." Said the Governor: "Who wrote that editorial in the *World*?"

Cornelia was escorted to her seat in the torture-chair, and the automatic smile and the cold agate eyes were fixed upon her. Other eyes also: Mr. Joseph Wiggin, the Governor's personal attorney, and Attorney-General Reading, and another lawyer. They never left him alone now, there must be witnesses to every word he said, and expert football players to employ what was known as "interference"—jumping in and protecting him, to keep him from revealing his ignorance about the case.

It was as Henry had said—he was a Roman senator, and did not want to talk about mercy. He wanted to pin this old lady down, and vent his exasperation at the trouble she had caused him. He did not say in so many words that she was to blame for all the lunatics carrying placards outside on the street, but that was the meaning of his attitude. Since his decision had been announced, he no longer had to pose as openminded; he might be the bitter advocate, asking questions, and not paying any attention to her answers. "If Vanzetti was an innocent man, why didn't he take the stand at Plymouth? Why leave his alibi to a twelve-year-old boy?"

"He produced eighteen alibi witnesses, Governor, and he could have got more if his lawyers had worked. We have found a dozen since."

"If Sacco and Vanzetti were good men as you say, why were they intimate with a man like Boda?"

"But what have you against Boda, Governor?"

"I have sources of information, Mrs. Thornwell."

"Boda was brought into the trial, and even Judge Thayer had to throw him out. They dragged in all that tale about the Coacci shed, and about Boda's little Overland car—on purpose to make the jury think they had a bandit-gang—"

"I don't understand you, Mrs. Thornwell; there is nothing in the record about Boda's Overland car."

"Why, Governor, of course it is there! I heard it in court, and I have read it a hundred times."

"You are mistaken, I am certain." It was a great man speaking. "Wiggin, is there anything in the record about Boda's Overland car?"

"Nothing, Governor, that I have ever seen."

What could Cornelia say? She could challenge him, of course, demand the record, and show him; or she could offer to send him the citation in a couple of hours. But what effect would

it have, except to annoy him? Several persons had had this
same experience, and had told her about it. Three times in the
course of a brief interview, Cornelia would have to let him
make incorrect assertions about the record. She must be tactful, and try to keep him smiling; for he was a man, and a
Roman, and he did not like women butting in, arguing, cor-
recting. Woman's place was the home!

XIV

The salesman of motor-cars rested upon the authority of
greater minds than his own. "Mrs. Thornwell, I appointed a
commission to investigate this case, and I assure you, if a
single one of those gentlemen had thought there was a doubt
of the men's guilt, I would not have taken this stand. But
here you have three impartial referees—"

"Judge Grant had expressed a belief in their guilt before
you appointed him, Governor."

"I have heard that gossip, but you should not repeat such
a thing unless you know it to be true."

"But Judge Grant has written his opinion of Italians—he
practically called them a nation of pickpockets."

"Where do you get that? I never heard such a tale!"

"I have the book upon my table at home, Governor, and
I will send it to you if you wish."

But what he wished was to change the subject quickly. "I
have had witnesses coming to this room for two months—
person after person, assuring me of their identifications—"

"But Governor, even Judge Thayer had to throw out the
identification testimony before he got through with this case!"

"What do you mean—throw it out?"

"I thought you had studied Judge Thayer's decisions. In
his 1924 decision he said: 'These verdicts did not rest, in my
judgment, upon the testimony of the eye-witnesses.'"

"What did he say they rested upon?"

"Upon the consciousness of guilt." So then the Governor
hastened to talk about the consciousness of guilt. Sacco and
Vanzetti had lied when they were arrested, and they had lied
on the stand, and their lies were manifest and had been exposed, so that no sensible person would dispute them.

"Granting your argument, Governor—"

"So you are prepared to admit that there was perjury in the case?"

"I am trying to find out where the argument leads us. If both sides made up testimony—and certainly we know that there was a great deal of it on the side of the prosecution—"

"I don't know anything of the sort, Mrs. Thornwell."

"You must know that Erastus Corning Whitney perjured himself."

"Erastus what? I never heard of any such witness. Do you know of any such, Wiggin?"

Cornelia broke in. "Pardon me, Governor, I was not setting a trap for you. Erastus Corning Whitney is the real name of the man who took the stand and swore that his name was Carlos E. Goodridge, and thereby manifestly perjured himself. So, as I say, if we assume perjury on both sides—"

"Then we can say that one cancels the other."

"Pardon me if I point out the fallacy, Governor. To begin with, the prosecution has to establish a case. When you wipe out the witnesses of the prosecution, one by one, as we have done by our new evidence, there is no case left, and under the law the men are innocent—quite regardless of whether some of their Italian friends may have taken the stand and made false alibis for them."

"Why should innocent people have to be defended by perjury, Mrs. Thornwell?"

"For only one reason that I know, Governor—that they know positively the other side is preparing a perjured case against them. We have established that, but we have never had any judgment upon it, except that of Judge Thayer."

One of the lawyers here considered it advisable to justify the high fees which the Governor was paying him out of his private purse to sit day by day and listen to these wrangles. "Mrs. Thornwell," he interposed, "you overlook the fact that the Supreme Judicial Court has passed upon Judge Thayer's rulings. As good citizens, we must have some belief in the competence and disinterestedness of our highest court."

Cornelia turned her brown eyes upon him. These eyes had somehow lost their softness, and had a sparkle that might be malice. "Are you going to advance that doctrine in your new brief on the Jerry Walker case?"

"My God!" thought the legal gentleman, and it took all his blue-blood inheritance and Harvard training to keep his annoyance from showing on his face. He relapsed into dignified silence, and pretended not to see the look of mischief which his enemy Henry Cabot Winters shot at him. Truly a comical situation: This gentleman, who was counsel for the Governor in the Sacco-Vanzetti case, also was one of the counsel for Jerry Walker, and was on the point of filing before the Supreme Court of the United States an application for a writ of certiorari, to take that case away from the highest court of Massachusetts and reverse its decision. In that application the lawyer and his associates were going to make the most outrageous charges—implying that the Supreme Judicial Court of Massachusetts had become a "house of refuge for the rich and powerful," and declaring flatly that the judgment of the Full Court was "made in bad faith," and that "there is nothing more odious than judicial favoritism," which in this case had been "exercised in favor of bankers." A marvelous thing, that flexibility of the legal mind, which can hold two diametrically opposite opinions at the same time; sorting out truth and error into two baskets, as it were, and carrying both to market, one in the right hand and one in the left!

XV

But it didn't do Cornelia a bit of good to score points like that; it only made these gentlemen hate her. She must swallow her indignation, and come back to beg for mercy. "Remember, Governor, you must be *sure*. You are doing something that can never be undone. There is an old saying—I don't know who is the author—that 'only an infallible judge should pass an immutable sentence.' "

"Do you know that those men are innocent, Mrs. Thornwell?"

"Of course I don't know that; how could I know it—unless I had been with them at the time? But I have been studying the case for seven years, and I believe that they are innocent, and certainly I know this—that they have not been proved guilty. I know all that I need to know—that they did not have a fair trial."

"Well," said the Governor, "I know that they are guilty, so I don't care whether they had a fair trial or not."

Cornelia stared at him; she was so taken aback by the remark that she could hardly believe she had heard it. "You know they are guilty, Governor Fuller?"

"I know it."

"But how can you know it, unless there was a fair trial—somewhere, somehow—to establish it?"

"I have sources of information, Mrs. Thornwell, which I am not at liberty to reveal. You should find out what the Italian colony thinks about this case."

"Governor, what are you saying? Some one has come and whispered into your ear, and you have been willing to believe it!"

"You cannot expect witnesses to tell all they know in the face of such peril as has been created in this community, Mrs. Thornwell."

"So then, it is exactly as Vanzetti said to me—for weeks he has been saying it: 'We are being murdered by the whispers of unknown men!' Boston has gone back to the days of Russia under the tsars, of Turkey under the sultans, of China under the mandarins! Spies come and whisper secrets, and our rulers execute men upon words which they cannot or dare not produce in open court!"

One of the lawyers thought he had better justify his fees again. "Surely it is not quite so bad as that, Mrs. Thornwell—"

"It is so bad that it cannot be worse! And I implore you, Governor Fuller—consider, before you take this fatal step, which will blast the rest of your life! You are executing men upon secret testimony—but I tell you, the world will insist upon knowing what that testimony is! History will never let you alone until you tell what it is! And when mankind has learned that it was the whispers of spies—the gossip of what you are pleased to call 'the Italian colony'—then you will face such a blast of indignation as no man can face and live!"

After that they did not want to listen to her any more. After that she was a distracted old woman who had fallen under the influence of sinister "Reds," and lost entirely her mental balance. All they desired was to keep her from wasting the time of a busy and important public man. They would be polite, of course—even in Russia and Turkey and China the high officials were doubtless polite to old ladies of the ruling caste. "Glad to have seen you again, Mrs. Thornwell. I will give my best consideration to what you have said." So Cornelia made her way out through the crowds, with tears in her eyes for all the newspapermen to see and report.

"Henry," she asked, when they had got by themselves, "what can those whispers be?"

Said the lawyer, "There's a man in that State House crowd who will talk with me, and I'll see if I can find out."

XVI

Michael Angelo Musmanno was in Washington, haunting the empty chambers of the United States Supreme Court. The justices were on vacation, but he lodged in the office of the clerk the two appeals from the Massachusetts courts. He entered the formal appearance of Hill and himself, paid the docketing fees, and the only thing remaining to perfect the appeals was the record of the case, which the clerk of the Dedham court had promised to send but which had not yet arrived. This was later secured, and duly filed.

But this procedure did not of itself postpone the execution, and Monday midnight was the hour set. Would any judge order a stay of execution? The lawyers were rushing to this one and that; it was a free-lance matter now, every man for himself—but still they found time to form opinions of one another. The Boston lawyers thought they knew Boston; they were conservative, and did things in a dignified manner, and held newspaper reporters off at the end of a ten-foot pole. The New Yorkers, on the other hand, were radicals, fighting in the open, and welcoming the reporters as allies. They accused the Boston crowd of being jealous about the case— "acting like a bunch of prima donnas!" said one.

Also among the committee, the frantic last-hour antagonisms between those who wanted to save Sacco and Vanzetti as human beings, and those who wanted to make them into symbols of the class war. Hardly a telegram could be sent, or a statement given to the press, that did not involve the controversy. The differences of ideas had become embodied in personal antagonisms. The communists were collecting sums of money for the defense, and the committee charged that this money was not coming to them, but was being used for communist propaganda. The communists replied with charges that the committee was wasting its funds upon high fees to capitalist lawyers. Charges and counter-charges—to the great glee of the enemy. The whispering gallery which was the State House buzzed and hummed with gossip. The spies came running, and the Governor's advisers were on tip-toe. "What are they doing now? What do they say about this? About that?"

The "New York nuts" organized another "death march." This time it was led by Captain Paxton Hibben, diplomat, war correspondent, and army officer; dapper, erect, and with sharp little military mustaches. He knew all about marches and parades, of course, and Boston knew him because the *Transcript* had slandered him and then had to retract and apologize. Hibben was a Harvard master of arts, and with him came Dos Passos and Hapgood, bachelors of arts, and therefore subordinates; also James Rorty, the poet; and Clarina Michelson, from Greenwich Village, a tireless soul who did the hard work; and several humble wage-earners with names never heard before on Beacon Street. They marched their allotted time— one-two-three-four-five-six-seven—with a captain of police holding a watch on them; then they were led off under escort, with the crowd hooting, and a few cheering.

At the corner of Joy Street, Captain Hibben, being in advance, commanded, sharply, "Files right!" The huge police sergeant who had him in charge looked at him, and said, "Were you in the service?" The answer was, "I was a captain in the 332nd Field Artillery in France." "Well, Captain," said the sergeant, "this is a strange place for you to be!" "If you knew as much about Boston as I do, you would be with me," said Hibben; and in the old Joy Street police station, so oddly named, they had a chat. Hibben had more than one man's share of adventures to tell; he had been second secretary in the American legation in old St. Petersburg, he had been a war correspondent in the Near East in the early days of the war, and secretary of the Russian Red Cross for the Bolsheviks; a Chevalier of the Order of St. Stanislaus (Russian), an Officer of the Order of the Redeemer (Greek), and of the Order of the Sacred Treasure (Japan). "Holy smoke!" said the police sergeant; and on Monday morning in court he was wholly unable to remember that he had seen this starred and beribboned diplomat on the picket-line, and so Hibben was discharged. The sergeant meant it for a favor, but it was a cause of vexation to the prisoner, who had prepared a ringing statement to read in court—and now it was a dud!

XVII

The three condemned men—Madeiros always with them!—had been moved back into the death-house; into the three little cells with clean, smooth white-tiled floors, and doors that were never opened—no guard ever entered and no prisoner ever came out, except to die. Six feet in front of the cells ran a painted line, beyond which no visitor was permitted to step; at least, it had never yet happened in the history of Massachusetts, which lives by precedent.

But now Luigia Vanzetti arrived in Boston, followed by a stream of reporters, eager to make the most of this human interest story—"sob stuff" is the technical name. A frail, pathetic woman, weighing not more than a hundred pounds, and looking for all the world like a New England school teacher—she was coming to the prison to meet her brother, whom she had not seen since he was a youth. She had come all the way from Villafalletto to help him die, and naturally she would wish to step over the painted line and clasp him in her arms. To obtain this favor all the eloquence of the ladies of the Sacco-Vanzetti defense was concentrated upon Warden Hendry. They came to his office and wept, and prayed, and stormed and scolded, until at last the Commonwealth of Massachusetts broke a precedent, for the first time in its three hundred years of history.

Bart was led out from his cell, and allowed to sit in a chair on the other side of the painted line. The warden himself brought Luigia, and two guards stood by to see that she did not give the condemned man any poison, or a revolver, or an

Italian stiletto. They tottered into each other's arms, sobbing; and in a moment more the woman collapsed, and one guard had to catch her, while the other brought a chair. Bart sat, patting her gently, and for an hour they talked about all the things which might interest a brother and sister who had parted in their teens, and met again in their middle thirties, with only two days more of life upon earth together.

The twelve-year-old Dante Sacco had come with Rosina and paid a last visit to his father; a terrible ordeal for a child, to pass that canvas-shrouded death-chair, and sit listening to a faint voice, and peering at a wasted shadow of a man through narrow steel bars which must not be approached. The boy and the mother went out sobbing, the latter hardly able to walk; each one of these visits was like a spell of illness to her. The father set himself to his last task, of writing the promised letter to the "bimbo"; to leave him some permanent message which he might study when he grew older. Pitiful, rambling words of a man trying to hold his faculties in the midst of torment, and to write in a foreign language—because the "bimbo" spoke that language, and was going to an American school. "Much I thought of you," wrote the father, "when I was lying in the death-house—the singing, the kind tender voices of the children from the playground, where there was all the life and the joy of liberty—just one step from the wall which contains the buried agony of three buried souls. . . . Yes, Dante, they can crucify our bodies to-day as they are doing but they cannot destroy our ideals that will remain for the youth of the future to come. . . .

"Well, my dear boy, after your mother had talked to me so much and I had dreamed of you day and night, how joyful it was to see you at last. To have talked with you like we used to in the days—in those days. Much I told you on that visit and more I wanted to say, but I saw that you will remain the same affectionate boy, faithful to your mother who loves you so much, and I did not want to hurt your sensibilities any longer, because I am sure that you will continue to be the same boy and remember what I have told you. I knew that and what here I am going to tell you will touch your feelings, but don't cry, Dante, because many tears have been wasted, as your mother's have been wasted for seven years, and never did any good."

XVIII

The Great Novelist who makes up history had brought it about that while Sacco and Vanzetti were lying in the death-cells, there preceded them to the land of shadows a great American lord of steel and finance: Elbert H. Gary, chairman of the board of directors and chief executive of the United States Steel Corporation, with resources of two billions of dollars. A great Christian he had been, helping to build that mighty university of Methodism from which Dean Wigless had assailed Felix Frankfurter; holder of eight honorary degrees from church universities—the most pious plutocrat who ever split his strikers' skulls and set thousands of spies to cow their souls. Before he left for his mansion above, he also wrote a message to his beloved ones, giving his *vade mecum* as a follower of the gentle Jesus. His last will and testament it was, and all the capitalist newspapers of America featured his exalted words:

"I earnestly request my wife and children and descendants that they steadfastly decline to sign any bonds or obligations of any kind as surety for any other person, or persons; that they refuse to make any loans except on the basis of first-class, well-known securities, and that they invariably decline to invest in any untried or doubtful securities or property or enterprise or business."

At this same time two anarchist wops, one of them an avowed atheist, the other a vague deist of the old-fashioned sort, were writing their last words to their beloved ones, and these words also were published. Said Nicola Sacco, with one foot in eternity:

"So, Son, instead of crying, be strong, so as to be able to comfort your mother, and when you want to distract your mother from the discouraging soulness, I will tell you what I used to do. To take her for a long walk in the quiet country, gathering wild flowers here and there, resting under the shade of trees, between the harmony of the vivid stream and the gentle tranquillity of the mother nature, and I am sure that she will enjoy this very much, as you surely would be happy for it. But remember always, Dante, in the play of happiness, don't you use all for yourself only, but down yourself just one step, at your side and help the weak ones that cry for help, help the persecuted and the victim because they are your better friends, they are the comrades that fight and fall as your father and Bartolo fought and fell yesterday for the conquest of the joy and freedom for all the poor workers. In this struggle of life you will find more love and you will be loved."

Also Vanzetti left his message for Dante to study in after years. One day before he died he wrote a letter to a little boy whose school friends jeered him because he was the son of a murderer. Said Bart:

"I tell you all this now, for I know well your father, he is not a criminal, but one of the bravest men I ever knew. Some day you will understand what I am about to tell you, that your father has sacrificed everything dear and sacred to the human heart and soul for his faith in liberty and justice for all. That day you will be proud of your father, and if you become brave enough, you will take his place in the struggle between tyranny and liberty and you will vindicate his name and our blood.

"Remember and know also, Dante, that if your father and I would have been cowards and hypocrites and renegades of our faith, we would not have been put to death. They would not even have convicted a leprous dog; not even executed a deadly poisonous scorpion on such evidence as that they framed against us. They would have given a new trial to a matricide and habitual felon on the evidence we presented for a new trial.

"Remember, Dante, remember always these things: We are not criminals; they convicted us on a frame-up; they denied us a new trial; and if we will be executed after seven years, three months and seventeen days of unspeakable tortures and wrongs, it is for what I have already told you; because we were for the poor and against the exploitation and oppression of man by man."

CHAPTER 22

THE CITY OF FEAR

I

"This is our career and our triumph," Bart had proclaimed; and assuredly never had "a good shoemaker and a poor fish-peddler" caused such excitement in the world. On Saturday, two days before the execution, there was an order for a general strike in Buenos Ayres; in Berlin a protest from the trade unions, and the first radical meeting ever held in the former House of Lords of the Kingdom of Prussia; in London a mob of ten thousand in front of the American embassy; in Geneva a call for the boycotting of American goods; in Russia enormous protest meetings in every city; in Paris a hundred thousand workers parading, carrying red flags and huge placards denouncing American justice; tourists being greeted with shouts from thousands of throats, "Pardon! Pardon!"— and as a rule finding it prudent to reply, "Vive Sacco et Vanzetti!" The workers were bewildered by the spectacle of Puritan severity, and helpless in the face of it. Pierre Leon, editing a French communist paper, cabled to Joe Randall: "What can we do?" Joe's answer was: "Repudiate the debts." But that, alas, was not an immediate program; the best the French could do was to fail to pay them.

Only in Massachusetts itself was silence. Boston under the iron heel, and civil rights subject to revocation. One simple rule, easy for all to understand: do what the police tell you and keep your mouth shut. Superintendent Crowley had requested the mayor to cancel all the eighteen speaking permits on the Common, and thus free speech was dumped out of the "cradle of liberty." The defense committee was trying to hire a hall for a last minute protest-meeting, but the police made a round of the halls and warned the owners; if they rented to the Reds, they would lose their license. It was a trick which

"Mickey the Gunman" had been working for several years; by means of it he had suppressed a young Lithuanian named Bimba, who proclaimed himself an atheist, and annoyed the Catholic priests. The police would close up halls, on the ground that they violated fire ordinances; something which, in an old city like Boston, a great many buildings did.

At the last minute the defense committee succeeded in finding a hall, and on Saturday evening a pitiful meeting was held, with almost as many "cops" as audience. A speaker started to describe what was going to happen in Charlestown prison on Monday midnight, and a police official stepped forward, saying, "No more of that, or we'll shut you up." So the orators discussed the case in abstract terms, not saying anything rude about governors or college presidents, nor using bad words like "anarchistic bastards." Paxton Hibben spoke, military and incisive; Powers Hapgood, fiery and determined; Alfred Baker Lewis, who seemed like a big but very serious boy; then Betty Alvin, for the Back Bay; and—miracle of miracles—a Catholic lifting his voice for two infidels! The members of the Boston police force rubbed their eyes as the Reverend Francis Xavier Regan took the platform, and told the story of Caleb Cunningham, the wealthy resident of Milton who had shot and killed the Swede, John Johnson, for cutting wood on his land, and had been so considerately treated by the authorities of Norfolk County. One Catholic remembered the humble origins of his Church—even in the diocese of His Eminence, "Big Bill"!

A call had been issued for labor union delegates to meet on that same Saturday evening, to consider plans for a general strike. Since it was manifestly too late, the police did not interfere. About fifty workers attended, mostly from the Italian barbers and the Jewish needle trades; the American workers present might have been counted on the fingers of one hand. The American workers were out on the roads in second-hand cars with their families, eating hot-dogs and drinking soda-pop; they were at the movies, watching poor girls marry millionaires and poor boys make fortunes overnight; they were shooting craps and playing poker and drinking home brew. Assuredly they were not out on the streets, getting their heads broken for any wops.

Michael Gold went about listening, and reporting public

sentiment in Boston. A young sailor prowling in Scollay Square, on the hunt for women: "They ought to be burned; they insulted the flag." A clerk drinking ice cream soda at a fountain: "All them Italians look like murderers to me." A timid little groceryman expressing himself over the counter: "Yes, maybe they are innocent, but we gotta bump 'em off, or we'll all be bombed in our beds." A telephone girl, hearing an Italian voice complaining of a wrong number: "Aw shut up, you Guinney rat, wait till you see what we do to you on August 22nd!"

All this they had got out of their newspapers, of course. For a brief time there had been a break in newspaper solidarity regarding the Sacco-Vanzetti case; an editorial writer of the *Herald* had won the Pulitzer prize of 1926 for an editorial demanding a new trial. But now his voice was silent. The department-stores were clamoring to have an end to the public anxiety; business had fallen off, because women, who do most of the shopping, were afraid to go about. The only industry which was thriving was that of riot and bomb insurance; the companies wrote it to the amount of eight hundred million dollars, and didn't have to pay one cent! A net profit of a cool million to the companies, and a corresponding loss to Boston merchants. Preposterous that two wops should cause such trouble! The newspapers, which thrive upon department-store advertising, made one sweet harmony: "Stand by the Governor and the courts." In the profession, Boston was known as "the poor-house of journalism."

II

Cornelia, splashing around frantically for a straw to catch hold of, bethought herself of Cardinal O'Connell. Luigia Vanzetti was a faithful daughter of the church, and a pitiful figure; perhaps she might be able to tempt the great man into making an appeal for clemency. So Jessica Henderson came with her limousine, always there to help the Sacco-Vanzetti defense, and they drove the anxious, fearful little woman out to the summer home of the great prelate at Marblehead. He was on the lawn with his dog when the party arrived, and Mrs.

Henderson's daughter went to ask if he would see Luigia. "Bless her heart, of course," he said.

He was cordial, charming, as he knew how to be when it was worth while. He served tea himself, and remarked to Cornelia, "It may be a long time before you have a cardinal pouring tea for you again." He chatted with Luigia in Italian, and Cornelia could understand enough to know that he was sympathizing greatly, and doing nothing. Afterwards he wrote and gave to the papers a statement on the subject which was a masterpiece of diplomatic piety: "Human judgment is fallible at best. . . . But the judgment of God is perfect and in the end He and His ways, mysterious as they are, are our hope and salvation." Said the sarcastic Betty: "Now we know why God was invented—so that princes of the church may dodge their moral responsibilities!"

Futile to try to make headway in Boston, with the weight of such authority against you! The local liberals were hamstrung by the Lowell report. If Mr. Lowell said it, it must be so, and who are we to set ourselves up against him? Likewise Bishop Lawrence had clambered onto the bandwagon. Having asked the Governor to appoint an impartial commission, he now accepted the impartial decision, and commended the Governor for his firmness and courage. He did this in a letter, which appeared in the press.

There they stood, the three intellectual and spiritual guides of Boston: the Cardinal of the Holy Roman Catholic Church, the Bishop of the Protestant Episcopal Church, and the President of Harvard University. When a stranger inquired concerning them, he was struck by a curious fact: the first statement about any one of the three would be that he was an efficient administrator of enormous properties. This was not his fault, of course; the properties were there, and must be administered; but the automatic effect was this, that if you were to go to any one of the three administrators, and make a remark suggesting that he should act upon the creed he taught, he would begin to watch you to see whether you were the dangerous kind.

The Cardinal of the Catholics was exiling rebellious spirits to the backwoods, and raising up a generation of young clerics who were at once preachers, politicians, and real estate ex-

perts; you could know when one of them was in favor by
the fact that his mother and father, brothers and sisters, cousins
and aunts, moved immediately into expensive residences. As
for the Bishop of the Blue-bloods, he had a father who
helped to finance John Brown's expedition to fight slavery in
Kansas; the son was known as the best money-raiser in New
England, and had turned his vast organization into a school
of social propriety. When it was a question of a blue-blood
church official accused of undue intimacy with choir-boys, you
would see this well-bred bishop as anxious to have the law
not enforced as he was to have it enforced against anarchist
wops.

As for President Lowell, he would boast that every professor in his great institution enjoyed complete freedom of
speech, and when some one asked him how he could manage
anything so dangerous, he would smile and say that it was
easy if you were careful whom you allowed to become a
professor. When it chanced that a Harvard lecturer dared
to attack the electric light and power interests, whose directors
and bankers compose the governing body of the university,
President Lowell would "fire" him, and incidentally lie to him,
with exactly the same heartiness as a "wop" standing by a
friend accused of banditry, or a blue-blood banker trying
to save fifteen million dollars.

III

Bugles in the streets; a regiment of the state militia marching, with grim set faces—the answer of the Commonwealth to
the challenge of anarchy. Airplanes flying overhead, watching for bombers in the sky. Military squads on duty at every
public building, suspicious of every foreign face, and now
and then stopping a passerby to search a bundle or open a suitcase. Every policeman on twenty-four hour duty again; sitting in the station-houses, and now and then called out for
a wild ride or a gallop, on account of a bomb-scare. The firemen also on twenty-four hour duty, and all armed. The American Legion mobilized to guard the homes of the rich and
the great. Every judge, juror, prosecutor, witness, or official
who had ever had anything to do with the Sacco-Vanzetti case

was being protected, and there was no foolishness about the protection.

A man hopped out of an automobile at the home of President Lowell, and started towards the rear entrance, carrying a heavy black bag. They did not stop to ask him who he was or what he wanted, they hit him over the head and laid him out—and then ascertained that he was delivering a load of that heavy aluminum ware which is the latest fad in fancy cookery for the rich. A young Catholic priest stepped off the train in South Station, arriving from the west for a holiday; he went to the information bureau and said, "Will you please tell me the way to the State House?" "Certainly," replied the clerk, and called a policeman, saying, "This man wants to know the way to the State House." The kind-hearted policeman said he would escort him, and led him to a patrol-wagon, and drove him to the nearest station-house, where they held him "incommunicado" for twenty-four hours.

The great Commonwealth had told ten thousand lies; and now for every lie there was a club and a bayonet. If you wished to oppose the lies, there was just one way—put your head under the crashing clubs, throw your body onto the gleaming bayonets. This was not merely the law of Massachusetts, this was the law of life, the way by which lies have been killed throughout history. The friends of the defense confronted this crisis, and either went forward and took the punishment, or shrunk back and sneaked away with a whole skin and a damaged conscience.

Terrible scenes in the Thornwell family. In "Hillview," Great-uncle Abner storming, because the Governor had been browbeaten once, and might yield again; Abner declared that he would wheel himself all the way to Boston, thirty miles or so on the public highway, and present himself at the Governor's office to demand the death of the two anarchists. On the other hand, in the tenement on the north side of Beacon Hill was Deborah pleading and praying to her daughter, not to throw away her life, not to disgrace herself and her innocent and helpless family.

Cornelia was not going to get arrested; she was motoring with Mrs. Henderson to make an appeal to Justice Brandeis of the Supreme Court. But Betty had pledged herself to carry a placard on the Common, and Joe also. They had sent out a call for a thousand demonstrators, and at least two were going to respond. Nothing that Deborah could say would have any effect; no tears, no prayers. "They are surely going to arrest me once," said Betty, and laughed, a trifle hysterically. "They are not going to murder Bart and Nick without arresting me at least once!" When Deborah brought in the sacred names of little Rupert Alvin Thornwell Randall, the unnatural mother made reply: "The best thing that could happen to him would be for me and Joe to be clubbed to death, so that you and Father could raise him to be respectable!"

That was late Saturday night, after the meeting in Scenic Auditorium. Deborah stayed in town that night, and telephoned to Rupert, who gave up a service in his new private chapel, the joy of his life, to come and add the immense weight of his authority. But Betty did not even wait to see him; she went off to a gathering of the "New York nuts," who were making cardboard signs to wear while undergoing martyrdom. Her Uncle James Scatterbridge came upon her in the lobby of the Hotel Bellevue—most fashionable of hostelries, adjoining the State House, where a group of the leisure class "nuts" had made their headquarters, to the great dismay of the management.

Uncle James came there, with blood in his eye, looking for his Josiah, intending to take him captive by force if necessary. But James's Josiah was hiding, and when his father actually found him, he was walking on the outskirts of the Common, with a policeman holding each arm, and a jeering crowd all around. James pushed his way through and took charge, to the relief of the "cops," who had been told to make as few arrests as possible. There followed painful hours for both father and son; but do not worry too much, for it will turn out happily in the end—the great cotton-master will be able to keep his son's name out of the papers, and also be able to make his Josiah into a mildly successful young business man. They will look back on this adventure some day, and the older will be secretly rather proud of the younger's nerve. "A damned fool, of course; but then, we're all damned fools when we're young."

IV

Boston Common is an irregularly shaped park, comprising, with the Public Gardens, about a square mile. It is laid out with rambling paths, and has a Monument Hill, with cannon and other trophies; there are greenswards, groups of trees, a band-stand with benches, the "Frog Pond," and in the Public Gardens a little lake for boats. The State House with the golden dome overlooks it from one corner; the Park Street Church, the Union Club, and many of the homes of the old families on Beacon Street. On the other side is Tremont Street, with the fashionable shops; and from the end of the Public Gardens starts Commonwealth Avenue, where the Alvins lived. All very fashionable, in a dignified way, mixed up with history and tradition, taking itself seriously. In the old days, this Common had been the place where the villagers pastured their cows; now it was a place for nursemaids to flirt with sailors from the ships, and for out-of-works to study the "help wanted" ads in the newspapers. On Sunday afternoons all the religious cranks, the holy rollers and the Salvation Army, shouted under the trees along the mall; also the atheists and the socialists and the single taxers, and those who refuse to believe that the earth is round.

But this Sunday, August 21st, all that was off, and for a year to come. There was a band concert and a radio concert to keep the crowds occupied; also two ball-games, and two impromptu dog-fights. Twenty-five thousand people came —having read in the papers that some new-style martyrs were going to feed themselves to the lions.

One thousand had been called for, and fourteen came. The lawyers were in part responsible for that, having strenuously urged against it. The demonstrators would be sure to get their heads clubbed, and could only do harm to the case by cheap notoriety. Those who were troubled by the former considera-tion were glad to have the latter for an excuse. The few stub-born ones who insisted upon coming were troubled by both considerations, but of course would only admit the latter. They brought little rolls of cardboard, printed with Sacco-Vanzetti protests, to wear over their shoulders, and made their ren-dezvous in a corner drug-store, eyed suspiciously by the proprietor, because they looked fidgety and queer, not at all "Boston." The job had fallen mostly to the "New York nuts."

There was John Dos Passos, faithful son of Harvard, and John Howard Lawson, another one of the "New Playwrights" from Greenwich Village. There was Clarina Michelson, ready to do the hard work again, and William Patterson, a Negro lawyer from New York, running the greatest risk of any of them, with his black face not to be disguised. Just up Beacon Street was the Shaw Monument, with figures in perennial bronze, of unmistakable Negro boys in uniform, led by a young Boston blue-blood on horseback; no doubt Patterson had looked at this, and drawn courage from it. To uphold the high traditions of the city, there came Betty Alvin and Joe Randall, considered a Bostonian-in-law; also James's Josiah, more scared of his father than of the police; and Margaret Hatfield, whose father was a prominent Republican, treasurer of Middlesex county. Margaret had taken the precaution to "dress the part," so she was safe, though she couldn't be sure of it. Her mother was behaving exactly like Betty's mother, wandering about the Common twisting her hands together, and moaning to herself, "Oh, *why* do they have to do it?"

V

"Come on, you sons-of-bitches, do you want to live forever?" So, according to army tradition, a sergeant shouted to a squad, going "over the top" in the Argonne forest. It is an idea which, with or without the language, has animated martyrs through the ages. They have walked to the lions, they have walked to the stake and the gallows and the guillotine, and other forms of terror; now they walked to the clubs and the bayonets—a little group from the corner drug-store, quaking inside, and trembling in the knees, but setting their teeth and holding their heads high. As it happened, none was to be seriously hurt, but they could not know that; pain is pain, and a cracked skull, or the hoofs of horses in your stomach, are as unpleasant as any other form. Come on, you New York nuts, do you want to live forever?

The Common stretching before them. The mall, where the speaking should have been, is closed by a cordon of police; no use to try it there. They get out on the concrete walk, and then look at one another anxiously. Are they in a good place, among the crowd? Some one says yes, and with trembling fingers they unroll the placards and put them over their shoulders. The bystanders see, and cheers go up. Crowds begin to gather; they have been wandering about, waiting for something to happen, and here it is! "Hurrah for Sacco and Vanzetti!" "Save Sacco and Vanzetti!" At once a counter demonstration: "Down with the Reds! Lynch them!"

The little band of martyrs walk on, seeing nothing, hearing nothing; a trifle dizzy with the excitement—that rare mood of martyrdom, more wonderful than drunkenness. You walk upon the air, into the clouds; the earth and the limitations of the flesh no longer exist; you have transcended them all, you belong to the ages, you speak to God. "Wir sind all des Todes eigen," sings the German poet—"we all belong to death." We have seen such wickedness upon earth that we choose rather to die than to let it prevail.

"All right," says the world, "if you want to die, we are willing!" The lions roar; if you want to be eaten, their stomachs are made for the purpose! Here come the police, clubs drawn. "Enough of that now! Take off those signs and get out of here!" They try to grab the signs, and the marchers dodge this way and that, to protect them as long as possible; bystanders grab at the signs, others try to block the way of the "cops." The clubs begin to fall; a disagreeable sound, the thud of hickory on human flesh and bone.

Here come the mounted men, riding through the throngs. "Look out for yourself!" Women shriek; the horses charge straight ahead, knocking people down. A strange experience for a daughter of the best families—Betty can hardly believe it; she thinks the horse will swerve at the last moment; then she realizes that the rider means to run her down, and she leaps too late, the shoulder of the passing horse strikes her and sends her spinning.

The trooper speeds on; he has spied the black face, and wants that most of all. The Negro runs, and the rider rears the front feet of his steed, intending to strike him down with the iron-shod hoofs. But fortunately there is a tree, and the Negro leaps behind it; a man can run round a tree faster than the best-trained police-mount—the dapper and genial William Patterson proves it by making five complete circuits before he runs into the arms of an ordinary cop, who grabs him by the collar and tears off his sign and tramples it in the dirt, and then starts to march him away. "Well," he remarks, sociably, "this is the first time I ever see a nigger bastard that was a communist." The lawyer is surprised, because he has been given to understand that that particular bad word is barred from the Common; Mike Crowley was so shocked, two weeks ago, when Mary Donovan tacked up a sign to a tree: "Did you see what I did to those anarchistic ————? Judge Thayer." But apparently the police do not have to obey their own laws.

The "Black Maria" is in readiness, and comes with clanging bell, and the prisoners are loaded into it—all but the "nigger bastard." He has to be walked to the police-station—because it would not be decent for him to ride in the same patrol-wagon with his friend Clarina Michelson! The others are driven off— and when they get to the La Grange Street station-house and compare notes, they discover that they have lost their blue-bloods! Betty is missing, and her husband, and her cousin James! Margaret Hatfield is missing! Even in the midst of that excitement, the police have found time to consult the "social register"! A little later they turn loose John Dos Passos— no Harvard graduates wanted! The only ones they arrest are five workers, two named Sansevrion, one Schulman, one Amari, and that Cosimo Carvotta against whom they have a special grudge, on account of having lied about him in the police court after the previous Sunday's arrests.

VI

In the La Grange Street station they found Paula Holladay, waiting for some company. No story of that last Sunday would be complete without the Odyssey of Paula, who had made a parade all by herself—and a long one! She was the founder of "Polly's," a Greenwich Village café renowned in song and story; that summer she had been running a restaurant in Provincetown, on Cape Cod. Her conscience began to gnaw at her, and she decided to do what one woman could to express a sense of injustice. She turned her business over to a friend, and put on a sign reading, "Is justice dead? Save Sacco and Vanzetti," and set out to walk from Provincetown to Boston, a distance, as the "nut" walks, of a hundred and twenty-five miles.

Now and then on the route, women working in their gardens would see that sign, and follow along on the other side of the picket-fence, saying, "I wish I had a shot-gun in the house, I'd show you what I'd do to you!" Ladies in automobiles would stop to express the same sentiment. But apparently the shot-gun is an obsolete instrument in Massachusetts, for Paula reached Boston with a whole skin, except for a blister on the heel. She joined the other nuts, and learning that the police were destroying all banners and signs, she painted her message on a red "slicker," or waterproof coat, and sallied forth onto the Common thus garbed.

She was passing the bandstand, when the first "cop" spied her, and took her in tow. A crowd gathered quickly, and there were waves of shouting, some for, some against. The police-man's hand began to tremble on the woman's arm. "Why are you so nervous?" she said—after which he managed to control himself. Another came to his aid, and then two mounted men, who kept her between them, safe. When she told them that she was determined to stay on the Common, they conducted her to the police-station. "What is the charge?" she demanded; the answer was, "Oh, never mind that, just lock her up."

Presently came "Mike" Crowley, having kissed the Blarney stone that morning. "Now it would be too bad for a nice-looking young lady like you to get into any trouble that might get her on the books here." The answer of Paula was, "I am neither so young nor so good-looking, and I am not afraid to get on the books. I want to know whether I am kept here by force with-out any charge." When he wouldn't answer, she said, "I will find out," and started to leave; so then he put his hand upon her shoulder, and she was there by force. They kept her until evening, when there were no more crowds upon the Common, and no more harm to be done by the wearing of a red "slicker" with the question, "Is justice dead?"

The lawyers were making another attempt to open the Department of Justice files, and they appealed to Governor Fuller for a respite until the documents could be studied. Arthur Hill asked also for time to permit the United States Supreme Court to consider his application. The Governor followed his usual policy of declining to say what he would do; so the lawyers were racing about from one country-place to another, trying to persuade some judge to order a stay. In those last hectic days they put the matter before a dozen different judges, representing the Superior Court and the Supreme Judicial Court of Massachusetts, and the District Courts and the Supreme Court of the United States.

Mr. Hill journeyed to see Justice Holmes at his place in Beverly, on the North Shore: Oliver Wendell Holmes, son of the poet, eighty-six years of age, respected by all liberals, because he and Brandeis invariably wrote a minority opinion when the court made further restrictions upon human rights in the interest of privilege. The old gentleman now said that he did not think he had the power to interfere, but wished them luck with some other justice who might think differently. "Unofficially," he said that Sacco and Vanzetti could not have got a fair trial in 1921.

They went to Louis Brandeis, their last hope. A Jewish lawyer of great ability, Brandeis had begun practice in Boston, and made a fortune early, and then turned against the system, and became an advocate of the public interest, and therefore one of the most hated men in the city. When Woodrow Wilson had named him for the Supreme Court bench, there had been a howl from State Street, and no voice louder than that of President Lowell of Harvard. Nevertheless, the radical Jew had got in; and now he had the greatest chance of his career —and missed it.

The Court was composed mainly of hard-boiled corporation lawyers, selected by President Taft—now the Chief Justice— and by Harding and Coolidge. Undoubtedly these men would have reversed any action that Brandeis might have taken; but at least it would have been a gesture, and a crown upon a great life. Cornelia spent Sunday afternoon arguing and pleading with the justice, but in vain; telegrams came raining upon him, in vain. He was bound, like all other judges. It so happened that Rosina Sacco had occupied a house belonging to Mrs. Brandeis in Dedham, and this constituted "prejudice." The justice could not be persuaded that prejudice in favor of mercy was different from prejudice in favor of one interest against another. Vanzetti commented upon this singular situation in a letter to Harry Dana—almost the last words he wrote:

"So it is coming to pass that some justices repel our appeal because they are friendly with us, and other justices repel our appeal because they are hostile to us, and through this elegant *Forche Caudine* we are led straight to the electric chair."

These nine elderly gentlemen who did the real governing of the United States were overworked, and in dread of taking more upon their bowed shoulders. They had the task of telling the American people what laws they might pass and what laws they might not pass; what their laws meant, or ought to mean; in short, what served the propertied classes, and what threatened them. An enormous task; and the old gentlemen contemplated with dismay the idea of opening the sluice-gates and letting in more work upon themselves.

They dealt with the law, they said, and never with the facts. But when there came an emergency where it seemed necessary to deal with facts, they would find a way to do it. The Supreme Judicial Court of Massachusetts had just shown that in the Jerry Walker case, where the jury had decided the facts against the interest of the fellow club-members of the Court. The Court had stepped in and considered such facts as they pleased, and like all special pleaders they had stated the facts on their own side, and suppressed the facts on the other side. But in the case of Sacco and Vanzetti there were no vast sums of money at stake—only the lives of two wops. "It were better that you be ruined than that the law be changed for the likes of you!"

VIII

Cornelia came back to her apartment on Sunday evening, beaten and exhausted. Betty was over at defense headquarters, helping to organize the new arrivals and plan the last demonstration. Poets, writers, artists—all persons, old and young, with an urge to martyrdom—were pouring into Boston, and in front of the State House they would have their chance. Betty was lame from her effort to upset a horse, but was sticking to her desk; she had not been to bed the night before, and was not going to-night. "Plenty of time to sleep after Monday midnight," she said. "Bart and Nick will keep us company."

Joe was at the headquarters of the new "Citizens' National Committee, which was concentrating its efforts upon trying to persuade the Federal authorities to accept their responsibility in the case. The committee was sending and receiving hundreds of telegrams every day: obtaining signatures to a petition to the President of the United States, asking him to intervene, according to the precedent set by Woodrow Wilson, when the State of California had been on the point of executing Tom Mooney. But there was an important difference between the two cases; Mooney was an A. F. of L. man, and labor had to be handled gingerly in war-time. But now there was what capitalism calls "peace," and Sacco and Vanzetti had no standing in the court of power-politics.

The President of the United States was that "Cautious Cal," whom we saw shot up on the Massachusetts escalator. "Keep cool with Coolidge," had been the slogan which had got him the greatest vote ever given to a wizard of prosperity. Now the wizard was keeping himself cool upon a high mountain peak in Yellowstone Park. He knew the way to do nothing, and do it more systematically, than any man who had ever held the office. He had as much idea of dipping his fingers into that boiling Boston caldron as he had of spending his vacation in the mountains of the moon. Hundreds of dollars were spent collecting signatures to a petition, and thousands were spent by individuals telegraphing direct. The messages came by the basketful, and served to start the evening fires for a chilly and frugal New Englander.

Musmanno was at Hill's office, trying for a long-distance telephone connection with Chief Justice Taft. This elder statesman was in Canada, where he could not legally sign a writ; it was Musmanno's idea that he might come to the border, and there at least hear a petition. The young lawyer had an airplane ready, and would start that Sunday night. He sat at the telephone from seven in the evening until four the next morning, but the great jurist was able to find some perfectly good legal reason for staying where he was.

IX

Deborah was in the apartment, waiting for her mother, to plead with her not to kill herself in this dreadful crisis. Cornelia was hardly able to get up the stairs without help; yet unwilling to go to the Alvin home, where there was an elevator. She could not sleep; she must lie on the bed, with the telephone receiver to her lips, asking for news. She would sink back, and Deborah would think she was resting—but no, she was getting ready to call Mr. Moors, to see if he could not induce Mr. Lowell to induce the Governor to grant a few more days! She was appealing to Hubert Herring, a young Congregational clergyman who had risked his job, getting a dozen other clergymen to sign an appeal to the Governor!

Mother and daughter shouted to each other across an abyss, and just now the abyss was full of thunder, and it was hard for voices to get across. "Mother! Mother!"—Cornelia heard a faint cry—"You think more about two Italian anarchists than you do about any member of your own family!"

"My dear"—Cornelia shouting back—"no one is planning to murder any member of my family."

Deborah would take a sentence and meditate over it, until an answer became so urgent in her bosom that she would try once more. "Mother, there are other kinds of unhappiness, almost as bad as being murdered."

"My child, that is God, trying to break the hard shell of your pride."

Cornelia phoned to Arthur Hill's office. His daughter-in-law was in charge of the phone, and would tell her if there was any more news. There was none, and Cornelia hung up, and sat staring before her with a face of torment. Deborah's heart ached, but the only way she could help was to diminish her mother's interest in those dreadful Italians! "Mother, Henry has become positive that both those men were dynamiters." And again: "Mother, I believe you really prefer dynamiters to law-abiding people!"

Make allowances for Cornelia. These family disputes, that go on for years and years and never get anywhere, are hard upon the nerves. Said the mother: "I prefer the dynamiter who cares about justice to the most law-abiding person in the world who doesn't!"

The telephone rang; Deborah's older daughter, Priscilla, asking if she might come round. This had been one of Deborah's schemes—her daughter would keep Cornelia's mind occupied with news about the great-grandchildren. But Priscilla had better not mention that her mother had suggested the visit. Deborah was forever devising such little plots—always, of course, for the other person's good; and she had trained her older daughter to coöperate.

Cornelia began asking about the wife of Governor Fuller— what sort of woman was she? It seemed that Jessica Henderson and Cornelia were planning to motor up to Rye Beach, New Hampshire, the next day, and implore the help of this much-troubled lady. Deborah told what she had been able to judge from one dinner-party. Mrs. Fuller was a Catholic; and Cornelia asked, what would that mean? Could she possibly be made to understand that Jesus was to be electrocuted in Boston to-morrow midnight?

So Deborah burst out again: "Mother, do you think Jesus ever used dynamite?"

"No, my dear, it wasn't invented in those days. All he had was a whip, to drive the moneychangers out of Trinity Church." And after Deborah had expatiated upon the extreme charitableness of Trinity Church, her mother shocked her by exclaiming: "Oh, Boston, Boston, thou that givest the prophets a ride in the patrol-wagon!"

x

Priscilla came, a tall and distinguished young matron now; but she did not get any chance to tell the news about her three children. She found the poor old woman lying back on her pillow with her eyes closed, speaking in whispers which might have come from a death-bed. She took Priscilla's hand, and said, "I talk to your mother, and it means nothing to her. Let me try the next generation!"

"Yes, Grandmother," said Priscilla, obediently. "What is it?"

"Your mother cannot understand how anarchists come to be in Boston. So I try to explain to her. When I was a young married woman, about your age, I used to look out of our back windows and see pitiful children of the poor, going about in winter-time with ragged shawls over their shoulders and holes in their shoes, rooting in the frozen garbage in alleys behind the Back Bay homes. I was told that it was the will of God, so I did nothing. But now I have discovered that it is a social system. All those miles of slum tenements down in the South End, falling into ruins, with filth and litter in the alleys and mangy cats prowling—that hideousness which is the underside of our proud and pious city—that is not God, that is blueblood old ladies and gentlemen holding acres and acres of land, inherited from their great-grandfathers, and letting the tenements fall into ruins while they wait for an increase in land values which they do nothing to produce. Is that so hard to understand, Priscilla?"

"No, Grandmother."

"Well, that is one detail out of a hundred. Your husband owns millions, because he was allowed to inherit a mountain of copper, which he did nothing to earn, and which others manage and work for him. You will inherit millions because your father is allowed to manufacture the credit of the country and keep it for his own use—no, Deborah, don't argue with me, for I know you haven't studied our banking system, even though you are a banker's wife. Mr. Lowell is a multi-millionaire because he is allowed to exploit the labor of thousands of slaves in cotton-mills—even though he never tended a spindle or managed a factory in his life. Governor Fuller is the richest of all of us, because he is allowed to sit like a robber baron of the Middle Ages, and fine everybody a thousand dollars for the privilege of driving a Packard car in New England. He talks about bandits, and really thinks they should all be executed! All of us sit on top of our privileges, and haven't the least idea of getting off; we use all the powers of society to seduce or destroy those who resist us—if necessary, we kill them for a crime, whether they committed it or not."

There were many questions that Priscilla would have liked to ask, and many objections that her mother would have liked to register. But both of them were frightened, thinking that Cornelia might gasp out her life on that bed. So they sat silent, with distress in their eyes; and presently the poor soul was whispering again:

"My children, I have followed this case for seven years, and here is what I know about it, a frightful thing to say—from first to last there has not been one honest man who had anything to do with it on the government side: not a single one, from the policemen who lied on the witness-stand to your three blue-blood commissioners who doctored the record—every man has been seeking a pretext to carry out his will upon two fanatics whom he considers dangerous. That is the truth about the Sacco-Vanzetti case; and there lie those two men in the death-house, one of them a self-taught philosopher, a man of genius who has managed under the pressure of affliction to make himself into the most beautiful character I have ever known in my years on this earth—"

There came tears from the wrinkled old eyelids. "Sacco, too!" she exclaimed. "A man with the heart of a child!" She put out her hand and took some papers from the lamp-stand by her bed, and began turning them over. "Listen; he is writing to Inez, his six-year-old daughter; a letter which the child may have in after years, to tell her what her father was like:

" 'It was the greatest treasure and sweetness in my struggling life that I could have lived with you and your brother Dante and your mother in a neat little farm and learn all your sincere words and tender affection. Then in the summer time to be sitting with you in the home nest under an oak tree shade, beginning to teach you of life and how to read and write, to see you running, laughing, crying, and singing through the little verdant fields picking the wild flowers here and there from one tree to another and from the clear vivid stream to your mother's embrace. The same I have wished and loved to see for other poor girls and their brothers, happy with their mother and father, as I dreamed for us. But it was not so and the nightmare of the lower classes has saddened very badly your father's soul. The men of this dying old society brutally have pulled me away from the embrace of your brother and your poor mother. But in spite of all, the free spirit of your father's faith survives.' "

XI

On Monday morning, the last day, Governor Fuller came to his office in the State House at half past ten o'clock; rosy and smiling, greeting the newspapermen: "Good morning, boys; a fine day. I'll be here at my desk until midnight, boys, doing my duty." Already there were deputations waiting for him, lawyers from New York, editors, writers, labor leaders, society women —he would see them all, in batches, all day long; he would greet them with his marble smile, listen with politeness, and say: "I will take what you have said under consideration."

Some came to urge him on the other side; including the newly elected officers of the American Legion, which was holding a convention in the State House that morning. Returned soldiers who hadn't had enough of war, they were keen for this as for all other killings. They were singing the "Star-spangled Banner" at noon, when the first group of pickets began their march on the street outside.

All day long the pickets would come, one batch after another, ten or twenty at a time, with their placards of polite protest, all bad words barred. They would walk their appointed number of paces, and then the police would close about them, and take them in tow, and march them to Joy Street, and then—"Files right!"—to the police-station. The men were packed, eight into a cell, and the women in the guard-room, waiting for their bail.

There were well-known names among them. Edna St. Vincent Millay, from Rockland, Maine, home of her ancestors for many generations. Loveliest of women poets, she would find this a devastating experience; life would not seem the same after a rendezvous with murder. "My personal physical freedom, my power to go in and out when I choose, my personal life even, is no longer quite so important to me as it once was. . . . The physical world, and that once was all in all to me, has at moments such as these no road through a wood, no stretch of shore, that can bring me comfort. The beauty of these things can no longer make up to me for all the ugliness of man, his cruelty, his greed, his lying face."

John Dos Passos again, and John Howard Lawson; also Clarina Michelson, and Paula Holladay—still with her red slicker. And Paxton Hibben—still with his speech. Alfred Baker Lewis of the Socialist Party, Harry Canter for the communists, and Margaret Hatfield, who might be taken as representing the Republicans, since her father was county treasurer. Professor Ellen Hayes of Wellesley College, seventy-six years of age, marching with a cane, and holding her head up high—the most serious hour of a scholar's life! A picturesque figure she made, in a Norfolk jacket and skirt, square-toed shoes, a little flat hat, and white hair bobbed to her shoulders; bright, eager eyes and sensitive face, now grim—the New England conscience working. "What is your occupation?" asked the clerk. "Professor of astronomy and applied mathematics." They did not book these very often!

Others to uphold the honor of "Old Boston": Catharine Huntington, who lived on Pinckney Street, with ancestry going back three hundred years in New England; Helen Peabody, and Helen Todd, suffrage workers; Lola Ridge, the poet—all these New England born, with forefathers on the *Mayflower*, or the *Fortune*, the second-best boat. This was true of Edna Millay, of Margaret Hatfield and of Dos Passos. The committee had sent out a call for everybody "with a background"—the polite Boston phrase. Nothing would count so much with the newspapers; the humble Jews and Italians and Slavs—Frishman and Pogrebisky, Chiplovitz and Chasanovitz, Pulcini and Magliocca and Spognodi—these must be content to have their names listed wrong. "What is fame?" say the British army officers. "To die in battle, and have your name misspelled in the *Gazette*."

Betty and Joe had their chance now; the police were taking them as they came, blue-bloods and all; so near the end, they no longer worried about public opinion; it would all be over to-night, things would settle down, the dead wops would stay dead. Over in the office of the Boston *Herald*, on Tremont Street, they were putting into type an editorial, kissing the case good-by. A year ago they had been heroically demanding justice, and winning a prize for it; now what they wanted was "Normalcy." "Back to Normalcy! The asperities which have attended the Sacco-Vanzetti case in its long and tedious journey through the courts are greatly to be regretted, and should be forgotten as quickly as possible. Let us get back to business and the ordinary concerns of life, in the confident belief that the agencies of law have performed their duties with fairness as well as justice. . . . The chapter is closed. The die is cast. The arrow has flown. The voice of the department store advertising agent has been heard in the office of the *Herald.*"—They did not publish that last sentence, of course. That was the truth.

XII

Betty and Joe marshaled all the others, and then joined the last contingent, a group of needle-trade workers, risking their jobs to go to jail. The little party came into Beacon Street, and saw a mob of thousands on the side adjoining the Common. The great iron gates in front of the State House were closed and chained. The policemen were an army, the reporters and photographers and plainclothesmen were another. The pickets were accused of obstructing the sidewalk, but really it was these others who did it.

The little group exposed their signs and began to walk. The cops closed round them, not much formality or delay; the guardians of order were tired, and the seven-minute provision got scant attention. The pickets were told to disperse, and when they walked on, paying no attention, they were shoved against the railing and closed in. "Christ, my arm!" screamed a Jewish boy, not yet out of his teens.

"What are you doing?" cried Betty, to the policeman. "You don't have to twist his arm like that!"

"Shut up, you bitch!" was the answer.

"I don't have to! I'll take your number, and make it hot for you, if you don't let up on that boy!"

"Shut your trap, and go back where you came from!"

"I came from Commonwealth Avenue, and my father is Rupert Alvin, president of the Pilgrim National Bank of Boston."

"Holy Jesus!" said the pious cop, and stopped his torture.

The reporters came running; a story for the last afternoon editions. "Have you anything to say, Miss Alvin?"

"Yes, I have a whole speech to make, but your papers won't print it."

"Give us a try!"

"Well, I'll say that the men we are murdering to-night will have a statue in front of the State House before you and I die. I'll say there are two judges whose names will be linked together in history—Pontius Pilate and Webster Thayer." Thus Betty, trembling with rage, the white and pink in her lovely cheeks coming and going like Northern lights in the sky.

"Come on, Miss," said the scared cop; and Betty walked down the street, remarking, "My husband is back there—Joe Randall; he's got a statement written out."

So the reporters went to Joe, who gave them a copy of a cablegram he had sent that day, in answer to one from Pierre Leon in Paris: "Tell the workers of the world that the way to punish Boston for this crime is to repudiate the debts. Cancel every dollar owed to America, both publicly and privately. When the first nation does that, Boston will be sorry it committed murder. When the second nation does it, Boston will take steps to bring Sacco and Vanzetti back to life." Needless to say, that did not appear in any Boston newspaper!

The old Joy Street police station, so oddly named. The main room crowded with tired and disgusted-looking policemen, and young ladies from sheltered homes, getting their first lessons in profanity. "Take these god-dam bastards to number nine." "Take them bitches to the detention room." "What the hell we going to do with this new bunch?" There were more than a hundred and fifty in all, and the old place had been built before the program of "loitering for liberty" had been thought of. The walls shook with cheering, and waves of revolutionary song:

> *Arise, ye prisoners of starvation,*
> *Arise, ye wretched of the earth!*

Outside in the crowd there were Reds who joined in. Boston was honeycombed with sedition, so the patriotic societies declared.

The women sat on the benches lined against the wall. They spread newspapers, for the place was in a state of filth not to be described in print; the walls against which you wanted to lean were covered with dark smears, the blood of that creature which Vanzetti termed the "bed-buck." If a woman asked for a toilet, she was taken to a place of filth in an open cell among the men. If she asked for a drink, she was pointed to a faucet with a dipper so dirty that she would not take it in her hand. If she complained, the word would be, "Why don't you go back to Rooshia?" When your time came to be bailed out, you put up two dollars extra for the bailer; graft in Boston had become a system, a vested right. You could even have got a drink of the best liquor, confiscated from the unlicensed bootleggers, if you had looked like the right sort, and had the price. But you could not get the windows of this hellhole opened— not unless everybody would agree to stop singing Bolshevik songs.

XIII

Mary Donovan came, with bail for Powers Hapgood. He was to be her husband before long, and she had reason to be concerned about him now, for he had won special enmity. This was his fourth arrest. After the Sunday demonstration, a fortnight ago, the police had come with a warrant and arrested him again upon the more serious charge of "inciting to riot." "A bare-headed youth leading women into danger," said the police sergeant in court, and the judge said, "Six months."

Powers was nowhere to be found, and there was great alarm. For several hours nobody could find out what had become of him; then came a "tip"—he was in the "Psychopathic." That had been the bright idea of the captain of the state police. The shortest time in which anybody could get through the "Psychopathic" mill was ten days; and meantime Boston would be "back to normalcy." It was all for the prisoner's good, to keep him out of danger, said the police; the most considerate lot of sluggers that ever filled their stomachs with bootleg whisky and their pockets with bootleg graft.

A weird experience for a member of the Dickey and the Hasty Pudding Club and the Harvard Memorial Society! He was a handsome, athletic young fellow, but he looked less impressive after they had stripped him of his clothes, and put him in a dirty bathrobe. They took him to one of the wards, and put him in the very bed in which Sacco had once lain! Next to him was a man who believed himself to be God; on the other side a man who sat with his head in his hands and never moved for hours. The attendants apparently desired to get Powers excited, so that they could put him "on the ice." They would come and make provocative remarks; a woman nurse started to express her opinion of Sacco—an ugly wop, and she pounded the bed as she said it; worse than that, he was an atheist. Powers was aware of the importance of keeping cool without any ice; he answered amiably, and with his charming smile. One attendant whispered that he was in danger, and offered to phone a doctor for him. Doubtless that was the source of the "tip."

Doctors came to examine him; all the regulation mental stuff. You believe that Sacco and Vanzetti are being framed? Are you yourself being framed? Have you a mission from God? What are your dreams? Please take this pencil and write, how much is fourteen times fourteen? If twelve is greater than ten put a dot inside the circle which is not inside the square. Did your mother have a hard time at your birth? Explain this little story, how the Pope was crowned and so the little boy died of gilt paint. If you can explain it, then it is established that you are a "nut"!

They must have found this Harvard graduate an interesting specimen, for they put him up before the whole staff that evening. They made him put on his bathrobe backwards; which he thought was to make him look crazy, but doubtless was to keep a lunatic from committing any indecency. There were forty or fifty persons, men and women; doctors, nurses and students, many flappers. They put him on the platform and asked him to explain his ideas about reforming the world; so he made them a little socialist speech, ten minutes at least. They began asking him questions: a flapper wanted to know why he thought Sacco and Vanzetti were not guilty. What did he think about the McHardy bomb—the one which had blown out the front of the juror's home? That was a catch, of course; he would say it was a provocateur job, and then they would all know he was a "nut."

He said it. He fitted perfectly into their categories. And yet— a singular development—he began to expand before their eyes, and before he stopped, he had smashed their categories. A distressing experience to scientific minds—to have their categories smashed! Some one had said of Herbert Spencer that "his idea of a tragedy was a generalization killed by a fact."

Powers had many facts, all deadly. The strike-breaking agencies planted bombs all the time, nothing simpler. It was the accepted technique of class war in the mining districts; one bomb, and the militia came and broke up the strike. It had been done right here in Massachusetts, by the great Mr. William Wood, president of the American Woolen Company; it had been proved in court, the men he had hired had been sent to jail for it. Too bad that Bostonians didn't know their own industrial history!

After this session, fifteen alienists turned in a report to the effect that the former member of the Dickey, the Hasty Pudding Club and the Harvard Memorial Society was sane; one of them added that he had better be got out of "Psychopathic" as quickly as possible, or he would make socialists of the whole staff! They held him overnight, in Sacco's bed, and in the morning they turned him loose—the first man who had ever got through the mill in one day. A triumph for a Harvard education!

XIV

Monday noon, with the execution twelve hours away, the Governor was in session with three lawyers of national repute: Arthur Garfield Hays, Frank P. Walsh, and Francis Fisher Kane, formerly a Federal prosecutor in Pennsylvania. These three were concentrating upon the subject of the Department of Justice files. They had traveled all the way to Vermont, to interview the United States Attorney-General. They had then proceeded to Washington, to interview a subordinate, and had succeeded in getting the admission that Sacco and Vanzetti were referred to in the files; also the written statement that the files would be turned over to the Massachusetts authorities, if these authorities would request it. Now the three lawyers endeavored, in vain, to persuade the Governor to make the request.

At this same hour, Arthur D. Hill was off the coast of Maine in a steamer, searching in a fog for an island eight miles out, where lived Justice Stone of the United States Supreme Court;

Elias Field, assistant counsel, was making a motion before another judge of the Superior Court of Massachusetts; Musmanno was waiting for a chance to appeal to the Governor with new arguments and affidavits of new witnesses; while Jessica Henderson and Cornelia were motoring eighty miles or more to the Governor's summer home to make their appeal to the great man's wife.

A stately home for a multi-millionaire, set far back from the boulevard, and well hidden by shrubbery. When the owner himself was there, a miniature army was on guard; twenty-six men, with several machine-guns, and seventy-five reserves in a near-by town. But apparently it was not feared that the enemy would harm the family, for now there was only one plainclothesman on watch.

The Governor's wife received the visitors courteously, and heard them to the end. Evidently the other members of the family resented the strain being put upon her, for three different persons came, seeking to cut the session short; but Mrs. Fuller would not have it so.

Cornelia knew something about the cares of office. She had realized that possibly the jauntiness of the supersalesman was merely a mask; it was his idea of being "game," the male courage which defies death and danger. Certainly it was not the same in his family; his wife had been ill, his son and daughter had been ill. "It has taken years from his life!" exclaimed the woman. "You can have no idea what it means. We, too, sit in the electric-chair." Cornelia, who had lived for forty years in a home of wealth, knew the whole story— even though in Josiah's day they had not thought about anarchists and dynamite. Somehow or other, great sums of money found a way to wreck the happiness of those who held them. Yet, no one would give them up, no one would cease the mad chase!

Cornelia poured out her story. It was one to move any woman's heart, and the Governor's lady sat with tears welling into her eyes. A little boy, her youngest child, played about the room and sat on the arm of Cornelia's chair; she told him about Plymouth, and about Trando, who had made himself a violinist; about Dante Sacco, who had bidden his father farewell in the death-cell, but had not been allowed to touch him through the bars. She told the mother about the framing of witnesses, and some of the new evidence they had found. But even while she spoke, she read in the face of her listener that her errand was a vain one.

"I can do nothing but this, Mrs. Thornwell; I will have the Governor see you to-day, so that you may tell him these things."

"I have already told him so much," answered Cornelia. "I was hoping you would go with me to the Governor."

"No, I could not do that; it would do no good, I assure you."

Mrs. Fuller would telephone, and see to it that Mrs. Thornwell and Mrs. Henderson had another interview that afternoon. The Governor must be made to comprehend those circumstances which made it so doubtful whether the men were really guilty. The Governor's lady put her arm about Cornelia as she led her out to the car; and Cornelia thought, if only the women would run the world! But no, she had seen it happen; women went into public life, and became as hard as the men. Could it be that, as Vanzetti said, there was something fundamentally immoral about the business of dominating the lives of your fellows?

XV

Three hours later they were back at the State House, having made no stop for lunch. There were larger crowds than ever in the corridors before the Governor's chambers, more than half of them secret service men and reporters. Mrs. Fuller had kept her promise; the Governor would see the two ladies, the secretary said.

Tom O'Connor sat with them while they waited; a reporter who was now with the defense, having given up a State House job a year ago. He would tell them the news.

Delegations to see the Governor, all through that day; there had been more than nine hundred telegrams received; few of them read. Musmanno had brought more affidavits; he had had word that his application for a writ had been docketed with the United States Supreme Court. Fuller had not said what he would do. A deputation of labor men from New York had been in a while ago; Fuller had said to one of them, "I know the men are guilty, so I don't care whether they had a fair trial or

not." "He said those same words to me," said Cornelia; and
then, "old Boston" speaking in her, "Don't quote me, please."

Never had there been so many sensations, piling one upon
another—not in the memory of the oldest employee at the State
House. The Springfield *Republican* had published a powerful
editorial, underscoring the doubts as to the men's guilt; Seward
Collins, publisher of the *Bookman,* had put up the money to
insert it as a full-page advertisement in every Boston newspaper. The *Globe* had refused the money; others had run the
ad that morning, and the State House gang was furious. Then,
bright and early, who should walk in but Waldo Cook, editor
of the *Republican*—sixty-two years of age, and the most respected journalist in New England. He came with a deputation
of editors to see the Governor, and the private secretary
tackled him. "I understand, Mr. Cook, that you got twenty
thousand dollars from the defense committee for that editorial." "It's a damned lie!" said the editor.

"I suppose they get used to taking money here in the State
House," said Cornelia; and O'Connor grinned. The Governor
himself was no better than his secretary, when it came to repeating charges without evidence. He had said to one deputation
that Professor Frankfurter had been paid great sums by the
defense; he would go on saying this, even though he had been
many times assured that it was false. He was obsessed with
hatred of Frankfurter, and blamed him more than any other;
he would accuse people of having read Frankfurter's book,
and if they admitted this crime, he would not hear them any
longer.

XVI

The two ladies were ushered into the presence: two persistent pests who had sneaked into a man's home, seeking to
undermine his domestic peace! Nevertheless, he would be polite.
He had set himself the task of remaining here until midnight,
and seeing every one who came; and one person was about the
same as the next.

He started at once on the aggressive. "My wife tells me
that you ladies still don't think the men had a fair trial. But
you must know they had three trials—one before Judge Thayer,

one before the Lowell Commission, and one which I have conducted in these rooms. I tell you that I would not ask for my own son any fairer trial than that which took place before Mr. Lowell."

Said Cornelia: "It is the first principle of our law that the accused shall be confronted by the witnesses against them. But Sacco and Vanzetti did not see many of the witnesses who appeared before Mr. Lowell."

"Surely you must realize the absurdity of such a proposition! How could those desperate anarchists have been brought every day to the State House?"

"All right, if it is too much trouble to conform to the principles of our law, let us follow our convenience—but then don't claim that it is a fair trial."

"The men were represented by the best counsel."

"Even the counsel were barred sometimes; they were not present at Judge Thayer's examination; they were limited in questioning Katzmann. Worse than that—they don't even know the names of all the witnesses. I understand that Mr. Lowell is saying that he had 'confidential information.' He is telling that to all his friends; and what place have secret whispers in a fair trial? You say that the trial before Judge Thayer was fair—yet the Lowell report admits that Judge Thayer committed 'a grave breach of official decorum.' "

"That was after the trial, Mrs. Thornwell."

"It was while he still had the various motions before him. He was still the judge of the case, and the sole judge, right up to the time he pronounced sentence last April, and automatically excluded any other judge from acting. Are not men entitled to have new evidence considered before an unprejudiced judge? And who else has considered that evidence?"

"I have, Mrs. Thornwell; and I think that I have common sense, even if I haven't legal training."

"Pardon me, Governor, but we have suffered much from inability to get you to consider new evidence. We brought you the express receipt for eels, but we are told that you say you know Vanzetti never got them. We bring you the Pinkerton reports, but we don't know if you know what is in them. They cancel Mary Splaine, but you still go on citing Mary Splaine. We bring you the son of Lola Andrews, and he tells you that his mother is not to be trusted, but you go on trusting her. You tell Musmanno that you don't believe Vanzetti ever sold fish, and Musmanno brings you an affidavit from Carbone, the wholesaler from whom Vanzetti bought fish in Plymouth regularly. We bring you all sorts of affidavits, but nothing does the least good, because you have some secret information that we are not permitted to know about, and that determines the whole matter for you. What is it, Governor—tell us now, instead of too late. Believe me, the world is going to know some day!"

Thus the little old white-haired woman; and with elaborate and patient courtesy the sorely tried statesman assured her that she had fallen victim to the machinations of dangerous and depraved persons. He had the duty of deciding this case, not she; and when he made promises to witnesses in fear of their lives, he would keep those promises. When she broke down and wept, and Mrs. Henderson began to plead for mercy, he said that Massachusetts was in the grip of a crime wave, and that to pardon guilty men would set a dangerous precedent. He had refused to pardon the "car-barn bandits," even though they were native Americans, one of them a World War veteran. No, he was not troubled by the clamor from outside, the pleadings of what people said were "great minds"; they might be great in their own line, but they didn't know about the Sacco-Vanzetti case. This clamor would pass quickly. When Cornelia started to argue against capital punishment, his answer was: "You and I both sleep better in a state which has capital punishment."

Cornelia gazed at him, with a look of dismay. She could not reply to such words. Men had killed their fellows for fear and for hate, for piety and for glory, for exercise, for sport, for food; but here for the first time in recorded history they killed for a soporific! The little old woman stood up, trembling.

"Governor Fuller, answer me this: What are you going to do when we find the real criminals? Somewhere in the world are two men who really did the Bridgewater job; somewhere are four, or five, who did the South Braintree job. And rest assured, we are going to find them—we are never going to rest until we have found them—and then, how will you be able to face life? What will all you gentlemen do—judges and governors and college presidents—knowing that you sent two innocent men to their death? What will there be in the world for you—but insanity or suicide?"

He did not answer, and she went out, with despair plainly written upon her aged face, for all the newspapermen to see and record. In the corridor they told her the news, right hot off the wire—Arthur Hill had telephoned to his office, Justice Stone had turned down his request. The lawyer was up in Maine, and could not get back to Boston until morning, so his work was at an end.

What had Mrs. Thornwell to say to that? What was she going to do? The reporters gathered about, eager for more story. A marvelous melodrama this was to them—a whole day packed full of thrills! Melodrama at the State House, with millionaires and blue-bloods and "headliners" of all sorts in a fourteen-hour stream! All over the city, with two hundred persons arrested, and tens of thousands looking on; with poets and hoboes, "Reds" and "scions of wealth," famous lawyers and judges, playing their lively parts! All over the world, with bombs exploding and plate glass shattering, mobs yelling and cavalry charging! And at the end death waiting, in the aspect of a chair with widespread, capacious arms, gaping for its victims! Monday, August 22nd, 1927, a date never to be forgotten in the history of the world!

CHAPTER 23

THE LAST ENEMY

I

In a room in the Hotel Bellevue, adjoining the State House, five lawyers from New York, all volunteers in the case, had worked all Sunday night and part of Monday, eighteen consecutive hours, concocting legal formulas and having them typed. On the roof of the hotel were detectives, and in the windows of the State House opposite; for the spectacle of lights burning all night in a room known to be occupied by Reds exercised an irresistible spell upon the authorities. "What are they doing now? Where are they going?" Half a dozen automobiles waited outside the hotel, and whenever one of the lawyers took a taxi, the august Commonwealth of Massachusetts trailed behind.

Now the Boston lawyers had failed, and admitted their failure; the New York lawyers had the field, with seven or eight hours to go. They asked for a hearing before Federal Judge Lowell, and he set the hour of six o'clock. A court session consisting of one judge, five lawyers, and a score of newspapermen. The judge resented the intrusion of "foreigners" into this case, and took occasion to say what all ruling-class Boston was thinking. He accused the strangers of "trying the case in the newspapers"; he interrupted them again and again to demand "law, not eloquence." When William Schuyler Jackson, ex-Attorney General of New York State, was showing the conspiracy carried on by Katzmann to deceive the jury at the Dedham trial, the judge broke in: "Did you ever see a Norfolk county farmer?" The lawyer, disconcerted, had to admit, "Not in reality." Whereupon the judge snapped out: "Well, if you had, you'd have a better opinion of that jury."

It made magnificent copy for the newspapers; the *Herald* put it in a "box"—"Judge Lowell Praises Norfolk County Farmers"—and all patriots swelled with pride. Wonderful beings were Norfolk county farmers, and wonderful also the Lowells, who spoke only to Cabots, who spoke to God. It was the hard luck of the ex-Attorney General of New York State that he was not familiar with the details of the case; otherwise he might have made answer to the arrogant judge: "The Sacco-Vanzetti jury consisted of two real estate men, two machinists, a grocer, a mason, a stockkeeper, a clothing salesman, a mill operative, a shoemaker, a lastmaker, and *one* Norfolk county farmer!"

The lawyers loaded themselves into an automobile, together with Isaac Don Levine, journalist, and set out for Beverly, to make a last appeal to Justice Oliver Wendell Holmes. Detectives trailed behind them, and more detectives met them at their destination. The very old gentleman sat in his parlor, talking with two very old ladies; a chaste New England home, everything antique, in the taste of a bygone age. The lawyers presented their petition, and the judge sat himself down to peruse it—four thousand words of "law, not eloquence." A dead silence; and Levine sat in the hall, listening to the ticking of a "grandfather's clock." "Life-death, life-death, life-death," it said; the listener shivered.

The old gentleman looked up. "I appreciate the general force of your argument," he said—and their hearts leaped. He was famous for the so-called "judicial mind," his ability to consider legal principles in a vacuum completely freed of human emotion. He went on: "I am of the opinion that the petition is covered by the principles stated in my decisions upon the former applications for habeas corpus and certiorari, and therefore I am compelled to deny the writ."

The lawyers excused themselves, and got into the car again, and whirled back to Boston. One more hope; Federal Judge Anderson, who was not quite so free from human emotion. Seven years back, he had condemned the Red raids in an exhaustive and scorching decision. Now he was attending the Institute of Politics at Williamstown, two hundred miles away, and Tom O'Connor had arranged at the East Boston naval airport to charter an airplane to take John Finerty, a leading lawyer of Washington, formerly assistant counsel for the U. S. Railroad Commission. It would be a risky journey at night, but they had worked for eighteen hours over those four thousand words of "law, not eloquence," and wanted to make it count if they could.

The nearest landing field was in Albany, New York, fifty miles from Williamstown. O'Connor had arranged with a taxi company to have a cab waiting at the landing field. All was ready; but alas, some one tipped off the authorities at the airport as to who these nefarious persons were, and a naval officer ordered them off the premises. "It would give me pleasure to shoot you," he said to the ex-Attorney General of New York State; and next day the newspapers reported that the Commonwealth of Massachusetts has been asked to put a special guard over the airport, threatened with seizure by the Reds!

II

From a window of the Hod Carriers' Union in Salem Street, Ella Reeve Bloor was explaining the case as an episode in the class struggle to a crowd of some hundreds of solemn-faced workers. "Mother" Bloor, they called her; sixty-five years old, she had raised a brood of five children, and turned them loose in the radical movement, and so was free to wander over America, wherever workingmen on strike called for a martyr. A little round jolly figure, full of laughter, brown as a hickory nut and as solid, she said her say, until the policemen forced their way into the union headquarters and dragged her out. "Inciting to riot," was the charge.

At the same time Paula Holladay was getting arrested in her red "slicker" again; they took it away from her this time! Over near Charlestown prison another group were preparing to walk into the den of blue-coated lions; their leader was Helen Peabody, one of those "with a background," who conceived it her duty to be in jail when the execution took place. In an obscure hall near defense headquarters, Betty and Joe were speaking to a somber crowd. It would not save Sacco and Vanzetti, but it would save their message, as Joe pointed out. Let the workers learn, and organize to defend themselves against ruling class murder.

A curious instance, then going on, to illustrate Joe's message. Everywhere in Boston the workers had been dragged to jail for attempting to voice their protest; but in the town of

Peabody, some twenty miles away from Boston, there was now going on a meeting in the public square, at which ten thousand workers were voicing their feelings unmolested. How came that? Quite simple; the workers of Peabody had taken the precaution to elect themselves a Socialist mayor. Yesterday, Sunday, the chief of police had broken up a mass meeting, in the regulation Mike Crowley style; the mayor had been on vacation, and hearing the news, had hastened back, and removed the chief of police from office, and taken charge of to-night's meeting himself, and introduced Alfred Baker Lewis as the principal speaker. Would the workers of Boston learn anything from that?

Governor Fuller was in session with Congressman La Guardia, who had flown all the way from Washington in an airplane; an Italian, he pleaded for mercy for two men of his race. Musmanno, having presented four new affidavits in vain, waited outside for a chance to present one more. He argued with Attorney General Reading, counsel for the Decimo Club and the "L.A.W.," seeking to persuade him that it would be a discourtesy to the United States Supreme Court, to take the life of two men, when their appeal was actually on file before that high tribunal. Mr. Reading did not answer Musmanno's argument; neither did he say what he would advise the Governor. Death was only three or four hours away.

Over in the death cells, Sacco was bidding a last farewell to his wife, and Vanzetti to his sister. The men stretched their arms through the bars; the women broke down, and had to be carried out, sobbing wildly. They belonged to a demonstrative race—one of the reasons why stern New England did not like them. Nevertheless, New England would read about it—column after column in the next morning's papers—"sob stuff," that sold best of anything.

Rosina and Luigia decided to try one last appeal to the Governor. They had not intended to do it; they knew in their hearts that they would fail; but they had several hours to pass, and it was easier to do anything than to do nothing. Friends telephoned and made the appointment, and at nine o'clock they arrived at the State House, a fortress surrounded by armed men, the searchlights which usually illuminated the golden dome now turned upon the crowds in the streets. They ascended in the elevator, and Rosina walked ahead, through the rows of silent newspapermen; Luigia followed hesitatingly, bewildered by this strange environment. Musmanno was there to act as interpreter, and they were shown into the private office, where so many had sat and poured out eloquence in vain.

Rosina Sacco spoke first, in English. She told of her faith in her husband's innocence. She told about the trial; about Lola Andrews, the hysteric; about Captain Proctor, who had admitted his trick; about Goodridge, the many-times convicted crook; about Mary Splaine, and what the Pinkerton reports had revealed about her. She told about Judge Thayer; over and over, she insisted that the trial had not been fair. She asked for mercy. The Governor was a father, and he was sentencing two children to lose their father, and to wear a dreadful brand all their lives.

The great man listened with politeness—his store of the commodity was inexhaustible. He turned to the frail worn sister of Vanzetti, who began speaking in soft musical Italian, the young lawyer translating sentence by sentence. She had just come from her brother in the gloomy deathhouse; his protestations of innocence were ringing in her ears. He had asked her to convey a message to the Governor. Some weeks ago Bartolomeo had shaken hands with the Governor in the prison, and he thought that he had demonstrated his innocence; the Governor had given him that impression; now he could not understand how the Governor would let the death sentence stand. If he could have one more chance to talk with the Governor and answer his objections, he, Bartolomeo, was sure the death sentence would not be carried out.

For more than an hour the salesman of motor-cars listened, without interrupting. At last the two women said that they were through; and then, leaning forward slightly in his chair, he gave his answer. He appreciated the feelings of both of them, and was sorry for them. But he had taken an oath to uphold the constitution and laws of the Commonwealth of Massachusetts, and his conscience dictated that he should permit the law to take its course.

But still, he would be polite. Excessively so; as if he were paying compliments at a social function; or as if he were selling a Packard limousine. To some final argument of

Musmanno's he replied: "What you have said impresses me greatly. But even that is nothing compared with the eloquence of these ladies' presence." Was this one of the dreadful perversions of Puritanism? A kind of sadistic pleasure in inflicting torture with a smile? Whatever it was, it failed to make a hit with Rosina Sacco. "Let us go," she said, coldly, and they rose, and walked slowly from the room.

The newspapermen besought Musmanno to tell them what had happened, and he tried to do it; he touched upon a few of the arguments which the women had presented, but before he had got very far the tears began to run down his cheeks, and he had to stop. He went over to a chair and sat down and buried his face in his hands and sobbed. It was then half past ten, and the grandfather's clocks which kept the time for all Massachusetts were ticking steadily, with fifty-four hundred seconds still to go.

III

At six o'clock Cornelia had gone back to her home. The chauffeur had to help her up the stairs; and there were Deborah and Clara with the Negro maid, ready to come running, and lead her to the bed, and make any amount of fuss; to bring her tea or coffee, or a glass of milk, or a poached egg on toast. No, she could not eat; they pleaded, and wanted to phone for Dr. Morrow. The tears ran down their cheeks; they would do anything, abase themselves, agree with her wildest words, in the effort to quiet her, and persuade her that their love meant something. They were terrified at her appearance and her attitude; ashamed because they had shown so little sympathy in the past. Yes, no doubt there were very fine and good qualities in anarchists—anything, anything—so that their mother would stop killing herself!

Clara's precious youngest had got poison ivy all over him, and was shut up in the house with a poultice over his eyes; her oldest, who was just out of Harvard, was suspected to be on the verge of getting engaged at Bar Harbor; the oldest little fat treasure of Priscilla had got a bee sting over one eyelid, otherwise his mother would have been here. Quincy Thornwell had won a chess match—such items of family gossip Clara poured out, in a premeditated torrent—only to discover that her mother was not hearing a word. "Please, Clara, I can't think about anything now. Let me be quiet."

Deborah had taken the precaution to get a prescription from Dr. Morrow; it was his advice that Cornelia should take a strong sleeping powder and forget the ugly world and everything in it for at least twelve hours. But Cornelia said no. When her oldest daughter tried to insist, she said, "I was talking with one of the lawyers from New York, and he offered me a quart of whisky. If all hopes fail, he will retire to his hotel room and get drunk." The silence of Deborah and Clara said plainly, it was what everybody in Boston had known about that New York crowd! Cornelia, reading their thoughts, remarked grimly: "The whisky might give him pleasure, so that is immoral. But a sleeping powder is strictly business!"

The women decided to call in Henry, who understood the insides of this crisis so much better than they. So Henry put off dinner with an important banker from New York, and came over to sit by the bedside and tell his mother-in-law how it was possible for Boston to do this dreadful deed; how it was possible for such wickedness to be organized, and in control of society. "With all that new evidence before them, Henry! And with an appeal to the United States Supreme Court actually docketed!"

"Docketed doesn't mean anything, Mother. It simply means that you have put your request on file; it doesn't mean that it will get anywhere. In this case I assure you it wouldn't."

"Henry, if we could manage to keep those boys alive until October, we could really get the public to understand about this case, and they would never dare to execute them."

"Well, I guess that's just it, Mother. Fuller can't afford to let the case go on growing and growing."

She pondered that. "I have just heard that Quincy has won a chess match; and now the Governor is winning one, with human lives for pawns!"

IV

She told about her last interview, and the things that had been said. She told about the trip to Rye Beach; it was quite a story, and helped to pass the time without whisky or drugs. Deborah and Clara refrained from breaking in; there must be no arguments, nothing to excite the patient; each minute that passed was a danger escaped. Deborah ventured to make some remarks on the subject of Mrs. Fuller, and the problem of Catholic wives and Protestant husbands. The Governor was such an ardent Baptist, he wanted to teach a Sunday school. Was he letting his children be brought up as Catholics?

But no use; Cornelia could not be diverted from the main topic. "Henry, did you find out what is that 'confidential information' that Mr. Lowell and the Governor are talking about?"

"There's a lot of it, Mother; they keep quoting the Italian colony and what it thinks about the case."

"The 'Italian colony'! Do you stop to realize what the words mean? There are as many differences inside the Italian colony as in any other part of New England. The ruling group is Fascist; they hate Sacco and Vanzetti exactly as Judge Thayer does—only more so, because they know them better. The majority of the colony is Catholic; and when Bart was arrested he had on him a letter in which one of their priests was described as a 'pig.' Of course all the Italians know who that priest is. Does the Governor take the opinion of the priest? Or of his parishioners?"

"The story runs something like this, Mother: one of the Italian anarchists got drunk and talked, and admitted that Sacco had been in the bandit car at 'South Braintree."

"I've heard that," said Cornelia. "I've heard many such stories. But of course I couldn't guess which one the Governor of our Commonwealth and the President of our University would elect to believe. What do they say about Bart?"

"They don't think Bart was in the car, but they think he knew about it, which made him an accessory before the fact."

"Before, or after, Henry—are they sure which?" A pause. "And so that is what Mr. Lowell meant when he said that he thought Vanzetti was guilty 'on the whole'! I am solving the riddles which have tormented me for weeks! Who do they say was actually in the car?"

"Boda and Coacci and Orciani."

"Mike Stewart's theory complete! Have they overlooked

the fact that Orciani punched a time clock that day in the foundry where he worked?"

"The story is that he got somebody else to do it for him."

Cornelia sat, gazing with her inner eye into the face of Massachusetts statesmanship. "So that is why our boys have to die! Somebody got drunk and talked, and the talk came to the ears of our great men! Stop and think what this means, Henry—the breakdown of our legal system and our moral codes! Was it one of the guilty men who got drunk and talked?"

"No, that is not what I understand."

"It couldn't very well have been Sacco or Vanzetti, since they have been in jail, and couldn't get liquor in our model prisons, and anyhow, they don't drink. It couldn't have been Coacci, who was deported before the arrests took place; nor Orciani, nor little Mike Boda, who are sitting out on a barren rock somewhere in the Mediterranean, as prisoners of the Fascist government."

"Fuller doesn't claim it was the guilty ones who talked; it was one of their comrades."

"That is what I am trying to get straight. One of the bandits told a comrade, and this comrade got drunk and talked! Did he talk to Governor Fuller?"

"That is not the way I heard it."

"Hardly! There are automobile salesmen who get people drunk, I suppose, but not ardent Baptists, with Sunday school inclinations. We have to assume that some government spy got the anarchist comrade drunk, and then the anarchist comrade talked, and the spy told the Governor about it. Or maybe even that is too undignified for a Governor—surely it would have been for Mr. Lowell! Deborah, do you think Mr. Lowell would stoop to listen to a spy?"

Deborah understood that this was a rhetorical question, and prudently made no reply; Cornelia went on, working herself into a cold fury.

"Our dignity requires us to assume that the spy talked to some police official, whose business it is to know spies. So then we have this: Sacco or Vanzetti or Coacci or Orciani or Boda told an anarchist comrade that they were guilty; this comrade got drunk and told a police spy; this spy told the police; the police told the Governor; and the Governor told Mr. Lowell and Mr. Stratton and Judge Grant! So they have 'confidential information,' and decide that 'on the whole' they think Vanzetti was guilty! That is how our laws are enforced, that is our police system and our legal system and our judicial system and our political system and our educational system! Such are the masters of our youth and the guides of our intellectual life!"

"Mother—" began Deborah; but Cornelia exercised the privilege of age, to do the talking when she wanted to.

"There is a saying—all three of our educated commissioners know it, and possibly told it to our Governor—'in vino veritas.' But proverbs are false more often than they are true. Think how many circumstances there might be under which you would get falsehood from drunkenness, instead of truth. Suppose there was some personal grudge; or some vainglorious fool, taking pride in knowing a secret that was baffling the whole world! Suppose it was some one who had heard a rumor, and turned it into knowledge; suppose the talker were a Fascist agent, a spy himself—such things have happened. Anything in the world can happen, where men make their living by betrayal, and their rewards depend upon the tales they bring in. I know enough about the anarchist movement to say that you will find every sort of disordered mind in it; also, you will find every kind of rascal among the men who are trying to destroy it. From such a situation there arises a poisonous mist, a gas cloud of gossip and scandal. I thought that the whole purpose of our judicial system was to deliver men from such terrors; to force accusers to come out into the daylight, in open court! But here our great Commonwealth has proved itself worse than one of the Sewing Circles!"

V

Cornelia sat up, with an announcement which terrified her family. "I am going to see those boys before they die!"

"Mother! Mother!" All three of them started to protest at once. Impossible! Not to be thought of!

"I went Saturday, and the warden wouldn't let me see them. I wrote them letters; but that is not enough, I refuse to accept it. I am not going to let them go out of this world without bidding them good-by."

"Mother, the strain would kill you!"

"It is less than the strain of lying here doing nothing. I am only two or three miles from them—"

"A difficult two or three miles, Mother." It was Henry speaking. "The bridge is closed, and the streets roped off—"

"Governor Fuller can write a dozen words, and the road will be clear. He is going to do it for me! I am going to have a talk with Bart—and ask him to tell me the truth! I know that I can help him, and Nick, too. I am going to see the Governor—phone for me, Henry, and make sure he is still at his office."

Cornelia got up, in spite of all protests, and began to arrange her hair and put on her hat. Henry phoned, and got the information; then, when he saw that all argument was futile—that she was going to call a taxicab and go alone if necessary—he said: "Stay here, Mother, and rest. I will go and get the pass for you—if Fuller will give it."

"He *must* give it! I will not take a refusal! It will cost him nothing, it will do nobody any harm. Deborah, you go with Henry; you gave that creature a dinner party, now make him pay for it!"

All right, Deborah would go; anything to keep the poor soul quiet for another half hour. "It is a mad idea, Mother, but I will do the best I can."

"I know that you can do it! Promise me that you will do it, Henry—I will never forgive you if you play me a trick."

"I wouldn't do that, Mother—"

"You might think it was for my good. But I know myself better than you. I have a right to say good-by to those friends who have taught me so much. Tell the Governor that maybe they will confess to me—he'll be fool enough to believe that, I am sure! Tell him that you are very important persons, that he will shine by your reflected light! Telephone me the moment you get the answer—because I am coming myself if you fail!"

The State House lies just over the top of Beacon Hill, and it took Henry's car only five minutes to get there. Being large and expensive, it went past the guards without delay, and very soon there was a ring of the telephone by Cornelia's bed; she took the receiver with trembling hands, and heard the voice of her son-in-law: "All right, Mother. The Governor has been so kind as to give his consent." She could tell by the phrasing and the tone of his voice that he was speaking from the great man's office.

She got up and got herself ready, with Clara's help, and in a few minutes Henry's chauffeur was at the door, ready to assist her down the stairs. Clara went along—they would all go, expecting her to collapse, fearing she might die of the strain. Since opposition only made things harder, they must turn themselves into slaves of her whim; at the same time agreeing in their hearts with the Governor, they would be glad when this was over!

VI

There sat a strange man in the seat by the chauffeur; a police official in civilian clothing, who had been at the State House, and whom the Governor had assigned as an escort. They came quickly to Prison Point Bridge, across the Miller River to Charlestown, where the old prison stands. At the bridge entrance the lights of the car fell upon officers waving the traffic to a detour; behind them a solid line of blue-coats, with riot-guns in hand; behind these latter a group of mounted men, and behind them iron gates. A couple of motorcycle officers shot out towards them, blowing a shrill warning to bring them to a halt.

So began the tedious process of breaking down the barriers which the stern Commonwealth had set up against anarchists and bomb-throwers that night. The police official produced the paper with the golden crest at the top and the magic signature at the bottom. "To police officers of Boston and Charlestown: You will permit Mr. Henry Cabot Winters and party to drive to Charlestown prison this Monday evening. Warden Hendry will permit Mrs. Thornwell to converse with Sacco and Vanzetti for one hour, subject to his convenience, and without interference with his plans. Alvan T. Fuller, Governor." It was a signature familiar to all Bostonians, being regularly attached to advertisements, telling the eagerly expectant motor-world the latest wonders which "Packard" had to impart. "This will prove to be the most popular model which Packard has ever offered to sons and daughters who may have their own cars. . . . When may we show you this latest offering?" It did not seem to the Commonwealth at all humiliating to have a Governor who wheedled; neither did it trouble the sons and daughters of the rich who were able to have their own luxury cars that the same signature was attached to advertisements and to death warrants.

The fact that the police official was not in uniform may have accounted for the delay. One of the motorcycle men took the order back to the group, to show to his superior; after which he rode out to the car again and ordered it forward. The blue-clad lines gave way, the gates swung open, and the car rolled through. But half way across the bridge, there was another pair of gates, with another line of guardians, and the same procedure to be repeated. It was like the German entrench-ments—the Hindenburg line, the Siegfried line, the Wotan line. In the river, below the bridge, were speed-boats of the harbor-patrol, their searchlights sweeping the docks and the tracks of the Boston and Maine Railroad. Along the tracks were searchlights, three in a group, weaving futurist patterns on the night.

A third line, strongest of all, at the Charlestown end of the bridge. The military formalities were complied with, and the car started up Austin Street, when the revolving searchlight on the prison tower picked it out, and seemed to be a signal to a score of mounted troopers to come galloping from every direc-tion. Other searchlights, mounted on the prison wall and sweep-ing up and down the streets, brought out their figures, shining white for moments, then lost in semi-darkness.

"Why don't you send a man to pass us through?" demanded the police official, with some irritation; but apparently they hadn't intended to pass any one through. They had a dead-line, three hundred yards from the prison walls, blocking every street, and running over the tops of houses, where men sat with machine-guns, and stores of tear-bombs. The inhabitants of houses within the barred area were confined indoors, not even permitted on the steps; they could lean out of windows, and the searchlights shone upon rows of faces, staring white.

The instructions had been for the car to go to the warden's

home, which constituted a separate entrance to the prison enclosure. "No publicity, if you please, Mr. Winters," the Governor had said; and this was to the taste of a blue-blood family. The warden would be notified by telephone to expect them, and would smuggle them in, with no reporters crowding about, and no picturesque stories in the morning: "Widow of Ex-Governor Visits Condemned Men in Last Hours!" The car had to make a part circle of the aged fortress, and it gave even high-up Brahmins a realization of their importance, the favor which was being granted to them. Eight times they were halted and investigated; every foot of the way the searchlights followed them suspiciously, revealing bright bayonets and heavy riot guns, firemen with high pressure hoses ready for action, rows of horsemen drawn up against the prison walls, and motorcycles darting suddenly forth. Once a bomb went off—but not a dangerous one; only newspaper photographers taking photographs of the line of cavalry defending the main gate of the prison. Earth, water, even air were being guarded; searchlights played in the sky—a spiritualist medium having called at the prison, announcing that she had had a vision of an airplane dropping bombs. The Sacco-Vanzetti case had started from crystal-gazing, so it was reasonable that it should end with clairvoyance.

VII

They came to the warden's home and drew up at the curb. More parleys, after which the police official assisted Cornelia out of the car. The chauffeur was told to stay in his seat—no unnecessary chances taken. Deborah and Clara and Henry would sit where they were. The armed men stepped back, and the door opened, and prison guards met the visitors, and silently led them through the house and into the yard, past the cell-blocks, oblong brick buildings with rows of narrow barred windows. The lights were out, and the prison was supposed to be asleep, but the searchlights made the scene as bright as day, and nobody slept. There were white faces at the windows, and now and then a chorus of cries: "Let them out! Let them out!" Wild beasts, barking, howling, roaring in their cages!

To Cornelia it was as if she had taken Dante's place, in a journey through the various stages of hell: all this elaborate display of killing power, a thousand intricate and ingenious inventions, all the arts and sciences which civilization had contrived, applied to the wholesale and instantaneous wiping out of human life. The fact that this military force was for Cornelia's protection, that it gave back respectfully before the magic of her name, only filled her with the greater abhorrence, only proved her thesis, that its purpose was not justice, but the comfort and safety of the rich.

The death-house: a square brick building, immediately under the prison wall, a highly unstrategic position, which in part accounted for the need of a miniature army. Upon the wall with its wooden walk stood a line of machine gunners, and men were lined up several deep upon the sidewalk of Rutherford Avenue below the wall. Across the street were firemen with four high-pressure hoses.

There was a group of guards at the door of the death-house, and the warden came out, and took over the task of escorting the privileged old lady. A dreadful ordeal: Cornelia had to pass through the execution-chamber, and the canvas cover was off the chair; the heavy leather straps at the hands and feet dangled and called for their victims. One glance, and then the warden half lifted Cornelia and walked her swiftly on. He had had to do that same thing for many women, relatives of the condemned. It was not a jolly job this plump and round-faced old Scotchman had found himself.

The death cells, three in a row, opening upon a corridor; each cell a narrow little room with steel-barred door; in each a cot, a table, a little bureau. A neat, white-tiled floor, and on the outside, running the length of the corridor, a painted line, six feet from the cells, beyond which no visitor might step. Cornelia knew the lay-out, the lawyers having described it to her. In the first cell was Madeiros, in the second Sacco, in the third, the farthest from the death-chamber, Vanzetti. It was the order in which they were to "go."

Cornelia tottered to the last cell. A light inside; the occupant was sitting on his cot, with the table drawn up before him, writing one of his farewell letters. He heard a faint cry, "Bart!" and started and shoved the table away. "Nonna!" A second more and he was at the door, his arm through the bars; Cornelia ran to him—it was automatic, no way to help it—

and anyhow, the warden was holding her, and not trying to hold her back. She clasped the outstretched hand and wrung it; that hand which so many times she had held in friendship, which had performed for her so many services of love; a hand toil-worn and bruised, now emaciated, but still warm with life. Three hours more and it would be cold, a piece of death and corruption. She let it go, and sank into the chair which had been placed for her, behind the painted line.

"Bart, I had to see you to say good-by!"

"I am so glad, Nonna! It is the one more thing I wanted."

"We have done everything we could, Bart, but it is no use."

"I know. Mr. Thompson was here, he has just been going. We had a long talk."

"I have an hour to stay with you, Bart; the Governor granted me that favor."

"I will leave you, Mrs. Thornwell," said the warden. "I will have to ask you not to cross the line again. You understand, we have rules, and they must be enforced."

"I know," said Cornelia; "I will respect your wishes." She had heard the prison stories—they had permitted one condemned man to receive a roast chicken from a relative, and it had contained a loaded revolver. "Thank you, Mr. Hendry." She was as sorry for him as for his captives.

VIII

A guard sat at the entrance to the corridor, fifteen feet from Cornelia's chair. He could hear everything that was said, but neither she nor Bart heeded him. This was like being alone with God; this was different from human life, where people met, and would meet again by and by. "We have failed, Bart," she whispered, and he said, in a voice without a quiver: "Do not worry for me, Nonna, I am ready. Nick also is ready. We will die as anarchists should."

The light in Sacco's cell had been out; he turned it on, and lay on his cot with his face to the bars, so that he could hear the conversation. "Hello, Nick," said Cornelia. He answered, with his quick sympathy and consideration for others: "You are too unhappy for us, Nonna. Take it more easy! Plenty fellow have die." She imagined the twinkle in his eyes—even though now she could see only one eye through the narrow slits. She could see Vanzetti's whole face, because he was standing at the door, and at that height there was a bend in the bars, making an opening through which he could look.

"Nonna," he said, "it is more easy to die than to look out through bars like a beast for seven years."

"Bart, I am going to fight for your good name the rest of my time."

"Fight for the workers, Nonna; fight so they be free, that other people do not live idle on their hard toil."

"I will surely do that," she answered; "but most of all I want to be able to tell people about this case. Tell me the truth, Bart, now that it is the end."

Said Vanzetti: "I will speak like I would if it was God. I am an innocent man, Nonna; I was never at the South Braintree crime, I was never at the Bridgewater crime. I tell you that in solemn words, for you to say to all the world, all the time, forever. And Nick, he is innocent, he was never at South Braintree like they said. This is the truth, as I hope for joostice, I did never take a umane life, I did never anything that would take umane life, and I work with all my soul for those day when it will not be possible ever for one umane being to kill any other, when all such wickedness and machines for killing lives will be destroyed from the earth. It is because I know that the class system and exploiting of labor is what make such machines to be that I am anarchist. I am against all government, because I know it is tool of exploiting classes, it is not to make joostice in this world, but to make slaves, and to punish the libertarians—as they prove this night upon the bodies of Nick and me."

There was a pause. When Cornelia spoke again her voice was grave, and her words came slowly, carefully. "Bart, I mean to write what you tell me, so the world will know it. May I say that with reflection and these many years of study, you have changed your views about violence in the class struggle?"

Vanzetti's answer also came slowly. "You may say I do not wish vee-olence, Nonna. All my life I suffer torture when I think of vee-olence committed upon one body or one soul. But I read the history of all, and this I see, never have the slaves been free because the master was generous; always it is because the slave made some struggle, he made fight for his right. Is it not so?"

"It has been so in the past. But may we not hope for some better way? Think, Bart, before you answer that."

"I think always, Nonna, it is one thought that I have all my life. I look at the great cruel capitalism—do I think that will give way without fighting? Look this night—Mr. Thompson has told me what he see outside. They make so many thousands, millions—machine-guns, bullets, gas bombs, artilleries—every day new inventions—you think they do not use them? You wish me to say to the worker, 'You need no fear, you need no preparing for slaughter?' Shall I say to the young worker, 'You do not need arming your souls for martyrdom, like Sacco and Vanzetti; Sacco and Vanzetti will be the last martyrs'—can I say that? No, Nonna, I have to say, it will be thousand of martyrs, perhaps millions, it will be most bloody slaughter, before the master class is thrown down, before the workers own the tools and the riches without any master."

"So that is what I must tell, Bart?"

"That is what all must tell, else I would be traitor, and not good guide for workers; else they would say, 'Vanzetti has lost his nerve, they have broke him.' Never will they say that, for me or for Nick."

"Never!" cried Nick, with his mouth to the bars. "They say we died anarchista."

"There may be some who wish to avenge your death, Bart, and that would be a dreadful thing, nothing would set back the cause so much. What shall I say about that?"

"Say that I want no such thing, Nonna, we are not such a man to be revenged; we are humble for our cause. What we want is joostice for the worker, freedom for all men on this earth, and we want every libertarian work for that, and not for us, nor for vengeance, which is a wicked thing."

"May I say that you forgive your enemies, Bart?"

There was a long silence. "Is it a thing that should be forgiven, Nonna—what men has been doing to us?"

"Men are ignorant, Bart—"

"These men are not ignorant, Nonna! Do you think that Judge Thayer is ignorant of what he did? When he call us foul name such as I not like to say before lady, is he ignorant?"

"I think so, Bart; he is one of the most pitiable of human creatures. Think if I were to put it to you, would you have your body free, and be shut up in the narrow dungeon of that man's mind? Would you consent to be mean, to be a cheat, and eaten up with hatred? When you realize what a blessing has been yours in life, to have the vision, to know the future as you do—can you not pity the poor wretch who lives in darkness of the soul, and behaves like some cruel animal, not a man?"

There was a long silence. Cornelia looked at the face, with its frame of steel bars; it was emaciated, deeply lined by suffering; the dark-brown walrus mustaches drooped, and were partly hidden by the bars. "Remember, Bart, what Comrade Jesus said. He forgave the men who nailed him to the cross."

"Sure, Nonna, that I can do! Poor fellows in this prison, who are workers too, they have maybe wife and children, how can they stop the evil thing? Many man in this prison knows what I believe, many do not like to take life for the big capitalistas."

"But the big capitalistas, the men who give the orders, Bart? The judge, the governor, the college president?"

Again a long pause. "I will think about it, Nonna. I would not tell you anything but truth, and it is not easy thing for me to say what you want to hear."

IX

They talked about the fearsome yet fascinating question of where Bart was to be in two or three hours. "I don't know, Nonna," he said. "It is strange idea. If I wake up somewhere, I be very much surprised. What you think?"

"I cannot guess," she said.

"I think we go back where we come from. It is like a bubble that go back to be water again. This face, this voice, this what you call Vanzetti, I do not think it will be like that anywhere."

There came a voice from between the next row of bars: "That is all bunk!" (Sacco had not been in America for nineteen years in vain.) "When you are dead, you are dead, you no wake up. For us it come quick, I like quicker. It is what I beg them long time ago."

Cornelia turned to the speaker. "Is there anything I can do for you, Nick?"

"Take care of wife and kids."

"You may be sure of that; they will not suffer want."

"I don't worry for that," said Nick, the free-spoken. "If all I want was easy time for them, I would made it myself. Teach the kids what we die for, make them some sense. That is it."

A pause, and then from the far cell a timid voice: "Good-by, lady."

"Good-by, Madeiros. Can I do anything to help you?"

"I am not like these fellows," he said. "I done what they got me for, I deserved it. But they don't, they are good men; some day it will be known." The voice was slow and drawling, marred by only a slight accent. Cornelia did not see the speaker, but she had met him before: a thin, undernourished young fellow with a weak but amiable face and small dark mustache. He was only twenty-one, and the doctors said he was a half-wit; the job for which he was to die was the killing of a bank-cashier in a robbery. He admitted it, and some other crimes.

Had he really been at South Braintree, or had he just climbed onto the Sacco-Vanzetti band-wagon at the last moment, with a faint hope of respite? Cornelia had never been able to make up her mind about that. She had watched a curious little drama going on—Madeiros looked up to Sacco and Vanzetti, as to social superiors; they were great men, celebrities, and he was proud to be associated with them. Sacco accepted his homage, but Vanzetti was extremely reserved. The young Portuguese never stopped insisting that both were innocent, and that he was the only guilty man.

Vanzetti spoke about Luigia, and what a joy it had been to see her—but hard for her; such crowds, such excitement, and a terrible end. He had tried to explain to his sister what it was to die as a martyr, not the same as a criminal. She ought to have been able to understand, because she believed in Jesus; but Jesus to her was something far away and terrifying, to be dealt with by the priests. A wicked thing, that ecclesiastical system, which enslaved the minds of the poor, and made the name of God something which libertarians could not speak.

The prison authorities had been pleading with Sacco and Vanzetti to let a priest or some kind of clergyman administer to them. It seemed to the authorities dreadful to kill men and have their souls go to hell! It was the first time the thing had happened in eighteen years, so they said. But the three men stood firm—Madeiros taking a chance with the others. They would never surrender the integrity of their minds. "Giammai!" cried Nick; and added: "That says, 'Not on your life,' Nonna." He was gay, being soon to get the freedom which he had craved for so many years. Impossible to crush that spirit of steel springs; and for the body, even though weakened by confinement and fasting, they would need an extra voltage.

X

Cornelia wore a wrist-watch, and every now and then her glance would be drawn towards it. The minute-hand seemed to be stealing time from her, it would take jumps when she was not watching. Vanzetti sat on his cot, and peering with one eye through the bars, saw a tear stealing down the old woman's cheek. "Nonna," he exclaimed, quickly, "I want you do something for me."

"What is it, Bart?"

"Something very great, a last thing—something hard."

"Tell me."

"I want you to not be sad."

"Oh, Bart!"

"It is easy to die. It is little thing—only for friends, for so many women, grieving, weeping. It is—what you say, futile. Is most futile thing in the whole world to have grief. Is it not so?"

"Yes, Bart—but—"

"Listen. I speak for all three. We are soldiers. It is our business to die. What for do you weep? It is our job."

"I will try, Bart."

Vanzetti's voice had taken on a note of sternness that Cornelia had heard a few times, when in his imagination he was going to battle with the capitalist class. "You remember, Nonna, we publish book, our gruppo, 'Faccia à Faccia col Nemico.' All right. It is what we are now. It is our dream, it is our life. What for do we ask you to weep? Coraggio! Coraggio!" He went back to his childhood language when he was deeply moved; and his voice stiffened Cornelia's bent spine.

"Amica mia, you have been good soul to us. You have done more than help, you have onderstood. Now onderstand once again—is it too much?"

"I will do my best."

"We choose this death. Long ago we know it, we see him come. You be anarchista militante, you die. You die by hangman of capitalist class. All right, we choose. Every man have got to die, it is no great news, it happen each day. Poor workingmen, rich capitalistas, all. But to live forever, that is not so easy; to speak to all the world—how many time do it happen to poor workingmen? To a couple of wops? Did ever you hear such thing?"

"No, Bart, you are right."

"Our life, it has been success; it is victory, like never we have dream. Men stop, they say, 'What is this anarchist? What is this men believe, that they die so glad? What is this joostice? Have I got it? Have I got freedom, or am I slave like they tell me?' He ask, and he begin to think—million men begin to think—it is something your great Go-vérnor give us, something he cannot take! Our crown, our victory! Is it not so?"

"Yes, yes, Bart!"

"Viva l'anarchia!" came the voice of Nick.

"Our bodies they kill, they make our souls immortal. Young workers take up our cry—you see, Nonna, only wait, it grows all over the world, the revolt of the worker, the message that men be free, that they work for joostice, not for parasite. And we have helped, we have done a part. Only one thing more to do, is to die brave; to walk to the chair, smile, speak the truth to the end. So, amica mia, help us; no sad thought, only coraggio! Tell our friends it is joy, not grief, it is success, not failure."

There is a contagion that spreads in human souls, and shakes the thrones of emperors and kings. Cornelia's hands were clenched and her teeth set. "All right, Bart, I will do what you say. I will be with you to the end, and afterwards."

The warden stood in the doorway; and Cornelia rose to her feet, not waiting for him to help her. "All right, Mr. Hendry, I am ready. I have had a worthwhile hour. May I shake hands with my boys once more?"

"Yes, Mrs. Thornwell." He came to help her, but she did not wait for him. She took Vanzetti's hand in a firm, strong grip. "Good-by, for the last time, Bart. You have taught me more than any of the great persons I have met in my life. I shall remember every word you said to me."

"Good-by, Nonna. I thank you. Thank you for the good help."

"Good-by, Nick. You have been a brave fellow. You have done your job."

"Good-by, Nonna. Good-by to wife and kids. Teach them for me—what I believe."

Then Madeiros. He put out his hand, and Cornelia made no difference between a hero and a criminal. "Good-by, my son. I hope the next world treats you better than this one."

"Good-by, lady." He was a timid bank robber, who found this an incomprehensible world. Anarchists sought to overthrow the rich, and then the rich came to shake their hands!

Cornelia went to the door. The guard had risen, ready to help her if need be; but she was doing her stunt. "Thank you, Mr. Hendry, these three soldiers have given me back my strength." She turned, and called: "Good-by, dear friends! Good luck to you—and to your cause!" To a chorus of good-by shouts in English and Italian she walked through the death-chamber, past the chair with the gaping arms and the dangling leather straps; her little head held high, her steps firm and proud. Through the prison yard she went, steady, amid the beams of the drunken searchlights, staggering this way and that; past the cell-blocks, with white faces looking out, eight hundred and eighty-one human beasts, roaring now and then, "Let them out!" Into the warden's home, and through the front door; through the group of policemen, and into the waiting car with the anxious women.

"Mother! Mother!" They started to make a fuss, after the fashion of families. She sank back in the seat and whispered, "Let me be quiet! I have been talking with God."

That happens also to families in Boston now and then. They

thought, "It has been too much for her mind!" and were frightened into silence. They could not realize how this strange idea would haunt the minds of men all over the world in this dreadful hour. John Haynes Holmes, a clergyman, formerly of Boston, was writing at that moment a "Ballad of Charlestown Gaol":

> *There's a chair for you, Vanzetti,*
> *In a cold and empty room;*
> *A chair aloof and lonely,*
> *Like a spectre in the gloom;*
> *A chair with open arms and wide,*
> *To welcome you to doom.*
>
> *They've made this chair, Vanzetti—*
> *Good men, and strong, and true—*
> *To manifest the will of God*
> *On poor men such as you;*
> *To show the Lord Christ lives again—*
> *And dies, the Lord Christ, too!*

CHAPTER 24

THE TRIUMPH

I

EVEN at that late hour there were men and women who could not make up their minds to let Sacco and Vanzetti die. There were protestants who would not cease marching. In Salem Street, in the North End of Boston, a thousand or more Italians gathered, declaring their intention to march to the Bunker Hill monument and hold a meeting during the execution. Mike Crowley's mounted men charged into the midst of them, scattering them in every direction, crushing many. The same thing happened in Thompson Square, and in the roped-off area near the prison. Here seven men and women broke through the police lines, singing the "International," and lifting their printed protests, in defiance of all that military might. "Hail, Sacco and Vanzetti! The élite of the world salute you as heroes!" One of the seven was a war veteran, and when the police fell upon him, "Oh, boy," they cried, "wait till we get you in jail!" A traitor to the army system, they would teach him a lesson he would remember! They beat three men, one of them insensible, the others nearly so.

Also there was another campaign before the Governor—at half-past ten at night. William G. Thompson had come down from his vacation in New Hampshire, and was making an appeal, based on the Governor's fixed prejudice concerning Vanzetti at the Plymouth trial. Over and over again, for months, Fuller had been talking about the fact that Vanzetti had not taken the stand in his own behalf. That very morning he had voiced dark rumors about Vahey and Graham, the lawyers who had defended Vanzetti at Plymouth; if they were not bound by the code which forbids lawyers to betray a client, they could tell dreadful things about Vanzetti.

730

The substance of this proposition had been telephoned to William G. Thompson, up in New Hampshire, and he had motored to Boston, and gone to see Vanzetti early in the evening—a long conference, the substance of which he later published in the *Atlantic Monthly*. He asked if Vanzetti would be willing to permit Vahey to tell the truth about the case, and his dealings with his clients. The answer was Vanzetti's usual charge, as to how his case had been conducted, which he was certain had cost him his life. Now the lawyer came to see Governor Fuller, bringing Vanzetti's message, that he was willing for Vahey to say anything he knew, provided that the interview took place in the presence of Thompson, or some other friend in whom Vanzetti had confidence. So now the way was open to a "show-down," and would the Governor follow his own suggestion? Surely fair play required that!

The answer of Fuller was to make no answer—a trick which public personages have to learn. Silence! Out there on the other side of the Charles River was a miniature army on duty, and a prison staff about to put those wops out of the world, so that Fuller and his class could "sleep better." All traffic stopped over main highways between the two cities; thousands of persons, living near the prison, illegally shut up in their homes for the night; a million dollars invested by Boston merchants and manufacturers in riot and bomb insurance; the newspaper wires run into the prison, the witnesses summoned, the traveling expenses of the executioner incurred for the second time—and all that trouble and expense to be brought to nought, while the Governor carried on a debate with a bunch of "meddlesome Matties" in secret sympathy with terrorists! In the formula which had been current in the sporting world when "Allie" Fuller was a bicycle-racer: "Not on your tin-type!"

II

At a quarter before midnight William G. Thompson came out from the Governor's chamber, and to the waiting reporters expressed his solemn conviction that innocent men were about to be executed. A strange event—a great lawyer breaking the rule of his lifetime, defying Boston legal proprieties and "trying the case in the newspapers!" He would give a long interview, defending his clients, and telling the Vahey episode, and much of what Vanzetti had said to him in prison.

Meantime—even at that hour—one more protest! Francis Fisher Kane, former U. S. Attorney for Pennsylvania, had been waiting for two hours to see the Governor to make one last appeal concerning the Department of Justice files. He persuaded the doorman to take in his card, and the Governor granted five minutes. Mr. Kane presented a fact which had just come to his knowledge; President Lowell had stated to a friend that the files were of no significance, and could not have affected the decision of his Commission. Mr. Kane now strove to make this matter clear to the Governor. The files would show that the Department of Justice had been watching Sacco and Vanzetti by means of "informers," considering them as dangerous anarchists. Mr. Kane himself knew exactly what that meant, having been a Federal prosecutor, in charge of the watching of certain anarchists; he had resigned his position, in protest against the things he saw being done during the "Red raids." He could certify that Sacco and Vanzetti had had good reason to be afraid for their lives on the night of their arrest; and thus that famous "consciousness of guilt" theory of Judge Thayer was knocked out. The arrested men had a kind of guilt to be conscious of, entirely different from that of the South Braintree crime!

So the lawyer argued; and it was like water falling upon a granite stone. For seven years the authorities of Massachusetts had had these facts before them, and had resolutely shut their eyes; the reason being that, in their secret hearts, they desired the death of anarchists quite as ardently as the death of bandits.

The telephone ringing; the group of New York lawyers who had set out to try to reach Williamstown by motor-car, but realized that it was too late. John Finerty on the wire, to beg the Governor, in the name of common decency, to put off the execution for just a couple of hours, until they could reach Judge Anderson and see if he would act upon their appeal. The Governor's answer was that Mr. Finerty should communicate with Attorney-General Reading, who was in charge of legal matters that night. Mr. Finerty called Mr. Reading's office and learned that Mr. Reading had gone to the Governor's office about the matter. He called the Governor's office and

learned that Mr. Reading had gone back to his own office. He
called Mr. Reading's office and learned that Mr. Reading had
not arrived. Astonishing agility on the part of a high official,
in spite of his pockets being stuffed with the money of the
Decimo Club and the "L. A. W." and other corporations which
feared trouble from the legal department of the great Commonwealth! Mr. Finerty was not able to hear Mr. Reading's
voice.

The weary Governor rose from his desk, and put on his
hat. It had been a strain; his face was drawn with exhaustion—
impossible to conceal it now. "No statement, boys," to the newspaper men. His guards closed about him, and he went down to
his Packard car, under the Mt. Vernon Street arch of the State
House, closed all that day to traffic. The guards saluted, they
fell back and dropped the ropes; a police-car in front, another
in the rear, with riot-guns ready for instant action—the little
procession rolled out into the night, on its way to the summer
home in New Hampshire.

III

Cornelia, returned to her apartment, found Betty waiting.
So she sent off her daughters and son-in-law. "I am perfectly
all right now. That visit was what I needed. No use to keep
you up. Thanks for what you did, it made everything all right."
She lay on the bed, and told Betty about her visit, and every
word that had been spoken. Betty told about the meeting she
had attended, and how the crowds were behaving. It was like
war time, tens of thousands of people in front of the bulletin
boards; and when some item of bad news came, you would
hear a moan, a sob of mass-agony. Apparently the public was
beginning to realize—at the last moment—too late!

"I am going to be able to stand it, Betty. I have got to
stand it, for Bart's sake." Betty was glad to hear it; she was
prepared to carry her own burden, but no more. "Yes, yes, it's
all right," the old woman went on. "It is what Bart and Nick
wanted." But even as she said it, there was a trembling at the
lips, and a look of terror in her eyes.

An hour and more still to be passed. Betty began hastily
to tell the news. She had stopped at headquarters: she told

who was there, but dodged away from describing the weeping and anguish. Powers Hapgood had been missing for hours, and word had just come that he was shut up in "Psychopathic"; Joe Randall had hurried off to fetch Dr. Myerson, to get Powers out. Creighton Hill had made a trip to Maine, with two clergymen, to get another clergyman to make an affidavit concerning Thayer's prejudice. But Fuller wouldn't pay any attention to it, of course.

Cornelia was only half hearing. "Betty, do you suppose the Governor can be meaning to put it off again?"

"I don't know, Grannie. How can you tell, with that beast?" Never if they lived a thousand years would the women of the defense forgive him for the night of anguish he had caused them, by withholding the reprieve until twenty minutes before the time for the execution.

Gossip wouldn't do, Betty realized; she must tap the deeper layers of the human soul. "Man's extremity is God's opportunity," so the evangelists tell us; now Betty Alvin, hard and grim little realist, must become a prophet and a saint, like Bart! She must point out that stone walls do not a prison make, and how they that kill the body only glorify the soul. She must make real to both her grandmother and herself what this night's events would mean to the future; a consecration to the radical movement, a purifying of the faith of all of them, a spiritual rebirth for Boston. "Oh, Betty, is it really so? Won't they forget all about it, and go back to their radios and their jazz?"

"Some will, Grannie; but some of us aren't going to forget this long fight."

"Seven years!" Cornelia whispered. "Seven years!"

Betty answered that it had taken those years to make the case; to get public attention centered on it, to get the great ones of Boston to notice two wops. "Don't you see what it's for, Grannie—to dramatize the class struggle! To make it so plain that every child can see it! To make it into a formula, that you can say in three words, and have everybody understand it —everywhere, all over the world, for all future time! 'Sacco and Vanzetti!' And right here in our great and prosperous America, that is making so many automobiles and bathtubs and books of etiquette! Right here in Boston, that is so moral!

Don't you see how important it is to have the capitalist class electrocute its own lies?"

"Betty! Betty! When will men stop killing?"

"When we end exploitation, Grannie dear; and Bart and Nick are doing the job! Don't you see the glory of this case—it kills off the liberals! Before this, it was possible to argue that injustice was an accident, just an oversight—in a country that was so busy making automobiles and bathtubs and books of etiquette! But now here's a test—we settle the question forever! We take our very best—not merely cheap politicians, but our great ones! Our biggest business man! Our most cultured university president! Our supreme court judges—even the liberal ones! We prove them all alike—they all know what flag they fight under, who serves out their rations! They all take their places in the ranks, with every button in position, and all of them washed behind the ears! They all obey the great capitalist drill-sergeant, and not a man deserts to the enemy—not one single man!"

A quarter to twelve. "Betty, if they were going to put it off, they'd have had to say so by now."

"Yes, blessed dear, I'm afraid so."

"And somebody would have let us know!"

"Yes, surely they would."

"They'll let us know when it's over?"

"Joe promised he'd phone at once." Then, in desperation: "Grannie, did you hear about the necklace which Bart gave to Mr. Thompson? He took the ten dollars you sent him, and bought some things the prisoners had made, and gave Mr. Thompson a necklace of beads for his wife, and Mr. Thompson broke down and cried. They say he can't talk about it without crying. It'll ruin him as a lawyer."

"Bart and Nick were right about it all along," said Cornelia. "They knew more about Boston than we did."

"That is something that touched Mr. Thompson. Nick had insisted he'd never get anywhere with the courts, and to-day Mr. Thompson thought that Nick would remind him of it. But Nick didn't say a word; he knew how much it would hurt."

Twelve o'clock. Cornelia, white-faced, her hands clasped together, and her voice a faint whimper. "Betty, they must be in the death-chamber now."

"Yes, I suppose so. Remember what you promised Bart!"

"I know, I know—but I wonder—how long does it take?"

"Not very long, dear, they make it quick, they are as polite as Fuller."

But somehow that wasn't the right thing to say. Betty caught the poor trembling hands, and began to whisper: "Grannie, dear, don't let yourself go! We all need our strength, we have a whole world to change."

"All right, I won't, I won't! How long does—how long do they keep the current on?"

"I don't know, two or three minutes. But the victims don't know it, so what's the use thinking about such things!"

"They must be doing it now! Oh, Betty—tell me something to think about!"

"They are brave men, Grannie. They have lived the life they wanted to live, and they don't want us crying over them. Think of all the people who get killed—so many in needless ways—that we can put a stop to when we have learned what Bart and Nick have to teach us." So Betty, rushing on, a little stump-speech—but all in vain. She had to keep squeezing the poor frail hands, and saying over and over again the simple elemental idea, that Bart had forbidden Cornelia to grieve, and she had promised not to. After all, Bart's life was his own, and if he chose to become one of the world's great martyrs, who had a right to object?

IV

Cornelia could be got to listen to that, to sit staring, like a hypnotized rabbit. The trouble was that the clock on the mantel-piece became hypnotized, too, and the hands refused to move; all time stood still, there was no way to get it past. The world hung suspended in a void of suffering—that very hell which Father Murphy, the prison chaplain, had been telling about, where pain endured forever.

Some magic spell had been woven over the minds and souls of tens of thousands, perhaps millions of persons, scattered over every part of the earth; never had there been such a phenomenon since the world began. They sat in rooms and stared at each other, they stood in front of bulletin boards and clenched their hands, or maybe bit their finger-nails; they went walking blindly about the streets, not knowing where. In whatever part of the world they might be—in Boston or Los Angeles, Buenos Ayres or Paris or Tokio—they had figured the time, and were saying the same words as Cornelia Thornwell: "They must be doing it now! They must have them in the chair! How long does the current take?" And one and all they noticed that extraordinary phenomenon—time stood still, minutes refused to pass as they normally should.

The telephone ringing; Betty had to let go of her grandmother's hands to take the receiver. Cornelia watched her face, reading the fates there. No need to hear a word; Cornelia knew it was Joe, and he was saying, "It's all over." "Yes, sweetheart," said Betty, in a voice as even as if she were accepting an invitation for lunch. "Yes, we're all right. Grannie went over and had a talk with them both, and she's feeling stronger. But you'd better come home right away—yes, dear, we might need you. Please do." She hung up quickly, so that Joe might not hear the dreadful burst of anguish from the poor old woman on the bed.

Betty dug under the wasted body, and got hold of the hands, and made the agonized soul sit up and look at her. "Grannie, listen to me now! You don't realize—it's all over! Stop and think what that means—Bart and Nick can't suffer any more! Nobody can punish them, nobody can torture them—ever again! They aren't in jail! They are free!"

So on and on, until the idea did actually penetrate Cornelia's mind. The sobbing ceased, and she sat staring ahead of her, as if at an apparition in the room. "It is really so! They can't do any more to them!"

"Grannie, blessed dear, it is what Nick has been saying all along, and we never had sense enough to realize it! Their job is done, and they are all right!"

v

At ten o'clock the chief electrician and his assistant had tested the death chair and pronounced everything in order. Then came the executioner, to make his inspection. Elliot was this gentleman's name; he preferred a retired life, on account of anarchist bombs, but the clamor of newspapers had brought him into the limelight; they published his picture, and a list of the human beings he had killed. The "false execution" of twelve days ago had compelled him to make a journey for nothing; very annoying, and he was hoping that now there would be no hitch, he would get his seven hundred and fifty dollars.

Father Murphy came to the death cells, to make his last offer of eternal life. Absolutely without charge, and merely by a few passes of the hands and the speaking of a few words, he was willing to deliver these three men from the otherwise certain fate of perpetual roasting upon a brimstone and sulphur fire. Nearly three hundred years ago the philosopher Pascal had presented an unanswerable argument on the subject: the procedure would do you great good if it were valid, and no harm if it were not valid. But Vanzetti answered that it would do harm to those whom he left on earth, to be more tightly riveted in the chains of superstition. So, a few minutes before midnight, Father Murphy went to the officers' club of the prison and remarked to the newspapermen, "There seems to be nothing for me to do, so I am going home."

That clubroom was like the "pit" in the stock exchange, with more than a hundred reporters scrambling for every scrap of news. Many telephones were installed, and eighteen telegraphers sat at eighteen machines, to feed the curiosity of a ravenous world. The service included direct cable connections with all the other five continents. The representative of the Associated Press had been honored by an invitation to witness the execution, and was pledged to furnish the details to his colleagues.

There were, according to law, a number of official witnesses, whose duty it was to certify to the Governor that his orders had been carried out. They were in readiness, and the warden now led them to the death-house. Chairs were lined against the wall of the execution chamber, facing the electric chair, and the worthies took their seats. The big warden, with plump round face and little black mustache and narrow slits for eyes; a well-known Boston surgeon; the physician of the prison; the surgeon general of the national guard, who looked like a college professor; the medical examiner of Suffolk County, who looked like a romantic poet with tousled hair; the sheriff of Norfolk County, a bald-headed, stern-faced old Puritan, who had had Sacco in charge for seven years, and Vanzetti off and on, at great expense to his office—he was one of those who had expressed their sentiment by piling up the desk of Judge Thayer with flowers, on the day that learned jurist delivered his charge to the Dedham jury, and explained the nobility of loyalty.

There was a telephone against the wall of the execution chamber, and the representative of the Associated Press took his stand by it; the wire ran to the warden's office, and from there a telegraph operator would relay every word to the crowd of reporters. In this way they would learn when each man entered the death chamber, when the current was turned on, and when the death was officially announced. Later the "A.P. man" would go over to the officers' club and give the details.

The executioner stood behind a screen in one corner, to the left of the death chair; he could look over the screen, and see when it was time for him to earn his money. Two guards stood by the door leading to the cell corridor, and when the warden signaled that all was ready, they stepped back to the first cell, and unlocked the door. Madeiros lay asleep—not setting much value upon his last moments. The guards awakened him, stood him on his feet, and led him, half dazed, into the execution chamber, closing the door behind them, out of kindness for the occupants of the other two cells.

The victim had on short gray trousers, with a slit cut up each leg, and a blue shirt with short sleeves, made especially for the occasion. He was seated in the chair, and as quickly as possible the deputy warden and a guard buckled the straps which would hold his hands and feet immovable. The electrodes, from which the current was to enter the body, were fastened, one to each leg, and a third, the headpiece, covering the entire top of the head; they contained wet sponges, to afford perfect transmission.

They tied a bandage over the victim's eyes, and then stepped back; all was ready. It was the warden's part to signal with his hand to the executioner, who would then move a switch. Since this did the actual killing, the theory was that the executioner alone was responsible, and for carrying this heavy responsibility the Commonwealth paid him the sum of two hundred and fifty dollars for each of three motions of the hand—plus traveling expenses from his retreat in New York.

He made the first motion, and there was a whir of the current, and the body of Madeiros gave a sudden leap, which would have jerked it from the chair if it had not been that the straps were heavy. Human flesh became of the rigidity of steel, and stayed that way for several minutes, with a current of nineteen hundred volts passing through it. A ghastly odor of burning hair spread through the death chamber.

The current was turned off, the body sank back limp into the chair, and the warden signed to the medical examiners, who stepped forward with their stethoscopes. At nine minutes and thirty-five seconds past midnight they pronounced the Wrentham bank robber dead, and the body was lifted from the chair and carried to one of three newly painted slabs hidden behind a screen in the death chamber. Nothing could exceed the sense of propriety of the great Commonwealth of Massachusetts, or the decency with which it prepared for the elimination of its enemies.

VI

The door leading to the cells was opened again, and the two guards went in to the second cell. Nicola Sacco was not asleep, but waiting, to do his last duty as a revolutionist. He walked out between the guards; he entered the execution chamber, and looked about him at the row of solemn witnesses, the deputies, the chair, and the screen with the face peering over it. His own face was white and haggard, his lips set, his whole expression that of defiance. He walked directly to the chair and sat down; then, as the guards began to adjust the straps, he lifted himself slightly, raised his voice, and said, in what came as a shout in that still brick-walled chamber of death: "Viva l'anarchia!"

("You see!" said all Massachusetts, when they read about it with their morning coffee and codfish balls. "We told you so! We knew it all along!")

The guards paid no attention to any words. They went on with swift fingers, as if they feared that some one might come to stop them at the last moment. When they were through, and stepped back, Sacco opened his lips again, and the warden withheld the signal. "Farewell, my wife and children and all my friends!" Then, as the warden was in the act of lifting his hand: "Good evening, gentlemen. Farewell, Mother."

The cue was given, and the executioner moved the switch, and the body leaped so that it was like a blow against the straps. Twenty-one hundred volts was the executioner's estimate of what it would take to rid Massachusetts of this wiry peasant; the amperage was from seven to nine, and it was nineteen minutes and two seconds after midnight when the medical examiners pronounced the duty done. The body of Nicola Sacco was lifted from the chair, and carried behind the screen and laid upon the second slab.

Then for the third and last time the door into the cell corridor was opened, and the guards entered. Bartolomeo Vanzetti had sat upon his cot alone, knowing what was happening in the adjoining chamber, but it had not shaken his nerve; he had had seven years in which to work out his system of self-discipline. "This is our career and our triumph." He rose from his cot, and walked with firm steps, the guards holding him, one by each arm. When they entered the execution chamber, the guards released him, and he looked at them—men whom he had known for a long time, and whom he had taught to respect him, no longer to call him a wop. They were poor fellows, who maybe had wives and children to keep, and could not help what they were doing; so he turned to them first, as became a proletarian martyr. "Good-by," he said to each, and held out his hand to each in turn, and shook their hands firmly.

Then he turned to Deputy Warden Hogsett, and took both his hands and wrung them. "Good-by, I thank you for your courtesy to me." And then to the warden, a big towering figure. Vanzetti was quiet and at ease, as if he were welcoming visitors to his home. "Warden, I want to thank you for all that you have done for me." He held out his hand, and the warden took it.

("Jesus!" he said, to one of the reporters afterwards. "He shook my hand, and then I had to raise it to give the signal!")

Vanzetti walked to the chair and sat down. Then he spoke—

words which he had made the subject of much thought. "I wish to tell you that I am innocent and never committed any crime, but sometimes some sin. I thank you for everything you have done for me. I am innocent of all crime, not only of this one, but of all. I am an innocent man."

The guards, well trained, went on with their work, paying no attention to eloquence. The electrodes were adjusted, the straps made fast. As a guard started to apply the bandage to Vanzetti's eyes, he spoke again; it was the question which Cornelia had asked him, and to which he had promised an answer. He gave it with all the world for an audience. "I wish to forgive some people for what they are now doing to me."

The guards stepped back, and the warden gave the signal; the executioner moved the switch, and the body of Bartolomeo Vanzetti leaped as the others had done. Nineteen hundred and fifty volts were estimated to be sufficient for this less robust person, a dreamer and a man of words rather than of action. Many, many words he had both spoken and written, but now no more. The current was turned off, and the medical men made their examination, and at twenty-six minutes and fifty-five seconds past midnight they pronounced that the last spark of anarchism had been extinguished from the august Commonwealth of Massachusetts. The warden had a solemn formula to recite, but his voice almost failed him, and not all the witnesses heard the words: "Under the law I now pronounce you dead, the sentence of the court having been legally carried out."

The third body was laid on the slab, and the doors of the execution chamber were opened—it had grown very hot, with the many volts of electricity and the tense emotions of martyrs. Also, the odor of burned hair made one ill; the night breeze was very welcome. The guards and witnesses went outside, and wiped the sweat from their foreheads, and from the backs of their wilted collars. "Christ!" said the deputy warden. "Did you hear what he said? He forgave me! Now what do you make of that?"

VII

The representative of the Associated Press hastened to the officers' club. Not often does one man carry a message to the whole world. He entered the room with the hundred ravening reporters, and had to mount a chair so that all might have an equal chance to hear. "No features," he said. "Entirely colorless." The proper professional air; if his "assignment" had been Mount Calvary, he would have said the same. If Jesus had raised a row at the last moment—if he had tried to escape, and had knocked down the captain of the centurions—that would have been "hot news." Or if he had cursed God, instead of merely asking why God had forsaken him. Obvious enough that God would not pay any attention to the leader of a Jewish rabble, a common workingman, born in a stable in the flea-infested village of Bethlehem!

So likewise this death of Sacco and Vanzetti—"no features." No, they hadn't confessed—except that Sacco had confessed to being an anarchist. He had cried: "Viva l'anarchia!" ("How the hell do you spell it? Has it got a 'k'?"). No one had collapsed, or made what you would call a scene. Sacco's complexion had been white, you might almost say green. ("The way Mary Splaine described him—I remember at the Dedham trial.") Vanzetti had shaken hands with everybody, very politely. ("Anarchist propaganda! A grandstand play!") He had said—the bored correspondent consulted his bunch of papers, on which he had jotted down a few words—he said that he forgave everybody—no, it was "some people." ("The little infant Jesus! Ain't they lambs, these Reds?")

The room was gray with tobacco smoke, an inferno of heat—the windows having been boarded up, for fear somebody might "throw something in." The clamor was deafening—the clicking of eighteen telegraph keys, and the voices of men shouting over the telephones, each trying to hear himself above the uproar—that competition which is the life of capitalism. Men standing against the wall scribbling, or writing on their knees, each hoping to file his words the first. The three big press associations would take care of the main outlines of the news for all the papers of the country; they had already sent three "flashes" on each execution; now they would follow with details. But a hundred papers had sent special correspondents, and these pleaded for "human interest stuff," hounding those who had witnessed the events.

The warden had gone to his office; he was gray, and the

perspiration could not be kept from his forehead, nor the trembling from his whole body. He invited his deputy to have a drink with him, and opened his cupboard for the purpose; but there entered Mike Crowley with the police commissioner, a blue-blood, appointed by the Governor. The warden didn't think it quite right for that high-up personage to see him indulging his appetite at this moment, so he hastily shut the cupboard door again. He had to sit down in a chair. The deputy kept saying: "He shook both my hands! And he forgave me! I never saw such a thing! I couldn't conceive of it!"

The news was spread by a thousand telegraph wires, and in a hundred cities great crowds learned it from the bulletin boards of newspapers; for the most part in silence, but sometimes with groans and sobs. The Boston *Evening Transcript* had kept its broadcasting station open—radio WBET—entertaining the listeners with music and miscellaneous news all evening. The comfortable population of New England sat in their easy chairs and absorbed the easy entertainment: the WBET Troupers in "Not Quite Such a Goose," a comedy in one act; Boots and His Nighthawks, dance music; the Klassay Boys; the Handy Instrumental Trio; Doc Wassermann's Orchestra; and the Correct Time.

In the news that day all kinds of thrills: Ed Farrell's hitting had been a large factor as the Braves won three straight from the Cubs; two school boys were leading the field in the first half of the qualifying round for the amateur golf title; a girl tennis queen had won an impressive victory in New York, and the French Davis cup team had arrived in Boston. More serious items: St. Mark's Church had benefited by the will of a millionaire manufacturer of extracts; eight hundred Catholic teachers from a hundred and thirty-five parochial schools were in convention; the city council had voted three hundred thousand dollars for a golf links; the wife of a moving picture favorite had obtained a divorce from her husband, after charging him eight hundred and fifty thousand dollars for his freedom. The flappers of Boston listened, and reflected: "If I could get to marry somebody like that, I could live on the alimony the rest of my life." Radio central station WBET, the Boston *Evening Transcript*: "The juice was turned off, and Vanzetti was officially pronounced dead at twelve, twenty-six, fifty-five. The orchestra will now play, 'The End of a Perfect Day.'"

VIII

In every great capital of the world there were mass meetings and protests that night. In London a mob marched upon Buckingham Palace, and had to be ridden down by mounted men—quite as if it were Boston Common. In Berlin there were a score of meetings, ending with parades. In Geneva the demonstrants raided the American embassy, and when clubbed away, broke the windows of the League of Nations Palace. Even in far-off Tokio the American ambassador had to receive a deputation of labor leaders, and explain that he had no control over executions in Massachusetts.

In Paris there had been a general strike, and on the night of the execution there were street demonstrations, with mobs shouting curses at Americans whenever they met them—which was frequently. An American playwright and his wife asked for police protection, and when the official learned that they knew German, he advised them to speak it for a while. An odd freak of history—only ten years since the battle of the Argonne, and here was a man who had taken part in it, being told to speak the language of the Boche!

It was dawn when the workers of Europe got the news, and they went to their tasks with hearts blazing. To them it was a personal matter, for they had friends in America, and knew the attitude of native New England to its foreign workers. There were guards before all American embassies and consulates, and few escaped without broken windows. In London forty persons were injured in the rioting; in Australia eighteen hundred were discharged for taking part in a strike; in South Africa the American flag was burned on the steps of the town hall of Johannesburg.

On the evening of the 23rd in Paris huge masses of workers were driven about the streets by the police. They would scatter, and then reassemble, wherever Americans were to be met. They raided the cabarets of Montmartre, and showered the patrons with broken glass. The "Moulin Rouge," shrine of tourist culture, was demolished, and when the panic-stricken patrons got outside, they found their automobiles overturned and the tires cut. Unkind and inexplicable it seemed to amiable globe-trotters, who had sent over their boys and won the war for the French, and now, finding that the French could not pay their debts, were permitting them to work it off by entertaining several hundred thousand bond-holders every summer. Large round gentlemen in golf-pants, with horn-rimmed glasses and rosy cheeks, ate the best food in the country, and drank the best wines, and had the best dress-makers to decorate their bouncing jolly wives, or the lean tall ones who took culture seriously. They rode about in rows on large motor-buses, with guide-books in hand, admiring indiscriminately; they scattered money to right and left, paying double prices, determined to have the best of everything in the world.

The wage-slaves of French factories, half starved for generations, read in their socialist and communist papers of the death of Sacco and Vanzetti; and in the same issue they read how the wife of an American millionaire was introducing a new fashion in carved emeralds from India, of which jewelers in the rue de la Paix had a few rare specimens. The Chicago harvesting-machine queen had paid approximately eighteen million francs—the life-time earnings of several hundred French workingmen—for a necklace containing eighty-nine such jewels, minutely carved in relief to represent events in Hindu history. She had been the sensation at Biarritz when she appeared on Baron Fascini's yacht, wearing this necklace as the sole ornament on her newest Oxford bags pajamas suit of natural colored pongee, and a royal blue jacket with gold buttons. Such munificence made prosperity for all Paris, and kept many thousands of workers alive; yet they refused to love their benefactors, but called them dirty names, and threw stones through the windows of the cafés which exhibited the depravities of Paris to the Puritan trade.

The wisest of Frenchmen had written a letter to Governor Fuller. "I say to you, beware of making martyrs. This is the unforgivable crime that nothing can wipe out and that weighs on generation after generation." But alas, the name of Anatole France meant nothing to a salesman of motor-cars who read the *Saturday Evening Post;* that letter had doubtless been burned in the furnaces, along with all the others. And now

Massachusetts had made her martyrs, and stood upon her pedestal of self-righteousness. The more the world hated her, the more proud she would be, to be right while everybody else was wrong. "Massachusetts, there she is!" said Daniél Webster, darling of the "golden mob." "Behold her and judge for yourselves. There is her history; the world knows it by heart. The past at least is secure." So the golden ones would continue to orate, while the names of her two martyrs swelled to a battle-cry of the disinherited of the earth. Until that day when the workers of Europe began to take Joe Randall's advice and repudiate the debts!

IX

The corpses were in a mortuary, still held by the authorities. Then, horror of horrors, the friends of the defense learned that the bodies were being mutilated, the hearts and brains of both men were to be turned over to a medical school—of all places, Harvard University! It was a custom with the bodies of executed men, not a special indignity planned for these two—so the newspapers explained. Did the authorities have a right to do it? Or did they just do it? Nobody seemed to know. To the friends of the two martyrs it was the final insult—they could not have been more outraged if they had seen the august president of Harvard thumbing his nose at them.

"What do they want with their hearts and brains?" cried Cornelia; and Betty, the ferocious, explained matters. Harvard had so many millions upon millions of endowments, and had not succeeded in producing a great man for at least a generation. So many hundreds of professors, of every kind of subject on earth, and they couldn't teach anything worth while! Now they wanted the hearts and brains of two wops, to see if they could find out the secret of greatness. If they studied Nick's heart, they might learn about courage; from Bart's they might find a clew to social idealism, and the chemical constituents of faith. This fancy gave great joy to Betty, who went on to picture the medicos peering through microscopes, and making analyses in test-tubes, to find out the ways of genius. Mr. Lowell studying blood-counts, to learn how to put a little human interest into a speech or an essay! The heads of the English department making drawings of the cells in Vanzetti's cortex, to find out how a wop had become a great master of English prose!

The mutilated bodies were turned over to the relatives at last. Thousands of persons wanted to view them, and pay their last tribute; but the proprietors of the building in which the defense had two dingy rooms refused to permit it to happen there; to make sure, they nailed a joist up and down through the middle of the entrance to their building, which they figured would keep out coffins! So arrangements were made with an Italian undertaker on Hanover Street; and the moment it was known that the bodies were there, ten thousand persons gathered, and the police had to rope off the entire block, and let in only a few at a time.

Also they had to start clubbing and jailing again. For Mary Donovan came with another placard, containing those words which three or four weeks ago she had nailed to one of the elm trees of the Common: "Did you see what I did to those anarchistic ——? Judge Thayer." She set that placard in front of the two coffins, while the newspaper photographers prepared to take pictures of it. And of course the police wouldn't permit that; had they not abolished free speech in Boston in order to prevent those words from being put before the public? A policeman grabbed Mary's placard, and she, being Irish like himself, was not above fighting for her own. Other "cops" came running, and dragged Mary off to jail; and then of course they had to club the crowds, to keep them from crying "Shame!"

The friends of the defense desired to have a parade to the crematory where the bodies were to be burned. Many persons desired to go, and why should they not walk? So began negotiations with officials of this city of terror, for the right to walk eight miles to a crematory. The first stipulation was that the walkers must go by the most direct route, which would take them through obscure streets for the most part, and past no precious public buildings. The second stipulation was that the caskets must be carried in a hearse, and not upon the shoulders of men. The third was that no signs or banners should be borne. No word about "anarchistic ——"!

"Back to Normalcy," said the Boston *Herald;* and put all

this news on an inside page. The *Post* discussed such topics as "The Sunless Summer" and "Vegetarians and Shoes." The chiefs of the moving picture industry, whose orgy with drunken prostitutes had filled the Boston newspapers while Sacco and Vanzetti were on trial, now held their meeting in New York and passed a resolution that the case was to be barred from the screen forever, and that all films of it should be destroyed. Said Betty, the ferocious: "The great American whore covers us with her skirts!"

Said Cornelia: "They must have found out what Bart thought of them! Do you remember, Betty, what he wrote in 'Events and Victims'?" She looked up the manuscript, and found the passage in which Vanzetti had described the entertainment which American capitalism was supplying for its wage-slaves. "That ought to be published!" exclaimed Betty, and Joe made a copy of it; but alas, there was no paper in Boston which could be lured into printing such blasphemous words!

x

Sunday the day of the funeral. The crowds in Hanover Street made all movement difficult; they were so great that people were pushed through plate glass windows, and when these crashed there was a panic, because the crowd thought the police had started shooting. In the roped off area were two hearses and several limousines; oh, crowning insult—they were Packard cars! The supersalesman, now enjoying his hard-earned vacation, was making money as usual! In one car, with curtains drawn, rode the widow and children of Sacco and the sister of Vanzetti, both women in a state of collapse. It was an Italian funeral, with great floral wreaths borne by mourners, and the undertaker marching in a Prince Albert coat and top hat, in spite of a drizzling rain. State police— the "Cossacks"—rode ahead and alongside the hearses, to see that the procession followed the prescribed route. In the rear followed several open cars full of flowers, and several with mourners, among them Cornelia Thornwell.

The authorities had given the necessary permit, and had not limited the number of persons who might march in the procession; but they dared not let it be too big, for the sake of the moral effect. So the entire march was a series of battles between those who were determined to march, and the police who were trying to break them up and shunt them off into side streets, even if some had to be killed in the process. The members of the committee and friends of the defense had provided themselves with red arm-bands, reading: "Remember Justice Crucified. August 22, 1927," and the wearers of these arm-bands were singled out for the fiercest attacks.

The procession moved down Hanover Street, and fifty thousand people fell in behind after it had passed. So when they came into Scollay Square, mounted policemen rode into the middle of the throng, and tried to form a line across the street, barring the bulk of the procession. The crowds dodged this way and that, to get by; the policemen began to wield their clubs, galloping their horses, and trampling men and women beneath the iron-shod hoofs. But a frenzy possessed the mourners; it was their last chance to express their loathing of the crime that had been committed, and of the criminals who had done it, and thousands were ready to die rather than be cut out from the parade. They broke through again and again, and screaming and cursing people were knocked down, or jammed through the windows of stores; the younger and more fleet-footed went racing around the block, so as to catch the procession farther on.

The hearses continued down Tremont Street, and came to Park Street, the corner of the Common, where the State House with the golden dome may be seen upon the hill. To march up Beacon Street and past that State House had been a fond dream of the friends of Sacco and Vanzetti. To keep them from realizing it, the police had not merely made a solid blockade of trucks across Park Street, but had a gang of laborers come and take up the paving blocks from sections of the street. The laborers stood watching the show, until the hearses and the crowd had passed; then they replaced the paving!

The procession moved along Tremont Street; on one side the Common, on the other the fashionable shops. A solid mass of people all the way, filling the sidewalks; the newspapers estimated that two hundred thousand saw the hearses go by. The marchers would have taken all day, if the police had let them alone. But at Charles Street they had another device;

line after line of empty taxi-cabs drawn up, waiting for the hearses and the little group of mourners to pass; then the taxis broke out into the throng. It was against the law to break into a funeral, but there was no law in Boston except the will of the police. Who was paying the taxi-cabs for the service was not known. Their efforts were futile, for the people kept breaking through at risk of their lives.

No order was possible to the marchers; they just walked as they could; the crowds fell in behind, mostly with bared heads, in spite of the heavy rain that had begun to fall. Betty and Joe, Mary Donovan, Powers Hapgood, Alfred Baker Lewis —all the leaders were there. They were spreading flowers on the street—but that was against a city ordinance, said Mike Crowley, who rode with the procession, greatly astonished to see how many men and women were willing to get soaked for the sake of two anarchist wops.

Out through the South End; the friends of the defense now forming lines with linked arms for protection against the police. By the time they came to Roxbury Crossing, they had a military formation, and were able to keep the traffic from breaking them up, in spite of all efforts. The traffic police would signal for traffic to break into the procession, and cars would force their way a few feet amid cat-calls and screams; then they would give up, and Sacco and Vanzetti would have their way for the first time in Boston. One policeman forced a seven-ton truck into the crowd; the truck driver was attacked with umbrellas, and when the policeman tried to draw his club, he was swept aside.

It was in that part of Boston called Jamaica Plain that the orders came to break up the parade at all hazards. A small army of patrolmen charged into the crowd, wielding their clubs right and left. One patrolman made his attack in an automobile—darting this way and that, running people down, a new sport. Others climbed into the cars of the sympathizers, and clubbed the drivers, and drove the cars out of the line. Even the hard-boiled newspaper reporters were astonished by the sights they saw in that battle, and were permitted by their city editors to write a few plain sentences telling the incidents:

"One officer was to be seen beating a woman in the face with his fist. A girl was standing near the coal company office, her

face buried in her hands with a split chin. . . . A policeman
stuck his pistol at the window of a taxi-cab, then turned suddenly, went to another car, dragged a man out to kick him
toward Boston. Persons who were riding on running boards of
autos and taxi-cabs were dragged off and beaten or booted in
the direction of Boston. By this time the main body was in
flight toward Boston, pursued by a line of policemen who still
used their clubs. Women were given no mercy in the panic.
. . . While one man was being beaten by a sergeant with an
umbrella, his hat was knocked off and, stooping to pick it
up, he was booted by a patrolman. He went down and the
patrolman kicked the hat high in the air."

It was the process known as "Americanization."

XI

Ten thousand persons were crowded about the Forest Hills
cemetery, with hundreds of policemen to keep them from getting inside. The hearses were passed in, and the cars with the
reporters and photographers, and a little group of mourners;
the rest of those who had marched eight miles to attend the
ceremony had to stand about outside—unless they were lively
enough to climb the hedge and the iron picket fence. Inside the
little chapel a hundred persons were gathered, and the two
coffins were set upon a dais, covered with flowers, and Mary
Donovan took her place beside them, white and trembling. For
two years she had made the cause of Sacco and Vanzetti her
life; she had given up her religion, her friends, her job; and
now it was her opportunity to speak the last words which the
defense had to say to the rulers of Boston.

She lifted her voice; and then—a miracle, such as happens
when martyrs are made in this world! It was discovered that
the heart and brain of Vanzetti, supposed to be in the possession of the medicos of Harvard, so that they might probe
into the secrets of how to be noble and how to be eloquent and
how to be a master of English prose—that heart and brain
had escaped from under their scalpels, and were here in the body
of a frail Irish girl, a reformed Catholic, speaking words which
would be woven into the texture of the new religion of humanity, and learned by school children under the new dis-

pensation. Said Mary Donovan, addressing Boston's martyrs:
"Nicola Sacco and Bartolomeo Vanzetti. You came to
America seeking freedom. In the strong idealism of youth you
came as workers searching for that liberty and equality of opportunity heralded as the particular gift of this country to
all newcomers. You centered your labors in Massachusetts,
the very birthplace of American ideals. And now Massachusetts
and America have killed you—murdered you because you were
anarchists.

"Two hundred and thirty-five years ago the ruling people of
this State hanged women in Salem charging them with witchcraft. The shame of those old acts of barbarism can never be
wiped out. But they are as nothing beside this murder which
modern Massachusetts has committed upon you. The witch-
hangers were motivated by the superstitious fear of an emotional religion. Their minds were blinded by their selfish passion
to reach heaven.

"The minds of those who have killed you were not blinded.
They have committed the act in deliberate cold blood. For more
than seven years they had every chance to know the truth about
you. Not once did they even dare mention the quality of your
characters—a quality so noble and shining that millions have
come to be guided by it. They refused to look. They allowed
the bitter prejudice of class-position and self-interest to close
their eyes. They cared more for wealth, comfort and institutions than they did for truth. You, Sacco and Vanzetti, are
the victims of the greatest plutocracy the world has known since
ancient Rome.

"Your long years of torture and your last hours of supreme
agony are the living banner under which we and our descendants for generations to come will march to accomplish that
better world based on the brotherhood for which you died.

"In your martyrdom we will fight on and conquer.

"Remember Justice Crucified. August 22. Remember."

XII

Those who had strong nerves were privileged to go back into
the crematory, and look through a glass plate into the "retorts,"
and see the two bodies being resolved into their original ele-

ments—dust unto dust, ashes unto ashes. Those who could not stand the ordeal by fire, went out to face an ordeal by water; a downpour of rain such as Boston had rarely seen, almost a. cloudburst. A more superstitious age would have said that the heavenly powers desired to wash the city clean, the blood from its streets and the blot from its name. One of those natural portents, like the rending of the veil in the temple, which accompany the making of martyrs!

Yes, Boston had rejected the advice of the shrewd old Frenchman, and made two martyrs. Mystic beings, with supernatural virtues, destined to become a legend; to expand like the genii released from the bottle, until they spread over the sky, completely overshadowing the city and its fame. No more would Boston be the place of the tea-party and the battle of Bunker Hill; Boston would be the place where Sacco and Vanzetti were put to death!

And those two, the shining ones, the holy, who died to make freedom for the workers! Already one saw the history of martyrology repeating itself: the process of two thousand years crowded into one. Already they were canonized beings, concerning whom it was forbidden to speak any word but of praise; already there were men who worshiped their ashes, and imprisoned those who followed their example!

And yet, obscurely, the symbol was working in the souls of men. A hundred million toilers knew that two comrades had died for them. Black men, brown men, yellow men—men of a hundred nations and a thousand tribes—the prisoners of starvation, the wretched of the earth—experienced a thrill of awe. It was the mystic process of blood-sacrifice, by which through the ages salvation has been brought to mankind!

A hundred million workers, shackled and blind, groping in a poison fog manufactured by their masters, learned that two of their fellows had been put to death for lifting the banner of freedom. In spite of all the wrangling of the radical sects, that was a fact the meaning of which could never be obscured; a fact which shone like a pillar of fire in the workers' night. Bart had succeeded in the purpose he had declared, to give a meaning to his name. "It mean joostice, it mean freedom, it cannot mean nothing but!" To a hundred million groping, and ten times as many still in slumber, the names of Sacco and

Vanzetti would be the eternal symbols of a dream, identical with civilization itself, of a human society in which wealth belongs to the producers of wealth, and the rewards of labor are to the laborers. In the words of the prophet Isaiah:

"And they shall build houses, and inhabit them; and they shall plant vineyards, and eat the fruit of them. They shall not build, and another inhabit; they shall not plant, and another eat; for as the days of a tree are the days of my people, and mine elect shall long enjoy the work of their hands."

THE END

THE COMMONWEALTH OF MASSACHUSETTS

EXECUTIVE DEPARTMENT

STATE HOUSE　•　BOSTON 02133

MICHAEL S. DUKAKIS
GOVERNOR

Report to the Governor
in the Matter of
Sacco and Vanzetti

To: Governor Michael S. Dukakis

The accompanying Report has been prepared under the auspices of the Office of the Governor's Legal Counsel* in response to your questions: first, as to whether there are substantial grounds for believing — at least in light of the criminal justice standards of today — that Sacco and Vanzetti were unfairly convicted and executed, and, second, if so, what action can now appropriately be taken. It is my conclusion that there are substantial, indeed compelling, grounds for believing that the Sacco and Vanzetti legal proceedings were permeated with unfairness, and that a proclamation issued by you would be appropriate.

DANIEL A. TAYLOR
Chief Legal Counsel

July 13, 1977

---

*Invaluable assistance was rendered in the preparation of this Report by, among others, Alexander J. Cella, Esq., Alan M. Dershowitz, Esq., Thomas Quinn, Todd D. Rakoff, Esq., Deborah M. Smith, and Lewis H. Weinstein, Esq.

Report to the Governor

August 23, 1977, will be the fiftieth anniversary of the execution by the Commonwealth of Nicola Sacco and Bartolomeo Vanzetti. Controversy has surrounded the Sacco and Vanzetti case ever since its inception. The continuing doubts as to the legitimacy of their convictions and executions have prompted reconsideration. Two issues are raised: (1) are there substantial grounds for believing that Sacco and Vanzetti were convicted and executed without a fair trial demonstrating their guilt of murder beyond a reasonable doubt and without an adequate appellate review of that trial; and (2) if so, what action should appropriately be taken in the present circumstances:

1. WERE SACCO AND VANZETTI CONVICTED AND EXECUTED AFTER A FAIR TRIAL DEMONSTRATING THEIR GUILT OF MURDER BEYOND A REASONABLE DOUBT, AND AFTER AN ADEQUATE REVIEW OF THAT TRIAL?

(a) *The Basic Chronology**

On April 15, 1920, at about three P.M., Frederick Parmenter, paymaster of the Slater and Morrill Shoe Co., and his guard, Alexander

---

* See Attachment A for full chronology.

2

Berardelli, were robbed of the payroll they were carrying, some $15,000, and shot to death, in South Braintree, Massachusetts. At least two men did the robbing and shooting, leaving six bullets in the dead men's bodies; having seized the money, they jumped into an approaching get-away car, containing several other men, and sped away. The murders have always been undisputed; the only issue is who the guilty group of men were.

Nicola Sacco and Bartolomeo Vanzetti were arrested while travelling on a street car on the evening of May 5, 1920. They were indicted for murder on September 14, 1920. (Vanzetti in the meantime had been convicted, separately, of a holdup which took place in Bridgewater; his conviction of that crime was based on identification evidence that Felix Frankfurter, then a Professor at Harvard Law School and later a Justice of the United States Supreme Court, said "bordered on the frivolous," and in the teeth of very substantial alibi evidence. Frankfurter, *The Case of Sacco and Vanzetti* 7 n. 1 (1962 ed.).) The trial for the South Braintree murders began on May 31, 1921, and lasted until July 14; with but a few hours of deliberation, the jurors returned a guilty verdict.

In the succeeding five years various motions for a new trial based in part on newly discovered evidence and in part on alleged improprieties of the prosecution were made. All of the motions were denied by the trial judge. On May 12, 1926, the Supreme Judicial Court overruled all of the exceptions which had been taken after the trial and after denial of the various motions. *Commonwealth* v. *Sacco*, 255 Mass. 369 (1926). Various other motions, denials, and fruitless appeals followed. *
In May, 1927, Vanzetti petitioned Governor Fuller "not for mercy but for justice"; the petition was denied on August 3, 1927, in part on the basis of Governor Fuller's own review, and in part on the basis of a report the Governor had received from a specially established Advisory Committee composed of A. Lawrence Lowell, president of Harvard,

---

* *Commonwealth* v. *Sacco*, 259 Mass. 128 (1927); *Commonwealth* v. *Sacco*, 261 Mass. 12, *cert. dismissed*, 275 U.S. 574 (1927).

3

Samuel W. Stratton, president of M.I.T., and Robert Grant, a former Probate Court judge.*

Early in the morning of August 23, 1927, Sacco and Vanzetti were executed at the Charlestown State Prison in Boston.

(b) *The Grounds For Continuing Doubt*

Despite, or, perhaps in part because of, the very considerable attention paid to the Sacco-Vanzetti case prior to the execution of the defendants, there have remained, ever since, several grounds for doubting that Sacco and Vanzetti were fairly proven guilty, beyond a reasonable doubt, of the South Braintree murders. These grounds encompass both the conduct of the trial itself, with the consequence that there is doubt whether the jury's verdict represented only its consideration of rational proof of the crime charged, and also the effect of later-discovered or later-disclosed evidence, with the consequence that even if the trial jury rightly decided the case placed before it, there remains a substantial doubt whether a jury in possession of all of the facts would have returned a guilty verdict. As will be discussed subsequently, the refusal of the Supreme Judicial Court to overturn the verdict does not answer these doubts.

Of course, many of these bases for doubt are fully intelligible only upon a complete explication of convoluted evidence, but some of the more serious points can be briefly summarized.** A more detailed

---

*Governor Fuller's decision and the Report of the Advisory Committee are reproduced in *V The Sacco-Vanzetti Case: Transcript of the Record of the Trial of Nicola Sacco and Bartolomeo Vanzetti in the Courts of Massachusetts and Subsequent Proceedings, 1920-1927* (New York, Henry Holt & Co., Inc., 1928-29) at 5378a *et seq.*

**Even beyond the specific points, the mere fact that for the last fifty years countless authors have debated the merits of the case, without a clear victory either for the proponents of innocence or for the proponents of guilt, is in itself a reason to think that a miscarriage of justice may have occurred. Extensive bibliographies are included in Russell, *Tragedy in Dedham* (1971 ed.), and Ehrmann, *The Case That Will Not Die* (1969).

4

outline of the more significant instances of unfairness, together with a reference to appropriate standards currently applicable to criminal trials and appeals, is appended to this report.

(1) "The Sacco and Vanzetti case," wrote Samuel Eliot Morison, "was an offshoot of the . . . whipped-up anti-red hysteria" of the period just following World War One. Morison, *The Oxford History of the American People* 884 (1965). The defendants were aliens, poor — and espoused a political ideology — anarchism — which struck fear in the hearts of many Americans; that fear was later exacerbated when various left-wing movements embraced their cause. Whether prejudice against anarchists influenced the verdict, and the denial of new trial motions, is perhaps open to debate; that a strong possibility existed for that to happen is irrefutable. It was said at the time, and has been said since, that the defense itself made political beliefs central to the trial. In the sense that the defendants' explanation for their behavior, including the various falsehoods told at the time of their arrest, was that they were afraid that they and their friends were to be persecuted for being anarchists, that is true. Whether that justified the extraordinary, indeed brutal, cross-examination of the defendants, especially of Sacco, is another matter. Many of the questions asked, and many of the responses elicited, seem to have been devoted to making it ring in the jurors' minds that the defendants were radicals — which is, of course, precisely what they claimed — rather than to establishing that their justification for their actions upon arrest was trumped up, which was the point the prosecution ostensibly wished to prove. Whether, in permitting this line of questioning, the judge properly balanced the probative value of the answers produced, as against the potential for prejudice necessarily involved, may be seriously questioned. The Supreme Judicial Court ruled only, not that the questions were proper, but that the trial judge had not abused his discretion in permitting such questions within the traditionally broad scope allowed to cross-examination. *Commonwealth* v. *Sacco, supra,* 255 Mass. at 439.

5

Whether the trial judge was as impartial as the reliance by the Supreme Judicial Court, here and elsewhere, on his discretion would indicate, has also been seriously challenged. In the years following the jury's verdict, many claimed to have heard the trial judge make statements, which if indeed made, would indicate a fixed prejudice on his part, both during the trial and later, against the defendants. The Governor's Advisory Committee, even while not fully crediting some of these statements, concluded that the judge had been guilty of "a grave breach of official decorum" in his discussion of the case; and further felt that his judicial qualities had been sufficiently called into question as to make it advisable for the Committee, on its own, to reconsider the merits of the discretionary new trial motions. Report at 6, 8. In themselves serious, these judgments were mild compared to the conclusions reached by other qualified commentators. Professor Frankfurter, writing at the time, described the judge's opinion denying a new trial as "a farrago of misquotations, misrepresentations, suppressions, and mutilations." *The Case of Sacco and Vanzetti, supra,* at 104. Professor Morgan, writing with 20 years' added perspective, described the judge as a man "whose prejudices made him overlook misconduct of the prosecutor, made him determine every discretionary matter against the accused, and permeated the proceedings from beginning to end with its vicious influence." Joughin and Morgan, *The Legacy of Sacco and Vanzetti* 157 (1964 ed.).

Whether the judge was prejudiced to that degree, or whether, whatever his prejudice, his biases had that great an effect on the course of the proceedings, is beyond our now knowing. Nevertheless, there is a substantial possibility that some prejudicial influence was imparted to the trial, and an even greater probability that the judge's hostility to the defendants influenced the exercise of his discretion, particularly in such critical matters as deciding the motions for a new trial. The other

6

problems present in the proof offered against the defendants have to be considered in the light of these possibilities.*

(2) The overwhelming fact about the South Braintree crime is that the crime itself remains unsolved. Even if for the moment it is assumed that Sacco and Vanzetti were participants, there were still several other participants; at trial, nothing was offered to identify who these other bandits were, or to connect the two defendants to the rest of the gang. Similarly, it is undisputed that the robbers made off with more than $15,000, a substantial sum even now, and a relatively much greater amount in 1920. No part of this money was ever traced to the defendants, and at trial the prosecution offered no explanation whatsoever as to what had happened to it. Further, six bullets were found in the bodies of the two victims. Leaving aside, for the moment, the question whether one of the bullets was successfully shown to have been fired from a gun in the possession of Sacco at the time of his arrest, no account was ever offered at trial as to the source of the other five. Numerous more minor points also remain unresolved; and, of course, the Madeiros statement, which specifically exonerated Sacco and Vanzetti and served to implicate the Morelli gang of Providence, was never adequately investigated. In short, this was not a trial where the evidence adduced served to explain the entire event in such a comprehensive fashion that each detail gained persuasiveness from being a composite part of a complete whole. Rather, the jury was asked to find that, even though it could not on the evidence know all that had happened,

---

* Allegations were also made that one of the jurors, prior to his selection, had indicated his firm intent to hang the defendants. The trial judge denied a new trial motion based on this information, and the Supreme Judicial Court overruled the exception thereto, stating that the judge had the discretionary power not to believe the underlying affidavit. 255 Mass. at 450-51. The Advisory Committee also rejected the contention on the basis that "it is extremely improbable that Ripley was so different from other men that he desired the disagreeable task of serving on this jury, and he had only to reveal what he had said to be excused." Report at 10. Whatever the truth may be, that reasoning is surely a supreme example of begging the question; if the juror wanted the men hanged, of course he would want to serve on the jury.

7

or even most of it, the jurors still could know beyond a reasonable doubt that the two defendants were guilty. While juries must, of course, often make such judgments, the fact that the full story was not known doubtless increases the likelihood that the conduct of the trial influenced the result; that fact also serves to highlight the importance of the accuracy of each specific piece of evidence that was offered.

(3) At trial, the prosecution offered several witnesses who purported to identify one or the other of the defendants as participants in whichever aspect of the South Braintree robbery they had witnessed. Large parts of several books have been written dissecting the various identifications. Without reviewing all the details, it has been asserted that several of the witnesses did not have an adequate opportunity for observation; that some had previously stated that they could not identify the men they briefly glimpsed, or, worse yet, had previously identified photos of others than the defendants as depicting the assailants; that some described details of the defendants not, in fact, true, or inconsistent with the details reported by others; and that at least one had an undisclosed motive for testifying favorably to the prosecution. The defense offered several witnesses who placed Vanzetti in Plymouth and Sacco in Boston at the time of the South Braintree affair. Thus, at the core of the trial there was a direct conflict of mutually exclusive identification testimony.

If that were all, it would be unwise to second-guess the jury's determination as to which witnesses were truthful; even then, it would still be troublesome that the trial judge passed over the bulk of the defendants' evidence in but one sentence of his extensive charge. (The material portions of the charge are set out at 255 Mass. at 388-403.) But that is not all. After the trial an additional witness, Roy Gould (who had not testified although he had spoken to the police), affirmed that he saw the bandits, and that they were not the defendants. Gould, who had had a bullet put through his lapel by the robbers, "certainly had an unusually good position to observe the men in the car," in the words of the Advisory Committee. Report at 9. The trial judge denied the motion for a new trial based on this evidence, stating

8

that "these verdicts did not rest, in my judgment, upon the testimony of the eye witnesses"; and the Supreme Judicial Court held his denial not to be an abuse of discretion. 255 Mass. at 457-59. The Advisory Committee dismissed the importance of this evidence as well, on the basis that it was "merely cumulative" and was balanced by two new witnesses supporting the prosecution's claim. Report at 9. Neither of the prosecution's new witnesses was as impressive as Gould; but even if the point be granted, the need to weigh the testimony of one eyewitness against another confirms the need for a new trial rather than supporting its denial.

(4) Apparently the trial judge, having said that the convictions did not rest on the testimony of the eyewitnesses, was of the opinion that what had convicted the defendants was the "consciousness of guilt" shown by their actions and statements on the night of their arrests. Since the arrests took place fully 20 days after the crime, and since the defendants were not informed of the grounds of their arrests, this is hardly solid proof of their guilt. More particularly, it was precisely this proof concerning the motivation of their actions at the time of arrest that had been so thoroughly tainted by the prosecutor's cross-examination, and which most clearly invited the jury to exercise its emotions rather than its thoughts. The jury may well have decided on this basis, and was indeed almost invited to do so by the heavy emphasis placed on the arrest, rather than the crime, in the judge's charge. If that was the sole ground of decision, the case against the defendants was certainly not proven beyond a reasonable doubt.

It seems more likely that the jury also based its decision on certain other circumstantial evidence purporting to show the defendants' participation in the crime. The trial judge's charge picked out three pieces of such evidence: the identification of one bullet; the identification of one revolver; and the identification of one hat. 255 Mass. at 391-93. In the light of the evidence discovered after the trial, the tendency of each of the three to prove the guilt of the defendants is doubtful.

9

Whether one of the bullets taken from Berardelli's body was fired from the gun found in Sacco's possession at the time of his arrest remains one of the most hotly disputed points of this hotly disputed case. It is beyond the competence of this memorandum to attempt to determine which of the many ballistics tests that were made, if any,* reveals the truth. It suffices to say that the jury did not have the whole story put before it, and may indeed have been misled. The prosecution's chief expert testified only that his opinion was that it was "consistent" that the bullet had been fired from the pistol. After the trial it developed that this expert, if asked whether he had found any evidence that the bullet had passed through Sacco's pistol, would have answered in the negative, and that the prosecution knew that he would have so testified. Yet his testimony, not further developed, may well have been thought by the jury to be virtually conclusive on this issue; at least the judge appeared to think so in his charge that the testimony was that "it was his [Sacco's] pistol that fired the bullet."

The prosecution also tried to prove that the gun in Vanzetti's possession at the time of arrest was connected with the crime, having been the gun carried by Berardelli on the fatal day. The testimony was, at best, confused. Even the Advisory Committee, wanting forcefully to state the case against the defendants, could go no further than to state that Vanzetti had in his possession a pistol "resembling" the pistol "formerly possessed" by Berardelli. Report at 19.

Finally, the prosecution attempted to show that a cap had been found at the scene of the crime which was Sacco's cap. Quite apart from the disputes as to when the cap had been found, and as to whether it fit Sacco, it was developed after the trial that what may

---

*The bullets and gun passed out of the custody of the Commonwealth sometime after the trial. Subsequently, in about 1960, the bullets and gun believed to have been the evidence introduced at trial were located at a personal residence in Massachusetts. There was no trail of continuous custody, nor any witness who could reliably establish these bullets and gun as the bullets and gun put into evidence. See, Russell, *Tragedy in Dedham, supra*, at 315-17.

10

well have been the crucial identifying feature of the cap for the jury, a tear in its lining, had been added to it by a police officer while the cap was in his custody.

In sum, the overall effect of these three pieces of evidence may well have been to convince the jury that it had more definite proof of guilt than in fact it had.

(5) In light of the foregoing, a serious question exists and will continue to exist whether the guilt of Sacco and Vanzetti was properly determined. The jury was invited to decide the case on the basis of appeals to prejudice; the eyewitness testimony was conflicting and even the judge apparently thought it to be an inadequate basis of decision; many of the facts which might have altered the jury's conclusion were not presented at trial, including further eyewitness evidence and other important pieces of evidence concerning identification; and the evidence concerning the defendants' "consciousness of guilt" at the time of arrest was overblown, and may well have been viewed through the perspective of a cross-examination as much calculated to damn the defendants as to advance the cause of truth. While a jury's verdict in the normal case settles the facts once and for all, a verdict rendered on such a basis, and with such vital consequences, calls for much more careful scrutiny.

It is precisely for cases of this sort that procedural devices such as motions for a new trial, and especially review by a different and superior tribunal, have been fashioned. When the trial proceedings have undergone careful review, the confidence that may be placed in the verdict is much greater. Unfortunately, the system for reviewing murder cases at the time of Sacco's and Vanzetti's convictions and executions failed to provide the safeguards now present, safeguards which might well have prevented a miscarriage of justice.

To acknowledge that mistakes occur is not to challenge the importance of the criminal law in the protection of society, nor to denigrate in any fashion the criminal justice system of the Commonwealth. It is the very possibility of mistake that is one of the strongest grounds for the existence of a well-developed appellate system of justice. And it

11

was the possibility that a mistake was committed in the executions of Sacco and Vanzetti that led to a strengthening in the system of appellate review of capital cases in this Commonwealth.

(c) *The Review Of The Case By The Supreme Judicial Court*

It is sometimes thought that the Supreme Judicial Court, in failing to reverse Sacco's and Vanzetti's convictions, and in failing to order a new trial, endorsed in their entirety the proceedings below. This description of what the Supreme Judicial Court decided is incorrect, and deficient in crucial respects.

In its main review of the case, including the review of some but not all of the motions made for a new trial, the Supreme Judicial Court considered separately, in thirty-three numbered sections, each of the exceptions raised by the defendants; its final decision was merely to overrule those exceptions. *Commonwealth* v. *Sacco*, 255 Mass. 369 (1926). Both in this opinion, and in a later opinion considering other exceptions to the denial of further new trial motions, *Commonwealth* v. *Sacco*, 259 Mass. 128 (1927), the Court at many places grounded its decision on the basis that various matters, including the decision whether to grant a new trial because of newly discovered evidence, rested within the discretion of the trial judge. The standard of review used was that set forth in *Davis* v. *Boston Elevated Ry. Co.*, 235 Mass. 482, 502 (1920), a civil case many times cited in the *Sacco* opinions, which reads as follows:

> "The question is not whether we should take a different view of the evidence or should have made an opposite decision from that made by the trial judge. To sustain these exceptions it is necessary to decide that no conscientious judge, acting intelligently, could honestly have taken the view expressed by him."

12

Both the language and the purpose of this standard of review indicate that little short of proof of sheer incompetence or corruption would have persuaded the Supreme Judicial Court to reverse matters it considered discretionary.

The consequence of this narrow standard of review was that on many vital issues, including especially whether a new trial was warranted on the basis of new evidence or because the prosecution had prejudiced the defendants because of their political beliefs, the lives of the defendants were completely committed to the judgment of the trial judge acting alone. This was the same judge that even the Governor's Advisory Committee described as having been "subjected to a very severe strain" by reason of "the criticisms made upon him," which resulted in his being "in a distinctly nervous condition." Report at 8. However, even assuming the judge fully competent, it may fairly be asked whether the lives of defendants should be so fully placed in the discretion of one man, and whether one man should be asked to bear by himself such an awful burden.

It is no criticism of the Supreme Judicial Court, acting under the procedures then lawfully in force, to point out that at almost all other times in the history of the Commonwealth greater protection for defendants in capital cases has been required. For nearly one hundred years, the full bench of the Supreme Judicial Court directly heard trials for capital crimes. Not until 1872 was this practice altered, and even then the power to hear trials for murder was given to two or more Supreme Judicial Court justices. St. 1872, c. 232. In 1891, jurisdiction over capital crimes was transferred to the Superior Court, but trial was to be before three justices. St. 1891, c. 379, §§ 1 and 2. In 1894, the number was changed to two or more, St. 1894, c. 204, but it was not until 1910 that a single justice of the Superior Court was given the power to hear by himself a trial for murder. St. 1910, c. 555, § 1.

Following upon the decisions in the *Sacco* case, sober citizens concerned with the administration of justice in the Commonwealth perceived the error of giving a single judge such great power over the life of a defendant. In November, 1927, the Judicial Council of the

13

Commonwealth recommended the enactment of new review provisions in capital cases. Commenting specifically on the proceedings in the Sacco and Vanzetti case, the Council stated (13 Mass. L.Q. No. 1, at 40-41):

> "A single judge of the Superior Court now presides over murder trials and passes not only on questions of law included in the trial of the indictment, but upon mixed questions of law and fact arising on motions for a new trial. The Supreme Judicial Court on appeal passes only on questions of law. As the verdict on such an indictment involves the issue of life and death, we think the responsibility too great to be thrown upon one man. If he errs in any matter of discretion as distinguished from law, the result is irreparable. . . .
>
> "It is true that the decisions of the trial judge upon matters of discretion may be reversed if there has been what is called an 'abuse' of discretion. . . . It is needless to say that such an abuse will so rarely be found by the Supreme Court to have existed that there is no real appeal from that judicial act."

Following renewed recommendations by the Judicial Council, 23 Mass. L.Q. No. 1, Prelim. Supp., at 28-30 (1937); 24 Mass. L.Q. No. 1, Prelim. Supp., at 14-16 (1938); the General Court enacted the desired legislation, St. 1939, c. 341, which, as amended, is the present M.G.L. c. 278, § 33E. This statute provides that in reviewing capital cases the Supreme Judicial Court shall consider both "the law and the evidence" and further provides that the Supreme Judicial Court may order a new trial, or direct the entry of a verdict for a lesser degree of guilt, if the verdict below "was against the law or the weight of the evidence, or because of newly discovered evidence, or for any other reason that justice may require."

14

The protection for a defendant in a capital case is thus greatly increased. Of substantial import for considering the questions raised by the Sacco and Vanzetti case, the statute now empowers the Supreme Judicial Court, not only to review the trial judge's decision on a motion for a new trial for "abuse of discretion," but also to exercise for itself the very powers given to a trial judge. Even more broadly, the statute requires the Supreme Judicial Court to investigate the whole case to see if there has been a miscarriage of justice. *Commonwealth* v. *Gricus*, 317 Mass. 403, 406-07 (1944); *Commonwealth* v. *Cox*, 327 Mass. 609, 614 (1951); *Commonwealth* v. *Harrison*, 342 Mass. 279, 297 (1961); *Commonwealth* v. *Baker*, 346 Mass. 107, 109 (1963). Thus, the Supreme Judicial Court now considers, in capital cases, not only the specific assignments of error, but also the record and evidence as a whole.

This change in procedure has changed results as well. For example, in *Commonwealth* v. *Cox, supra,* the Court found, in its consideration of errors of law, no error in the denial of defendant's motion for a new trial. 327 Mass. at 614. Yet, upon review of the entire case under M.G.L. c. 278, § 33E, the Court concluded that "the verdict was against the weight of the evidence, and there should be a new trial." 327 Mass. at 615. Of like import, in *Commonwealth* v. *Baker, supra,* the Court found that there was sufficient evidence to warrant a finding of premeditation, and yet ruled that "justice will be more nearly achieved" if that finding were not made, and thus ordered entry of a verdict of manslaughter. 346 Mass. at 119.

Had the Supreme Judicial Court of the 1920's been authorized to take this wider view of Sacco's and Vanzetti's convictions, the evidence already recounted suggests that the Court, in passing on the record as a whole, including the motions for a new trial, might well have ordered a new trial. Indeed, Professor Morgan concluded that under these later-enacted procedures "these defendants would certainly have had another trial." Joughin and Morgan, *The Legacy of Sacco and Vanzetti, supra,* at 177. At least, the narrow standard of review present for that short period in the Commonwealth's history has long

15

since been abandoned. That a review process adequate to insure that the ends of justice were served by Sacco's and Vanzetti's executions was unavailable at the time should not prevent the Commonwealth from once again addressing the question whether those executions were proper.*

2. WHAT ACTION SHOULD APPROPRIATELY BE TAKEN IN THE PRESENT CIRCUMSTANCES?

(a) *The Pardoning Power*

The normal way in which relief is granted after conviction of a crime is by exercise of the pardoning power. This power is set out in the Constitution as follows, Amendment Article LXXIII:

> "The power of pardoning offences, except such as persons may be convicted of before the senate by an impeachment of the house, shall be in the governor, by and with the advice of council; provided, that if the offence is a felony the general court shall have power to prescribe the terms and conditions upon which a pardon may be granted; but no charter of pardon, granted by the governor, with advice of the council before conviction, shall avail the party pleading the same, notwithstanding any general or particular expressions contained therein, descriptive of the offence or offences intended to be pardoned."

---

* Little need be said about the procedural implications of the reviews conducted by the Governor and his Advisory Committee. Whatever might be said about the particular evidence relied on, or the particular arguments made, the fundamental point is that advisory review by an *ad hoc* committee is no substitute for a new trial before a jury, and was never intended so to be.

16

The statutory "terms and conditions" upon which a pardon for a felony may be granted are those provided in M.G.L. c. 127, §§ 152-54, see St. 1945, c. 180. Together these provisions define the pardoning power, and such lesser powers as those of granting conditional pardons and commutations of sentences. *Juggins* v. *Executive Council to the Governor*, 257 Mass. 386 (1926); *Opinion of the Justices*, 210 Mass. 609, 610-11 (1912). However, while the powers so defined are suitable to usual cases, they appear not to be applicable to the present one.

First, as a procedural matter, M.G.L. c. 127, § 152, authorizes the Governor to grant a pardon "with the advice and consent of the council . . . upon the written petition of the petitioner." This requirement of a petition appears to be an integral part of the statutory scheme. See M.G.L. c. 127, §§ 152-54. Assuming that by "petitioner" the Legislature meant to denominate the convicted person, the statute would seem to indicate that posthumous pardons cannot be granted; or, at the least, that the pardoning power in its ordinary course is not the appropriate vehicle for addressing a matter such as this.

Second, in present day circumstances there are no legal consequences to conviction for a felony that last beyond the death of the felon. Compare 4 Blackstone, *Commentaries on The Laws of England* 402. Accordingly, the only purposes that could be served by a pardon in the present case are to right a wrong, by now historical, and to remove the stigma placed on Sacco and Vanzetti by their conviction and execution. Whether a pardon would in fact accomplish these aims is doubtful.

Judicial interpretations of the premise of the pardoning power are mixed and conflicting. The Supreme Court has stated that "when the pardon is full, it releases the punishment and blots out of existence the guilt, so that in the eye of the law the offender is as innocent as if he had never committed the offense." *Ex parte Garland*, 4 Wall. (71 U.S.) 333, 380 (1867). However, in a later case the same Court stated that the grant of a pardon carries "an imputation of guilt." *Burdick* v. *United States*, 236 U.S. 79, 94 (1915). Whether a pardon implies guilt, or, in some circumstances at least, implies innocence, has also been much debated among the legal commentators. Williston, *Does a Par-*

17

don *Blot Out Guilt?*, 28 Harv. L. Rev. 647 (1915); Lattin, *The Pardoning Power in Massachusetts*, 11 B.U. L. Rev. 505, 519-20 (1931); Weihofen, *The Effect of a Pardon*, 88 U. Pa. L. Rev. 177 (1939). The Supreme Judicial Court has defined the effect of a Massachusetts pardon, in at least the usual case, as removing only the consequences of the conviction per se, and not as obliterating "the acts which constituted the crime . . . which, despite the public act of mercy and forgiveness implicit in the pardon, ordinary, prudent men will take into account in their subsequent dealings with the actor." *Commissioner of the Metropolitan District Commission v. Director of Civil Service*, 348 Mass. 184, 194 (1964). Accordingly, the Court held that a pardon from this state does not restore the "good character" of one who has been convicted of a felony.* Other courts, although not uniformly, have reached the same conclusion. Note, *Presidential Clemency and the Restoration of Civil Rights*, 61 Iowa L. Rev. 1427, 1432 (1976), and cases there cited. Whether the Supreme Judicial Court would rule differently if presented with "[a] pardon clearly granted because of the wrongful conviction of an innocent person," 348 Mass. at 193, n. 8, it would not say; but even this phrasing of the contrary issue suggests that it might not give any different answer were the pardon granted only because of "reasonable doubt" as opposed to clearly established innocence.

In any case, the present situation raises issues neither of the direct nor collateral legal consequences of a conviction, but rather of the more general social implications. Professor Williston has stated that "[e]verybody knows that the word 'pardon' naturally connotes guilt as a matter of English," Williston, *supra*, 28 Harv. L. Rev. at 648, and this statement was quoted with approval by the Supreme Judicial Court, 348 Mass. at 193. Assuming that the statement is correct, if not for "everybody," then at least for the bulk of the population, to grant Sacco and Vanzetti a "pardon" would not only not have the desired consequences, but would in fact be taken to be the expression of a sentiment precisely contrary to that intended.

---

*Compare M.G.L. c. 276, § 100A (relating to sealing of court files).

18

Third, because the granting of a pardon is often thought to reaffirm guilt, if not legally then at least in the eye of public opinion, it has been adjudged that a pardon is not effective unless accepted. As stated by the Supreme Court, in *Burdick* v. *United States, supra,* 236 U.S. at 90-91:*

"Circumstances may be made to bring innocence under the penalties of the law. If so brought, escape by confession of guilt implied in the acceptance of a pardon may be rejected, — preferring to be the victim of the law rather than its acknowledged transgressor, — preferring death even to such certain infamy."

The law of the Commonwealth appears to follow the same rule. In *Commonwealth* v. *Lockwood,* 109 Mass. 323 (1872), the Court considered the effect of a pardon granted after a verdict of guilty had been rendered, but while exceptions were pending in the Supreme Judicial Court. In addition to ruling that a pardon could be granted at that time, the Court held that the defendant had the power and the obligation to choose whether he would rely on the pardon and waive his exceptions, or whether he would waive the pardon and rely on his exceptions. 109 Mass. at 339. The implication must be that the defendant had the choice of accepting his pardon or of attempting to establish the invalidity of his conviction. While the setting was of course far different from the present one, it may well be that the granting of a pardon to Sacco and Vanzetti after their deaths would be a null act, because the pardon is void without an acceptance, and no power of acceptance exists.

Fourth, in light of the foregoing it would be presumptuous for the Commonwealth to pardon these men fifty years after their execution by the Commonwealth. Sacco and Vanzetti maintained their innocence

---

* *Biddle* v. *Perovich,* 274 U.S 480 (1927), did not overturn *Burdick,* but only refused to extend it to the commutation of a death sentence to life imprisonment.

19

throughout their ordeal, and their protestations are a frequent reminder of the very real possibility that a grievous miscarriage of justice occurred with their deaths. A pardon, carrying the connotation that they were in fact guilty, and appearing as but a merciful act, with the implication that they would have, even now, welcomed it, would serve not to dignify, but rather to denigrate, their own claims to innocence.

In short, a pardon, or any of the forms of clemency bespeaking of a pardon, is not the proper remedy.

(b) *A Proclamation*

The fact that use of the pardoning power would not be the appropriate remedy for this situation should not mean that the Commonwealth is wholly without power to take any action. It would be outrageous to decide that no power exists to give whatever redress is possible at this late date.

Since Sacco and Vanzetti suffered the supreme legal punishment, there are no lingering legal consequences of their conviction. The only thing that can be done is to attempt to remove the stigma placed on them by their conviction and execution. It is, however, of great importance that that be done, both as a simple matter of justice to them, and, equally important, as a matter of clearing the record of the Commonwealth insofar as that is possible. Even though no relief with substantial legal effect is possible, at least a statement should be made.*

The necessary statement should take the form of a proclamation issued by the Governor. The Governor is the supreme executive magistrate of the Commonwealth, Const. Pt. 2, c. 2, § 1, Art. 1, and

---

* There is at present a healthy trend in the direction of a dignified closing of unfortunate incidents of history. The pardon of Tokyo Rose and the restoration of citizenship to Robert E. Lee and Jefferson Davis represent this trend for the Nation. In Massachusetts, the Legislature has resolved that "no disgrace or cause for distress" exists for Ann Pudeator, executed in 1692 for witchcraft, and her descendants, c. 145, Resolves of 1957; and Governor Dukakis on August 25, 1976, by proclamation revoked the 1637 banishment of Anne Marbury Hutchinson.

20

as such may take the lead in voicing the position of the Commonwealth on a matter of great public moment.

While there is no direct precedent for what is by its very nature a unique situation, Massachusetts Governors have long issued proclamations to call public attention to important matters and occasions. Furthermore, there is some legal precedent that bears directly on the matter at hand. In *People* v. *Bowen*, 43 Cal. 439, 13 Am. R. 148 (1872), a convicted felon sought to establish his competency to testify by producing a proclamation of the Governor declaring that "whereas it is desirable for the ends of justice that he should be restored to citizenship; now, therefore, I . . . do hereby restore [him] to all the rights of citizenship possessed by him before his conviction . . .." *Id.* at 441. After a discussion of the power provided for by the California Constitution — which is similar to that of Massachusetts — the Court concluded that while the Governor could have pardoned the individual, ". . . the executive act under review is not a pardon, nor was it intended to be such." *Id.* at 443. While the California Court held that the disability to testify remained since "there is [no] known relation between the competency of a witness and his 'rights of citizenship'," *id.*, it nevertheless recognized that the Governor's order had the effect of restoring the rights of citizenship.

Thus, a proclamation intending to remove any stigma and disgrace from Sacco and Vanzetti, from their families and descendants, and, as a result, from the Commonwealth of Massachusetts, should stand at least on the same footing as the California gubernatorial proclamation and have effect in accordance with its terms.

21

Appendix

SACCO AND VANZETTI: TRIAL AND APPEAL UNFAIRNESS

I. *Prosecutorial Abuse*

A. Knowingly utilizing false evidence to mislead the jury.

1. At the trial, Captain William H. Proctor, head of the State Police, testified in substance that his opinion was "consistent with" one of the recovered bullets having been fired by Sacco's gun. Proctor, in an affidavit (Vol. IV, 3641-3643),[1] subsequently stated that District Attorney Frederick G. Katzmann and Harold P. Williams were aware that Proctor could not definitively state that the bullet in question came from Sacco's gun. Proctor said he was repeatedly queried about this and repeatedly made his opinion known to the prosecutors. He also affirmed that the prosecution prearranged a question to which Proctor could say that his investigation of the bullet produced results "consistent" with its having gone through Sacco's gun, thus creating the impression in the jury's, judge's and defense counsel's minds that Proctor's opinion was that it had done so.

(a) Katzmann's response: He did not deny his prior knowledge of Proctor's real opinion or the connivance of the trick question, but merely stated that Proctor had not repeatedly been queried on the matter (Vol. IV, 3681).

(b) This subterfuge had immense impact on the trial's outcome because the three principal bases of the state's case were the alleged identification of the fatal bullet as being fired from Sacco's gun, the alleged identification of Sacco and Vanzetti as being present in South Braintree, and their alleged consciousness of guilt. The defense counsel even characterized Proctor's testimony as stating the bullet passed

---

[1] References to volume and page number refer to *The Sacco-Vanzetti Case: Transcript of the Record of the Trial of Nicola Sacco and Bartolomeo Vanzetti in the Courts of Massachusetts and Subsequent Proceedings*, 1920-27, Vols. I-V and Supplemental Volume (New York: Henry Holt 1928-29).

22

through Sacco's gun (Vol. V, 5054). Judge Thayer did likewise in his charge to the jury (Vol. III, 3422). One juror later reported that the expert testimony of Proctor and Van Amburgh was the deciding factor in the case (Russell, 212).[2]

2. Standards violated:

(a) The government may not knowingly rely on false evidence; it may not rest its case on testimony which it believes to be incorrect. *United States* v. *McGovern*, 499 F. 2d 1140 (1st Cir. 1974).

"If 'the State, although not soliciting false evidence, allows it to go uncorrected when it appears,' the defendant is entitled to relief." *Commonwealth* v. *Hurst*, 364 Mass. 604, 608 (1974).

The Fourteenth Amendment cannot tolerate a state criminal conviction obtained by the knowing use of false evidence. *Mooney* v. *Holohan*, 294 U.S. 103 (1934); *Napue* v. *Illinois*, 360 U.S. 264 (1959). In *Mooney*, the conviction was obtained by presentation of testimony known to the prosecutor to be perjured.

(b) ABA Standards Relating to the Administration of Criminal Justice (1974); The Prosecution Function:

> (i) "3.3. Relations with expert witnesses. A prosecutor who engages an expert for an opinion should respect the independence of the expert and should not seek to dictate the formation of the expert's opinion on the subject . . .."
>
> (ii) "5.6. Presentation of evidence. (a) It is unprofessional conduct for a prosecutor knowingly to offer false evidence, whether by documents, tangible evidence, or the testimony of witnesses, or fail to seek withdrawal thereof upon discovery of its falsity."

(c) ABA Code of Professional Conduct, canons and disciplinary rules, incorporated in the Rules of the Massachusetts Supreme Judicial Court,

---

[2] Russell, *Tragedy in Dedham* (1971).

23

Rule 3:22 (359 Mass. 787, 796) in 1972. The Code states that the disciplinary rules are "mandatory in character . . . and state the minimum level of conduct below which no lawyer can fall without being subject to disciplinary action."

(i) "DR 7-102. Representing a client within the bounds of the law. (A) In his representation of a client, a lawyer shall not: . . . (3) Conceal or knowingly fail to disclose that which he is required by law to reveal . . .. (4) Knowingly use perjured testimony or false evidence . . .. (6) Participate in the creation or preservation of evidence when he knows or it is obvious that the evidence is false."

(ii) "DR 7-109. Contact with witnesses. (A) A lawyer shall not suppress any evidence that he or his client has a legal obligation to reveal or produce."

B. Making use of unfair and misleading evidence.

1. When the prosecution's eyewitnesses initially identified the defendants, no line-up was utilized and counsel was not present. Prospective witnesses observed the defendants in jail, standing by themselves (Vol. I, 248, 252, 404-06, 509-10, 606-16). The defendants were forced to assume the crouching and shooting positions of the bandits to assist eyewitnesses in their identifications (Vol. I, 473-74). The method of identification was prejudicial and leaves the validity of the eyewitness testimony in grave question.

2. Standards violated:

(a) "The practice of showing suspects singly to persons for the purpose of identification, and not as part of a line-up, has been widely condemned." *Stovall* v. *Denno*, 388 U.S. 293, 302 (1967). To support this statement, the Court cited several law review articles and books, including Justice Felix Frankfurter's analysis of the Sacco-Vanzetti

24

case. See, *Foster* v. *California*, 394 U.S. 440 (1969); *Neil* v. *Biggers*, 409 U.S. 188 (1972).

C. Withholding exculpatory evidence.

1. The name and address of an eyewitness, Ray Gould, who stood within five to ten feet of the fleeing car after the fatal Braintree shootings (Gould affidavit, Vol. IV, 3504) was in the possession of state officials throughout the trial. Indeed, Gould was interviewed by Braintree police immediately following the murder (Officer John Heaney's affidavit, Vol. IV, 3508-09), but the prosecution made no further investigation (Gould affidavit, Vol. IV, 3504). The prosecution instead relied on eyewitnesses who had less opportunity to view the assailants. Gould's identity was subsequently learned by the defense through a defense witness. Defense counsel then attempted to locate him without success (Moore affidavit, Vol. IV, 3499-3500). During this time the Commonwealth did not forward the identity and address of Gould to the defense, nor did the prosecutors secure Gould's attendance at the trial. Following the trial, the defense located Gould, who definitively stated, after observing Sacco, that Sacco was not the assailant who had been at the scene of the murders (Gould affidavit, Vol. IV, 3505).

2. District Attorney Katzmann requested that the Department of Justice determine whether the anarchist radicals in New York, some of whom were associated with Sacco and Vanzetti, had received any large sums of money following the South Braintree robbery. The Department of Justice reported that the group had not. This was revealed in a summary of the Department's files on the Sacco-Vanzetti case released August 22, 1927, to W. G. Gavin, Washington correspondent for the *Boston Traveler*. The story appeared in the *Traveler* at 3 P.M., nine hours before Sacco and Vanzetti were executed (Ehrmann, 61).[3] Had this information been made available to the jury, the defendants' apparent motive for the crime would have seemed improbable.

---

[3] Ehrmann, *The Case That Will Not Die* (1969).

25

3. The prosecution utilized the minutes of the official inquest following the murder during cross-examination of defense witnesses at the trial. The minutes were not made available to defense counsel until July 21, 1927, when they were released to the Governor's Advisory Committee (Vol. V, 5251). The minutes revealed discrepancies in prosecution witnesses' testimony and contained information that corroborated the Madeiros confession. By withholding prior inconsistent statements made by prosecution witnesses the day after the murders, the prosecution denied to the defendants evidence critical to effective cross-examination.

4. Standards violated:

(a) Fair use of evidence by the prosecutor is required "accompanied by a duty to disclose evidence materially favorable to the defendant." *United States* v. *DeLeo*, 422 F. 2d 487, 498 (1st Cir. 1970).

". . . The Government is not forbidden to call witnesses whose reliability in one or many particulars is imperfect or even suspect. Its obligations are to make a clean breast of any evidence it has which may contradict such witnesses or undermine their credibility and not to rest its case upon testimony which it believes to be incorrect." *United States* v. *McGovern*, 499 F. 2d 1140, 1143 (1st Cir. 1974).

(b) ABA Standards Relating to the Administration of Criminal Justice (1974); The Prosecution Function: "3.11. Disclosure of evidence by the prosecutor. (a) It is unprofessional conduct for a prosecutor to fail to make timely disclosure to the defense of the existence of evidence, known to him, supporting the innocence of the defendant. He should disclose evidence which would tend to negate the guilt of the accused or mitigate the degree of the offense or reduce the punishment at the earliest feasible opportunity . . . . (c) It is unprofessional conduct for a prosecutor intentionally to avoid pursuit of evidence because he believes it will damage the prosecution's case or aid the accused."

(c) ABA Code of Professional Conduct adopted by the Massachusetts Supreme Judicial Court, 1972: "DR 7-103. Performing the duty of public prosecutor or other government lawyer. . . . (b) A public

26

prosecutor or other government lawyer in criminal litigation shall make timely disclosure to counsel for the defendant, or to the defendant if he has no counsel, of the existence of evidence, known to the prosecutor or other government lawyer, that tends to negate the guilt of the accused, mitigate the degree of the offense, or reduce the punishment."

(d) "It is well understood that the duty of a district attorney is not merely to secure convictions. It is his duty to secure them with due regard to the constitutional and other rights of the defendant." *Smith* v. *Commonwealth*, 331 Mass. 585, 591 (1954); *Berger* v. *United States*, 295 U.S. 78, 88-89 (1934).

D. Failure to investigate new exculpatory evidence.

1. In November, 1925, Celestino Madeiros, a convicted murderer whose appeal was pending before the Supreme Judicial Court, confessed to participation in the South Braintree robbery, and exonerated Sacco and Vanzetti. Based upon his statement (Vol. V, 4416-18) a motion for a new trial was filed May 26, 1926. Winfield M. Wilbar, then District Attorney of Norfolk County, rejected defense counsel's request that a joint investigation of the new evidence be undertaken (Vol. V, 4536-37). No independent investigation was undertaken by the District Attorney's office (Ehrmann, 409). Assistant District Attorney Dudley P. Ranney's response: "We have been criticized for failure to investigate this matter jointly. That is the explanation. We believe we have found the truth, and in our judicial capacity — there is some to a District Attorney — having found the truth, nothing else can matter. And that is our honest conviction. And if that is so it is a case not for investigation, and we justify our position by that alone. We will answer, but not investigate, because we know or believe that the truth has been found." (Vol. V, 4390.)

2. Standards violated:

(a) "Good faith and reasonable belief in the guilt of the defendant do not necessarily measure the duty of a prosecuting officer to secure a fair

27

trial to the accused and to bring before judge and jury all that ought to be brought before them." *Smith* v. *Commonwealth*, 331 Mass. 585, 593 (1954).

(b) ABA Standards Relating to the Administration of Criminal Justice (1974); The Prosecution Function: "3.11. Disclosure of evidence by the prosecutor. . . . (c) It is unprofessional conduct for a prosecutor intentionally to avoid pursuit of evidence because he believes it will damage the prosecution's case or aid the accused."

E. Appeal to jury's prejudice and biases.

1. During the cross-examination of Sacco, Katzmann dwelt upon Sacco's trip to Mexico to escape the draft, even though the trip bore no relationship to the crime. He ridiculed and unfairly distorted the political beliefs of Sacco in a manner that appeared calculated to rouse any anti-foreign animosity the jury may have had toward the defendant. This line of cross-examination was admitted by Judge Webster Thayer as testing the credibility of Sacco, who had earlier testified under direct examination that he "liked a free country" (Vol. II, 1818). The following excerpts are indicative of the tone of the cross-examination:

Q. Don't you think going away from your country is a vulgar thing to do when she needs you? A. I don't believe in war.

Q. You don't believe in war? A. No, sir.

Q. Do you think it is a cowardly thing to do what you did? A. No, sir.

Q. Do you think it is a brave thing to do what you did? A. Yes, sir.

Q. Do you think it would be a brave thing to go away from your own wife? A. No.

Q. When she needed you? A. No. . . .

Q. You love free countries, don't you? A. I should say yes.

Q. Why didn't you stay down in Mexico? A. Well, first thing, I could not get my trade over there. I had to do any other job.

28

Q. Don't they work with a pick and shovel in Mexico? A. Yes.

Q. Haven't you worked with a pick and shovel in this country?
A. I did.

Q. Why didn't you stay there, down there in that free country
and work with a pick and shovel? A. I don't think I did sacrifice
to learn a job to go to pick and shovel in Mexico.

Q. Is it because, — is your love for the United States of America commensurate with the amount of money you can get in this
country per week? A. Better conditions, yes. (Vol. II, 1869.)

2. The prosecutor's appeal to the jury's post-World War I prejudice
against draft dodgers and alien anarchists was intensified by Judge
Thayer's opening remarks to the jury and by the first words of his
charge. At the beginning of the trial, Judge Thayer said: "Gentlemen, I call upon you to render this service here that you have been
summoned to perform with the same spirit of patriotism, courage and
devotion to duty as was exhibited by our soldier boys across the seas
. . ." (Vol. I, 15). In his charge to the jury, he said: ". . . The Commonwealth of Massachusetts called upon you to render a most important service. Although you knew that such service would be arduous,
painful, and tiresome, yet you, like the true soldier, responded to that
call in the spirit of supreme American loyalty" (Vol. II, 2239).

3. Standards violated:

(a) "Language ought not to be permitted which is calculated by . . .
appeals to prejudice, to sweep jurors beyond a fair and calm consideration of the evidence." *Commonwealth* v. *Perry*, 254 Mass. 520, 531
(1926).

(b) ABA Standards Relating to the Administration of Criminal Justice
(1974); The Prosecution Function:

(i) "5.7. Examination of witnesses. (a) The interrogation of all
witnesses should be conducted fairly, objectively and with due

29

regard for the dignity and legitimate privacy of the witness, and without seeking to intimidate or humiliate the witness unnecessarily. Proper cross-examination can be conducted without violating the rules of decorum."

(ii) "5.8. Argument to the jury. . . . (c) The prosecutor should not use arguments calculated to inflame the passions or prejudices of the jury. (d) The prosecutor should refrain from argument which would divert the jury from its duty to decide the case on the evidence, by injecting issues broader than the guilt or innocence of the accused under the controlling law. . . ."

(c) ABA Code of Professional Conduct, adopted by the Massachusetts Supreme Judicial Court, 1972:

(i) "DR 7-106. Trial Conduct. . . . (c) In appearing in his professional capacity before a tribunal, a lawyer shall not: (1) State or allude to any matter that he has no reasonable basis to believe is relevant to the case or that will not be supported by admissible evidence. (2) Ask any question that he has no reasonable basis to believe is relevant to the case and that is intended to degrade a witness or other person."

II. *Judicial Abuses*

A. Prejudicial Behavior

1. Following the earlier Plymouth trial of Vanzetti for the attempted Bridgewater robbery, at which Judge Thayer presided, he requested Chief Justice John Aiken assign him to preside at the Sacco-Vanzetti trial in Dedham (Ehrmann, 159; Russell, 127). Such a request was and is a radical departure from usual judicial decorum and indicates Thayer's intense personal interest in the outcome of the trial. It is also highly probable that after presiding at the Plymouth trial and sentencing Vanzetti to fifteen years for attempted robbery, Thayer could not claim total impartiality toward the defendants at the Dedham trial.

30

2. In an article appearing in the *Boston Herald*, nine days after the South Braintree murders, Judge Thayer angrily denounced a Norfolk jury for acquitting Sergis Zagroff, a self-admitted anarchist indicted for violating the Criminal Anarchy Statute (see attachment B). The evidence indicated that Zagroff had merely expressed his views but had not violated the law.

3. Judge Thayer is reported as having made numerous disparaging comments about the defendants and their counsel outside the courtroom. Judge Thayer reportedly said:

(a) "Did you see what I did with those anarchistic bastards the other day?" Judge Thayer to Professor James P. Richardson (Richardson testimony before the Governor's Advisory Committee, Vol. V, 5065).

(b) When speaking about defense counsel Fred H. Moore, Judge Thayer to several reporters, "I'll show them that no long-haired anarchist from California can run this court!" On several occasions Judge Thayer said, "Just wait until you hear my charge." (Sibley affidavit, Vol. V, 4924-25.)

(c) "Mr. [Loring] Coes said [but later disavowed saying] that Judge Thayer had referred to Sacco and Vanzetti as bolsheviki who were 'trying to intimidate him', and had said that 'he would get them good and proper' . . . that he 'would show them and would get those guys hanged.'" (Benchley affidavit, Vol. V, 4928.)

(d) Judge Thayer to newspapermen: "You wait till I give my charge to the jury. I'll show 'em!" (Beffel affidavit, Vol. V, 4929-4931.)

(e) A motion for a new trial based on Judge Thayer's prejudice was filed August 6, 1927. The motion was argued before the judge who, after he refused to withdraw, denied the motion. The Supreme Judicial Court overruled the defendants' exceptions to Judge Thayer's denial on procedural grounds (Vol. V, 5500).

(f) The Governor's Advisory Committee concluded: "From all that has come to us we are forced to conclude that the judge was indiscreet in conversation with outsiders during the trial. He ought not to have talked about the case off the bench, and doing so was a grave breach of official decorum. . . ." (Vol. V, 5378L.)

31

4. The significance assigned to evidence by Judge Thayer varied dramatically, as it became necessary to deflect defense counsel's attempts to upset the guilty verdict. The judge's treatment of Proctor's testimony illustrates the judge's strong desire to prevent a new trial and uphold the verdict. During the trial, Judge Thayer instructed the jury that the fatal bullet had been shot from Sacco's gun, according to the expert witnesses for the prosecution which included Proctor (Vol. III, 3422). When faced with the Proctor affidavit stating that this was not Proctor's opinion, Judge Thayer dramatically minimized the testimony and its importance and belittled Proctor's expertise (Vol. IV, 3702). Later, when confronted with a motion for a new trial based upon the Madeiros confession, Judge Thayer once again maximized the weightiness of the expert witnesses' testimony to illustrate that a new trial was not necessary in view of the impressive evidence indicating the defendants' guilt (Vol. V, 4766).

5. Standards violated:

(a) ABA Standards Relating to the Administration of Criminal Justice (1974); Fair Trial and Free Press: "2.4. Recommendation relating to judges. It is recommended that, with respect to pending criminal cases, judges should refrain from any conduct or the making of any statements that may tend to interfere with the right of the people or of the defendant to a fair trial."

(b) ABA Standards Relating to the Administration of Criminal Justice (1974); The Function of the Trial Judge: "3.7. Prejudicial publicity. . . . (b) The trial judge should refrain from making public comment on a pending case or any comment that may tend to interfere with the right of any party to a fair trial. . . ."

(c) ABA Code of Judicial Conduct (1972):

(i) "Canon 2. A Judge Should Avoid Impropriety and the Appearance of Impropriety in All His Activities. A.) A judge should respect and comply with the law and should conduct himself at all times in a manner that promotes public confidence in the integrity and impartiality of the judiciary."

32

(ii) "Canon 3. A Judge Should Perform the Duties of His Office Impartially and Diligently. A.) Adjudicative Responsibilities. (1) A judge should be faithful to the law and maintain professional competence in it. He should be unswayed by partisan interests, public clamor, or fear of criticism. (2) A judge should maintain order and decorum in proceedings before him. . . . (6) A judge should abstain from public comment about a pending or impending proceeding in any court, and should require similar abstention on the part of court personnel subject to his direction and control. This subsection does not prohibit judges from making public statements in the course of their official duties or from explaining for public information the procedures of the court. . . . C.) Disqualification. (1) A judge should disqualify himself in a proceeding in which his impartiality might reasonably be questioned, including but not limited to instances where . . . he has a personal bias or prejudice concerning a party . . .."

33

Attachment A

SACCO AND VANZETTI CHRONOLOGY

April 15, 1920	Murders of Berardelli and Parmenter at South Braintree.
April 17, 1920	Inquest at Quincy with regard to South Braintree murders.
May 5, 1920	Arrest of Sacco and Vanzetti.
May 6, 1920	Interview of Sacco and Vanzetti by District Attorney Katzmann.
September 11, 1920	Indictment of Sacco and Vanzetti for South Braintree murders.
May 31-July 14, 1921	Trial of Sacco and Vanzetti at Dedham before Judge Webster Thayer.
November 5, 1921	Motion for new trial as against the weight of the evidence argued before Judge Thayer.
November 8, 1921	First supplementary motion for new trial filed.
December 24, 1921	Motion for new trial as against the weight of evidence denied.
May 4, 1922	Second supplementary motion filed.
July 22, 1922	Third supplementary motion filed.
September 11, 1922	Fourth supplementary motion filed.
April 30, 1923	Fifth supplementary motion filed.
October 1, 1923	Supplement to first motion filed.
October 1-3, 1923 November 1, 2, 8, 1923	All five supplementary motions argued before Judge Thayer.
November 5, 1923	Motion relating to Proctor affidavit filed.

34

October 1, 1924	Decisions by Judge Thayer denying all motions.
November 18, 1925	Madeiros confesses to South Braintree murders and exonerates Sacco and Vanzetti.
January 11-13, 1926	Argument of appeal of Sacco and Vanzetti from conviction and from denial of first, second and fifth supplementary motions.
May 12, 1926	Conviction of Sacco and Vanzetti affirmed by Supreme Judicial Court.
May 26, 1926	Motion for new trial based on Madeiros statement filed.
September 13-17, 1926	Madeiros motion argued before Judge Thayer.
October 23, 1926	Decision by Judge Thayer denying Madeiros motion.
January 27-28, 1927	Appeal from denial of Madeiros motion argued before Supreme Judicial Court.
April 5, 1927	Denial of Madeiros motion affirmed by Supreme Judicial Court.
April 9, 1927	Sentence of death imposed by Judge Thayer on Sacco and Vanzetti.
May 3, 1927	Petition for clemency addressed to Governor Fuller.
June 1, 1927	Advisory Lowell Committee appointed by Governor Fuller.
July 11-21, 1927	Hearings held before Advisory Committee.
August 3, 1927	Decision by Governor Fuller denying clemency.
August 10, 1927	Petition for writ of habeas corpus denied by Justice Holmes of the United States Supreme Court, and by Judge Anderson of the United States District Court.
August 19, 1927	Exceptions overruled by Supreme Judicial Court.

35

August 20, 1927	Petition for writ of habeas corpus denied by Judge Morton of the United States Circuit Court of Appeals.
August 20, 1927	Petition for stay and extension of time in which to apply to the United States Supreme Court for writ of certiorari denied by Justice Holmes of the United States Supreme Court.
August 22, 1927	Similar petition denied by Justice Stone of the United States Supreme Court.
August 23, 1927	Sacco and Vanzetti and Madeiros executed in Charlestown prison.

36

37

Attachment B

Boston Herald
April 24, 1920, p. 1

"JUDGE SCORES JURYMEN FOR FREEING 'RED'. Prosecutor Refuses to Try Any Further Cases in Norfolk Court. ZAKOFF ACQUITTED ON ANARCHY CHARGE.

"A verdict of not guilty, returned by a jury in the Norfolk county superior court yesterday afternoon in the case of Sergis Zakoff, charged with advocating anarchy, brought forth a severe arraignment of the jury by Judge Webster Thayer, who was presiding, and a refusal on the part of Asst. Dist.-Atty. William Kane, who was prosecuting the case, to try any further cases.

"'Gentlemen, how did you arrive at such a verdict?' asked the court. 'Did you consider the information that the defendant gave to the police officers when he admitted, according to the three police officers, that he was a Bolshevist and that there should be a revolution in this country? Upon his own testimony he said to the officers, in the conversation they had with him, that he believed in bolshevism and that our government should be overthrown. Didn't you consider the testimony given by the police officers when you were deliberating, before you agreed upon a verdict?'

"THOUGHT ACTUAL VIOLENCE MEANT

"In reply to the court's questions, the foreman said: 'The jury came to the decision of not guilty after they had interpreted the meaning of advocating anarchy, as explained by the court, as that of one who actually used violence and not a person who expressed his opinion and talked of overthrowing the government.'

"Zakoff was one of the alleged 'Reds' rounded up last January by the department of justice officers and allowed to go later. Chief Harry Swift and Officers William Barrett and Peter Curran testified that

38

Zakoff said to them that the government in this country was no good and that the only true form of government was the soviet government established in Russia. He also asserted, they testified, that the best thing for this country would be to have a revolution, and he advised Officer Barrett to become a Bolshevist himself."

The Commonwealth of Massachusetts

By His Excellency
MICHAEL S. DUKAKIS
Governor
A PROCLAMATION
1977

WHEREAS: A half century ago next month, Nicola Sacco and Bartolomeo Vanzetti were executed by the Commonwealth of Massachusetts after being indicted, tried, and found guilty of murdering Alessandro Berardelli and Frederick A. Parmenter; and

WHEREAS: Nicola Sacco and Bartolomeo Vanzetti were Italian immigrants who lived and worked in Massachusetts while openly professing their beliefs in the doctrines of anarchism; and

WHEREAS: The atmosphere of their trial and appeals was permeated by prejudice against foreigners and hostility toward unorthodox political views; and

WHEREAS: The conduct of many of the officials involved in the case shed serious doubt on their willingness and ability to conduct the prosecution and trial of Sacco and Vanzetti fairly and impartially; and

WHEREAS: The limited scope of appellate review then in effect did not allow a new trial to be ordered based on the prejudicial effect of the proceedings as a whole; and

[797]

WHEREAS: This situation was later rectified as a direct result of their case by the adoption of Chapter 341 of the Acts of 1939, which permitted the Massachusetts Supreme Judicial Court to order a new trial not merely because the verdict was contrary to the law, but also if it was against the weight of the evidence, contradicted by newly discovered evidence, or "for any other reason that justice may require"; and

WHEREAS: The people of Massachusetts today take pride in the strength and vitality of their governmental institutions, particularly in the high quality of their legal system; and

WHEREAS: They recognize that all human institutions are imperfect, that the possibility of injustice is ever-present, and that the acknowledgement of fault, combined with a resolve to do better, are signs of strength in a free society; and

WHEREAS: The trial and execution of Sacco and Vanzetti should serve to remind all civilized people of the constant need to guard against our susceptibility to prejudice, our intolerance of unorthodox ideas, and our failure to defend the rights of persons who are looked upon as strangers in our midst; and

WHEREAS: Simple decency and compassion, as well as respect for truth and an enduring commitment to our nation's highest ideals, require that the fate of Nicola Sacco and Bartolomeo Vanzetti be pondered by all who cherish tolerance, justice and human understanding; and

WHEREAS: Tuesday, August 23, 1977, will mark the fiftieth anniversary of the execution of Nicola Sacco and Bartolomeo Vanzetti by the Commonwealth of Massachusetts;

NOW, THEREFORE, I, Michael S. Dukakis, Governor of the Commonwealth of Massachusetts, by virtue of the authority conferred upon me as Supreme Executive Magistrate by the Constitution of the Commonwealth of Massachusetts, and by all other authority vested in me, do hereby proclaim Tuesday, August 23, 1977, "NICOLA SACCO AND BARTOLOMEO VANZETTI MEMORIAL DAY"; and declare, further, that any stigma and disgrace should be forever removed from the names of Nicola Sacco and Bartolomeo Vanzetti, from the names of their families and descendants, and so, from the name of the Commonwealth of Massachusetts; and I hereby call upon all the people of Massachusetts to pause in their daily endeavors to reflect upon these tragic events, and draw from their historic lessons the resolve to prevent the forces of intolerance, fear, and hatred from ever again uniting to overcome the rationality, wisdom, and fairness to which our legal system aspires.

Given at the Executive Chamber in Boston, this nineteenth day of July in the year of our Lord, one thousand nine hundred and seventy-seven and of the independence of the United States of America the two hundred and first.

By His Excellency the Governor
s/**MICHAEL S. DUKAKIS**

s/**PAUL GUZZI**
Secretary of the Commonwealth